The Green Deal Quartet

By

Jim Lowe

Published in 2023 by JRSL Publications

www.jimlowewriting.com

2084

New World Man

Book One of the Green Deal Quartet

By

Jim Lowe

PROLOGUE 1 Of 3: THE QUIET REVOLUTION

They never caused anybody any trouble. They led quiet lives and lived in peaceful communities. They were tolerated in the world's harshest regimes because they were hard-working tenders of the land. They didn't engage in local politics or harangued people about environmental issues, even if this was the only topic they felt passionate about.

After the collapse of the Climate Change Summit in 2050, they reasoned that talking had achieved little and that nobody wanted to listen to their preaching or bleating as it was more unkindly described. So they shut up and closed themselves off from the rest of society or the Traditional Cultures as they labelled the rest of the humanity.

The masterstroke was that they announced their utter surrender and proclaimed that they were no longer concerned about how others chose to live their lives and enjoyed their freedoms. They only asked that they could be left in peace to care for their small plots of land. Even when corporations or totalitarian governments stepped in to buy or claim their repaired lands, they didn't protest or demonstrate. They didn't organise TV or internet campaigns. They simply asked, politely, for another place to go and start again. Because they were so nice about it, even the dictatorships agreed. After all, they always improved any landscape they were relocated to. If they did an exceptional job of this, then this land could always be confiscated later.

The Green communities lived simply. They had computers that ran on Sattva Systems FusionCell™ batteries which were prohibitively expensive and generally incompatible with the rest of the world's high performing technology. Their communication speeds were deliberately ponderous. However, it was portable and environmentally sound. Sattva Systems™ gave this technology freely to the Greens, as a quiet thank you to the gentlest of people for looking after their patch of Mother Earth.

From the 2050 withdrawal of the Green radicals and environmental activists, they faded from view except for the occasional bemused and humorous TV reports of the strange behaviours of these nomadic people. They were treated as a drab version of a cheap Hare Krishna cult. They walked or cycled around areas of outstanding natural beauty, untouched land and critical green spaces still untouched by humanity. The thing that caused much comment, from gentle ribbing to ridicule, depending on the network coverage, was that this meandering trek went around the outskirts of these areas. They didn't bother to explore the wondrous sights within them.

Soon this became an old joke, and even the press tired of talk of the crazy but harmless activities of these Green Mother Earth Freaks.

Of slightly more concern was the activities of another group of Greens. They didn't walk around the outer areas of green spaces. Instead, they walked around the external sites of the key installations of every country in the land. This alarmed all nations' defence and secret service agencies, but the Greens were willing to be searched. - there was no tech, cameras or smart devices ever found on them - and as they never attempted to break in, this reduced the concern about terrorist threats.

Usually, after a Green Disciple had asked - with all humility, to simply be left to complete their walk around the outside of the walls and fences as part of their pilgrimage. And with the promise that they would never return. Even the most hardliner of personnel would let this happen for a quiet life, and a negation of paperwork would acquiesce.

Some would insist on accompanying and monitoring these shabbily dressed Greens. They always complied and the Traditional Culture representative would be thanked for watching over them as they walked.

For more than three decades, they cycled and walked.

Their shoes pumped out micro amounts of Nanoparticles around the perimeters of the green spaces to be preserved. And NanoSpray™ was applied to the walls to be destroyed. Every step released particles from shoes, and every revolution of the bicycle wheel pumped out more. Every one of the nine hundred million Greens who had resigned from the Traditional Cultures across the globe made at least one pilgrimage a year, spraying as they went.

The Nanoparticles replicated and spread unseen, forming the basis of the Green Shells waiting for the New Green Day to be activated. The NanoSpray™ eroded the walls at a molecular level. With impeccable sequencing, the walls would not show the irreparable internal damage to their structures.

Glenarvon Cole had received a message on his DumbSatt™ that China had fallen. He told the hundred-thousand Greens surrounding the Kremlin that they must remain calm and implacable, and he reminded them that they were wearing the Red.

It seemed likely that Russia and America would be the last to fall. He reasoned that this might go smoother now that word had reached President Maxim Yashin that no weapon on Earth could harm or move the Green protestors. When they released their chemical and biological weapons, they only risked harming themselves.

It still didn't stop the Russian soldiers from firing into the Green crowd at will. Because the RedSuits™ could anchor deep into the ground, even tanks couldn't move them. When the tanks fired their shells, they ricocheted harmlessly off them.

A hastily erected machine gun from the Trinity Tower fell silent. Glenarvon Cole pulled up his megaphone and announced calmly in Russian and then in English, 'Please leave the tower. We don't wish to harm anyone. It's over for you. Don't waste your life. Go home to your loved ones - while you still have a chance.'

He heard the same message relayed in a clockwise manner all around the Kremlin until the final warning was heard at the Middle Arsenal Tower to his left. Then with depressing familiarity, a man appeared holding a child and threatening to kill her unless they backed off. Glenarvon spoke calmly through his megaphone to the Greens, and they would pass the message on to the adjacent sections of his GreenRevs army. 'We will not harm anybody. If the Trads wish to harm their own, then that is for them and their consciences, not ours. If we don't do this, everybody and every living creature will die. You are at liberty to avert your gaze if you don't wish to witness yet another act of futile barbarity.'

The man who Glenarvon guessed to be GRU slit the girl's throat and then dragged up another to replace her.

Glenarvon Cole gave the order. The Greens marched forward one slow step at a time and marched up to the walls and towers surrounding the Kremlin and its grounds, and they placed their hands upon them and pushed. After years of erosion from the replicating NanoSpray™, the walls crumbled from the bottom. They fell inward with ease, and the towers collapsed. The Greens moved silently over the rubble. Not one of them gloated or cheered. They walked with dignity to within a few feet of the Kremlin Palaces.

Glenarvon Cole announced with calm authority. 'You are free to leave. Your families are waiting for you. If you delay, then you'll be cut off from them forever. This is not a threat. It's just the way it's going to be.' He paused to let this information sink in. He then added the information that would mean more to some of them, especially President Yashin. 'If you don't leave now, your homes will be unavailable to you. You will still be free, but you will have to make your living off the city streets and whatever land you can use within them.'

His reply came in actions and not words, as he heard engines running, and then the motorcade approached slowly and then stopped. The rear blacked-out window rolled down, and President Yashin smiled his acknowledgement and wound the window up.

Glenarvon Cole moved to one side, and the crowd parted to let him leave. Seeing their leader go, the evacuation of the Kremlin began in earnest, and the war in Russia was over with minimal casualties.

He dialled the number for Bodhi Sattva at the Sattva Systems ™ HQ in Boulder Creek, California. 'Hi, Bodhi. Russia has fallen. With the news from around the world, self-interest won the day for them.'

Bodhi said, 'I have a proto-type FusionPlane™ on its way to pick you up and fly you back to America to fulfil my promise to you. Are you sure you didn't want to make the big announcement in your homeland of England? Big Ben and the Houses of Parliament would make a more dramatic backdrop.'

'It doesn't feel right. New Hope made more effort than many in going Green, es-pecially under the decades of stewardship of Samii Trudeau. I want to do this for my Moppa. They always hated the inequality of corrupt capitalism. This is the moment I have always dreamed of.'

'By the time you return, there will be only one working TV station left on Earth. You will have a global audience as The Green sponsored Free TV News is the only one that avails itself of our FusionPower™.'

Glenarvon Cole laughed as he looked upon his brick dust coated clothes. 'I'm not dressed for a TV appearance. Not that it bothers me in the slightest.'

Bodhi chuckled but then fell quiet for a moment, 'I have a request.'

'Anything. You know that.'

'I am sending a reporter to conduct the final interview. I want you to recruit her. I want her to be the last recruit to the Green cause.'

'She works for Free News, and she's not already Green. I don't understand.'

'I need her - or someone like her for the One-Hundred-Year Plan to save the planet. She has the unique ingredients I need.'

Glenarvon Cole still didn't understand, but he didn't need to. Bodhi had delivered the tools needed to win the Green Revolution. 'Who is she, and why her?'

'Her name is Rhea Laidlaw. She was a child star and a social media influencer known the world over. She made headlines around the world when she gave up the glamorous world of Hollywood to join our dowdy and distinctly lo-fi TV station as a lowly reporter.'

'I haven't had time to watch much television - I've been kinda busy. What's she like?'

'Her image for Free News is dressed down and trying hard to gain some street credibility. But in her previous incarnation, she was quite the beauty with long red hair - My mother would have liked her. They'd have been two green peas in a pod.'

'I don't like the sound of this.'

4

'Why?'

'I don't want to stroll in and claim I'm helping to save the planet and then give the impression that I'm somehow getting the girl. It feels crass. It could give my fellow comrades the wrong impression.' He felt guilty about refusing Bodhi's request. He'd had rather he had asked him to risk his life on some daring mission.

After an awkward silence, Bodhi said, 'Don't worry. I understand. If you or your, our comrades come up with an alternative, then we'll use them instead.'

'Thanks, Bodhi. I'll put the word out. What are you looking for precisely?'

'Somebody who was clearly a Trad, but recently converted to our Green cause but is recognisable the world over.'

'Does it have to be right away?'

Bodhi laughed. He wanted to diffuse the tension. He didn't want to spoil Glen's moment of victory. 'No. Anytime in the next hundred years will be fine.'

'No problem. Look out for me on the TV when I get to Wall Street.'

Brady Mahone rubbed the beads of sweat from his cropped black hair on this sweltering midsummer day in California's Modern Ridgecrest Supermax Penitentiary. The Exercise Yard had been closed for no apparent reason. The Human Communal area was packed with hot and bothered inmates. Lucian 'Lucky' Lopez stayed close to his friend. Trouble was brewing, and everybody could taste it.

Lucian said, 'Something strange is happening, and I can't figure it out.'

'Yeah, the guards have changed shift patterns. I ain't seen Guard Askew for days, and they've put in some new faces.'

'When did it become legal for them to put a sniper in situ with shoot to kill orders? I can't believe they shot Johnson with no warning.'

Brady grimaced, 'Straight between Joachim's eyes. He was only acting up, breaking balls. What do you think, Lucky?'

Lucky looked up at Brady, who towered over him. 'Sending a message. It's the only thing that makes any sense. But if they want to keep order, why don't they let us use the Exercise Yard. They've even cut off the TV from us. I know they only allow us to watch soap streams. However, you still pick up hints at what's happening in the outside world, even if it is just the clothes and the cars.' He added 'I never realised how educational rampant product placement could be.'

Brady laughed, 'I seen ya getting all engrossed on whether Simmons was going to marry Holly.'

Lucky laughed, maybe a little too loudly, 'I see you've been keeping up with the plot.'

Brady gave the signal with his eyes to Lucky to warn him. Luca and Georgio Cesare were making a move in their direction. They moved into Brady's bubble as if he didn't have a say in the matter.

Georgio prodded Lucian aside. Lucian showed his palms and stepped respectfully aside while Luca got up close and personal with Brady. He was six-foot-plus, but he still had to look up into Brady's pale Polynesian face. 'You made ya mind up, Brady boy?'

Brady said calmly but with equal menace, 'You seen what I can do if you mess with me. I only likes my own company and my buddy, Lucky.' He looked over at the patch of lingering bloodstains on the nearby wall. 'That's all that's left of the last man who tested me. Even you daren't take on the Cartel.'

Giorgio grabbed Lucian's ear, and Lucian grimaced in pain.

Luca continued, 'We ain't scared of nobody Brady Mahone. Your little baby friend here might just find that out first. Remember, anybody, can be got in here.'

1.ALL CHANGE

'This is the end of your world.'

The TV screen captivated its captive audience. The last station on-air informed them with authority that it was the end of the world - so it had to be true.

Those lingering in the Communal Recreational area, were momentarily shocked into silence as they watched the statement's confirmation in the flashing images. There were scenes of rioting in the so-called free countries, and there was mayhem in the dictatorships, but of particular interest to this audience was the anarchy in the USA. The smooth-talking TV reporter was harassed but also, maybe a little excited at her scoop. It was a shame about the timing - the last ever transmission.

The leader of the GreenRevs thrust his face into the screen. 'This is it - the Promise has been fulfilled. We are making this world Green again.' He pulled away from the screen to give it back to his fresh-faced interviewer and the jubilant Greens behind her. They laughed as bullets ricocheted off them. They were unmoved by tear gas and other chemical repellents. They didn't even flinch as the grenades exploded around them.

'You are watching Free News, and I'm Rhea Laidlaw reporting from Wall Street.' A female GreenRev pushed past, yelling into the camera, 'Bodhi! We did it!' She hugged her GreenRevs leader, and Glenarvon Cole smiled, but that wasn't enough. There was a message to the people to give. His supporters leapt for joy. Another shot rang out, and the bullet glanced by Glen's face. Rhea screamed, and Glen grabbed her to stop her falling. The GreenRevs cameraman who had commandeered the equipment zoomed in. Glen examined Rhea's wounded arm, before applying some material, 'It has NanoHealing™.' He said, 'You'll be ok - I promise.'

She grimaced, but said with professional urgency, 'Can we carry on with the interview?'

'You're a brave one - perhaps you should join us.' He laughed. 'You've got nothing left to lose. You're broke. Everyone in the world is broke.' He pointed into the camera lens. He was pointing at every Free News viewer - whose ratings had gone from thirty thousand to hundreds of millions in the last two hours; as all its competition, including the Internet, dropped off the airways, 'Even you. Do you still want to carry on?'

Rhea looked to her new lensman. He nodded. It didn't matter if the cameraman was giving her a cue - this was a once in a lifetime opportunity. 'Yes.' She moved the microphone to her right hand and winced at the throbbing in her wounded left arm. 'What my viewers would want to know is - how did you know that the Internet would crash? Did you cause it to happen?'

'Bodhi knew all along. He prepared us for this moment for years. He saw it.'

'What did he see?'

'The future.'

Rhea scoffed, 'Utter rubbish. He might be a GreenTech™ giant, but he hasn't built a time machine.'

'All I know is he said this would happen. He told us that the whole system couldn't withstand the cocktail of viruses within it. He said, "Wait for the predicted 2080 solar storms, and it will collapse irrevocably." We spread the message, and they came.'

Rhea challenged him. 'That was another *end of the world* conspiracy theory.'

Glen smiled and gestured to the rioting crowd and re-stated to the camera, 'The end of your world.'

'Surely, this isn't going to be of any use to you or your followers either. There will be mass unemployment and poverty. This is a disaster of global proportions.'

'You don't get it. We've been planning this for years. Sattva Systems™ has been developing GreenTech™ for decades, but the old industries with the governments in their pockets wouldn't let it overtake them. They made all kinds of promises for 2050, but it didn't happen. They lied and cheated and ignored the climate crisis for the sake of their own profits and material wealth. Well, now the wealth has gone. A virtual world of transactions has been wiped. The new currency is going to be Green. Our people earn Green Credits. The Trads will just have to start again and muddle their way through - like they always do. This is the New Green Deal.'

'You can't just take people's savings and belongings from them.'

'Yes, we can. All you've ever owned is gone. Capitalism is dead. Welcome to the new Green World. This isn't a return to feudalism. This is a future of high-tech developments to take us into the twenty-second century. Our friends and early adopters will be well rewarded with new homes, jobs and re-education.' Glenarvon Cole wasn't entirely telling the whole truth - Rhea could tell - but he had to play the political games, like his opponents of old. He knew the places in the new communities had mostly been self-selected already.

'But what if the Trads - as you've named them - as you've labelled me, I suppose - what if they come to claim it all back and storm your Green Communities with force?'

'You've seen what our NanoArmour™ can withstand. It has survived nuclear attacks in Pakistan, chemical weapons in Russia, and everything our government can throw at us. We know how to defend ourselves. The future is not a scary place for those that want to help Mother Nature restore Herself back to health.'

And perhaps it wasn't. But the inmates at the Modern Ridgecrest Supermax Penitentiary would never know.

The interview was cut short as a chair smashed through the TV screen. A Nazi inmate yelled, 'Those Green pigs have stolen my money.'

Brady Mahone, six feet six inches and eighteen stone of muscle made a quick-fire decision to make his retreat. He wasn't scared - he usually enjoyed a good ruck - but he could see where this was heading. He grabbed his diminutive partner, Lucian, aka Lucky Lopez, by the arm and dragged him back to their cell, closed the barred doors and pulled the curtain over. It was a hot, muggy, midsummer day, and tensions among their fellow inmates had already been running high before every prisoner was informed that they had just lost everything. The fucking Green Credit was the new dollar - and they didn't have any fucking Green Credits.

As the inmates were absorbed in the acts of assault, battery and murder, two of the guards had just discovered they'd lost everything they had ever worked - or been bribed for - decided to give them what they should have had all along - death.

The two guards sprayed bullets in all directions. The mayhem continued for minutes. Brady shielded Lucian with his massive frame at the back of his cell. The angle of the firing was upwards, and the hundreds of bullets spilt crumbling masonry upon them. Then the shots took on a more deliberate rhythm. He guessed they'd now entered the execution phase. Brady rooted through the rubble until he found a piece of solid concrete which fitted comfortably in his massive hand. He squeezed it to make sure it wouldn't crumble to dust.

Brady said, 'Lucky, take a peek, and tell me what you see.' Brady saw his animal and insect sketches shot to pieces within the dust and concrete. *I loved those pictures - I spent hours on them.* He thought. Lucian's glamour girl photos were also in the rubble.

Lucian inched back the curtain, 'I see one guard executing the injured prisoners in the Communal Area.' He stuck his head out a little further. 'Shit! Guard Askew is coming up the stairs.'

'Which stairs?'

'To the right.'

'Ok, sneak into Croker's cell on the left, and make some noise.'

'But he'll see me.'

'Shuffle along on your belly, like a soldier.'

Lucian took a deep breath. 'Ok, and when I get there, do I call him or something?'

'Act like you're injured, nearly dead. I don't want him running.'

'Ok.' Lucian slithered along like a snake, not realising that he'd left a trail in the dust from the bullet-ravaged walls.

Askew's heavy boots thudded and clanged on the steel floor. At first, the rhythm was steady as he passed the rows of barred but open cells. They were all empty because their inmates were on Human Communal Time before the massacre - no one stayed in their cells for a minute longer than necessary. Askew spotted the trail in the dust, and he slowed down. He looked warily ahead, and then he heard the groan. He inched forward. *I guess he's dying, but where's the blood?* Askew thought, crouching down to examine the tracks.

That was the last thought he ever had. Brady punched the rock through his skull. He took the antique gun off the dead body of Guard Askew and went through his pockets, removing keys, passes, and even his wallet.

Lucian returned to his side as Brady examined the dead guard. Brady turned to him. 'He's big and overweight - strip him, and we'll use whatever clothing we can. I'll see if his jacket will fit me, maybe even the pants. You can roll the sleeves up and use his shirt.'

'The other one is still down there - and he's a bit smaller.' He smiled. 'His stuff might fit me better.'

'Sneak down the left stairs and watch for me coming down the right. When I get close - distract him - without getting yourself shot in the process.'

'Aye-aye captain.' Lucian whispered, and then he scampered away.

Brady changed into the guard's clothes. They were on the small side but at least the boots fitted. He stayed low as he moved efficiently past the cells and down the stairs. The shorter guard seemed to be double-checking that there was no one left alive. Occasionally, he would fire another shot into a barely twitching body.

Lucian waited for his moment. He watched Brady reach the bottom of the stairs, and he saw him check his weapon. The smaller guard sensed movement behind him. Lucian threw a rock across the floor before the guard turned. The guard's eyes followed the sound - just as Brady jumped him. He put the guard in a chokehold and lifted him off the floor and held him until his last breath left him.

He looked at the Tommy Gun and the Revolver, 'What the fuck are these things?'

Lucian picked them up and examined them, 'Antiques. This is less the twenties - more like the 1920s - and it's out of bullets. That's why he used the old Revolver.' Lucian wiped the guns where he had touched them on a dead inmate's T-shirt, then dropped them back near the guard. He looked over the guard's body and admired Brady's latest kill, 'I think he's new. I don't recognise him.'

'I don't think he was employed for his welfare skills - he was a sick fuck.' Brady issued his instructions. 'We take our time. Think about what we are going to need. Grab keys, money, clothes. If we can't find transport, it will be a long trek. We might have to rough it.'

'You do know this is unfair.'

'What is?'

'That you ended up with the brains as well as your brawn.' Lucian said knowingly.

'I must have come from a good gene pool. Let's move - no time for chatting.' He sighed, 'This is fucked up. I had fifty thousand bucks waiting for me when I got out, and now it's gone. That's my whole life savings - my emergency fund.'

'If we manage to get out of here, at least we'll be free.'

Brady pulled off the dead guard's boots and passed them to Lucian. 'I hate these places. They always stink of sweat and defeat.'

Lucian changed into the small guard's uniform but left the weapons. 'Have you touched them?'

10

'No. You must be thinking the same as me - we'll be in enough trouble if we managed to escape - don't want to be blamed for a massacre as well.' Brady remembered he still had Guard Askew's gun. 'Wait here.' He took the gun back, cleaned it, and then placed it in the dead guard's hand. From the upper floor, he checked for any further threats before returning to Lucian.

They both left the Communal Area and searched rooms to the left and right. Their newly acquired Guard's key cards were useless, so they used the old-fashioned bunches of keys to open any *Restricted Access* doors. When they found the guards' locker room, they grabbed holdalls. 'There are only two bags,' Brady said. 'These probably belong to the two we just killed. I'm guessing the others legged it when they realised that they were now unemployed and penniless.'

'Those two psychos obviously had other things they wanted to do before they signed off.'

'See if you can find car keys. I'm guessing there will be at least a couple of vehicles outside that don't use fingerprint locks. If not, then we'll have to chop off...'

'Let's hope we can find keys...'

They rummaged through the abandoned lockers. Lucian found some chocolate bars and cans of Coke, and they both consumed them greedily. When they found the car keys, they made their way through the deserted building to the control room. 'That was easy.' Lucian said, apprehensively.

'They didn't think there was going to be anybody left alive. After they've checked their loved ones are ok, they'll start to realise they're broke. That means they'll return to scavenge for anything of value. We'll take a car each if we locate them - then follow me - and don't drive like a granny.'

They moved methodically through the prison. Brady was calm and alert. They filled their requisitioned holdalls with as much as they could carry. In Lucian's case, a little, but with Brady - a lot. They even picked up old toothbrushes and toiletries like an eerie game of the Supermarket Sweep.

Before they reached the outer areas of the building, they came to the CCTV room. Lucian located the keys which would unlock the door, and Brady swept past him, ready to kill any remaining occupants. But there was nobody there. Brady checked the CCTV monitors, and it was clear the place was deserted. He wondered if they had left hours ago. Maybe the last two guards wanted a bit of sport before they left.

He thought about the chain of events leading up to the bloodbath. They hardly ever put on the news, it usually got the blood of the rival gangs or political allegiances up. He remembered Guard Askew yell before switching over from the daytime soaps they were allowed to watch. 'Boys, we got a real treat for you today. We are going to switch on Free News, so y'all can see what you're missing in the big world out there.' At that, Brady had instinctively known trouble would follow.

In the CCTV control room, he asked Lucian to confirm that the Internet was indeed dead. Lucian was in here because he was guilty of being in the wrong place at the wrong time for him, but precisely the right time for a corrupt Police Department to make a positive impression on that quarter's crime statistics. He had worked in Hollywood as a computer graphics assistant for one of the streaming giants. It didn't take long for Lucian to confirm the deceased status of the Internet and the whole of social media. 'Godammit - my education and career has gone down the drain.'

'Talking of drains, make sure you use the toilets before we leave. We don't want someone using your bony ass for target practice when you wanna stop by the side of the road for a dump.'

'At least, they would have the challenge of trying to hit mine.'

Brady laughed. He rubbed his fingers through his stubbly black crew-cut hair - he hadn't shaved it bald for more than a week - while examining the array of equipment in the room. 'Is any of this tech worth taking with us?'

'Only the Dumb Satts™ - Satellite Phones still should work, and they are Fusion-Powered™. They are supposed to last forever.'

Brady packed them away. They were surprisingly heavy. They both moved out, taking in the heavily wooded areas which surrounded the Modern Ridgecrest Supermax Penitentiary.

There were a few cars in the parking lot, and they soon found a couple of keys that worked without needing fingerprint technology to open them. 'You know what.' Lucian said, 'A lot of products are going to be fucked without the Internet.'

'Not our problem.' Brady found a car he liked, a *Twentieth Generation Ford Mustang*, while Lucian chose a *2045 Mid-Engine Mini*. 'Thank fuck we don't have to trek through the forest.' Brady said, dumping his heavy bags into the trunk. 'I've got a place we can lay low in McFarland. It's about sixty miles west of here. Keep up and keep close.'

2.ARCHIE'S RANCH

McFarland wasn't the town he'd remembered. Brady had only been inside for ten years, and McFarland wasn't the sort of place which attracted investors, but it had received quite the makeover. He slowed his driving down to a crawl to take in the details. He wondered how his stolen car could travel on the Highway, but Lucian's car seemed to be blocked by an invisible barrier. Brady had tried, and it worked fine for him, but Lucian was blocked. Lucian drove behind Brady but stayed off-road to the edge of the Highway.

There wasn't another vehicle in sight, but he noticed curtains twitching as he passed people's homes. *Maybe, it's the economic collapse. Or it could be that news of the prison break has reached them,* he thought.

He wondered how many of the prison guards and workers lived here. The prison was only twenty years old. Maybe they had brought a measure of prosperity to the town. He was anxious to get to his old Foster Daddy, Archie. He had a bunker, and he was a sucker for conspiracy theories. As he drove through the town centre, he noticed a common theme of environmental messages and sponsorship by Sattva Systems™ - they seemed to be the most significant player in this place.

He glanced in his rear-view mirror to check if Lucian was still behind, in his Mini, and then indicated right, heading to the more rural east side of town and the small ranch where Archie lived. It was well to the south of McFarland's more populated east side, but not far from the west side. However, Archie was on the other side of Highway 99, which formed a formidable barrier to anyone deciding to investigate his ranch. Archie chose it for privacy from the east and the convenience of the west.

After making their way down a dirt track, past the few cattle Archie still owned, they pulled up just outside Archie's ranch. Brady got out of his Mustang and went to the gate. Lucian wound down his window to check for potential threats. A couple of shots rang out as Brady approached the entrance to the ranch. Brady shouted, 'Hey! You old fucker, it's me, Brady.'

There was a pause before a raspy voice replied, 'Brady! Well, come on in.'

Brady opened the big gates wide open. He turned to Lucian, 'Let me drive in first. He don't like strangers.'

They parked up, got out of their cars, and Lucian stayed back as Brady gave the old man a warm hug. 'Hey, Foster Daddy, how ya been keeping?'

'I tell ya now.' Archie Mahone rasped, 'Some of those young fuckers are gonna git it - if they try to steal my ranch.' Archie was deeply tanned after years of working in the Californian sun, and his thick silver chain glinted in the light, nestled in the bush of his white, wiry chest hair.

'And who's gonna try and do that, with fierce old Archie Mahone guarding it?'

'The Greenies! I knew they'd try and take over the world.'

'You old fool,' Brady teased, 'I thought it was the aliens or the Deep Cons in the government who were going to do that first.'

'I've seen the townsfolk eye up my bunker.'

'I'm surprised you're not down there now - I half expected it.'

'Well, boy, I had to defend the ranch, and I couldn't do that from down there, now could I?' He looked him over, 'Boy, you haven't aged a bit, and there ain't a mark on ya.' He took in his boy's bronze skin. He never did know where he came from. Archie remembered telling him to tell the townsfolk he came from Hawaii to explain it. Archie used to convince himself: *Well, he has got that kinda South Seas islander look about him.*

'I've had my fair share of scrapes, Pops, and you know I take some hurting. And even when I do, I heals real quick.' Brady looked over at the vintage machine gun, ready and waiting with its glittering array of bullets dangling from it. 'You got Old Marvin out. I used to have so much fun playing with that as a kid.'

'The new machines don't work no more.'

'Seven or eight years ago, all weapons had to be fitted with a disabler.' Lucian interrupted, 'You had to activate a stream-switch to use it. It was a compromise with the gun lobby. You could use your weapons as much as you want, but it had to be the owner or authorised user, and all firings were logged.'

'I was inside.' Brady said, 'I must have missed it. Pops, this is Lucian, but I call him Lucky, cos he's my *lucky* mascot. He saved my ass inside Ridgecrest.'

'And for that, Brady here, literally saved my ass!' Lucian laughed.

Archie wheezed, 'I can see that - you're no bigger than a boy, son.' He looked at Brady, 'Really, he saved you?'

'Even I don't have eyes in the back of my head.' He added, 'We need a place to stay, to stay low for a while.'

'Of course. I'll be glad of the company, and you can do me a favour.'

'What can we do for you?'

'You can help me protect the place until things play out.'

Brady placed his massive arm around Archie's shoulder, and Archie almost buckled under the weight of it. 'Be our pleasure. If someone out there wants to play at target practice, then I'll show them that Brady don't miss with Old Marvin.'
When Brady moved his arm from Archie's shoulder, Archie returned to his previous six-foot height. He brushed his fingers through his long, thinning white hair and then stroked his white beard. 'You boys, grab your things and get settled in while I go and get us some grub.'

Later, around the table, they devoured the assorted fries and grills greedily. Brady and Lucian talked animatedly about their exploits and near misses in their Supermax home. While Archie enthusiastically tried to claim every conspiracy theory known to geek-kind was correct all along.

'What are your buddies saying about it all?' Brady said,

'I don't know. All my tech is useless. I spent a fortune on it over the years. I kept up to date with every development - but even the Black Web has gone. It shouldn't be able to happen. That's why it must be alien technology. Must be from space to git the whole world in one go.'

'What about mobiles? Surely, the phones still work.'

Archie flushed, 'You gotta understand. That must have been the masterplan, to communicate through the phones. They left them standing for a reason - right?'

'Ok, that kinda makes some sense if it's human overlords taking over the planet - but you said you thought it was aliens - from outer space and all.'

'Couldn't be too careful. The last calls I had said was to prepare to defend yourself to the death, for all that's sacred. They were going to destroy the masts. They ain't gonna spy on us no more.'
'Is that it? That's the plan for the uprising, the fightback?'

'In fairness, it all happened so fast.'

'But you and your conspiratorial buddies have been planning for decades for a moment such as this, surely?'

'We had our bunkers…'

Brady laughed, but Archie saw the warmth within it. 'I notice you ain't in your bunker.'

Archie started to form an answer. 'I got my eyes peeled for them no good, piece of shit Hodgsons. They ain't got no bunker, and they never prepared like me. They just steal what they wants. One man alone can't defend two properties…' But then he roared with laughter, he was so happy to have his boy back again, 'Truth is, son, it's more than forty years old, it stinks and ain't fit for purpose no more. To tell the truth, boy, I'd rather live in Ridgecrest than that piece of shit, hole in the ground. But I didn't think of that when I made it my control centre.'

Lucian spat out the meat he was chewing and erupted in laughter, and Brady and Archie couldn't help but laugh along with him.

After Archie and Lucian went to bed, Brady stood on watch all night. He had never needed much sleep, even as a boy. He wondered if it was because he was always sent from one foster home to another - until he finally settled with Archie and Edie. At least it was quiet here. He thought about his ten years in prison, ten years gone and not being able to sleep. He never did like listening to the sounds of the men inside, snoring, farting, and masturbating all night long - never mind the quiet violence and the noisier rapes. He hoped to erase those thoughts from his mind - given time.

He wandered around the ranch, not too far from the homestead, and looked up at the glittering stars. It was easy to imagine for a moment that the world hadn't changed - but it had. Now was the time for planning not only how he could survive it but also, how he - how *they* might be able to thrive in it. The decking creaked as he rocked in his Pop's old chair. He watched the FusionPlanes™ glide through the skies intermittently. A few of the HeavyLoader™ Planes were coming into land at the nearby Airport. He thought *they* weren't supposed to fly over the town after midnight.

Then something strange appeared. He didn't get up, feeling as though he was catching a glimpse of something that could disappear if he changed angles. *It looks like one of those aurora type things, except I'm sure you don't see them down in these parts.* He knew there was nothing wrong with his eyesight. The prison doctors were amazed at the ease in which he passed his optical evaluation - they didn't have any other charts with smaller lettering to test him. This ain't like no aurora I've heard of. It's coming from the ground up and not from the skies. The translucent green glow moved to envelop the town of McFarland at first, and then it rolled, like mist, down the Highways and even the dirt roads surrounding Archie's ranch and the neighbouring Hodgsons. In a matter of moments, the glow faded, and Brady wondered if he had imagined it. *I can't leave my watch, not with the Horrible Hodgsons down the way. I'll check it out in the morning.*

As the first rays of dawn broke over the horizon, Archie appeared with hot coffee for them both. He sat down on the porch next to Brady. 'I still got all your old things, and looking at you boy, I'm guessing you could still get into your old clothes.' He smiled, 'Your little buddy is in the kitchen - says he can't wait to make us all a big, cooked breakfast.'

'Thanks, Pops. I need a shower first, then get changed. I must say I'm looking forward to some proper home-cooked food myself.' He gulped down his coffee. 'The town has changed a lot since I was last here. They didn't let us keep up with the news in Ridgecrest - they considered it a mood agitant. It looks a lot more prosperous than I remember.'

'That was all the corporate sponsorship - part of the New Green Deal. They persuaded the townsfolk to join a scheme where if they let them take over the running of the town, they could get virtually free Green energy and other benefits.' He laughed. 'The Internet ran as slow as if it was moving through treacle, and everybody but the Greens got real mad about it and upped and left.'

'But you didn't go for it - no doubt.'

'Nah, too good to be true, if you start to believe in some corporation's bullshit, then it's the beginning of the end for the freemen of the west like me - like us.' He looked into Brady's face to make sure the years inside hadn't changed him.

Brady smiled. 'I just remembered, we picked up a bunch a Satts™ before we left - could you find a use for them?'

'More Sattva Systems™ stuff - they were worth fucking trillions of dollars, and you can't go barely a mile without seeing a sign of theirs. Having said that, now that the Internet and the Cell Phones aren't working, maybe the old-fashioned Satellite Phones might still work. I might take them, even if it does kinda go against my principles.'
'I need to know more about what I've missed. How did this Sattva Systems™ make their money?'

'It was after the third pandemic of the Twenties and the crash of Twenty-Nine - that fucking crash looks like a walk in the park compared to this one. Anyhows, Sattva was already a highly valued company, even though it was massively in debt - these fucking tech companies never did make financial sense - they must have had something over the government...'

Brady laughed, gently, 'Pops, give me the details first, and we'll talk about the conspiracies later - I promise.'

'Alright, alright. Anyhows, the aviation industry was decimated, but Sattva had developed clean energy with FusionPower™, which solved some of the climate issues. That was probably, just after you were jailed for the jewellery heist in Bakersfield. The trouble with everything Sattva Systems™ did with Fusion-this and Fusion-that is that it was all expensive, slow and total fucking crap, and nobody wanted that shit except the Green Communities - who got it for free - if you call giving up on living *free.*'

Brady guessed that Archie would rather talk about that instead, but he needed to catch up with the rest of the world. 'I thought they were Green, this Sattva Systems™ - surely, the environmentalists would have been happy to see the back of airlines altogether?'

'You said I couldn't go into conspiracy theories, so, let's just say, they musta come to some sort of arrangement.' He smiled as if he had won a point. 'Ya see, boy, they made them all their money by solving the pandemic issues with flying. I'm guessing the Greens still needed to travel to plot against the rest of us good ol' boys.'

'How did they do that?'

'It was their fucking NanoTech™. Trust me, son, if there's an end to the human race planned - it'll start with that invisible Green goo.'

Brady sighed. *I'm just going to have to let him tell it his way, conspiracy theories and all. It's going to be challenging to pick out the facts from all this.* 'Hey Pops, I thought you said it was invisible.'

'Do ya want to hear my story? Or are ya just goin' to pick holes in everything I say? Look around ya, boy, the world has changed. We have new rulers. They just haven't issued their demands yet - but it's coming, you mark my words, and when they do, I betcha we all gonna have to pay a high price - maybe not today, but at some point.'

'Ok, Pops. You're right. Things have changed big time. I can't deny what I see with my own eyes.' He thought again about the green glow he saw last night. He reached over and grabbed his Pop's arm. 'I hear you, Pops.' He could sense Archie's stress levels coming down. 'You were saying about planes and the pandemic issues.'

'Yes, I was, before I was rudely interrupted. Anyhows, they put NanoTechFilms™ - think of it like when you used to blow them bubbles as a young 'un - they put this Film over the entrance to the FusionPlanes™. Passengers had to agree to all this and acquire enough Green Credits from the Sattva Systems™ Reps - to prove their environmental credentials. The devil is always in the fucking details.' He muttered, 'If the passengers did all this, then they would go into the plane and be covered in Green goo...'

'But you said it was invisible. Could the passengers feel the goo on them?'

'Well, I never went on them planes, but apparently, no - they didn't know it was on them. Now, that is scary. It could be all over us right now.'

'Carry on, Pops.'

'What it did was individually isolate them from any viruses or infections of any kind. They were literally in their own bubble.'

'Sounds like a good thing.'

'That's how they get ya, son. They came back from their holidays and their business trips, and they all said they never felt better, renewed, turns out, this Green goo...'

'Do they call it *Green goo*?'

'Sattva Systems™? Of course not. Who markets anything that's the truth? They, and the sheep who follow them to the slaughter, call it NanoFilm™.'

'I didn't think Green goo was a good name.'

'Good enough for me, boy. Anyhows, as I was saying, not only did these passengers say it relieved them of some of their ailments - they also said it acted as a sunblock. Remember the Thirties when the weather got biblical? Record hurricanes, tornadoes, rain and heat - almost all the time?'

'Yeah. Come to mention it. I had noticed the weather calming down since I went inside. Out in the Exercise Yard, I started taking it personally.' He let out a big laugh, but Archie was frustrated because he had made Sattva Systems™ sound good, and that wasn't his intention. He decided to skip telling him about the Intense Renewable Projects and the trillions of investments into Sattva's New Deal.

Archie went for the big conspiracy. 'You know what else these returning travellers said about the effects of the Green goo?'

'What did they say, Pops?' Brady knew conspiracy was coming. Inside he shrugged wearily, but outwardly, he gave his Pops his full and undivided attention.

'That it was also, a contraceptive. Nobody ever got pregnant while they were away, after travelling on those planes.'

'Come on, Pops. How could anybody prove that?'

'I had loads of stuff on it before the Great Internet Crash. There were studies and all sorts.'

'Presumably, people had kids after?'

'Yeah, after, but not during.'

Brady thought about it, even though he thought this was pretty damn trivial for a conspiracy theory. 'Even if this was true. Did the Nano - Green goo just wear off when they returned?'

'No. On arrivals, they would pass through security and the Green goo was recycled. Made more and more people want to fly - for the so-called health benefits and the Green Credits, even though they weren't worth anything, they were just some liberal greenies badge of honour. They were always showing off how many fucking credits they achieved. Sattva Systems™ ruled the skies - and now they want to rule the whole fucking world.'

Brady laughed, 'I don't suppose you've got any of those credits, Pop?'

'Damn right, boy - none. That's my badge of honour.'

3.DISCIPLE

Brady helped Lucian clear up the breakfast dishes - it was the least he could do after Lucian had prepared a breakfast feast of epic proportions. He felt clean, back in his old jeans and a starched white T-shirt and had found the DeNine DeLuxe Sneakers™, he'd hardly had time to wear before his incarceration. And now he was fed and watered; he felt ready to take on the world.

His Pops waited for them next to the log fire. It was spring, warm and sunny outside, but Brady took this as a sign of Archie's oncoming old age that he felt the cold more. It made him a little sad to think of his Pops no longer apparently indestructible.

They all chatted for a while; Brady and Lucian gave Archie all the gory details of their time inside. He especially liked the stories about the old-timers locked up in Ridgecrest - some of them he knew from his old days. By lunchtime, Archie was becoming sleepy. Brady reached out and touched him on the arm, 'Hey, Pops. I'm going to walk over to the town to see how the land lies.'

'Are you sure that's a good idea, boy? Won't folks be looking for you?'

'I can look after myself. Anyway, I don't think anyone's got a job at the prison anymore.' He looked his Pops in the eye, 'I need to check things out for myself.'

'Ok, you be careful, boy. If there ain't no prisons, they might decide to take you dead and not alive. You catch my drift?'

'I've set up a couple of the Satts™.' Lucian said, 'If you take one, we could still communicate. You never know, we could get you to pick up some shopping,' he added laughing.

'Yeah, sure, with no money and none of that green currency?' Brady said. 'I'll ruin my rep if I go from heists to shoplifting.'

Lucian handed him a belt with a holster for the Satellite phone. Brady put it on. 'You'd have thought they'd have made these things smaller by now.'

Brady marched the twenty-minute walk along the dirt track past the Mahone Ranch and around the Hodgson Ranch. As he came to the first major road - McFarland was his hometown, but this road was new, so he didn't know its name - he saw a couple of the Hodgson Mob, throwing rocks which bounced off thin air. They were yelling as the rocks seem to hit an invisible wall and drop dead to the floor. They threw the stones at passing drivers, who ducked and swerved, expecting the hit, but the rocks never got anywhere near them - until one car veered off the road and headed straight towards Brady. He leapt out of the way just in time as the vehicle hurtled past him, skidding until it came to a halt.

Brady went to rescue the old woman inside, but the Hodgson duo had other ideas. 'Hey, Brady! She's ours - we fucking did the hard work. We want what's coming.' Alan and Gary Hodgson had grown up a lot since Brady had been inside, and they were not the little roustabouts he remembered.

He looked over the old woman. She didn't seem to be injured. 'Are you ok, ma'am?' She looked as terrified of him as she was about the two Hodgson boys.

'Yes, thank you. Please get me to the road, if you would, please…sir.' She thought it might humour him.

'Stay behind me. I'll hold them off.'

He shuffled backwards as Alan danced and dodged his way behind Brady while Gary pulled a knife, ready to attack. The plan seemed to be to distract Brady while Alan grabbed the woman. All the while, Brady fended Gary off while the woman frequently screamed as the knife whipped past.

After a few minutes, Brady reached the edge of the road. Knowing this was their last chance of securing their prize, and whatever this woman owned, they rushed Brady. He staggered backwards and the old woman started to fall. She tried to get out of his way, she twisted and tripped, but it was enough for her to find the edge of the road. An oncoming car swerved to miss her, as did the next car as one only just avoided Brady. He pulled her to the kerbside. He turned back to see Alan and Gary only inches away from him, but they were punching the invisible wall, uselessly trying to get to him. Gary tried to hack and slice at it but to no avail.

They soon lost interest in them and instead turned their attention to the vehicle. Brady watched them closely as they tried and failed to start the car. Then they just took anything of value they could find within it.

He checked on the old lady, but she'd crossed the road while he was watching the boys. She looked back and screamed at him, 'Don't come near me. You shouldn't be able to get in here. I'm going to report this to the Disciple. This isn't part of the deal.'

Brady decided to let her go. *More trouble than it's worth.*

He brushed himself down - he'd liked the feeling of being clean again after his time inside. He wandered around the edge of the new road, which appeared to encircle the town. He thought about testing this invisible wall by trying to leave and then coming back in again but decided against it. *It might have been a fluke when I fell in at the same time as her.*

He came to McFarland Park and decided to remain there while he considered what to do next. People passed him and paid him very little attention. It was as if they didn't have a care in the world - they looked at ease. *How could they feel so safe in the middle of a revolution?* He listened to their chatter until he heard an old couple talking about a meeting for residents at the New Green Hall. *That's as good a place as any to find out what the fuck is going on.*

If he didn't know any different, the town would be going about its daily routines as if nothing extraordinary had happened. He listened discreetly to conversations - mainly about family, friends, and everyday happenings. It surprised him that there were no mentions of prison breaks and murderers on the loose. There were no digital displays or wanted posters to be seen. He took a closer look at all the signs and businesses owned by Sattva Systems™. They all had a theme; how business and environmental activism could come together to save Mother Earth. Brady liked to sketch any creatures he came across, from beasts to critters to insects, and he appreciated the high-quality designs and images of these advertisements.

Physical cash had disappeared from society, even before he went inside, which was why he had turned to jewellery store heists. He had been highly successful until he was undone by pure bad luck. The police were booked to advise on new security measures, just minutes after he and his crew had moved in to rob them.

He watched as people paid for their goods with things that looked like old-fashioned micro-chips - these were in different shades of green. Before handing them over, the customer placed them between the thumb and forefinger and when they glowed, the business owner put them in the top of a small tube, which flashed green as it swallowed it up, as if some kind of transference had been completed.

A new phone store was opening - also owned by Sattva Systems™ on the old First Street. *No surprise there.* The queue snaked back for a few hundred yards, past where the old McDonald's had been, before his time away. He wondered if the whole chain had disappeared. The potential customers didn't look excited - unlike the old days when a new tech product was launched. *This ain't new tech - this is old except for the fancy Sattva logos. They don't want them - they need them.*

He instinctively patted his own Satt™. He spotted an old man sitting on a bench, with a satchel by his side, watching the world go by. It was time to ask one of the residents a few questions, but it would be tricky. The questions he wanted to ask were so fundamental, they'd almost certainly give him away as an outsider. He sat beside the old man and said nothing. He tried to appear relaxed. He rubbed his head. He had got used to shaving it bald when he was at Ridgecrest, but now he felt the stubble sprouting through. The old man watched him. Brady continued to rub his head, fascinated by its rough feel.

The old man spoke first, 'I used to have a lovely head of hair, it was my crowning glory, the ladies used to say, and then it all started to go, almost exactly when I hit sixty. I thought I was going to keep it.'

Brady smiled. 'I think I'm going to grow mine back - make a new start.' He thought about using an assumed name, but he thought it would be a waste of time. He was too recognisable to hide his identity, with his size, pale-brown skin, physique, and dark brown eyes. Only the old natives of McFarland would recognise him, and as he was last here, more than twenty years ago... He reached out his hand, 'I'm Brady Mahone - pleased to meet ya.'

The old man shook his hand, weakly, 'I'm Gus. We're all making new starts, even at my age.'

'I can't get used to this new way of working. What about you?'

'I lost my life savings in this crash. Fortunately, I'd built up a lot of Green Credits over the years...and kept them alive with consistent Green living.'

'What's the deal with those? I've been abroad for the last few years.'

The old man looked at him suspiciously. 'Where could you have been that you hadn't heard of Green Credits?'

Fuck! This really is a worldwide phenomenon. Where the fuck could I have been? He remembered the old wildlife books he read voraciously in Ridgecrest and how he used to copy the pictures and pin the sketches to the wall in his cell. 'I've been deep in the Amazon rainforest, keeping a census of animals which are nearing extinction, like the Pink Amazon dolphin and the White-Cheeked Spider Monkey. If you've got a pen and paper, I could draw you one.'

He expected Gus to decline the offer, but instead, he pulled out a leather-bound notebook and a pencil from his satchel. He handed it to Brady. 'I'd like to see that monkey of yours.'

Brady started to sketch, taking his time - sketching always relaxed him. He began with the monkey's sad eyes. He had to pick out every detail before he could move on to the next feature.

Gus watched on as though he had nothing else to do with his day, and this was worth savouring.

Brady moved onto the grim expression of the monkey's mouth.

Gus laughed. 'Are you sure you're not drawing me there, fella?'

Brady laughed heartily, but then resumed his concentration. After the mouth and the short pencil strokes deployed for the button nose, he opened out the rest of the face, the brandished white hair nearest the main features, and then fanning out extravagantly - the darkening strands which looked like fireworks jetting away in all directions. He handed the notebook back to Gus.

He looked at it closely. 'I love it, thank you.'

'You're welcome.'

'Could you write its' name on there, so I don't forget. My memory ain't what it used to be.'

Brady wrote *White-Cheeked Spider Monkey* in neat, small print, but slowly. He didn't write very often - he added to *Gus from Brady.*

'If you ain't built up any Green Credits, then you'll have to start from scratch. Seems unfair to me. If you've been looking after animals in the rain forests, then you deserve to be a Green Credit Millionaire in my mind.'

'Where did they start?'

'Sattva Systems™ started issuing them for every time you did something good for the environment. They told people to look after them, to nurture them because one day they might be used as an unofficial currency like Bitcoin.'

'I suppose Bitcoin has gone as well.'

'No Internet, no cyber-currency. People started to treat them like a collector's item, a badge of honour in the war against climate change - and because they were a physical thing, it kinda fulfilled an old-fashioned desire. Well, it did for me.'

'Surely, they would try to eliminate manufacturing things first, especially money, seeing as we had already gone cashless.'

Gus thought about this for a moment, 'Sometimes, you only see things with hindsight. It was as if they were planning for the final crash.'

'Do you think they knew it would happen?'

Jim Lowe

'The GreenRevs and Sattva Systems™ claimed they *guessed* that it would happen - viruses, solar storms - but they've never stated that they were responsible. People tend to admire visionaries - when their visions come true - but not terrorists.'

'So now, people are using these Green Credits as currency. Why aren't people stealing it - or other companies buying them up?'

Gus smiled, 'Because they can only be used by people who believe in helping the environment and have a track record on trying to save the planet, and they can only be given *freely*, and *freely* taken, with an open heart and mind.' Brady laughed, but Gus added, 'And they are only issued in small denominations, a hundred Greenback file is the highest - at least for now.'

'Ok, let's say a mugger robs the purse off an old lady, or there's a stick up at a liquor store…'

'Can't see there being any more liquor stores.'

'Whatever.' Brady took a deep breath. He was starting to become agitated and was in danger of losing the trust of this old-timer. 'What happens next?'

'For the old lady in question, she would be proud of her environmental record, and these, enzymes, hormones, whatever they call them - I ain't a biologist, would be in her body, and when she gives them over to somebody else, she holds them in her forefinger and thumb, and this checks for any stress levels, and sleep agents. The chip glows when it's ready, and the same process happens with the receiver. They said the chips, or Files as they are called now, ensure that we buy what we need, and not through the stimulus of acquiring *things*. It reduces over-consumption.'

Brady knew he would need time to let the implications of this sink in. 'Is there anything that people buy with these Green Credits that aren't just bare essentials?'

'Not that I know of - but I bet it's only a matter of time before somebody finds a workaround. That's what humans do. Someone will spoil it, either for greed or just for the hell of it.'

If I can figure this out first. Brady thought, *then I could make an absolute killing.*

An old woman's voice called out from across the street. 'Gus, honey, I got it.' She waved her Sattva™ Satellite Phone, still in its box, at Gus. 'Now, we can call our baby Claire in Montana.'

Gus smiled at Brady, 'Got to go. Nice meeting ya fella - and thanks for the drawing.'

Brady watched the old couple stroll away. He wasn't hungry after his colossal first breakfast after escaping from Ridgecrest. He had a sense that his morning world was like a different planet, instead of being only about a half-hour walk from where he sat right now. He was feeling thirsty, though. He looked around - most of the shops were closed, apart from the odd GreenGrocers™. He laughed to himself. They are actually called the GreenGrocers™. He checked the area for cops or security, but he couldn't see any. He was in jeans and a T-shirt. *I shoulda worn something to hide stuff. I don't even have the money to buy a carrier - probably don't have none of those either.*
He spotted a sign above a small fountain indicating that this was a drinking station.

He stood from his bench and went to check it out. He leant over the little jet of water and drank. As he straightened up, he heard a whirring sound, and at the side of the plinth, which caught the overflowing water for recycling, a slot emerged with a Green chip with a number 1 printed on it. He could only retrieve it by picking it up using his thumb and forefinger. As he did so, it glowed green in his grip. He also noted that the slot glowed green as if it was happy to deliver the One Green Credit File to him. A young teenage boy waited behind Brady - wanting to use the fountain.

Brady moved aside. 'Does this give you free money every time you take a drink?'

'You're funny, mister. It assesses how much you drank already. It read you when you took the Greenback. When it re-assesses that you need rehydrating, and you've chosen an eco-method of replenishment, then it will issue another, as a thank you from Mother Earth.'

'The locals call these Files, Greenbacks?'

'The kids do. My history teacher says this slang originated from more than two centuries ago when the commoners called their paper dollars Greenbacks.'

'What do you kids do for fun now? Y'know, now there's no Internet?'

'It hasn't been down for long.'

'Do you think they will get it back up and running?'

'I don't know. There's no way of communicating with anyone. I lost my friends in the UK to it first, and then we went down. My Dad says it will never recover - he says it's completely destroyed. He used to work in Cupertino. He knows about this stuff.'
'So, what are you going to do?'

The kid looked around. 'When the weather is good, we ride our GreenBikes™ and hang out down the park.'

Brady was determined to pick up intel on what the future markets could be. 'What do you miss doing?'

'Hologames. 3DI…'

'I heard of 3D Immersive games.'

The kid said, 'You haven't heard of Hologames?'

'I'm guessing it's to do with Holographs, Holograms, whatever.' Brady wasn't in the mood for taking grief from a kid. 'What about music, movies, TV, y'know, things like that?'

'Who's gonna do that if they ain't being paid? All the streamers are down - and out. They were all falling foul of the GreenRevs anyway. Love songs are binary - even World Music reinforced stereotypes. There's only the GreenRevs TV station left, and that is showing the Trad riots.'

'Trad riots?'

'The Traditionalists, the Non-Greens. They are outside the Green Safety Zones. It's great fun watching them loot, riot and fight each other over stuff that ain't gonna work no more. I saw this guy stagger out into the street carrying this massive TV - I wish I could see his face when he plugs it in and can only find one channel still going. It will be even funnier if he hasn't had an old-fashioned aerial installed to receive it!' He laughed, and Brady remembered what it was like at this kid's age. He would have found it funny as well.

Brady wandered over to the GreenGrocers™. He was going to see what One Greenback could buy him. Maybe, he could buy a bag and then steal whatever he needed. Brady went inside. He wasn't inspired. It was full of fruit, vegetables, and most of it proudly *locally sourced.* There were health foods and other essentials. But what there wasn't, was a sales assistant. He went to the pay station and picked up a biodegradable rice bag. He was alone in the store at the moment. He checked for CCTV. He couldn't see any, but he couldn't be sure - they had become tiny over the years. He decided to move quickly before another customer came into the store. He loaded his bag with snacks, drinks, and some assorted fruit and then made his getaway. As he tried to leave, he found he couldn't. He tried again, and his foot stuck at the edge of the doorway.

A robotic female voice said. *This is NanoSecurityFilm™, a trademark of Sattva Systems™. You appear to have forgotten to pay for your goods and services. Please return to the Pay Station to complete your purchase. Have a wonderful Green Day and thank you for saving Mother Earth.*

Brady angrily threw the shopping across the floor, and it scattered across a wide area, with apples and pears rolling away, some under the shop fixtures. He then strode angrily to the exit but was stopped again.

This is NanoSecurityFilm™, a trademark of Sattva Systems™. You appear to have forgotten to pay for your goods and services. Please return to the Pay Station to complete your purchase. This is the second helpful message. If you have changed your mind, then please return all goods to their original place of sale, and ensure they are in the same condition as when you selected them. Consideration of other customers is paramount to us here at your friendly and local GreenGrocers™.

Brady considered destroying the place with his bare hands. For a moment, he wondered if there was another exit out the back. But he was already convinced that these Green bastards would have thought about that. He gathered up the stuff on the floor, checked for damage, and placed them back on the shelves. Then he got down on his hands and knees and searched under the fittings. He retrieved the pears, rubbed them over with his biodegradable rice bag and placed them carefully back onto the display. He then retrieved the apples. One was just out of reach, so he had to lie on the floor to make his fingertips reach the edge of it. He struggled to tickle it into a position where he could grab it. 'You, absolute bastard piece of shit!' Finally, he flicked it against the back wall under the fixtures, and it bounced back far enough for him to take hold of it.

He slid back on the polished floor and stood up, holding his prize. He examined it. He noticed the bruising on the apple's skin. He went to the apple display and placed it into the array of fresh apples with the bruised side hidden.

He put the bag back on the pay station and went to leave.

This is NanoSecurityFilm™, a trademark of Sattva Systems™. You appear to have forgotten to pay for your goods and services. Please return to the Pay Station to complete your purchase. This is the third helpful message. If you have changed your mind, then please return all goods to their original place of sale, and ensure they are in the same condition as when you selected them. You need to pay for one damaged apple. Please deposit One File at the Pay Station. Consideration of other customers is paramount to us here at your friendly and local GreenGrocers™.

Brady screamed, 'Aaargh!' He remembered his One Green File, and he marched to the Pay Station. He put the File into the slot. The Pay Station said, in a male voice this time.

This is your NanoPayStation™, a trademark of Sattva Systems™. Your biological readings suggest you are at an elevated stress level and might be under pressure to deposit your File. This is a polite customer notice. Please be aware that one biodegradable bag has been removed and not paid for. Please return when you are willingly able to deposit your payments. Thank you for shopping with GreenGrocers™.

Brady knew it wouldn't work, but he was blazing. He charged toward the door, wondering if his power and bulk would punch a hole in the film. It didn't work. The NanoSecurityFilm™ enwrapped him, it even made him stand up straight and pushed his arms down his side and held him there, like a human statue.

This is NanoSecurityFilm™, a trademark of Sattva Systems™. You appear to have not understood our helpful messages intended to help you improve your shopping experience. Please wait until one of our representatives comes to assist you. Your custom is always our highest priority with your friendly and local GreenGrocers™.

4.ON DISPLAY

Brady had to endure the strange looks of other customers as they came and went. Some avoided looking at him. A father and young daughter were the first to openly discuss the Brady exhibit. The girl, a precocious child of about eight years old, asked her Daddy, 'Why is that man standing there?'

'That's what happens when you do bad things,' he said, 'He was probably stealing the food.'

'Shouldn't somebody call the police? I mean, he looks scary.'

'Don't worry, sweetheart. He can't hurt you. We shouldn't need the police anymore. Not here. This is a place of hearts and minds.'

The girl teased her Daddy, 'You used a binary term of endearment. You said, sweetheart. The teachers say we shouldn't use them anymore. Will you be trapped like the naughty man?'

He ruffled her hair and laughed, 'I think that wouldn't register on any level of criminality, but you're right, us older folks have still got a lot to learn. Now come on, let's pick up the food.'

Brady wondered which was worse, the public shaming or having to listen to, over and over again, the Pay Station thanking every shopper for their custom, followed by the doors thanking them for their honesty and wishing them a nice day.

A couple of bored teenagers, a boy and a girl, toyed with him for a while. As she stroked Brady's frame, the girl informed her male friend, 'He's quite a specimen - look at that physique. Are you sure he can't hear or see me?'

'He's in stasis. It happened to the Crow when he tried to burn down the school. He was stuck like that for hours until the caretaker found him. He still had the petrol can in his hand. And the NanoSecurityFilm™ had even sealed the petrol that had spilt from his can.'

'I heard about an attempted arson. What happened to him?'

'He was expelled from the community and sent to some members of his Trad Family on the outside. Apparently, if they didn't take him, then he would have to fend for himself. No second chances.'

Brady couldn't feel the girl stroking his arm. 'Look, his tattoos are fading.' This news alarmed Brady, but he couldn't move his eyes enough to look down. The boy moved in closer, 'But not all of them.'

'Why is that do you think?'

'I think it's cleaning out the synthetic materials.' He jabbed his fingers into Brady's arm, 'These look like traditional tatts - they are probably made with natural plant dyes.'

'Do you think he can feel me touching him?'

The youth traced his hands up through Brady's inner thigh, but then a voice announced:

This is NanoRespect™, a trademark of Sattva Systems™. A sexual act without the permission of the potential survivor has been detected. Please refrain. This is your first warning. The welfare of our consumers is our highest priority.

She laughed, 'You might get a File Note and fine for that.'

Brady had enough lateral vision to watch them leave the store hurriedly but laughing together. He fretted about his fading tattoos. *I paid a fucking fortune for them. It's part of who I am. They've no right to remove them from me.* He was then left again with the shoppers and the Sattva Systems™ announcements.

He caught snippets of conversations, an elderly couple complaining about machines talking to them, instead of being served by humans. He whole-heartedly agreed with that sentiment. He also heard a large group of eco-warrior types complaining about why they need technology of any description anymore until they listened to the warning of increased stress levels detected, asking them *if they were feeling ok*, followed by a *thank you for being a part of our Green Journey.* They hushed to whispers and completed their shopping, but he could tell, as they passed him on the way out, they weren't as happy about the situation as they should have been.

No pleasing some - they got the whole damn world, and it's still not enough. Spoilt fucking brats.

He wondered whether the Nano-Fucking-Whatevers would be picking up his own stress levels. He guessed he'd been here for about four hours. *I should be tiring, but I don't feel it.* He checked himself over, in his mind, wandering over every inch of his body. *I think, if anything, I'm feeling better than before.* He remembered the bit about the travellers and the planes and the disputed health benefits. *If I ever see Pops again, then I'll tell him about this.* However, this thought embarrassed him. *Getting caught in a heist is manly and something to be proud of - a badge of honour. This is pathetic - caught stealing groceries.*

Suddenly he heard a lot of noise from outside of the shop. He couldn't see, but he could hear it from further down the High Street. He heard slamming vehicle doors, and then it sounded like a riot had broken out. He couldn't make out clearly what they were shouting. There wasn't any coherent chanting like there would be at a demonstration. This was more like a round-up. He picked up snippets of angry voices. 'Fucking get your hands off me. You've no right...I live here, you sonofabitch...You can't make me leave...' The only responses from the Green side he could pick up on was the mention of, 'A Green Adjudication Panel will assess your claim...You are not Green...It is not a family membership deal...' He wondered why the clingfilm wasn't working on them. *Maybe I'm special.*

There was more slamming of van doors, and then Brady picked up on the demonstrators pounding from within the vehicle. This went on for about an hour before calm and then eerie silence descended - apart from the incessant robotic shop announcements. Brady began to wonder if he'd been forgotten about amid all the drama.

Brady was held in suspended animation for six hours when at last, somebody turned up and started talking to him as if she might free him from his GreenGrocers™

28

nightmare. She was a petite slender black woman, in her early twenties, he guessed. *I'll break her in half like a twig if I must.* Then he thought better of it. *If they have this level of security for a fucking bruised apple…*

'Hi there. I'm Lizzie. I'll Unfilm you, but you'll have to be assessed by the Disciple. I'm not convinced you are one of us, but we don't judge people on their appearances. The Disciple will decide if you are eligible to stay here or whether you belong in the Trad world.'

Brady tried to answer but couldn't move.

'All you need to do now is bring your anger and stress levels under control, and the Film will leave you and return for recycling.'
She waited patiently. Brady was still dwelling on the lost investment of his tattoos. The Pay Station and the Exit were making their Sattva Systems™ announcements for the hundredth time. It was not conducive to bringing Brady to a calm state. A dog caught his eye, a mangy old mutt to most people, but Brady thought it might help him calm his fraught emotional state if he imagined sketching it. He pictured a fresh sheet of paper and a stick of charcoal, and he began to draw, starting with the eyes. Within a minute, he noticed the weight being retaken by his feet as he was placed back on the ground. He wondered at the strength of the SecurityFilm™ - as he now assessed that he had been held a few inches above the ground the whole time. He had a tingling sensation as he sensed the Film was leaving his body. He couldn't explain how he knew, but he intuited that it departed from within him, and not just layers on his skin.

Lizzie smiled, 'Much better. Welcome back.'

'Am I under arrest?'

'No. We haven't got a suitable or humane place to detain you. Only people who want to be here, in the spirit of saving Her, can stay. Those who don't - simply have to go and make their way in the old world.'

'Great. Then I'll be off then. I don't want to be here a minute longer than necessary. Bye.'

He went to walk out of the exit when he was stopped - again.

This is NanoSecurityFilm™, a trademark of Sattva Systems™. Your shopping indiscretions have not been rescinded by the Disciple of your community. The Nano-Markers™ in your system need to be assessed before you can travel freely within the Green Community. Have a happy and Green Day.

Lizzie smiled, 'We won't hurt you. We haven't harmed you - have we? We just need to follow the protocol. Please, walk with me. This won't take long, and then you can go on your way.'

Brady felt like he was with a parole officer. *There must be some way to fool that SecurityFilm™ stuff.* 'I suppose if I had been in a vehicle or a confined space then that thing couldn't have got to me. Is it just a shop security system?'

She knew he was pumping her for information, and he wasn't particularly subtle about it. 'The Film is made up of the finest, tiniest NanoBots™ imaginable. If you were in a vehicle, they would secure the entire vehicle - if you were driving. On the other hand, if you were a passenger threatening the driver, they would seep into the vehicle almost instantaneously and secure you - the Security Protocols™ would track the vehicle. There is no escape because there is nothing small enough to prevent the Security Protocols™ from entering and securing the transgressor.'

Brady knew she was right. *There's no escaping these Security Protocols™ Machines.* He related it to being in jail, and the period after exploring all means of escape - and concluding that there weren't any - and then the acceptance that followed. 'Ok, how did they know to attack me?'

'The Security Protocols™ didn't attack you. They don't spy on you. They are here for everybody's safety and mental wellbeing.' She looked at him and could see him attempting to work out the puzzle. She wasn't sure if he could understand scientific rationales but tried to enlighten him. If she could convince him, then he would be less of a problem to West McFarland in the long run, 'It detects signals in movements, signals given off in the air, hormones and pheromones. After millions of experimental trials and decades of research, they can spot signals that the human body emits. If you even thought about harming someone, even an animal, the Security Protocols™ would pick up the signal before you even had the time to act on this impulse.'

Brady considered Lizzie's explanation and what it meant to his predicament as they walked.

He knew they were heading south. It brought back a lot of memories. They passed the High School, where he learned how to be a gang member. As they ventured further southwards he looked, with a mixture of pride and regret, at the places where he graduated, the Central Valley Modified Community Correctional Facility and the Golden State Correctional Facilities. He laughed when he thought about them completing a new build, just for him to live in later, the Ridgecrest Supermax Prison.

Lizzie watched him chuckle to himself as he passed the Correctional Facilities.

He pointed at the buildings. 'What did you do with the inmates?'

'We let them go.'

'Surely, they created mayhem before they left?'

'We gave them a demonstration of our SecurityFilm™ and said if they left the city limits immediately, then we wouldn't come looking for them. They chose freedom.'

'And the Supermax?'

'The prison officers had their own ideas about what should happen to hardened criminals. They acted before we could - unfortunately.'

'This SecurityFilm™. Is it well known, y'know, what it can do?'

'Sattva Systems™ and the GreenRevs, have been preparing for the Revolution for decades - some developments were held back until the Glorious Green Day arrived. They thought we were conspiracy theorists and a cult, but we had trillions of dollars backing our cause. Sattva Systems™ had to play their games - to look like any other greedy Corp - even we had doubts, but Bodhi's love for Her was beyond doubt, and now that love has been realised. We are the Green Revolution, the GreenRevs, and the hundred-year plan has begun.'

30

He rolled his eyes. 'Good luck with that.'

She ignored his sarcasm. 'We are nearly there.' He saw a modern structure - he didn't have to guess that it would be environmentally friendly, and eco this and that. They entered the compound, and banners lined the pathway: *Welcome to your New Green Town Hall.*

A man in a robe left the hall and came out to meet them. He had crystal clear green eyes, his bare feet glided across the dusty path, and the Sun seemed to glow around him. *Fuck. This guy has really got the Jesus look nailed down.* He laughed at his own unintended pun. *I see how this is gonna go. He's going to try and sell me his magic potions. I've seen these con artists do their tricks a thousand times already. Well, Brady Mahone ain't goin' to fall for this crock of shit.*

The Jesus figure gasped at the sight of Brady. He inspected his tattoos. 'My God.'

'Cain - what is it?' Cain flashed Lizzie a look which she took to mean as later. He called out, 'Hey, Siddha.' A slender Asian man came over. Brady looked around. He hadn't noticed before that all the people here seemed to be of slim build. *Must be all the vegan shit they eat that makes 'em all so scrawny.*

'Siddha, I want you to look after our guest for a short while. Get him food, drink or whatever else he needs.'

Siddha turned and said sarcastically, 'And what do you require, sir?'

'The name's Brady, no need for all the phony pleasantries. I need the bathroom.'

'Of course - Brady. If you'd care to follow me.'

Cain watched Brady follow Siddha and waited until he was inside the Town Hall. He whispered to Lizzie, 'What do we know about him? I notice he has a Satt™.'

'He shouldn't be here for starters. Mrs Wilson said that he saved her from some troublesome youths on the wrong side of the Shell™.'

'And why was she there?'

'They were throwing rocks at her car - she forgot that she was safe. She panicked and veered off the road - there is a lot of last-minute travel before the old vehicles stop working. They tried to attack her, but Brady intervened. The problem is that he managed to go through the SecurityFilm™ as if it wasn't there.'

'He must be Green, then?'

'I don't think so. He had no Green Credits. He attempted to steal from the Green-Grocers™ - but there, all the SecurityFilms™ and Protocols™ worked perfectly. Unless the NanoShell™ let him in because he saved Mrs Wilson?'

Cain thought for a moment, 'No. It isn't that. It doesn't work that way.'

'What do you think?'

'I'm going to contact Sissy or Bodhi with this. It's important. I just can't figure out why.'

Lizzie gasped, 'You know Bodhi!'

'I've had dealings through an intermediary for years, but I have never been in direct contact with him. Our business had to be conducted in the utmost secrecy.'

'But you are a Disciple; therefore, you must have been granted an audience for him to bestow the status upon you.'

'I didn't meet him individually. I was one of an audience of more than a thousand Initiates - and there were thousands of these Green Initiations. I am a Disciple, but that is not unusual. One day, we will all be Disciples. All I have that marks me out as different from the other townsfolk is that I receive the next version of NanoSuit™ ahead of them. I am in line for Orange™, whereas they will all - very soon - be given a chance to buy the Red™. I am not a chosen one - I am simply an early one.'

Lizzie was a believer but still found his quasi-religious demeanour a little pompous at times. Still, he had access to the future plans of Sattva Systems™, which nobody else in McFarland had. *And what we have achieved already has been pretty fucking awesome.* 'So, you've seen Bodhi. What was he like, y'know, in the flesh, like?'

Cain looked at her with his crystal green eyes. 'He looked remarkably like this man who calls himself Brady.'

'It can't be him. This Brady creature is a Trad-Alpha-Male. He's exactly the kind of man we would have been afraid of - before the Green Revolution.'

'Bodhi did say we would be tested. There were always going to be anomalies in the implementation phase, and he said we would have to watch, learn and report back.'

'Is that what you are going to do?'

'Yes. I want you to talk with Brady and find out more about what he wants from me - us. Bring him along to the Town Hall meeting later this evening. In the meantime, I'll Satt™ someone at Sattva Systems™ about this development. You never know - even Bodhi himself might want to discuss this with me.'

'Wow, holy shit! Can you imagine? He's like the King of the World right now.'
'He is just one step ahead of the Disciples at the moment. He has developed and taken the Yellow™. He has promised that by the end of the one-hundred-year plan, Bodhi will have no more power or Green Credits than any other man, woman, or child. We will have saved Her, and we will live out our lives serving Her. He is only a guide.' He paused, 'Is there anything else I should know?'

'He says his full name is Brady Mahone, and there was another weird thing - his synthetic tattoos were erased exceptionally quickly. As you know, it usually takes weeks. He had natural tattoos which were completely unaffected.'

'You used to have tattoos. You are more of an expert on this than I am.'

'They are the sort which Readers - spiritual tattooists' design. They read the receiver and then decide upon designs which will protect or guide the recipient.'

5.TOWN HALL MEETING

Brady made the most of Lizzie's hospitality during the afternoon. He ate a lot of fruit but gave the vegetables, beans, and rice a miss. 'I'm not into all this rabbit food nonsense,' he had informed her, as politely as he could muster under the circumstances. He enjoyed the ice-cream though, as long as he didn't ask what was in it. As they chatted, Brady assumed they knew everything about him, but still gave absolutely nothing away - he could spot a good-cop interrogation from a mile away.

He asked her about the meeting, as they watched the volunteers placing out the chairs. 'How many are coming tonight?'

'We are preparing for twelve thousand - should everyone decide to attend.'

'The population of McFarland is bigger than that, isn't it?'

'The West Side of Highway 99 took the Green Incentives in the fifties. Those who didn't like the culture slowly moved over to the Traditional East as the decades moved by. They thought they were wealthier because of their accumulation of material goods. It sped up the migration when in the last few years, the West Side began to reduce its reliance on the Internet. We operated on slow speeds to aid the withdrawal symptoms. That was tough, but worth it in the end. They had their chance to do it our way - now they can have the Wild West – or rather, East - they always pined for.'

But Brady had travelled West from Ridgecrest. He knew he shouldn't have been able to be here at all - if all Lizzie was saying was true.

She continued her spiel as though giving him a guided tour. 'This was the blueprint for most towns and cities across the globe. The powers that be saw communities that were impeccably behaved towns, which used up very little of the local resources, and were becoming less reliant on the Internet - as a curiosity but ultimately harmless. Better still, as this was happening all over the world, the problems created by climate change receded dramatically, saving them billions in the currencies. What's not to love?'

Brady didn't take the bait. He would let them complete their investigations on him, and only return when he had figured out a way to make it pay.

'Do you want to give them a hand with the chairs?' she said. 'It'll keep you busy.'

'What's the pay?'

'Nothing. Except for the warm glow of knowing that you helped our community.'

'Yeah, all the same darling - I think I'll pass.'

She thought for a moment. It wouldn't do any harm to test him out. 'There are a few broken wooden chairs where the legs have come out of their sockets. With a bit of brute force and natural glue, you could probably fix them.'

He looked disdainfully at the sad-looking chairs beyond the stage area, near the fire exit. *I could escape, I suppose - but I could gain some valuable intel if I stick around.*

'I could give you two Green Credits for your contribution to our community.'

'Ok. Deal.' *It won't hurt to have some currency, and two Greenbacks would have got me out of the shop bind.*

He wandered over to the broken chairs. He spotted the store cupboard and found some wood glue. He saw craft tools but decided against trying to steal any of them. He'd had enough excitement for one day. He sat cross-legged on the floor and put glue into the round holes. He did need a firm grip to generate enough force to jam the legs into the holes.

Just as he'd finished Lizzie returned. *This is no coincidence – she must have had me watched.* Still, he gave nothing away. 'All done. They should last for years.'

She examined them and nodded. She closed her right hand, then looked into his eyes. She then closed her eyes as if she had gone into a momentary trance. When she opened her eyes again, she opened her right hand and revealed a Two Green File chip, which Brady thought looked like one of those old-fashioned SD cards. She put it between her thumb and forefinger, and it glowed green. Brady took it off her, with his big fingers struggling to grasp the part of the File left showing. As he did, it glowed once more.

'I give this *freely* to you, for a job well done.' She smiled mischievously. 'This can only be given or redeemed by another Green Community Member - it has no value to Trads or outsiders, but you already know that - don't you?'

'Of course,' he lied. 'Everybody knows that.' He made his ignorance evident to her when he asked, 'It doesn't have to be used in this community though - does it?'

'No. It can be used in any Green Community - anywhere on Mother Earth.'

Brady put his Two Greenbacks in his pocket. 'Here, I'll get you a Distor™,' Lizzie said, wanting to laugh at his incomprehension. 'It stands for Dispenser and Storage. It will keep your Green Credits from being damaged. It keeps a tally for you.' She added, jokingly, 'Don't worry, they are free of charge.' She briefly went into the storage cupboard and returned with a small tube and handed it to Brady. 'Don't be concerned about its small size. You can transfer small change to larger File amounts as you attain more.'

He held it and then dropped his Files into it. 'Hold the top of the tube with your thumb and forefinger,' she said. When he did, a luminous green display stated: TWO GREEN CREDITS. *They put the fucking Green word on everything. It's fucking brainwashing, that's what this is.*

'Great. Thanks. I'll have fun spending them.'

She laughed and took his hand. 'The Meeting will be starting soon. I'll show you to your seat. You'll be at the back, as you seem a little unsure of how things work around here. Plus, we want our audience to be as relaxed as possible, and you are a bit intimidating - if you don't mind me saying…'

'Fine with me. What happens afterwards?'

'Cain wants to have a chat with you. He wants to know more about you. I'm going to organise a place for you to stay overnight, and tomorrow, you can do whatever you want to do.'

'You mean I can leave if I want?'

'Of course. But if you want to stay, I think you might need help assimilating into our way of life.'

Fuck that, he thought. *This isn't how I want to live my life. I'm not changing one prison for another.*

She showed him to his seat and then rushed off as though she had a lot to do - or organise. Brady sat back, putting his feet on the back of the chair in front of him. *It's not like there's anybody sittin' there yet.* He looked around at the very ordinary-looking people slowly filling the hall. There were no reservations, so it was hardly surprising that no-one sat anywhere near Brady. For something to do, he checked off in his mind the odd person he recognised in the crowds. The old man, Gus, smiled at him, but mostly, anyone who had seen Brady earlier pretended not to notice him. Siddha beamed at him beatifically, and Brady smiled back at him sarcastically. *I know a snitch when I see one.*

The lights dimmed a little, and a few test shots lit up the big screen and the few smaller screens that surrounded the audience. They were followed by a few sound tests, as each individual set of speakers were checked. *They obviously want everybody to get the message.* Then the lights went back up. It was 7:50 pm. Brady looked in the direction of the projectionist. *I know him. I did time with him at Juvie.* He unhooked his legs from the chair in front and pulled himself to his full imposing height and walked over to the scrawny white guy who operated the projector. Brady stuck out his big hand. 'Hey man, I'm Brady - remember me?'

The fear in his eyes told Brady that he did, even before he could answer. 'Yeah,' he said, extending a nervous hand in return. 'Vance. Uhhh, look. I've been going straight for five years now. I don't want no trouble, and the movie will be starting soon. So, you can see I'm…'

'Hey, calm down, man. I just want to ask you a few things.' Brady didn't want to make friends with this low-life – a mugger, if he remembered right - and he was aware he would have to get to the point. 'What do people want around here that the regime doesn't allow them?'

'It's early days sir…err, Mister…too soon to tell.'

He moved in menacingly. 'Well, give me an idea.'

'If you stress me out, I might not be allowed to operate the projector - you must know how the SecurityFilm™ works.'

Brady did, all too well. He backed off - a little. 'Look, Vance, quit acting like a baby and just help a brother out here.'

Vance looked around, to see if anyone was watching, but the crowds had their eyes trained onto the stage area - waiting for the show to begin. 'I only know what I deal with.'

Brady picked up a blank black file and examined it.

Vance gulped and said, 'People are already missing the pre-crash stuff - the kind of things that will be banned here. Things that could be put on those, the Information Files.' He looked at the clock. He couldn't be late, and he had his final checks to carry out. 'Sattva made these files in the last few years. The general public wasn't that interested because everything was streamed. I now know, of course, that Sattva had transferred millions of acceptable items from the Internet to use in this environment.'

'Like what, exactly?'

'Stuff for educating the kids. Lots of scientific things and approved entertainments.' 'And it's all boring, and some of these whining Greens still want a drop of the good stuff - ain't that right.'

'Yes - yes. They are worried that the kids will get bored once the novelty of the Revolution wears off...'

'And you can supply them?'

'Not from in here. They should have old machines on the outside for manufacturing the Bootleg Files. I'm an Inner, you see. If you have a non-approved criminal record, but have proved your Green credentials, then you can remain, but I'm not allowed to come and go out of the Community Perimeter.'

'What's an approved criminal record?'

'Political activism - arrested at demonstrations, hacking for the cause...'

'Ok. Let's cut to the chase. If I could get this stuff, would it be worth my while?'

'Yes. People here would give a lot of Green Credits for high-quality Bootlegs. I could be your middleman,' he added, weakly.

'Yeah, sure - so you could rip me off. You'd buy them from me, and re-sell them for a fortune, or maybe you'd pirate them and start your own business – right?'

'No. Not at all. The Green Credit system won't allow it. It works on a system of give and receive. A purchased Black File turns to Green when the transaction is completed between you and your buyer. The newly formed File can only be used by the person who bought it from you. The only Files allowed to be replicated and passed on are the Green Community Information Films.'

'So, what's in it for you?'

'I thought you could pay me in stock. Y'know, you could give me a spare copy for my own use. I love old movies, that's why I've taken this role to earn my own Green Credits. It's that or farm labouring, working on the Highways or Operation Clean-up - this is a dream job compared to that.'

Brady frowned, 'I've had that SecurityFilm™ attack me. Is this legal enough for me to get away with this kind of activity?'

'Yes. As a culture, our community was generally against manufacturing. I say, generally, because there was a lot of things that they took a pragmatic approach with. There were pockets of physical software around - very little, to be fair - but it did enable people to trade, and there was no blowback from the Security Protocols™. It didn't even issue any warnings.'

Brady placed a big hand on Vance's shoulder and smiled, though there was still a hint of a threat in his eyes. 'Write down your address - and if I track down some of this stuff, I'll come find you.'

Vance wrote his address in his notebook and ripped the page out and gave it to Brady. 'It's a warzone out there – I mean, so I've been told - and only the conspiracy freaks were into this stuff. It was old-fashioned tech, but some wanted to keep their stuff off-grid - especially the more disturbing entertainments, shall we say. They'll be hard to track down and they won't trust you - they're paranoid.'

'That's my problem, not yours.' *It's one thing getting to be a Green Credit millionaire,* he thought, *but what the fuck have they got here to spend it on?*

'Hey man. If ya don't mind me asking? How did you get in here?'

'Just lucky, I guess.' Brady looked up and spotted Siddha coming toward them. He said, 'Is everything ok, Vance?'

'Yes, Siddha. Everything's workin' just fine.'

Siddha looked at both of them, and asked, 'Do you two know each other?'

Brady smiled broadly. 'I was just checking out his equipment. I was getting a bit bored, sitting all on my lonesome.'

Vance held out his hand and offered Brady a Blank File. 'Here, take this as a souvenir.'

Siddha watched closely as Brady took it. It didn't turn green. 'It's not a Green File,' Vance said. 'It isn't part of the system, until it's activated. You're going to need a lot of these.'
'Can old used or pre-recorded Files be overwritten?'
'Not here, but they should be in the Trad world.'
'Thanks, man.'

Brady returned to a seat. Other people had taken his, and the ones nearby. He didn't need to check, but he knew Siddha would be keeping a close eye on him from now on. He wasn't happy. He felt hemmed in by the people around him, and his seat was too small for his frame. He shuffled and fidgeted. He knew he was annoying the people around him, but also knew they wouldn't have the nerve to challenge him.

The lights went down, and the Jesus-like figure of Cain glided across to the centre of the stage. A spotlight picked him out, and he spoke gently into the tiny microphone affixed to his white robe.

'Welcome - all of you. Welcome to the Green Community of McFarland, California in the United States of America, and now a member of the Green World Alliance. Over the next few days, there will be meetings, just like this, to introduce the New Green Deal for Mother Earth. Our goal is to repair the damage to the planet caused by toxic humanity over more than two hundred years in the false name of progress. We are not a backwards-looking society. We are a future-forward society - and this is just the beginning.'

The front rows of the audience stood up and clapped and cheered. Brady guessed these were the activists of the GreenRevs. Brady observed the audience he could see in the semi-darkness.

I notice the liberal lefties aren't quite as enthusiastic. They just want to know what's in it for them - same as it ever was.

Cain continued with his quiet but authoritative speech. He was preaching from the pulpit to his Green believers. 'We will be implementing the cutting-edge technologies which have been available for the last fifty years but weren't utilised because governments took the bribes of the dirty businesses and corporations to suppress the Green developments. They left us no choice but to ruin them and do things our way. The right way.'

Brady wondered whether everybody here knew they were going to lose everything they owned. He could tell by the clothes they were wearing that they weren't poor. *They musta really believed in this shit - and fair-play to them, they backed the winners. I could do with finding out what made them so sure to bet that big.*

'We are going to show you a movie from our partners at Sattva Systems™,' Cain announced, 'and afterwards we will have a Q & A.' He nodded toward Vance, and the lights went down. The screens in front of, and around, the audience flickered into life. Brady spotted Vance load the Black File into the side of the old-tech projector.

'Sattva Systems™ have always dedicated ourselves to leading-edge...' Brady showed some interest in the action sequences at the start of the movie. There were scenes from all over the world - of governments using every kind of military, chemical and biological interventions to try and rid themselves of the GreenRevs, but they were impervious to all attacks. *I thought the guy on the TV had been hit in the face by a bullet*, he thought. *But he didn't even seem to notice.* The audience only gasped when one government started to threaten to kill the children they had put in place as human shields - and there were tears when that threat was carried out - but it didn't deter the GreenRevs. There was a map of the world, showing all the countries changing from the pink and blues - to Green.

The film lost Brady, though, when they began the tour of the labs at Sattva Systems™. He didn't often sleep, but if there was one thing that could do it, it was being sent back to school.

The NanoTech™ Division pioneered the purification and filtration systems which could prevent and protect any attacks on the water delivery into your Green Communities...Exotic properties...vaccine delivery...Diamonoid shell...
Brady began to doze off while the jargon fell into white noise at the edge of his senses. Nanoscopic level...quantum effects...analyse electrons with colliding photons...frequency of light.

He had leaned back in his chair, and he awoke with a start as it was just about to tip over. The people he could see around him looked like they were in a trance. *I can't say I find this particularly fascinating*, he thought. 'Einstein's photo-electron effect where direction, speed and energy...' Brady mocked the narrator out loud in a whiny voice. 'Einstein's photo-electron effect where direction, speed and...' He heard a woman shush at him. 'Fuck you, Lady Know-it-all.'

Still, Brady did quieten down. Typically, somebody would laugh with him, if he had said something like this in a cinema - but not here. *I also don't want any more of that fucking SecurityFilm™ on me*, he thought. *I suppose that means that Brady gotta be good and stay out of trouble.*

He endured more of the Sattva Systems™ propaganda. Superconducting cube levitation…magnetic train…target individual cells…self-replicating cells…life enhancement.

Brady missed the movie ending, his mind having wandered. He noticed the audience around him, clapping politely, and the cheering from the distant front-of stage dwellers. And then the lights went up. Cain returned to the stage to take questions. There were a number of fear-based questions. What if they try to attack our communities? What if they try to steal our Green Credits? What do we do if we get sick? Cain reassured them - they had thought of everything. He repeatedly referred his questioners back to a portion of the movie, to explain in technical detail, how the NanoTech worked to protect them.

A girl of about nine-years-old asked 'Will the animals in Africa be protected?'

Cain beamed. 'What a marvellous question. I'll tell you the truth. Our Nano-Shells™, like the one which protects our community of McFarland, have been activated around Nature Reserves and National parks all over the world and especially in Africa. Our GreenRev explorers installed them - it took twelve years to complete. There is a short-term issue, and that is with the poachers who are still inside the perimeter. This means, some animals will die, but as the poachers leave the perimeter then they won't be able to get back in. Only those with the Green Credentials and Green Credits will ever be allowed to go into this land.' He looked up from the girl to address the whole audience. 'This thinking is at the heart of everything we do.'

An old woman asked cynically, 'Who out of all of us here will benefit most from this revolution? You look like you are doing ok from this - being our self-appointed leader and all.'

'You raise a valid point - and one in which I will answer fully.'

This I gotta hear, Brady thought.

'We are progressing through the Nanowear™ Colours. I will always be one colour ahead of you, but at the end of the process, we will all - each and every one of you - will all be on the same highest level, and all at the same time. We will all be equal.'

'That's all well and good,' the old woman said. 'But how long before this dream comes true? I haven't got long left in this world. Not that I'm ungrateful. I've lived to see this day - but what about my children and grandchildren?'

'Gloria – is it Gloria?' She nodded. 'Even your InfraRedPrimer™ NanoWear™ will give you some limited life-preserving and life-enhancing properties. Could I be so bold as to enquire about your age? It is so hard to tell with the effects of Nano-Wear™?'

'I am eighty-four.'

I woulda guessed around sixty, Brady thought.

'You should comfortably go beyond one-hundred years old,' Cain said, 'but you

39

might only attain the Orange™ by that time - which is where Bodhi Sattva is now. Put another way, you could reach the levels of the Leader of Sattva Systems™ within twenty years. Bodhi only experiments with new developments on his own body first. He does not agree with animal or human trials. He considers this deeply unethical. When he is satisfied that the latest developments are safe, and working as they should be, then he moves all the Disciples up to his previous level, and then you all will move up a level.'

He peered intently into Gloria's eyes. 'Alas, you may not see the end - but after many more years of a healthy and active life, I'm hoping you will see just how wonderful the future will look for your family.'

An audience member shouted, 'What will we need to do? How much will the next level cost?'

'You are InfraRed™, and I am Red™,' Cain laughed. 'What I have is the NanoArmour™ you saw in the movie. All the activists received this, like so many of my comrades down in the front rows.' Again, more cheers. 'You will all have to earn one-hundred Green Credits. You earn these with your environmental good works - this helps Mother Earth. Some of you good people have already acquired this amount from before today, but you cannot buy the RedNanoWear™ early. We don't want a society of haves and have-nots. You all have to have the Green Credits earned and then use them. When you have the Red™, you will be safe to travel anywhere, even in the lands left to the Trads. They will be unable to harm you.'

Now, I know what to get those Green Credits for, Brady thought. *I gotta have me one of those Suits™.*

'And after, you can all save up for the Orange™. I can't give you the details but trust me - you are all going to want that. It's amazing.'

6.CLOSE CALL

After the meeting had finished, Brady searched out Lizzie. He needed some action and thought he might be able to persuade her to join him for the evening. When he found her, he started helping the nearby volunteers to stack away the thousands of chairs. He didn't need to know why they were doing this or what they were going to use the space for. *This will impress Lizzie – women like her like a strong, helpful guy.* He looked her up and down, watching the way she moved. *She keeps herself in good shape - I like that.* Lizzie sensed Brady was watching her, but her job was to keep an eye on him, so she wasn't overly concerned.

After showing off his power and strength - compared to the other volunteers - and not too subtly - he made his move. 'Interesting movie tonight.'

She smiled. 'I'm glad you thought so. I hope you learned a few things.' Even though you looked half-asleep through most of it - *you're not exactly the brightest star in the sky*, She thought.

I hope I don't have to pass a fucking exam to get in her pants, he thought. 'Yes, I did. This Nano stuff is everywhere. Is it watching us twenty-four-seven?'

'Of course not. We would need streaming for that, and that doesn't work anymore.'

He carried on stacking chairs, and Lizzie did the same next to him. He noticed that it seemed easy for her. 'So, how does it happen to be around at exactly the right time?'

'It monitors the physiology of all living things. It reacts if there are heightened neg-ative stress markers. There will come a time when it will work internally - this will be a leap in medical advancement. But it can already work, externally.'

'Like repairing sunburn.'

He does know something then, she thought. *I was beginning to wonder.*

'Somebody mentioned a place for me to stay tonight?' he said.

She knew where this was going. 'I believe Siddha is arranging your accommoda-tion.'

'Couldn't I stay at yours?'

'Well, you don't waste any time.' *I'll string him along first and see if he has any-thing interesting to offer,* she thought. *It could be a good opportunity for intel.* 'You can walk back with me when we've finished here. I live in the same house as Siddha and Cain. We'll see how we get along, first.'

As they walked back, Brady tried to be as charming as he could, although he let her do the talking. *These liberal-lefty girls love the sound of their own voices, which is fine by me, as I don't have a lot to say - and they are tricky, all too easy to say the wrong thing,* he thought, zoning out. *Keep nodding and smiling Brady-boy. She'll think you're one of those good listeners. Don't lose her now - she's wriggling on the line.*

'Nearly there now,' she said. 'Just a few hundred yards to go.'

He struggled to keep his self-control, but there was a question bothering him – and he needed an answer. 'Why are you living with Siddha and Cain? Don't you get your own place here?'

'In the Green Communities,' she said, 'there is no more property ownership. Technically, in the Trad areas, there shouldn't be, as all the electronic deeds have been wiped.'

'I know plenty of people that won't give up their homes that easily.'

'We're not concerned with them. They can fight over their petty possessions if they want to.'

They'll fight to the death over them, he thought. *But maybe that's the plan.* He knew he'd hinder his romantic prospects if he opened up the debate, so he asked, as calmly as he could, 'So, who owned the place you're staying in before...y'know?'

'It was Siddha's. We are happy for people to stay in their original homes because they are emotionally attached and connected to them, but now, they have to let others move in where they have spare bedrooms. It's environmentally sound, and they pick up extra Green Credits for their generosity.'

'Why would they willingly agree to do that? It just doesn't seem very... American.'

'Risk and reward. If the NanoWear™ develops as hoped - then the life expectancy of every Green Community dweller could double, or even triple - especially for today's and tomorrow's children.'

Brady never wanted kids, so this was an abstract concept for him, but he could understand the price to pay for decades more life was worth it.

When they arrived, the front door wasn't locked. He could see Siddha, Cain and about a dozen others in deep but seemingly informal conversation in the lounge as Lizzie led up the stairs. *Straight to the bedroom is an excellent sign*, he thought, *and I don't have to talk to the weirdos first.*

As soon as the bedroom door closed, he grabbed her, and kissed her and then they tumbled onto her bed. He half-expected to be covered in SecurityFilm™, but he wasn't. *I'm good to go.*

She began to hurriedly undress. Brady was hungry for her. She watched him take his T-shirt off. *This should be interesting*, she thought. *Fucking an alpha-male Trad. At least he's in good shape.*

'I haven't got any - y'know – protection,' Brady whispered.

She smiled. 'That's ok. I'm Filmed, and I'm Red™.'

'Will I notice it?'

'Only one way to find out.' She kissed him, and then they made love.

Later that evening, they made love again. Afterwards, Brady felt more tired than he could remember. He yawned. 'Sorry babe. I don't usually fall asleep.'

'I've heard that one before.'

'No, really. I hardly sleep at all, but since I've been in this place...'

'Lack of stress. You've probably spent your whole life looking over your shoulder for the next threat - but here, there aren't any.'

He didn't need to give this much thought. 'It's true - you're right. It's just a bit boring.'

'You're saying I'm boring?' she teased. She grabbed his cock, and it responded. 'I think you're answering in your own way.'

He flung her over and entered her hard. He had been reasonably restrained, out of something like politeness, before - but he might not see her again after tomorrow. *I'm going to take what I need,* he thought. *I'm going to have you the way I want. I'm going to fucking enjoy this.* He fucked her as hard as he possibly could, and he held her in a bear hug, squeezing her to the point of hurting her.

But she didn't struggle or even seemed to notice his power. He looked at her face. Her eyes were closed, and she was panting softly, gently moaning. She opened her eyes slowly and smiled, then closed them again. As he powered into her, his arms squeezed her with such force that any average woman would snap. He squeezed her until he was exhausted, and he climaxed for the last time that night.

He fell away from her, breathing hard. She kissed him on the cheek. 'I'm going to sleep now,' she said.

Within minutes, Brady fell into a deep sleep, too.

At around 3am, Brady stirred. He could hear noises. There was a ringing sound in the room, and in the distance, he could hear gunfire. In his sleepy state, he was confused. Lizzie woke up. 'It's your Satt™ phone,' she said, rubbing sleep from her eyes.

Brady hadn't received a call on it - Lucian had looked after the set-up. He retrieved it from within the pile of discarded clothes. It kept ringing until he figured out how to answer it. 'Hello - who is it?'

'It's me - Lucky. The Hodgson Boys are attacking us. Archie's holding 'em off with the old machine gun, but they've split up. We can't hold out for long - even with a weapon.'

'How many are them?' Brady heard Lucian shouting over the machine gun noise to Archie.

'Archie said there are the two boys. Their Daddy is disabled and can't get out of the house without their help - and one of them's got a wife and baby.'

'Ok. Hold them off. I'm coming over.'

'What is it?' Lizzie said.

'You could say it's Trad problems. I don't want that fucking SecurityFilm™ to stop me going to help my Foster Daddy. I'm finding it fucking hard to keep my stress levels down.'

'Get dressed, stay calm. I'll go and get Cain. He's the appointed one and can stop the NanoTriggers™ if he is with you.'

Brady took a deep breath and dressed calmly. *I guess stealing knives from here is out of the question*, he thought. *I'll have to pick them up at the ranch.*

Cain stood in the doorway looking like a vision from the Bible, with his robe, beard and crystal green eyes.

'Thank you, Cain,' Brady said. 'I owe you one - we gotta hurry.'

'Where are we going?'

'The Mahone Ranch.'

Cain climbed into a bland, cream-coloured, ceramic FusionPowered™ vehicle, and Brady squeezed in beside him. He noticed Cain inserting a Green File which glowed green as the car whispered into life. 'The Mahone Ranch,' he said, 'with urgency.'
Brady watched him drive in conjunction with the car. *I wonder if the Satnav systems have been unaffected. It was as if they were working together.* 'If it's in emergency mode,' Cain said, 'it can sense my intentions with regard to cornering and braking.'

They quickly reached the point on the road where Brady had first entered the town. *These are clever bastards I'm dealing with*, he thought. *This could be some kind of ruse to get me to leave.* But Brady was beyond caring. He leapt out of the car, and Cain effortlessly kept pace with him. The unmistakable sound of Old Marvin the Machine Gun grew ever louder - the bullets pulsing, presumably every time some movement caught Archie's eyes.

Brady hadn't noticed that Cain had split away from him. *Fuck him,* he thought. *He probably wants to negotiate with the Hodgson Boys - ain't no point in that.* He could see Archie now, with Lucian behind him, peering into the darkness. 'Hey Lucky,' Brady hissed, between shots. 'It's me, Brady.'

Lucian looked around, picking him out in the gloom. 'Hey, man. Good to see you. We need help.' Brady noticed Lucian whispering to Archie, and then he patted Archie on the shoulder and left him nursing Old Marvin. Lucian made his way over nervously to Brady. 'One of those boys is trying to distract us by making movements near that fallen tree about a couple a hundred yards away. I think the other one has made it to the little wood on our right.

'I'm gonna grab a hunting knife and see if I can find him,' Brady said. 'You two concentrate on keeping the one in front of you nailed down.'

Brady went into the ranch and grabbed one of Archie's old hunting knives and circled back around the house toward the wooded area. He knew every square inch of this place, as he used to play there every day when he was a boy. For a hulk of a man, he was exceptionally light on his feet, unlike Gary Hodgson, who crunched his way along the narrow path between the trees. Brady crept up behind him.
Gary stopped, as if some instinct was trying to warn him, but it was too late. Brady

grabbed Gary and slashed his throat so hard that it almost removed his head. Brady dropped the body on the floor and set off to locate Alan Hodgson. As he approached the edge of the treeline, he heard another round of machine gunfire. For a moment, he wondered if Archie had spotted his movement and mistaken him for one of the Hodgson Boys, but then he heard Archie cry out in anguish, 'Jesus Christ - I've gone and shot Jesus Christ!'

If he had shot Cain - and he could hardly have missed him with that many bullets from close range - then Cain didn't seem to notice, as he strolled toward the fallen tree where Alan might have been hiding. Archie cried out again, 'Did you see that? Ya did see what I saw, didn't ya? That was one of those bona fide fucking miracles, that's what that was.'

Brady knew this would make it much easier for him now. If Alan saw it, then he would be utterly distracted. He ran around the area to the back of the fallen tree. He could see Alan, and he watched Cain approach him with his arms open wide, his white robe glowing in the darkness. Alan stood and looked into Cain's crystal-clear green eyes, ready to receive his forgiveness. 'I come in peace,' Cain said, in a soft voice.

But then, he spotted Brady creeping up behind Alan. 'No!' he shouted. He wasn't too late, as such, as Brady would never have let this lifetime threat to his Foster Daddy live. But Cain was appalled as he watched Brady hack his victim to pieces.

'It's over Pops,' Brady shouted in Archie's direction. 'Hold your fire.'

The three remaining Hodgsons left their home to come and make sense of the slaughter and the image of Christ before them. A grizzly old man led the way in his wheelchair, and a young woman, with her baby in a pushchair, trailed behind him. 'You ain't gonna get away with this boy,' the old man growled. 'There's laws about killing my boys - you know that.' He pointed at Cain. 'And you...'

An axe plunged through the old man's skull, cutting him off mid-sentence. 'I prayed for this day - you sick fucks,' the young woman screamed, dropping the axe and wiping the blood from her face. 'You answered my prayers.' She fell to her knees. 'Every day they raped me, used me as my slave, they did.' Amid her tears she pointed at the old man, slumped and oozing blood. 'And that old bastard used to get off on watching them do that to me – so you have to forgive me.'

Cain was horrified at what he saw and wondered if scenes like this were playing out all over the world. She then noticed her blood-spattered baby. She picked her daughter up and hugged her tightly. 'Oh, my poor baby. Mommy had to do it, or you would have replaced me when I got old. You must forgive Mommy.'

She made her anguished plea to Cain. 'Tell me that you forgive me - please.' He didn't answer - he couldn't. He was still digesting the horror of the scene before him until Brady nudged him. 'Won't hurt to tell her - will it? The baby's too young to remember. All it takes is a few words. Even if it's a lie - it's a good lie.'

Cain was reeling. He thought about the government forces killing the people they used as human shields in the name of preserving their way of life. *Have I become one of those people?* He also looked at Brady and considered the awful test that Bodhi - the great Bodhi - might be putting him through. He then looked at the young woman and her child, and her words. The hell she must have gone through. He knew that she would never be allowed into his world, the Green Communities, as they were now sealed to newcomers. *The future holds little in the way of comfort for those like her.* He looked again at Brady, who nodded in a way that suggested that Cain should just get on with it. *If all it takes is a few simple words from me to give her comfort,* Cain thought, *then who am I to deny her?*

'What is your name?' he said.

'Mary-Lou, my Lord,' she sobbed.

He transfixed her with his green eyes. 'Mary-Lou. Your God forgives you.'

'Thank you. Thank you.' She picked up her daughter. 'My poor Amie. Mommy will clean you up and make everything better - I promise.'

Cain turned away, appalled at the enormous falsehood he had committed. He was close to tears. Brady put his muscle-bound arm around Cain. 'I think you'll feel better back in your own place. Thanks for your help. I'll walk ya back to your car.'

As they ambled back to the New Road, both Cain and Brady seemed eager to grab some nuggets of information from the other. 'What's going on here, with my Pop's place?' Brady said. 'Is he trapped here?'

'When the NanoShells™ were activated, everyone was sealed into the boundaries they were in at that moment.'

'I think I saw that yesterday morning. It was like one of those aurora things they teach you about at school.'

'You must have been mistaken - you cannot see NanoTech - it's too small.'

'I got good eyes. I saw the Green goo rolling on down the road, and you can't say I didn't.'

Cain laughed. 'Green goo. Good God, is that what they call it now?'

'My Pops calls it that. I hadn't heard of it before.' 'It's a corruption of the ancient conspiracy theory from the dawn of the Millennium - they called it Grey goo back then. Supposedly, it was going to destroy the human race, instead of saving the world.'

'Sounds like one of my Pop's theories - except you haven't involved extra-terrestrials - yet.' Brady laughed heartily, and Cain relaxed.

'Like all good conspiracy theories, it starts with a few facts and then twists them out of shape. There was a massive oil spill, and Sattva Systems™ cleaned it up by applying NanoTechnology™ to break down the carbons in the oil. It was a huge success. Everybody was happy except for the lunatics...' Cain could see that offending Brady's Father wasn't helpful – so he changed his angle. 'The conspiracy theorists, however, put it all over the Internet that this was in fact, a trial run, to exterminate, all carbon-based life forms. Unfortunately, these theories spread like wildfire, and yes, even alien invasions were involved.'

Brady still wanted an answer to his earlier question. 'I watched this Green goo move around the boundaries of these two adjoining ranches - my Pop's and the Hodgsons - does that mean we are trapped in?'

Cain looked uncomfortable. He knew Brady couldn't harm him. It was that he was supposed to be the giver of good news to his people. 'No, they will never be able to leave this place.' He tried to soften the blow, and justify the decisions. 'But they are lucky. They have a green space to work and plant. It's much harder for those in the cities. And if there hadn't been anyone living there, the NanoShell™ would have claimed their land as well. It's programmed to take all unoccupied natural land - the fields, the farms, as it protects Mother Nature. The City Trad dwellers will not be allowed to gain access to plunder Her, anymore.'

'So, you'll let them starve.'

'I don't think it will come to that - do you? We know the kind of men and women that are left. They are avaricious and cunning - they'll think of something. You would think of something, wouldn't you?'

Damn right, I would, he thought. *I would take or persuade your goody-two-shoes people to give me what I need - you self-centred pious bastards.*

Cain went on. 'From what I've witnessed here tonight, there will no doubt be violence, lawlessness - it will be a survival-of-the-fittest situation. I'm glad that our communities won't be a part of it.'

'What about the Government, the army, police - the President?'

'Anybody still loyal to the President has lost everything and will not be paid. They won't stick around for long - especially those with families, who may be in grave danger. The President will hide in his bunker, but when he decides to venture outside, he will never be able to leave the White House grounds. He will be in the same fortunate position as your Pops. He will have some green spaces to plant crops, although his stores should have enough food and drink to last him for years - possibly.'

Fuck - it's going to be hell in these so-called Trad areas, Brady thought. Still, he tried not to let his reservations show. 'But I can still get me one of those RedSuits™?'

'It would appear so. If you were to come up with the required one hundred Green Credits, then I would be duty-bound to apply it to you.'

They reached Cain's blandly designed car. 'I want to put my mind at rest before I leave. I hope you won't feel insulted. It's not my intention.'

Brady was intrigued. 'What do you want?'

'I want to see for myself whether you can still enter the Green Zone.'

I could do with checking this out myself before I make any further plans, Brady thought.'Sure thing.' He crossed the New Road - as Brady had christened it. Dawn was lighting up the horizon. He slowed, as though he expected to walk into the invisible barrier - but if it was there, he didn't feel a thing. He walked a further fifty yards into the Green's territory and then wandered back to Cain, who didn't look entirely happy at the result.

7.NEW DAY - SMALL WORLD

Once Brady had returned to the ranch, everybody relaxed - a little. Brady didn't need sleep, but he knew all this late-night drama wouldn't be good for his Pop's health, so he encouraged Archie and Lucian, to head off to bed for some shut eye. *I'll give them the bad news later in the morning,* he thought, though the sun was already rising before they went to bed. Still, he hoped they would sleep. *Poor old Lucky, he goes and breaks out of one jail, and now I gotta tell him he's ended straight up in another one.*

He looked over to the Hodgson homestead in the distance and wondered about Mary-Lou and her baby. *Someone gonna have to tell her, as well. Ain't gonna be easy, the girl is already at her wit's end.*

He waited for them to wake up naturally. Lucian was first to arise. *He's still adjusting to the time outside of prison,* Brady realised. While Lucian poured himself some cereal, Brady made them both coffees. Brady wanted to speak to them together about what he had discovered the previous night, so he left the significant issues alone, for the time being.

'How ya feeling Buddy?'

'Still sleepy. It was quite a night.'

'Feels like the world's gone crazy - we were only inside for ten years, weren't we?'

Lucian laughed. 'For you, it was ten, for me, it was five - remember?'

Brady knocked back his first hot, black coffee, 'Seems like a lifetime ago, already. What do you want to do today?'

'It'd be nice to just chill the fuck out, y'know? Catch my breath and all.'

'Amen to that.'

Archie must have woken up and smelled the coffee, as he shuffled in to join them. He hadn't bothered to dress; he had slung his old and worn-out dressing-gown on. 'Pour the old man a coffee, would you, son.' He paused. 'I wasn't dreaming last night. I saw Jesus.'

'Was that before or after you raked him with Old Marvin?' Brady roared, and they all laughed. 'He's one of the Green's Disciples - as they call themselves,' he said, once they'd calmed down.

'Well, I know I hit him,' Archie said.

'He was wearing what they call a RedArmour™ NanoSuit™. It's how those Green-Revs deposed the governments. They claim it's worldwide.'

'Well, it won't be for long. The good ol' boys will soon regroup and kick their Green asses back to where they belong.'

'I don't think so, Pops. Looks like they've got it pretty sewn up to me.'

'We'll soon see about that - once the Internet is back up and running, we'll organise. That's if it ain't one big hoax - some kinda publicity stunt.'

Brady paused and looked at Lucian, then his Pops. 'In the meantime, you've got something closer to home to worry about.'

'What, man?' Lucian asked, nervously.

'You're fenced in. You can get as far as the edges of the roads which surround yours and the Hodgson's ranches, and that's it.'

'For how long?'

'Cain seems to think forever. He also made out that if you weren't here at the time of this *Green Takeover*, then you would already have lost this land already - to them.'

'Fuck them!' Archie spluttered. 'They can't do that - this is the fucking United States of America - the Land of the Free. Me and Old Marvin will soon sort them out.'

'Like you did with Cain last night? I've seen first-hand what their NanoTech™ can do, and it's pretty damn scary.'

'But we can't just sit here and wait to die, and then hand over my land. We have to do something.'

'Brady, you're the one for plans,' Lucian said. 'Is there anything we can do about this? I mean, this is better than prison and all, but...'

'I've got nothing. They've won. We might just have to count our blessings for now. Pops has got his bunker, with supplies to last a hundred years.' He turned to his Pops. 'Gotta say it. You were right, old man. You always said there'd come a time when other folks would have wished they'd have prepared like you.'

'Can't say it's bringing me a great deal a comfort, boy. I was hoping to pass the ranch on to you when it was time to meet my maker.'

'Sorry Pops. I didn't want to be the bearer of bad news.'

'Not your doing, son.'

'What are your plans, Brady?' Lucian asked. 'From what you're sayin' you can come and go as you please.'

'It would appear so. Those Green weirdos are none-too pleased about it - they treat me as if I'm some kinda freak.'

'You see?' Archie said. 'Already things aren't going to their plan. There might be others like you, and then you could band together, and fuck 'em up big time.'

'You never know, but for now, I think we need to concentrate on our survival and immediate needs.'

'Such as, boy?'

'I was thinking about earning some of their Green Credits to help buy you fresh food. Your stores are basic and designed for surviving - not living.'

'Fuck boy, I'd rather see you die like a man than do these environmentalist's bidding for a few lousy pieces of their fake currency.'

'It's the only money in play, now - but it's not just that. I want a hundred Green Credits to get myself some of that RedArmour™. It makes you pretty damn indestructible.'

'I don't know, boy. That's how the aliens infect you. They give you something they think you want, and then you end up volunteering for their tests and probes voluntarily. They'll put those Nano things inside you, and then they'll take you over from the inside out. You mark my words.'

Brady slumped in his seat. 'Fuck. You know what, Pops, I think you could be right. They did seem awful determined to get everyone to buy into it. You were spot on about the bunker - still not sure about the aliens though...' He smiled, but he wasn't mocking Archie. *He has got a point,* he thought. *I should steer clear of those Suits™ until I've seen what happens to the others. This does feel more like End of Days, rather than the New Beginning these Greens are selling us on.*

Brady noticed that Lucian seemed distracted, he was gazing in the distance, in the general direction of the Hodgson Place.

'We still need extra supplies and other stuff to make life more bearable here. I had picked up an idea, but I'm not sure about how I can put it into action.' Brady pulled the Black Blank File from out of his pocket. 'Are you familiar with these things?'

Archie took it from him. 'Sure. Blank Files. A few of my buddies - not many, mind - used them to store away some of their more personal pleasures - ancient tech - antiques, truth be told.'

'I know it's a long-shot, without the Internet, but do you know where I could find some of these old buddies of yours?'

Archie smiled weakly. 'You'll have to accompany me to my control room - down in the bunker.'

'Are some of your electronics back up and working?'

'I wish, boy. I'm going to have to resort to ancient methods of my own.'

'Are you coming, Lucky?'

'Nah, I'll rest my head, and look out over my new home, if ya don't mind?'

'Sure thing.'

Archie had already opened up the entrance to his bunker. Brady caught him up and followed his Pops down the stairs. Brady hadn't been down here since he was a kid, and those damp cellar smells brought the memory of those happy days immediately back to him. They were only about twenty feet under the ground, but he could remember the younger Archie, and his wife telling her all about the place, excitedly.

It could withstand a nuclear blast…three-inch-thick steel…encased in a foot of concrete. He remembered his Pops getting into computers at this point, and then down the rabbit holes of his conspiracy theories and secret organisations. He was shaken out of his reverie when he spotted the table-tennis table. His old bats were still near the net, next to an old ping-pong ball.

'Come on, boy,' Archie said.

'Pops, you still got the old table-tennis gear? Remember when we used to play down here for hours in the winter?'

'Sure do. I used to keep you entertained when your Foster Moms used to complain that you were becoming a real handful. You recall how boisterous ya used to be back then?'

I never thought about it before - I was always on the go, he thought. *Didn't sleep much back then, either.* 'Yes, Foster Moms was a fine woman. I really should've appreciated her more while she was still with us.'

'She loved you like her own son - that I do know.'

Brady noticed the climbing wall. I used to love playing there – though it seemed so small to him, now. He went past the small bedrooms and living quarters, to the back of the bunker to Pop's inner sanctum. There was a wall full of electrical equipment of all the twenty-first-century vintages. Most of them were switched on and blinking away. Brady thought of a taunt he used to use on the slower kids at school, and he smiled, ruefully. *The lights are on but there ain't nobody home.* 'Any activity, Pops?'

'No. Not a peep.'

Archie used a screwdriver to open a ventilation grill. He reached inside and pulled out a black leather notebook. 'Things like this you couldn't put on the web - not in one place.' He handed it to Brady.

Brady scanned through the passwords to his accounts and secret groups. *No Internet - not much use to anybody now.* He turned the pages until he came to the A-Z tabs. These revealed names, addresses, mobile numbers, web-addresses, handles and other notes.

'Some of the folks in there are still alive, I think - I hope,' Archie said. 'Goes back years, my little black book does.'

Most of the physical addresses were all over the world. 'I don't think I'll be able to travel far. I got the impression that most of the infrastructure has been compromised.'

'That'd be the plan of it. We used to debate this kind of stuff all the time, we did - about destroying the systems which held the countries together at source. Come to think about it, there were some environmental activists on these online forums…'

'What do you mean, Pops, when you say, at source?'

'Don't nobble an airplane, destroy the airport - better still, sabotage the fuel. You could do the same for motor-vehicles, power-stations, even the fuel for generators… Thank God I got my reserve fuels years ago. Otherwise, I couldn't even keep my bunker going.'

'And you think they've thought about all this?'

'Fuck, I remember we even talked about fucking-up the economy. When the whole cashless society came in, we joked at how easy it could be.' He clicked his fingers. 'Bingo, hello!'

'What is it, Pops?'

'Sattva Systems™ overtook mASSIVE as the biggest company in the world about ten years ago. They were worth fucking trillions already, but you know what they did next, boy?'

'What?'

'They borrowed trillions more. Everyone was like - what the actual fuck? Why would they need to do that? But it's obvious now...'

Everything's always obvious when Pop gets on board his conspiracy train.

'...We have fucking funded this take-over of the world - they gone and did it... I kinda admire them, in a strange way. They got us to pay for our own takeover, and they don't have to pay the money back - because all their loans have been written off.'

Brady thought he understood - but he wanted to be sure. 'So, you're saying that Sattva Systems™ and the GreenRevs got together years ago to plan for a time when they guessed the Internet would crash, and in that time, they went around the whole planet, planting their NanoBots...'

'I think they did more than guess... The viruses and the solar storms were real, and we all knew it would cause massive disruption. In the Twenties, we had the Fave Wave virus, and the Thirties, the Doom Trilogy - China Virus, combined with another solar flare, and a mercifully small, but still significant asteroid hit. We were all paranoid, this time around - we were primed - but the GreenRevs were laser-focused. It's gotta be, boy.'

Brady shook his head. 'Well, it's too late now. I've gotta focus on what's in front of me. Can you pick out a couple of local-ish leads in your book who might be able to help me?'

'What you are looking for, exactly?'

'I'm thinking about making Black Files, with stuff I can sell in these Green Communities. They have strict content rules of what they can view - y'know, worthy stuff, science, education, authorised musical and film content.'

'You think there's a black-market demand?'
'Yeah. So I need to trade for a bulk load of blank Black Files, then find old mediums of storage, if any exist still.'

'You mean tapes, discs, physical formats? You'd need working hardware from back in the day.'

'That type of thing, yeah. I'd also need to know what our people would want from the Green Communities in return. You can't steal from them because their security systems are impenetrable - so, I would have to buy from the Greens, and get it back to my dealers.'

Archie thought it over. Brady could see he was troubled, torn over whether to tell him or not. 'Come on, Pops. I need this. The world has changed. Even your old friends are going to be looking after their own needs now.'

Archie winced, and then sighed. 'There are one or two possibilities reasonably close to here, and lots in the wider California area. - there's a guy in Bakersfield who fits the bill. He's a creep - he used to deal in kiddie porn - he specialised in off-line mediums.'

'I ain't dealing with nonces - I'd rather crush him with my bare hands.'

Archie frowned. 'You ain't gonna get the luxury of choosing. The other guy has been off-line for so long that he must either be dead or in prison. I would use his resources first, and then crush him,' Archie said, laughing uncomfortably.

'Is there a phone number? Maybe a landline or whatever - something might still be working. You could call him, and at least let him know I'm coming - and check if he's still around.'

'He don't deal with phones, not even Satts™ - especially not Satts™. Paranoia kinda comes with the territory, y'know.'

Brady shrugged. 'What's this guy's name?'

'Small Hand Don - on account of his withered left hand.' He opened the notebook to P for Don Pickerstaff. 'He won't trust you. You'll have to say that the Arrow sent you and quote the code in the book. Be careful, boy. He has a thing for Chloroform.'

'What the…? Honestly Pops, you worry me with the people you know.'

'If ya want to find dirt, sometimes ya gotta get dirty.'

'Why Arrow?'

'Easy for me to remember, and it sounded kinda cool… Archie… Archer… Arrow.'

'Let's hope he can get me what I want,' Brady said, darkly, 'but I'd rather die in hell than deal with child porn. It ain't me, Pops…'

'Don't think that… I never done anything like that. I won't lie, a lot of the people on these forums were into collecting it - there were women as well as men. I know you might find it hard to believe. But I don't want you to think worse of me. I wouldn't have wanted you to know anything about this, but you'd struggle to find…'

'I know Pops. They would never have let you look after me when I was a kid - they would have run their checks…' He paused. 'I love you Pops.'

Archie was embarrassed, Brady could tell. He changed the subject. 'Thank for this, Pops - better get back and check-in on Lucky.'

'I'll just stay down here for a bit longer. If you don't mind.'

Brady left the bunker alone and went over to the porch. It would be a beautiful day if the world hadn't gone to hell in a handcart. Lucian was staring into space.

'How are ya feeling? There's a lot to process - gotta admit it's been one helluva fucked up couple of days.'

Lucian had never felt so small as he did today. He was more than a foot shorter than Brady and probably half his weight. *If Brady is a bear,* he thought, *then I'm a rat.*

He had been catching a few rays of the early afternoon sun, as he sat back in his chair on the decking. He sat up, he pushed back his lank, greasy black hair, and then brushed his thin black moustache down with the edge of his index finger. 'If I'm going to be locked up, there are worse places than here, I suppose. Are you planning on leaving soon?'

'I don't know whether it's better to try to go into the towns early before the looters have picked the place clean or to wait until all the carnage has calmed down. One thing I do know is the ones who get organised the quickest will be the ones who prosper.'

Lucian brooded. He didn't want to see his friend leave - he might not return. *Even Brady might not survive out there,* he thought. *Not that we've got any evidence - even the Free News channel wasn't working on Archie's TV. It might have calmed down already - for all I know.* He felt guilty, though - because there was another part of him that wanted Brady to leave before it was too late. 'What are you planning to do if you do go?'

'I might have to break into some places and look for old-style entertainments - hard copies. It's likely to be old folks' places - maybe a thrift stores.'

'It's a shame that I can't come with you - even if I could, I suppose I'm still on the run, technically.'

'Ancient history, now. Seems odd that no-one is coming looking for us.'

Lucian laughed. 'Yeah, we're the world's most unwanted criminals.' But then, he stopped laughing - abruptly. Mary-Lou had appeared outside the Hodgson Home-stead, she was hanging out the washing. *She's probably trying to wash out the blood-stains,* he thought. *That was the dress she had on before.*

'What is it, brother?' Brady said. 'What's troubling you?'

Lucian sighed heavily and closed his eyes. 'If it's true - that we ain't never gonna leave this place - then she is the only woman left in the world. And I likes her, but she ain't never gonna choose me over you.'

Brady glanced at Lucian, and then looked over at Mary-Lou. She seemed to spot them watching her, and she hurried back inside the house. 'Hey, I haven't even been thinking that far ahead, yet.'

'That's because you got all kind of exciting things to look forward to. You can go where you please and have other women out there. I ain't got nothing.'

'It ain't my fault, man.'

'I know. I know.'

Brady thought about the situation. *I don't want Lucky to be a problem, and I owe him. Pops ain't gonna be happy if he gets stuck with the boy, especially if he's gonna be moping about the place.*

'If you're planning to get it on with Mary-Lou, then you're gonna have to come on all sensitive, like.'

'You mean you won't try and get in there first?'

'I won't try and get in there at all. She ain't my type,' he lied. 'Remember, she's probably traumatised, and she's killed, now. It's always easier, the second time,' he added, 'only half-joking. Just in case you're thinking of just rushing in and taking her.'

'I ain't no rapist,' Lucian snapped.

Brady raised his palms. 'I'm kiddin', man. But she probably hasn't figured out she's trapped here yet. That's a bit of information someone needs to tell her... Sensitively.'

Lucian sighed, looking resigned. 'Thing is, I've never had much luck with women. What would you do? Y'know, if you were me?'

I'd probably do something to make Brady Mahone look bad and Lucky look real good. 'Well, there's three bodies to bury.' *And I don't want to be the one to bury them,* Brady thought, suppressing a laugh.

'Should I go over there, and offer our help?'

'*Your* help. Don't bring me into this. Anyways, it'll be better, if you just do it - otherwise, it will look like you are doing a deal with her - y'know, you saying and all - if I buries your kin, then maybe you can...'

'But that will take hours of back-breaking labour - that's worse than fucking prison, man.'

'Do you want to win the girl, or not?'

'Like you said, I could just take her.'

'You could, but don't blame me if ya wake up one morning with a splitting headache.'
Lucian stood up sharply. 'That ain't funny at all - that just ain't fucking funny.'

'Calm down, come on, I was just joshing with ya. Y'know I love you, man. Just think it through. She will see you, working hard, doing something for her, and she didn't even need to ask - and if she looks at me, she will see a lazy, arrogant and selfish son of a bitch. She'll think the Lord has sent her a real good man to take the place of the Hodgson Boys. You gotta play it cute.'

Lucian thought it over. *It sounds like a lot of hard fucking work, but Brady is stepping aside*, he thought. *I better be grateful, or he might change his mind.* 'You're right. I can see how that might work. I've got to win her over.' He tried to change the subject. 'What's the deal with these old-style entertainments?'

'The Greens are going to be starved of unauthorised movies and stuff. I'm going into bootlegging. My plan is to find old-formatted items, then arrange to have them converted onto the Black Files by dealers in the Trad districts. Like this one.' He pulled out his blank Black File and passed it to Lucian. 'And then I'm going to trade them for Green Files - I can then use these to buy anything we need or want, from the Green communities.'

'What sort of things do we need?'

'It's early days, I don't really know yet. All I know, from years of listening to Pops, is that things that were worthless in one time can become super valuable in another and vice versa. He used to talk about olden times when men travelled the world hunting for spices, sugar and even tea. All I gotta do is figure it out, what the next big things might be.' He looked at Lucian, 'I owe you, man - anything I do, I will do it for you, Archie...and Mary-Lou. Y'know I'm nothing, if not loyal.'

Lucian laughed. 'Look after yourself, man. I don't want to lose you.'

'Thanks. Now go get that girl.'

8.THE HIGHWAY

Brady left the ranch. He had decided to travel light. He had his jeans, white T-shirt, and black leather jacket - a plastic bottle of water poking out of a pocket, and Archie's contact book in one inside jacket pocket. In the other, he had his Satt™ - it bulged out, ruining the cut of his jacket. *That was one thing about the older tech – at least it was small.* He had a large hunting knife in a leather sheath which hung from his belt adorned with a skull and crossbones silver buckle. He couldn't see why he would need a wallet, but he'd borrowed one from his Pops, complete with an old credit card and Driver's ID. The only other item he had was the car keys for his stolen Mustang.

As he came to the New Road, the first thing he noticed was that he had wandered into the Green Zone without a problem. *I still got it - whatever it is.* The second thing he noticed was that his Mustang had moved. Moved wasn't the right word – been dumped was more appropriate. The Mustang appeared to have been picked up and dropped near Lucian's Mini. The bumpers of the two cars were entangled.

Won't be a problem to get it free, he thought. *Just need to rev it up and blast it into reverse.* He got into the Mustang and turned the key. The car spluttered and then let out a loud bang before dying on him. He saw a cloud of blue smoke in the rear-view. *Fucking great, must be thirty miles to Bakersfield. Just as well I'm not in a hurry. I won't get there until nightfall now.* The Mustang gave a strange odour, and Brady wondered if it might be toxic, so he jumped out of the car - sharpish.

The New Road seemed eerily quiet as he marched along looking for the signs for Highway 99. *If all the cars are fucked like Pops guessed, then I'll walk as the crow flies.*

As he approached the junction to the Highway, he heard the roar of vehicles in the distance, but it didn't sound like regular traffic. He walked onto the Highway, and the road was empty, clear of obstructions - but off to the sides of the Highway, the hard shoulders were littered with abandoned cars and trucks. *I'm starting to get the hang of this fucked up world,* he realised. I bet they triggered something in the fuel to stop the traffic in its tracks. He also noticed the Highway looked… Clean. He passed a pothole which looked newly repaired, and the inside lane had white bicycle signs painted on the tarmac.

The Greens have commandeered the Highways. I'll bet they've taken the airports around here as well. He remembered his first night of freedom when he had watched the FusionPlanes™ and HeavyLoaders™ flying through the Green Glow. *If those lanes are marked for bikes, then the other lanes must still be used for vehicles. I'll walk down there for now.*

Brady noticed that some of the vehicles had broken up, having failed to withstand the fall after whatever it was had dropped them at the roadside. He glanced through some of the scattered possessions but didn't want to be weighed down on his travels. One truck had split open, and there were hundreds of taped up packages that must have fallen through the floor of the truck. *That sure is one big haul of cocaine, heroin - or something like that,* he thought. *I suppose it could be worth a lot of dough to somebody.* He then tried to work out if it was worthwhile taking this instead of messing around with his bootlegging plan. *If it was valuable, then they woulda come back for it…* He saw another painted bicycle sign. *Or the workers would've retrieved it.*

He marched along at a good pace for a few miles. The exercise was doing him good, giving him time to think. As he approached Famoso, the industrial noises grew in intensity, and in the near distance, he understood what had happened to his Mustang, though he wasn't without regret. *I liked that car; it was going to be my trademark - something to impress the ladies with.* Still, he watched in quiet awe as two ceramic looking vehicles used giant magnets to lift the abandoned cars up, and then drop them unceremoniously on the hard shoulder. The second vehicle was much larger, with a crane to remove the lorries and tankers. Upturned domes sprung out from the opposite side to the hard shoulder and acted like suckers onto the Highway, to give it stability. *Pops would have loved this*, he thought. *They really do look like aliens.*

He watched the vehicles for a while. They fascinated him. He used to love the Demolition Derbies and the Monster Truck events when he was a kid. A couple of trucks passed him. He noticed them giving him the eye, suggesting he shouldn't be here. *Maybe, the road is closed while this work is being done.*

They stopped a few hundred yards in front of him, behind the other working vehicles. One group of people jumped out and fixed up the potholes with a substance which seemed to set exceptionally quickly, while the other team painted their bicycle templates on the chosen lane. He heard laughter from them, they seemed happy and motivated. *They ain't messin' about*, he thought. *They're really goin' for it.*

As he closed in on the workers, one left the group to come and check out Brady. He was a big guy, too, dressed in moss-green overalls - not unlike military garb. On his cream-coloured ceramic looking hard hat, the words seemed to proudly proclaim that he worked for Sattva Systems™.

He reached out his hand and shook Brady's, firmly. 'What are you doing out here, buddy? It's not safe until we've done the full clean up - unless you are already Red™?'

'No, I'm not Red™ yet - gotta save up.'

The big guy looked him over. 'I could see if I could get you on the team. We could always use big strong guys like yourself.'

'What's the pay?'

'Five Green Credits per day. I'll soon have enough to feed and keep my family, and to save up for the RedSuits™ for all of us. After that, gotta start saving for the Orange™. I'm hearing they could cost a thousand apiece - but still, talk about affordable Healthcare.'

Five Green Credits for a day's back-breaking work. It didn't seem a fair deal to Brady. 'Thanks for the offer, but I think I'll pass this time.'

'Suit yourself, buddy. Where are ya heading?'

'I've got an old uncle in Bakersfield. I just wanna check he's ok.'

'If he's in the non-Green area, that could be tricky. It's gone fucking mental in there.' He looked at Brady, closely. 'There's a couple of things that are troubling me. Do you mind if I check out a couple of things with you?'

'Sure. Knock yourself out.'

'I'm assuming you are Green. Otherwise, you wouldn't be here - but you didn't know to keep away from the Highway this week - it was well publicised, everyone shoulda known. Also, there were supposed to be Town Meetings today, to warn people to stay out of the cities until further notice, unless you were Red™ - which only the GreenRevs and the Disciples are.'

Brady felt his Amazon rainforest story would be a bit weak for this guy. 'I'm checking things out, as an independent. Then reporting back to Sattva - another pair of eyes kinda thing.'

'And who do you report to?'

'Do you know Cain and Lizzie from McFarland?'

'Ah man, you should have said so in the first place. I love Cain. Is there anything I can do to help?'

'I've been in some remote areas for the past few years - securing borders.' *I'm sure there was a question from a kid about animals and parks.* 'Anyways, I'm a bit out of the loop with what's been happening closer to home, so Cain said to just ask any Green friend I came across.'

'Of course – shoot.'

'What's the deal with the vehicles at the roadside?'

The big guy looked over toward the hard shoulder. 'They'll remain there for a few weeks – to give the Trad folks a chance to recover any belongings from them – seems only fair.'

Only fair? Brady thought. *You've wrecked their vehicles - in the grand scheme of things…I suppose.*

'There's a no-mans-land corridor,' the big guy went on. 'Beyond the hard shoulders, which will remain open for a while.'

'And why's that?'
'To give the Trads a chance to get to their vehicles for a short while - kinda goes without saying - and there's likely to be an exodus as families attempt to reunite from different areas. It'll only be temporary, mind you. Once the vehicles have been collected for recycling or decontamination, then the hard shoulders will become Green Zones, and then the no-mans-lands will revert to us.'

'We are going to keep the roads then? Y'know, you'd think they would be the first things to go, if you care about the environment, and all that.'

'I hear where you are coming from, buddy, but once we are done, the road networks are going to be sprayed with NanoRepair™ and NanoProtect™, so that means they will be designed to last forever, even after the buildings have gone. They've clearly got plans for them… But I'm not privy to them, not at my level.' He wondered about the flimsiness of Brady's story, but he was Green, and he knew Cain, so he put it down as a test of some sort. He decided to give as many correct answers as he could.

Brady heard something which sounded like coaches turning into the Highway from the direction of Famoso. They pulled up to a gap between the abandoned vehicles. He watched as families were forcibly removed off the buses and marched beyond the hard shoulder of the Highway. The Greens returned to the coaches, as though they were busy - and had many more trips to do. The families tried to return to the road but couldn't break through the invisible wall. They were distressed and agitated, and obviously yelling, but the wall shut out the sound of them.

'What's going on?' Brady asked.

'It's another strand of Operation Clean-Up. Those folks didn't qualify to remain in the Green Zones. They may have been hanging out with friends or even other qualified family members. You can't go feeling sorry for them, though. They had plenty of opportunities to lead a more sustainable lifestyle, but they chose to keep on exhausting Mother Earth's precious resources. They made a choice. We are sending them to live out days in the hell they created - the Trad ways. Good luck, and good riddance to them.'

Brady recognised one of the teenagers who teased him when he was strung up at the GreenGrocers™ in McFarland.

He saw the figure of Siddha alighting the coach and heading his way. Brady braced himself for capture - he knew he couldn't land a blow on a RedSuit™. *I wonder if I could restrain him - a bear hug, perhaps?* He then followed his thought through. *I just can't see what good it would do me.*

Siddha glanced at Brady, suspiciously – but spoke to the big guy beside him. 'Hi Bill. Any trouble here?'

'I was just chatting to Cain's friend here. Sorry buddy, I didn't catch your name.'

'Brady. Brady Mahone.'

'Brady told me that Cain okayed us filling him in on what's happening here – he's been doing good things for the Green cause in some pretty remote places.' He sensed the tension between Siddha and Brady. 'I haven't done anything untoward, have I?'

'No, my friend,' Siddha smiled. 'You have done a superb job on the Highway. Thank you. I'm sure Brady won't hold you up any longer.'

'Cheers buddy. I'll get back to the crew.'

As Bill strode away, Siddha hissed: 'If it was up to me, I'd wrap you up in Film and dump you in a ditch, but Cain seems to have plans - or orders to follow - with regards to you.'

'And you know better than Cain? Are you jealous of him? Do you want to play at being a leader?'

Siddha refused to engage. Brady should have known the plan was to have no leaders - eventually. 'Where are you heading?'

'Bakersfield. I'm going to visit my uncle - check he's ok.'

Siddha wanted Brady far away, and fast – so he smiled in a phoney attempt at cordiality. 'At the old Police layby - a few hundred yards past the Green Highways Team - you'll find some GreenBicycles™. You could use one of those.'

Brady scoffed. 'I ain't ridden a pushbike since middle grade.'

More evidence of his ignorance, Siddha thought. 'They are protected by Green-Shells™ - meaning if you were riding through Trad areas, then nobody could harm you - not as foolproof as a RedSuit™, but still very useful. Also, only a Green could use it. It's a rental - if you leave it, then it's available to others to ride.'

Brady thought of the fountain and tried to disguise his sarcasm. 'I suppose I get to earn some Green Credits?'

Siddha smiled, falsely. 'Yes. If you ride it for more than ten miles in one day, then you get to earn a One Green Credit File, for your use of sustainable transport, and the commitment to your physical fitness, and mental wellbeing.'

I suppose it would be quicker, he thought, *even if I'll look like a fucking dork.* 'Well, consider me sold.'

'Better be on your way then, but there is one more thing.'

'And what's that?'

'I don't trust you, and if you return to McFarland, I'll be keeping a close eye on you. Am I making myself clear?'

'Crystal.'

9.GRAND TOUR

Brady strode passed the Highways Team, and Bill gave him a wave. *Seems like a nice enough fella,* he thought. *Not like that Siddha creep.* He examined a few of the stranded vehicles at the roadside. Brady liked his cars but had become a little out of touch with the latest designs since his time inside. *Some of these are electrics and hybrids. I don't get the problem they would have with these babies.* He even wolf whistled as he came across a top of the range supercar. He peered inside, for old times' sake. The glove box was open. *I bet he took his gun with him,* he thought - *assuming it was a him, of course.*

He took a swig of water. It was hot in the desert-like sunshine.

A hundred yards further on, he came to the Police Patrol Car layby. There was an abandoned Police vehicle here, as well. He spotted the racking containing the GreenBicycles™. *They must be new - there was no reason to have bikes next to the Highway, before.* He pulled one out - it was feather-light. He didn't feel confident about it carrying his weight. He carried it down to the Highway and then started to ride it. Brady wasn't a natural cyclist, but the bike seemed to keep itself upright - as if it had invisible training wheels. He began to move more quickly, and a digital display appeared across the handlebars, which showed his speed, distance covered, and his progress toward earning a Green Credit.

After five miles, he came up against a traffic jam. The hard shoulder was relatively unobstructed, because the Highways Team hadn't reached this part of Highway 99, yet. He weaved, slowly, around the cars that had slid off onto the hard shoulder, and into the bulk of the stationary traffic. All the vehicles were deserted. There were no dead bodies – or at least, none that he saw. He noticed the silverish sheen to the road, and he could make out footprints, and small-wheeled tracks.

I guess these tracks could be made by suitcases or pushchairs, he thought. *Make way boys, Inspector Mahone is on the case.* He hopped off his bike, the vehicles increasingly close together as he approached the front of the queue. He carried his bike, grateful that it was light. There were a lot of heavy vehicles obscuring his view into the distance. Looking down, he noticed the silver sheen was everywhere. Whatever had happened had happened to every vehicle, not just selected ones.

After slowly making his way through a further mile of traffic, he came to the head of this traffic jam. There were jack-knifed articulated lorries, which had been slammed into by many other vehicles. *I'm guessing the momentum carried them forward even if the engines cut out.* Brady did find some dead bodies in this carnage – though they didn't shock him. He'd seen plenty before. He entertained himself by imagining cops picking through the wreckage – solving the puzzle, piece by piece.

Looks like after the engines cut out, then the car filled up with something which smelled like poisonous gas. This made the occupants flee the scene. 'And then what happened Inspector Mahone?'

I'm glad you asked me that. My deduction would be that they fled the scene, taking the things they could grab real quick with them.

'Oh, Inspector Mahone, you are so clever.'

Yes, I am, but that's not all I deduced - my sexy sidekick babe. You see, I'm guessing they ran into the no man's land, maybe there was smoke on the Highway, and then they walked southbound to Bakersfield, or wherever because they were heading that way in the first place. Having said that, I suppose some might have headed back - if home was that way.

'*That's amazing, I love the way you think.*'

I know, I have got excellent powers of deduction...I also, have tremendous powers of seduction.

'*Oh, Inspector Mahone, I have to make love to you right now.*'

He laughed. *I'm already talking to myself,* he thought. *Clearly this fucked-up world is gonna take some getting used to.*

There were a few hundred yards of clear road ahead before the next set of traffic chaos awaited him. The same scenes were playing out across the median strip. An accident had crossed the divide, affecting both sides. He wondered if the median strip had a GreenShell™, and if not, had people been able to cross the Highway on foot to either side.

He hopped on and off his bike, depending on the obstacles before him. His handlebar display flashed at the ten-mile point to alert him to his Green Credit award. He stopped. *I may as well take it. Lord knows I needed it in that bastard GreenGrocer™ shop.* The end of the right-hand-side handlebar glowed green, and a Green File emerged, encouraging him to use his thumb and index finger to retrieve it. He took it out and placed it in his Distor™, the display informed Brady that he was now the proud owner of three Green File Credits.

10.BAKERSFIELD

Brady rechecked the details in Archie's notebook. *I know roughly where to find Lakeside County Road, he thought. It's near a Lagoon, but that ain't in Bakersfield, that's in Castaic. I think Pops musta got that wrong.*

It still troubled Brady that he would be in contact with a lowlife like this Don Pickerstaff. He reflected upon his time as a small boy when he was taken in for fostering. He could remember being scared because the woman who handed him over seemed to have utter contempt for the Mahones. *Looking back, I would've expected them to tell me how fortunate I was that a wholesome family would want to take me in.*

His Foster Daddy did most of his day-to-day upbringing, while his Foster Ma drank herself to death. *But I always felt loved by Pops - he didn't do anything that wasn't right by me.* He racked his brain for any signs of abuse he may have suffered. *In those early months, Pops spent an awful long time down in his bunker.* He thought about what those kiddy porn perverts were in to. He had overheard plenty of disgusting conversations from in jail - the things they did to them. He also remembered the justifications that it was out of love. Mostly, it was about the movies, photos, and the sharing of information. *Pops isn't like that. He's not one of them.*

He also tried hard to remember if there was anything suspicious about Pop's use of the camera or the family camcorder. *I can't say I recall anything inappropriate, just the usual birthday pictures, and movies about the festive season, and the fireworks for the Fourth of July celebrations.* He knew he was going to have to remain calm and controlled with this Small Hand Don and give his Pops the benefit of the doubt. *He always says to me, 'Treat people as they treat you.' And Pops has always treated me real good.* He thought again on his Pops friendship with this man. *It could be that Pops didn't know at first about what this guy was into. Knowing Pops, he just met him on a group that was discussing UFOs.*

As he arrived at the outskirts of Bakersfield, Brady tried to shake off his reflective mood. Even in prison, he hadn't spent this much time alone with his thoughts. Now, once again, he needed to be sharp. He knew he was wandering into a highly volatile situation. It wasn't long before he noticed the looted shops, but it seemed relatively quiet in the early evening sunshine. He guessed that the oncoming night would bring out the hardened troublemakers.

The more defensively minded people seemed to be struggling to form into groups - for support and protection. They congregated around their churches and other meeting places. Over in a nearby park, there was a speaker with a megaphone imploring a crowd to take back control of the neighbourhoods. The one thing they had in common, from Brady's perspective, was that they all looked at him with a mixture of distrust and apprehension - this aggressive looking hulk of a man, pushing his GreenBike™. Was he a Green? Was he indestructible like them? Or, if he was one of us, then how did he manage to steal one of their bikes?

All the roads were littered with broken-down vehicles as he made it to the heart of Bakersfield. A half-hearted attempt had been made by someone to break into an old-fashioned bookshop. Brady finished the job, ramming his shoulder into the door. He succeeded in knocking the door off its hinges.

Brady realised that there weren't any alarms sounding anywhere. There wasn't any power or lighting here. *Come to think of it*, he realised, *I haven't noticed any traffic signals.* He remembered the advertisements on TV for the new Green Communities, extolling local, sustainable power. He remembered the pathetic tagline: *Sure, it's more expensive than oil and gas, but what would you pay to help save the planet?*

The press ridiculed them - labelled them as a regressive cult. The reporters mocked these *environmental headcases* volunteering to live in areas where power was more expensive, and broadband was deliberately slowed down to the point of being practically useless.

They never saw it coming.

He took his bike with him into the shop and went straight to the Travel section. He grabbed a local atlas and went through the index. He was right, there wasn't a Lakeside Canyon Road in Bakersfield, but there was one in Castaic. That meant another day's riding and walking. He wondered about the prospect of sleeping rough in the freezing night to come. *Desert nights could be fun*, he remembered, *but they were always cold.* He ripped out a few pages, folded them up and pocketed them. He didn't want the whole atlas, as he didn't want to be marked out as a stranger in a strange land when he got there. Looking like a tourist could mark him out as a potential victim - even though trying him would be a very unwise move on their part.

When he found a camping store, he realised he wasn't the first to plan ahead. It had been picked clean of tents and sleeping bags. He spotted the locked storeroom. He looked around for a suitable chunk of metal to prise the door open. The looters were content for some instant gratification and didn't want to work too hard for their booty – but he wasn't afraid of a little fight.

It wasn't easy, but he managed to break in, and he went through the racks until he found a sleeping bag big enough for him, but also designed to be easily carried. He might not sleep much, but he'd welcome a little warmth while he rested.

He decided to push beyond the south of Bakersfield before finding a place to rest.

He came to Alameda. Usually, he wouldn't have given the place a second thought, but the lights were on. He guessed this was another Green place, like McFarland. He left the Highway and ventured a few hundred yards across some farmland until he found a disused barn. He figured that he was protected by the GreenShell™ surrounding the town. He propped his bike up, shook out his sleeping bag, undressed and slipped inside.

But he couldn't sleep. There was too much for his mind to process. He wondered whether the Greens had left the whole of Bakersfield to its own devices. He guessed they would take the Highways and the Airports, but it seemed unlikely they'd want the University. *Those layabout hippies are no goddamn use to anybody.* He wondered about the rest of the world for a moment, but Brady had never lived or moved outside California, so he soon gave up on that. His education began with the things he learned from his Pops and ended in the finishing schools of various correctional facilities - but that didn't mean he wasn't intelligent. He knew what made him - and the people like him, tick.

He pondered on how McFarland split into two sections. He guessed that a lot of folks would move away if their neighbourhood was invaded by undesirables, but most wouldn't want to go too far from the town they considered home. He remembered how the prices of real estate soared on the East Side but fell on the Green side of the Highway.

Brady wondered about Pops but guessed he would be holding up ok. He'd spent his whole life preparing for days such as these. And he laughed as he imagined Lucian digging those three graves. *That'll be the hardest damned work he'll have done in his whole life.* He hoped Lucian would find a way to make it work with Mary-Lou and the baby. Before he drifted off to sleep, he vowed to provide for them – somehow.

He was awoken at dawn by the sound of footsteps and conversation. He slipped out of his sleeping bag and snuck out the barn, dressed only in his underwear to check the situation. He watched an old couple walking their dog and chatting about their simple plans for the day as if they hadn't a care in the world.

After they had gone, he heard the sound of water from nearby. It was a fast-flowing creek, but the water looked fresh and inviting. He took off his underwear and went down the bank and immersed himself into the freezing cold water. He was invigorated and repeatedly dunked his head under the water.

He went back to the barn and got dressed. He packed away his things, and Brady felt refreshed and ready for the challenges ahead in this new world.

He made good progress down the Highway on his GreenBicycle™. The opposite carriageway was clogged with abandoned vehicles, but there were relatively few on the southbound side. He couldn't be bothered to try and figure out why that would be the case. That morning, he'd decided not to overthink things, and just deal with whatever lay in front of him.

Brady rode past those weird ceramic-like Road-Clearers - as Brady had christened them - and then climbed off his bike again, picking his way through miles more of littered vehicles of all shapes and sizes.

It had been slow going, but he finally made it to Castaic in the evening. There were familiar scenes of looted properties, and the loose associations of people trying to work out how they were going to make things work for their mutual benefit and survival.

Castaic was a small town compared to Bakersfield, but as far as Brady could see, it was a day further on in its evolution. Gangs had formed and begun hanging out menacingly on their chosen turfs. The atmosphere was just like entering a new prison as an inmate for the first time.

Brady picked up his bike, effortlessly, exuding power and potential violence. He strode down the streets, confidently. He knew someone would be goaded into challenging the big guy, the new guy. It was how the system worked. And so, he wasn't so much as irritated when a brash young white guy, with jet-black crew cut hair, stepped into his path. Brady watched the assorted pack of youths and teenagers gather behind him. *Some of them look like they could be handy, but most are just a bunch of scared kids.*

Brady smiled a broad, self-assured smile. 'Hi, buddy. I'm Brady. Brady Mahone - and you are?'

'Vincent Cesare, my family, runs this neighbourhood - I assume you know who we are.'

I could say I haven't, just to fuck with them, he thought – but decided it wasn't worth the trouble. 'Yeah, I know the name. I hung out with a couple of your crew when I was in Ridgecrest. I just got out, a couple of days ago.' He laughed. He didn't know why - it just sounded funny.

'What were you in for?' He paused. 'Or were you a screw?'

'Armed robbery. I'd served ten of my thirty-five. Is this some kinda interview?'

'You think you're funny. I'll show you funny.'

Brady already had his hunting knife to hand. This guy wouldn't be a problem for him, but he had to be prepared for the next one, so he had to choose carefully. There was a fearsome man with a face full of tattoos. Brady decided that he would be next - this would send the others fleeing for their lives, with a bit of luck.

An older man came out from the shadows. He was stocky and wore an immaculate Italian suit. He moved in close to Brady, but Brady didn't move. *I've seen this move before.* 'I'm Abramo - what were their names?'

Brady was being tested. He answered, 'Luca and Georgio.'

'And how come they haven't returned home?'

He thought it wise to leave Lucian out of this story. 'I was the only one who survived the massacre.'

There was a sense of shock among the gang. Abramo looked to Vincent, who Brady assumed must be his son, before returning his attention to Brady. 'How did it happen?'

'A couple of the guards didn't think it was a fair and equitable solution to let the cons have a quiet and peaceful death by, say, leaving us to starve. They had other ideas.'

'What other ideas?'

'They had an antique Tommy Gun and pistol, and they shot the place up. They killed everybody, including Luca and Georgio. Apparently, antique weapons didn't have the whatchamacallit...I'm a bit out of touch...Kill Stream switch, is that right?'

He could see Abramo trying to figure out where he might find these old weapons. He didn't say this, of course. 'So, how come you escaped?' he asked, after a moment.

'I hid.' There was mocking laughter from Vincent which triggered a wave of sniggering from the rest of the crew. Abramo wasn't laughing. 'But then I killed both guards and left.'

'And what brings you here?'

'Nothing. I'm just passing through - putting some miles between me and Ridgecrest. I wouldn't be here - I'd be somewhere else if you hadn't gotten in my way.'

Abramo smiled. He liked the way Brady handled himself. He wasn't remotely intimidated, he appeared calm, and in control. 'Come inside, and we'll talk some more.'

'The thought of going inside - anywhere - doesn't exactly appeal to me. I'm sure you understand.'

'I just want to talk, learn a few things, and then, maybe you could continue on your journey. We could eat, I'm sure you could do with a hot meal?'

Italians and their hospitality, he thought. *But a hot meal would be nice, I guess.* 'Sure. Why not.'

He entered into the dark house, which was dimly lit by candles. *Add that to his shopping list for his boys - more candles, to go with the Tommy Guns.* Abramo invited Brady to sit at the dining table. He then barked out orders for food and drink. Brady watched the bald-headed chef, struggle to cook with a couple of camping stoves. 'When did the power go out?'

'Last night.'

'I don't think it's going to ever come back on. Do you?'

Abramo shrugged.

I wonder if the power at Pop's house has gone, he thought. *I best not stay away too long. He might need me to help to figure something out. I'll give him a call when I get out of here.*

They chatted for about an hour, as Brady gave a detailed account of everything he had seen and done since his escape while he was travelling down Highway 99. He described the machines, the traffic carnage, the Highways Teams, and the eviction of the non-greens from the villages. He didn't mention anything to do with his time in the Green Community in McFarland. *I don't know whether there are lots of people who can pass through the Green's SecurityFilm™ or if I'm the only one,* he thought. *I don't want to give these guys another reason to think I'm useful to them.* He ensured he mentioned the packets of drugs he'd seen. That would definitely distract Abramo, while at the same time demonstrating his own lack of interest in this area of crime. He wouldn't be seen as a threat if they weren't in competition.

'We are in the middle of the biggest turf war in history,' Abramo said. 'I could use someone like you.'

'You wouldn't want me,' Brady lied. 'I've got issues.'

'What kind of issues?'

'I breakdown a lot. It's in my head. It makes me unreliable.'

Abramo believed him because of the detail of his account of his time from Ridgecrest to here. Still, he wanted to use him as a sounding board before deciding whether he would let him leave or not. 'How do you think this turf war is going to pan out?'

'I can only go on what happens in prison.'

Abramo was intrigued. 'Please, go on.'

'We have our enemies - the rival gangs, and we spend a lot of time, energy and blood, in fighting them. Trouble is - the real enemy is the system which keeps us locked up. We should have joined together and taken on the guards and the governors.'

'And who are the guards and the governors now? Is it me - should the people take on me - is that what you're saying?' Abramo said, contempt creeping into his tone.

'It's the Greens. They'll march in and take anything they want. Even armies couldn't defeat them.'

'I don't believe you. They're hiding away, enjoying their victory, with their lentils and soup.'

'You think that, and you might be right. But if I were you, I'd be spreading rumours about what those Green bastards are planning next. Make them come to you for protection - it's what you do best. The alternative is to fight your war. Sure, you'll kill a hundred, for the loss of every one of your gang, but there are hundreds of thousands of people out there. Who knows - maybe the Greens want a turf war between y'all?'

Abramo considered this. 'So, you're saying I should be going on a recruitment drive?'

'If you don't, some politician will, and when people are scared, they head to the biggest flock. It's one of those safety in numbers deals.'

'And what will I get out of it?'

'Anything you are going to need in this new era - skills, services… I don't know what's going to be valuable anymore.' *I'm getting the Green's market*, he thought. *I might just have that all to myself. This Trad business is going to be absolute chaos.*

Abramo reached out his hand, and Brady shook it confidently. 'Thank you, friend. You've been excellent company. I'll let you go on your way. Pop in and see me if you're passing this way again - it will be good to catch up.' He called for Vincent to show Brady out. 'Escort my friend out of the area and ensure our people know that no harm must come to him.' Vincent nodded, though it was clear he wasn't happy about it.

They left the candlelit hallway and headed out into the cold night. Vincent's friends were attempting to use Brady's bike, but they couldn't get near it. It stood, immovable, where Brady had left it, leaning against a wall. They were throwing rocks at it and using knives to attempt to stab and slice their way through the invisible fence, but it was impenetrable.

I need to think quick.

'You must be one of those Greens,' Vincent said. He slashed a blade at Brady, and it grazed his forearm, beginning to bleed.

'You couldn't draw blood from a Green,' he said, his palms raised.

'He's right,' one of Vincent's crew called out.

'How come you can ride their bikes then?'

'I jumped a Green exactly at the same time he touched the bike. He fell off, and I stayed on. I must have fooled it into thinking I was the Green. Since then, it's been mine. You should try it - it might work for you.'

'Vincent!' Abramo barked, 'What did I say?'

Brady pointed to the wound on his arm. 'You got anything for this?' Vincent nodded, and one of his crew came forward with some cloth and tied it around the cut, to stop the bleeding. Brady knew it would soon heal - his wounds always did.

11. SMALL HAND DON

Brady pocketed the pages from the street atlas and stood looking at the three-story house on Lakeside Canyon Road. The bright sunlight sparkled off the vehicles from the car park to the right, forcing him to raise his hand above his eyes. He knocked lightly on the door. He didn't want him to think it could be the authorities.

From across the road, he heard someone shout, 'Fucking paedo!' Brady turned, and saw a middle-aged man on a pushbike, with a trailer attached behind it, probably carrying all his worldly goods. *He's accusing me of being a child-molester,* he realised. The middle-aged man knew he had committed a life-threatening error when he saw Brady turn to confront him. The pushbike man tried to peddle, but his bike moved slowly as it was dragged down by the trailer. Brady made as if he was going to chase him, and the man finally got the bike moving. Brady laughed - it looked like the guy on the bike was close to having a heart attack. He let him escape. He looked up and noticed the twitching of a curtain from the second-floor window.

He knew that Small Hand Don was at home. He listened at the door. He heard heavy footsteps coming down two flights of stairs, and then he heard the padding of bare feet until Don stopped at the other side of the door. A soft male voice answered, though the door remained closed. 'Who is it?'

Brady pulled out Archie's black leather notebook from inside his jacket - marked at P for Don Pickerstaff. 'The Arrow sent me.' He then spelt out the code *A F T 729.*

There was a pause before Don replied. 'What do you want?'

'Archie's my Foster Daddy. He reckons you are the man to help me locate some old tech.'

The door opened. They looked at each other, suspiciously. Don was checking out the apparent threat of this hulk of a man in front of him. Brady let his muscles loosen in an attempt to look relaxed - his shoulders dropped, his hands open. Don's round and flabby body was only covered by a garish blue silk robe with large flowers embroidered on it. He looked like he had stepped out of a bath, but he was dry. Out of curiosity, Brady looked for the deformed hand, but it was hidden within the flapping sleeve.

'Come on in. Make yourself at home.'

'Do you mind if I park my bike in your hallway?' Brady said. 'Nothing's safe anymore.'

'Of course. Follow me.'

'What does the code stand for?'

'Didn't Archie tell you?' Don said. 'Well, I don't suppose it matters anymore. It's *All Friends Together* - member seven-hundred and twenty-nine.'

He led Brady to the lounge, through the hallway adorned with signed framed photographs of famous children's TV presenters from the distant and recent past. The lounge was full of soft furnishings, but Brady instantly clocked the large display of children's toys near the TV. He tried to not make it obvious that he was checking the place out.

'So, you're Brady, if I'm not mistaken. I haven't been in touch with Archie for...' He was trying to work it out. 'Well, it must have been more than thirty years ago. Would you like a coffee? I'm having to use a camping stove. They're hot property - no pun intended.'

'Yeah - a coffee would be great.' Brady watched Don head off to the kitchen. He listened to him padding down the hallway, gauging where the kitchen was – and he heard a key turn in a lock before the padding continued. *It's no surprise that he's securing his secrets while a stranger is in his home,* he thought. *But I want to know what it is before I leave.*

As he listened to the sound of coffee being made, he turned to his immediate problem with his business plan. *I can't create files without power. The Greens have a power supply. I could make them in McFarland, but that's going to get complicated. I probably should have picked up those free drugs at the roadside.* He then returned to his original reasoning. *They would have been too heavy.* He didn't have any knowledge of dealing drugs, and he knew the narcotics industry required certain skillsets he wasn't sure he possessed. He also knew he would have had a hard time getting beyond the Cesares with a load of dope on him. They wouldn't have taken kindly to a drug dealer encroaching on their turf.

Don returned with the coffee. 'You're deep in thought for one so muscular,' he said. 'What's perplexing you?'

Brady stuck with his last thoughts, hoping it would come across as truthful, and establish trust. He knew he didn't want to bring up the subject of child pornography – and certainly didn't want to explore his Pop's relationship with this toad. 'I was wondering what would happen to the drug market, now.'

Don's tone was superior, overly intellectual. 'The drug market is flooded. In my line of business...' He paused. Brady knew he should ask, but he didn't. He acted like he wasn't concerned. Don went on. 'I deal with the major players - you could say our specialities cross.' He leaned in as though he were letting Brady into a secret. Brady could smell the man's body spray and aftershave, and he tried not to show his discomfort as Don's dressing gown slipped off his leg, exposing the absence of underwear. 'They tell me the Greens are dumping huge quantities of smuggled drugs from abandoned vehicles on our side of their invisible walls.'

Brady remained composed, despite feeling strangely intimidated. 'Why would the Greens do that?'

'It's been done before.'

Brady put aside the knowledge that Don was a predatory paedophile - and if he was a friend of Pops, then he was more than likely an obsessive conspiracy theorist. He felt more comfortable dealing with this version of the perfumed man in front of him. And sometimes Pops was right with his predictions.

He sat back in a deliberately relaxed pose and drank some coffee. Don mirrored his guest's posture - it was a well-practised move. Brady encouraged Don to continue.

'Over a hundred years ago, the government feared an uprising from the Black civil rights movement, but instead of sending in the military, they sent in the drug dealers.'

'I don't follow.'

'They flooded the area with ample supplies of super-cheap heroin. They sent the opposition into a drug-induced haze.'

Brady weighed up - as he always did - stories like these before he came to his conclusion. 'I can see how that would apply to our current situation.'

'While the dealers, were fixated on the loss of their cash, cars and rushing off to secure their substantial properties in the suburbs - the addicts were swarming at the kerbsides like flies on roadkill. They've got more than enough to take themselves and all their friends to oblivion.'

'The dealers are saying that?'

'Yes. Also, they don't know what to ask for payment if they did still hold the poor unfortunates in their grasp. There's no money, nothing seems to have any value at all - except for the pleasures of the flesh.'

Brady knew there was no point in being coy with this man. 'And how is your business?'

'Like everybody else in this current catastrophe, it has slowed, somewhat. It didn't help with the fucking Internet crashing, never mind the loss of power. I've lost my contacts list - they were all in encrypted files online.'

'Why does that matter?'

'In a business which relies on the utmost discretion - we would discuss our more tactile, shall we say, arrangements and trades in secrecy.'

Brady didn't want to help Don with his business venture - but he did have Archie's contact book. Don shuffled in his chair, straightening his robe. Brady saw Don's withered hand for the first time, before he tucked it back into the silk sleeve of his dressing gown.

Brady considered the usefulness of Archie's contact book to Small Hand Don. *It's more than thirty-years-old,* he thought, *and surely most of them have either moved on or died in that time.* He considered Don and his Pops. *But they haven't moved. Pops has his secret bunker. Don's got his area which required locking before he let me in. The nonces in Ridgecrest, all had secret places in their houses for porn stashes and even hostages. I wouldn't know if they were still at these addresses, but Don would. He's active, and even if only half of them were still valid, that could still be valuable to him.*

Brady needed to find out if his Plan A was still a viable option. 'Don, I value your opinion. Do you think they'll ever get the power back on? I'm thinking that it's fucked, forever this time.'

'I never underestimate the endeavours of the human species to triumph over adversity. However, considering the comprehensiveness of the destruction of the infrastructure on our side of the fence. I would say your succinct conclusion is appropriate - it's completely and utterly fucked - forever.' He paused. 'Normally, you could tap into somebody else's power supply, but the only people who have that are the Greens, and they live beyond walls of indestructibility.'

Not for me, they're not. 'Is tapping into power supplies an easy thing to do?'

'Well, not for me - I mean, could you imagine me scrambling up to a power line?'

Brady did not want to imagine Don, in his bathrobe, climbing anywhere.

'Not a problem for Archie the Arrow in his younger days, though,' Don added.
This information gave Brady some hope, but also, fear. He hoped Pops wasn't going to try to climb trees or pylons to attempt to sort out an electrical supply. He didn't know how high they've built these Green Fences – he was almost certain they were entirely enclosed, but Pops might not believe that.

He changed his story a little, looking for a new angle to deal with Don. 'I promised my Foster Daddy that I'd bring home some old tech. It seemed important to him, as he's... He's been unwell even before all this. But now, with the loss of the power supply and all, I can't see how useful it would be to him. The thing is, I made a promise. Who knows, it could be his dying wish.'

Don looked at Brady closely, and Brady wondered whether this man could tell he was lying. Still, he went on. 'And if the power has gone forever - like you say - you might not need it. Of course, I wouldn't expect you to give it away - I would have to offer you something in return.'

Don slavered and looked Brady over. He could barely disguise his desire. 'What are you looking for? I don't believe for one minute that you haven't got a plan for how to get it working. But let's assume that the only value it might have for me is what it's worth to you.'

Brady finished his coffee, then relaxed back in his chair. He needed to play his part in this game. He thought this was the right moment to bring Archie into the deal. Brady believed he had Archie all wrong, but Don saw Archie's motivation through his own prism. 'We need machines to overwrite Black Files with music and movies, and maybe even games. We're looking for the ones who didn't use the Internet.' He watched Don thinking over the proposition. Brady licked his lips as Don studied him. 'We also need a large supply of Blank Files to make copies with.'

'I have the tools to satisfy your requirements. I don't believe you have the benefits in kind to satisfy all of mine.'

'I don't know... You haven't seen what I have to offer.'

'And what's that?' Don reached over and clasped Brady's knee. He wanted confirmation. He stroked Brady's thigh. Brady reached down and gently moved Don's hand away.

'How about, I'll show you mine if you show me yours,' Brady whispered.

'You want to see my equipment first?' Don said, teasingly.

'Yes, and if you do… I'll give you something to satisfy your desires for the rest of your life.'

Don was wary, but intrigued. 'You'll have to accompany me to the second floor.' He reached out his hand, offering to help Brady out of the chair. 'When did your Foster Daddy first love you?'

In normal circumstances, the inference of a question like that, and in the way that Don put it, would have seen him dead already. 'I can't remember, I was only five when they took me in.'

'Yes - so young. I wish I could remember the first time my Daddy loved me.'

Brady had heard these conversations before. In Ridgecrest, they were heavily protected for services rendered by some of the more psychotic inmates. Some used these topics to wind the other inmates up, while others were wishing for an understanding of their motivations. Ridgecrest inmates weren't known for their empathy. *I can't remember that far back,* Brady thought, *but Archie has only shown me the love and support of a good father. Surely, I would remember something like that happening.*

Don unlocked the second-floor room. It was a familiar scene that greeted him - almost a home from home, except here it was in a second-floor room in Castaic, and at home, it was in a bunker in McFarland. All the expensive computer equipment covered a whole wall - and all of it was dead. Don opened a walk-in wardrobe, which had been converted into a storeroom. Everything was neatly stored, from the old-fashioned CDs, DVDs, computer games, SD cards and files. Other boxes contained an array of every kind of old-fashioned cables. He also noted there were items which were of no use to him, like old hi-fi equipment and vinyl records. More chillingly, there were young children's toys, dolls and teddy bears.

Don adjusted his dressing gown and brushed back his mousy-brown hair to cover a bald patch. 'I've shown you mine.'

Brady reached into his jacket pocket and pulled out his Archie's contact book. 'This is my Pops' contact book. It's how I found you. It has hundreds of other names, and codenames - and lots of other details. Will this do for payment?'

Don tried to grab it from Brady, but Brady whipped it away. 'Ah, ah, ah - you can look, but you can't touch.'

'Ok. Let me see.'

Now it was Brady's turn to tease. He opened the pages, slowly, at random. 'If you package up what I need, and with a thousand Blank Files, then… Will you consider our trade complete?'

'Only if you have dinner with me tonight. I'm starving for company. I'll have everything ready for you by the morning.'

He's playing for time, Brady thought. He's up to something. Brady considered the practicalities of his situation. He might need more of Don's stuff in the future, and he could only carry with him a bike full of gear at a time. He remembered the guy on the bike with the trailer.

'The guy who heckled me,' Brady said, 'the one with the bike. I know you saw him - is he from around here?'

'He's a small-time crook. I had the misfortune to deal with him, once. He lives at number 483. He's set himself up as a courier.' He changed the subject, eager to obtain an answer to his more pressing question. 'So, are you staying for a little sleepover?'

'I can do that. But just so we're clear - I'm sleeping alone.'

It was freezing cold in the dead of night. With a working power supply, Brady wouldn't have noticed the desert-climate temperature drop, but without power, Brady felt he was trying to get some shut-eye in a stone-cold mausoleum. He pulled his sleeping bag around him, but he didn't get inside it. He didn't want to restrict his movements.

Earlier, he had heard Don creeping down the stairs, and padding around softly in the hallway. He half-expected Don to come into the lounge to try his luck seducing him, but instead, he heard the sound of a key unlocking a door, followed by the sound of it locking again behind him. A couple of hours later, the reverse happened. Brady wondered if he had a bunker underground like his Pops had, back home.

Next came the sound of Don moving up and down the stairs. Brady got up to investigate. He didn't want to engage Don in conversation, so he peered through a crack in the door which looked out into the hallway. He watched as Don dutifully brought down another cardboard box of equipment and accessories, to add to the two he had brought down earlier. A few minutes later, Don brought the fourth box down - and then, it went quiet.

Brady went into the hallway, feeling like a kid at Christmas having a peek at the presents before the big day. Don had kept his side of the bargain. There were neatly tied cables to keep them from entangling, along with the hardware secured in bubble wrap, and a tray of blank Black Files complete with batches of sticky labels for them.

Brady was delighted with the result of his negotiation, but he knew his dilemma. He had his criminal code of - a deal is a deal, but this was his Pop's property he was offering up as his stake. Also, there was the guilt about enabling his paedophile host, to re-establish his ring. *The world is shot to shit anyways,* he thought. *Why is one more fucked up situation my concern?* But his inner voice couldn't quell his disquiet. *Just because the world has changed shouldn't mean I have to change with it. What kind of man would I be if I helped scumbags like Small Hand Don out? I mean, I steal stuff, but I ain't never put kids in harm's way. I'll string him along, but he ain't getting his slippery hands on Pop's book. End of.*

He reasoned that he should try and at least get a couple of hours shut eye - he wanted to put in the miles on his journey back to McFarland. Still freezing, he wrapped his sleeping bag around him, and finally managed to drift off into an uneasy sleep.

An hour later, in the darkness of the lounge, he heard something – something in the room. He listened intently. There was no sound at all. He closed his eyes again but still listened. He heard the sound of breathing coming up behind him, and then an arm snapped tight around him, and he smelled something chemical, his eyes adjusted to the darkness in time to make out Don's withered left hand bringing a white cloth to his face.

Brady jerked his head from side to side to avoid the cloth, but Don was stronger than he looked. Don managed to press the cloth on his face, but Brady inched away enough to bite down hard on Don's withered hand. Don squealed as the cloth fell to the floor. Brady was light-headed. The chloroform made him feel like he was fighting in a dream - but he was still much stronger than Don. He flung himself to the floor, taking Don down with him. He managed to get on top of Don, holding his hands around Don's throat until the life was squeezed out of him.

Brady lay next to Don's dead body for long minutes, as the effects of the chloroform began to clear from his brain. He wasn't thinking straight, obsessing about Don's secret room. He needed to know what was down there before he left. He wasn't the kind of idiotic criminal who would take the small prize and leave a jackpot in the cellar for someone else to have.

He noticed Don was fully clothed, he felt around trying to locate pockets, but everything he touched felt rubbery. *He obviously had plans to dispose of my body,* he realised. *I guess that's why he's dressed in fisherman's waders. He was going to dump my dead body in the Lagoon.* He removed Don's waders and checked his jeans. He found a wallet, with a Driver's ID and some now useless credit cards - but he didn't find keys. Fuck it, he thought. *Who needs keys anyway?*

He found the locked door. He tapped on it, to check its construction - he wasn't going to bust a shoulder trying to break it down if it was reinforced. But it was wooden. He took a couple of steps back and launched into the door. Then, he kicked out at the lock area of the door, and the door came off its hinges, clattering down the concrete steps.

Brady walked down the steps and entered Don's bunker. It wasn't like his Pop's. There was a bed in the centre of a room, with an en-suite shower, toilet and washbasin. He noticed the filming and lighting equipment around it. He could guess what this room was used for. There were four locked doors. He undid the bolts, rattled the locks, but the doors didn't budge. He looked around for the keys. He went to a medicine cabinet above the washbasin and found four keys hanging up, above the shelves of condoms and assorted lubrications.

He heard a voice. 'Take me. Leave the young ones alone, please, I beg you. Have you killed Mr Jell-O? Is that why you've broken in? Please Mister, let the young ones go. You can take me, instead.'

Brady followed the voice to the fourth room. He fumbled with the keys until he found the right one. He opened it, and a girl of about fourteen stood before him. He expected her to be bedraggled, but she was clean and wearing silk pyjamas. She was slim and pretty with her long blonde hair. He noticed the teen magazines on a bedside table, but even he could tell they were decades out of date. 'Are you the police?' she said, nervously.

Brady laughed, 'No, but you are free to go. What's your name?'

'I can't remember my real name, but... He calls me Angelique. I was kidnapped when I was five.'

Brady felt awkward as a hulk of a man comforting a young girl after all she had gone through, and he was concerned his attempts at sympathy might be misunderstood. He put a respectful arm on her shoulder. 'You're in safe hands now. I ain't gonna hurt ya.' He smiled. 'I'll let the other ones out.'

'They will be scared. I'll do it - they trust me.'

Brady handed her the keys but said, 'Don't get their hopes up. The world has changed since you've been in here. You'll never find yours or their parents. Unless you live very close to here.'

She began to cry, and Brady put his big arm around her, but she moved around and sobbed heavily into his chest, as years of bravery and resolve dissolved into a pool of tears. Brady held her close, knowing that a hug was all he had to give her. Eventually, she pulled away from him, wiped her tears away and put on as happy a face as she could muster, before freeing the other captives. Brady stood back and watched as two boys were released - Brady guessed they looked about eight to ten years old, and then a girl of about seven completed the freed hostages. Angelique hugged them all, whispering softly to comfort them all as best as she could. He looked into each of their rooms and saw the same set up as Angelique's - but in place of the magazines there were assorted toys, games and children's storybooks.

Brady couldn't - or didn't want to - take them under his wing. All he could do is offer words of advice about possible next steps. He justified his lack of chivalry. *I can't stay because my Pops needs me*, he told himself. *I can't take them with me because they can't travel through the Green Walls - and in any case, I'm no good with kids.*

'Hey, Angelique,' he said, finally.

She went over to him. 'Yes, Mister.'

Brady was happy with Mister - he didn't want his name associated with a place like this. 'I know this is a big ask but… Keep the kids down here for about an hour. I've got to get rid of the dead body of your Mr Jell-O.'

'Will you come back?'

'Yes, but only for a little while. I'll think over your situation, and what you can do next. Maybe you could do the same. Maybe get the kids involved – it might give them something positive to think about.'

'We're free - what could be more positive than that?'

Brady smiled, though a dark thought crossed his mind: *You haven't seen the fucked-up hell hole of a world you are about to re-join.*

Brady returned to the body of Don. He slipped Don out of his waders and put them on himself. He picked the body up in a fireman's lift and carried him outside. There was no point disguising the fact he was disposing of a body – there wasn't any law enforcement left, anyway.

As he walked a few hundred yards to the Lagoon, he noticed the odd curtain twitching. One old woman smiled from across the street, and she had some children in tow. 'Now, now. Stop crying, we'll soon be at St Stephen's, and you'll be safe and warm there. It's not far…' The woman had a pink sash around her with *Save The Children* emblazoned on it. She seemed disinterested in Brady and whatever he was up to. When they had gone, he guessed she feigned this, so as not to attract attention from a man like him, with a drunk or worse on his shoulders.

Brady splashed into the Lagoon, and as soon as he found the deeper waters, pushed the body of Don in, watching him float away. As he emerged from the Lagoon, he removed his waders. The thought of being this close to Don Pickerstaff's slimy, rubbery clothes made his skin crawl. He dumped them on the bank.

Before heading back to the children, he decided to complete another errand.

He wandered up the road until he came to number 483. He rapped on the door. 'Police! Open up.' He stepped away from the peephole and as the door opened slightly, he was delighted to see the same guy who had called him a paedophile earlier in the day. Brady pinned him up against the wall, roughly, and the guy cried out in pain. 'I need the trolley from your bike, and you're going to give it to me.'

'But what if I haven't got it anymore?'

'Then I'll take your life instead. So, what's it going to be fuck-head?'

'It's out the back, but it's got my stuff in it.'

'Show me.' He rammed his arm up his back - close to the point of dislocating his shoulder.

Outside, he used the quick release on the trailer. He looked inside and saw tinned food, toilet rolls and pasta. Brady tipped it up, sending the contents scattering. 'You can keep this. And stay away from that house. The nonce that lived there is dead, and it's a Mob House now. Am I making myself clear?'

'Yes.'

'Repeat it back.'

'It's a Mob House, and I've got to stay away from it.'

Brady wheeled his trailer back to Don's home and went to check-in with the kids.

'It's ok,' he called into the cellar. 'You can come up now.'

Angelique led the kids up, and they huddled behind her nervously. Brady had already started to load his trailer, with his files and electrical equipment. 'What are you going to do?'

'We want to find our parents. Will you help us?'

Brady frowned before answering quickly, he didn't want to offer them false hope. 'No. I've got things to do, and where I'm going, you wouldn't be allowed to enter.' He thought about their plan, he guessed they would have an overwhelming desire to go home. 'The only people I can think of to help you would be the church.' They looked at him, hopefully. 'I think there's a place nearby, where they could help you better than me.' He looked at them all, they were scared. The youngest were putting on a brave face. 'Ok, wait here. I'll see if I can find help.'

Angelique stood up straight, as though she were preparing herself for hard times ahead, but with a sense of purpose. 'Ok, that's what we'll do. We need to get home. Our parents will be worried sick.'

Assuming they're still alive, he thought. 'There is another option. The owner of this place is dead. You can have it. It will be safe for a while, even if it's just while you get fed and watered.'

'No. No,' one of the young boys cried out. 'Please don't make me stay here.'

Angelique turned around and cuddled him. 'We are only a few steps away from escaping our nightmare - our hell. Surely, you can understand that, Mister?'

Brady knew exactly how that felt. 'Of course.' He sighed. 'I'm packing up my things. I'll keep guard, while you get ready and gather up anything you might need. It's going to be cold at night, so make sure you've got plenty of warm clothes and blankets - and grab stuff to eat and drink.'

Angelique smiled a *thank you* for the advice, and then led the children to the kitchen. Brady continued to load his tech into the trailer. He'd already raided the kitchen for food and drink for the journey - anything left over he would give to his Pops. He grabbed some bags that the children could carry, and he went back to his trailer to fill them up with the sort of things the kids would like to eat and drink. Small Hand Don had plenty of supplies with these kind of guests in mind.

He used the elasticated straps attached to it to secure his chosen items securely into place. When he had finished, the children had returned, loaded up with little toys and teddies. He wondered if they had been sensible and practical in their selections, but guessed, if what they had chosen had made them feel better, then that would have to do.

Angelique stood up on tiptoes and kissed Brady on the cheek. 'Thank you for rescuing us - you saved our lives.' He was surprised and thought she should have feared him, but if she was afraid, she didn't show it.

They left the house. Brady pushed his bike and trailer with the kids in tow. It didn't take long to find St Stephen's Church. Even though Brady had brought the children to their door, they eyed him suspiciously as if he was dumping his own children or rounding others up in the hope of a reward. Brady wasn't interested in obtaining gratitude or approval. The women took the bags off the children and ushered them inside the church, and then closed the door to keep them safe from the monsters outside.

12.LIZZIE

Lizzie welcomed her pupils to class on the Third Green Day - as the third day after the Green Revolution would come to be known. The pupils sat at their desks, each inlaid with a Sattva Systems™ Green File computer. The launch of the Sattva-Green™, as it was abbreviated to, was a much-ridiculed machine. Its' primary benefit was its exceptionally low energy usage. However, it had the slowest Internet processing speed of any comparison model - almost to the point of being useless. It also used a backwards-looking slot for work with the defunct Black File Chips. They were ridiculed for being a so-called Green Company who manufactured physical files. Their devotees, however, bought them with old money and were allocated Green Files to add to their collection as a reward. They sold well in the revisionist new Green Towns and districts.

The Greens, in these places, drew the kind of quiet disdain that used to be reserved for communities such as the Amish - but they weren't hurting anybody.

Lizzie's Junior Ecology class today was for the eight to ten-year-olds. Every child was expected to learn at their own pace, and certainly not to be in competition with each other.

'Now children, please put in your Files marked New Day.'

The children put in their files, and the screens lit up with a picture of a verdant green tree with the sparkling rays of dawn splintering between the leaves.

'To celebrate the beginning of the saving of all Mother Earth's vegetation and animals - we will be giving you a Green Credit to take home at the end of each school day to your family. Your families will be so proud of you.'

An excited murmuring of children filled the room.

'In your second slot, place a blank Green Credit with your thumb and index finger.' There were slots on both the right and left sides of the screens, so as not to appear to discriminate against those who were left-handed. Lizzie helped a disabled girl with her File. All the Files glowed green.

'I will authorise them at the end of class when I put my Group Award File in.' She held it up for the class to see.

The children enjoyed the lesson, which focused on the animals that might now be saved from the ravages of mankind. Much was made of the ringfencing of the rainforests, national parks and any other significant green spaces.

Her final class for the day was Senior Humanities. She knew this would be challenging, and the offer of a Green Credit wouldn't stifle the expected more incisive questioning. She asked for their attention during the lesson, with the promise that she would answer any questions they had for her at the end, to the best of her ability.

She gave the class a potted history of the last hundred years - not because they were unaware of it, but to try and remind them of the context, and how they had made it to this point. 'Decade after decade, we warned them of the consequences of Climate

Change, but they never took it seriously,' she said, closing the lesson. 'Even when all hell was breaking out around them, with the mega-storms of the late thirties and early forties… We tried to communicate in a civilised manner, but the people who held the levers of power wouldn't listen, or would pretend to listen if the voters and consumers could be won over. This is why it had to come to this. They left us no choice but to save Mother Earth and bypass the Traditional Cultures.' She smiled. 'Does anyone have any questions?'

A hand went up, and she laughed. 'Daryl. I thought you'd have something to say.' The class chuckled.

'You indicated that they wouldn't use the technology invented by Sattva Systems™, and yet they ended up being the largest tech conglomerate in the world. That doesn't make sense to me.'

'When Sattva brought a product to market which had no competition, like the Human NanoBubble™ in the Twenties, which solved the public transport issues after the third great pandemic of the decade. It made financial sense for governments to let it freely come to market. But when Sattva developed FusionPower™, the dirty energy producers were threatened, and they used their lobby powers to encourage governments to impose punitive tariffs on its supply. The same happened when Sattva introduced Intense Recyclable Energy. So, yes, Sattva made trillions of dollars, but it was forced into the niche markets in Energy and Transport.'

'Niche markets?'

'Yes. The tariffs made FusionPower™ energy supplies and vehicles expensive. Only the Green Communities, who were prepared to sacrifice other material possessions were prepared to live in them.'

'But my parents were poor.'

'Your parents were good people, and hard-working, and they collected lots of Green Credits for their assistance on projects to help the environment. The Green Credits had no value to the Traditional Cultures, then, but they collected them as a matter of faith. This is what helped them to become part of our McFarland Green Community.'
Another hand went up. 'Dawson - what would you like to ask me?'

'I disagree with the way we are treating the Trads. I know they were mean to the Greens, but I worry about the people I used to know. We all have extended families out there, and I think it's cruel to take away their basic needs.'

The rest of the class murmured their support for Dawson's question. Lizzie had been dreading this - but she knew it needed to be addressed. 'For over a hundred years we have warned about Climate Change. We have made suggestions, offered to help them, and with Sattva, we even offered solutions. They always promised much but delivered little. It might have carried on that way if it wasn't for the irrefutable evidence that the Earth was entering into the Runaway Greenhouse Phase.'

Dawson slumped. 'I kinda know all that, but surely I should have been able to take my family, and my girlfriend, in. I should have tried to save them - or at least have been allowed to try.'

Girlfriend, she thought. *That's the crux of his angst.* 'I'm sorry Dawson, I know this is upsetting. I, too, have had to leave old family and friends behind. But here's the deal: the planet was going to die, and eight billion people and every other living thing were going to perish. The GreenRevs, working alongside Sattva Systems™, have saved more than nine hundred million people across the globe, and they will live in low energy and sustainable communities. We are preserving all of Mother Nature's creatures. But we had no choice. A line had to be drawn over who to save, and who to leave behind.'

'But couldn't we have made exceptions?'

'No. If they weren't Green, then they would soon start up the old ways to hoard material possessions. And we haven't attacked anybody,' she added. 'We could have developed the technology to do it, but our ethos is not to deliberately harm or hurt anybody. The Traditional Cultures are cunning and inventive and will soon learn to forge new societies and new ways of living - and that's absolutely fine. But we will put our time and effort into healing Mother Earth.'

She looked to the only hand left raised. It was Martina, whose cheery and constructive disposition was always a relief to Lizzie. 'Yes. Martina.'

'My parents always told me that the thought of returning to pseudo-feudalism was an unattractive proposition but were enthralled with the prospect of saving the planet with cutting edge technology. Do you have any insight about what the future might have in store for us?'

Thank heavens, she thought. 'At the moment, you are confined to the community for your own safety. There is a lot of turmoil beyond the NanoShell™. However, when you attain the Red™, you will be completely protected. That will be the point you could visit your old friends and family.' *By then, though,* she kept to herself, *you'll be heavily dissuaded from dealing with any Trads, but we can cross that bridge later.*

'But after that? What then?'

'The Orange™ is an exciting prospect. It will enable NanoBots™ to patrol your body, working in conjunction with your antibodies to target sources of illness. You could be cured before even becoming aware that you were ill. Also, this will vastly improve your quality of life as you grow older. I know that doesn't seem important now, while you're young and healthy, but trust me - it will matter a lot when you approach middle age and beyond.'

The class eagerly asked for more, their questions crowding into each other. 'Well,' she said, 'this is just at the early planning stages, and there's no guarantee that the clever people at Sattva Systems™ could pull it off, but a little bird told me they're trying to get rid of the need for the textile industry, due to its heavy use of the environment's resources...'

'We are all going to get naked in our Red™ see-through suits,' Daryl called out. 'You won't need clothes with those on.' The class burst into riotous laughter.

'Technically, that's true,' Lizzie replied, 'but I'm not going to start strolling around naked.'

'Shame!'

'Daryl - that's enough. You know what happens if you stray close to verbal sexual assault?'

Daryl knew about the SecurityFilm™. They all did. 'Sorry, Miss.'

'You can still call me Lizzie.' She smiled. 'As I was saying, the Yellow™ upgrade might make the RedSuits™ take on any appearance you would wish to adopt, literally, second by second. For instance, if you were to go to the Trad areas, you could have your appearance set to blend to make you or your old friends feel more at ease. Another application might be simply allowing you to appear in what makes you feel good or how you feel at that moment - though I'm not sure I'm looking forward to those classes,' she added, playfully.

The bell rang for the end of the day's lessons, and her class departed. Some were discussing the YellowSuits™, but one or two of the class were patting Dawson on the back.

As she made her way back to her communal home, she reflected upon the day's lessons, feeling contented - she had done a satisfactory job.

The smell of cooking from the kitchen greeted her as she entered the lounge area, where Mollie was chatting with Cain. They looked remarkably relaxed considering the tumultuous events taking place in the world, and on their proverbial doorstep. Siddha called out from the kitchen. 'Hi Lizzie. We're having Fried Wontons followed by Thai Basil Eggplant - is that ok with you?'

'Sounds wonderful - can't wait. I'll just go and get changed.' She smiled as she mused on the sharing of her insights on the YellowSuits™ with her class. Getting changed might become a thing of the past - but how stressful might it be to have an infinite choice of clothes. She changed into her jeans and a flowery blouse. *I should have mentioned that people wouldn't be able to class themselves by how expensive or desirable their clothes were anymore,* she thought. *They would have appreciated that - I'll have to remember to mention that in the other Senior Humanities Group.*

Back in the living room, she slumped into the armchair. 'How's your day been?'

'Good,' Cain said. 'Though I thought there would be more drama.'

Mollie nudged him. 'Tell Lizzie about your phone call with Bodhi. I still cannot believe you've actually spoken to him.'

'I know. It's like getting through to God - and he wants me to call him once a month.'

'Oh, wow!' Lizzie gasped. 'How did that come about?'

'Well, I put a message through about this Brady character, and he phoned me back, personally.'

'What did he say?'

'He said that we should monitor him if he returns - and he's certain he will, after I told him about his family situation on the farm just off the New Green Road.' Cain omitted to tell Mollie and Lizzie about the carnage on that night at the farm, but he had informed Bodhi of every detail - Bodhi had insisted on it. 'He wants him monitored, but not prevented from doing anything he wants that doesn't break the SecurityFilm™ Protocols™. He informed me that he has told other districts to do likewise. He thanked me for help and promised that I might be one of the first to take the Orange™.'

'That's wonderful news,' Lizzie said. 'I'm thrilled for you.'

'You had a close encounter with this Brady,' Mollie teased. 'I heard you two together - you know - intimately. What was he like?'

Lizzie laughed, a blush appearing on her cheeks. 'He was ok.'

'Only, ok?'

'Yes. That's an accurate appraisal of his skills. He's a bit one-dimensional - typical alpha-male Trad, all force and strength, but lacking finesse. Still, a pleasant enough experience.'

Cain changed the subject, without trying to conceal it. 'Siddha said he spotted Brady on his way down Highway 99 en route to Bakersfield. He apparently, had no trouble crossing through the Green Zones there, either.'

'He's quite the anomaly,' Mollie said. 'But Bodhi believes he is the only one.'

'I get the impression that Bodhi knows he is the only one, but still, Bodhi might want us to think that way, so it doesn't spread any panic.' He fixed Lizzie and Mollie with his crystal green eyes. 'After dinner, I've asked Mrs Wilson over for a chat. I want you to lead the conversation, Lizzie, as I might be a little intimidating for her.'

'No problem, Cain. What do you want to find out?'

'The precise details of how she came into contact with Brady and how he came to go through the NanoShell™ with her.'

After dinner, Cain cleared the dishes and washed up. It was how things were organised - there were as few hierarchical structures as possible, while still maintaining a chain of command for communication purposes. He brought in herbal teas. As he passed a cup to Siddha, he said, 'Are the Hodgson and Mahone Ranches without power?'

'Of course.'

'I want you to restore the supply - off our grid.'

Siddha frowned. 'Why would we possibly want to do that?'

'Bodhi's instructions. He said Brady would, in all likelihood, try to tap our power lines. He doesn't want him to even try. He said it would be dangerous to us.'

'When do you want it done by?'

'As soon as possible. Could you do it while we are dealing with Mrs Wilson?'

'It'll be dark by the time the FusionPower™ team have eaten with their families, but I'll do it. It wouldn't do to disappoint Bodhi,' Siddha added, smiling.

They heard a knock at the door. Lizzie answered and ushered Mrs Wilson in. Cain offered her tea, but Mrs Wilson seemed too overawed to agree. Still, Cain insisted that it would be his pleasure, so she asked for a Peppermint tea.

Siddha smiled at Mrs Wilson as he passed her on his way out.
As Cain headed back to the kitchen, Lizzie took over. 'Am I in trouble - for letting that man come into the village?' Mrs Wilson asked.

'No, not at all. We just want to ascertain exactly how he managed to breach the Shell™. It may be that he has the right to be here.' Mrs Wilson was about to answer, but Lizzie invited her to sit down on the sofa. Cain brought in the tea, and Mollie and Cain left the room together, though remaining within earshot of the conversation. Lizzie sat beside Mrs Wilson, twisting around in her seat to face her.

'Would you mind if I called you Margaret instead of addressing you as Mrs Wilson?'

'Maggie. You can call me Maggie.'

Lizzie smiled. 'Now Maggie - exactly what happened on the day you met Brady?'

'I was driving over to visit my sister - it was a low powered electric car...'

'Honestly Maggie, we know you are an honourable member of the Green Community of McFarland. We are only interested in this Brady character. Please, be at ease.'

She sighed. 'I was distracted by some boys who were throwing rocks at me - I know I shouldn't have been concerned, but it was the first day of the NanoShell™ being activated, and it was just instinct to swerve away from the rocks... And I lost control of the car. I was terrified, I thought I was going to die when the car left the road. Then those boys came over, and I could tell they had bad intentions.'

'And did you see Brady at this point? Was he with these boys?'

'No, I don't think so.'

'Then what happened?'

'Wait - I just remembered something. When I lost control of the car - I nearly ran somebody over - it might have been the man you're calling Brady - I saw a figure for a split second.'

'Was this on or off the New Green Road?'

'It was definitely off the road.' Maggie sipped at her Peppermint tea, and Lizzie mirrored her – one of the many interview techniques she had learned. Maggie went on. 'I was shocked, but Brady came over to see if I was ok. I think I was rude to him - all I could think of was getting back to the safety of the Shell™.'

'What did Brady do?'

'He was chivalrous. Actually, he shielded me from those animals – though those two give animals a bad name. They came at him with knives, but he protected me. He edged backwards toward the road, with me behind him. These thugs moved in for the kill when they realised that I might reach the safety of the road, and that's when we both fell. As we did, we nearly got run over. I didn't wish to be ungrateful, but while Brady was distracted by the oncoming cars, and looking back at the thugs, I crossed the road and left him behind. He might have saved me, but I still thought he looked terrifying.'

Lizzie placed her hand upon Maggie's. 'That's completely understandable. Now, I want you to think carefully before answering. When you both fell through the shield, did you fall first? You said he was in front of you - or did you fall through at the same time?'

Maggie thought hard, her lips pursed tightly together, and she pulled up her right hand to her chin. 'We stumbled. I remember thinking he was going to fall into me, and he was a big man, but he swerved at the last second as he was falling...' She pulled her hand away from her chin and looked straight into Lizzie's eyes. She seemed pleased to be able to give her the definitive answer she desired. 'We both fell through the Shell™ at the same time. We were very close together. I'm sure that's how it happened.'

'Thank you, Maggie, you've been very helpful.'

Maggie was embarrassed to ask her next question, but she knew this would be her only chance. 'I lost my car. I don't know if it's recoverable, now that it has left the Shell™... I don't suppose...?'

'I'll have a word with Cain. I'm sure he will be able to help you out.'

When they had finished their tea, Lizzie showed Maggie out, Mollie volunteering to drive her home. Lizzie returned to the lounge to discuss the situation with Cain.

'We cannot rule out the possibility that he somehow acquired a free pass through the Shell™ by saving her,' she said.

'I don't believe that, but it can't be ruled out,' Cain replied, 'The opacity of the Shell™ has always been a tricky thing. If it had been opaque, then Maggie wouldn't have seen the Hodgson Boys, and they wouldn't have been able to see the road. But it would have made the Community feel claustrophobic, and that wouldn't have helped their mental health. It's not like this transition period isn't already tough enough for our people to get their heads around.'

'What about the semi-opaque version of the Shell™?'

'When I saw that, my first thought was how my younger children would view it. I have to say the visions of blurred out people seemed quite nightmarish. I think the only option was to go for the Clear View, it gives the impression of having nothing to hide - and natural light is always the healthiest option. You mustn't blame yourself.'

13.GREEN BEACONS

Brady locked up Don Pickerstaff's home and kept the key. There might be other resources he could plunder from here in the future. *Although*, he thought, *next time I hope I have some kinda vehicle instead of a bike to travel back and forth.* While it was out of his way, by heading southwards at first, he wouldn't have to pass through the Cesare's territory. He had a loaded trailer on the back of his bike, and knowing criminals, even if the contents were of no value to them, they would confiscate them anyway - just in case they were missing something that he had thought of.

There were other advantages to going this way. The land to the left of him was barren, so carried little in the form of hidden threats. He hadn't thought to check out if this was under a GreenNanoShell™, but also, he would soon reach Highway Five, which he knew was Green Protected.

In standard times - like just a few days ago - he wouldn't be able to access Highway Five, as this road ended up as a bridge that went over it. Now, though, he could scramble down the bank, carefully picking out a path that would accommodate his bike and trailer and cross the almost deserted road to pick up the northbound carriageway.

The newly painted cycle lane was smooth and easy to travel on, even with a heavily loaded trailer, and Brady was beginning to enjoy his newfound hobby of cycling. He made good progress through the early evening, and it struck him that the sound of the world had changed. He was on Highway 5, soon to hit the busy intersection to join Highway 99, but all he could hear was birdsong and the sound of cicadas. Even the nearby urban areas seemed quiet. He noted the lack of police sirens and wondered if the Police Department still existed. Brady chuckled at the thought.

Later, deep into the night, he stopped for a while, to gaze in wonder at the glittering stars in the heavens. Around him, the power-cut areas were enshrouded in darkness, but in the distance, he could see the ethereally lighted green domes encasing towns, districts and other protected areas. He watched in awe as he saw one small dome merge into another. *I guess that's another Trad area being reclaimed by the Greens*, he thought. It also increased his concern for his Pops.

After a couple of hours, he suddenly heard the sound of rumbling and popping in the distance. He could just about make out a couple of creamy, ceramic looking flying vehicles cruising at an almost impossibly low altitude, one travelling south, and another crawling up behind him travelling north, both very close to the sides of the Highway. He quickly moved his bike and trailer to the central reservation, as this felt like the safest place to be. He hadn't seen a car pass him by for hours.

These planes seemed to be shaped like petrol tankers - except about four times longer. As they gradually moved closer, he noticed they were suspended in the air by giant drone-type propellors. They were about a hundred yards away from the edges of the Highway, but they had stiff hoses pointing in the direction of the road. *Looks like a whale with a hard-on*, he thought.

As they passed near him, and he could see that they were spraying the vehicles which were placed at the sides of the Highways by the road crews a couple of days ago. When they were travelling away from him, in their diverging directions, he went over to the abandoned off-road vehicles to investigate. He spotted movement as people scurried away into the nearby trees and undergrowth. Brady guessed they had been going through the vehicles and picking them clean for anything useful.

The silver-ish goo covering the vehicles wasn't wet, like he guessed it would be. Instead, it was a dry illuminated Film. After a minute or two, he began to notice tiny holes appearing in the vehicles, and even on the tyres. Then he heard the popping and banging of bursting tyres all around him. He instinctively lay on the ground for cover, until he realised what was happening. He saw the tyres' shrapnel bouncing off the GreenShell™ and, encouraged to take another look, he saw the vehicles slowly crumbling away.

Reassured, he mounted his bike and continued his journey back to McFarland. He whooped and hollered every time another tyre exploded. He figured the further he travelled northward, the longer ago the vehicles were doused in what he guessed was some kind of Nano Technology. *All I've heard from those Greens is Nano-this and Nano-that,* he thought. *They probably take Nano-shits, too.*

He didn't mind the noise. It took his mind off the pedalling, and he barely noticed the miles he was clocking up. He appreciated the work out his leg muscles were getting. *Feel the burn man, feel that fucking burn.* There was the sound of creaking metal, as if it was collapsing under its own weight - and then came the enormous bangs of lorry tyres exploding all around him. *Woohoo! Hell yes!* And then there was an explosion the size of which Brady had only ever dreamed of witnessing, as an oil tanker blew up. As the flames rose hundreds of feet into the air, Brady watched the NanoShell™ rise up with it, as if it was magnetised to the flame; then the Nano-Shell™ formed an archway over the Highway to block the debris from falling onto the road. *Wow! This is like a hundred Fourth of July's rolled into one.* He watched in awe as the silver goo completed its tango with the jet-black smoke. *Oh, my fucking God - it's eating the smoke - it's eating the fucking smoke. This is amazing!*

The oil tanker explosion seemed to trigger a chain reaction in the other vehicles as one-by-one they all blew up. Brady road the bike with no hands, he stretched out his arms to welcome the fiery devastation. He felt like a God as he bellowed, 'Sattva Systems™ - You fucking raaaaaawwwkkk! Woohoo! Yeah!' Then, up ahead, where the northbound plane had overtaken him, the scene played out again, and Brady pedalled quickly to make sure he was in place for the encore performance. *You couldn't have a show as good as this for all the money in the old world.*

Eventually, the explosions only went off intermittently, and the fires and smoke were doused as if God Almighty had a heavenly fire extinguisher. It was mid-morning, and the sun was getting hot. Brady's legs were sore and painful from the build-up of lactic acid, so he decided to rest up for a while. He did some stretches and some cool-down exercises, and then strolled along the edge of the carriageway. He saw the slow but unmistakable signs of the cars and trucks dissolving away, and more disturbing, he spotted the same thing happening to the occasional dead body – some of which, he realised, were children. He thought about what might have happened to Angelique and her brood of broken kids. *It seems I'm having a mental cool down as well,* he thought. *Poor little bastards.*

He had stopped at a bend in the road. He worked out where the sun was likely to be in the next couple of hours and checked the position of the trees at the side of the road. The goo hasn't affected the trees, bushes, and grass at all. He listened to the sound of birds for a moment. *This will do to get my head down,* he thought. *There'll be shade for the next few hours.* Even the sound of far-off explosions couldn't prevent Brady from falling into a deep sleep. He dreamed of all the explosions he had witnessed the night before, and it was the best dream he had ever had.

14.HOME ON THE RANCH

It was night, and Brady left Highway 99 and picked up the New Road to McFarland. The lights from West McFarland were aglow, but the Eastside had disappeared in the darkness. He was alarmed to see the unmistakable signs of a power supply from the Hodgson and Mahone Ranches. He pedalled quickly - he needed to know that nothing untoward had happened.

A few hundred yards from the homestead, he saw three graves marked with simple wooden crosses. Brady called out, 'Hey, Pops. It's me, Brady. I don't want to be mistaken and get myself mown down by Old Marvin.'

He was relieved to hear Lucian reply. 'Hey man - did ya have a good trip?'

Brady walked his bike up to the homestead and hugged his buddy, slapping him on the back a couple of times. 'Oh man - I wish you could have seen what I've seen, but that can wait. How have y'all been?'

'It's all good, man. Your Pops is sleeping. He's even insisting that I call him Pops as well. That's if you don't mind, of course. I don't want to look like I'm getting my feet under the table.'

Brady smiled. 'You're stuck here, man. Don't you worry. You're like a brother to me now.'

Lucian beamed. 'Come on in. You want coffee or something to eat?'

'Coffee would be good, but give me a hand bringing the stuff in from the trailer first, would ya?'

'Sure thing.' Lucian helped unload the trailer, making quips about it looking like the worst antique heist in history as he examined the hardware and cables.

'You've still got a power supply,' Brady said.

'Yeah. It went off for a day, and we all thought - oh shit, here we go. Your Pops, I mean, Pops was trying to show me how to try and tap into the neighbour's supply - but they've got this - I dunno - an invisible wall of some kind. Anyway, we were trying to come up with another plan when - hey presto! The power just up and came back on.'

'Well, that will save us a lot of trouble.'

Lucian yawned, the long night's watch showing on his face. 'Hey,' Brady said, 'I slept in the day, I ain't tired. I'll take over the watch. I'm used to it.'

'If you're sure - I am beat.'

'No problem, we can catch up in the morning.'

Lucian smiled, yawning again. 'Maybe we could all get together and plan what we're going to do over a meal tomorrow night. I could invite Mary-Lou...'

'Sure. Why not?'

Brady had reason to take his time in the shower. He had just returned from his gruelling few days of travelling on foot and by bicycle. Lucian, however, seemed to take forever, readying himself as though he were attending a wedding. Archie took care of the meal arrangements, with enough frozen meat in his bunker to last for decades, he had been panicking about his freezer supplies when the power went off, as his generator had broken as well.

The evening air was fresh and cool, and the dining table was set for four adults. Archie had even scrubbed up an old highchair - which had been abandoned in the barn, along with other junk that Archie couldn't part with - for the baby.

There was a light tapping at the door. 'Hey, Lucky,' Brady called out, 'you have a visitor.' Archie's laughter roared from the hot kitchen. Lucian brushed himself down and straightened himself up and went to the door. As he opened it, his jaw dropped. Mary-Lou had dressed up to the nines for the occasion. He held out his hand, and she took it. 'Welcome to the Mahone Ranch,' he said, formally. 'And you too, little Amie.' He looked at Mary-Lou. 'Do you mind if I take her?'

'No, sir.'

Lucian unstrapped Amie from her pushchair and held her close to him, before placing her carefully in the highchair. He pulled out a couple of toys - Archie had also retrieved them from the barn - which Amie promptly began to chew. 'She's teething,' Mary-Lou said, softly.

As they ate until they were bursting, they chatted enthusiastically about the events from the past few days. The only thing Brady didn't cover in detail was the line of business Small Hand Don dealt in. Brady talked about him as if he was a small-time antique dealer. He also didn't mention the freeing of the children – which didn't fit the narrative he had created.

Once the past few days had been thoroughly picked over, Archie broke out his once-famous moonshine, and they began to brainstorm their plans for the future in more detail.

Archie brought up the subject of securing the premises. Brady hadn't even thought about this. In his mind, they were trapped here forever - end of story. 'I'm saying, son,' Archie said, 'that if your business venture is successful, and they love your Files of movies and stuff - what's to stop those Green sons of bitches from just strolling on over here and stealing all your stock? After all - you make out like they are invincible. Even you and Old Marvin couldn't stop them. Ya see what I'm getting' at?'

'I never thought of that Pops. They seem so Goody Two Shoes - but you're right, that's what I'd do. What can we do to stop them - or at least make it more difficult?'

'I've got big strong fences surrounding most of the place, and the Hodgsons have got barbed-wire on top of theirs.' They all thought about it for a few moments. 'We could dig ditches, that'd slow 'em down.'

Lucian looked distraught at that idea. 'It took me a day to dig three graves, and I still got backache.'

'It won't stop 'em Pops,' Brady said. 'We might be ok. They might not be like that. They might be law-abiding, God-fearing folk.'

'Now come on, son, you ain't making sense with your own logic. You want them to buy your contraband, don't you? If so, you better hope that lots of them are exactly like us.'

Mary-Lou spoke up. 'Do you mind telling me what you are planning to sell to them?'

Lucian wanted to be the one to answer. 'Entertainment files. Brady figures they will get bored or just miss the stuff from the old days - y'know, the nostalgia market.'

'So, you would take the stuff over to them and let them pick out what they want?' Brady leaned in. He was curious, and Mary-Lou was obviously either shy, or her personality had been beaten out of her by the Hodgson boys. 'What's the point of barricading us in here, if you are going to carry your goods into West McFarland, anyway? It seems to me that your strength and demeanour is not much of an asset there.'

Brady wasn't used to having his manly power questioned. 'Don't get sarcastic with me,' he said. 'You ain't no more than a mere slip of a girl.'

'Brady, man,' Lucian interrupted, 'I don't think she meant you to take it like that. Mary-Lou is trying to help.' He turned to her. 'Ain't that right, Mary-Lou?'

She didn't answer. She withdrew, looking away in quiet defiance. Brady remembered the way she slammed down the axe into the old-man Hodgson's head. *I might be underestimating her*, he thought.

'I'm sorry, Mary-Lou,' he said. 'I'm not used to the sort of company that questions my plans.'

She looked around the table. 'I was concerned that you might get robbed.'

She paused, to see if Brady would object again. 'I know,' he said, softly.

'We've got the power back on, and I'm guessing you've got a printer - one that doesn't need the Internet or Wi-Fi?'

Archie laughed. 'Well, I've at least got that covered in my plans for End of Days.' They all laughed with him.

'Well, I could make a catalogue of your goods and services. My granny used to do that for a living. She would travel door-to-door, selling her wares. The customers would place an order, and then the company would deliver it later.'

'That's a damn fine idea, little lady,' Archie said.

'There are other advantages with doing it this way, too,' she added.

'Like what?' Brady said.

'You don't need to make any spare copies - you just make a copy at a time, when a customer orders it. You won't have to waste unsold stock.'

The men looked at each other and laughed. 'Welcome aboard Mary-Lou,' Brady said. 'You're the new Marketing Director here at Mahone Enterprises.' He raised his glass. 'I propose a toast to Mary-Lou.'

Mary-Lou had other ideas, too – she'd thought about making sample copies and trailers for Brady's wares, for instance - but she didn't want to impose any further. She was content for a happy mood to have been returned to the group. She saw too many similarities between Brady and the Hodgsons to ever feel that she could be truly comfortable with him. She feared his innate criminality. *I'm stuck with these men for the foreseeable future*, she thought, *and I have to survive for the sake of Amie.*

They all knocked back their moonshine, and Brady and Archie slammed down their glasses in celebration. Brady noticed that Lucian was deep in thought. He wondered if he was worried about his intentions toward Mary-Lou. 'Are you ok, buddy?'

'Yes. I'm still thinking of the original boundary problem.'

'I can see your mind whirring, I know you too well, my little friend.'

'I'm trying to look at our problem by putting myself in their shoes. From what you've told me, they're quiet, well-disciplined and, for want of a better word, good people - honest citizens at heart. You're hoping they might go for a little low-level criminal activity, like bootlegging, but nothing more serious than that, or they risk being expelled - and look how long they've sacrificed to get to this position. It shouldn't take much to put them off any bad intent they may have towards us.'

'I'm listening,' Brady said. They all were.

'We just need warning signs around the place.'

'You mean like: Trespassers Will Be Shot?' Archie said. 'We already got them, boy.'

'I was thinking something scarier - to them, anyway. I was thinking Sattva Says…' Lucian smiled and continued with his idea, 'I know how to build billboards. If I copy the Sattva Systems™ Logos, then I could put official warnings and consequences for encroaching on our land. They will think we are some kinda test facility for Sattva Systems™. It might work.'

Brady slapped him on the back. 'If you can do that, then it's worth a fucking try. We'll start tomorrow - but tonight, we celebrate.'

15.MAHONE ENTERPRISES

Over the next few weeks, the Mahone Family, of which Lucian, Mary-Lou and Amie were now honorary members, worked hard setting up their new business. Brady helped Lucian build and erect the fake Sattva Systems™ Billboards, placing them all around the Mahone and Hodgson Ranches - while Archie and Mary-Lou began work on putting the old electronics hardware together and testing it until they were confident in how to use it efficiently.

Archie had a few old CDs and DVDs from the early part of the century to use as test pieces, though certainly not enough to launch a business with. Mary-Lou practised putting snippets of his collection onto the Blank Black Files, then improved her skills to organise them into chapters, content groupings and overall indexing. Archie loved working with Mary-Lou, and his mood brightened with every passing day. It was beginning to feel, to him, like there was a future worth living for in their Brave New World.

Archie selected a couple of feasible computers and printers which had the potential to work off-line. They were basic models even back in the day, so they were brilliant for this technological scorched earth.

Once up and running, Mary-Lou began working on a catalogue design. At night, sometimes she would be alive with possibilities, potential layouts and designs buzzing around her head. Her initial fears of being trapped forever with such a collection of misfits changed to hopes for her - but she couldn't see what kind of life existed for her toddler Amie in the future, unless someone, someday could find a way of destroying the Green barriers that kept them boxed in. Sometimes her thoughts travelled into the outside world, worrying about the millions of people who were worse off than her.

Brady had become used to being on the ranch, but he felt he had become too comfortable there. Even he had begun to worry about venturing back out into the Trads territory. He didn't like that term until Lucian had said it was actually quite polite, in the circumstances - in keeping with the Liberal-Eco's branding. If some of the Nazi Fucks in Ridgecrest had have won, they would have called them all vermin or cockroaches.

Brady knew he had to go and find stock for his venture. He wasn't used to feeling this sense of responsibility. *I can't believe how much work they've put into making my idea work,* he thought. *I'm responsible for a team of people, and if I let them down...*

He thought about saving up for one of those RedSuits™, but his Pops' words still rang alarm bells within him. *That's how they get ya, son.* He took out his Distor™, which lit up with his three Green Credit Balance and put it back. *Still, a long way to go before I get to one hundred Green Credits, anyhows.*

He didn't want to return to Castaic just yet, as he didn't want to travel that far again - not yet, anyway. East McFarland was metaphorically on the doorstep, so it made sense to try and find the stock he needed there. He considered the old thrift stores, thinking they would be a good starting point. *I ain't no Robin Hood,* he told himself. *I'm going to be stealing from the poor to give to the rich fuckers on the west side. I suppose business has always been this way, and I'm a capitalist pig now.*

For a few days, he went into training. He needed to be prepared to fight - he didn't know how things were going to be organised over there. He planned to stay close to the Highway where it split the town from North to South. He could always head to the NanoShell™ for safety if he was outnumbered.

Brady was going through Archie's coats, when the old man asked, 'What are you looking for, boy?'

'I don't want to take the bike and trailer with me. They're too conspicuous and might slow me down. I was thinking of a coat with a lot of deep pockets.'

'I got a poacher's jacket - one of those wax ones that's good for keeping out the rain. Except it don't rain here much, and it's too warm to wear in the sun.'

'Let's see it anyways.'

Archie opened a closet and retrieved the black wax jacket that was as long as a trench coat. He unrolled it - it hadn't even been hung up. 'It will do the job, and it will be warm at night,' he laughed, 'but you sure ain't gonna be inconspicuous wearing that during the daytime.'

Brady tried it on and explored it. It fitted him ok, and it seemed to have pockets on the inside and out. 'It's perfect Pops. Do you mind...?'

'Take it, boy, it's yours.'

Brady decided to head north to East McFarland later that evening. He figured that, in this coat, he wouldn't look too out of place on his first day there. He had a jemmy in one of his pockets, and Archie gave him a glass cutter, in case he needed a quieter way to break and enter. Then, there were the other objects he took around with him, his hunting knife and his Satt™. He wondered if he should bother taking the satellite phone with him, as he hardly needed it since he had it. He remembered being chided by ex-girlfriends in the past for never using the phone. *I just ain't big on conversation*, he thought. Still, he put it in a pocket, just in case.

He took a walk to the Highway, staying under the Shell's™ limits beneath West McFarland. He half-expected to be challenged, especially when he spotted Siddha looking up and down the Highway with binoculars, but even he acted like Brady had every right to be there.

He paused when he left Highway 99. He took a deep breath as he left the sanctuary of the NanoShell™ and headed over the Highway back onto East McFarland side of town. He could smell the remnants of barbecues in the air. *I suppose they've figured that out.* He wondered if the gas was still usable in the canisters or whether they had gone entirely back to basics. As soon as he passed the first houses, he heard a whistle, and then another. It made him feel uneasy - he was being watched by unknown assailants in the dark. He wandered north into the town centre, not surprised to see the looted supermarkets and the burned-out shells of other now unrecognisable buildings. In the centre of town, he noticed the whistles had become less frequent. He heard another whistle, and he looked up, almost able to make out a figure from a window in a block of apartments dart back into the shadows. Brady moved on, warily.

He noticed a pattern as he walked past the businesses. The chain stores were the ones which were wrecked, whereas the family businesses had been boarded up. He moved into the back streets, and the whistles continued to follow him. He looked up above the boarded-up panels, to the shop signs above the entrances, stopping outside a likely business: Old-Timey Marvels and Curios. He removed his jemmy and was about to go to work on the protective panels when the whistles merged to form an alarm. In the light of facing a faceless foe, Brady stopped, put away his jemmy and strolled on. The whistles only resumed as he began to glide past another set of buildings.

He sat on a bench in a deserted taxi rank, relieved, at least, to find the whistles had stopped. He considered other places he might find old stuff. He considered breaking into people's homes. *They couldn't stop me, they wouldn't dare.* But then, he guessed the whistles would start-up again. *The fucking Greens spent a fortune on that fucking NanoSecurityFilm™ or whatever the fuck it's called*, he thought, *and all they had to do was whistle.*

But then, he had an idea. He thought about the small industrial estate, near the Medium Correctional Facility of which he was once a dishonourable member. There were storage units - *and no fucking homes nearby*. It was back over the Highway on the opposite side to the Mahone Ranch. *It's worth a try - I'm guessing the Greens wouldn't have put their Shell™ over a prison. I wonder if there are prisoners still in there.*

He walked southbound down the Highway and wandered into the Bell & Sons Storage Facilities. It was dark, which meant it wasn't under the GreenShell™, and there was nobody around - no whistles. He jemmied his way through the outer door, and as there was no power - there were no alarms. It was a noisy process and breaking into the storage lockers would generate more noise, so he closed the door behind him.

He went to work on the doors, but the locks were more substantial than he anticipated. He went back outside and rummaged around the industrial complex. He found some metal bars, which looked like they would give him the required torque to break locks. He tried it out on the nearest lock-up - and it worked. He rooted through the various treasured possessions, which looked like junk to Brady's eyes. He tried another, and another, with similar results. All he was finding was clapped out gym equipment, old books, photograph albums, pathetic collections of knick-knacks - usually decorated with cartoon characters, or cutesy animals - and musty old clothes. Brady was sweating from his hard work, even in the cold desert-climate night.

Finally, he hit pay dirt. There were hundreds of CDs and DVDs - obviously a whole family's collection, adult titles mixed with children's music and movies. He remembered seeing a granny shopping trolley on wheels in one of the previous lockers, big enough to hold a lot of stuff. He went to retrieve it and loaded it neatly - he could get more in that way. He grabbed a cardboard box, filled it with more DVDs, and put it across the top of the shopping trolley on wheels.

He rolled his motherlode back to the highway - wishing the sound wasn't so loud from the little wheels rattling along on the concrete. Luckily, he wasn't disturbed, and he completed his first shipment by getting Archie off his night-time watch with Old Marvin to help him unload his haul into the barn.

'That's a great start boy, me and the young 'un, what's her face - ah yes, Mary-Lou - will work through them in the morning.'

'The night is young,' Brady said, 'so I'm going back to get the rest. The more choice we get, the better. We could make a fortune in those Green Credits - I just don't know what we'll spend them on.'

'I've prepared for this as best I can, but you can't really solve the problem of fresh food and water - for those Greens that's going to be their speciality. It won't come cheap, of that I'm certain.'

'That's all well and good, Pops, but I'm hoping they'll have some things that might be a little more fun - or at least useful. I've ridden on their pushbikes, and they got working vehicles, so I could do with earning enough for a car. Then I could go down to Castaic and get the rest of Small Hand Don's belongings.'

Archie shuffled, awkwardly. 'You never did say what happened with you and him.'

Brady frowned. He knew he was going to have to tell him everything that happened down there. 'He had four kids held hostage - either using them as sex slaves or pimping them.' He remembered the film studio set-up. 'Probably making kiddie porn movies as well.'

'So, you killed him?'

'Not before he tried to kill me first. He was desperate to get his hands on your little black book.' Brady still had it in his pocket. He handed back to Archie. 'Thanks, and all that - it did come in useful for the equipment and all - but I don't want to have anything more to do with your... Friends.'

'I'm sorry, boy. It's a long story, and I don't think you'd understand it. I gotta lot to answer for when I go to meet my maker - not least driving your Foster Moms to an early grave by drinking herself to death. It was on account of the shame of being married to someone like me, it was.'

Brady knew this was an admission, if not a confession. He didn't want the sordid details about other children, for now - all he could deal with was finding out about himself, and whether Archie had ever abused him. 'How come you ended up fostering me?'

'Your Moms wanted to foster children after she'd been refused permission to adopt. I tried to persuade her not to, but she went ahead and did it anyway. I knew they'd find out about my record - and when they did, they put a halt to the proceedings. And then, nearly a decade later, you were virtually delivered to us, without us even asking.'

'Did, they say where I came from? Who my real family was?'

Archie didn't want to admit that he wasn't interested at the time - all he was concerned about was how long they could keep him. 'They never said. I asked of course, but they just said that you'd had a troubled upbringing and that you were likely to be a challenge - a real handful, that's the term they used.' He squirmed. 'They told us not to spare the rod, and that we could do whatever we saw fit to make you shape up and fly right.'

'I don't get it, Pops. That sure don't sound like no carer type talk that I ever heard. Normally, it's all, love, nurture, educate and all those ten kinds of crap.'

'I know boy, but we wondered if we were picked because they believed we were unsuitable for nice children. Your Moms was deeply suspicious, and being the God-fearing woman she was, she thought you might be the Son of Satan.'

'What?'

'Well, after she found out about my past, she thought she was being punished. If it was one of those reverse psychology deals - ya know, the government is always up to all kinds of tricks - then I decided those bastards weren't going to fool me. So, I decided to show them that we could bring you up real good - and I did.'

Brady roared with laughter, but Archie knew his son's intent - there was warmth within it. 'I'm sure the authorities think you've done a grand old job with old Brady Mahone. I've been in and out of juvie and ended up in Ridgecrest Supermax.' He laughed again, and Archie laughed with him. 'And all for crimes I did actually commit...' Now they laughed uncontrollably. Every time one of them tried to control the laughter, it only made them laugh even more, until tears rolled down Archie's cheeks.

'You do know what I mean, boy?'

'I do. I love ya Pops, and I'm grateful to ya.' He put a big arm around Archie and then added, 'How come I stayed with you, for like, forever?'

'They never came back - and we never complained. I always suspected I was being secretly monitored by the Deep State and later by the Deep Cons, I got me a kinda antennae for that kind of activity.' He noticed Brady's eyes glaze over. *He doesn't need this right now,* he thought – more perceptive than Brady ever realised. 'Your Mom kinda came around - just a little, before her death. I think it surprised her how much you and me bonded. God rest her soul.'

16.JUDGE AND JURY

Over the next few nights, Brady completed his search and collections from the Bell & Sons Storage Facilities. He only found a handful of additional titles to add to his collection. On the last night, somebody connected to the owners - maybe even the owners themselves - came over with dogs to check out the damage which Brady had inflicted on their business.

He knew he had to try East McFarland again if he was to find enough to make his Green fortune. *First up - I'm gonna raid the Old-Timey Marvels and Curios shop,* he thought, *and I ain't gonna be a pussy about it. If they want to try and stop me with their scaredy-cat whistling, bring it on. I'll teach 'em not to mess with Brady Mahone.*

He cut a curious figure as he marched up Highway 99, with his long-waxed poachers coat - the trench coat-length version was fashionable back in the days of the Mega-Storms, all of forty or fifty years ago. The label suggested this one was an imported version from England. Here he was dressed like a Gamekeeper, pushing along a granny's shopping cart. He strode into East McFarland with purpose. He ignored the whistles, occasionally pausing to give them the finger.

He was just about to march into the street where the Old-Timey shop was located when a gang appeared and barred his way. This wasn't like any gang he had ever encountered before. There was a mishmash of ages - some of them were kids, there were different races, but there was no mistaking the self-appointed leader. He was huge and, Brady assumed, Mexican. He was dressed like a biker - whereas his gang were not - and he carried a fireman's axe. He did notice that a lot of this guy's bulk wasn't muscle—the result of too many hours sitting on a bike and not getting enough proper exercise. He heard the whistles increase in intensity and regularity. The Mexican yelled, 'Shut the fuck up!' But the whistling continued. *The whistlers aren't with these guys - and girls.* He noticed.

Brady slowly reached into his pockets, and with his right hand, he fingered his jemmy. With his left, he secured his grip around his hunting knife. Brady was in no mood for negotiations with this fathead. He placed his feet, ready for action, and he revealed his weapons. He said, 'I just got out of Ridgecrest Supermax. I was serving life for murder,' he half-lied. 'You better be real sure you want to do this because if you don't get the fuck out of my way, then I kill you. I'm the real deal - I ain't no poser like you.'

He could see the fear spread through the gang, but the Mexican's plans for the future depended on showing his followers that he could deal with this. He said nothing - only swung his axe around, before lunging at Brady. Brady watched the motion and smartly eluded him. Brady continued to dodge as the biker kept coming at him. He only came at Brady with right-handed swings, and quickly, Brady could sense he was tiring. One of the gang members tried to creep up behind him, but Brady kicked him away, sending him tumbling to the ground, moaning. The biker tried to use the distraction to bring the axe downwards at Brady's head, but again he side-stepped him. The next attempt was the biker's last.

He swung from the right, trying to decapitate Brady, but he stepped inside the axe's arc and swung the jemmy's hooked ends into the biker's skull. In the instant that followed, he used the jemmy to pull the biker towards him and onto his hunting knife, which Brady thrust deeper and then sliced upwards.

He let the biker's dead body fall to the ground, but Brady wasn't finished. He knew from the first day he'd ever spent in prison that the performance - the show of power - was everything, when it came to getting the other inmates to stay out of his fucking way. He picked up the axe and forcefully chopped the head off his rival. The axe clanged into the concrete, and the head jumped as the jemmy buried in the skull bounced off the road before the dead biker's head went spinning across the street.

Some of the younger members of this nascent gang ran away into the shadows, but he also heard the sound of scuffles, as though they were being captured. He turned to the seemingly more brave or foolish ones with his axe still dripping with blood, and he roared, 'Who's next? Come on fuckers, if you want it, come and get it.' He took a quick step forwards and stamped his foot down, and the rest of the gang ran from the ghoulish figure with the dripping axe and the long dark coat.

Brady wiped his hunting knife on the clothes of the decapitated body. He retrieved his jemmy from the road. He was picking out the bits of skull, blood and brains from the hook ends when he realised he had been surrounded. He looked around, pretending not to see them. He inspected his jemmy and then returned it to its pocket.

He casually looked around and decided that if the gang were the prisoners, then these guys must be the guards. He recognised the black middle-aged woman who stood before him – they'd almost grown up together.

At every step of her judicial career in McFarland, from lawyer to District Attorney to Judge - Audre Jefferson was there to put Brady Mahone out of harm's way for the good folk of McFarland.

Brady said, 'Good evening Judge Jefferson. Is this one of those Kangaroo Courts I heard about? I can see you got people taking notes and all.' He stared menacingly into the eyes of the two women who were writing in their notebooks. *There may be a lot of them,* he thought, *but these are ordinary citizens, I could take half a dozen out before they've even thought of how they'd take me down.* He studied the crowd which amounted to about fifty people. There was an old Chinese man who was whispering in her ear. He had to be someone smart if the Judge was listening to him.

'Good evening, Mr. Mahone. I recall your defence lawyer asking for leniency as he claimed you were a thief but not a danger to society.' She looked at the decapitated body on the ground. 'I never rated him a good judge of character.'

'Just doing his job. I think circumstances have changed since then, don't you?'

'You are correct.' She stepped out from the crowd toward Brady, and the old Chinese man followed her. Brady thought, *I'll give them bonus points for bravery.* 'This is Professor Yuan Chu, he studied and later taught at Stanford University.'

Professor Chu stepped up to Brady to introduce himself. He reached out his hand. Meanwhile, Judge Jefferson had a discreet word with a couple of people in the crowd, and shortly afterwards, they brought over blankets to cover the body and the head of the deceased Mexican gang leader.

Brady thought. *I'm watching you.* Brady looked for somewhere to wipe the blood from his hands. He reached down and used the blanket covering the body, then stood back up to his full height, towering over the Professor. He shook hands with the old man, whose grip was feeble, and Brady assumed he didn't have long to live.

'We may be able to come to an arrangement,' Yuan said.

'We could have you detained,' Judge Jefferson said – though Brady noticed she didn't say *arrested*. 'But that would mean some of our community will be injured in the process - and they've gone through enough hurt, wouldn't you agree?'

'I suppose so.'

'And the resources we have are precious. We don't want to waste them on attending to prisoners.'

'So, what's this agreement?'

'We want you to stay out of East McFarland - for good.'

'Can't do it, Judge. I live here.'

The crowd murmured, but Judge Jefferson was undeterred. 'Don't play games with me Brady - you know exactly what I mean. Stay out of this area.' She looked at him and asked, politely, 'What are you looking for?'

'If I told you - the price would go up. Do you think because I'm a criminal that I don't know how deals work? You tell me what you want first, and then I'll tell you.'

'You've travelled, since the Green Revolution,' Yuan intervened. 'You have an ability that I cannot fathom. You are a source of valuable information for our community. All we want from you is your story, and for that, we would try to meet your price.'

Brady was intrigued - and flattered. He was talking to a professor from a world-renowned university, wanting to find out what Brady Mahone knew. He laughed. 'I think you picked the wrong guy, man. What did you study, anyhows?'

'I studied the use of Nano-Technology and its use with fertility treatments, particularly in the field of IVF.'

'Then what are you doing on this side of the fence? You should be with your Green friends.'

Yuan smiled. 'Many of my colleagues did indeed end up working for Sattva Systems™ and were handsomely rewarded for doing so - but my area of expertise was considered of little value to them.'

I hope I don't get a technical explanation for this, Brady thought. 'And why's that?'

'Because I was working on helping people have babies. Sattva Systems™ believed that the human race was already the biggest polluter on the planet. Adding more little humans didn't fit their overall goals.'
Brady's demeanour changed. He understood. 'What are your plans for East McFarland? This isn't like other places I've seen, so far. I ain't seen many, mind you.'

'We have a lot of different skills available to us. For instance, we're analysing what has happened to the old infrastructure - although the damage done seems to be substantial, down to a molecular level. This fits in with a Nano Technological attack. And we're experimenting with a mixture of old ways of generating what we need and maybe coming up with some brand-new solutions of our own. What we need is time and information. I don't think you are a man who wishes to harm us. The man you killed was the biggest threat to our community. We should thank you.'

Brady laughed, but it was suffused with warmth. 'The pleasure was all mine.' He added, 'I'll tell you what I know, but I can't see how it will be that useful.'

Professor Yuan Chu smiled and thought, *I'll be the judge of that.* 'Now, what was it you were searching for?'

Brady now wondered if he would appear foolish. 'Old entertainment, CDs and DVDs.'

'And how many of these - if we have them - would be enough to have you agree to leave us be?'

Brady thought about it carefully. 'One thousand. But all of them have to be different titles - I don't want lots of the same things. They'd be useless to me.'

Judge Jefferson addressed the crowd. 'Let's see some hands if you have any old CDs or DVDs at home. Come on, I can assure you, your assistance will be duly noted, and when we get back on our feet, your help with this matter will be subsequently rewarded.' More hands went up. The notetakers jotted down the names in their books. Brady wondered why they had more than one notetaker but didn't have enough interest to try and work it out.

'Well, Brady Mahone,' she said, 'it looks like we have a deal.'

Brady told them his story. 'There was a riot at Ridgecrest Supermax, but the guards started it, in a way. They put the TV on with them telling everyone was fucked. The place went up, but the guards shot and killed everyone with fucking antique weapons. I didn't kill the prisoners, your honour, but I did kill the guards - but they started it, it was a self-defence thing.'

'Duly noted. Carry on.'

'Well, then, I went home.' *I'll leave Lucky out of this in case they arrest him and claim they had a deal with me, but not with him,* he thought. *You can't trust these bastards.* 'To cut a long story short n'all, the Hodgson boys were throwing rocks at the cars, but they were hitting an invisible wall - they call it a NanoShell™. I rescued an old woman, I did, but we fell through the shield at the same time. I think that's why I can go into the Green areas.' He noticed a look on the Professor's face as if he was dubious. 'Then I tried to steal some food from the Grocery, but I got trapped in all this SecurityFilm™. I couldn't move. They released me...'

'Who released you?'

'Lizzie, Cain and a guy called Siddha. I'm a bit hazy on that.' He tried to remember but then decided it didn't matter, anyway. 'I went to this Town Hall meeting, and they showed a movie about the Revolution, and they did this science bit...'

'What was that?' Yuan said, eagerly.

'I fell asleep. I was never into that school crap.'

'Never mind. This is all very helpful, please, continue.'

'They all got to earn one-hundred Green credits to buy themselves a RedNano-Suit™. Everyone's going to get one. Apparently, it will make them indestructible.'

'They were developing Diamonoid Technology before even I was a mere student.'

'Next up, Professor, they will have to earn a thousand Green Credits for an Or-angeNanoSuit™, and that will check them out for infections and diseases.'

'Who told you that?'

'A guy I met from the Highways Department. He was shoving abandoned vehicles off Highway 99. They were making Cycle Lanes - would you believe?'

'And this was after you'd left West McFarland?'

'Yes. I was heading down to Castaic - for business purposes.'

'It must have been important business to walk to Castaic.'

'What can I say? I'm an entrepreneur now. Anyhows, I got myself one of their GreenBikes™ - that took a load off. Then, after that, I came home.' *No way am I mentioning little black books and Small Hand Don,* he thought. 'Oh man, I nearly missed out the best bit. On my way home, there were these flying Green tankers. Well, they weren't green coloured, they were cream-coloured, not that that matters. Anyways, they were spraying every vehicle that had been shoved to the side of the road, and this silver goo was slowly rotting them away, and then POW - the tyres blew, like machine gun fire, and then BOOM the petrol tanks blew up, and man! You shoulda seen it when the petrol tankers went up - it was like the end of the world. And the NanoShell™ mirrored the flames and the debris, and the silver goo ate the smoke - it ate the smoke, man.'

He looked around, expecting his audience to love his crazy story, but they looked dejected.

'We heard the explosions,' Judge Jefferson said, 'and what we thought was gunfire. We hoped that the military were fighting back.'

'Ain't no military, ain't no police. You are the nearest I have seen to law and order anywhere. Sorry, your honour.'

'How are the other places you've visited coping?' Yuan asked.

'Bakersfield is chaotic - I don't think anyone's taken over yet. Castaic is probably ruled by the local Mafia by now. Alameda looked like a Green Town.' Brady was getting bored of talking, especially given his story about the exploding vehicles fell flat. 'Are we done here?'

'Thank you,' Yuan said. 'Your words have been insightful.'

'Do we have your word - for what it's worth - that you'll stay away?' Judge Jefferson said.

'When I get my stuff, yeah.'

'There's an old bus shelter, about half a mile north of your ranch. We'll collect up the CDs and DVDs, sort them out, and leave them for you by tomorrow evening.'

Professor Chu seemed to be deep in thought. He looked up. 'Brady, are you going to be doing a lot of travelling in your new business venture?'

'I guess so.'

'I would be most grateful if you could do me a personal favour.'

'And what's that?' *I like this guy*, he thought. *He treats me with respect.*

'Could you leave me notes about where you've visited and what the place is like? I don't need an essay, just a symbol to represent the area - with a tick to say it's like us, here in East McFarland, a cross if it's like Castaic, or a G to indicate that it's a green town. You see, if we find a way of communicating or travelling again, it would be nice for us to know where our future allies might be. You could leave your notes at the bus stop...'

'I get it. Yeah, I don't mind doing that - you can call it my civic duty.' He turned to the Judge. 'I hope you are going to get your little scribes to put that on the record.'

Judge Jefferson smiled warmly. 'Your assistance will be recorded.'

'One more thing. I was told that if a green space or maybe a whole block was vacated, the GreenNanoShell™ would claim the land. I saw it happening before my very eyes when I was travelling back.'

Some of the crowd were alarmed at this prospect and began scurrying back to their homes.

'Thank you, Brady,' Yuan said. 'You've been most helpful.'

17.KING OF THE ROAD

The townsfolk of East McFarland were as good as their word. Brady took along his bike and trailer to pick up the thousand CDs and DVDs. He could tell instantly that they looked clean and had been sorted into various categories. He felt as though he was evolving from a thuggish criminal into a semi-legitimate businessman.

When he got his stock back to the ranch, Lucian was ready and waiting to help Brady to unpack his stock. He removed Brady's overcoat and began transferring the stock into repurposed fruit trays. 'Hey, man,' he said, when he had finished, 'you'll never believe how hard everyone's worked to help set you up. Come with me, and I'll show you.' Brady followed Lucian into the barn. 'Here, we have the racking, and it's all, in alphabetical order, so we can find everything real quick. Archie sorted out the fixtures, while I put the stock in place - but that's not all. Mary-Lou has done an amazing job on the catalogue - the only trouble is that it's quite big. Take a look.'

He handed over a red binder to Brady. It was in sections divided by categories, and he could see that it couldn't have been made any smaller. He noticed each item had a reference number. He pointed at one. 'What does this mean?'

'Mary-Lou wanted to save you work when you got an order in.' He handed over a blue binder. 'And this is to take your orders. It's laid out so you don't forget anything. She took the inspiration from her Mom's business. It's got spaces for the name, address and payment information, but also, it's got a space for the reference number, so you don't have to write the whole thing out. Mary-Lou says that a lot of the descriptions can be very similar, so this will help us to pick you out exactly the right copy.'

Mary-Lou appeared and went over to Lucian's side. 'She's pregnant y'know,' Lucian announced proudly. 'She's having our baby. Can you believe that?'

Brady hugged his friend. 'Fuck me, you didn't waste any time. Congratulations Lucky, my best buddy, and to your good self, Mary-Lou.' She smiled bashfully, and Brady could see that Lucian hadn't prepared her for this moment. He diverted the subject away, a little. 'And thanks, Mary-Lou. The work you've done to help me is fantastic. I'd have never thought about all that. It's not as though I'd ever gone to business school y'know.'

Mary-Lou smiled. 'It's the least I can do after all you're doing for us here. I'm glad I can help.' Lucian put an arm around her and kissed her on the cheek. 'This baby is a sign of new hope. Amie needn't be alone if she has baby brothers and sisters to play with.'

'Whoa, how many kids are you planning to have, little lady?'

'I want loads and loads; I want to fill these ranches with children.' She laughed joyfully, and then she blushed as she realised that Brady would know what she was planning to do with Lucian.

Brady smiled. 'I mean it. I'm so happy for the both of you. It's going to make all the difference around here.'

Brady retrieved his coat which he had used to cover and secure the stock in his bike trailer. He put it on and then checked to see if the binders fit into the huge pockets at the base of his coat. 'They just about fits, one on each side, so they balance out. That's great if I'm walking and I need to keep my hands free. Otherwise, the binders would have to stay in the trailer.' He took out the binders and flicked through the pages, then put them into his bike trailer and removed his coat, placing it protectively over them. 'You know what I fancy - to celebrate?'

'What's that?' Lucian said.

'A barbecue. I'll be the chef-meister.'

The whole family ate heartily from Archie's freezer stock. He had been keen to use this food since the power cut in the early days of the Green Revolution. It was a sunny afternoon, and they talked excitedly about plans for the future. Amie toddled around and picked daisies, which Mary-Lou made into a daisy chain. Towards late afternoon the clouds gathered in, and an almost inaudible droning sound could be made out when the trees stopped rustling. Then a delicate mist descended. It wasn't enough to make them head for shelter, so they continued their conversations. Brady rubbed the mist which that settled on his muscular arms, and noticed it felt dry to the touch - not wet, as he expected it to be.

'Fuck me,' Archie exclaimed. 'Did you see that?' He was pointing upward, but all they could see was low grey clouds.

'What did ya see, Pops?'

'A fucking alien spacecraft - that's what?'

'Oh, come on.'

'No. No. I seen it, I tells ya. Just keep looking.'

And then they all saw it. A long cream cylindrical vessel, with two hoses, swaying slowly underneath, and just as quickly as it emerged, it glided behind another bank of clouds.

The mist that settled on them didn't hurt them. Mary-Lou instinctively went to her daughter Amie and took her inside to bathe her and herself. Archie rubbed it and tried to smell it, but it was odourless. Brady prepared for the pain he expected to follow. He observed Lucian and his Pops carefully, wondering whether he might be immune as an honorary Green. He waited for a few minutes, as they all peered upwards, straining to catch another glimpse of the alien vessel.

Brady worried about the others. He remembered the bodies at the side of the Highway - the ones who were picking clean the vehicles, and who probably sheltered in them when the Highways Department and their vessels went by. *I wonder how long it took the goo to take effect*, he thought. And more darkly he considered. *How long did it take them to die?*

He looked over in the direction of West McFarland, and he was sure he could see a smearing effect on the NanoShell™.

'There it is!' Brady and Lucian followed Archie's outstretched arm pointing in the distance. It must have been a few miles away. It looked like a giant, slow-moving flying mammal taking a piss over everyone beneath it.

They watched it in silent awe for long minutes until it was too small a figure in the distance to see anymore. 'I've seen them before, or something very similar,' Brady said. 'It was breaking down the vehicles which were abandoned on the Highway. It ate into them. It wasn't like acid, but it killed people too.'

'Oh, fuck.' Lucian checked himself all over. 'I don't feel anything. I haven't even got it on my skin anymore. Do you think we're going to be ok?'

'It ain't just physical you got to worry about.' Archie said, pointing to his temple. 'It's up here as well. They might be pouring some of that NanoShit over the population to mind control us. That was crop spraying - pure and simple.'

Lucian tried to keep himself from panicking. 'You might be right about looking like it was crop-spraying, but maybe it was a health thing. Y'know, to protect us - or to stop the spread of disease.'

'Come on, boy. Those Green fuckers don't give a damn about us. There are only two options here. They're either trying to destroy us - or control us.'

Brady believed his Pops' version of events was closer to the truth. *We'll know it isn't about destroying us if we are still around by tomorrow*, he thought.

Brady couldn't sleep at all that night - not even for a few moments of shut-eye. He patrolled the grounds and listened nervously for sounds of pain - but his companions slept soundly. He then fretted about whether they were sleeping too soundly - but was put at ease when his Pops went for a piss just before dawn, before returning to his bed.

He might not have slept a wink, but by morning when all the family had woken up and were heartily tucking into a fried breakfast, he felt mighty fine as the weight of worry left his broad shoulders, leaving him with a profound sense of relief. He was looking forward to putting the strange events of yesterday behind him and embarking seriously on his new business venture.

Over the next few weeks, Brady travelled up and down the Highways from McFarland and all the way down to Los Angeles, where he uncovered a lucrative market for his wares in the former Hollywood set. He was surprised that some of the wealthiest enclaves had turned to Green and not to rust – he'd always thought the rich were the most responsible for the planet's climate troubles. Instead, he discovered large communities of the old Liberal elites who seemed to have acquired a fortune in Green Credits in the run-up to the Revolution. As an added bonus, he seemed to find plenty of women who were as interested in him as they were in his catalogue. It certainly added motivation to his days of cycling to ply his trade this far south.

The more impoverished areas were the most troubled he had seen so far, as it had descended into anarchy and gang warfare, and large tracts of the city were left in a burned-out trail of destruction. Brady wanted to keep his tally of the state of play in various districts for Professor Yuan Chu. Brady, through a mixture of analysis and gut instinct, began to predict, with some accuracy, which towns and districts would fall into a particular category. If he saw offshore Intense Wind Farms, or the equally Intense Solar Farms, these would be a good indicator that they had turned Green – which meant the tiny villages nearby had a good chance of being next in line to be swallowed by the neighbouring NanoShell™. As he got closer, the Sattva Systems™

logos were the biggest giveaway. These were where his target market lived. The smaller towns contained the gentler systems like the one that was forming in East McFarland. The Highways and river boundaries often split the communities into two different types. The larger cities were the ones which struggled the most with the transition to the new order.

He got off to a slow start with his orders, as there was resistance to his pricing strategy. In the smaller towns, the people were busy saving for the RedNanoSuits™ at one hundred Greenbacks - as Brady began to call the Green Credits - apiece, and then faced the prospect of earning a further one thousand for the Orange™ health upgrades. He had three tiers of pricing dependant on the quality and quantity of the content of the item. He tried to go for five, ten and fifteen, at first. If using a water fountain was one Greenback, then five was cheap. But when he dropped the pricing structure to three, five and ten, he had more joy, and his order book began to fill up nicely. When he reached the old affluent coastal areas, west and south of Los Angeles, he reverted back to his original pricing structures, and he soon had an order book with a potential turnover of more than six-hundred Greenbacks. All he had to do now was head back to the ranch, fill up his trailer and return to his customers, fulfil the orders and collect his Greenbacks. Occasionally, he worried about running out of stock – but decided to give more thought to this problem when he had endless hours to pass on his days of cycling home.

He made a detour to Castaic, to Small Hand Don's place. He had a virtually empty trailer to fill. He travelled there by night and went through nearby Green Communities, then took the most rural routes to get there. He was wary of the Cesares and how things might have developed in the time since his last visit. He had predicted that things were unlikely to have gotten any better.

He let himself in and headed quickly upstairs. He knew what he needed most urgently, and that was as many Blank Black Files as possible. He went to the storage area and rifled through some boxes.

He was in luck. He found a few boxes which he estimated contained around five thousand Files. *This guy was running a fucking industry from here,* he thought. He then found almost double that many with reference numbers on, not unlike the system which Mary-Lou had designed for his wares. *These must be already recorded on but maybe they can be overwritten. Won't do any harm to take them as well.* Back in the main bedroom, he noticed an old camcorder set up. He went to press the camcorder on, as it wasn't plugged into the dead electrical system, but the battery was flat. There were a few other Files placed near the camcorder, so Brady threw these into a box of tightly packed Black Files, and these were strewn over the top.

Flickering orange light lit up the road from outside. He looked out, and he thought he recognised some of the members of Cesare's crew. They were patrolling the area as though they were the new law enforcement. He instinctively knew that he shouldn't hang around for a second longer than necessary. He had what he'd come for. When the patrol had turned the corner and was out of sight. Brady loaded up his trailer and moved his GreenBike™ and trailer from the hallway of Don Pickerstaff's home and back onto the road towards the safety of Highway 5.

He had started his journey home when his Satt™ went off. He pulled over and took the call. There were only a handful of cream cars which passed him by and a few bikes. 'Mary-Lou has had a miscarriage,' Lucian said, as he answered.

'I'm real sorry, buddy. Is there anything I can do? Anything you need?'

Lucian cried. 'No. I just ain't got no-one else to talk to. It's messed up, man.'

Brady encouraged Lucian to talk. *I ain't big on sharing feelings and all*, he thought, *but he is my best buddy. I'll let him do all the talking, and I'll be the good listener type.*

The ride back to McFarland seemed endless to Brady, and the thought of the atmosphere of sadness set to greet him back home took the edge off his feelings of success around his order book.

As he reached the outskirts of McFarland, he decided to drop in on Vance, to see if the middleman experiment was worth continuing.

He tracked him down to his home. He rapped on the door, and a young girl answered. 'Does Vance live here?'

'Yes sir. Who shall I say is calling?'

He noticed she showed no fear of him. 'Tell him it's Brady. Brady Mahone.'

Vance came to the door. 'Come in, man. Come up to my room, and we'll talk there.' A few people were chatting in the lounge, which had a similar vibe to the place where he shared the night with Lizzie.

'How's it going?' Brady said.

'Brilliant. I've made three hundred Green Credits in orders. It pays to know your audience, and not going door-to-door with only hope on your side.'

Brady wasn't going to divulge how much he had made himself, but he was impressed with the figures Vance was quoting - and all done without much effort. *I gotta admit,* he thought, *other people are better at business than me. What I need is a Vance in every town. I'll recruit when I deliver my products. I'm sure that some will work for my entertainments rather than pay me Greenbacks for them.*

'You've done well,' Brady said. 'Have you got the order details?'

'Sure thing, man.' Vance handed him wads of paper of assorted shapes and sizes.

Mary-Lou was right, he thought. *That's how I would have done it, and it's a mess.* 'I've got a proper order book. I'll bring you one to use. You'll find it easier to manage.'
'That's why you're the boss. Hey, so, I'll get my copies, y'know, as my payment - right?'

I'm going to need a bigger supply of Black Files at this rate. I might need Pops' little black book again, after all. 'Sure. A deal's a deal.'

'Great.' Vance smiled broadly, but Brady knew the relief of a fellow criminal when he broached the subject of being paid.

He held all the aces in this game, but he needed to cultivate his empire in these early days. He didn't like the guy, all the same.

'I need a vehicle,' he said. 'If I'm going to expand, I need to travel. Plus, I can't spend the rest of my days riding a bicycle like a fucking dork.'

'A Green Car, or FusionCar™ as we must call it, will put you back about two-thousand Green Credits.'

'What the fuck? For eleven hundred you can get both a Red™ and an OrangeNano-Suit™, but a car costs two-thousand?'

'It's three thousand for a FusionVan™.' Vance flinched as if expecting Brady to explode. 'They want you to obtain the Suits™. They don't want to encourage people to own vehicles. They say it's the vehicles that caused so much pollution.'

'Don't these cars run on…whatever power?'

'Yeah, but there's not many FusionPowered™ cars, so they're hard to come by. But the GreenRevs said that once we've got through the initial phases, more will be produced and then they'll become more affordable, and afterwards, they said that they will reintroduce FusionPowered™ consumer air travel, because they understand the human need to explore and feel free, blah blah blah. Right now, though… it is what it is.'

'Can you take me to an auto dealer?'

Vance shrugged. 'There's no point, man. There are only two designs available. One is a car like the one Cain has, the other is a van that's shaped like a hearse. You can have any colour you like as long as it's Ceramic Cream.' Vance laughed at his own joke. 'This isn't a material world, anymore. You can't change the design or customise them. Pride in ownership isn't encouraged.' He looked at Brady, who clearly was unimpressed. 'The good news is that they can run almost forever. No filling up, and no need for gas stations. Though they're not too quick - mind you.'

Brady had stopped listening. He was working out the fastest way to make more money. He thought about the notes he had made for Professor Chu and guessed they were of value to him. *But it's kinda one of those unwritten deals, a gentleman's agreement,* he thought. *I feel bad asking him for more stock. I always hated it when people did that to me.*

He then thought of another item which could be useful to a man like that, maybe valuable enough for the whole town to contribute - if the Professor could persuade them. *But how do I get around the lack of working technology?*

'Hey, Vance. You know that movie you showed about the science stuff. Have you got a copy of that?'

'Every household has. Information is free to all.'

'Can I borrow a copy? I'll bring it back.' Brady peered straight into Vance's eyes, daring him to negotiate.

'Uhhh… Yes. Ok.' Vance went downstairs. Brady listened as Vance tried to explain to his housemates who Brady was, and how Cain had instructed him to keep Brady happy. *Why would Cain say that?* he thought. *Are they scared of me?* Vance returned with a Black File with a tiny label marked: The New Green Deal.

Brady took it from him and pocketed it. 'Thanks, man.'

After leaving Vance, Brady went to the bus stop near his ranch, and removed the old service information poster behind a soft plastic cover. He put in his notes and observations of the places he had visited or seen. It covered dozens of districts between here and slightly to the south of Los Angeles. He heard footsteps. By now, after all his travelling, he didn't want another confrontation. Brady just wanted to go home and check-in on his Pops, and to see how Lucian and Mary-Lou were coping. He went to get on his bike and started to ride away when a voice called out to him. 'Brady - please, wait.'

Brady stopped and looked back to see Professor Chu walk to the bus shelter. He was walking an old black Labrador dog. He watched as the Professor retrieved the notes he had left behind. The Professor sat down on the bench in the shelter, and the black Labrador sat beside him, obediently.

As Brady approached the bus stop, the Professor said, 'I was walking Bessie, and I saw you. I guessed what you were doing, and I wanted to say thank you - while I still had the chance.'

Brady bent over and stroked the old dog, while Professor Chu scanned Brady's notes. Brady said, 'Is it any use to you?'
'Yes, very much so - not in a practical sense just yet, but it's good to have a feel for what's going on elsewhere. It looks like a mixed bag.'

'Yeah. But it seems to be the more rural and isolated places are already Green - or at least more civilised.'

The Professor smiled warmly, not taking offence at the unintended slight. 'I agree. That's an insightful assessment.'

'Why is it that there are a lot of rich people around Los Angeles who live in Green areas? I thought they were the worst polluters, the most materialistic. Why save them and not people like you?'

'That is an excellent question. In another life, you would have had potential.' Brady laughed sarcastically, but the Professor added, 'No. I mean it.' He looked like he was thinking deeply. 'If I were to judge the venerable Bodhi Sattva - not his real name, by the way - as a human and not as a guru, or a cult-leader, I would suggest that he has protected the area where he was raised as a boy, and by extension, the family and friends of those who were close to him.'

'Makes sense,' Brady said, without irony. 'That's what I would do.'

The Professor stood up, as did Bessie. 'I better head back. I don't want them to send the search parties out for me. Thank you for these...' He held up the notes. 'And continue to have safe journeys.'

'To tell you the truth, it's not a happy place where I'm going home to. My friend's partner has had a miscarriage.'

'It's happened all over town. The GreenRevs are sterilising the population. I can't see there being any future pregnancies.'

'Holy fuck! They can't do that, surely?'

'It's their world to do with as they please. I'm not wholly surprised at what they are doing - just the speed of it. It's the opposite of my field of expertise – they're using Nano Technology to end reproduction.'

'Why didn't they just kill us all and be done with it?'

'They need to keep their own people on board. The Green Communities will be unaware, for the most part, though the leaders will undoubtedly know the plans. In their minds, the human race has always been the biggest risk to the welfare of the planet and its eco-systems. In time, the old ways of man will fade from existence, and the Greens will be a population who will be dedicated to using mankind's skills to help Mother Earth.'

'You almost sound like one of them.'

'It was the sort of topic we used to discuss at length. I just didn't foresee that they would acquire the means to implement it.'

Brady sensed an opportunity, but it seemed utterly selfish under the circumstances. Still, he couldn't resist. 'I feel bad saying this. I know I'm not a good person and all…'

'Go on. You can say it - the truth is powerful - or you can ask it, and I can always say no.' He smiled.

'I want to make another deal. I want another thousand CDs and DVDs.'

'I don't think there are that many left in the town. What are you offering to trade?'

'I'm not sure. I have some information that you, personally, could use, I think - as you could make sense of it - but you don't have the means to access it, so, it might be useless.'

'Tell me what you have, and I'll make the proposal to Judge Jefferson - if I deem it worth the price.'

Brady went to his trailer and rummaged around in the pockets of his crumpled Poacher's coat and retrieved the Black File. 'This is the movie they played for the Greens - not just in West McFarland, but in every Green Community across the world. It has all the scientific stuff they used in the Revolution and the plans for the future. You haven't got the power, or the hardware to play it on if you did have electricity, I'm guessing.' He paused for a few seconds. 'But would you want it?'

Professor Yuan Chu thought over the potential benefits of acquiring this information over the costs of handing over out of date, and useless discs. He also considered the problem of extracting the data from it. 'I can't promise you one thousand discs, but I could give you my word to give you every last disc in the town. I also wouldn't know if you already had a copy. You might receive duplicates.'

'Ok, but I'm not dealing for any less than five-hundred, minimum.'

'Let's say we have a deal. You would need to do some work to make it acceptable for me. The only problem is that it would mean a lot of writing, and I don't mean to be disrespectful...'

'I don't write much, but I have somebody who could do that. What are you thinking?'

'Somebody would have to play the movie and write down, word for word, everything that was said. Also, add in a brief description of the scenes.'

Brady didn't know how smart Lucian was in the words department. He'd had a computing job, once, but Brady wasn't sure if you needed writing skills for that. But Mary-Lou might be able to do it. 'I'm good at drawing,' he said. 'It would take time. But I might have someone who could write it out.'

'We would have to work harder to find the required CDs and DVDs than we did last time. I suggest that we leave each other notes, in this bus shelter, on our progress over the next couple of days - and when we are ready, we make the exchange. How does that sound?'

'Sounds good to me. Let's shake on it.' Brady was careful not to shake the old man's hand too hard.

18.CODE BREAKERS

Brady's mood had darkened by the time he arrived home. He wondered about whether he would ever be able to have children. He considered Amie. Her future seemed over before it began. He decided against telling the family what he had learned. He thought about his Pops and how he hadn't been that far away from the truth, in his skewed worldview.

He put on a smile and used exhaustion as an excuse for his pensive mood. He hadn't intended to hug anybody, but they all hugged him, one by one, even Mary-Lou. He hadn't known a time in his life when he had been missed by anyone like this before.

'I'm sorry about, y'know, your news and all,' he said.

'Thanks, man,' Lucian replied. 'You look whacked. Let's get you inside and give you a chance to acclimatise. We'll get some food on, and we can all catch up over dinner.'

'I was going to put away the Files from my trailer.'

'I can do that for you - least I can do.'

Brady smiled. 'The ones with serial numbers are pre-recorded, and might not be any use, so put them away from the Blanks. If we get desperate, then we'll see if they can be wiped and re-used.'

They ate well - sat around the rough-hewn dining table in Archie's rustic but spacious kitchen area. 'Hey, Archie, old man, you certainly weren't planning on starving through the apocalypse,' Lucian said. 'You've got enough food to last you a hundred years at least.'

They all laughed as Archie's cheeks turned faintly red. 'When I was planning all this, I had a growing boy to cater for, and Jesus, it's just as well I did. Look at the size of him, now.'

Brady was relieved that the mood wasn't as gloomy as he'd feared. 'I know this ain't the right time and all,' he said, 'but I've got a job for Lucian and Mary-Lou - it could bring in up to another thousand discs. I'm sorry if I'm being insensitive, I'm not good in these, y'know, situations.'

'I can't lie,' Mary-Lou said. 'I'm feeling real low, but my life is so much better than the hell I lived in before. I'll always be grateful to you. In all honesty, I love the work, and if I can help you some more, then it will help to take my mind off things.' She looked away - Brady always made her blush a little, but she tried to recover quickly. 'What do you need?'

'I need somebody who's good at writing. I've got a movie the Greens played, showing how they made all this happen, and what they've got planned for the future. I met this Professor Chu guy over on the East Side, and he will pay for this in discs. Now they ain't got no power or equipment, so he asked for it - word for word.'

'A transcript,' Lucian added.

'Yeah. I can do the drawings because I remember a lot of diagrams were shown, and I think Professor Chu would appreciate that.'

'You always were good at sketching. I loved all those insects and animals you drew.'

'Thanks, Lucky.' Brady looked around the table and smiled. 'Can you do that?'

'How long was the movie?' Mary-Lou said.

'About an hour, I think. To tells you the truth of it, I fell asleep during it - I felt like I was back in school.'

Archie laughed. 'You ain't never been too good in the studying department, boy.' He reached over and ruffled Brady's black hair, which was beginning to grow out of the prisoner's crew cut. 'I sure would like to watch this movie of yours.'

Brady laughed. 'It was probably made just for you, Pops.'
'It'll take a while to do,' Mary-Lou said. 'There'll be lots of stopping and starting. And you'd have to stick around to do the drawings.'

'Not a problem. I'm sticking close to home for a while. The bike riding is killing me.' He looked around the table, 'I'm going to make enough money in the nearby town to buy one of the Green's vans. It means I won't be putting the Green Credits into here for a bit, as I got to save hard. I need three thousand Greenbacks. You'll be doing the work but getting no reward for a while.'

'I ain't got nothing better to do, buddy,' Lucian said.

Archie added, 'I ain't ever asked nothing from you, boy. You just make sure you stay safe.'
'Thanks, Pops. It will be worth it, eventually.' He turned to Mary-Lou. 'If we can get this transcript together, I'm thinking we could make lots of photocopies. Then I could sell it to other Trad areas when I take the orders back out.'

'That's a brilliant fucking idea,' Lucian shouted, before pausing. 'Sorry, Mary-Lou, I slipped up, again.'

Over the next few days, Brady and Professor Yuan Chu exchanged notes on their progress towards a deal.

Finally, Mary-Lou, Lucian and Brady finished the work on their document, and Brady settled for the eight-hundred and fifty-seven discs which exhausted the stocks in East MacFarland.

Brady travelled on his GreenBike™ with his trailer - the half-mile to the old bus stop to meet Professor Chu for the exchange. He saw he was accompanied by Judge Jefferson and a couple of men. He was wary of this apparent ambush, but not overly concerned. Still, he was hoping for a friendlier meeting. He dismounted his bike. 'Hey, Professor - what's all this?'

'It's nothing to worry about, Brady. I needed assistance with carrying this - I'm not as strong as you.' He smiled, warmly. 'Audre wanted to make sure everything went smoothly.'

'Hi, Judge,' Brady said cheekily.

'Hello, Brady. I never thought I'd be checking you've done your homework assignment.' She turned to her men. 'You boys can start loading the discs into Brady's trailer, if you wouldn't mind.'

'Yes Ma'am,' one replied, and began stacking the trailer neatly.

Brady handed his notes to the Professor, and the Judge moved in close to examine the documents with him. From Brady's perspective, they couldn't possibly be reading the pages that quickly, while talking at the same time.

'It seems the other thing they were spraying was fire retardant,' the Professor said, matter-of-factly. 'I'm guessing they were worried we would try to burn down our own buildings.'

'It's been done before, I suppose, in the good old days of riots and looting.' Brady laughed, in a needless attempt to show he was joking.

'I think it's their way of stopping us eating meat, and rearing cattle,' the Professor added. 'And reducing the risk of forest fires.'

Brady watched the way the Professor switched between the chat with him, and the intense scanning of the documentation. Professor Chu pointed to items which clearly fascinated him, and the Judge nodded in agreement. 'This is an excellent piece of work,' he said to Brady. 'Please, pass on my thanks to whoever did this.'

'Mary-Lou did the writing, and I did the drawings.'

'Really?' Audre said, glancing at the intricate drawings of Nanostructures. 'Truly remarkable - talk about hidden talents, Brady... I never knew you were so talented. I wish I had - I might have been inclined to punish you more constructively, instead of simply locking you up.'

'Water under the bridge, now. At least, you'll be reassured that I'll keep my word not to return to East McFarland. I know you haven't got any more CDs and DVDs.'

'I wish you no harm, Brady Mahone. Good luck in your business endeavours.'

The men had finished loading up Brady's trailer and backed away. Brady turned to Professor Yuan Chu. 'Give Bessie a pat from me - and thanks for not putting me down, and all. You're alright, y'know.'

'You too, Brady Mahone.' He held up the documents. 'This is straight A work and very much appreciated.'

19. SATTVA SYSTEMS™

Bodhi Sattva was the model of self-sacrifice. If his dreams of saving the planet from destructive climate change were to come to pass, then his home would be the most undesirable place in the world to live in.

He had little sense of pride in his massive industrial chemicals complex. The cream-coloured ceramic buildings, laboratories and enormous vats would have taken a day to walk around.

Bodhi managed his business by walking around. He was keen to be seen.

The old ways of doing business were an anathema to him, and he would only countenance them when it would have been utterly impractical to do it any other way. Bodhi Sattva's style was not to hold court in skyscrapers with highly polished tables with leather seats and giving his employees a bird's eye view of the kingdom he surveyed. Bodhi's style was pared back to all kinds of minimums. If there were trappings of success he enjoyed, then even his closest colleagues would be hard-pressed to name them, except for the unconditional respect and awe from his followers. His brand was an anti-brand, and yet it dominated every country in the world.

He walked for two hours, alone. He smiled and greeted every employee. He wore the same Sattva Systems™ overalls and hard hat that his workers wore - emblazoned with the moss green Sattva S. If they stopped and asked him a question, he replied truthfully - there was no sensitive information to protect in a world without competitors. He only held back if his management team needed to know first, as that was a matter of courtesy. He explained the need for civility to them when he denied them an answer. It was the civilised way to conduct his business. It only made them love him more.

Finally, he reached the transport hub of his Boulder Creek base. His visitors had requested permission to land near the Main Entrance of the Sattva Systems™ HQ, but he was eager to keep the trappings of hierarchy away from his front door. Bodhi held no possessions or trinkets of wealth to himself. He slept in a pod in the HQ, and he ate with the workers in the cafeteria.

The first of his visitors arrived in their private FusionPlane ™. Bridgett Tarnita brought the vehicle down vertically into the pre-allocated space. She was a continental Disciple for Europe, although her official title was only that of the Disciple for Green Malmo. Bodhi didn't want labels to become the new measure of wealth or self-worth - that was the Trad way of doing business.

Bridgett had been his person on the inside of the EU. She had first given him the indication that the climate change summit in 2050 would renege on all the climate change promises it had made a decade before. She effectively sealed the fate of the Trad world with her inside information, and she was now one of the most influential people in the new Green World except for Bodhi. Today she represented the Earth's Northern Hemisphere as she met with Bodhi Sattva to receive an update on the one-hundred-year plan.

The representative for Earth's Southern Hemisphere parked her private Fusion-Plane™ next to Bridgett's. Precious alighted her vehicle and went and stood beside Bridgett. They had to wait for two more visitors to arrive, and Bodhi would not want his next arrivals to appear to be at a disadvantage, so they all knew that he would greet them when they were all together. The tracking systems informed them that everything was on schedule, and they were due at any moment.

Precious hugged her ally while they waited for Glenarvon Cole and Rhea Laidlaw. Precious was the Disciple for Green Cape Town of Green South Africa - officially, but to Sattva Systems™, she was the continental Disciple of Green Africa.

Two more FusionPlanes™ came into land. Their gentle subsonic booms played like two heartbeats in competing rhythms. Glenarvon Cole was one person in the world who couldn't conceal his true stature. He was the Leader of the GreenRevs and the one person on the planet who could outdo the great Bodhi Sattva in the charisma stakes. He wore combat fatigues and yet seemed almost homely in his demeanour. The love of his fellow green warriors came from the knowledge that there was nothing he wouldn't do to protect them. He loved his soldiers, and they worshipped him in return.

Bodhi couldn't have completed the Green Coup without him, and Bodhi loved his revolutionary comrade. Glenarvon Cole was a man of his word, just as Bodhi Sattva was.

Rhea left her own FusionPlane™ and parked it next to the other three. The four vehicles looked precisely the same with their cream-coloured livery. The only difference was that Rhea's was a rental and not a private FusionPlane™. She could have had one, of course, but she played a winning card with Bodhi by eschewing ownership. Rhea had been given the small town of San Martin - a stone's throw from Boulder Creek - to administer as its Green Disciple. Its proximity to the Sattva Systems™ HQ enabled her to be Bodhi's eyes and ears in the outside world. She would jokingly describe herself as his Special Ops.

Bodhi smiled beatifically, and his arms outstretched, 'Welcome, friends.' They moved in for a group hug. This is how things worked when Bodhi held court.
'I'm going to give you the updates on the one-hundred-year plan. This means taking you to our esteemed Green Project Manager, Professor Pinar Dogan - you don't need me to tell you how difficult she can be.'

They laughed. Bridgett said, 'You provided us with the inspiration and the resources, but this is all hers.' She spun slowly around with her arms open wide to take in the surroundings.

'Ugly, isn't it?' Glen laughed.

Bodhi said, 'An unfortunate necessity.' He led them away, and he made a point of smiling at every worker, and the others followed his example in this silent training session.

It began to rain heavily, but the group hardly noticed, as the RedSuits™ repelled every water droplet.

Walking deliberately at the back of the group, Rhea over-rode her auto-settings by wanting to know what the rain felt like and instantly, she felt the cold rain in her hair and on her skin. Once it became uncomfortable, she turned the auto-settings back on again just by wanting it to happen. She still splish-sploshed through every puddle. *They all work so damned hard on being so self-effacing,* she thought, *I must remember to keep my sense of self within this Green cult.* Rhea knew there was little need for security, as the Greens were exceptionally well behaved, but it still perplexed her how they could enter any door at will. If there were warning signs, then that was considered ample to keep people from entering. Many doors informed them of hazardous or toxic materials, but workers wandered in and out of them without any protective clothing. She had to remind herself that she was now Red™ and that she had nothing to fear, but it was a hard habit to break.

I've never liked Bridgett, she thought. *Bodhi must have his uses for her - as her ruthlessness is way off the brand narrative of Sattva Systems™*. Rhea recalled Bridgett stating that eradicating the excess of humanity was the simplest solution to the climate change crisis. *She may as well have shrugged at the prospect for all she cared*. She considered Precious in her African Print Rotta blue dress, she wasn't in Bridgett's fanatical league, but she was a skilled politician and arch manipulator. Rhea was never privy to the private discussions they had with Bodhi, but she shuddered at the breadth of topics under consideration. *It's unusual for Glen to be here. He always gives the impression that his work is done. The GreenRevs delivered the world to Bodhi, and now Bodhi's job is to fix it.*

She had a trained eye for picking out details, but the Green logistics were clever within their simplicity. Everything they designed was the same colour schemes of cream and moss green, even the office walls. It was proposed as being anti-Trad, anti-capitalist, and anti-materialist, and yet it was the branding of the highest order. The rooms had no tell-tale signs of whether they were more important than the next. One room could be working on a revolutionary new product, while the next could be a storage cupboard. Again, this was sold as anti-Trad, but in a complex of this magnitude, she decided it was a brilliant way of hiding secret operations.

They went through a door that opened out into a vast laboratory. She recognised the Turkish-looking woman in her trademark black leather clothes in deep, some might say, aggressive conversation with a couple of her colleagues.

Professor Pinar Dogan peered across at her visitors disdainfully and then continued to berate her subordinates. She marched over to Bodhi. 'I haven't got time for this.'

Bodhi smiled, 'Now, Pinar. Play nice. Our friends have travelled a long way to see you. This is a need-to-know situation. There is a big world out there to keep on board with our plans. These are the people to make it happen.'

'Fuck you, pay me.' She added at the looks of bemusement from the group. 'I won't allow the fucking Security Protocols™ to come within a mile of me. They are mine. If he…' She pointed at Bodhi, 'wants me to alter the settings, then he has to ask me, and then I decide - after I've made him grovel first.'

Rhea was glad she stayed at the back of the esteemed visitors because she wanted to laugh, and here, nobody could see her smile. Bodhi was non-plussed, he was either used to this; or could hide his discomfort with consummate ease.

'All in good time.' Bodhi said. 'Your selections have historical merit, and we can't allow them to become shrines to the Traditional Cultures.'

'You didn't say that.' She barked, 'I'll tell you how it's going to be from now on. I'm gonna be paid up front. Every time you want something from me, here's what I'm gonna say: Fuck you, pay me…'

'I thought you would be able to work that out for yourself. How could you reconcile your choices with our desire to relieve our followers of the need for nostalgia and painful memories.' He turned to the group and gestured an apology. 'We'll take that off-line if that's ok.'

'Fuck you. No.' Pinar moved in nose-to-nose with Bodhi.

Glenarvon Cole broke ranks and ushered Pinar away. 'After the Red Ceremonies, I will take you with me, all over the world, to help you select suitable properties. You have my word.'

'You, I trust. But him…' She made a dismissive sweep of her hand. 'Ok. Let's get this over with. I'm busy.' She called out to one of her colleagues. 'Have the reports ready on my bench.' Pinar's choice of standing around a bench in a laboratory was all the hint she needed to give that she had no intention of dragging this meeting out a moment longer than necessary.

She marched to the bench, and her VIPs were reduced to ducklings trailing the mother. She whipped a report open. 'We have manufacturing plants running across the world at full capacity to generate enough Red Nanomaterials for the Red Ceremonies. For the life of me, I cannot fathom why all the poxy Green peasants need to receive it at the same time.'

'For the sense of theatre.' Bodhi said softly.

'I always hated the fucking theatre. I didn't get it.' Rhea laughed, and Pinar laughed in response. Pinar's mood softened. 'We've had to manufacture enough for more than nine-hundred million RedSuits™ it's taken a vast amount of resources. At the moment, I have to say, our victory hasn't helped much in the impact of climate change.'

Bridgett intervened, 'There are still more than eight billion Trads in addition to the nearly one billion Greens populating Mother Earth. This is an unsustainable amount in a potential runaway Greenhouse situation. We could consider the possibility…'

'No.' Bodhi said. 'There is to be no direct harm to any living creature. Nature will take its course now that we have loaded the dice in Her favour.'

Pinar said. 'Just as well. I wouldn't have agreed to that. I'm a scientist, not a genocidal maniac.'

'Neither are we.' Glen stated.

'The sterilisation programme will cap the Trad population…'

Precious said, 'I need to work hard to sell this. Some have said that this has always been a white man's plan to reduce the population in Africa.'

'Do I look like a fucking white man?' Pinar joked aggressively.

'I'll work with you to recalibrate the Security Protocols™ to ease your burden. I agree we need to address all concerns of our Green colleagues with the utmost sensitivity. Historical and Traditional issues are of little help to us in Her hour of need.' Bodhi placed his hand on Precious' shoulder.

'Can I continue?' Pinar said.

121

'Please do.'

'The massive reduction in energy consumption will soon feed through into the statistics. There is no more Trad power, no electricity or power plants of any kind. All vehicles have been deactivated. There will be little capacity left to even create fire once our NanoFireRetardents™ complete their spread. However, we are continuing to allow the water system - as we don't want to spread diseases that could enter the food chains or harm the environment further. While this will allow the Trads to grow crops, this will be offset by the difficulty of surviving the winter months, especially in the harsher climates. Life expectancy will fall dramatically in the coming decades, and without the prospect of repopulation through childbirth, then within twenty years, there will be a massive improvement in the climate. But please, don't be fooled. This is still a race against time…'

Bodhi said, 'She's right. The one-hundred-year plan is sacrosanct. It has been precisely calibrated and signed off by myself and Pinar. We can do this if we all work together as a team.'

'What do you want me to do?' Glen said.

'You, our Green Hero. I can't think of anybody better to select the most Devout of our Green colleagues to help save the planet for thousands of years to come.' Bodhi flicked over the pages of the reports to a map of the world. 'There are twenty-six million square miles of hospitable land on the planet, and I want you to allocate the most Devout Greens to take a square mile each…'

'You want me to recruit twenty-six million volunteers…'

'Yes. It's a big world that needs micro-managing if we are to protect Her for eternity.'

'Ok. I'll start with the original GreenRevs and begin building from there. I was wondering about what their role could be after winning the war. When do they start?'

'June 2184.'

'But that's a hundred years away. You are confident the technology…'

'Yes.' Pinar interrupted. 'It would be a huge investment of resources, but my team are working on a NanoSuit™ variant which could enable its users to live for a thousand years - minimum. Why do you think I want to have plenty of places to stay in around the world?' She laughed, but nobody else did. They were stunned at this development, everybody except Bodhi Sattva.

Rhea asked, 'The Brady Mahone anomaly - are there any others like him?'

Only Glenarvon Cole, among this select group, seemed not to understand the question. 'Who is Brady Mahone? Have I missed something while I've been away?'

Bodhi said, 'It's nothing.' Rhea flashed a look of apology to Bodhi.

Glen looked at Bodhi, suggesting that this wasn't an answer.

'He's an escaped convict, a Trad. However, he can enter Green territory seemingly at will.'

Bridgett turned to Rhea. 'There have been no reports of any breaches in Europe or Asia.'

'Nor any from any of my territories. It seems he's a one-off. My guess is that he is Green, but maybe he doesn't know it.'

'Let's discuss the evidence,' Glen folded his arms, 'I don't like information being kept from me. I want to hear what you've got.'

'He's from California. He escaped from the Modern Ridgecrest Supermax Penitentiary on Revolution Day. He's a career criminal. However,' Bodhi attempted to appear serene, 'he wandered into the Green town of West McFarland unimpeded, but the Security Protocols™ apprehended him for attempting to steal groceries. He's nothing to worry about. In fact, he's become a little pet project of mine.' He touched Glenarvon Cole on his arm. 'Let me handle it. It's all under control.'

Glen looked at Pinar. 'How is this possible? The Shells™ have been tested for decades.'

'My team have their theories, but he seems to confound us at every turn.' Pinar laughed heartily, 'He's brought us much amusement. He's started up his own business selling entertainment to the people.'

Bodhi smiled, 'He's no threat. We have to learn from this specimen.'

'That's not enough.'

'It's not one Green area,' Pinar continued, 'nowhere is off-limits to him. We have evidence that he had been wounded on his travels. This would suggest that he is a Trad and, that he hasn't adopted a NanoSuit™. He is looking after a Trad family. However, he has murdered since his release…'

'And you say he's not a threat.' Glen said pensively.

Rhea watched on taking mental notes of the conversation.

'How old is he?'

'Forty-two? He was adopted by Archie and Edie Mahone - utterly unremarkable people.'

Glen said, 'The Security Protocols™ only intervene to save Greens. That's the whole point of the calibration of them. They prevent unlawful and disrespectful behaviour from one Green to another.'

Pinar laughed sarcastically, 'Of course. If we tried to rule over the Trads bad behaviour, the fucking things would explode in seconds.' Bridgett, Precious and Bodhi laughed along, but Glenarvon and Rhea didn't seem to find this observation particularly amusing.

Rhea smiled a little when she noticed Bodhi looking at her.

'So, the Security Protocols™ activated on the signals emitted by the Trad, Brady Mahone, to prevent him stealing…' Glen was thinking out loud.

'They also intervened when they detected sexual interference.' Pinar added.

'What the fuck was this animal up to?'

'Brady Mahone was the victim. He was touched inappropriately while suspended in NanoFilm™.' She shouted, 'Ha-ha! I got you. You should see your faces.'

'I don't think this is a laughing matter. It's a breach of security. We could…'

'No.' Bodhi said. 'We have a new world order. We cannot alter our core beliefs and principles for one man. We do not harm a single creature. He is one of Mother Earth's sentient beings. He should be allowed to try and survive like any other of Her creations. I will watch over Brady Mahone. I'm just trying to find a way where his uniqueness could be of use to me.' Bodhi smiled before adding, 'If he does anything to suggest he is more of a threat or indeed a potential enemy to our cause, then I'm sure that I'll have the wherewithal to deal with him.'

Pinar had lost interest and was flicking through her files, she still had to inform them about Destructive NanoEnzymes™, and they had already derailed the session with the talk of one rogue Trad. She wanted to bring this waste of time meeting to an end. She muttered, 'When a man plays God, is his enemy the Devil?'

20.ORDER FULFILMENT

Over the next month, Brady worked hard to supply his customers, and to deal his photocopied transcripts. He had set himself the goal of buying his FusionVan™ by Thanksgiving, and he achieved that and more. He checked his Distor™, and it informed him that he was now the proud owner of three-thousand and seventy-one Green Credits.

He went into West McFarland to pick up his van. He'd ordered it two weeks previously, as there was very little stock available anywhere in the state, apparently. He paid the GreenAutos™ owner the three thousand Greenbacks by dialling up the small ratchet on the Distor™ until the three-thousand glowed green. *I have to give this willingly,* he reminded himself. A green chip emerged from his Distor™ with the figure of three-thousand glowing on it. He picked it out between his thumb and forefinger, and it flashed as he handed it over to the owner who, in turn, placed it into his own Distor™.

'All done,' he said. 'She's all yours. She'll only respond to you, and she will send out sub-sonic signals when you are within range to ensure you don't lose her, or if you need to find her within a host of other FusionVans™. And you have full Nano-Shell™ protection within her, even if you go into the Trad areas.'

Brady examined his new car. It was an elongated van shape which Brady had already nicknamed the Hearse. It was ceramic cream, even the wheels and what he assumed were tyres. *It's an ugly sonofabitch fucking car,* he thought, *but now I can expand and make some real fucking money.*

He drove it back to the ranch. *It doesn't drive real fast, but it seems to know what to do before I do.* He celebrated having his new car at the family's Thanksgiving dinner, and even if he wasn't particularly proud of how it looked, he was proud of the fact that he had earned the money to buy it. He felt good about loading his stock in the Hearse. There was room in the back for his bike and trailer, which he figured he would still need in the Trad areas with barricades and roadblocks. There, he would leave his car in a green area and cycle.

He announced to the family that he would be gone for a few weeks but hoped he would be back for Christmas. He also asked Archie for his little black book. He didn't tell his Pops that this time he wouldn't be messing around trying to negotiate. He would take what they had and kill them if necessary. It was the obvious course of action, and if Archie was the only one to mourn them, then so be it.

Those fuckers don't deserve no mercy.

He appreciated the long drives down the almost uninhabited Highways. He also noted more towns had turned Green, though it was mostly the small hamlets at this point. He left the Highways to see how the streets were, there - and spotted the same patterns as on the Highways. The roads were cleared, the vehicles were *eaten,* (as Brady described it), and the buildings were sprayed, some already showing early signs of decay. Only the road infrastructure appeared to be protected. *It looks like they don't even want the Greens moving in there,* he thought, *although it's excellent for shortcuts.*

Brady switched into different personas as he went from place to place. He was threateningly charming as he recruited his Sales Reps, friendly and amenable as he sold his stock to new customers, and as upright as a citizen could be as he dealt with the great and the good when selling his documents. *I know these folks see me as nothing more than a snake-oil salesman, but as long as they pay me…*

He took his time exploring the formerly wealthy coastal areas. Some he had already visited as he now fulfilled his orders from a few weeks earlier, but now he explored further in search of the more well-heeled Green customers.

He was on his way back to the Hearse after a successful day's orders in Malibu when an old man in a suit - which gave him the appearance of a servant, rather than a businessman - approached him.

'Excuse me, sir. Libby Berrington requests an audience with you.'

I know the name, but I just can't place it, he thought. 'Is she buying?'

'I don't know, sir. She only said that she was sure you would want to meet her.'

'Where does she live?'

The old man pointed high up a cliff-top to something the size of an estate, rather than a home. 'I've got a lot of potential business down here,' Brady said. 'I'll see if I can head over this evening.'

'But sir, she said you would want to meet her. She sees very few people, and she is one of the most important people in California, maybe even the world, now.'

'I ain't got time for meets and greets,' Brady said. 'It'd better be worth it. Who is this dame, anyway?'

'Libby is the Mother of Bodhi Sattva. I trust you've heard of Sattva Systems™.'

'No fucking way am I walking into a trap. You must think old Brady is a stupid fuck. Step away old man, I ain't got time to be put away for bootlegging.'

A robotic voice stated from the ether - or from a speaker in a palm tree:

Increased stress levels detected. You may be contemplating committing an act which is not permitted in the Green Zone. Please accept our apologies if this is not the case. This message was brought to you by the Security and Protection Division of Sattva Systems™. Please enjoy the rest of your day.

The old man seemed ruffled. 'Oh, dear. Sir, I truly believe Libby only wants to meet you. I detected no trace of ill intent. Shall I inform her that you will meet her shortly?'

Brady tried to control his breathing and temper. He didn't want to end up wrapped in SecurityFilm™ again. 'Fine.'

'When you arrive, the guards will be expecting you.'

Brady drove up the snaking roads to the cliff-top mansion, and the gates opened without him even having to stop. The first thing he noticed was the fleet of ceramic cream cars. *In the old days, they were Ferraris and Bentleys*, he thought. *I miss those days - those cars had style.*

The threat of SecurityFilm™ reminded him that no one would be remotely scared of him in this place, not even the old woman who came out to greet him. She opened her arms. 'My dear Brady Mahone. Bodhi said that I really should meet you if ever you came to Malibu.'

The Palm trees stood like sentries as they walked together, down the long driveway to the main entrance, lined by garages on either side - with exclusive chalets above them. In front of him was a huge, glass-panelled entrance, and at the centre of the lobby was a spiral staircase of marble with ebony bannisters.

'So, which room are you staying in?'

Libby laughed. 'It's all mine, my dear. Trust me, I earned it.'

He studied her like he would an animal before he began to sketch it. He couldn't work out how old she was. Her hair was grey, but it was sleek and shiny, with traces of remaining jet-black strands running through it. She was slender and tanned, and her clothes were stylish and undoubtedly expensive. *And,* he thought, she smells amazing.

She guided him up the staircase to the gallery, which appropriately was lined with artworks from the late twentieth century. The place was so large that Brady lost his bearings, until he spotted the driveway he had walked down beneath him, the Pacific Ocean visible through the Palm trees. He looked down, and steps led to a sizeable open-aired jacuzzi only covered from the elements by a sloping glass ceiling.

Libby walked down the steps and her clothes melted away and now she was in a black swimsuit. Brady blinked, amazed by what he'd just seen. She entered the hot, bubbling water. 'Would you care to join me? We could get to know one and other a little better.'

After showering nude every day in prison with every kind of criminal, being naked with this old woman held no concerns for him – so he stripped. Libby looked at him approvingly as he sploshed down the steps, before lying in the pool like he was the master of the house.
'Could I get you anything?'

'A drink would be nice.' He chuckled. 'I don't suppose you've got any cigars lurking around the place?'

She rang a tiny bell which tinkled in the soft winter breeze. The old man appeared. 'Hunter, kindly bring Champagne for my guest and I, Brady...'

'Mahone. Brady Mahone.'

'And cigars. I think you'll find them in Freddie's old room.' She turned to Brady. 'One of my ex-husbands. I've had four - quite the collection. He was small for a Hollywood actor - but perfectly formed.'
The champagne and cigars arrived. Hunter helped Brady to light the cigar, and waited until Brady was content, then placed them on a wooden shelf which overhung the edges of the jacuzzi. Brady chuffed away at the cigar, blowing smoke rings. He gulped down a glass of champagne before retrieving the bottle from the ice bucket and pouring himself another. He positioned himself for the best view of the ocean, and then breathed out a contented sigh.

Libby sipped her champagne and smiled. 'I do like a man who can make himself at home. It shows confidence - and there is nothing more attractive in a man than confidence.'

'You have to take what you can while you have the opportunity. I'm not going to miss out on this. I've never been on vacation,' he added. 'I'm guessing this is what it would be like.'

'Yes. I suppose it would.'

They lay in the jacuzzi for more than an hour, barely uttering a word. Brady concentrated on the hot bubbles swirling around his naked body while drinking his champagne and smoking his cigar. The old man, without needing to be asked, brought out fresh bottles when required, and helped Brady to light his second cigar. Brady loved this place. The winter sun began its late afternoon descent, and he probably wouldn't have moved, even if Libby had suggested it. All he wanted to do was to feel the warm California breeze on his face and to watch the hazy sun sink into the sea in a display of fire-red against the backdrop of the wispy blushing clouds.

'Are you glad you came to visit me now?'

'Yes. I'm super-chilled.'

Libby laughed. She climbed out of the jacuzzi and was instantly dry, then instantly dressed in another set of clothes, as though she was about to attend an exclusive restaurant in the city, and Brady detected the scent of another sensuous perfume which was different to the last. Before he decided to leave, she returned with a white luxury bathrobe and slippers. 'I don't want you to slip on the marble floors.'

He pulled his naked body from the jacuzzi, and she held open the dressing gown for him to slip his arms into, and she tied the robe as if she were dressing a child.

Hunter appeared. 'Have Brady's clothes washed and take him to Xavier's bedroom,' she said. She turned to Brady. 'He was about your size when he was younger. Pick out what you want, and you can wear them this evening. Hunter will have your old clothes ready to take with you when you leave. Anything you choose - you can keep,' she added, smiling mischievously.

'Can your friend Hunter give me a tour of the place?' *I won't be able to steal anything,* he thought, *but there's no harm in scoping out the joint.*

'Of course, but don't be too long, as I was hoping you'd have time for dinner with me. Is there anything in particular you'd like?'

'Steak - well-done, with fries, mushrooms, onion rings and pepper sauce.'

Libby laughed. I should have guessed, she thought. 'I'll have my chef attend to it.'

As Hunter showed him around, Brady asked lots of questions. 'So, who's this Libby broad?'

'She was one of the most famous and glamorous actresses in Hollywood. I'm most surprised you hadn't heard of her.' Hunter changed direction and headed down another hallway, 'This way is Libby's bedroom.' All along the corridor was framed photos and movie posters. There were semi-naked poses in her youth, intermingled with costume dramas and serious poses through her middle-age.

'How many bedrooms does this place have?'

'Twelve, sir.'

'There seem to be as many lounges.'

'Yes, there are. There's also the games room, the cinema, the gymnasium, of course, and the kitchens. And before you ask, there's a private beach, four swimming pools and tennis courts.' He changed direction to head back to Xavier's room. Brady noticed a children's playroom, and it was full of toys and games for all ages.

'Who's that for?'

'It's for the visitor's children, to keep them amused while Libby is entertaining.'

'On the way back, I want to see the other bedrooms,' Brady said. 'The one Libby sleeps in, and the ones where her ex-husbands did as well.' While in Libby's bedroom he was struck by the beauty of one large movie poster. It was called the Virgin and was billed as an epic masterpiece. Libby was dressed in gossamer white and looked like an angel. She was playing the Virgin Mary. Brady gasped. 'Wow!'
'Everybody said she should have won her Oscar for that role,' Hunter said. 'It was a travesty. John Kane believed so and he used this to seduce her. She was outstanding in that role - utterly compelling.'
'So, why didn't she win?'
'The conspiracy theorists believe there was pressure bought to bear by the Catholic church. It is Libby's personal favourite image of her,' he added. 'John and Xavier loved it also. Xavier used to gaze upon it, just like you are now.'
Brady looked at it for a moment as if he was an art critic studying a masterpiece. 'I want to see the rest.'

'As you wish, sir.'

After a few minutes, they arrived, and Hunter opened the door for Brady. 'Here we are, sir. The walk-in wardrobe is over there.' He gestured to the left. 'And if you need to freshen up, then the en-suite bathroom is off to the right.'
Brady flopped down on the enormous bed and moved his head from side to side to take in the vast bedroom. There were a few photos of Libby - some with her son, and presumably, Xavier - AKA Bodhi's father. He got up, and went to the en-suite - another cavernous room with a golden bath at the centre, a sink area and a mirror above that both spanned the whole length of the room, as well as a gold toilet. If he'd had more time, he would have taken a bath, despite having spent all afternoon in the pool. He washed, and shaved, and then went over to the display shelves and put lots of aftershave on - just like he used to do with the tester bottles at the local drug stores.

He went to the walk-in wardrobe and flicked through the suits. He picked a dark one - this would be more practical in the outside world where he lived. He chose a silk shirt, but didn't want to wear a tie. In the drawers, he found expensive underwear and socks, and in a cupboard, he found expensive footwear of all kinds. He knew he should have chosen shoes to go with the suit, but the exclusive limited-edition sneakers took his eye, and they would be more comfortable to travel in.

When he was dressed, he left the room, and found Hunter waiting for him. 'Shall we continue the tour, sir?' he said stiffly, clearly disapproving of Brady's sartorial selections. He showed him the bedrooms, as Brady checked out whether there was stuff left behind in these vacated rooms, and he also took notice of any photos of the exes, especially the size and shape of them as they posed with Libby or Xavier.

Hunter guided him through the banqueting hall and through to a smaller dining room where the table was dressed as if Brady was a visiting royal. Hunter pulled out a chair for Brady, and he waited impatiently for Libby to arrive. *This is all good n'all,* he thought, *but I could have made some sales.*

He fiddled around with the heavy cutlery and ran his finger down the razor-sharp blade of the steak knife. He scanned the room and looked at the photos and expensive artwork. He saw Libby walk in with Hunter, who pulled out her chair. She sat, and whispered her instructions to Hunter. She didn't say anything to Brady, just gave a small smile of acknowledgement.

Then there was a burst of activity as waiters attended to them. She smiled at Brady. 'I didn't want to start a conversation, only to be interrupted by the staff. I do hope you understand. I think we should get to know one and other better.'

Brady drained a glass of wine with indecent haste, and a waiter refilled it immediately. 'Fine with me. Can I interest you in some of my Entertainment Files? I've got a catalogue in my Hearse - I mean, FusionCar™.'

How delightful, he's going to play the part of a low life travelling salesman, she thought. *My dear Xavier, what have I done to deserve this?* 'Sounds enchanting. I will peruse your delights after dinner.'

Brady ate well and drank a lot, but he didn't display any obvious signs of drunkenness. *I have to admit,* he thought, *that was the best steak I ever had.*

Afterwards, Hunter escorted them down in the elevator, which Brady hadn't noticed before. They walked over to a lounge area which overlooked the ocean. Brady gazed over the dark water and watched the moonlight fragment on the gentle waves.

Hunter was given his instructions, and a drinks cabinet was wheeled over, a cigar box was opened and left on the table, and some soft jazz music played in the background. Brady noticed the lights dimming. *If I didn't know better,* he thought, *I'd guess the old broad was trying to seduce me.*

'I can't say I ever saw many movies,' he said, 'so I can't flatter you by saying I loved a film you were in.' *It's now, or never,* he thought. *I need to make some sales before I leave.* 'But speaking of movies, I'll grab my catalogue and order books from my van.'

After a couple of wrong turns, he found his way back to the entrance, and then to his Hearse. He took a few deep breaths of the refreshing ocean air and fixed his eyes on a bright star until he could tune it from a blur in his eyes into a sharper focus - it made him feel like he could control his oncoming drunken state. *Whatever we are drinking, it's strong stuff. It's going to my head.*

He went back to join Libby and placed his Mahone Enterprises catalogue, with its amateurish-looking logo, designed by Mary-Lou, on the ebony and glass coffee table. Libby picked it up, and flicked through the pages, chatting in a distracted way, almost to herself. 'Nobody kept any hard copies. Everything was streamed, and to such high-quality - even my cinema is set up for streaming. I must get Xavier to arrange installation of some old-fashioned hardware. It would be lovely to use the cinema again.' She added, 'If ever you use my son's name be sure to pronounce the X as in X-avier, some try to say it as Zavier.'

I'll call him what the hell I want, he thought. Still, he played along. 'Why's that?'

'He was John's Project X. He used to joke that learning human nature was as easy as X, Y and Zee. Then he would say X marks the spot for perfection, Y is for the triers, and Zee is for life's losers. I can't say I understood him.' Libby looked away as if this was a memory she craved to delete. She moved back gratefully to a subject she could be distracted by.

She browsed his catalogue until she came to a section rich with movies which interested her. Brady moved next to Libby, with his pen poised over his order book. She looked at him, and her eyes sparkled as if she had transformed into the Hollywood starlet of her youth. It was as if another version of her had been switched on.

She continued her monologue while pointing at her selections, and Brady hurriedly copied the reference numbers into his order pad. 'Oh, such memories... She was such a sweetheart, but I couldn't say the same about her... That was one of my favourite performances... I was nominated for an Oscar in that role... That was where I met Freddie, we had such fun.' Libby continued her trip down memory lane for more than an hour, and Brady ended up with more than seventy orders in his book. He took the unusual step of asking for payment upfront. *She's loaded*, he thought. *She can afford to take the risk.* He wondered if the SecurityFilm™ would wrap him up if he displayed any bad intent in his vital signs, anyway. *It would be bad for business if I didn't deliver, as she would tell those wealthy friends of hers not to buy from me.*

Libby was merry from the alcohol, and in a dreamy state. She rang her tiny bell, and Hunter appeared with her Distor™. *He must be listening. She didn't even ask him for it.* She duly paid Brady the seven-hundred and fifty Green Credits. 'I'll bring them over in a couple of days,' he said.

She nodded. 'What kind of movies did you like?'

'Action movies, things with cool special effects. I used to like those Marvel comics ones. Were you in any of those?'

'No. My area was complex studies of relationships, and the occasional costume drama.'

'When was that?'

'At the turn of the century and through to the late twenties. The three great pandemics curtailed my career, somewhat.'

'So, how old are you then?' he said, bluntly.

'I'm one-hundred and fourteen years old.'

'Wow. I wouldn't have had you as a day over seventy.'

He would never know how much of an insult this was to Libby. 'One of the benefits of having a husband and son who led the world in cutting edge technology.'

'Like the clothes changes you do. What colour are you? That's what you Greens are into now, isn't it?'

She looked at him, still angry at his assessment of her as a woman - an old woman - but she had her assignment to complete. 'What have you learned about the Nano-Suits™?'

'The Red™ one makes you indestructible. Professor Yuan Chu - nice guy by the way - said something about Diamonoid Shells. That kind of makes sense, y'know - diamonds and all.' *I miss those jewellery heists.* 'And then everybody has to save hard or work hard to grab one of the OrangeSuits™, which will look out for germs, and keep everybody healthy.'

'You've been keeping company with Professors?'

'Just the one. He treated me with respect.'

'And where was this?'

Brady didn't want her to know - he knew a potential undercover approach when he heard one. He wouldn't just lead her to the Professor, he would be leading them to his new family. 'Castaic - just south of Bakersfield. So, what colour are you?' He changed the subject as quickly as he could.

'Yellow™. It comes after Orange™. The textile industry uses so much water and resources... We just won't need it anymore. Personally, I welcome the return to freedom of expression through appearance - I was beginning to wonder if they were planning to eliminate style as well - which would have been quite unbearable.' Libby laughed at her own joke. Brady didn't think it was all that funny, but he smiled, anyway.

They talked for a couple of hours over brandy, while Brady chuffed away at his huge cigars. She spoke of her early childhood memories of London before moving to the States when her Hollywood career hit the heights. Occasionally, she mentioned how she met her ex-husbands, in no particular order, all were fellow leading actors in the movies she made with them. She discussed the merits of her movies, punctuated with, *I was nominated for this or that award, but I always just missed out...* And then she began to mention her first husband more, Brady guessed that the drink was talking now, *I thought this OrangeSuit™ would at least come up with a hangover cure.*

'I was Libby Skye, in my Hollywood glory days - such a lovely name. Then I became Libby Kane. John insisted that I take his surname. He was an industrialist with a vast fortune, and a man who was used to getting his own way.' Brady wanted to smile when she began to slur like an angry drunk as it revealed a Trad trait... 'But I drew the line at changing my name to Sattva. Libby Sattva, I mean, come on. I couldn't stop him changing Xavier's name to Bodhi.'

'Why did he do that?'

'John had one of those midlife crises and went all "Buddhist" on me. He wouldn't hurt a living creature, but he sure didn't mind hurting me.'

Brady thought about this. 'I noticed you don't have any of those Sattva Signs any-where - not in your home, or in this part of Malibu at all.'

'This is my home. It's mine, I earned it. My home is not a damn corporation.' She closed her eyes, like a drunk trying to find a moment of clarity to re-join a conver-sation. 'Him and his visions, I thought meditation was supposed to bring peace. Anyway, after one of his interminable meditation sessions, he believed he was chosen to save Mother Earth and that a boy would be born at the turn of the Millennium to guide us to the New World.' Her demeanour darkened further. 'You look like him. He's playing games with me. How old are you? Where did you come from?'

'Me? I'm forty-two, I think.'

'You think?'

'I was abandoned as a baby outside a drug rehabilitation clinic. It was February time in 2042. Then I was in care, I was told, until I was fostered when I was four. I was kinda forgotten about, and just left there.'

'Nobody visited you?'

'Apart from the police, when they came to arrest me for something I *did* do.' He laughed. 'I hate it when the inmates squeal about the injustice done to them. I did it, I deserved it, but I got away with most of the stuff I did. When they caught me, I was unlucky, not because I didn't plan it right.'

'What did you do?'

He knew she wasn't scared – she was wearing a RedSuit™, and the NanoFilm™ would get him if a bad intention so much as crossed his mind – so he didn't mind telling her the truth. 'I was in for armed robbery, grand theft auto and assault. But I have committed murder, too. I just ain't been to jail for that - yet.'

She didn't seem at all fazed by his crimes. 'And nobody visited you - to check up on how you were doing?'

'Only my Foster Daddy from time to time. My Foster Moms drank herself to death when I was a young 'un.'

'I could look after you,' she said. 'I could pay for your NanoSuits™, all of them. Or any colour you like.'

Brady began to feel as if he had been suckered into being here. He heard his Pops' voice in his mind: *That's how they get you, son.* 'No. Thanks,' he said. 'I'm just fine as I am.'

'As you wish. Bodhi ensured I was a Green Credit millionaire before his revolu-tion. I made sure my friends and neighbours were well compensated. I wasn't going to live here as a pariah. I need my friends.'

Brady made a mental note of the other Greenback millionaires he had to track down around here. 'What happened next, after the visions your husband had?'

'Pass me another drink. I think I'm going to need it.' Brady poured her another large Brandy. She sipped it elegantly, but Brady noticed that half the glass had been drained. 'John was a perfectionist. He wanted to run all kinds of tests on me to see how feasible it would be to conceive and have a son - it had to be a son - as close to midnight on the Millennial day as possible. You can probably deduce that John wasn't a particularly romantic person. I, of course, refused. I was a Hollywood Star in my own right. I had signed his prenup, and there weren't many upsides for me. Even if it had been possible, I didn't want to miss out on the party of the century to go into bloody labour.'

She took another sip of brandy. *He told me to tell him everything,* she thought. *He told me he could have anything he wanted, and if I refused, I would be punished.* 'John promised me anything I wanted, one thing - he specified, up to one hundred million pounds - which was a lot of money back then.' She laughed again at her own joke, but Brady didn't get it. 'And it would be entirely in my name and outside the scope of any future divorce proceedings. I did mention that he was a romantic, didn't I?'

Brady laughed. He was intrigued. He reflected upon all the things he might have chosen - the luxury high-performance cars, the massive gold chains, 'So, what did you choose?'

'This place. This home is mine, and mine alone. Even after the Green Revolution, Bodhi had to honour his father's promise to me. I gave him life. He only exists because of me. I have my home, and my friends and I earned it.'

Brady scoffed. 'You missed a party - you had a baby - but you earned all this? Get real, lady.'

'Let me tell you about that night. Pour me another.' Brady did, pouring himself one as well. 'I had been through all kinds of tests. My eggs had been engineered to ensure I would have a boy. The doctors and nurses had been well-rewarded for working on the Millennial Eve, but what I didn't know was that they were offered bonuses that would make them rich for life if they induced me to have the first baby in the world born on the Millennial Day. They even had a registrar ready. I should have wondered why I had to go to Tonga to deliver the baby. You could say that they were highly motivated. The only rule was that I couldn't have a Caesarean section, I must have a vaginal birth.'

Too much information, Brady thought.

She pulled her left hand to her face and breathed heavily into her palm. 'They were brutal with me. As the clocked ticked down, they tried everything to bring Xavier into the world, and then as the clock was about to strike twelve, the surgeon butchered me. He sliced me up. They used a ventouse and pulled him into the world on the first second of the new Millennium. I cannot find the words to describe the agony they made me endure. I suppose I should be grateful that they stuck around for the emergency surgery I needed afterwards. If I'd have known what John's plan was, I would never have agreed to it, not even for this place. I have massive scarring to this day - even after the best cosmetic surgery you could buy back in those primitive times.'

Brady wasn't overly interested, but he had learned that information had some value to the Trad areas, and it would give his business legitimacy if he could claim to be friends with Bodhi Sattva's mother. He thought it wise to keep her talking. 'What happened to Bodhi?'

At first, she scowled at the lack of interest in her welfare. *I suppose I shouldn't be surprised*, she thought. *He's a man, after all - and an uneducated criminal.* 'Xavier's education began even before he was born. John had his teachers come and talk to the baby inside me. Can you imagine how weird that was, having to let complete strangers hover over my stomach and recite science and business lessons to a foetus? Every single day I had to let them do that to me.'

'Was there nothing you could do about it?'

'I wasn't allowed to prevent this under the terms of our agreement. I did rebel in my own little way - I always do.'

'What did you do?'

'I talked to my unborn baby. He could hear me day or night. I used to say, "Xavier, this is your Mother. Whatever anybody should say to you, you must always protect your Mother." I must have looked like I was insane, but I talked to my boy, all the time, day and night. I had to keep my bond with my baby.'

'Did you have any other kids?'

'No. I tried. Freddie, in particular, was desperate for a child with me. That's why he left me, I believe. In no time at all, he was playing Daddy with my best friend. They were very dark days for me.' She sighed. 'I didn't even have Xavier for long. John took complete control over his upbringing. He was Daddy's little science project.' She waved her hand dismissively as if she were physically shooing away her memories.

Brady excused himself to go to the bathroom. Libby called Hunter over.

Libby was drunk. *I suppose I'd better get this over with,* she thought, *God only knows why Xavier insists on putting me through this ritual humiliation to play his little games.* She whispered to Hunter, 'I know I'm supposed to offer him the run of the place, and I'm not to suggest limitations, but I think I can bend the rules a little.'

'What would you like me to do?' Hunter said.

'Let him think that my personal and sentimental items are Film protected.'

'Which items?'

'Diaries, jewellery, artworks and photos…'

'I hope I won't be impacted.'

'Just do this for me, will you?'

'Yes, Libby.'

'Get others to help you. This one is going to be greedy.'

Hunter marched away, smiling at Brady as he returned. Libby stood up to greet him. 'I do believe it's Christmas in three days. We are not allowed to celebrate traditional date related festivals, here in the Green world – they're synonymous with materialistic indulgences and the depletion of the planet's resources. But no-one said anything about giving things away. I assume they are still planning Christmas festivities in the Traditional Areas?'

'Yes. Why wouldn't they?'

'Why, indeed. Hunter will escort you, but please feel free to take any items I own that could be of use to you. That will be my Christmas gift to you.'

I'm glad I asked for payment upfront, he thought. *Otherwise, I might have felt under pressure to give her the Files she ordered, free-of-charge.* 'Great, I mean - thanks.' He acted casually, but he was cautious, he glanced around for signs of a trap. However, the lure of free stuff was too tempting to pass up.

As Hunter and Brady left the room, Brady instantly began deciding how he'd make the most of this opportunity. He had robbed homes before, and he was thinking of the valuable items he could ram into his car. *The bike and trailer are taking up valuable space,* he thought. *I could leave the bike and pick up another rental later. But the trailer could be filled up. I need to organise the items. I could use sheets...*

'Sir, there is a trap within the request that you should be aware of,' Hunter said.

'Trap? Fuck.'

'You'll be able to take anything, but the artwork and jewellery are Film Protected, as are her personal objects, like diaries and photos. It wasn't intentional, but I think in her inebriated state, it slipped her mind. Bodhi had those things additionally covered.'

Brady was disappointed, but grateful for the information. He noticed a couple of men and a woman approaching.

'Michael, Jasper and Holly,' Hunter said, 'please assist Mr Mahone. He is very dear to Libby, and she has given him the freedom of the house to take away with him anything he needs. You can help take the items to his van.'

'Yes, Hunter,' they said, in unison.

'First off, I need a dozen sheets, some cords and cable ties, and a Magic Marker,' Brady said. 'I want you to lay them on the floor so I can sort things out. Is that clear?'

'Yes, Mr Mahone.'

Brady began with Xavier's room and rifled it for clothes, shoes, toiletries and aftershaves. He poised at the jewellery but left it untouched. He proceeded onto every other bedroom, followed by the kitchen. After three hours, his van was packed with wrapped up sheets, each full of luxury items. Then, he realised: he had more room on the passenger side. He asked for pillowcases and headed to the kitchens and utility ro oms and stuffed these with food, alcohol, cigars, and even cleaning materials and detergents.

He finished packing the car, convinced he had used up every square inch of space when Hunter handed him his Catalogue and Order Book. He placed them under the driver's seat. *I should have thought about that before,* he thought, *but at least I don't have to give anything back.* 'I better go in and say thank-you. Goodbye, and all that.'

'There's no need, sir. Libby has retired to her bed. I fear she is going to have quite the hangover in the morning. Have a safe journey, Mr Mahone.'

21. HIDDEN WEALTH

Brady returned to the ranch; it was just before dawn. Archie heard Brady's car coming up the driveway and went out to greet him. There hadn't been any need for late-night watches, as the Trads couldn't enter, unable to pass the roads which surrounded the ranch, and the Greens had shown no interest in entering their land - the Sattva warning billboards of Lucian's seeming to do the trick. Archie was in his long johns, with a dressing gown wrapped around him, 'Hey, son, didja have a good trip?'

'Sure did, Pops. I would say get back to bed, but there is something you can help me with.' Brady pulled out the pillowcase sacks of food and homewares. 'I don't want this to go off. Could you help me to get it into storage and the freezers?'

Archie whistled when he saw what was inside. 'God damn it, son. This is some mighty fine shit you have here.'

When they had finished, Brady persuaded his Pops to go back to bed. He reversed his Hearse back to the barn, and then unloaded the rest of his goods into a corner, covering them with tarpaulin.

The next day was Christmas eve, and Mary-Lou was making an effort to make it memorable for Little Amie, as she was becoming affectionately known. Archie had dug out his old Christmas Tree, and Lucian and Mary-Lou had decorated it with tinsels and baubles. Mary-Lou was reading Amie Christmas stories.

As there was no TV stations or newspapers, everyone was desperate for news of the outside world and hung on every word of Brady's trip to Malibu. He tried not to make them too jealous, as he worried about them being hyper-aware of what they were missing, and what they had lost, but it was impossible. His story - to their ears – couldn't sound anything but glamorous. Archie seemed especially interested in Bodhi's parents - John and Libby Kane.

There was a time, with so many distractions in the old world, when the life story of Bodhi Sattva might only have interested Archie and his conspiracy theories - but not now. They questioned every morsel of information and extrapolated it all into theories of what it could mean for the future. Brady knew he had a valuable commodity on his hands, and that if he chose carefully, he could gain a lot from the key influencers in the Trad Areas. *As long as I'm careful and don't get myself in a position where someone might choose to beat it out of me*, he thought, warily.

Archie spoke of the food and drink that Brady had brought home, and how they would have a proper Christmas feast tomorrow. Spirits were high at the Mahone and Lopez Ranches. It seemed no longer appropriate to call it the Hodgson Ranch, now that Mary-Lou and Lucian Lopez lived there.

Later, Mary-Lou and Lucian used the cleaning materials to scrub every surface clean. They had decided that the risk of infection was the most significant danger, but even the detergents were a welcome reminder of olden times.

Mary-Lou put Little Amie to bed, before drinking wine on the porch with Lucian. They had worked hard and talked themselves out after this busy day. They soon retreated into their homestead to get some much-needed rest.

Brady let Archie talk for hours. He had now decided that the doctors at Bodhi's birth were aliens, probing Libby and injecting her baby with alien DNA. That explained how he could do all this. 'It's all about alien technology. They've had it since Roswell, they were just waiting for the signal. I bet they ain't no real solar flares, that was their spaceships signalling the beginning of the invasion...'

Brady wished his Pops sweet dreams as he helped him to bed, but deep down, he knew his Pops' dreams would be like the sci-fi movies he was selling. He was happy for him – he guessed his Pops loved those dreams.

Brady went out on the porch to see in Christmas. In the very far distance, he saw a few fireworks explode. There couldn't have been many - as the display was over in a matter of seconds. He figured they must have found a few which hadn't been sprayed by the Greens. He kept his eyes peeled in case there were more. He saw a small ceramic cream airplane fly rapidly and quite low down and he assessed it was only a little bit larger than his Hearse. *I haven't seen one of those before*, he thought. He had a drink on the porch and reflected upon his life since escaping Ridgecrest. *It ain't been too bad really - not for the businessman of the year Mr Brady Mahone.*

After about an hour, everywhere seemed quiet and peaceful. Brady got up and went over the barn and quietly rolled his trailer to the tarpaulin in the corner. He removed it and then loaded up six loads of goods contained within the pillowcases. He checked his Magic Marker symbols and rubbed his fingers over the silk sheets. Even they would be useful for bedclothes, now they'd served their purpose. He didn't have his bike – he'd left it behind at Libby's Ocean view home - so he pulled it like a human workhorse. It was heavy, and the sheets looked like they were housing dead bodies as they hung over the edge of the trailer.

When he got to the Lopez ranch, he knew the door would be unlocked - there was no need to lock the doors anymore. *This will be a test of my skills. It's like a reverse robbery.* Before he went any further, he went from room to room to ensure everyone in the house was sleeping. He crept back to his trailer and then took the silken sacks one at a time and placed them at the bottom of the beds. He arranged them, with two on Lucian's side, two at Mary-Lou's and then he crept into Little Amie's and placed two outside her crib.

He headed back with his empty trailer behind him. *I still got it*, he thought, smiling to himself. *Not a peep from any of them. Just the old man to do and that completes another successful mission for top commando Sergeant Mahone.*

He knew his Pops was a light sleeper, but he also knew his single malt whisky should have knocked him out for the night. He had no problems completing his special delivery. His final act of the evening was to put the two sheet loads of goods at the bottom of his own bed. *I can't wait to check these out myself in the morning*, he thought. *I picked this stuff out in a hurry.*

It took a while for Brady to drift off to sleep, the adrenaline still pumping around his body - but when he did, he dreamed of being the richest man in the world, with a home like Libby's and his own private jet.

In the morning, he was woken by excited voices. He had slept heavily. Mary-Lou had bought over Little Amie holding a teddy, and in new night-clothes, which Libby had obviously kept aside for sleepovers, if her friends and family visited. Mary-Lou was in a new dress and shoes, and the smell of expensive perfume was almost overpowering. She had also made herself up with the cosmetics he had grabbed for her, while Lucian was in his smart clothes which Brady had assessed would fit from one of the photos of Libby's ex-husband. They were ecstatically talking of all the other luxury and practical items he had selected for them.

Archie came to join them in his designer and probably rare Levi jeans, and his new sneakers. 'These are the most comfortable sneakers I ever wore. Thank you, son - merry Christmas.'

They all joined in, 'Merry Christmas, Brady.'

'You all really came through for me when I needed you,' Brady said. 'You worked hard for me, and it was my way of thanking you - but I can't promise this every year. I just made the most of a one-off opportunity.'

'This is delicate,' Archie said, 'and it don't matter to me one way or another, I just wants to know. Did you steal these?'

Brady laughed. 'You know I'd tell you if I did, but no, I didn't. Libby said I could take what I needed, so, I did. She gave them freely. You can't steal from the Greens. They wraps you up in SecurityFilm™ if you even try.'

Archie made them all breakfast as they talked excitedly about every item, and how much they would have cost in the old world. Brady went to help his Pops with the dishes, but his Pops sent him away. 'It's the least I can do, son.'

Brady went to his bedroom to put away his own things. He hung up the suits and silk shirts, and he displayed his array of luxury aftershaves on a bedside cabinet. He tried on an expensive full length Italian black leather coat which went down to his ankles. It had a large collar and deep pockets. He rummaged around in the pockets and pulled out a pair of calf-skin black gloves, and then a sizeable manly ring dropped on the floor with a thud.

He bent down and picked it up and tried it on, and it fitted on the third finger of his right hand. Brady knew his jewellery; it was his former profession, after all. It sparkled in the late morning light. There were many diamonds and inset was a letter S in the same font as that of Sattva Systems™, and this was made up of emeralds. *That Libby and her old creep Hunter fucking lied to me,* he realised. *I could've loaded up on all their jewels. They robbed me of my dream heist.* He paced the room as he plotted his revenge. He still had to deliver her movies. *I'll be ready if they give me another go.*

After a while, he heard the sounds of the family preparing the Christmas feast. *It doesn't seem that long since breakfast.* He looked at his old watch, and this irked him, as he had left behind a whole collection of vintage and designer watches. He realised he had been in his room for more than four hours, dwelling on his anger at missing out on his jackpot. *I got to get a grip. What good is jewellery in this world anyway?* He told himself. *There's no market for it.* He tried to make himself feel better by trying to convince himself that he had done right by the rest of them, but even that didn't entirely do the trick. *I still could have just replaced the one load, maybe, took one bagful of toys instead of the two. Little Amie would have been none the wiser, and you can get a helluva lot of jewellery in one of those sheets.*

Two days later, Brady drove to Malibu in a sullen mood. He knew it was going to be challenging to maintain his composure to keep off the threat of the Security-

Film™. To calm himself, he went around the other large houses and found a willing market for his wares. He soon picked up on the competitiveness of Libby's friends and acquaintances. They seemed to choose all the same movies as Libby - once Brady had informed them of her orders - and then chose one or two others, as though this would give them an edge of exclusivity. He had a full order book, which would mean another return trip in a couple of days. *I need a system or strategy to cut out all of this wasted time on the road. I've got my sales teams in the Green Communities, but I need to do something about the manufacturing side.* He laughed at himself, thinking like a big-shot businessman. *That would mean cutting out Lucky and Mary-Lou to a degree, but they are good at this kind of thinking - the strategy stuff.*

He put this to the back of his mind as he drove up the snaking roads to Libby's place. He arrived at the main entrance, but it was locked, and a security guard came over and asked why Brady was there.

'Libby is expecting me. I have her Entertainment orders.'

The guard said nothing but went back to his sentry point. He spoke into an old-fashioned walkie-talkie, before turning back to Brady. 'Someone, will see you shortly.'

Hunter came to the gates. 'Libby has requested that you give them to me.'

'I'll give them to her myself.'

'That won't be possible. You are to give them to me, freely, and then she requests that you never return.'

Brady handed over the Entertainment Files through a gap in the railings. As Hunter turned away, Brady shouted. 'Hey, Hunter. You fucking lied to me, man.' Brady held up his right hand with the Sattva ring on his third finger. Hunter turned ashen. Brady knew fear when he saw it. 'Seems you've made an enemy of more than just me; wouldn't you say. You have a nice day and all.'

After Brady walked away, Hunter smiled as if he was relieved. *I hope the ring is enough to save me.*

22. TIBERIUS

B rady kept his promise with Professor Yuan Chu and dutifully placed his update on the new areas he had visited. Usually, it would be the name of the district, with a tick against a place he had designated as civilised and well-ordered, a cross against the name if it was predominantly lawless, or a G to establish it as a green community - like the one on the west side of McFarland. For Malibu, he went so far as to give a further update.

He wrote:

Malibu - G. The place is full of liberal elite, wealthy bastards including Bodhi Sattva's Mother, who lives in a house that cost a hundred million dollars back at the turn of the Millennium. So much for principles - they can screw everybody else as long as they look after their own.

Look after yourself, Professor and give Bessie a pat from me.

Brady Mahone - Businessman of the Year!

He returned to his bland ceramic cream vehicle and directed it to home, having discovered the Sattnav™ and semi-autonomous functions. Once he fell asleep at the wheel, and it slowed itself. When he awoke, he felt the car avoiding obstacles and even wildlife on the road.

He explored the car, and as he moved his hands over the smooth, unblemished cream dashboard area, a cache of Files ejected. The current one installed had an inscription of Western United States of America with a small Sattva Systems™ logo underneath. Alongside this was a batch of other files with areas such as Mainland Europe, China, Australia, and dozens of others, which he guessed covered the entire planet. *Does that mean Satnav is operating?* he thought. *I suppose the Satellite Phones still work.*

By Californian standards the weather was miserable, the slate grey sky soaking everything with its cold drizzle. Brady strode into the house, not in the mood for idle chit-chat. 'Hey, Pops. I've got a full order book. Can you go and bring Lucky and Mary-Lou over? I need them to get on with making the next batch.'

'Boy, have you seen the weather out there - it's real miserable.'

'I'll do it myself then, shall I?'

'No. I'll do it.'

Brady watched in gloomy silence as Archie retrieved a rarely used raincoat and trudged across to the Lopez Ranch. He then went to his van and retrieved his order book. It was raining harder now, and the cold wind picked up. He went to the barn and waited and waited.

After about an hour, Archie, Lucian, Mary-Lou and Little Amie arrived. 'Why the fuck did it take you so long?' Brady snapped.

'Little Amie was having her bath - we had to sort her out first. We came as fast as we could,' Mary-Lou answered. She wanted to show her anger at being treated like this, but she was grateful for everything Brady had done for her. 'Sorry, Brady. We didn't mean to keep you waiting. What do you want me to do?'

Brady smiled grimly. 'There are hundreds of orders to do. I need the Files completed for me to deliver tomorrow.'

Lucian gave Brady a look of concern, but he followed Mary-Lou as she scurried away to begin work.

Brady turned to Archie. 'I want that book back - the one with your contacts.'

'But you said...'

'I don't want to fuck about. They've got what I, no make that we, need.'

'Ok, boy. No need to get all uppity about it.' Archie left Brady alone in the room. 'Jesus, what's eating him?' he muttered to himself on the way out.

Brady made himself a coffee and sulked. He took out his Sattva ring and examined it, squinting as he looked for hallmarks or other tell-tale signs, but he couldn't find any.

After a while, he realised Archie hadn't returned. *He's had second thoughts,* he thought. *I wonder if he's looking through that fucking book checking if there's anything even more incriminating in there. Does he think I wouldn't know he'd do exactly that? Anyways, they couldn't possibly be any worse than Small Hand Don.*

He went outside to check that Lucian and Mary-Lou weren't slacking. They weren't. The machines were blinking away, and the barn rang to the sound of spinning discs. Lucian looked around, having been engrossed in the DVD filing system of the racks, and smiled at Brady. Brady gave him a thin smile in return and then returned to the kitchen table.

He took out the ring and fiddled with it for a few more minutes before decisively placing it back in his pocket.

Archie returned clinging to his little black book. He gave it to Brady. Archie turned to leave, but Brady stopped him. 'Hold on there, Pops.'

'I got things to do, son.'

'You can do them later. Sit down.'

Archie scowled. 'What's gotten into you, boy?'

Brady said nothing. He flicked through the pages, one by one. He examined the seams minutely before moving on to the next page. This process continued for a few minutes. 'Hand it over, Pops,' he said, finally.

'Hand what over?'

Brady moved his chair next to Archie. 'Look, here, see that? It's a fresh tear in the page. You ripped it out. Judging by the letters, I'm guessing it's a J or a K.'

'You're mistaken, boy. That page coulda fell out years ago. This book is at least sixty years old by now. C'mon, give your old man a break.'

'Do I have to search you, for it?'

'No. Of course, you don't.'

'Then fucking hand it over. Now.'

Archie reached into the back pocket of the Levi jeans Brady had given him for Christmas and gave Brady the missing page. The first names on it would usually be significant enough - there was Judge Almeida, followed by Justice Santos, but it was the final name Brady's eyes narrowed on: John Kane.

'What the actual fuck, Pops? John fucking Kane. You ain't going to tell me it's not the same one - like it's some kinda fucking coincidence, are you?'

'No.' He looked away, as though he thought Brady might peer directly into his brain and see all his darkest secrets.

Brady slammed his fist on the table. 'I think it's high time you told me the whole fucking truth, you degenerate old bastard. Otherwise, I'm outta here, and I ain't coming back. You can rot for all I care.' Archie looked at him, tears running down his face. 'And don't think you can come on with all the waterworks. It don't work when some girl tries that on with me, and it sure ain't gonna work with you, you old fucker.'

'Ok. Ok. John Kane was the money man. He was a cold fish - lordin' it about over us, like he was something special. If he wanted something -particular, like. Then we could get it for him. I don't like to go into details…'

'I've been locked up for fucking years, with every kinda criminal you can imagine,' Brady snarled. 'You don't think I haven't heard stories about the fucking paedophiles who were in the same jails as me. Just spit it out. It's not like any of you lot are going to be brought to justice in this world - is it?'

Archie grimaced and licked his old lips. 'Oftentimes, it was runaways we'd collect, or we'd have people placed in care homes or even schools - the church was good hunting ground. However, sometimes kids were stolen to order. John Kane had the money to pick any kind of kid he needed when he was hungry - like.'

'Hungry?'

'Sorry. It was a term we used.'

'Go on.'

'Well, we were kind of immune. If one of us got caught, then we always had connections to get us out of trouble, and John Kane had deep pockets.'

'And what was in it for you?'

He sighed. 'Ok, son. I'll tell you it all, but you ain't gonna like it. You'll probably leave anyway no matter what I says. But when I tell you that I left it all behind me, and I did nothing since I had you, you gotta believe that too. Do you promise to believe that?'

Brady reflected on this. He went back as far as he could, searching for signs, but he couldn't find or recall anything. 'Ok. I promise.'

'I used to make money from the kids I found - big money, and a percentage of the earnings, you know, porn films, prostitution... And I used to get a taste... Y'know - of the action.'

'Why did you tear this one piece of paper out? Is it because I mentioned his name?'

Archie sighed, and his shoulders sagged. Brady knew this look. He did it himself when he knew he was outplayed by a detective, and he was ready to confess, just to get it over with. 'It was a big story, back in the day, big shot industrialist vanishes. It went on for years, it did.' Brady practised what the police used to do to him - he didn't say anything, just leaned in, encouraging Archie to speak more. He did. 'I did it. I killed him. I garrotted him with a cheese wire. Damn near took his head off, I did. And then I buried him, deep in the forests. I knew the cops would be swarming all over this.'

'Why'd you do it?' Brady's tone was cold, still imitating police procedure, and not showing signs of understanding - which Archie hoped for.

'He came here to take you away from me, boy. He wanted you, but I loved you, and I wasn't going to let that happen - not for all the money in the world. I ain't ashamed to say it, but I loved you, son - always have - always will.'

Brady's mind was in a whirl. Pops... John Kane... Libby... Bodhi... Take what you want... Unexpectedly fostered... Foster Mom's drinking herself into an early grave...

A loud scream came from the barn. Brady followed more slowly as Archie rushed out to investigate. Brady guessed his Pops would have used any excuse to pull himself away from this interrogation. When Brady reached the barn, he found Lucian consoling Mary-Lou. She was shaking. 'What is it?' Brady said, rushing over. 'Has there been an accident?'

'Your Father is a monster,' Mary-Lou yelled. 'Keep him away from my child.' She sobbed, tears of rage streaming down her face. Brady was utterly confused. *Was she listening?* he thought. *But if she was listening, why did she go to the barn to start screaming? Maybe it was because Lucky was there...*

Lucian held her tightly as she buried her face in his chest as if she couldn't bear to look at Brady. 'We ran out of blank Black Files, so, we checked out the pre-recorded ones you brought back. On the top of the box were a few scattered about. Mary-Lou thought that maybe they weren't as important as the neatly stacked ones, so it wouldn't matter if we broke a couple by using a screwdriver on the button which looked like a flip switch...'

'But she wanted to see what was on them first,' Brady said, filling the gaps. His mind went back to Don Pickerstaff's place, he recalled the camcorder and the Black Files next to it. *He must have been watching them the night I was there until the battery died.*

'She was doing it for you and the business - there might have been something useful on there. She wasn't going to just destroy them without checking.'

'I can never unsee that filth,' she yelled, 'but at least I'm aware of the monster who lives here. He is a threat to my child, my poor baby.' She was weeping, but Brady could sense her disgust. He didn't want to ask her what she had seen, and he didn't want Lucian to let her go.

Archie had listened and watched what was happening through a crack in the door. He didn't want to inflame the situation. He watched Brady with an overwhelming sense of dread as he wandered over to the Black File player.

Brady stopped. He went through a box of accessories and found a pair of headphones. He plugged them into the player. Brady positioned himself to block the screen from Lucian and Mary-Lou. He pressed Play from Start. The title credits rolled, but it was evident to Brady that the names were pseudonyms, and then a banner appeared stating proudly that this was an *All Friends Together* production.

Then a serious-looking black screen with writing appeared. *In Ancient Rome on the heavenly isle of Capri, Emperor Tiberius is entertaining guests from the senate...* Brady guessed the delay was a ruse to make it look like a historical costume drama if the viewers needed to explain what they were watching. *Just hit Play from Start and it makes you look like you're watching the History Channel.* There was more historical context before the first punchline for the dickless wonders - he knew these nonces had an awful sense of humour to match their god-awful personalities. *Do I think that about Pops? I know others would - and I wouldn't blame them.* Brady ground his teeth as the title appeared: *Orgy Porgie Pudding and Pie.*

The faux movie opened with Emperor Tiberius declaring that today's indulgences were open, but he must take the virgin first. There must have been thirty or more children, and as many adults. Of course, they were nearly all men, but there were a couple of women present. He watched a boy of about seven being selected and being stripped and presented to Tiberius. Brady turned away as the boy was about to be raped, but he couldn't escape the sound of it happening and the encouragement of the crowd.

Outside the barn, Little Amie toddled over from her playpen and was heading to the barn, she smiled at Grandpops, as they were teaching her to say. He smiled grimly.

Brady wanted to stop watching, but he had to know whether Archie was there. There had been only rapid cuts of the crowd so far. *Maybe he wasn't there? Perhaps it only looked like him? What if he was there but didn't take part - could that be excusable? For the love of God give him plausible deniability.*

After the red-faced Tiberius had finished, he looked at the crying child and smiled broadly as if was reliving his sexual gratification. He raised his arms and declared: 'Let the games begin!'

The adults rushed over and grabbed the children. Some fought over the same angelic girl. And then he saw a close up of one of the child molesters slobbering over a young girl. It may have been more than half a century ago, but the face which leered into the camera proudly couldn't be denied.

It's Pops.

He didn't need to see anymore. He ejected the File and put it in his pocket, almost absentmindedly as he fought to control his emotions. *Should I try to explain it to Lucky? Comfort Mary-Lou? Confront Pops? What do I do first?*

Little Amie tottered into the barn. Mary-Lou broke free from Lucian's loving arms and picked her up and hugged her protectively. 'My baby, what was I thinking? Leaving you to play with that monster on the prowl. I'm so stupid.'

'It's ok,' Lucian said. 'She's fine.'

'No. It's far from fucking ok. I can't leave. I can't take Amie out of harm's way, and he will be waiting and watching, every day and night, waiting for his moment. He'll be fantasising about her until one day he will act - and do those terrible things to my daughter. That is my life from now on, dreading the moment he takes her for another one of his victims.'

Brady observed Mary-Lou and put himself in her position. *I'd think that if I was her, he thought. I can't change her way of thinking. If it was me, I'd kill him.* He then remembered that Archie wasn't in the barn - but he should have been there before him. *Where is he?*

Before he reached the house, he scanned the ranches - but if Archie was out there, he couldn't see him. He went into the homestead, and searched from room to room, but Archie was nowhere to be seen. Then Brady went into the bathroom. He found Archie in the bathtub lying fully clothed but in a pool of blood.

'Pops! No, Pops!' He tried to lift him, and Archie groaned. 'What have you done, you...?' He was a dead weight, and in an awkward position, so he put him back down. He went to the airing cupboard and tore off strips of linen to bind his wrists. He spotted the cut-throat razor which had slipped beneath Archie when he had attempted to lift him. The wounds on both wrists pumped out the blood at an alarming rate, and as he tried to clear the blood away, Brady realised how deep the wounds were. Archie had sliced through the veins and arteries the whole length of his forearms.

Archie gasped. 'Ain't long to go now, boy. Nothing you can do for me. Don't blame...' His eyes closed, and Brady already feared he was dead, but Archie made an effort to open his eyes. It looked to Brady like his Pop's eyelids were heavier than any lift he had done in the gym. Archie whispered, with his last dying breaths, 'Tiberius...' He gulped. 'Is John Kane.' And then he slumped into Brady's arms.

23.NIGHT ON THE TOWN

Only Lucian and Brady attended the burial and funeral of Archie Mahone. Brady had dug the grave alone. It was an act of penance, though for what, he wasn't quite sure. *I should've done something. It was my fault bringing those Files back from Castaic. I should've checked them myself.*

He thought about what he needed to do next. *I'll deliver the completed orders to Malibu tomorrow, and then I've got to dig out some Blank Files - I might have to start exploring north of here - up to San Jose. I'll make a plan for the new year.*

He went to the barn and gathered up the box of pre-recorded Files, retrieving the ones that lay next to the File player and taking them back to his bedroom. He intended to keep them from causing any further damage until he had checked them out. He knew what John Kane looked like. *I ain't looking forward to going through them, especially if Pops is on them, but they could provide leverage if I'm in a tight spot.*

One thing's for sure, they ain't for sale.

He went through to Archie's bedroom. He ached to cry when he saw the pile of presents, he had given him. *I ain't crying,* he told himself. *I don't cry for no one.* He took a deep breath and set about tidying up his Pops' room for one last time. After he had finished, he sat on his Pops' bed and tried to compose himself, but he felt like going out and getting drunk and picking a fight with someone. He wanted someone to fight back, just so he could feel something, but the options were virtually non-existent around here. *I don't want to hurt Lucky or Mary-Lou - it ain't their fault.* He thought about going into the Eastside, but he experienced something he rarely had for anything or anybody - respect. *I like it that Professor Chu treats me like a real person. I don't want to let him down.* He then thought about the Green community on the west side, he considered Vance. *I don't like the guy, he ain't got a RedSuit™, but surely that fucking SecurityFilm™ would activate and then I'd be fucked. In any case, it ain't good for business.* His anger rose when he thought of Siddha, Cain, and Lizzie. *They would just stand there laughing in their indestructible Suits™ - smug bastards.*

He took a last look at Archie's room before closing the door gently. He considered checking in on Lucian, Mary-Lou, and Little Amie, but decided to let them have some space to deal with the day's events. He thought about Lizzie. He didn't want to be alone this evening. *Not tonight. Not here.* He laughed bitterly. *Make love not war - isn't that what those fucking hippies always used to say.*

He shuffled to his own bedroom. He picked up the Sattva ring and fiddled with it until it caught the light and sparkled. *I'm gonna get dressed up for a night on the town and take the car.* He selected the most expensive and luxurious of Bodhi's old attire. The handmade black suit, the silk shirt and even a bowtie, even the underwear and socks exuded quality. He had showered, shaved, and sprayed himself with deodorants and lavished on large quantities of aftershave. He laughed. *They could smell me coming from here.* He didn't care that he would look insanely out of place in the understated to the very soul of West McFarland. *That's the whole fucking point. Let them see me in all my glory. A successful Trad with all the trappings of success they left behind. I'm going to strut my stuff. Let them laugh if they want. I can outsmart them. I am Brady, Brady Mahone. King of the new frontier. They'll rue the day when they decided to fuck with me.*

He wasn't going to spoil the look this time by wearing sneakers with a suit. He selected a pair of shiny black shoes. He examined the label which informed Brady that these were limited edition handcrafted Italian leather by Gucci. He put them on, and they fit perfectly. In the full-length mirror, he pasted back his black scrub of hair with moisturising hair cream from a golden pot. *I never looked so good, and on a day when I never felt so bad*, he thought. *Wish me luck, Pops.*

As he cruised West McFarland unhindered by any other vehicles, he pulled up frequently to check out what was passing for entertainment in this joyless fuck-hole. He saw plenty of recruitment centres. They advertised jobs ranging from wildlife census clerks to a myriad of work under the banner of Operation Clean-up. He liked the idea of a HeavyLoader™ FusionPlane™ operative. *That woulda suited me.* He saw other signs as he passed more recruitment centres, they seemed celebratory as they implored:

You've earned the Red™ - now go for the Orange™.

He drove down to the New Green Hall. He watched dozens of volunteers putting up environmentally friendly banners and bunting, for the *Freely Giving of the Red Ceremony. All are welcome. This is the New Green Years for the New You.*

He reflected darkly on their New Year, a stark contrast with the tough times for those not in the GreenShells™. It seemed a good time to wander around in and among the volunteers. He looked like a visiting President, and the volunteers weren't sure how to react. His aftershave wafted after him. He looked wealthy, whereas, by comparison, they appeared poor. Some smiled politely, but nobody laughed. Even though their minds informed them that they were protected, they couldn't reconcile this powerful looking Trad wandering around showing not one shred of fear, though he could be stopped in a heartbeat. Brady owned the room. He had star quality, and the spotlights of their eyes followed him everywhere until he, and not they, decided it was time for him to go.

He got back in his car and headed over to Lizzie's place. When he arrived, he knocked on the door, and she answered. Her frown was enough to let him know he wasn't welcome. She looked him up and down and smirked. 'Sorry we aren't buying anything. Goodbye.'

He put his foot in the door before she could close it. A teenager was walking up the road and called out, 'Are you ok, Miss?'

'Yes. Thank you, Dawson. Have you completed your homework assignment?'

'Nearly. I'll hand it in before the Red Ceremony tomorrow - promise.' Dawson smiled and headed on his way.

'Who is it?' a voice called out from the lounge.

'It's Brady.' She sighed. 'You may as well come in - seeing as you've obviously gone to a lot of trouble.'

Cain came out to the hallway in his white robe and bare feet. He looked over Brady. 'Business is obviously going well. Congratulations, my friend.'

You ain't no friend of mine. 'Thank you. Us Trads aren't beaten, yet.'

'We are not in competition with you. I wish you every happiness,' Cain said, without a hint of sarcasm. Siddha came out to investigate but said nothing. He looked over Brady's clothes and bowtie without disguising his utter contempt. Cain said, 'Come, Siddha. Let's take an evening stroll and talk about our plans for the next few days. We'll give Lizzie some privacy.' Lizzie glared at him as if she'd been given an order she wasn't allowed to refuse.

She went up the stairs without offering Brady a tacit invitation, knowing Brady wouldn't wait for the courtesies of polite company. *One thing I like about these Green Girls is that they are so easy - no messing*, Brady thought.

Lizzie did her duty and let him make love to her. She even adjusted the settings on her RedSuit™ to set her own stimulation levels to maximum. *If he deems me to be exceptionally responsive, it will play to his ego and vanity*, she told herself. *If I'm doing this, then I may as well extract as much information from him for Cain and the cause.*

Brady left the bed and showered without asking or waiting for permission. The soap was basic and reminded him of the bars they were allocated in prison. He wished he hadn't washed his aftershave away. He began to get dressed when Lizzie said, 'So, you're not planning to stay?' Lizzie was naked but had pulled up a sheet to cover herself.

'I didn't think you'd want me to.'

She knew she was intellectually light-years removed from this thug, and yet here he was treating her like a groupie. He carried on dressing, he fiddled around with his bowtie until he gave up and shoved it in his pocket. Then, he made a show of putting on his ring. He looked up - knowing she would be curious. 'I'm sure you recognise the design,' he said. 'Isn't this where you ask me how I got it?'

'And why would I do that?'

'Come on, lady. I know you think I'm some kinda dumb fuck.'

'That's the most insightful comment you've made. Congratulations. I'll give you a B+ for effort.'

She expected Brady to get angry and storm out, maybe even to slam the door behind him, but he didn't. He smiled. 'Maybe you're right. After all, this whole Green mess proves it. You've won, and now you get to treat the losers like shit.'

There was a glint in his eyes which made Lizzie wary. 'No. We don't gloat.'

'Are you sure? There was a guy on the TV. I remember - Glenarvon Cole. He was with a pretty red-headed reporter. He was surrounded by some of your GreenRevs - that sure looked like some heavy-duty gloating to me.'

'That was in the heat of celebrating the victory. I can assure you, we are far too busy repairing the damage left behind to spend precious time on pontificating and gloating.' Lizzie enjoyed debating. It was a specialism of hers in school, and it felt good to cross swords with someone again, even if it was with an old-fashioned meat-head jock like Brady Mahone. First, she had to get him off balance and lower his guard, and then she would be well placed to go in for the kill. 'Why, apart from the obvious, did you come over here tonight? And what's with the dressing up for the occasion? You didn't think it would impress me - surely?'

Brady sat on the bed next to her as he was lacing up his shoes. When he had finished, he swivelled around on the bed to look at her. 'My Pops died today.'

'Oh,' she said, briefly taken aback. 'I'm sorry. I'm sure he will be a significant loss to society, I mean, he brought you into the world, and that's quite an achievement. What happened to him?'

'I'd rather not say.'

Ooh, he's displaying sensitivity, she thought. *I'm not sure how I feel being his sympathy screw for the evening.* 'Did you love your father?'

'Yes. Pops wasn't a good man, but he was to me.'

'I'm sure he was.' She paused. 'What's your earliest memory of him?'

Brady thought for a moment, and then lied. 'There was this nursery rhyme he used to sing to me, but I can only recall the first line.'

She smiled. 'I used to teach kindergarten; I might be able to help.'

'Ok, it went something like - Georgie Porgie...'

She picked up the rhyme. 'Kissed the girls and made them cry. When the girls - or boys...' She laughed. 'Came out to play, Georgie Porgie ran away.'
'What does it mean?'

'I wouldn't want to say. It might tarnish your precious memories of your Father, and I wouldn't want to do that.'

'Please, I insist.'

'Well, let me say firstly, your Father wouldn't have looked into the rhyme in any other way than it just being a popular children's rhyme. However, it was banned, quietly, because of its potential body image connotations, and of course, due to its hints at shaming children for having latent homosexuality traits. Of course, no decent person would agree with that in these more enlightened times, but back then...'

'It was seen as being kinda funny,' he said.

She nodded and smiled. Brady frowned and considered his next move. 'Where are Cain and Siddha going?'

'Nowhere in particular. Cain often takes one of us out in the night for a long walk and a chat. He likes the peace and quiet; it helps him to concentrate. When I'm with him, I find I listen more intently, without the distractions of the daylight hours. I wouldn't be surprised if they headed to the Town Hall to see how the preparations are going for the Red Ceremonies,' she added.

'That's where the rest of the people get their RedNanoSuits™, the things which make them kinda indestructible?'

'Yes.' She wondered if she had given something away, but then she remembered the SecurityFilm™. In the old world, this would have been the time to plan a terrorist assault, before the population was fully protected. However, the SecurityFilm™ would detect any ill intent, and why would anyone target an outpost like West McFarland and not the more significant Green Communities across the globe? *Nobody could plan an attack of that magnitude.* Lizzie was shaken that she still felt insecure, even in this impregnable fortress. She wanted to change the subject – even if it was only in her mind. 'It will take all night for Cain to give out the RedFiles™, but it will be part of the New Green Year festivities. The townsfolk are very excited, despite the hard work which lies ahead of them next year.'

'And then they'll all work like slaves to earn enough Greenbacks - I mean Green Credits for the OrangeSuits™ - like the one this Bodhi Sattva has?'

'You've been listening and learning. Well done, you.'
Her patronising tone was not lost on Brady. *That's just fine by me, Little Lady Lizzie.* 'And you are all equal under the Green sun and sky like some big happy-clappy collective. Everyone working together, sharing each other's homes, and eschewing the trappings of capitalism.'

'Eschewing is a big word for you. Have you been moving in educated circles?'

'Professor Yuan Chu is a mate of mine. He thinks I'm smart. I'm sure you know him.'

'Of course. Everybody in McFarland knew Professor Chu. He should have been with us.'

'He worked on NanoTech™, helping couples with fertility issues. He told me that his work went against the doctrines of Sattva Systems™, so his expertise wasn't welcome.' He peered into her eyes. 'You know that, though, don't you? You are happy to let Sattva Systems™ sterilise the planet - even me?'

'I'm sure you've sown your seed around the Western Seaboard, and I'm sure you haven't bothered to find out if there are any mini-Mahones out there,' she joked. Still, she was rattled. She'd underestimated him. 'The last thing this planet needs at this time of crisis is more humans using up the last of Her precious resources. We haven't hurt or directly harmed anyone…'

'My friend has had a miscarriage since being crop sprayed by your Green goo.'

'That doesn't count. Any babies who went to full term were unaffected.'

Brady laughed darkly. 'I'll go and give your condolences to Mary-Lou when I get back. My friend, Lucky - I mean Lucian - was the father.'

They both lay in silence. Lizzie was still under the covers, while Brady was in his expensive suit and shiny shoes, on top of the bedclothes beside her. She wanted him to leave but didn't make this request because Cain would need more information. She hadn't got to the bottom of his impeccable - though strange, on him - collection of clothes… or the ring. She had lost one round with Brady, but the fight wasn't over.

'Where did you pick up those clothes? I assume you broke into a tailor store on the Trad side?'

'I was given them - *freely.*' He emphasised the word to draw her in. He was still in the same wrecking mood as when he left the ranch. He couldn't wipe them out physically, but he was confident he could mess with their smug attitudes and assumptions. 'I know what you are up to. I've had girls like you, when I pulled off a big jewellery heist - who'd let me sleep with them, hoping to get something sparkly and nice out of me. You ain't no better than them, except you want Greenie points from your boss - or are you being paid in Green Credits to sleep with me and gather information?'

Bless him, he honestly believes that he has played his killer line in the debate - as if I care what this lump of Traditional Meat thinks of my motivations. 'Of course, you are right. I don't want this to come across as being laced with sarcasm, but yes - the only reason any woman would sleep with a lowlife like you is to get something out of you. For some, that might be jewellery or money. I mean, nobody in their right mind would want to have a long-term relationship with you. I mean, what have you got to offer but a life of pain and misery and punctuated with an occasional slap to keep the little woman in her place?

'So, in answer to your question, I am sleeping with you for information, though for the life of me - I don't know why, it's hardly likely you would have anything particularly insightful to bring to the party. And no, I am not being paid in Green Credits because I am a veteran GreenRev. I don't need Green Credits to receive my upgrades. I've witnessed, first-hand the hellish tactics you brutal Trads used to repel us. They were happy enough to use children as their human shields, so don't come at me with this *won't someone think of the poor children crap.'*

He was delighted she was getting angry. 'The clothes I'm wearing were given to me by a woman who is one-hundred and fourteen years old - her name was Libby. I can't remember her current surname - she seems to have gone through a few in her time - but she was married to John Kane. Am I ringing any bells?'

This did shock her, but she attempted to cover it up, 'Please don't tell me you slept with her, like some tawdry gigolo.'
'If I had, then I could have persuaded her to turn up her NanoSuit™ to maximum pleasure. I know when I'm being played. There's a Cain, Siddha and a Lizzie in every Green Town, except some of the Green Girls talk a lot - and I mean a lot - about the fabulous innovations the Suits™ have to extend sexual pleasure. Some of them seem very keen for me to get a NanoSuit™ of my own…' *That's how they get you, son.*

'Did you have sex with Libby?'

Brady roared with laughter. *I might leave that question hanging.* 'So, you do know her?'

'Of course, I know her. She's Bodhi's mother.'
He leered at her, 'And you recognise this ring, don't you?' He put his hand near her face and waggled his finger - the diamonds and emeralds sparkling in the dappled moonlight through the gaps in the curtains.

'Yes. That is the same font as used by Sattva Systems™. It must be either Bodhi's or John Kane's.'

'I'll give you a chance to escape now, with all your pretty preconceptions still intact,' he said, playfully. 'Do you want me to leave right now? Because I can – it's no skin off my nose. Or shall I stay, and tell you all the juicy stuff? Cain will probably take it quite calmly, but Siddha, he's a creepy bastard, by the way, he will go absolutely ape.' He sat up, as though he was going to leave anyway. He did it to toy with her.

There was no point in hiding her true intent, any longer. 'No. I've gone this far. Cain would never forgive me if I didn't find out everything.'

'Ok, but you have been warned.' He paused and then showed her the ring. 'This…' he said, like he was reciting a bedtime story. 'This is a magic ring.'

'Oh, please.'

'Ok, it might not make magic, but it does have the power to break spells. Is that magic?'

'It's a profound question, but let's just say I have no idea and cut to the chase.'
He exaggerated his disappointed slump, like was a child, and she'd told him she didn't want to play anymore. 'You've told me these fairy stories about your magical world, where you all share everything with each other, and in your Green World you don't see the need for the finer things in life because those things represent the Old Order of capitalism and materialism…'

'Thanks for the history lesson. I am a teacher, remember.'

'Well, this is where it begins to unravel for me. I was invited to visit Libby. I didn't stumble upon her by accident. She got her servant to seek me out and bring me to her.' He waited for the word servant to land. He knew precisely the effect each revelation would have on her. 'Anyhows, he accompanies me up to her enormous house in Malibu, set on a clifftop and overlooking the Pacific, with its twelve bedrooms…'

'I don't need the full realtor spiel…'
'This house was worth one hundred million dollars back at the turn of the Millennium, and it's still hers - I'm putting Greenbacks on Bodhi having kept the paper deeds to this one.' He went on. 'She wasn't sharing this palace with any other needy and worthy Greens - it was all hers. Oh, and she didn't lose any friends as they kept their luxury condos because Libby would be upset if she had lost her friends.'

Lizzie resorted to lying about how she felt. 'So, Bodhi is looking after his Mother. That's understandable, I suppose.'

'Did you look after your Mother?'

'That's none of your business.'

Brady snorted. 'I'll take that as a No, then.'

Lizzie was reeling. 'Why would she want you to know all this? It doesn't make sense.'

'Who cares? All I know is it was a very profitable day for me. And looky here - I've got Bodhi's ring or Xavier as his darling Moms insisted on calling him. And your SecurityFilm™, which you place so much faith in, is doing nothing at all about it.' He held up his hand triumphantly, and said to the darkness, 'Hello. I've got Bodhi's ring. Come and get it.' He paused, 'Nothing. It must be his night off.' He looked at her, like an opponent in a boxing ring, checking they were in precisely the right position to receive the knock-out blow. 'But you're right. Bodhi's a terrific guy, and upright citizen and all that jazz.'

'Is that it? Is that all you've got to tell me?'

'I'm curious. What would Cain, and Siddha make of this?'

She knew he wouldn't believe her if she tried to pretend it wouldn't be of concern to them. 'They would be disappointed, but I hope they would treat it as a human flaw with Bodhi. After all, he is a man and not a God.'

'I think you had him down as the Perfect Man. I've never heard any of you mention flaws before.' He deliberately slowed the pace. He needed to draw out the justifications from her now - to leave her spent, when the final moment came. 'I had a wonderful time at Libby's. She made me feel like an honoured guest. She gave me brandy and Cuban cigars and then invited me into the hot tub with her.'

'She sounds like a very nice woman. I wouldn't have expected anything less from Bodhi's Mother.'

'For a broad of one-hundred and fourteen, she didn't look a day over seventy. She kept herself in good shape. And by the way, I didn't have sex with her. She was out of my age range,' he added. 'There was something else. Something she said, which didn't make sense.'

Lizzie leaned in, sensing that this was she was meant to find out. If Brady didn't understand it, then it was probably something good. 'What did she say?'

'She said she was *Yellow*™.'

'She can't be. That's impossible. Even Bodhi is only at Orange™ - and he only tries the new NanoSuits™ on himself before letting anybody else have them. It's a matter of ethics. If there is any fault within the technology, then only he would be harmed. You're either lying or badly mistaken. You said it yourself. She's positively ancient. She might be coming to the end of her extended life…that's it, she's confused, and she got her colours mixed up. I mean, Orange™ is only a shade away from Yellow™.' She paused. 'The YellowSuits™ are still years away.'

'You're probably right. I've been in a few courtrooms in my time. I'm probably one of those unreliable witnesses. However, the sight of her did take my breath away.'

'What do you mean?'

'The way she was fully clothed one second, and then as she glided down the steps into the pool, her clothing transformed into a bathing suit.'

24.RED CEREMONY

Cain walked through the adoring crowds on New Year's Day. It was 2085 and the first New Year of the Green Revolution. They cheered him as they passed. It was the day when the Green Community of West McFarland would be issuing its citizens with their new RedNanoSuits™. Most had worked hard to earn enough Green Credits to pay for the suits, but for those who were less fortunate, through no fault of their own who found they had missed the deadline, others contributed the Credits for them to receive them on this auspicious day. It was an act of kindness and charity which was embedded into the very souls of these caring people. They were sacrificing everything to save the planet from climate extinction, but today, they would be receiving their just rewards for their generosity of spirit.

They were at one with all the other Green Communities from West McFarland to Malibu to New York, and from London to Singapore to Sydney, in celebrating the Year of the Red™.

Cain was contemplating the phone call he made at his allotted time the previous evening with Bodhi. He had been honest and brave as he informed Bodhi of every detail of Brady Mahone's encounter with Libby Kane - Bodhi's Mother. He expected denials, excuses and justifications, but all he received was praise. All Bodhi asked of Cain was that he should trust him and that it was all part of the overall plan. He also informed Cain that he should keep this to himself, for now, and that Cain would be rewarded for his work by being the first of all the Green Community leaders across the globe to be invited to receive the Yellow™ - when it was ready and available. Bodhi didn't state the obvious rebuttal regarding Libby's account. Cain was happy to be elevated, and he hadn't hidden anything from Bodhi - and therefore, he had nothing to fear. He had faith.

Cain wove his way through the bustling crowds of the New Green Hall, which the older residents still preferred to call, simply, the Town Hall. He went backstage to greet his closest friend and confidante Siddha. They hugged warmly. Cain patted Siddha heartily on his back. 'We have come through so much together and this year has been tumultuous, but now the hard work begins.'

There were no chairs - it was standing room only in the New Green Hall, with thousands more in the grounds outside. Lizzie went to Cain to affix a microphone onto his robe, while Siddha brought over the two RedDistors™.

'I'm sorry, Cain,' Lizzie said. 'I didn't expect him to be so brutal.'
'And I'm sorry for placing you in such an insidious situation. If it makes you feel any better, then Bodhi says that Brady has a function to perform, but even he admitted that he had underestimated Brady Mahone's intelligence levels.'

'I suppose even criminals have intelligence…'

'But he's hardly a criminal mastermind. He's been captured and detained on so many occasions.'

Lizzie laughed. 'We caught him stealing fruit from the GreenGrocers™.'

Cain held out his arms. Lizzie took this as a sign she had been forgiven. She moved in for a hug with the man she most admired in the world. 'I want you to be at my right-hand side today,' he whispered.

'Is Siddha ok with that?'

'Of course. He will be at my left.' He looked around the hall and through the open doors of the main entrance. The sun was shining brightly against the azure sky. 'I think we are ready.'

Lizzie moved to her position on the stage and Siddha gave her a warm smile as she passed him. 'I've dreamed so long of days such as this,' he said.

The applause and cheers were almost deafening as Cain moved to the centre of the stage. It was daylight, but still, Vance shone a spotlight on Cain before moving back to the edge of the crowd.

Cain opened his arms in the universal gesture of greeting, his white robe hanging from him like a holy man. He scrunched his Nano protected toes on the wooden stage. His crystal green eyes sparkled as he addressed his audience. 'Today is our Red Day. Are you ready to receive?'

The audience cheered. 'Yes. Yes.' They whooped and hollered, and this mixed with laughter in the jubilation of the day.

Cain waited until the din subsided. 'The next few years will not be easy. There is much work to do beyond the NanoShells™. We have to clean and rewild America, and our fellow activists across the globe will be doing the same in their lands. To-gether we will restore Mother Earth to full health. We will end, once and for all, the devastating impact of man on the planet. Remember this, when you are challenged by the Trads in the old world - the planet and every living thing that relied upon its bounty was in its death throes. The Trads would have destroyed not only us, but also, themselves. Just because they didn't understand, doesn't mean it wasn't so. We took direct action, and now we'll make the world a better place, not just for mankind but for all Her creatures. We – you – won!'

There were more cheers. 'To go out in the world you will need to be protected. The RedNanoSuits™ you are to receive today have been battle tested by our glorious GreenRevs.' The front rows of the audience were reserved for the GreenRev veterans, who roared and jumped up and down furiously like a mosh pit from the old rock con-cert days. Some waved at Lizzie, and she beamed and waved back. Cain and Siddha laughed proudly.

'With these Suits™, they cannot hurt you. They even anchor through the floor, so you are immovable. But they also come with responsibility. You cannot use them to hurt another living thing. You cannot even use them to deliberately embarrass an en-emy. We will not hurt the feelings of another. If you do, the Security Protocols™ will be alerted, and your Suit™ will be withdrawn. We are not here to harm - our whole reason of being is to save.

He let the warning hang for a second before continuing, he shouted at the top of his voice: 'Are you ready to receive?'

His audience clapped and cheered. 'I want all of you to hold the hand of whoever is next to you. Please look around and ensure that nobody is left without a partner. While you are doing this, the GreenRevs will form a human chain to Lizzie on my right and Siddha on my left.'

There was much shuffling, and quiet chatter as people linked up. They knew what to do - it was a similar ceremony they had taken part in a few short weeks after the Revolution, when they had all received the InfraRedPrimerSuits™. These were only an outer coating, but they did speed up the healing process if they were injured in any way. This gave them all the reassurance they needed - nobody had acquired any ill side-effects. In fact, quite the opposite was noted, as many had stated that they had never felt better. After a few minutes of checking and double-checking that nobody was left out of the human daisy chain - a reverential calm descended. All eyes were fixed upon the stage, where Cain stood as the only broken link. He held up the two red tubes - the RedDistors™. The crowd waited for the new holy words of the Green Revolution. There was utter silence as Cain built up the tension like a consummate showman.

'Our Mother.
Who art Heaven on Earth.
For what we are about to receive
May we be truly grateful
And lead us not into temptation.
Show us the way.'

The audience murmured in reply, 'Show us the way.'

Cain held the RedDistors™ above his head and then lowered them into the waiting hands of Lizzie and Siddha. There was a frisson in the air as a soft red glow passed slowly from one audience member to another, as if each were gaining a visible aura. Cain reminded the audience, 'Do not let go of your hands until everyone has received.'

They held hands in a meditative silence. Cain looked right, and then left at the RedDistors™ until a message in Red appeared. *All Given Freely.*

157

25.ALL IS QUIET

The Mahone Ranch didn't merrily greet the oncoming of the New Year. Lucian, Mary-Lou and Little Amie remained in the Lopez Ranch. They felt they couldn't conspicuously celebrate in the light of Archie Mahone's suicide - and they wanted to give Brady some space to grieve his Pops death.

Brady did mourn his Pops - in the time-honoured tradition of getting drunk. It didn't feel right to drink the alcohol he had acquired from Libby. Instead, he drank copious amounts of Archie's homemade Moonshine. He couldn't ever remember getting so drunk.

He awoke next day to the mother-of-all-hangovers. He scratched around for whatever breakfast would take the least effort to make, poured himself and chain-drank black coffee, and then he fell into a sleep full of headaches again. He dreamed of his Pops and his Foster Moms, even in this dream state he began to understand her attraction to the thought of drinking the pain away.

He roused himself at midday. He looked over to West McFarland and was sure he saw the barely detectable clear GreenShell™ turn to a reddish glow for a few minutes. *With a bit of luck, they've blown themselves up.* He smiled and then winced at the pain in his head. He walked around the Ranch to try and get a bit of fresh air. He then went into his barn and looked at the empty boxes which used to be home for his Blank Black Files, and then the DVDs and music CDs awaiting his next deliveries. He was taking stock.

He went to the catalogues and order books. *Jesus - he's a smart kid, that Mary-Lou. I still need her.* He looked at the strewn tarpaulin with which he'd used to cover his Christmas gifts. Already, that day felt like a lifetime ago. He shook his head ruefully.

I'll go and see Lucky tomorrow. I'm not up to it today.

He strolled back to the house, and he drew in deep breaths of fresh air, but instead of reinvigorating Brady, it only added dizziness to his list of drink-related symptoms.

He lay back down on his bed and stared up at the ceiling. In his pocket he toyed with the Sattva ring he now carried around with him. *I need to look after this,* he thought. *I can't wear it all the time, but I can't have it falling out my pocket.*

Brady wandered into to Archie's room and went to the bedside table. He opened the drawer and pulled out the thick silver chain he always used to wear around his neck. It was only then that Brady remembered that he wasn't wearing it when he slashed his wrists. He didn't know why Archie had done this. *He musta had his reasons.* He slid the Sattva ring over the chain and slipped it over his head. He went to the bathroom, and he checked to see how it looked. The ring seemed weighted to hang with the S the right way up.

He twisted the silver chain between his thumb and forefinger of his huge hand and then pulled the chain around until the catch was hidden at the back of his neck. He removed his T-shirt and examined himself, and even in this hungover state he concluded that he still looked good for his age - younger than his years. He looked over his tattoos from the weird Hawaiian guy in prison, and he examined himself for scars, but there weren't any.

I always did heal real quick.

Brady put his T-shirt back on and went to the porch and sat next to the Old Marvin machine gun. He playfully aimed it in the direction of the dissipating redness from the Shell™ over West McFarland. He knew this was just the beginning.

THE END

2100

Crime Of The Century

Book Two of the Green Deal Quartet

By

Jim Lowe

1.THE PROMISE

B odhi Sattva managed his sprawling industrial complex by wandering around.

It took the best part of a day of walking to cover all the research, development and manufacturing bases. Everywhere he went, he winced at the pain his machines had inflicted on to the surface of Mother Earth. He had instructed the diggers to break ground on the third area in Boulder Creek to supplement the two industrial complexes his Father, the industrialist John Kane had purchased in 2030. These were held behind moss-green walls to blend into the surrounding forests. The last units were built in 2042, nearly fifty-eight years ago. He still had nightmares about Her screaming as the steel jaws sliced through Her skin.

Sometimes you have to harm the environment to save the environment.

He sold his dream to the Revolutionary Greens, and they bought it.

After the Internet succumbed to infection, and then terminal death and the stock market crashed to zero - he manufactured his first trillion Green Credits. Sattva Systems™ was the central bank of the New Green World.

Boulder Creek was the focal point of operations for the New Green Deal. Bodhi Sattva was going to guide them to find heaven on Earth - it was here all along.

Forty-two years it had taken him to prepare the hundred-year plan to save the planet, and he enacted it in the Spring of 2084. Today, he was going to align his aims with the leader of the GreenRevs - Glenarvon Cole. Bodhi was to receive the ten-point list of demands from his GreenRevs members. In the past sixteen years, they had worked so hard for him, and their only tangible rewards were the RedSuits™ which enabled them to topple governments and bring an end to the Earth-ruining capitalist and industrialist eras. The RedSuits™ kept his people safe from external harm.

He followed this up seven years later with the mass distribution of the Orange-Suits™ which flooded the human bodies of the Green Communities with NanoBots™ to repair any internal organ damage or extinguish any signs of malignant cells. This increased the life expectancy of his followers by more than fifty per cent.

Of course, they also had the satisfaction of knowing they had saved the Earth from Climate Extinction.

Bodhi's team of scientists and Nano-engineers had been working to an almost impossible deadline of trying to ensure that the Yellow™ upgrade could be completed in time for the End of the Century celebrations. The Yellow™ would bring a new level of freedom to his people and extinguish the need for much of the textile resources, which drained so much of Her resources in the act of creating clothing.

Bodhi worked exceptionally long hours, and when he slept at night, his dreams were always about his project and the end result. His nightmares about the days of the Traditional Cultures fired him to complete his tasks to the satisfaction of *his* boss - Mother Nature.

He wasn't where he should be, the noise from the research facilities was almost deafening so he had ear-protectors emerge from his skull as part of his YellowSuit™ features. It would be two hours walk to return to the NanoTech™ HQ - and his meeting with Glenarvon Cole, his Worldwide Co-ordinator was just over two hours away. He made his excuses to the head of HydroPower and strode back through the FusionPlants™. There was a short-cut through the Intense Solar and Wind Developments that saved him a few minutes. He was never out of breath, he never sweated, and his moss-green overalls shifted their image to jeans, khaki T-shirt and sneakers as he strolled through the NanoTech™ HQ to greet his visitor and old friend.

His ethical promise was that he would only ever release a new version of the NanoSuit™ to his people once he had tested it on himself first. Some knew this lie had been exposed back in 2084. But such was the faith in him, they believed the story that his Mother, the Hollywood actor, Libby Kane, had acquired an early prototype from a disgruntled Nano-developer, and that she subsequently died of complications due to flaws in the Suit™ at the age of one hundred and twenty-four, only six short years ago.

She was always Libby Kane to Bodhi, as his Father was John Kane, but she came to Hollywood fame in the late twentieth century as Libby Skye - her stage name, and she died as Libby Berrington after taking the name of her fourth and final husband. She only ever had one child, and that was Xavier Kane, who his Father later renamed Bodhi Sattva. Xavier was born in Tonga, the very first child born in the Millennium.

After the lawsuits had been settled following his mysterious disappearance in 2048, Bodhi continued his late Father's project to pummel his industrial rivals into the ground and to save the planet as a by-product.

To Bodhi, the spin-off was the all-consuming project, politics and competitiveness never held any fascination for him. World politics and corporations between them were destroying the planet, and he had the means to level the playing field and give Her, Mother Earth a chance to fight back - a chance to recover.
He needed the outcast and much ridiculed Green activists and their communities of fellow idealists to bring about change, and to repair the damage of the Traditionalist Cultures on Her.

He found his ideal man in Glenarvon Cole. Glen was laser-focused on the causes and effects of human activity on the planet and was a natural leader of men. If Bodhi was the head of the project, Glenarvon Cole was the heart, and Bodhi loved him and trusted him without reservation.

He hugged his friend, 'Hi Glen, so good to see you - you're looking well.' Glen smelled like hard work and factories. 'Let's get away from all this noise,' Bodhi led the way and Glen kept pace with him.

'You too - it's been five years, and yet you never seem to age. How old are you?'

'I'm ninety-nine - I was born on Millennium Day.'

'You don't look a day over forty.'

Bodhi smiled at the flattery. 'Actually, thirty-three would be more accurate, as that was the day of my first fitting for InfraRedPrimer™ which my father, John Kane, organised for me. I'll let you into a secret. It actually didn't work as expected, and I could have died, but one of the side effects was that it protected me cosmetically. However, my near demise, meant that I couldn't experiment on another living creature or human first when I took over the company after my Father's disappearance. It made me feel more comfortable with the work we were doing.'

Bodhi could see Glen doing the math, Glen said, 'So, it took another nine years to perfect the InfraRed™?'

'Yes. I have been Yellow™ for ten years myself, and now I am trialling the Green™ phase. I can't tell you what the GreenSuit™ will achieve right now, but when I am able, you will be the first to know.' Bodhi put his arm on Glen's shoulder and smiled, 'You took on governments, and many of you died in the revolutionary protests back in eighty-four. I owe you for your bravery and your devotion to Mother Earth.'

'You gave us the Red™ version of NanoWear™.' Glen said, 'we were indestructible - it was amazing. Even when they learned that they couldn't shoot or bomb us into submission; and gassed our comrades to death - you solved that problem as well - we have much to thank you for. Without you, the Green Revolution could never have succeeded, especially in those totalitarian regimes.' Bodhi shuffled uncomfortably, but Glen continued in his gratitude, 'And now you are going to give us everything we have ever dreamed of. You don't have anything left to prove to us about your devotion to our cause. If you need volunteers, I have thousands who would give their lives to you - you know that - don't you?'

'Thank you, but I insist on being patient zero. I couldn't live with myself otherwise.' Bodhi changed the subject. He didn't take praise well and preferred to talk about business. He said, 'Have you got the list?'

Glen took out a piece of paper and handed it to Bodhi, 'You said to pick the top ten projects, but we couldn't get it to less than thirteen without upsetting people.' The paper was crinkled and stained as if it had been on a pocket for months. The places where Glen would go to sort out an issue wouldn't rule out this possibility.

Bodhi laughed as he read through it, many were as he would have predicted - and already had his team working on them, but there were a few he hadn't anticipated. *Hearts and minds.* He laughed kindly and said, 'I see we've got world peace on here as well.'

'No, I don't think...Oh, I see.' Glen laughed along with Bodhi.

'End hate thoughts and crimes. End binary identity and discrimination - I thought we were concentrating on Mother Earth and Her needs.' He already knew that Sissy would begin to challenge him on his language choice once she had this list.

'Happy humans equal committed volunteers - you don't have to...'

Bodhi interrupted him, 'No...no. We can do it, it will be a value-test for the rock star salaries I pay my top scientists and engineers. Although I have to admit, I'm not happy about how they spend their money on material things - such a waste of Her resources.' *Sometimes you have to harm the planet to save the planet.* 'I wouldn't usually waste my time and efforts on tracking down these old trinkets and artworks for them, but I can't do this alone.'

Glen said, 'Indulging a few is a price worth paying, although it does cause resentment in the ranks.'

163

Bodhi knew that his Mother's friends' protected status had the same effect until they were ejected from the Green Community of Malibu and put into the Trad Areas of Los Angeles. 'Did you distribute the Files of my requirements of the Disciples?'

'Yes. It helped, but it doesn't feel right.'

Bodhi spotted Genesis walking over to meet them, 'Hi Sissy,'

She smiled, and shook out her long auburn hair, 'Hi Bodhi - Glen - It's been a long time.' Sissy and Glen hugged.

He stood back and admired her, 'Another ageless wonder.'

Bodhi said, 'Sissy is my marketing guru, now. We've won the physical battle, but now it's time to win over the hearts and minds, but not in her old political ways - those days are over.'

Sissy said to Glen, 'Are the Disciples here?'

'Yes, the leaders of each territory, as specified.'

'Great, we've got a lovely presentation prepared for them.' She said to Glen, 'We've decided on the title of Regional Disciples, we think they'll be pleased with that.'

Glen said, 'Yeah, that's cool.'

'Is that the list?' Sissy saw the paper Bodhi was clutching. Bodhi passed it to her, and she scanned it instantly. Bodhi nodded, and she knew it had been agreed. She said, 'If you wish, I could have it blown up, and use it as a backdrop to the presentation.'

Glen objected, 'My handwriting is terrible, it's not even the same-coloured ink, and it's not straight - I had to squeeze the last request in - if I'd have known I would have written it out more neatly - or better still, have someone else do it.'

Sissy reached out and touched his arm, and he sighed. She said, 'No, it has authenticity, and blown up it will have an artistic quality. It will look great - don't worry.'

Bodhi said, 'I don't want it for the presentation. It wouldn't be perfect for the stage setting.' He said it with an air of finality that risked hurting Glen and Sissy's feelings, and he had designed the commandments to forbid the deliberate hurting of another's feelings, so he backtracked. 'Make it as big as possible and place it in the main entrance, so everyone can see it. It will be the mantra for all our endeavours.'

Glen shuffled, but Sissy smiled, and peered at him with her clear blue eyes, then hurried away with the revered note. Bodhi turned to Glen, 'Tomorrow the chosen ones will attain the Yellow™. They have nothing to fear, it's a saturated version of the Yellow™ so that you have more than enough to infuse the communities you watch over.'

'I'm sure we will feel all the better for taking it.'

Bodhi made a physical joke of standing tall and proud as he smiled. He said, 'In the spirit of trust, all our disciples will have free rein to visit anywhere in the complex.

Our teams will answer any questions, it's important they get the big picture. Obviously, they won't be allowed to enter anywhere that could be harmful to them, but even then, our people will give them open explanations as to what is happening.'

Glen said, 'Thank you. Industrial complexes are an anathema to them, but they understand the dilemma. The New Green Open Day was a great idea.'

Bodhi said, 'That was Sissy's idea.' He added, 'Tell them that our hundred-year-plan, of which we are now sixteen years in, includes the downgrading and rewilding of the Sattva Plant at the end of the project. I know I hurt Her in building this place - I hope She will forgive me.'

'I will - they get it.'

'Have you told them how important it is to bathe thoroughly ahead of the Yellow™ induction?'

'Yes. The Disciples can't wait to receive the upgrade.'

2.THE PRESENTATION

A group of excited Green Disciples, as the territory leaders were titled, gathered at the main entrance. They were watching the workers, in cream overalls in ceramic cream-coloured Cherry-Picker machines, hanging the giant fabric facsimile of Glen's thirteen requests - except to the Disciples they were demands.

Sissy and Glen joined them for a moment. The Disciples were happy and excited, and seemingly not at all concerned about the Ceremony. 'See, I told you it would look fab. Welcome to your exhibition.' They both looked on the draped banner which stretched for forty feet, and Glen had to admit that Sissy was right, as with his scrawled handwritten notes, blown up to this size gave the impression of it being a modern art exhibit from the old days.

Glen laughed, 'Now, you're mocking me.' But he did feel a tinge of pride.

'Come with me, I'll show you around. It's probably changed a lot since you were last here. Everybody here works exceptionally hard to bring our dreams to fruition. Even if they are rewarded in a way, we may find distasteful.'

'I do understand.'

They wandered out of the main entrance, and they hadn't walked for long when he had the feeling that parts of the complex seemed to have made a decisive leap into the future.' She said, 'It isn't always going to be about clean-ups and reparations. One day, in the not-too-far distant future, we will live a life of peace and harmony with the newly refreshed Mother Earth. This is why I want to bring children in the world to experience a kinder and gentler world.'

Glen said, 'I think I'm too focused on the work, but I do know that the freedom to travel has been warmly welcomed, and the new transport vehicles have opened up the world...'

'That's just the start. There are relatively small numbers of FusionVehicles™ available, but in time the whole infrastructure will be revolutionised and there will be enough transportation for all of the Green citizens. However, it will take decades for that to happen.'

'I know that people want the freedom to move around freely, to visit old friends and relatives or just to see the world, but I'm not keen on big infrastructure projects...'

'Don't worry.' She dug him in the ribs, 'You were always such a worrier. Bodhi isn't planning to add a single piece of new infrastructure, he would not slice into the Earth unless there was no other way. He is going to re-purpose the existing travel hubs in ways you could not imagine. I can't tell you, but you have to trust in him.'

Glen said implacably, 'I trust him with my life. If Bodhi asked for my life, then he could have it.'

Sissy smiled playfully, 'Anyway, how are you keeping? Is there a significant other who might have a say in what you do with your life?'

'No. I'm married to the cause - besides, over-population is bad for the planet.'

'You better not ask about me then?'

Glen flushed, 'I'm a bit out of practice with the social niceties. Please forgive me if I have offended you, you know I would never...'

'I'm teasing you. I had to work hard to generate enough Green Credits to offset my two, and soon to be three children. All of them will never have lived in the old world. They are the Green Seeds of the New Human Nature.'

'I can see why you are the Marketing hotshot around here. You could almost sell the idea of kids to me.'

Sissy laughed. They wandered over to the FusionPlanes™ parking area. There were hundreds of small ceramic cream-coloured crafts lined up, each identical to the next one. A few more were vertically landing into the neat but tightly packed spots, as other planes hurtled passed, high in the sky, noiselessly, but at incredible speeds. As each new arrival left their plane - they knew that they could choose any other vehicle for their onward journey, ownership and competition were relics of the past way of thinking. The internal NanoCleaning™ protocols would restore the machines to pristine condition in a matter of moments.

Glen knew all the veteran GreenRevs, and he looked forward to sharing the old war stories later in the evening with them all. He said, 'It's funny how it all worked out, in the end. I once feared futuristic tech, I mean, I was flat out against Genetically Modified Crops...'

Sissy agreed, 'I still am. It needed defeating. It was anti-nature.'

'But now, one of my closest friends is an industrialist at heart.'

'I know. At first, I was concerned about Nanotechnology. I was scared of nano-swarms and the potential of runaway self-replication wiping out the planet. But when it was the threat of the potential versus the real threat, well, it seemed like we had no choice.'

Glen said, 'Bodhi kept his word. You are closer than anyone to him. Is there anything to worry about?'

'I don't think so. It's the little inconsistencies which worry me.'

'Like what?'

'Well, on the day of the Revolution, you invited that TV reporter to join us, when nobody was supposed to have the opportunity to switch sides, but he let her in, at the death of the old world.'

'You're talking about Rhea, the TV reporter for...I forget the channel...'

'It hardly seems to matter now. But yes, the pretty red-head.'

'Bodhi had said to me that I should pick one woman on the day who represented the Old World. Bodhi instructed me. Then, when she got hit by a stray bullet while she was interviewing me, I felt that in that moment that Rhea had self-selected herself.'

'So, you didn't fancy her, and that was the only reason - you just left it to fate?'

'Yes. Bodhi was always clear. I must not succumb to temptation. I had to stay true to the founding principles of the project.' He smiled, 'She's done remarkably well since she did join though. She's been one of the most committed activists - for a Trad at heart. Rhea's not afraid of getting her hands dirty and is a Disciple of a small town near the Sattva Systems™ HQ on the back of her hard work. I've heard she's working on projects with Bodhi, and she's been given elevated access levels.'

'And you don't know what these assignments are?'

'No. Not yet, I've been promised full disclosure at a later date.'

'Does that concern you at all?'

Glen said, 'Not in the slightest. It's not my job to question Bodhi's judgment. I judge him on the progress of the project, and I do what I can to make it work for the Green communities of the world. The only thing that worries me, is if the Trads, or more to the point, one Trad in particular, sabotages the project from the inside.'

They strolled on together passed the vast warehouses, laboratory buildings and silos, their conversations occasionally punctuated by greetings with other Disciples - many of them overawed at meeting the legendary GreenRevs leader and Veteran #1. Glen turned to Sissy and asked, 'One of the troubling inconsistencies, is the blind-eye he is turning to the activities of Brady Mahone. That guy is running riot through the Western Seaboard. What do you make of the Brady situation?'

'Cain is now the Disciple for this area and has been in regular contact with Bodhi since day one. Bodhi does not seem the slightest bit concerned and has discreetly had Brady protected.'

Glen said, 'This Brady could protect himself. He has amassed hundreds of thousands of Green Credits, and I have it on good authority that he would be allowed to acquire the NanoSuits™ - if he freely chose to.'

Sissy said calmly, 'But he chooses to remain a Trad.' She endeavoured to alleviate the threat by sharing her insights on Bodhi's thinking and demeanour when receiving news about Brady Mahone. 'Bodhi is fascinated by Brady Mahone's progress - it's the closest thing to entertainment I've witnessed him indulging in. He looks forward to the reports of what he is up too next.'

'It sounds like a soap opera - remember those.'

She said, 'I haven't a clue what the deal is with Brady Mahone. All I know is that Bodhi does not view him as a threat in any shape or form.'

'Is he using him as a test of our Security Protocols™?'

'No. They work, flawlessly.'

Glen shrugged, 'I don't get it. I haven't come across this situation anywhere else in the world. He is a one-off. All I know is that I'd prefer it if he was eliminated.'

Sissy frowned, 'Well, we are not allowed to do that, not to Brady Mahone or any other living creature. If it's of any comfort to you, remember he has not taken the opportunity to attain any of the NanoSuits™, and therefore his life expectancy is considerably curtailed. He is fifty-eight and approaching old age in Trad terms. Having said that, he is ageing remarkably well. It must be the time he is spending with the Green Communities. He must be picking up some beneficial side-effects. After all, there are no diseases or infections there.'

'I suppose so. The Trads rarely live beyond seventy now, even those that have adapted well to their new conditions. And those that live in harsher climates than California barely make it past sixty…'

Sissy said, 'I sometimes feel a pang of guilt about that, but then I remind myself that the projections of Climate Change from the forties suggested that by the turn of the century, none of us would be around to witness it.'

Glen smiled broadly, 'But here we are, sixteen years into the hundred-year plan, and who knows, we may be here to witness the twenty-third century, never mind the twenty-second, with all the work going on to develop the NanoSuits™ further.'

Sissy looked at her cream-coloured ceramic watch, with its moss green strap and digital display. 'Come on. We'd better get back to the presentation ceremony.'

They both chatted happily on the way back to the Main Hall. Sissy was keen to hear about the gossip from all parts of the globe as Glen had flown from place to place co-ordinating the Disciples on behalf of Bodhi.

The Hall had filled up with Disciples. There was standing room only, but they were not uncomfortable as their NanoSuits™ supported them. They could stand for days if they needed to and feel almost weightless throughout the entire time. The Main Hall was egg-shaped with the stage area at the centre. In front of the stage and near the Entrance Hall was the audience. The rear of the stage area was empty and had lanes to the exits, which led to the communal showers and then onto the NanoPool™. The Main Hall had smooth cream-coloured walls which were ideal for projected images.

Sissy made her way to the stage while Glen took his seat at the audience's front and centre. It was one of the few times when a Disciple had an overt show of respect and allocated authority.

Sissy went to the side of the stage and exchanged words and completed a last-minute run-through of the presentation. She affixed discreet microphones to herself and Bodhi. She said, 'We are ready to freely give and receive.'

Bodhi strode on to the stage, his honey-skinned bald head shone under the soft lighting. He was dressed in a cream-coloured boiler suit with the S logo in moss-green positioned above his heart, and on the rear of the suit was the words Sattva Systems™ emblazoned in large letters. It was the same uniform worn by the technicians and workers at his industrial complex. He spoke softly, and his body language was open and inviting. 'It is so good to see you all. Please give your fellow Disciples next to you a hug and a pat on the back for a job well done. I am so very proud of each and every one of you.'

The audience turned left and right to ensure their neighbours were warmly congratulated, and there was an air of joyous brotherhood and sisterhood in the Hall. Bodhi waited until everybody had plenty of time to finish their hugs and excited chatter. He wasn't going to order them to stop - he didn't need to, as the Disciples wanted him to continue to deliver his message on this momentous day. He said, 'Before we start the Yellow™ Ceremony, I want Sissy to address you on the first baby steps on the journey for making all of your requests come to fruition.'

Clapping and cheering erupted from the faithful as Sissy moved to the centre stage. She had changed from jeans and T-shirt to the same boiler-suit design as Bodhi, within the time it took to take one stride. The Disciples collectively gasped. They knew this was what the Yellow™ could do, but they had never actually seen it before. Sissy said, 'I know you are all eager to get started, so I won't hold up the Ceremony for any longer than necessary.' She took a breath. 'I wish there was a NanoSuit™ upgrade for making public speaking less scary. On the list, there was a request to end binary thoughts and discrimination. Well, we are going to take the tiniest of first steps from today. I've spoken to Bodhi, and he is going to find this particularly difficult.'

Bodhi displayed a broad grin to the audience. 'We are going to change some of our descriptions of the cause, including our primary purpose. From now on, there will be no more references to mankind, we are now humankind. In addition, there will be no more Mother Earth, from now on we will be working for Earthkind, that means no more He, Her and She, Earthkind is for them.'

There was a warm-sounding murmur from the audience. She added, 'And I've set up a swear jar for Bodhi for every time he slips up. It should fill up rapidly as he will be attempting to give up the habit of a lifetime.'

Bodhi Sattva roared with laughter, as this wasn't in the script. He shook hands with Sissy and slapped her on the back before she left the stage. 'I might have more difficulty completing that particular challenge than all the others you have given me.' He laughed again and waited for the audience noise to subside.

The screens lit up with: *Loudspeakers activated in all Sattva Systems™ Industrial Units.* 'Today is the day when you will receive the Yellow™. My workers and technicians have all worked so incredibly hard so that you can deliver the YellowSuits™ to our beautiful Green Communities in time for the New Century celebrations. Please give them the cheer of your lives so that they can hear you all over the plant, and freely give them your thanks, as much as I freely give mine. My wonderful team, I thank you with all my heart.'

The audience roared, whooped and hollered. The high-pitched ululation came from some women within the room, and the cacophony was deafeningly loud. Glen roared along, and he had an overwhelming sense of pride in his fellow Disciples. They were the first to receive the NanoSuits™, and his mind swept back to those days of Revolution, when the fear was palpable within his Disciples, as they only had the faith, he had instilled in them that the Suits™ would withstand everything the Trads in the old world could throw at them. They had the fear of the suicide mission until they could feel for themselves that the Suits™ would withstand it all. Of course, the psychological damage the Trads caused proved to be unbearable to some, and he lost many close friends as a result. He remembered them deliberately at this point.

Bodhi said, 'You will all receive files with the full rules concerning the use of the YellowSuits™. Revise them before the Community Ceremonies as this is a leap in the use of your personal expression. However, I will summarise a few key points now.' He paused but continued to speak softly, 'They cannot be used to cause offence, ridicule or humiliation to another, not even to the Trads when you are working in their zones. Everybody can change appearance to the same level of ability, we do not encourage competition or one-upmanship - we would never want to inadvertently re-introduce any hierarchical structures within the Green Communities.' He smiled, 'Of course, there are rules and responsibilities, but we know you will have fun with the new abilities these Suits™ can bestow upon its wearers. You will receive a super-saturated infusion of the Yellow™, so as you can infuse your own Green Communities.' Bodhi moved to the side of the stage.

Sissy returned to the stage. 'Most of you know how the process works, but for the newcomers and newly promoted, here is what you have to do.' She pointed to the exit to the rear of the stage marked Magnetic Showers. 'You will have to remove your clothing, Distors™ and other possessions down to your OrangeSuits™, you will feel strangely vulnerable - I know I did.' She paused before continuing, 'You will then pass through the showers, it's imperative that you are magnetically cleaned. It will feel very much like a normal shower - don't rush through - take your time - use at least five minutes.' She looked around the whole audience to ensure they were all paying close attention to her words. 'Then you will pass through the NanoPool™. Ensure you will travel through the whole length of the pool - it's one hundred yards long, and it is very deep in the middle, but with the Red™ strata of your Suits™ you will still be able to breathe.' She added, 'By the way, do not worry if you swallow, inhale or any other form of ingestion, the NanoBots™ will magnetically find their own way to the appropriate parts of your body's internal structure.' She coughed and composed herself. 'There are different processes taking place at various parts and depths of the pool, so travel through it until you leave at the shallow end on the other side. Then I need you to return back here, to the Main Hall to give you a demonstration on how the YellowSuits™ work. As you enter the Main Hall, your Suits™ will blend to the default setting of a Yellow Silk robe.' She looked around the room. 'Any questions?' There weren't any - nobody wanted to halt proceedings. 'Let the Yellow™ Ceremony begin.'

As the Disciples filed passed the stage, Bodhi called out to one of them, 'Cain, my friend, could I have a quick catch up?'

Cain was dressed in his dishevelled white robe and sandals, and he peered across at Bodhi with his crystal-green eyes. 'Of course. What can I do for you?'

'How is everything on the Western Seaboard?'

'Pretty quiet. The Trad areas have become settled into the style of governance that seems to work for their own areas.'

'And your home community in West McFarland?'

'Peaceful, apart from the excitement of the New Century Day.'

'Lizzie and Siddha. How are they keeping?'

Cain smiled, but he knew that Bodhi was only really interested in Brady Mahone. 'They are happy and in good spirits.'

'Excellent, I'm very pleased to hear it.' He added, 'And any news on our unique friend?'

'Brady has continued to expand his business, but he's struggling to keep up with the demand, as he cannot find enough Blank Files. This is why he is extending his territory. Also, the Blank Black Files he does find are ancient now, as they were manufactured decades ago.'

'But the old DVDs and CDs don't suffer from the same degradation. They were never designed to be recyclable.'

Cain nodded, 'That's correct.' He added, 'Talking of recycling, Brady obviously knows about our YellowSuits™, and has already spotted another business opportunity.'

Bodhi laughed warmly, 'And what's next for our little criminal?'

'He knows the Green Community won't need physical clothing. He's purchased a FusionHeavyLorry™, and he's looking to go into trading these discarded clothes with the Trads.'

Bodhi put his hands to his face as if he were trying to figure out whether this would work. 'The Green Communities clothing is in good condition - we are installing the Yellow™ to run down the need for our textile industry. It is forbidden for the Green Communities to give to the Trads or face the risk of being banished and joining them. However, the Trads clothing from the old world is at least sixteen years old and mostly replaced by fairly primitive garments. Our friend Brady could be onto a winner.'

Cain said, 'As a Trad, he can do what he likes - and he does.' He added, 'At what point will you decide to do something about him? Surely, he's a threat?'

Bodhi changed the subject, 'Across the world we have banished just over two-thousand Green Community members for succumbing to the temptation to inappropriately interact with the old world. Out of the recently completed Census, that's not too bad an error rate.'

Cain shrugged, 'It's still two thousand too many in my opinion.'

Bodhi reached out and put an arm on Cain's shoulder, 'They self-selected. Just like the Trads did. They knew the rules but couldn't resist the temptation, they only had themselves to blame. If only they had the self-discipline of good people like you, my friend.'

'You're right. Of course. It couldn't be simpler than just to follow the rules that are there to help us all.'

Bodhi said, 'Thank you, Cain. Please continue to keep me informed. I always look forward to your monthly updates. Now, you'd better join the others and attain your well-deserved YellowSuit™.'

Cain went to the back of the line. As he got the Magnetic Showers, he disrobed. He hung up his white robe, with his Distor™ and his meagre possessions in his pockets, and then neatly placed his brown sandals underneath. Before him, some of the Disciples were utilising the Red™ and OrangeSuits™' blurring properties to hide their nudity, but Cain stepped into the showers, naked. The feeling was of a cold shower, but it didn't wet him. It left him with the vaguest sense of being coated in a gossamer film. He stayed there for nearly ten minutes, even though the last of the other Disciples overtook him. He then moved slowly, like a monk in a sombre religious procession to the NanoPool™. He stood at the edge of the glowing yellow liquid. He studied it and estimated that it might have had hundreds of different shades of yellow. He was at the lighter end of the spectrum, but it was a mustard colour at the furthest part of the pool and appeared more viscous.

He stepped into the shallow end and gracefully moved down the steps. He watched the people ahead of him disappear as they became submerged in the deep central section. He followed, serenely. He was aware that he was breathing in the perfumed yellow fumes, and he even felt as if the Yellow™ was entering his ears, he felt a pleasant tingling sensation as he went deeper and deeper into the pool. He looked up, and all he could see was yellow, he felt as if he were at the bottom of an ocean. He walked on until his head emerged above the semi-liquid until he saw his fellow Disciples emerge at the far end of the NanoPool™. They were exalted. They appeared to all be dressed in Saffron robes, and they all smiled like Tibetan Monks. As Cain emerged, he too became overwhelmed with joy as he hugged anyone and everyone around him. Cain was the last person to emerge from the pool.

Sissy's voice called out and urged everyone to return to the Main Hall. The Saffron-robed procession moved as one into the Main Hall, and they chatted and giggled excitedly as they walked. She addressed them all, 'And now for the fun part of the day. When you present this to your Green Communities via Green Community Leaders, I promise you, it will be a day you will never forget.' She paused. 'Please, I would like to draw your attention to the screens which will switch on around you.'

A hundred identical images appeared all around the audience. It was a photograph of Sissy in her Sattva Systems™ boilersuit. She said, 'I want you to look at the not-very-flattering image of me. Now you could choose, two settings, but first, I want you to think of the word Blend.

Sissy watched over the audience and laughed as she heard excited chatter punctuated by the occasional exclamation of 'Wow!' She said, 'Now we will put up a stream of photographs, and now I want you to think of the words Ongoing Blend. Over the next ten minutes, images appeared and disappeared, there were many images from the old world, ones of City investment bankers, police officers, military personnel and sports stars in team kits. Every time the picture changed, then the YellowSuits™ changed with them.

Bodhi interjected and joked, 'I think you are all getting the hang of this.' The Disciples laughed and pointed at each other until they realised, they had changed clothing themselves.

Sissy said, 'You will have noticed that the clothes have changed but not your bodies or facial features.' She waited for the murmuring to die down. 'All of this is in your training pack to give to the others.' She moved on to the next session. 'For this next section, I will put up a crowd scene, and then I want you to think of the words, Approximate Blend.' Over the next fifteen minutes, there were crowd scenes of many different Trad areas from all across the globe. The Disciples apparel changed with each one. Sissy intervened, 'You'll notice that nobody is displaying identical clothing to another. This is for when more than one of you are in the same Trad Area, the blending option will never match completely with anybody in the same vicinity, be that Trad or Green.' She then switched to a Mardi Gras Carnival and the Disciples' clothing turned into flamboyant costumes full of vibrant colours.

The Disciples danced and then examined each other and felt the texture of each other's clothing. Many even sniffed at the clothing, and it smelled authentic. It even seemed to smell like the location on the screens.

Sissy said, 'Here is the final lesson for today. On the screen will be a thousand different images of the day. Pick one and think of the words, Individual Blend. They each picked an image, and they changed into the clothing of the chosen one. Many picked the same pictures to tune into, and they noticed the discreet variations between them, while others who were more playful and confident, picked numerous shots and switched rapidly from one to another.

Bodhi spoke, 'With practice, you could imagine an image, and it will adorn you. This is the latest reward for your hard work and dedication. Pass this gift freely onto all our people.'

3.AMIE

Brady Mahone had been away for a few days, having completed his Christmas deliveries. His FusionCar™ or the Hearse, as he nicknamed it, was as new as the day he bought it from the Greens nearly sixteen years ago. *Gotta admit it - they knows how to make their vehicles reliable.* He pulled into the Mahone Ranch. He noticed the old Sattva Systems™ billboards which his old friend Lucian had made needed a lick of paint. As he got out of the Hearse, he checked his Distor™, its vivid green digital display informed him that he was now the proud owner of over eight-hundred and fifty thousand Green Credits. *Next year I'm going to be a Greenback Millionaire and then I can buy me one of those Mini-FusionPlanes™. The new century belongs to Brady Mahone Enterprises.*

He went over to Archie Mahone's grave and paused for a moment to think about the happier times he recalled from being with his Pops. He then marched over to the Lopez Ranch to see how the work was going in the East McFarland branch of his now sprawling business empire. His old friend Lucian got up out of his chair to greet him, 'Hiya, old buddy.'

'Hey Lucky, didja have a good Christmas?'

'Sure did. Just a shame you couldn't join us.'

Mary-Lou came over and gave Brady a hug, while Amie looked over at him from her armchair, and then she blushed and didn't say anything. Brady looked at her and winked. *She's one of the youngest people left in the Trad world. She's seventeen and cooped up here forever on the Lopez Ranch with only Lucky and her Moms for company. No wonder Amie keeps giving me those moon eyes.* He turned his attention back to Lucian, as Mary-Lou poured him a steaming black coffee without needing to ask Brady if he wanted one or not. He knew they were eager for him to tell his latest tales from his time in the outside world. Lucian would want to know if he had met anybody, they both knew from his travels - the list of known associates was dwindling over the years. Mary-Lou wanted to understand how people were coping in the Trad areas and was looking for every conceivable reason to count their blessings of living in reasonable comfort, peace and security, whereas Amie seemed to be enamoured by the glamorous - to her eyes - stories of the teenagers in the Green Communities. She overcame her shyness enough to quiz Brady on which Files they were using their Green Credits on. When Amie left the room to go to the barn-cum-workshop, Mary-Lou told Brady that she would be watching all those TV shows and movies, and dream about discussing them with children of her own age.

Brady had noticed all of them growing older, even if he seemed immune to the onset of old age. He still felt fighting fit - which was just as well as he had got into plenty of scrapes over the years. Lucian had recently entered into his fifties, which was now relatively old for a Trad nowadays, and he looked closer to sixty. Brady found himself dwelling on this more and more, especially as many of his initial contacts were beginning to die off. His remaining surrogate family at the Mahone and Lopez Ranches benefitted from a power supply and plenty of fresh food - courtesy of Brady's earnings. However, they still seemed to age quicker than the old days. Brady's theories as he travelled for long hours and days in the Hearse ranged from the effects of stress on them, having spent most of their adult lives isolated from the rest of the world - the sum total of human interactions between them were the three members of the Lopez family and himself.

The Trad areas depended on how society evolved, they seemed to have a different identity in every place he visited. In East McFarland, they worked hard to keep some kind of normality, they maintained a sense of law and order, no doubt inspired by Judge Jefferson's strong leadership. *That reminds me I'll leave them another update from the San Jose areas. The Professor loves my bulletins.*

He still tried to avoid Castaic, if he could, when he travelled south, as the Cesare Mafia were utterly ruthless with anybody who crossed them, and they seem to have had a system where if you didn't join them then you were eliminated. Then the Cupertino district adapted by fortifying the old MASSIVE™ complex and lived like blissful hippies and fully embracing their new feudalism ideals. This was the place he did most of his dealings for the old Blank Black Files.

Even Brady had found himself taken in by the tales of the secrets held in the hidden vaults. As with all the tall stories of an El Dorado of secrets, nobody ever knew precisely where these mysterious vaults were. *But trust the Cupertino Crew to spin a tale which would make them more special than any other of the Trad Areas.* Still, if the stories were true, then this would be a veritable museum of old tech as the CEO of MASSIVE™ in the 2040s had begun a mission to collect all the formats of the ages in her mad desire to be The One to convene with aliens that visited from outer space, one day soon.

Tia Cassandra reasoned that she would have the History of Mankind available in every possible format which an Alien Technology might be able to read. Tia Cassandra was ousted as CEO just three days before the Internet Crash of 2050 and supposedly went off to a remote retreat on the edges of the Mojave Desert. She told the world that she wasn't fired, but she was in fact, embarking on a top-secret project that would save mankind - whether they deserved to be saved or not. Most onlookers shrugged, 'She would say that - wouldn't she?'

I wish I'd have had the chance to take Pops to Cupertino, he would have been in conspiracy theory heaven.

His Pops had told him of every alien technology conspiracy theory ever mooted, so he was an expert when it came to dealing with the Cupertino Hippies. *Cupertino cunts, more like.* What fascinated him more were the stories of the bitter rivalry Tia Cassandra had with Sattva Systems™. They were effusive in their stories of how she, more than anybody else, stymied all the big ideas from John Kane, at first, and subsequently, the guru-like stylings of the poser Xavier Kane - the Cupertino Hippies, as a matter of principle refused to ever utter his pseudonym of Bodhi Sattva - that was just uncool.

Some loved Brady and took him in as one of their own, while others thought he was a collaborator with the Greens. Brady didn't look like them. They were long-haired, flowers in the hair types, whereas Brady was a hulking six-foot-six muscle-bound hulk of a man, and his jet-black hair was kept tidy and short, courtesy of the regular trims which Mary-Lou gave him. However, he used his stories of the favour-itism Bodhi Sattva had endowed onto his Mother, Libby Skye, and her cronies in Malibu to prove that he wasn't as golden as the Sattva brand suggested he would be, and when he told the story of John Kane being the money man behind a paedophile ring, they didn't know whether it was true or not. Frankly, they didn't care, it was a brilliant story and gave them bitter comfort that the Kane family was as corrupt as the rest of the business world back in the day, and not the perfect family who got into bed with the madder side of the Green debate. Even though the GreenRevs would have a lot in common with the new breed of Cupertino Hippies, they hated them like bitter sibling rivals.

No matter how different from each other all these Trad areas were, the one thing they had in common was that they all aged quickly, and the elderly were dying much younger than they would have done in the old days. *I wonder if it has something to do with that sterilising goo they sprayed on everyone, not long after they took over?*

Brady was confident that he would still live to a ripe old age. He felt good. Even after spending time in some hellish places on his extensive travels, he never seemed to fall ill. It concerned him that it might not be long before his surrogate family succumbed to old age, and he didn't want to contemplate his lonely life without them.

He thought of Professor Yuan Chu. He looked at his watch, and it was nearly 6pm. *I haven't seen him for a while, and he'll be passing the bus stop soon. I think I'll give him an update in person, for a change. I'm sure he won't mind.*

He walked over to the bus stop which the East McFarland Trads now called the Brady Stop. Nobody was there when Brady got there. He pulled out his latest communique, in recent times he was informing them more about places which had been lost to the Greens when the population had either died out or moved on. His latest entry stated: Los Banos XXX.

I'll head up there in the next few days to see if there were any scraps I can pick up. The basements and cellars of the abandoned homes have produced some rich rewards in the last few years. It's a closing down sale of epic proportions - the whole town must go.

He was smiling at his latest plans when the man, who was the nearest thing to a mentor in the life of Brady Mahone arrived at the abandoned bus stop. Brady lied, 'Hey Professor, you're looking good.' Brady struggled to keep his air of cheerfulness, as the Professor was the oldest man he knew, and positively ancient by Trad standards, Brady wondered if he was nearly ninety years old. Brady instinctively knew he was not long for this world.

'Hello, Brady. I wished I looked as good as you.' He laughed and said, 'Do you mind if I sit down. I'm feeling a bit weary, but the walk is beneficial to me.' He pulled the paper from behind the Perspex film, which used to provide protection from the elements of the old bus timetable. 'So, another town has been abandoned to the Greens. I used to have relatives in Los Banos.' He placed his walking stick between his leg and the wall of the shelter.

'I'm sorry.'

'Thank you. What do they do with the abandoned areas? Do they move in?'

'No. The Green Workers go into their Operation Clean-Up mode, they spray everything that doesn't move on the ground, and then the HeavyFusionPlanes™ move in and spray the buildings.'

'Even the old churches and historic buildings?'

'Especially those. The Greens have got a real hang-up about nostalgia for the old days. It's a real sin of theirs, y'know, all that Lead us not into temptation crap.'

The Professor nodded, 'And yet they let you wander into their homes and sell them all those images from the distant past.'

'I'm not knocking it. I gotta make a living, and if I spotted a loophole in their big plan then Go Me, that's what I think.'

'Do they draw any lines of what is fair game with historical artefacts?'

Brady shrugged, 'I haven't noticed any. It's all future-forward with these guys - no looking back. I suppose you gotta admire it, really.'

The Professor said solemnly, 'It will be of some comfort to me that I won't be around for much longer to witness it.' He changed the subject as it was not his intention to make Brady feel bad. 'I'm glad I had the chance to see you, as I wanted to thank you, personally, for all you have done for us over the years.'

'Me? No need to thank me. It's been good business. In any case, you've always treated me right. I've always appreciated that about you. You never looked down your nose on old Brady Mahone.' Brady laughed.

'You are one of the main reasons our community has held together over all these difficult years, and I suspect, many other communities in and around the old California State.'

'Now hold on Professor, I think you are giving me entirely too much credit here.'

'I'll try and explain. Our small community cannot move beyond the Green Perimeters. You told us not to abandon any land to prevent the Greens from acquiring it. This meant we could farm the green spaces still left to us. This kept us fed and with healthier food than we otherwise would have had.'

Brady wasn't used to taking praise, especially, when he felt he hadn't deserved it. 'I have said that, but I didn't see into the future, it was just what I'd seen on my travels, is all.'

The professor looked at Brady with his rheumy-brown eyes. 'Ah, let's discuss the effect of your travels. You'll never know the immensity of the value we put on your news from the outside world. When you bring us even the most basic information, it connects us to the outside world. You let us know that we are not alone. It gives us a reason to stick together and to struggle on. It keeps us civilised.'

'You're welcome. Just doing my job.'

'Brady, please receive my utmost thanks. I need to know you have received it in the spirit in which I give it. Even if you haven't saved us, in your own unique way, you have made our burden bearable.' A single tear escaped from Professor Yuan Chu's eyes, and Brady looked away. He put his hand back on Brady's shoulder and said, 'Will you accept my gratitude?'

Brady gulped involuntarily, but said, 'Yes.'

Professor Chu said, 'Now that you are aware of the importance of your visits, I would be grateful if you could promise to keep giving our people this information after I've gone.'

Brady wasn't going to give a platitude to the inevitable death of this old man, no matter how much he respected him. 'I will. For what it's worth - I give you my word.'

'Your word is more than sufficient.' He smiled, 'Now, I must return.' He laughed, 'I have been summoned by Judge Jefferson to help organise the New Century celebration.' He got up slowly, grabbed his walking stick and hobbled away.

His time ain't long. I'll do something nice for the next time I see him. I'm sure gonna miss him when he's gone.

4.OPERATION CLEAN-UP

Brady headed up to Los Banos. Whenever an area passed over to the Greens, he would usually be a little quicker off the mark as he didn't like searching the houses once the Greens had sprayed their Green goo over everything. But he figured that there would be little activity in the run-up to New Year, as they put a lot of store in the New Year as the focus of their celebrations. He had noticed that Christmas and other religious festivities hadn't been banned as such, but they were frowned upon as festivals of nostalgia. They also celebrated the material production age. The New Year was considered a future-forward event, and a time of renewal and therefore officially sanctioned, which meant the Green Communities could let their hair down without guilt. The fact wasn't lost on Brady that the New Year marked the birthday of a certain Xavier Kane or Bodhi Sattva as he liked to be known, though in an act of faux humility, he had stated to his people that the New Year's Day had nothing to do with him and was a mere coincidence - a statement which only endeared him even more to his people.

When Brady reached Los Banos, he was a little dismayed to hear the Green Clean-up crews already working. In the past few years, Brady liked this place and spent many a peaceful hour up here with his sketchbooks. It had waterfowl reserves, and he loved to draw the birds in exquisite detail and give them to Amie. It was a more peaceful account of the outside world. Sometimes, he would spot other exotic wild-life, and these he collected with his drawings like kids would collect baseball cards from so many years ago.

The town was a similar size to McFarland, but the climate was different, it had stronger winds and a distinctly colder winter, even though it wasn't that much further north from his hometown. He had wrapped up warm and had fingerless gloves for picking through any found product and a black beanie hat to keep his head warm. Otherwise, he still had his jeans, T-shirt, sneakers and his long Poachers Coat with its many pockets, to carry his treasures. He figured he'd take what he could from the place throughout January, after that the Green goo would begin to degrade anything worth reclaiming.

He kept away from the Green Workers and searched the houses. He found a few hundred old CDs and DVDs - some of which had been well cared for over the decades. He headed back to his cream-coloured hearse shaped FusionCar™. He emptied his pockets and put his newfound stock away before beginning his next round of searches.

He tried to figure out why this town had succumbed to the Greens, whereas East McFarland had survived as a Trad Area. *I suppose it's the waterfowl and wildlife parks, it would have attracted the Greens even before the Revolution in '84.* He had spotted a couple of remaining Trads in his search of the houses who had pleaded with him not to give them up. 'Brady Mahone doesn't snitch on anyone,' he informed them, but he knew he didn't have to - the Greens had their methods of detection, and these last Trads didn't stand a chance. It softened the blow that he knew they would only be moved on to other Trad areas and nothing worse would happen to them.

For the next couple of days, he had filled his Hearse and taken his stock back to McFarland, and then made the return journey to Los Banos to begin his search of the most likely places to acquire more DVDs and CDs. He began to believe he had developed a kind of sixth sense - or maybe it was the years of practice - to employ on picking out the most likely homes to creep into or break into, if necessary, and have a high chance of finding what he was searching for.

Brady decided to have a well-deserved break from scouring abandoned family homes and wandered around the local park. He listened, contentedly to the many different birds singing in the trees. He then heard a voice call out, 'You must be Brady Mahone. Come, join me for lunch, I have food to spare, as the Good Lord has over-provided for one such as I.' The guy was waving at him as if they were already friends.

Brady spied the black man, who was even bigger than himself. Even though the man was sitting down with his back to a tree, he could tell that much. *He's all muscle under that Green Workers uniform*, Brady noted.

Brady said warily as if he might be dealing with the law, 'Who's asking?'

'Please friend, let me introduce myself, my full name is Samuel Beardon the Third, some of my colleagues call me the Bear Down, as in I *bear down* on evil, but most of my friends simply refer to me as the Bear.'

Brady approached. *If this guy stands up, then I'm ready.* He looked all around him, as this felt like a trap. The Bear looked up and reached out his big right hand. Brady shook it, firmly. 'Why are you talking to me? You Green Workers usually try and pretend I'm not here.'

'Many are afraid that you will lead them into temptation, whereas I am comfortable with what the Lord provides.'

'I thought that Bodhi Sattva was your Lord.'

The Bear laughed warmly, 'I prefer to see him as a spirit guide on Earth, but my Lord is the one who will judge me at the end.'

Brady scoffed, 'Take a look around, Buddy. I don't think anybody's Lord is going to forgive you for this.'

'I understand your distress, brother. However, I take comfort in my duties with the words in the Good Book.'

'And where does it say you can ethnically cleanse billions of people. That's how a lot of clever people describe what you're doing.'

The Bear smiled, 'I haven't witnessed any killings, or even harm upon another living thing. The Bible says, "You shall not pollute the land in which you live, for blood pollutes the land, and no atonement can be made for the land for the blood that is shed in it, except by the blood of the one who shed it. You shall not defile the land in which you live, in the midst of which I the Lord dwell." He is with us now.'

Brady said, 'That doesn't make any sense to me, just sounds like it could mean anything you want it to.'

'I'll try something a little simpler, for the Good Book has many teachings, how about, "The Lord God took the man and put him in the garden of Eden to work it and keep it." The Trads wrecked the garden, but we are restoring it to its former glory.' He added, 'I don't want to debate with you, my friend, I only ask for your company. I'm keen to know more about you. You are a sense of much wonder and consternation. Come, sit, and let us break bread together.'

Brady sat down and accepted the Bear's offer. He tucked into the soft brown bread sandwiches filled with cheese, lettuce and tomatoes, and drank the piping hot coffee which the Bear poured him from his thermos flask. Brady soon relaxed, and the thought of traps receded. Brady asked, 'What's your job?'

'I am an Environment Sprayer. It pays well because of the potentially distressing scenes one may encounter.'

'I've seen that. You have one of those tanks on your back and spray Green goo over everything.'

'Yes. We don't call it Green goo, though.' He laughed as if he had heard the punchline from a brilliant joke. 'We return everything back to its elemental level and return it to God's green land. However, we have to leave the streets and highways for recycling and re-purposing - but that's a job for the Highways crews equipped with NanoFixant™ and NanoRepair™.'

Brady said, 'I don't want to argue with you, live and let live is my philosophy.' *Unless they get in my way.*

The Bear interrupted, 'A fine philosophy indeed, and one in which I concur.'

'But surely you are not happy about the destruction of the churches.'

'You are correct, brother. It does not fill my soul with joy. However, if we all decided on what we would want to save, nothing would change. I believed in my Lord, and not in the organised religions who coveted treasures and lands. The churches, in many instances, were memorials to their benefactors, rather than to God.' Brady was about to interrupt him, but the Bear raised his big right hand, 'I have to believe that - as my faith will always trump clever arguments. The Lord is behind all of this. This is His will, and I will put all of my strength into enacting it. The words of any man will not change that.'

'Not even the words of Bodhi?'

'He is doing the Lord's bidding, my friend. You will witness the New Eden. I can feel it. You are sent unto me. As many of my friends believe, you might undermine the Prophet, but you will not undermine the Lord. This is what I believe.' He looked at his watch. He said, 'It's two o'clock. I must return to my work.' The Bear looked into Brady's eyes as if he was searching his soul, 'I know you are searching out DVDs and CDs, but it's common knowledge that you need those old Blank Files. If you come along with me, while I work this afternoon, then I can ask my friends to get them for you.'

'How many Blank Files?'

'Thousands.'

Brady could hardly believe his luck. He *didn't* believe his luck. 'Where are they?'

The Bear smiled kindly. 'In the vaults of the old Library on Seventh Street. My good friends have the keys, but it's due to be sprayed tomorrow. After that, all the contents will start their decaying process.'

'And why are you doing this - for me?'

'I'm just helping a friend in need, as I would for any other Green friend.'

'But you know I'm not Green.'

'If Bodhi says that it is permitted to help Brady Mahone, if we encounter him, then that is Green enough for me. What do you say? I think you and I could be great friends if you allow yourself to get to know me better.'

Brady defaulted back to his usual criminal perspective. 'Sure, why not?' *I've got nothing to lose, and if there are thousands of Files, then it's more than worth it for an afternoon of my time.* He still didn't trust this Samuel Beardon the third, but equally, he was likeable enough.

The Bear put away his Tupperware boxes, thermos and spare cups into his duffle bag and left this on the floor while he readied himself for work. He picked up his substantial cream-coloured ceramic cylinder with its Sattva Systems™ logo and threaded the attached hose down the length of his right arm until the nozzle snugly fitted into his big right hand. He slung his duffle bag over his left shoulder and then walked away. Brady followed him. Brady couldn't remember the last time he followed anybody.

At the edge of the park, he went to a Sattva Systems™ FusionMiniBus™ and dropped off his duffle bag and then came back out with the air of a man determined to put a good shift in at work. They marched purposefully into a side street. Brady asked, 'How does the tank thing on your back work?'

'It contains compartments of Self-Replicating NanoBots™, and each compartment has a different function. If I click on the nozzle, I can change the settings.'
They strolled down the alleyway. There were overturned bins and dumpsters, which had been rifled through for anything of use. Brady accidentally trod in a black and slimy pile of rotting food. He shouted, 'Fuck this, man, these are top-notch sneakers.'

The Bear said, 'Sssh.' He whispered, 'I've pressed it five times to put it into pest control mode.'

'Why?'

'Because of the rats, brother.'

'So, you are going to kill them.'

'Of course not. We don't hurt God's creatures. I will spray them with steriliser, that way they can live out their lives but not ruin it for the other sentient beings by over-populating the area.' They both heard movement. Brady froze, but the Bear tiptoed his way to the back of a stinking dumpster.

Brady heard the hiss of spraying and then watched in horror as hundreds of rats raced past him. He tried not to sound scared, but he was shaken, 'Did you get them all?'

'I think so. They only have to catch a tiny amount of the spray for it to work, as even a speck of it contains billions of NanoBots™.'

For the next couple of hours, the Bear was in pest-control mode, and Brady could understand why this job would be a big Greenback earner in the Green Communities. 'Do you have to do this work full-time?'

'Not at all. We are all freelance. I could choose to do something gentler, like wild-life census, but I would have to do much longer hours. With this job, I get to spend more time with my friends. You would be welcome to join us.'

'I don't know...'

'There's wholesome food and coffee, and we like to laugh and tell tall-tales.'

In the old days, we would have got drunk and hit the nightclubs, but this is what passes for good entertainment, these days. 'Ok, why not? I was only planning to stay overnight in the Hearse.'

The Bear roared with laughter, 'I'm sure we can provide better entertainment than sleeping a Hearse my friend.'

In another alley, they heard a dog barking. They moved in to investigate. A teenage girl was lying on the ground, she was barely breathing, but rats were crawling over her prostate body. Brady spotted a lead tied around the girl's hand, and behind her, the dog was barking at a hole in the wall where the rats were pouring out. The dog's hind leg was bleeding, and its fur was covered in blood. Brady couldn't determine whether the dog was distressed because of protecting its owner or trying to fight off the rats.

He watched the Bear spray the rats and then he stepped over the girl to see to the dog. 'There's a good boy.' He stroked the dog and tried to calm him down. 'There's a brave boy. Calm down. I'm here to help. There's a good boy. Now, let me tend to that nasty wound.' He sprayed the dog's injured leg, and the dog jumped up and licked the Bear's face as if the effect of the NanoHealing™ had been instantaneous. The Bear untied the dog and set him free, but the dog went straight over to the girl and licked her face and then began to whine.

Brady said, 'Can't you use some of that spray on the girl?'

'No, my friend. I cannot interfere with the Trads. I shouldn't acknowledge her, at all.' Brady was just about to argue, when the Bear added, 'Nothing is stopping you attending to her. She only has moments left, in my humble opinion. However, I've seen thousands like her, and I haven't got the time to spare, but maybe, you have?'
Brady sighed and shook his head, and then he closed his eyes and heard the rattle of the girl's last dying breaths. He opened them again. He looked at the dog and felt some kind of empathy for the dog and the girl. He didn't really know what to do, so he moved in close to the girl and she tried to speak, 'My dog...My dog.' In between a few more breaths she uttered, 'Please, look after my dog.'

Brady thought he was lying when he said, 'I will. Don't you worry.' She attempted to smile but died at that moment. Brady picked up the Jack Russell dog, and thought it was some sort of crossbreed because its paws looked big. *I never get why people used to play around with nature and try and create crossbreeds themselves - it's kinda like playing God in my book.*

Jim Lowe

He picked up the dog and held it to his face and the Jack Russell licked at him - it also, seemed to implore him with sad eyes. It was then that Brady thought of the girl's age - she was about the same age as Amy. And that's when he had the idea of taking the dog home and giving him to her.

The Bear said, 'We don't agree with keeping domestic animals.'

Brady thought about it. He hadn't seen anybody in the Green communities with dogs, cats, or anything else for that matter. They had farm animals, but they weren't for meat, of course - they were for milk or any other functions they could perform. Brady said, 'I don't get it, why?'

'I know where you are coming from, as it caused a lot of consternation in the Green communities before the Revolution, but it was decided that these were Her creatures, and not to be owned by humans. They are not here to serve us and our pleasures. Many of our Green members left the community at that point, but the ones that stayed proved their devotion to Her, and not to their own emotional needs.' The Bear tried to lighten the subject. 'What are you going to do with him - our little friend?'

'I've got a girl at home - about her age.'

'You have a daughter?'

'No, no. She's my friend's girl, and she's about this girl's age. I'm gonna give the dog to her.'

'And have you decided the name for this dog?'

Brady looked at the dog, and the dog was wagging his tail. It was clearly recovering quickly from its injuries. 'I'm gonna call him Billy Big Paws. It's kind of a, say what ya see kinda thing.'

'I can tell you are a no-nonsense kind of guy.' The Bear said.

The Bear stepped up and sprayed the girl. 'It will help the decomposition process. Within a day or so, there will be no trace of her.'
Brady noticed that the rats lost interest in the girl. 'Why aren't the rats eating her?'

The Nanotech displays no odour, so predators are not attracted to any of the Greens because we are just like lumps of metal to them. We hold no interest to them, whatsoever. The same technology is applied to the dead bodies. From now on, animals will have no interest in her corpse, and pretty soon, she will melt away into the ground. We don't want the dead to spread diseases, and also, it has the side effect of keeping unpleasant odours away.'

Brady decided he didn't want to talk about it, anymore.

They walked in silence for a while. Brady struggled with his conscience, and more deeply, his concept of what humanity had become. The Bear finally said something, and Brady was shaken out of his melancholy. 'My friend. It is of little consolation, but I can offer a practical solution that might help your Trad friends. Especially for those communities which are losing their farming space to cemeteries.'

Brady had no idea what the Bear was talking about. 'I'm sorry, what?'

'This is going to sound heartless. I'm truly sorry. And it will generate high paying work for the Green Communities. But your people should consider it.'

'Why is it high paying work?'

'Because Trad Body Disposal pays a higher commission. I'm being honest with you. The GreenRevs don't want to waste valuable land on burying millions of bodies, and the Trad survivors need every green space they can retain for growing crops to continue to feed its people.'

This is the weirdest conversation I've ever had, and I spent ten years at Ridgecrest. 'You've completely lost me, man. What are you suggesting?'

'There are constant patrols from the air which specialise in detecting dead and rotting human flesh. I hate to inform you of this, my friend, but there have been increasing reports of cannibalism in some areas, especially where the food supplies are dwindling.' He shook his head in disgust, 'Anyway, these patrols inform workgroups like my own of the location of these carcasses, and we help with the decomposition. It's all part of Operation Clean-up.'

Brady snapped, 'Can you get to the point?'

The Bear could see that this was a difficult subject for Brady, 'Well, if you told the Trad leaders to leave their dead out in the open, at the edge of their districts, then we would dispose of the bodies for them. Then they could use their remaining green spaces for growing crops, instead of for burying their corpses.'
Brady threw his hands up in desperation, 'Well, that's fucking marvellous. That sure is going to be good for business, when I casually toss that into the conversation.' He laughed sarcastically.

'They trust you. You don't have to say it's your idea. Maybe, you could say that you've noticed other Trad areas doing this to save the living.'

'I know I'm a fucking lowlife criminal. I've never had delusions of grandeur, but even I can't answer this one now. I'm going to have to give this a lot of thought.'

'I won't mention it again, my friend. Let us talk about happier things. We'll head to Seventh Street next and meet my daughter and nephew and they also happen to be my co-workers Alicia and Tyrone. You'll want to meet Tyrone as he found the keys to the Library and has already checked it out.'

Brady desperately wanted to change the subject, as he couldn't get the images of the dying girl, cannibals and the thought of telling someone like Judge Jefferson of this crazy proposition regarding the East McFarland dead. 'How did he come across the keys?'

'Tyrone found them in a nearby home. After a cursory examination, he assumed it belonged to the Head Librarian.'

When they turned into Seventh Street, Tyrone and Alicia were already waiting for the Bear. Tyrone was black, tall and skinny with thick tortoiseshell glasses, and Alicia had her hair in a bun, and she looked tough until she beamed a white smile and hugged her Daddy. The Bear introduced them, 'Alicia is my daughter, and Tyrone is my nephew.' He held out his right arm to encourage Brady to move in closer, 'And this, my family, is the legendary Brady Mahone.'

Tyrone said, 'An honour to meet you, sir. We've heard so much about you. The only Trad who can pass through the Green Communities.'

Alicia intervened, 'Which means you must have some Green in you.' She said it flatly as if this was a fact that she wouldn't tolerate being challenged.

The Bear interrupted, 'We will have plenty of time to hear stories later. I've invited Brady to be our guest for dinner - but I've also promised him that we will be good company.'

Alicia said, 'I hear you, Daddy.'

They walked over to the misnamed minibus as it was the size of a tour bus which touring rock royalty might have used in those long-lost days. As Brady followed the family into the bus, he wasn't surprised to see that all the furnishings were in the Sattva Systems™ company colours of cream and moss green. Brady looked over the driver's cabin and noted that the controls were similar to his Hearse. There were luxury seats at the front, then there was a central dining area, and to the rear, there was the bathroom area complete with shower cubicles. He saw steps to the side, which he assumed led to the bedrooms on the upper deck.

The Bear said, 'We'll shower first as the work we do is not the most hygienic. You're welcome to use the facilities if you wish.'

'Thanks. I will.'

Brady was the last to shower, and when he emerged, The Bear and Tyrone were putting food on the table. Brady didn't ask what it was as it looked appetising and fresh. He sat next to Alicia and opposite the Bear and Tyrone.

The Beardon family closed their eyes and prepared for grace. Out of politeness, Brady did the same. *When in Rome…* Alicia led the proceedings.

'Our Mother.
Who art Heaven on Earth.
For what we are about to receive
May we be truly grateful
And lead us not into temptation.
Show us the way.'

The Bear and Tyrone answered, 'Show us the way.' The Bear smiled broadly at Brady, 'Eat up, brother, we have bountiful supplies.'

They ate, heartily and Brady listened to them talk about their respective days at work. He could sense their pride in working hard and completing their tasks to a high standard. He knew Greens of any shape, size, or age, didn't fear him, but he felt at ease with them. It helped that they weren't asking him any probing questions.

He expected that they would ask. He was suspicious of the Bear bringing up the subject of body disposals, earlier in the day. Once he had the time to mull over this, he wondered if he had been ordered to give Brady Mahone this information. It was his innate criminality which made him cautious about anybody attempting to befriend him.

The conversations were calm and relaxed, and even Alicia - who Brady had pegged as being uptight - was laughing softly at the stranger aspects of the day. The Bear was even telling them about his meeting with Brady as if he was hardly aware that he was still with them. He talked about Brady as if he was joyous at finding another new friend. Brady almost forgot why he was here in the first place as he drifted into the warmth of this family's embrace. 'When do we go and get the Files, you mentioned?'

Tyrone answered, 'First thing in the morning before I start work, if that's ok with you? I'll wake you, unless...'

'That works for me. How many are there?'

'I counted ten boxes, and I believe they each hold a thousand. Of course, I haven't opened them all, and some might not be full.'

'Amazing. What do you want for them?'

'Nothing. If they can be of use to you, and it's not a problem for our employers, then it's a good thing that they can be recycled.' The Bear placed a big hand on Tyrone's shoulder and smiled, warmly.

The Bear announced, 'I think we should play a game. I like games.

Alicia intervened, 'Daddy, I'm a bit tired of games. Couldn't we do the storyteller round instead?'

He laughed, 'Only if we tell scary stories.'

Alicia smiled, 'Ok, Daddy, I'll need time to think.'

Tyrone said, 'I'll sit this out. I don't like horror stories, and the skies are inky-black tonight. I want to take my telescope out.'

'If that's what you want to do. As long as you don't mind, Mr Mahone? After all, you are our guest.'

Brady checked out Tyrone, and said, 'You could do me a favour. Could you take Billy Big Paws for a walk while you are out there? I'm just wondering if he's feeling a little neglected - y'know, having lost his owner.

'Sure thing. Of course. My pleasure.'

Brady looked back at Alicia and the Bear, 'No problem with me. I'm just wondering if you could come up with a scary story if you are wearing those fancy Red-Suits™. They kinda reduce the thrills and spills.'

'Well, that's the challenge for today - to come up with a story that would scare a person, even if they were wearing the Red™.' Alicia had a puzzled look on her face as if she was already mulling over an idea. Tyrone returned from upstairs with his telescope and then went down the bus's steps, and the bus doors closed automatically behind him.

Alicia told her story first about the newfound craze among her Green friends who had taken up free-soloing mountain climbing to test the limits of the RedSuit's™

capabilities. She described the feeling of clinging on to the tiniest fragments of rock, thousands of feet up in the air. And then the sensation of losing her grip, millimetre by millimetre. She paused, to try and increase the tension, and she spoke slipping away and falling into the void, followed by the anticipation of crashing into the rocks beneath her. She lacked timing and her story didn't trouble Brady.

Brady said, 'But you knew you wouldn't die. There was pleasure within the fear - like a theme park ride.'

Alicia said, 'So, you wouldn't have been scared?'

'Maybe, the first time, out of my mistrust that the equipment would work properly. But after that, I'd jump off a cliff just to take a short cut.' He added, 'There's just no jeopardy in living life in a protective shell.'

'What's jeopardy to you?

'It's a rush.'

'A rush is just another word for fear.'

'Maybe. But I think fear is a negative, whereas to me a rush is a positive. It's a test to the limits of my life.'

The Bear seemed to be enjoying Alicia's gentle interrogation into the inner work-ings of Brady Mahone. She said, 'Give me an example.'

'I'm a criminal. I have to use my wits to commit a crime - to get away with it - and then, if I'm caught, to survive in prison. Even then, I am tested to the limits. I have to survive and succeed in the most hostile of environments. I have to assess the other convicts, the threat level who is in command, and carefully select my potential allies. Any wrong moves and I'm done for. It excites me. I never felt more alive than when I'm close to death. Whereas those RedSuits™ would take all the fun out of life for me. No offence.'

'None taken.' She smiled, 'When you are first in prison, what's going on in your head?'

'I have to own the room. I show no fear to buy myself time. If you are weak, the other inmates would be all over you in no time. But if you can exude a certain threat, then it will buy enough time to establish an alliance.'

'You mean - join a gang?'

'Could be, but I have a problem with that.'

'In what way?'

'I'm not the right colour. I'm not black, white or yellow. I'm not Latino or Italian. I haven't got a natural allegiance, and in prison, it's normal to fall into your colour groups for protection. Just like the Greens.'

Alicia laughed, 'We are not in prison.'

'You are encased in your Shells™ and your Suits™.' Alicia looked angry, and

189

Brady laughed loudly, before adding, 'I've got a talent for spreading doubt and fear - gotcha.' He was still smiling when he said, 'That's what I do in jail. I know that some of my trickiest potential enemies might not be the musclebound thugs - they might be the cunning and intelligent types. I have to throw them off-guard as well, or else they could cause a lot of trouble for Brady Mahone.'

Brady spotted the Bear stroking his chin. He wondered whether he was studying him or thinking about what his story would be. Alicia shook her head, but she asked warmly, 'What is your ancestry, Brady?' He seemed not to understand the question, so she asked more directly, 'What's your race?'

'I'm not sure. I was kinda adopted by my Foster Daddy. He was an old-school white man. He saw conspiracies in everything which wasn't white, from the Blacks and all the way to aliens from outer space.' Brady laughed at his own joke. 'He was a little bit embarrassed by my colour - but he did love me. Pops was good to me. He told me to say that I was Hawaiian, that way it was still a part of the good old U S of A.'

Alicia pressed him, 'When did you go, Green?'

'I'm not.'

'It's blindingly obvious that there is some Green within or about you. This bus wouldn't let you anywhere near it unless you were Green, It's an indisputable fact. Something I can witness and avow for with my own eyes.'

'I am not Green. Period.'

'Humour me. Let's say you are, but you don't know how it came to pass. Let's be friendly and play this game in a positive manner. We are no threat to you. I find you fascinating and would love to play. You have absolutely nothing to lose.'

Brady looked at the Bear and then back at Alicia. 'Ok. I'll go along with this, but I know, that I am not a Green from my soul. I'm a meat-eating survivor. The Greens see me as a threat, whereas the Trads only view me as a man. However, I can see with my own two eyes that I am not ageing much. That's something I put down to a better diet than the Trads because I eat food from the Green Communities and I work hard, most days.'

Alicia agreed, 'You have obviously given this matter some thought at some point, and your observations are entirely reasonable. What else is there about you which makes you special? And I'm entirely respectful, as you are a unique man.'

He stroked his chin and looked to the side as if inspiration could be found in another part of the bus, 'I've always healed real quick. I was a rough and tumble kid, always getting into scrapes, but Pops always said my scars didn't take long to heal over.'

'And your Mother - what did she think?'

These are the last people I'm going to tell that Moms drunk herself to death because she thought I was the Son of Satan or whatever. 'Foster Moms was a drinker and died young. I don't think she thought much deeper than the bottom of a bottle.'

'I'm sorry.'

190

'S'alright.' He shrugged, 'I've heard the stories. Most people think I can travel through both areas because of a coincidence, some piece of one-off timing. I rescued this old broad from a couple of hoodlums, and we both fell through one of those Green barriers at exactly the same time.'

The Bear said, 'The Lord works in mysterious ways. He forgave you your sins for an act of kindness. You could be Barabbas or the Good Samaritan, but the Lord has chosen you for a reason, brother.'

Alicia said, 'It doesn't answer the healing properties from when he was a child.'

The Bear smiled at his daughter, 'Children aren't the most reliable of witnesses, you used to play with dragons if I recall…'

She laughed and said warmly, 'Daddy, thanks for that.' She turned back to Brady, who was disarmed by the bond between the Bear and his daughter. She asked, 'Were there any other occasions when you were particularly close to a Green™ Ceremony.'

He laughed, 'I've slept with dozens of Green women if that's what you're getting at. You can't get much closer than that. Sorry sir, but she did ask?'

The Bear laughed, but Alicia didn't enjoy this latest turn in the conversation. She tried to change the subject, 'Was there anything else?'

'Only on that first day. I've been cautious since then, once I saw what it could do.'

'And what was that?'

'This is daft, but the master criminal here, Brady - Brady Mahone, got caught stealing fruit from a GreenGrocers™ and was covered in SecurityFilm™ for hours.' He added, 'And it erased nearly all of my tattoos. I still miss them. It was like they took a part of me with them.' Brady looked agitated.

Alicia was about to ask another question when the Bear raised his hand, 'I think our friend has been questioned enough. He is here to receive our good company and hopefully, to enjoy his evening.'

She said, 'Of course. If I'm not mistaken, it's your turn to tell a story.'

'Yes. I have given it some thought.' In the manner of a showman, he said grandly 'I will try to weave a tale that will terrify, and horrify our humble guest, Mr Brady Mahone. This is a tale of madness, of a man in a RedSuit™, who wishes he could die.'

Brady was instantly impressed by the persona of the charismatic preacher with the deep booming voice before him. *I would have sought you out to be a friend and an ally in Ridgecrest Supermax. You'd have survived.*

The Bear preached, 'There was a man called Rainer. He had a RedSuit™ which could protect him as he cleaned up the oceans. His Suit™ could help him withstand the pressures of the deepest depths of Gods blue depths, and his RedSuit™ helped him breathe underwater. And Rainer loved the ocean. He swam with the dolphins, and he rode on the backs of the Whales. He was the most indestructible creature in all of God's oceans. Soon, he hardly slept as he dreamed of spending forever in the seas. He asked God to make him able to reprocess his water and food so he could spend all his time in under water. He asked God to grant his wish that he could live forever in the bounty of his oceans. And the Lord God granted him his wish, but Mother Nature had not given any of her creatures the power to live forever. She was angry but couldn't challenge the will of God. Rainer swam for many years with the fishes and all the wonders of the oceans. He was at peace with the world. The rest of humanity had cleaned all the oceans and rested now that their work was done. Rainer understood his RedSuit™, he no longer needed to surface for air, food, or water, he had evolved into a new God of the Oceans. Creatures came to greet him as a friend, except for one of Her aquatic creations. As Rainer swam under the ocean one day, he saw an enormous Great White shark approach. Rainer was unafraid, he was indestructible in his RedSuit™.

The shark attacked Rainer, it chewed at him with his sharp teeth, Rainer looked on in wonder at this apex predator as twisted and turned, trying to break the figure in half, but Rainer was left without a scratch. He watched with a detached air of puzzlement as the shark's dead black eye rolled in its socket and turned white. Then the shark backed away, and Rainer was proud of his lack of fear, and the fortitude of his RedSuit™ against such a ferocious attack. But the enormous Great White shark studied his implacable foe in this underwater stand-off, and it powered through the water and swallowed Rainer whole. Rainer was awake as his arms were constrained parallel to his sides, and he felt the waves of rock-hard muscles and tendons pulse and pull him into the belly of the shark, and then he came to rest in the giant predator. He couldn't move. He wasn't blinded, and his eyes became adjusted to the darkness, and then he saw the remains of a fresh kill from the shark squeeze passed him. And then he remembered that he was indestructible in his RedSuit™ and that he didn't need fresh water or food to survive, and within minutes he went completely insane, but he lived forever.'

5. THE LIBRARY

Brady was fast asleep. He dreamed of being eaten and swallowed by sharks for what seemed like forever. He felt a light tapping on his shoulder, and he opened his eyes. He felt groggy as if he'd spent the whole night in battle.

'Mr Mahone. I've made you coffee.' Tyrone left the coffee on the bedside table. 'I've already fed Billy Big Paws and taken him with me for a walk.'

'Thanks Buddy. Call me, Brady. What time is it?'

'It's 5:30am. Venus is like a precious jewel in the eastern sky this morning.' Tyrone added, 'You said to wake you. I've got the keys to the Library on Seventh Street, but we must get going soon, as I start work at 7am.' Brady flung back his covers and Tyrone shuffled shyly, 'I'll just go and put my telescope away.'

Brady drank his coffee, got changed quickly and went to meet Tyrone outside the tour bus. It was cold, but the sky was crystal clear. As they walked, Brady noticed that Tyrone scanned the skies continuously. *At least he isn't boring me by telling me what all the stars are called.*

Tyrone watched the stars as he didn't know how to talk to somebody like Brady. They walked for long minutes with just the sound of their sneakers softly squeaking across the ground. It was Brady who finally surrendered to the silence. 'Boy, your Pops and his stories really got to me. I was having the weirdest dreams all night. I still can't shake them.'

'Yes. Uncle Sam will do that to you. He usually just repurposes old bible stories and fits them into a contemporary context. Which one did he tell you?'

'Something about a man being swallowed by a Great White shark.'

Tyrone stated, 'That will be Jonah and the Whale.'

'I don't know no bible passages, but he sure as hell woulda made one helluva preacher.' Brady said this without any knowing sense of humour.

'Actually, Uncle Sam comes from a long line of preachers.' Tyrone withdrew his gaze from the skies as he assessed that Brady wasn't as threatening as he first feared. 'He would dearly love for Alicia to continue in his footsteps, but she can't weave a tale like he can. Sure, he encourages her, but Alicia relays a tale more like a reporter giving the facts from a crime scene, rather than with the fire and brimstone treatment style of my dear Uncle.'

Brady thought about this, and remembered her story about rock climbing, and agreed. *She may as well have been talking about a roller coaster ride at Disney World - if that was still a thing.* 'And what about you? Have you got a thing for preachin' the gospel?'

'No. I'm into science and astronomy. I like to see concrete evidence and judge things on their merits.'

Brady tested him, the thought of Alicia's apparent interrogation of him still niggled him. 'And what do your concrete observations make of me, Brady Mahone.'

Tyrone thought carefully. Brady didn't scare him physically, he was protected from everything, but he had the self-awareness to know that he was sensitive to criticism and didn't handle conflict with any degree of confidence. 'I think you found yourself in an exceptionally complex situation, and you are just doing your best to take each day as it comes.'

Brady nodded. He liked this answer. He said, 'You say your Uncle came from a long line of preachers?'

Before Tyrone answered, he spotted Brady's FusionCar™, 'Is that your vehicle over there?'

'Yes.'

'I just thought we should drive it over to the Library and park up outside. There are quite a few boxes to carry.'

'Good idea.' Brady changed course and headed to the Hearse. He drove them quickly over the short journey and parked up. He laughed at the thought that he was illegally parked if this was back in the old days.

Tyrone pulled out the keys and opened up the Library. He said, 'Follow me, the stock you are looking for is located in the basement. I've brought a torch.'

Brady pulled out a larger torch from his Poacher's coat of many pockets. 'Never leave home without one.' He joked.

Brady searched the racking for anything useful, but they were full of old books. However, he decided that the racking itself could be of use to one of his many processing sites. *I'd have to ditch the books and come back for the racking later. I wouldn't want to offend the young scientist's delicate sensibilities.*

Tyrone went ahead and quickly located the boxes of old Blank Black Files. 'Here you are. There are more than I thought. Look, they are double stacked. There are approximately twenty-three thousand, not the eleven thousand from my first estimate.'

'Fucking ace! High-five me, baby.' Tyrone high-fived the big man with a mixture of relief and the pride of a job well done. Brady said, 'Why have they got so much of these here, do ya think?'

'Before the Internet Crash of 2050, we, I mean, the GreenRevs were putting enormous amounts of useful and authorised data onto Blank Files from the Web. They used selected local libraries from around the world to do this for them. The money from Sattva Systems™ kept them solvent. Of course, the libraries did all the work, they made a lot of money, but then went broke in the later crash, after all.'

Brady laughed, 'And you people think I'm the big criminal around here. I gotta hand it to them, there's been some clever shit going on. Still, their loss is Brady Mahone Enterprise's gain.' He slapped Tyrone across the shoulders. 'Good man. Now give us a hand with these and then I'll drive you to your work.'

They moved the boxes into the back of Brady's Hearse, and Tyrone noticed how Brady packed the boxes away while leaving plenty of room for more ill-gotten gains to come - but he wasn't going to ask him what this might be. He was content enough to be in the good books of Brady Mahone. Brady left his torch on the counter near the checking out area. Brady went to the car while Tyrone locked the building behind him. *I don't know why he's bothering to do that. It's all going to be decomposed in a matter of months.* Brady waited until Tyrone was settled back in the car, and then he said, 'Damn. I've left my torch in the Library.'

Tyrone said, 'Whereabouts? I'll find it.'

'No. I'll quickly retrace my footsteps, and I'll get it in no time. Can I borrow the keys for a minute?' Tyrone looked at him, nervously, but Brady added, 'I wouldn't want to make you late for work - not after all you've done for me.' Tyrone took out the keys and handed them over to Brady. 'Thanks, man. I won't be long.' Brady headed over to the Library. He picked up his torch and a piece of an old duster which he cut up with a nearby pair of scissors. He looked at the office scissors. *These could be useful.* And shoved these inside a pocket. As he left, he stuffed the material inside the lock-catch and then made a show of locking up after him. He held up the torch, triumphantly.

As he got back in the car, he changed the subject to stop Tyrone thinking over the events. 'You were saying about a long line of preachers in your family.' Brady sped away at a much higher speed than was necessary and smiled at the concern showing on Tyrone's face.

Tyrone stuttered, 'Yes. Samuel Beardon the First used to preach about the evils inherent on the Internet. He then met the Industrialist John Kane, and John Kane backed him financially, because he loathed the Tech Giants in Silicon Valley, as it was known back then. Have you heard of him?'

'Who?'

'John Kane?'

'No.' Brady lied.

Tyrone wasn't surprised, Brady hadn't even heard of Jonah and the Whale. 'Anyway, John arranged for all of Samuel the First's sermons to be filmed and shown on the Internet.' Tyrone laughed at the irony of this situation, but Brady smiled, politely. 'Sadly, Samuel the first died young, along with his wife. A car accident.'

'I'm sorry to hear that.'

'Samuel the Second was only a child, but John Kane, in his benevolence, took him into his personal care. He paid for his schooling, all the way to his Doctorate in the Effects of Climate Change on the Environment. Samuel the Second travelled the globe, preaching on the need to turn away from the Satans of Industry, and that if they formed communities to demonstrate the new way of Green Living, then they would be the beacons for others to follow.' Tyrone said proudly, 'With the backing of John Kane, my Great Uncle helped set up the Green Communities across the planet.'

Brady was deep in thought. He then asked, 'What happened next?'

'That's a bit of a mystery. Firstly, John Kane disappeared, and secondly, Samuel the Second fell out with John Kane's son and heir, Xavier Kane. Not long afterwards, Samuel Beardon the Second was charged with the disappearance of John Kane. He died in prison before he had a chance to clear his name. He was stabbed to death by a radical Green activist, who got it into his head that Samuel Beardon the Second was going to betray the Green movement.' Tyrone shook his head.

Again, Brady lied, when he asked, 'Who's he - this Xavier?'

'Xavier Kane is Bodhi Sattva.' He added, 'He had been friends with Samuel the Second. He wanted to bring Uncle Sam, sorry, Samuel Beardon the Third, into the inner sanctum of Sattva Systems™, as he had always been a close associate to the family, but Uncle Sam thought it wise not to follow the footsteps of his Father and Grandfather, so he said that he would always be loyal to the Kane family, and he would happily toil with his fellow Green workers, but he would prefer to follow the Lord on another path laid out before him.'

6.UNREQUITED

Brady would have preferred to have continued his search of the now deserted Los Banos but had promised his adopted Lopez family that he would return to East McFarland for the End of the Century and New Century celebrations. Brady wasn't sure whether there was much to celebrate. The Trad communities were set on using the occasion to boost their citizen's morale, whereas the Green areas were excited to greet the new century and receive their new YellowSuits™, giving them unparalleled freedom of visual expression.

Lucian greeted him as he returned to the Mahone Ranch. He also noticed that Amie had spotted his return but raced back to the Lopez Ranch.

Lucky is my old friend, and yet he is younger than me. He looks about seventy, and even Mary-Lou is looking like a pensioner. He thought about Amie and tried to calculate her age. *She must be about seventeen, but even she looks like she's in her mid-twenties. She looks at me like I'm only about ten years older, but I'm forty years older than her.*

Alicia's interrogation, coupled with the Bear's fish-tale, had played on his mind. He couldn't shake the feeling that he had been played his whole life.

'Hi, Lucky. Could you give us a hand to unload these? I hit the jackpot in Los Banos.' Lucian hobbled over to the Hearse, and Brady realised the selfishness in his request for the first time. *He's turned old and frail, and yet I'm still in my prime, and I'm asking him to do the heavy lifting.* 'On second thoughts, leave it to me. I'll do it later.'

'Are you sure, Brady? I don't want to be a shirker. You work so hard to keep us safe…'

'No, my friend. I owe you my life - remember?'

Lucian smiled, 'You've more than repaid any debt you may feel you owe me. You've been as good a friend as any man could dare to hope for.' He added, 'All I did was understand a bit of Spanish from my Dad's side of the family.'

'Enough for you to warn me that I was about to be shivved - and you tried to jump him.'

Lucian laughed, 'If I remember rightly, he threw me off like a rag-doll.'

Brady laughed warmly, 'True that - but you gave me the time to react.' Brady could still remember the sickening crack as he slammed the head of Miguel Alvarez into the wall, killing him instantly. 'He would have killed me. He was a hitman for the Cartel. If it wasn't for you…'

'Hey, Brady and Lucian - are you two going over your old war stories again?' Mary-Lou said with good humour.

'Hi, Mary-Lou, you're looking well.' He lied. 'I'm guessing Little Amie told you I was here.'

Mary-Lou laughed, 'I wouldn't let Amie hear you calling her that anymore. She's going through that troubled teenager phase and thinks she's a full-grown woman ahead of her time.'

'How are things on the road?' Lucian asked.

'Los Banos has gone. It's all but deserted. The Greens have started their clean-up operations. It's all a bit of a sorry state, but at least there are opportunities for Brady Mahone.' He pulled out a bag from the Hearse, and the clinking gave away the contents. 'Vintage alcohol. This should get us suitably shit-faced tonight.'

Lucian smiled, and Mary-Lou said in mocking formality, 'Well, Mr Mahone, as you have brought the bottles, would you care to join us at the Lopez Ranch as our honoured guest?'

Brady laughed, 'Why Mrs Lopez, I'd be honoured.' He bowed and then kissed her hand. He spied Amie watching from a distance.

Mary-Lou peered into the Hearse and asked, 'What's in the boxes?'

'Twenty-three thousand Blank Black Files.'

Lucian said, 'Wow! What a haul.'

'It was in a library stock room. I also had a load more CDs and DVDs from them and a ton of shelving which I dropped off to my contact in Hanford.'

Mary-Lou said, 'That's another reason to celebrate tonight.'

Brady showered and put on some smart casual clothes to mark the importance of the party. He also used up some of the last of the aftershave he had from the haul from Libby Kane's home. So many years ago. *I hope it's not gone off.* He sniffed as the sweet aroma wafted up from his freshly shaved face. *Still smells real good to me.*

He strolled over to the Lopez Ranch. Amie greeted him. She had dressed up and was wearing makeup, which hadn't been expertly applied. Brady was wary. Amie shook out her black hair and blushed, but then quickly reached up and kissed him on the cheek. Before he could react, she said breathlessly, 'Happy New Year, Brady.' She trembled as if her strength would fail her, but then rushed away.

Brady shook his head and cracked his shoulders as if he was trying to reset himself. He then went into the lounge where Lucian and Mary-Lou were cuddled up on the sofa. Brady assessed that they had already drunk heavily. *What the hell. It is supposed to be the party of the century.* Mary-Lou jumped up, she hugged and kissed Brady on the cheek. 'You smell gorgeous. Happy New Year!'

Lucian shook Brady firmly by the hand, 'Happy New Year!'

Brady laughed, 'I've been reliably informed that this is the best party in town.'

Mary-Lou turned the music up loud, and brought Brady over a tumbler full of brandy, 'You heard right mister, now let's dance.' Brady drained the glass and then joined

Mary-Lou and Lucian in dancing the night away. He watched Amie helping herself to the alcohol on offer, but as the night wore on, this didn't seem to trouble her parents, so he concluded that he shouldn't worry about her either.

They danced and drank into the early hours until they couldn't drink anymore. Brady watched Lucian and Mary-Lou become ever more amorous together until they hardly seemed aware that anyone else was there. The scene looked odd to Brady, as he was felt as if he was watching a couple of pensioners making out, even though he was older than both of them.

Brady staggered out of the Lopez Ranch ready to walk home to his own homestead, but he had to stop for a second as the fresh, biting wind assaulted his senses. His head reeled, and he grabbed a porch rail to steady himself. He looked in the direction of West McFarland and he caught sight of the saffron shimmer of the protective Shell™. He remembered that they were having their Yellow™ Ceremony from the stroke of midnight to celebrate the New Century.

He pointed himself in the right direction to home and concentrated on putting one foot in front of the other, in the hope of finding his way home on autopilot. He made it. He crashed through the door, taking his clothes off as he staggered, and leaving them strewn across the floor, until he was naked, and arrived at his destination. He flopped unceremoniously onto his bed and began to snore heavily.

Amie had also had too much to drink. She had danced with her family and had tried too hard to impress Brady with her moves. She watched with disgust, at first, the semi-public groping of her Moms and Lucian, but this turned to fascination, as she studied Lucian's hand slide up her Mom's dress. As they headed to the bedroom - giggling as they propped up each other, she followed them stealthily.

They pushed the door to the bedroom shut, but Amie edged it open millimetres at a time until she could observe them through a crack in the door. She watched as they pulled each other's clothes off until she saw them entirely naked for the first time in her life. She watched them kiss passionately, and then she watched their hands explore every intimate part of each other's body. In the semi-darkness, she believed she caught a glimpse of Lucian's arousal before he entered into her Moms. She listened, as they both grunted and moaned in pleasure, and then she was aware of her own breathlessness and feared she might get caught.

Amie rushed away. She went onto the porch. She looked over at the Mahone Ranch, and all she could think of was Brady.

She walked over, all the time thinking of being in the strong arms of Brady Mahone. *I don't know what to do - but I want him, and I know he loves me. He brought me a dog.*

When she got to Brady's door, she pushed at it gently and was almost giddy when it opened before her. She followed the trail of discarded clothing that led her to Brady's room. She picked up the white T shirt and breathed in the aroma of him. She edged into the room with a mixture of intense trepidation and excitement. On the first day of the New Century, the first rays of dawn cast a golden glow on the deep-honey-coloured naked body of Brady Mahone. *Oh, my word, this is so beautiful.*

Brady was lying face down on the bed. He was completely naked and still snoring heavily in his drunken stupor.

Amie crept over. The floorboards creaked, and she felt as if she was going to faint at every sound. She couldn't take her eyes off him as she moved. Her eyes swept over every square inch of him. She didn't want him to wake him - not yet. She wasn't ready. She toyed with the idea of getting undressed right there. She was excited about the thought of him waking and finding her there - waiting and prepared for him to take her - but she was too shy to do that. Her Moms was the only person on the planet who had ever seen her nude. She began to wonder if he might not find her attractive enough. She stood, helplessly, for moments which seemed like forever. All the while, she still gazed at Brady's body, trying to decide whether it was better to avoid the inevitable embarrassment or whether to let him take her.

Images of her Moms and Lucian's ecstasy began to crowd her mind until she finally dared to make her next move.

She tiptoed slowly around the bed. Brady stopped snoring, almost as if he had sensed a potential threat. Amie swooned. Her head was reeling from the alcohol. Brady shuffled around but appeared to go back to sleep. Amie waited. And then Brady began to snore quietly.

Amie was away from the potential gaze of Brady. She stood next to his bed. Brady shifted over onto his side - he was still facing away from her. From his tattooed shoulders of black-inked South-sea designs, she followed the line of his body, through the line of his back to his buttocks and then down his muscular legs.

She slowly undressed. She held her breath as she silently dropped her underwear to the floor. She then lay on the bed next to him, but not touching him. Again, she waited, as if she had reached the next level of her bravery. And then she moved her hand slowly to trace out the tattoos on his shoulder. She was a hairs breath away from touching him and the tension of her intake and the slow outpouring of her breath as she exhaled caused waves of pleasure to shudder through her. She closed the gap, and her fingertip touched his skin. She slid her fingers over him and then more fingers joined in caressing his back.

Brady was barely conscious. He was more than usually drunk. Even if Brady had been aware of a woman's presence next to him, he would not have been alarmed. He had taken many women as lovers in his life, and the post-coital caresses of a woman in his bed would be something to savour and required no further response than his simple allowance of it to continue. Amie needn't have been worried about Brady waking up from this night - he was dead to the world.

Amie traced her fingers slowly down the length of Brady's body all the way down to his ankles. As she reached out, she felt her whole body come into contact with him. Amie was past the point of no return so she pressed her breasts onto Brady's back, as this was the most erotic thing she could contemplate doing, and she wanted to cry out in exaltation at her own fearlessness. But as Brady moved decisively over in his bed to face her, she returned to the trembling shy girl she was, except now she was naked and in bed with this hulk of a man - a much older and experienced man.
She looked into his face. She wondered why he hadn't thrown her out of bed. She wondered why he hadn't taken her into his strong arms and taken her. She was a virgin, she wouldn't be expected to know what to do, even if she had dreamt of a time like this. This was real, he was a physical presence, not a figment of her imagination, this time. But Brady was still asleep.

She was still trembling. She couldn't stop herself from breathing out heavily, she put her face into the pillow to bury the noise of her breathing. She found her courage and desire again. She kissed him while barely touching his lips, she pulled slightly away again and then saw his unimpressive and flaccid manhood out of the corner of her eye. She instinctively looked away, but then she really wanted to look at it. She examined it. She then touched it. Something deep within the lost and loaded Brady responded. She felt it move. She watched in utter fascination, as she couldn't help but touch it again, and it began to grow in her hand, and Brady stirred.

'What the fuck is going on here. How dare you? How could you do this to my daughter? You monster - you fucking pervert!' Brady drunkenly woke up. He was startled to find Mary-Lou standing over him. He couldn't think of what he'd done to make her call him these things - and why was she grabbing at Amie? He watched in dumbstruck amazement at Amie attempting to cover up her nakedness. She continued to shout, 'And you, young lady, get dressed, now. I'll talk with you later.'

Amie was flustered as she tried to get dressed too quickly, and her clothes didn't go on correctly at the first attempts and all the while like a spider in free fall she slung out her silken web of lies to hide her shame, 'But Brady loves me...we will always be together...we made love, and we are so right together...'

Brady was hungover, if not still not utterly drunk. He wondered at one point whether he was dreaming this. He went over the events of the evening, but the last thing he could vaguely recall was the world spinning and the Yellow-ish glow over West McFarland. The criminal within him wanted to check for evidence, so he moved his hand to his penis to see if he could determine if he had actually had sex with Amie. It was dry to the touch, so Brady took this as meaning that he hadn't. At that moment, he hadn't thought about other people in the room.

Mary-Lou erupted, 'And now you are fondling yourself. In front of both of us. You Mahone's are all alike - like father like son. You stay away from us. Do you hear me?' She rushed out of the house, dragging Amie behind her before Brady could answer.

He pulled on his trousers and ran outside after them. He saw Lucian coming out to see what all the commotion was about. Mary-Lou shouted 'I don't want you to have anything to do with that monster. He raped my daughter - our daughter.'

Amie protested, 'He loved me. He didn't rape me.'

'Young lady - you are seventeen years old, and he is what...nearly sixty...Oh God, it gets worse. That certainly would have been statutory rape back in my day.'

Lucian looked over at Brady and smiled ruefully before joining his family as they headed back to the Lopez Ranch to continue the inquisition.

Brady just stood there, with the sun coming up over the horizon. Brady felt that even the sun was mocking him with its New Century greetings. He began to feel cold. He went back inside to put the rest of his clothes on to add to the jeans.

7.IN YELLOW AND DEEP RED

Brady needed to shake the events of this New Century morning. He decided not to take the Hearse over to West McFarland - he wasn't in the mood for dealing with customers. He just wanted to clear his throbbing head.

In the old days, a New Year would be one of the quietest days of the year. As the whole world would be nursing hangovers. If he thought West McFarland was going to be dead, then he was to be sorely mistaken. The sight which greeted him was if he had taken acid to add to his hangover. The streets were full of the townsfolk adorned in the craziest colours known to man. Every time he focused on a person, they changed into something new, and everybody seemed to be trying out the wackiest creations they could come up with in this carnival atmosphere. *For fuck's sake - I musta died and gone straight to hell.*

Lizzie passed him briefly, at that moment she was dressed as a tie-die flower child with a rainbow halo above her head. She looked at Brady in his jeans, white T shirt with his open Poacher's trench coat and said sarcastically, 'Happy New Century - it must be fun being you.' She moved on through the crowd before he could reply to greet Cain in a happy clown costume festooned with bright coloured bunches of paper flowers springing out from every loose fold.

Brady turned away from him in disgust. *I don't like this at all. The whole world is turning into a steaming pile of shit that some druid freaks have dumped on us from high.*

His thoughts turned back to this morning. *I'm going back out on the road when I've done here. Let's see how they get on without me. They don't deserve me. I'm a survivor. They've leached on my survival instincts for too long. They didn't even consider my side of the story - the ungrateful bastards.* He then shouted out loud as if thinking it wasn't final enough, 'They can all go and fuck themselves.' A few freakily adorned people looked at him as if he was the newly crowned King of the Party Poopers. He smiled and said, 'Just fuck off.'

He bustled his way through the crowds belligerently. It made him feel useful. *Someone should fuck with these smug bastards. They are always throwing these, 'Look how clever we all are, parties.' Well, they think they've seen what Brady Mahone can do, well, they haven't seen nothing yet.* He hadn't got any plans for what he might do, but the first name on his mind-map was being pencilled in. *I'll start with the smuggest bastard of them all. I'll have you Bodhi Sattva or whatever name you really go by.*

He then heard something which made him even angrier but then he had no choice but to calm down.

This is NanoRespect™, a trademark of Sattva Systems™. Your stress levels indicate a threat of violence has been detected. Please refrain. This is your first warning. The welfare of our consumers is our highest priority.

He shouted aggressively, 'Fine. Message received and understood. Fuck you Film Face!' He then closed his eyes and concentrated on his breathing. He listened as the throbbing in his head roared with his racing heartbeat. He focused on slowing his heartbeat down. He was conscious of the crowd pushing past him, but he kept his eyes closed. He breathed in slowly and deeply, and then let out a deep sigh. *It's not like I even remember where he lives anyway. I was doing ok, so why should I care. Having said that…*He concentrated on his breathing again, as he knew this train of thoughts would ride him into further trouble.

He opened his eyes. He tried not to let the ever-changing colours and costumes bother him. It couldn't have been more annoying to a man with a king-sized hangover than if they were pointing strobe lighting at him.

He spotted Vance in the crowd. Vance looked away as if Brady was the last person he wanted to converse with on this Day of Days. Brady glowered at him as he was in a suit which made him look like he'd been swallowed by a Rainbow Trout. Vance went to walk away, but Brady barked. 'You work for me - remember? Now get your fishy arse over here.'

Vance walked over, 'Hi Brady. I didn't see you there.' He added, 'It's still not too late. I could ask Cain to give you a YellowSuit™. It's not like you can't afford it. You are the richest person I know.'

That's how they'll get you, son. 'No. Don't want it. Don't need it.' He then said, 'Will you take that shit off. I can't do business with a fucking fish.'

Vance changed into a pinstripe business suit. Brady said, 'Are you mocking me?' Vance then morphed into jeans and a jumper. He wondered how Brady still had the ability had to scare him, even though he could not have been more protected than having a RedSuit™ layer.

Brady said, 'I want you to set up a business to collect all the unwanted clothes. It appears to me that you lot won't be needing them anymore. Am I right?'

'Yes. What does the…business model look like?'

'Preferably you'll pick them up for free, in the spirit of recycling. Otherwise, offer more entertainment product for them - but keep the costs down.'

'And what's in it for me?'

'We'll see how you do, and if you manage to get your hands on plenty of high-quality garments, then I'll make sure we come to a mutually beneficial arrangement.' Brady was still feeling distinctly ill-tempered when he added, 'Does that meet with your satisfaction.'

'Yes. Thanks, Brady. I'll get to it. But not today.' He looked around, 'I don't think that's on anybody's to-do lists at this moment in time.'

Brady's Satt™ went off, which was highly unusual as the phone was ancient and it hadn't rang in months. He only carried it around in case of emergencies nowadays. He dug around in his Poachers coat pocket and put the cream-coloured ceramic phone with its Sattva Systems™ logo to his ear. He watched Vance try to sneak away. He hissed, 'I didn't say you could go.' Vance lingered and looked on enviously at the people nearby who were enjoying the party.

'Hi Brady, it's Lucky. About this morning.'

'What about this fucking morning?'

'I know you probably didn't think what you were doing with Amie was wrong but...'

'Listen to me, you no-good piece of shit. Stay away from me and keep off my land, if you so much as set one foot on my property I swear I'll shoot you, and that fucking little bitch...'

This is NanoRespect™, a trademark of Sattva Systems™...

'Oh, for fuck's sake.' He shouted into the phone. 'We're through. You understand? Now fuck off.' He cut the phone off.

...Your stress levels indicate a threat of violence has been detected. Please refrain. This is your second and final warning. The welfare of our consumers is our highest priority.

Vance said, 'My God. I can see it.'

Brady was shoving his Satt™ away in a pocket. He looked at the amazement in Vance's eyes. 'See what?'

'The Security Protocols™ device. It's transparent. The technology dates back to stealth drone technology, but with the near weightlessness of Nanotechnology it...'

Brady looked at him angrily, 'If it's fucking transparent, then how can you see it?'

'I can't if I look directly at it. I can only make it out if I look at it kinda sideways.' He added, 'Nobody has ever seen it before. This is so cool.'

Brady's anger turned to concern, 'Where is it?'

'It's about three feet above your head. It's a skinny high-tech machine - it's shaped like a transparent hosepipe.'

Brady went through his anger-management regime while imagining the design of this SecurityFilm™ Dispenser. It was too high above him to reach, and he guessed it was designed to envelop him in any direction he should try to escape.

Vance watched what was happening as this would be a great story. He watched Brady close his eyes and take slow deep breaths until he reached a calm state. He caught the SecurityFilm™ Dispenser in the corner of his eye just in time to see it fly away at high speed. He said, 'It's gone.'

'Ok. Thanks.' Brady opened his eyes. He wondered if the SecurityFilm™ caught him again like it did on the very first day, post the GreenRevs Revolution, whether anybody would set him free this time. *I'm pretty damned sure Lizzie wouldn't, not now.* He looked at Vance and asked, 'Why do you continue to work for me? You must have your own copy of every piece of entertainment I have come across.'

Vance noticed how quickly Brady had changed his mood since being threatened with Filming. 'It's a collector's thing. I love the old TV Sci-fi series of the early twenty-first century; and the Space Opera movies of the late twentieth-century vintage.' He added enthusiastically, 'There are still a lot of gaps in my catalogue, especially when the formats changed. I think some were available on video and were never

204

made on DVD. And then there were the periods where DVDs weren't made any-more due to the new content only being made available through those old streaming platforms.'

Usually, Brady wouldn't be interested in nerdy conversations, but he had learned to listen, as enhancements to his business opportunities could be found with niche play-ers like Vance. 'I've noticed you are always eager to see the updates in my catalogue. So, that's what you are looking for?'

Vance felt he had given away too much information. Brady knew this, and he didn't want Vance to clam up on him now. Brady continued, 'It's ok. I won't change your rates. You've got an idea - let's hear it.'

'Like me, the serious collectors, would pay a premium price for the missing pieces in our Movie Files. I mean, there are connecting parts of series, which would be amazing to see.'

Brady thought it over. He smiled. 'In the future, I will bring any new DVD finds over to you for pricing. You can tell me how much I could get for them, but I will only charge you today's rates. Would that work for you?'

'Absolutely. Also, there are sought-after gaps in the Music Aficionado markets - tell you what - I could make you a list of the most wanted items…'

'Great.' *I need new ideas, especially seeing as Mary-Lou has outlived her useful-ness.* 'I thought that the catalogue and order books could do with a revamp…'

'My friends, I mean customers, are always complaining about the layout and in-dexing, especially when it comes to identifying specific versions and other details. I'd love to do that.'

Brady's head was clearing from his hangover, and his stress levels had reduced considerably. He patted Vance on the back to demonstrate friendship and trust. 'Will people be able to afford these inflated prices. They always seem to be working and saving hard for the next versions of NanoSuits™. What's it to be next time?'

'We don't know what the next one will actually do, but we have been told it is to be Green. Apparently, it won't cost nearly as much, maybe only four-hundred Green Credits.'

'Why are they lowering the cost?'

'Because it won't be a fun item like the Yellow™. It will be a direct benefit to the environment.'

'So, people might not bother with this GreenSuit™ then?'

Vance smiled, 'You have to get the Suits™ in the correct order. It's a bit like the collector's market we were discussing. You have to buy the Green to qualify for the next update.'

That's how they get you. son. That's how I'll get them. Brady said, 'What's the plan for you, y'know, long term 'n'all?'

'I want to get a FusionCar™ of my own, and travel to other Green Towns. I want to meet other movie buffs.' He added, 'I'd love to meet the other people who work for you. I feel like we are a team.'

Brady made an investment decision. 'If you do a good job for me. Then I'll buy you a FusionCar™.'

'Oh, man.' He hugged Brady, 'This is one helluva great way to start the New Century. Don't you worry, I'll do the best job ever for you - you'll see.'

8.TURNING OVER THE ROCKS

It was New Year's Day, the first day of the Twenty-second century. It may have seemed like a fresh start for the rest of the world, but Brady preferred the old century to this one. Until last night, he had a business he enjoyed, with the prospect of reaching his own personal goal of being a Green Credit millionaire. Shortly after meeting Bodhi Sattva's mother, Libby Skye, he chose that goal in her one-hundred-million-dollar mansion - in old money - in Malibu. She coined the phrase a Green Credit millionaire, and he decided that he would wear that tag one day.

He had wanted to look after his best friend, Lucian, for the rest of his natural life. With the splitting of humanity down Trads and Greens' lines, it was difficult to state with any confidence what a natural life meant anymore. Brady was proud at not only how he had survived this new world, but also how he had thrived within it. He had shaken off his lowlife criminal tag - in his own mind - and achieved the remarkable transformation into a legitimate businessman, as far as Brady Mahone, the Chief Executive Officer, Owner-in-Chief of the most successful Trad enterprise on the United States Western Seaboard. *Hell, I might even be the most successful businessman on the planet for all I know.*

Brady mulled over his lot as he meandered back in the general direction of the Mahone Ranch. *I've worked hard. I've never slacked. I looked after my friends. I've even done some things that people have thought of as being kind. Even Professor Chu treats me like I've been a good person - a real good person. And now, they falsely accuse me of rape at home. They even throw my Foster Daddy's bad stuff in my face. I didn't deserve that. Even when I go to the Green areas, they treat me like a bit-part-player in a freak show. I can't even be myself there without being threatened by that SecurityFilm™. I could understand it when I was robbing a store - that was kinda fair, but to threaten to wrap me up just for being angry - or was it because I had the audacity to even just think about getting mad about being treated badly. It sure beats the fuck outta me.*

He felt tired, even though he didn't usually need much sleep. *It must be stress.* When he returned to his home, he tidied up and thought about taking a nap, but then thought better of it. *If it's a Yellow™ Ceremony Day, there won't be anybody in Los Banos. It would be a good day to search the place.* His thoughts were tinged with disappointment that the Beardon family wouldn't be there. *I liked them, they treated me nice, and they didn't ask anything of me - not like those fuckers at the Lopez Ranch.*

He put his old Green Bicycle and trailer in the back of his empty Hearse. He was just about to go when he spied Old Marvin, his Foster Daddy's old warhorse of a heavy machine-gun. Brady had looked after it like it was a holy relic. Only antique guns without a Kill-stream switch could fire bullets in this world, and this was about one-hundred and seventy years old by Brady's reckoning. It was always loaded, just in case. He ran his fingers over the shimmering old black metal, the brass-coloured bullets glimmering in the belt-feed. He sat behind the tripod mounted beast of a weapon and set the gunsight on the billboard which designated the entrance to the Lopez Ranch. He steadied himself, and then he let the bullets fly. It ripped the billboard to pieces. Lucian, Mary-Lou and Amie ran out to investigate the commotion, but then hastily dived for cover as Brady aimed a barrage of bullets over their heads - some went crashing through the upper floors of the house and broke the first-floor windows. Glass was sent flying in all directions.

Billy Big Paws, the dog he had given to Amie, barked furiously in a mixture of fear and warning.

Brady stopped firing and then laughed loud enough for the Lopez family to hear. *Sometimes, actions speak louder than words.* He got up and strode to his car, and he drove away at the fastest speed his FusionCar™ could attain, spraying a cloud of dust upwards and behind him as it trailed in its wake.

On the outskirts of Los Banos, he noticed the array of parked HeavyFusionLorries™, parked up neatly along Highway 99. *It looks like they'll be spraying the buildings with their NanoShit tomorrow. Good job I came today.*

He parked up and took out his Green Bicycle and trailer. He loaded his bag of tools for breaking into the abandoned homes. It took him a while to figure out why the Green Workers were securing the premises. *They don't want any remaining Trads setting up home in them.* Brady searched the shops and houses using the Library as his starting point. He made a profitable start. The Library held cupboards of entertainment formats, some even older than the CDs and DVDs he coveted. He examined an old cassette tape, quizzically. He pulled out the tape like the entrails of a rat. Brady was on a roll. At the rear of an old domestic appliance store, he found a section with an old-fashioned Entertainment Department. He thought he would be out of luck when he saw it was the remnants of an old Video Rental Store, but when he searched a little more thoroughly, he came across a cache of DVDs that were probably the earliest versions of the format.

Brady found the tree where he had first met the Bear. He sat down with his back to it and ate his lunch and had his own thermos flask of coffee. In the warm afternoon sun, he found that work, had once again, lifted his spirits. He regretted, a little, his outburst in the morning of unleashing Old Marvin on his past friends and neighbours. *I'm still not going back on my decision. They kinda asked for it, and nobody got hurt.* He then reflected on his time with the Bear. *Was he trying to tell me something?* Brady took his time to think over everything that was said on his short time with the Beardon family. He was on nobody's clock but his own. *This family were suspiciously close to John Kane. It goes back a long way.* He continued to give the Beardon family his attention while he packed away his lunch and drove around Los Banos on his Green Bicycle. *If they were snitches and keeping a beady eye on Brady Mahone for the Big Man, then what would they do? There are always snitches waiting to trap Brady Mahone.*

He had selected his bike to travel as there were obstacles in the streets where the Operation Clean-up teams hadn't reached yet. Even while on his bike, he spotted more decomposing bodies as he weaved his way through the streets. He had to concentrate, and his mind left the problem of the Beardons for a time. He spotted a shop called Old Curiosities and struck more silver-tech. He also had luck at the Town Hall, where he found caches of pre-recorded files which had dates written on them going back to the dawn of the twentieth century. He rifled through the archive departments, leaving documents strewn over the floor in his wake.

I would try to be Brady Mahone's friend or Bodhi Sattva's enemy if I were them. That way, they could win my confidence. He considered this. *But I'm not really an enemy of Bodhi Sattva, am I?* He rode on. He spotted a ransacked jewellery store. *I know it's wrong, but I have a soft spot for the days when all I had to think about was the next heist to plan.* He saw a film poster through the front window of a house. It had the appearance of being student accommodation. Although they were usually poor in the traditional sense, they were often the source of rich pickings in these times. He broke in with ease and rifled through the front room's cupboards and drawers but found nothing. He found a pristine display of Sci-fi films in the bedroom - many of them in boxes of multi-disc sets. He noted the price stickers which were still affixed on them, most of them came from thrift stores. *These are worth their weight in Green these days.*

Brady's morning might have started badly, but the rest of the day rescued him from his dark mood. *I got the impression the Beardons had their issues with the Kane family, but they made a point about being loyal. Maybe all I've heard is all there is.*

His FusionCar™ was almost full. These last few days have been super-productive. Shame about all that crap last night with that lying little bitch. He then came upon the Los Banos Police Station. He looked at it deliciously. *Sweet. I'm gonna have me some fun here. I ain't never broken into a Police Station before. Let's wreck the joint.* He took out his tool bag and strode over to the entrance of the Police Station. *Who wants to be a legitimate businessman anyway? Time to make way for a bit of vintage Brady Mahone.*

He broke through the locks with ease and flung the doors back. The internal doors took a little longer to open, but he was now an expert burglar after breaking into thousands of abandoned homes and businesses. He swept through the rooms, trashing them as he went. He flung chairs through the internal windows, he kicked over anything that wasn't fixed to the floors. He came across a bank of disused Sattva Systems™ Satellite Phones, a newer version of the one he owned. They had a Fusion-Powered™ logo on them. He picked up one which hadn't been unboxed, he glanced over the specifications which stated that they carried a lifetime's charge due to Sattva Systems™ revolutionary design. The critical thing that Brady noted was that it was a dumb phone in the old technological parlance, but these would be an ideal addition to a Police armoury. He found a hard plastic crate and loaded it up with his new Satts™ and placed them near the exit for when he was ready to leave.

Finding the phones, alleviated his appetite for vandalism. He decided that he wasn't going to give the Lopez family a new phone. *I'll pass them on to my key associates in the other towns.* He moved onto the other rooms in the station. The interview rooms and holding cells were predictably empty. He then came across the Staff Lockers. He jemmied them all open, but he didn't find much of use to him. It took him back to his last day at Ridgecrest Supermax when the guards took everything they owned, to return to their loved ones on hearing about the Internet Crash and the subsequent riots.

He wandered through the Detective's Rooms and broke into the drawers. He found notes on the crimes they were investigating. He laughed as he spotted the names of some of his old friends, acquaintances and even cellmates from the old days. He guessed that many of them would be dead by now.

He found one labelled *Suspected Fraud and Embezzlement: Sattva Systems™.* He opened it and spotted that it came from the Police Department in Boulder Creek. He skim-read through the pages and saw a link to organised crime across the whole State of California. It wasn't an exciting report to Brady's eyes, as it was to do with funding and building regulations. *I'll read it later when I've got a little time on my hands.* He spotted a reference number on a document wallet which suggested that this was one piece of many in this jigsaw puzzle. He took the file with him as he passed through the Training Room and then onto Records and Dispatch. He perused the filing cabinets and racking system - which reminded him of the system back at the ranch devised by Mary-Lou. He pulled anything labelled with Sattva Systems™. He found a trolley and loaded it up as there was so much. He then found a file which had a potted history of Bodhi Sattva. At the back of this were photographs of him meeting with Glenarvon Cole. He didn't recall him instantly, but he had a nagging feeling that he'd seen this face before. He flipped over the photographs, where they had been seen together in various parts of the world. There were some photographs which had labels attached to them, indicating that these were from the CIA. He then remembered the face from the TV from his last day at Ridgecrest. He was Glenarvon Cole, the leader of the GreenRevs. Brady smiled at the recollection. *I was more interested in that pretty red-headed reporter girl with him.*

He changed his approach to search for files on Glenarvon Cole. There wasn't nearly as much information on him - and his known associates. *I suppose he was small fry compared to a famous industrialist like Bodhi Sattva.* He was just about to leave when he thought about searching for files on himself. *Might bring back some memories of the old days.* He also wondered whether the Bear was as clean as he appeared. He spent the next hour looking, and he did find plenty of documentary evidence of the life of crimes of Brady Mahone. He laughed heartily at his old mugshots, but he laughed, even more, when he saw the crimes in which he was in the frame for which had nothing whatsoever to do with him.

He did find a couple of slim files on Samuel Beardon the Third, which mainly concerned his association with Bodhi Sattva. He didn't appear to have been a suspect in any wrongdoing. That wasn't the case for somebody who he hadn't planned to search for - Samuel Beardon the Second had stacks of documentary evidence with regards to the disappearance of John Kane. He flicked through the files for several minutes until he came to the reason he was arrested. The last sighting of John Kane had been in McFarland. He had been travelling to his regional office in Los Banos, and he was scheduled to be at an important meeting at his industrial complex in Boulder Creek. Samuel Beardon the Second had been spotted by several witnesses in McFarland, who claimed he was following John Kane. A police officer had spoken to him, and Samuel Beardon the Second, denied the accusation and appeared to move on. *He probably lost him when John Kane went to visit my Pops.* He placed these files on his trolley, and he wheeled this back through the Police Station.

It took him several trips on his Green Bicycle and trailer to ferry all this documentation back to his Hearse, but he consoled himself with the knowledge that he had plenty of alone time now to immerse himself in this new hobby. This was an unusual investigation for Brady, as he knew who the murderer was. This was a project to connect up the web of the falsely accused.

As he drove back to McFarland, he began to wonder whether the Bear had deliberately engineered a meeting with him because he was still trying to clear his Father's name. *I wonder what he might have found out which could have led him to me?*

9.LOS BANOS RENDEZVOUS

Brady spent the next day going through the Los Banos Police records. Much of it bored him, especially the endless lists of documents relating to the Purchasing Departments of Sattva Systems™. There was also the incomprehensible legalese of the correspondence relating to the new Sattva Systems™ Industrial Units' permits. At a bigger picture level, Brady guessed that these would, with hindsight, unpick the pathway to the Revolution, but he was unqualified to understand these letters between Bodhi Sattva's people and the Governor of California and her legal team. *The Professor and Judge Jefferson would love these - they would have been of value to them - if only they had anything left to sell me.* He dwelled on the other areas where he might be able to trade these documents. *Cupertino has a lot of highly educated Trads. I'll try them at some point.* This was history, and history could wait. The information on the Beardon's seemed more personal and closer to home and therefore excited him. *I woulda liked to have more time to read them in more detail, but if I'm going to find the Bear again, I better do it before the HeavyFusionPlanes™ moves in and spray Los Banos to kingdom come.*

He needed to sort out in his mind, which he wanted to do first. *I'll leave a note for the Professor to meet me tomorrow evening. Going to Los Banos is more urgent, and Cupertino can wait - I hate those phoney Hippies.*

He got in his Hearse and stopped off at the bus shelter. He put a note in the time-table holder. He gave himself a few days to do some more digging into the secrets of the Beardon family.

Hi Professor. I got some real interesting stuff for you. Los Banos is being decomposed by the Greens. See you on Tuesday, 12 January 2100, at 6pm.

PS, by the way, you'll need a trailer and some helpers - I gotta lot of stuff.

Brady.

He drove his Hearse onto Highway 99. As he went, he recalled how busy this road used to be in the days before the Green Revolution. *I never thought I'd miss those traffic jams and all the crappy drivers on the road.* The busiest periods he encountered on his journey would be in the region of fifty vehicles within a couple of hours. *And the cars all look the same - you can have any colour you like as long as it's Sattva Cream.* The Hearse always worked in tandem with Brady as he drove it, and when on the Highway it seemed to learn his routes, and he could drift into his thoughts while the Hearse cruised Highway 99. *It's like my own private road nowadays. They oughta rename it the Brady Mahone Expressway.* He laughed heartily. Brady was proud of his sense of humour.

When he reached Los Banos, he saw the HeavyFusionLorries™ moving into the town. He overtook them - overtaking was now a rare manoeuvre, but he still did it without too much care and attention due to the scarcity of traffic he encountered.

He drove slowly around Los Banos looking for the Beardon family. The Green Workers were dressed in a variety of garishly coloured clothes. *They may have those fucking YellowSuits™ now, but they ain't got Brady Mahone's sense of style.* He couldn't fail to notice how much progress this small army of workers had made, as the roads were clear of all obstacles.

He couldn't find the Beardons, so he stuck around near the park where he first met the Bear and watched how the Green Community prepared Los Banos for its gentle destruction. He watched, as the Green Workers ushered the HeavyFusionLorries™ into the streets. He was surprised at how quietly these big beasts worked, and yet he could feel the power, as they hosed down the front of the buildings with massive hoses which seemed to defy gravity. They seemed to coat the front of a property in seconds. He looked around and spotted dozens of lorries across every viewpoint. As the lorries vacated the blocks, the HeavyFusionPlanes™ moved overhead at an almost impossibly slow speed - they appeared to be levitating rather than flying. The planes hosed down the roofs of every building in a block, before moving onto the next. They reminded him of the wonderful evening of explosions of the abandoned Trad vehicles back in '84. He smiled at the memory. *That was the Greatest Show on Earth.* He felt the soft sub-sonic booms from a distance as the HeavyLoaders™ ascended and descended over the differing heights of the buildings.

Brady knew the buildings would decay slowly, and he could see the reasoning behind it, as there was less risk to the Green Workers. He knew the Green goo wouldn't attack living creatures, so he felt safe. He rubbed off some of the goo that had drifted over him on the breeze. He knew the dry feeling to the touch, as this was a more common occurrence these days, as more areas became abandoned. *I've only just re-waxed my coat. I hope it doesn't break it down.* He took out a thermos flask of coffee and pulled out a packed lunch from one of his larger pockets and began eating while taking in the activity around him.

He then saw Samuel Beardon the Third walking through the park and headed to the tree that Brady was leaning against while sitting on the ground. Brady greeted him, 'Hey man, how're things? Didja have a good New Year?'

'It was a sight to behold. And you, my friend?' He added, 'Do you mind if I join you?'

Brady moved along and gestured for the Bear to sit with him. 'I had one to remember but for all the wrong reasons.'

'I'm sorry to hear that, brother. What happened?'

'The usual, too much to drink, followed by some girl trouble.'

The Bear laughed sympathetically, 'It's been decades since I last partook in alcohol-fuelled nights or girl trouble for that matter. Perhaps I should ask how you felt the day after.'

Brady laughed, 'Like every other New Year's Day for me. I had the hangover from hell.' He winced, then laughed again, 'But I'm over that now. Things are looking up again for Brady Mahone.'

'I'm very pleased to hear that.'

'What happened to Mrs Beardon - if you don't mind…'
'No, my friend. Marsha died in the chaos of the revolution. A driver lost control of his car. I'm guessing the engine cut out - it wasn't his fault. I didn't see him coming, and his car crashed into the sidewalk and took poor Marsha from us. Fortunately, Alicia was very small and can't recall that tragic day.'

'I'm sorry to hear that, man.' It was then that Brady noticed that the Bear wasn't dressed up in something weird. He still had on his Sattva Systems™ cream overalls with its moss-green logo. 'Hey, you are not wearing a YellowSuit™?'

The Bear was happy to return the present and leave the memory of that day behind him. 'I am, my friend. This is the Yellow™. I tend to believe in self-discipline, and I instil this same belief into my family. While in the employ of Sattva Systems™, we should attire ourselves accordingly, but when in our own time then we should dress as we please. I'm too old for treating clothes as a playbox.'

Brady said, 'I'd be the same. I've got a look that suits me.' He added, 'I'm glad I've run into you. I think we might have things in common and would like to get to know you better - as a friend.'

The Bear put a big hand on Brady's shoulder, 'Nothing would please me more. Maybe you could come and have dinner with my family this evening. We live in San Martin. Maybe you could follow us in your FusionCar™.'

'Yes. I would like that.' Brady thought for a moment, 'That's just off the 101, isn't it?'

'That's right. It's a small but perfectly formed Green Community. Cain is now the Regional Disciple after taking over the Western Seaboard area. He seems like an entirely reasonable fellow and a devout follower of Bodhi.'

'It helps with the whole Jesus look he has going on.'

The Bear said, 'So, you know Cain. How marvellous. We won't be short of conversation tonight.' He smiled, 'I'm going to do my speciality of deep roasted vegetables with my secret spice and herb sauce. Would that be ok with you? I know you are probably an old-fashioned meat-eating man.'

'I ran out of meat stores years ago, apart from the stuff my Foster Daddy hoarded in cans in the bunker. It's safe to say that I'm almost a level nine vegan by default now.' He raised his big fist and smiled as he shook it in mock aggression and peered straight into the eyes of the Bear. 'It sounds delicious. I can't wait.'

The Bear laughed heartily. 'You've given me much to look forward to, my new friend. It will be good to talk to someone nearer my own age, instead of having to try and teach my youngsters how to behave like good citizens in this strange world.'

'I hear you, man.'

They both watched the work continuing in the abandoned town of Los Banos, while they ate their food and drank their coffee. Brady said, 'I have to say - you Green people sure work damned hard.'

'There's a lot to be said for job satisfaction. We work for a kind and caring employer who rewards us generously for a job well done. It's a wonderful feeling to have all your efforts fully appreciated by the powers that be. But my friend, I get the impression that you are happy in your chosen profession.'

Brady said, 'Yes, it's true - I love my work. But for me, it's the running of my own business. I like being my own boss.'

'Well, everybody knows your name.' He shook his head slightly, 'I hope you won't be offended if I make just one tiny request.'

'Shoot. I ain't known for my thin skin.'

'I've always ordered my kin to not be tempted by your entertainments which recall the old days.'

Brady laughed, 'My friend, don't you worry. I'm just happy to be in your company. You have a good family, and you should be justly proud of them.'

'Pride is a sin, but between you and me, brother. I am, so help me, God.'

Brady wiped away more Green goo which had settled on his coat. The Bear said, 'You don't see a threat in the spray, my friend?'

'I've been covered in it so many times, if it was going to cause me harm, I would have known by now.' He thought for a moment, 'I'm guessing it's programmed to seek out only dead objects. I couldn't get my head around why it didn't attack my clothes, but when I sketched animals, I noticed it didn't attack their fur or even their habitats. It's some clever shit they got going on there.'

'Even I don't know the inner workings, but the stuff we use is particularly corrosive on man-made materials unless it's on a living being.'

'Have you known the goo to get it wrong?'

'Oh yes, especially in the early days, but they are constantly upgrading and evolving the Nanomaterials. You remember the girl, with the dog…'

'…And the rats. How could I forget.'

'Well, at first it attacked the flesh if a Trad looked dead or was playing dead. It was a horrific sight to behold. They were eaten alive. We downed tools. We didn't sign up for that.'

'So, they fixed it.'

'Yes. The Disciples had to demonstrate to us that it wouldn't happen again. It was a massive problem for them, but thankfully, they sorted it.' He added, 'You are stirring up some ghosts for me - my wife, and those troublesome days. I wish to talk about gentler things. You said you sketch?'

Brady could see the pain of those memories etched on the brow of Samuel Beardon the Third. He reached into an inner pocket of his coat and pulled out the latest of his nearly filled sketchbook. 'I carry this everywhere with me. I've always loved drawing.' He handed it over to the Bear, who took it eagerly from Brady.

The Bear took his time with each page as he looked at exquisite drawings of parrots and parakeets and even an albatross. He wondered how he had the skill to evade being noticed by a mountain lion. He flicked through dozens of pages with drawings from the smallest insects to the Tule elk. The Bear laughed when he came upon Brady's delightful depiction of a black bear. He said, 'You've travelled widely, brother. You have a sensitive soul.'

Brady roared with laughter, 'I have never in my whole life been described as sensitive.'

'You must let Alicia and Tyrone see these this evening.'

'Fine by me. I'm not exactly shy.'

The Bear stood up. 'My lunch break is over.' He smiled, 'I'll meet you here at 6pm if that's ok with you?'

'No problem.'

'I'll bring the coach to the park entrance and then you can follow us in your FusionCar™.'

10.SAN MARTIN

Brady hadn't visited the Green Community of San Martin very often. It was a small town with a devout Bodhi Sattva following. He followed the Beardon family coach, patiently, as the Bear was a careful driver, even on the virtually deserted Highway.

The Bear stopped near a large building. He could make out a faded sign which suggested it was once called the *Wings of History Museum*. Now, it was the *Green Revolutionary Hall*. There were lots of people milling around. Brady watched the Bear step down from his coach and go to greet an older man. They were in a friendly and excitable conversation. After a while, they parted, and the Bear came over to Brady's FusionCar™. Brady lowered the window. The Bear said, 'We could go home, or we could stop off here for a short while. I don't want to be a bad host, so please just say, I bet you are hungry, brother.'

'No. Don't mind me. What's going on?'

'Cain is here. He wanted to see me, but I have said that I have a guest with me.'

'I hope you are not in trouble for talking to me. I wouldn't want that.'

'No, my friend. I have some standing here, and I work closely with our Disciple of San Martin. This means she wants me to be involved in the discussions.'

Brady didn't trust the Disciples or their close associates. He couldn't help but know Cain, Siddha and Lizzie in his hometown of McFarland, but they had put him off making contact with any others - if he could possibly help it. When he dealt with his reps in other towns, he sensed they were trying to keep Brady's business away from the prying eyes of Disciples. Brady thought it was like being back in prison, where the screws would turn a blind eye to the low-level breaking of the rules, as long as it kept the inmates calm. *I don't want to spoil things for the Bear. I like the guy, and God knows I haven't met many people I like in this world.* He said, 'If being with me causes you any trouble at all, then just say so. I mean it. I'll tell them that you didn't have any business dealings with Brady Mahone. I'll say you were just being kind to me. Knowing you as I do - they'll believe me.'

The Bear smiled broadly. 'Spoken like a true friend, brother. If you want, I could introduce you to our Disciple.'

'I'm not sure, man. I don't think they like what Brady Mahone does in their Green Communities. I'm not one of them.'

'But Cain already knows you, and you know him better than I do. To tell you the truth, I'm nervous about meeting a man of Cain's stature, and would appreciate your company.'

Brady wasn't in awe of Cain at all. He was just another Green like all the others to him. 'Ok. Let's do this.'

The Bear went over to the coach, and Brady could tell that he was issuing instructions to Alicia and Tyrone. He watched as the coach drove away without him. He walked over to Brady's car. 'My home is only a few hundred yards from here. They'll prepare dinner while we meet up with Cain. It shouldn't take long. Cain is a very busy man.'

Brady got out of the car and walked with the Bear to the Hall. He had visited here before, but not for several years. He noticed he was picking up inquisitive glances, and he guessed it was directed at the odd pairing they made. They went to the backstage area, and Cain greeted them. In situations like these, Brady always knew he had to dominate the room. He shook Cain's hand firmly. 'No Yellow™ makeover for the Great Cain then, I see - still happy with the old Messiah look.'

Cain laughed and looked dreamily into Brady's face with his crystal-green eyes. 'I am comfortable in my own skin. How have you been? I trust your business is growing?'

Brady noticed a red-headed woman in the room. She was talking to a young Native American boy. He said, 'Absolutely. The nostalgia market grows with every passing year.'

'What do you plan to do with all your Green Credits?'

'I'm gonna get me one of those Green FusionPlanes™ of yours and expand my territories - y'know implement my business model across the whole of the United States of America.' He bragged. He was hoping the red head was listening.

Cain smiled beatifically, 'It would appear that the Green Revolution has made quite the businessman out of Brady Mahone. I'm pleased for you.'

Brady smiled distractedly as the red-haired woman continued to divide his attention. She placed a note into the boy's hand, and he scurried away. She turned, and when Brady saw her, he was captivated. He hadn't met anybody with her glamour for so long. Many years ago, he had seen her on TV - and to Brady that made her a TV star. He watched her move gracefully as she came to Cain's side. The Bear and Cain talked in hushed tones, but the fragments of the conversation he picked up seemed of little interest to Brady. He was engrossed in the image of the woman before him. He felt like he was in the presence of a time-traveller from ancient history. She also felt the pull of the old world, as there was a distinct look that someone had for her, back in the days when she was a celebrity - and Brady Mahone was giving her that look right now.

Cain finished his conversation with the Bear and then said to Brady, 'May I introduce Rhea Laidlaw - the Disciple of San Martin.'

Brady shook her hand and said, 'I know you. You used to be on TV.' He searched his mind for the station's name, 'Free TV News - you were a reporter.'

'That seems like another lifetime. Pleased to meet you, Brady.' He unashamedly looked her up and down. His eyes wandered over her neat and sober black and white trouser suit, and he then looked deeply into her blue eyes. He nodded as if he approved. *That was sixteen years ago, and she's hardly aged at all. She looks amazing.* He wondered if she was married, or whatever these Greens do. He remembered; it was something unromantic-like, partnership? Relationship? Oh yes, that's the term, *arrangement.* And then he wondered if she was in an arrangement with Cain.

The Bear looked at Brady, and then across to Rhea and Cain. He smiled, and said, 'We are having dinner tonight with Brady as our guest. You would be more than welcome to join us.'

Cain answered first, 'Thank you, Sam, but I have to be in Fresno by the morning.' The Bear nodded.

Rhea looked at Cain and then back to the Bear and then glanced at Brady. 'That sounds lovely. I haven't eaten since breakfast, and you know I adore your culinary skills. I'd love to.'

The Bear smiled broadly and slapped Brady on the back, 'Is that ok with you, brother?'

'Fine by me. I can't wait to get stuck in.'

They said their farewells to Cain and headed back to the home of Samuel Beardon the Third. They arrived at a large house just as a family, headed by an old woman was leaving the homestead. She said, 'Good evening, Reverend. We are attending a gathering at the Green Hall this evening, so you will have the place all to yourself this evening.'
Brady spotted the young Native American boy who was talking to Rhea a short while earlier. *This could be a setup.*

The Bear said, 'Thank you, Shako.' She smiled as she led her family away.

Brady made a show of his politeness at the Beardon's home door, and let the Bear enter first, followed by Rhea. He was watching her move when she changed clothes as she crossed the threshold. She was now dressed in a blue cocktail dress. The home was warm and spotlessly clean, but also it had a homely feel to it, with many chairs and sofas, festooned with cushions. There were cream-coloured ceramic radiators with Sattva Systems™ FusionEnergy™ logos on them. They seemed out of place to Brady, but he could feel the comforting heat emanating from them. He spotted the dining table, neatly laid out with silver cutlery, and the floral centrepiece. It reminded him of the old Thanksgiving dinners. He spotted Tyrone and Alicia laughing in the kitchen as they admired each other's flamboyant attire for the evening. The Bear changed appearance as if it was a completely normal thing to do. Brady watched the Bear's Sattva Systems™ uniform dissolve and re-emerge in slacks and a grey pullover, topped off with an apron emblazoned with the words: *The Best Cook in God's Kitchen*. He said, 'I'll add the magic to their culinary creation. Water? Fruit Juices?'

Rhea said, 'Lemon water for me, please.'

Brady joked, 'Water, straight - and make it a double.'

The Bear laughed, while Rhea gave a hint of a smile. She said, 'Samuel - such is the division of labour that Brady and I will wash the dishes after we've eaten.'

The Bear knew this but had forgotten that Brady might not know that this was normal behaviour in the Green Communities. 'Of course. So, shall it be.' He added more precisely, 'So, shall it always be.'

Brady said, 'No skin off my nose. Never let it be said that Brady is a shirker.' He smiled at them both, to let them know that he wasn't offended.

Rhea and Brady sat in awkward silence for a while. Brady struggled to locate a suitable chat-up line for the occasion. Then he remembered that Rhea was a Disciple and was probably not allowed to fraternise with the enemy. 'So, what's a Disciple, exactly? Do you have to worship the Earth, y'know, like Druids and stuff?' She laughed, softly and was just about to answer, before Brady added, 'Or do you serve your Messiah, Bodhi Sattva?'

It had been a long time since she had dealt with cynicism, but the old TV hack in her responded. She missed the old cut and thrust of political debate and bipartisanship. 'Our use of the term Disciple doesn't originate from the religious terminology. There are parallels, I give you that, but the religious term had more to do with faith and devotion. We, on the other hand, use the term as derived from the word, discipline.'

Brady played along, at least they were talking, 'So, you do as your told. You never misbehave?'

'Scientific discipline is essential. It is life-affirming and life-enhancing.' There was a hint of mischief in the way she looked at him. Brady loved this look.

'Do you mind if I ask you a personal question?'

'Fire away.'

'Are you in any arrangements with anybody?'

'Like whom?' She teased.

'I don't know, maybe Cain, or Bodhi?' He smiled as if he was treating these as jokes.

'Arrangements are quite rare. They can be viewed as an expression of ownership over another human. It's not my thing. As for Cain, or Bodhi - although I am close to both of them as friends and colleagues, I have spent intimate moments with them.' She then laughed, mockingly, 'My God, Mr Mahone, you don't believe I slept my way to this position, do you?' She looked down and examined his sneakers, they seemed well-worn and may need replacing soon. She then turned her attention to his Poacher's trench coat. The descriptions of Brady Mahone over the years often mentioned this apparel. She noted that it was hung up on a coat rack, and not in his bedroom as she'd expected.

Brady said, while Rhea scanned the room, 'No, that wasn't what I meant.' He was flustered, 'And of course, you could be gay...' *Please say that would be for me to find out.*

The Bear, Alicia and Tyrone entered with bowls full of food. The Bear said, 'They weren't sure what you would like, so they concocted a selection of vegan delights. Please, help yourselves.'

They all ate heartily, and the Beardon family dominated the small talk over dinner. Brady watched as Tyrone talked about his love of astronomy, and Alicia asked about the future of NanoSuits™, while the Bear seemed especially keen to impress Rhea as if she was an essential connection to a future career. The respect they gave her made him feel foolish about making a play for her. *I keep forgetting that I'm a Trad with all those old-fashioned ways of thinking from the good old days.*

Dinner was followed by fruit desserts and coffee, and then it was time for Rhea and Brady to clear away the dishes. He expected the Bear to offer, to ingratiate himself into her good graces, but it didn't seem to be an option. Rhea picked up the dishes in an unspoken demand that Brady should do the same. He complied.

As they went into the kitchen, Rhea said, 'Shall I wash, and you dry?'

Brady said, 'Shouldn't I be washing, as it's a dirtier job?'

'Practically, and hygienically speaking, it would be better for me to wash, unless you are RedSuited™?' Brady didn't understand, she could see this so she added, softly, 'If I wash, we can have the water temperature to a point which would scold you. Whereas I'm protected by the Red™.'

'Oh, I never thought. Ok, that makes sense.' He watched her pour the water until it was steaming hot, and he watched her plunge her hands into it, utterly oblivious to the heat. She washed each cutlery item, crockery and pans, meticulously, and passed each one over to Brady. She showed him where to put every item in the kitchen with the familiarity of someone who lived there. He also watched as splashes of water and specks of food landed on her blue cocktail dress, and her naked arms, only to disappear with the help of some kind of self-cleaning mechanism within the Suit™. He said, 'How did you get this job?'

She continued the washing up, absent-mindedly, 'I was selected by Glenarvon Cole. Have you heard of him?'

'Yes. I saw you on TV with him.'

'Bodhi had instructed him to choose one Trad to bring over to the Green side after the Revolutionary Coup was accomplished. He hadn't chosen one - I don't think he wanted to - but if you make a promise to Bodhi, you are duty-bound to keep it. I was the last Trad available - so he chose me.'

'You're a Trad?' He said astonished.

'At first. I'm told I still think like a Trad, as I wasn't an environmentalist before the Green Revolution. I was deeply sceptical about the whole thing they had got going on here. I thought I was an experiment for Sattva Systems™.'

'You mean, this Bodhi dude.'

She laughed, 'Oh my, that takes me back. That's just how I used to call him - until I got to know him better.'

'You do know him, then?'

'I've known Bodhi since 2085. Fifteen years - it's been. I love the guy. Not like that - I mean, I truly respect him.' She added, 'This is why I'm based here. He needs me close by, to give him counsel.'

Brady was stunned. 'Wait a minute. He's close by, and you give him counsel?'

She carried on washing and handed over a dessert bowl for Brady to dry. 'Yes. I have a unique point of view.' She said dreamily. 'I'm heading back there for a few days. We are discussing the ethics and morality of the next generation of Suits™.'

'Where are you going? Where is this place?'

'Boulder Creek.'

'No way, I've been there. I woulda known.'

She smiled, 'It's out of the way and hidden from view.'

Brady snorted, 'Makes sense. Industrial megalomaniac hides from his defeated foes who are out to overthrow him.'

She passed him some cutlery, 'Is that what you would do, Bigshot Brady Mahone?' She said it playfully and Brady knew that she liked him.

'I'd consider it. It kinda gives me a reason for why I'm different.'

Rhea laughed in a way that made Brady shudder with delight. She looked beautiful to him and so full of life. 'Brady Mahone, I do declare that you've been watching too many movies.' She pulled open the cutlery drawer. 'They go in here.'

The cutlery rattled as he sorted out the knives, forks and spoons and dropped them into their allotted slots.

She said, 'Any Green can go to the Sattva Systems™ Industrial Complex. I wouldn't be the slightest bit surprised if even you could. He only keeps it shrouded because industrial complexes are, by their very nature, ugly places, compared to Her undoubted glory. But there is another really boring reason, maybe something the intrepid Mr Mahone hasn't given a thought to for years.'

'And what's that?'

She threw her head back and laughed, 'Health and safety.' She said, 'They are always experimenting with new NanoTechnology™, and until it's proven to be completely safe, they wouldn't want any of our Green citizens harmed accidentally.' He watched as she sprayed a natural bleaching agent over the surfaces. She said, 'This is potentially corrosive to you.' He stood back as she wiped all the surfaces spotlessly clean.

He said, 'What would happen if I wandered into this place?' *Accidentally on purpose.*

'The same as anybody else. It happens quite often. They'd show you around, and answer any questions you might have, and some lucky ones have even been given an audience with Bodhi. He's not a recluse, he loves the planet and every living thing upon it.'

'But not the Trads. I'm a Trad.'

'The Trads - and I still am one myself, at heart - remember, had brought the Earth to the point of destruction. It was them or the planet. Some of the GreenRevs wanted to wipe them out, but it was Bodhi who stopped this. He took away their means of destruction but allowed them to live out the rest of their natural lives. That's more than the Trads would have done for them.' She added, 'Come. The Beardons are waiting, and we are their guests, it would be rude to stay here, chatting alone.'

Before he could challenge her, as he dearly wanted to stay and chat with her alone - she had already left the room. *I've never in my life wished there were more dishes to wash.*

After a convivial evening with the Beardons and Brady Mahone, Rhea made her excuses and left. She ensured she gave Brady a kiss on the cheek as she said her goodbyes.

Rhea waited until all the lights had gone out in the Beardon home, to signify that the occupants were going to sleep. She crept over to Brady's FusionCar™ and activated her special access privileges. With a slim FusionTorch™ in her mouth, she used her SattvaTools™ to undo the dashboard and insert a SattNav™ tracker unit. She checked the co-ordinates were correctly calibrated before sneaking over to the Beardon home.

She expertly undid the locks to the front door and moved silently to the living room. She took Brady Mahone's Poacher's coat from the rack and took it back outside to work on. She moved to a quiet spot which was out of sight from windows. She took out a heavy-duty sewing kit, which would have been strong enough to work on Trad shoes, but instead, it would be used on Brady's coat. She unpicked the stitching on the lining at the bottom of the coat, where he wouldn't feel the bump in the hem. She placed the miniature SattNav™ tracker inside. She needed to ensure this coat would not wear out, as the FusionBattery™ could last for a thousand years

11. DOCUMENTARY EVIDENCE

Brady frequently visited San Martin over the next few months, hoping to get another chance to meet Rhea, but she never seemed to be there. He was told by the Bear that she was often in Boulder Creek and that there was probably little for her to do as a Disciple in as small a town as San Martin. Brady didn't entirely believe him, although he valued the word of Samuel Beardon the Third. He still felt that Rhea had given him the brush-off. He had been turned down by women before, but it never felt like this. *I'm pining. Man, I never pine for no woman. I gotta shake off this feeling.*

He went to Los Banos a couple of times, but the town's decaying had taken root, and it left him feeling depressed. The Bear and his family had moved on to work in Oakdale, which was just on the outer edge of where Brady was prepared to travel. *I cleaned that place out of anything useful years ago, and I'm picking up more discarded Green clothes than I could ever need from elsewhere. I don't want to flood the market.*

He thought about Lucky, Mary-Lou and Amie, but he knew that if he tried to renew contact, that would be tantamount to confessing to a crime he didn't commit. Instead, he decided that the only person who might restore faith in himself was Professor Yuan Chu. He hoped he would be interested in the legal documents he had. Brady had given up on trying to decipher them, but someone of the Professor's intellect might be able to figure out something which Brady could make use of.

He left a note at the bus stop arranging a meeting for the following evening at 6pm, which had become a routine time by now, to save on any confusion. He also left word that Oakdale had been dissolved. In the early days of the post-revolutionary period, he would have declared it as Green, as back then, he thought the GreenRevs were capturing the land for their own use. Now, he knew different, it would be sprayed, and then once everything had been broken down, the re-wilding process would begin. There were some tiny towns he used to pass through, where he saw more spraying, several years after the initial destruction, and it reminded him of the muck spreading the farmers of old used to do - it certainly made the vegetation thrive in their newly prepared lands.

He knew the news of what was happening in Oakdale would be alarming to East McFarland's dwindling population, as places like Oakdale and Los Banos were of a similar size to them.

The next day, Brady loaded up his Hearse and stacked up legal papers beside him on the passenger seat. He joked to himself. *I am my own HeavyLoader™.*

He arrived at the bus stop a few minutes before 6pm, and Judge Jefferson was waiting for him. He also noted a couple of elderly ex-cops standing about fifty yards away. *I don't like the look of this.*

Judge Jefferson was sitting down with two walking sticks propped up beside her. She greeted Brady, 'Hello, Brady. I'm sorry to meet you in these unfortunate circumstances. As you can see, my health is fading, that's why I have someone to accompany me.'

'What's the matter with you, Judge?'

'Rheumatoid arthritis, it's a curse of the family, especially down the female line of my family. Of course, the living conditions don't help matters, none.'

'I'm sorry to hear that. I've seen a lot of folks with health issues out there. It's a tough life to endure.'

She smiled, 'But seemingly not for you, Mr Mahone, you appear to be in remarkable shape, and you don't seem to age. I'm guessing you found a way to go Green.'

'Not me. Not on purpose, anyhows. I'm still a Trad to the core.' He looked at her, and she looked defeated. He looked back across the ex-cops and then he spotted the wheelchair. When he saw how the elderly ex-cops shuffled, he realised that even these people were weak and infirm, and therefore of no threat to Brady Mahone. He felt troubled but couldn't grasp why. He guessed the situation was always going to come to this, but it didn't seem to matter until he was personally and emotionally involved. He said, 'If you don't mind me asking - I don't wish to cause you no offence, but why are you here?'

'Professor Yuan Chu is dead. He died peacefully in his sleep last week.'

Brady slumped onto the plastic seat in the bus shelter next to Judge Jefferson and started to cry. *Fuck this shit. Brady Mahone doesn't cry.* He tried to hold back the tears, but when Judge Jefferson put her arms around him and drew his head into her bosom, Brady Mahone sobbed his heart out. He couldn't stop, and he didn't want to stop. He hadn't felt this compassion for another, this pain, this human in his whole life. Even when his Foster Daddy, Archie Mahone, had died, he didn't feel anything like this, because the memory of his passing was tainted by his actions. For the last sixteen years since the GreenRevs Revolution, the only person who believed that Brady Mahone had goodness within him was Professor Yuan Chu.

Judge Jefferson continued to console him, and tears were rolling down her face as well. 'He thought a lot of you, Brady Mahone. He talked about you all the time and always looked forward, so much, to receive the latest missives from his intrepid scout, navigating his way through the new world.'

Brady sat upright and brushed his tears away with his coat sleeve. 'In all my travels, I've never met anybody like him. I'm not just saying that. He gave me something to think about other than myself.'

Judge Jefferson could barely utter the words through her own grief, 'He's a big loss to our community. He was my closest friend.' She wiped her own tears away, 'He made a request of me.'

'And what's that?'

'He asked me to see you in his place. I promised, on his death bed, that I would always be here for you, if you want me too, of course?'

Brady nodded slightly. He didn't want to discuss it. *I done enough blabbering for one day.* He said, 'I got some things in the Hearse. I brought them for the Professor, but you can have them if you want. Actually, being a Judge and a DA 'n'all, I suppose you might be better qualified.' It stung Brady that he said that, as nobody was more qualified than anybody than the Professor, in his opinion. 'You sit there, Judge. I'll back the car up.' Brady had started to call his vehicle a car while dealing with Trads, but he had to give everything it's proper title when in the Green areas, as they frowned if he didn't abide by their Green brand values. He knew it would be a hard habit to break, but business was business. He would have to train himself to say Fusion- this and Fusion-that, especially now that the Trads were beginning to die out.

He reversed the FusionCar™ to the bus stop, directly in front of Judge Jefferson. He opened the passenger door. He pulled out a few document wallets from the top of the paper mountain - he'd selected them because he suspected these had some more juicy information than the others. He handed them over to the Judge. 'I picked up these from the Los Banos Police Department. They were investigating Sattva Systems™. I suppose more accurately, they were assisting the FBI with their investigations. It looks like the CIA were involved in the overseas side of the business.' She shuffled through the documentation, she guessed Brady had made an effort to understand what he had here, as he had picked up on the difference of roles of the FBI and the CIA. Brady continued. 'I know there's nothing we can do now, but I thought you might find it interesting figuring it out how they gone and done it. If nothing else, it would pass the time.' He laughed.

She smiled, 'It's been so long. I would love to do this. And I promise to let you know of anything of interest that I come across.'

Brady laughed with a mixture of humour tinged with relief that he wasn't likely to start crying again. 'I suppose that's a great reason for Brady Mahone to keep visiting old East McFarland then.' He added, 'I could drive them over to your house if you want?'

She didn't want to embarrass Brady by refusing this offer, but she didn't want him to see where she lived. 'No. That's fine. Thanks for the offer, but there are obstacles and roadblocks. You wouldn't be able to get through. My officers will assist me.' They shuffled in closer at her signal.

Brady accepted her refusal. *I haven't been in the town for sixteen years. They are probably still scared of me.* He had a flashback of how he decapitated the wannabee Mexican gangster. The memory made him feel nostalgic. 'You better bring some trailers or something. I've got a whole car full of stuff.'

The officers went away to look for something to transport the loot of Brady Mahone.

Brady said to her, 'I've got a delicate and weird proposal for you. Being as you're the community leader and all. It was some information I picked up from a Green friend of mine. He said that if you leave any dead at the town limits, then the Greens will dispose of them ecologically.'

She looked at him, and she was clearly appalled at the idea. 'Is that what you would like us to do with the Professor's body?'

'No. Oh, God. I've probably not gone and explained it too well.'

She shook her head. The images of all the dead she had administered over piled up in her visions. 'Why on Earth would they want to do that?'

'My friend. He used to be a preacher. It's not a Green instruction. I believe he was giving me some inside information as a friend. I think it comes from a position of kindness.'

225

She softened. She didn't imagine any humanity within the Greens, but the Professor believed in Brady's judgment, and now she had promised to do the same. 'What kindness? I confess, I'm struggling to find it.'

'He says that the Trad communities are using up precious green spaces for growing crops, by turning them into cemeteries. I've seen the dead piling up, some of the places I've been to, they cannot cope with the volume of corpses.'

'How does this preacher dispose of them?'

'They spray them, and within a couple of days, they melt away into the Earth. They leave no trace.'

'I'll have to think about it. This is a very sensitive decision.'

'Ok, Judge. You don't have to make a decision. Just leave the bodies at the town boundary. They have things scanning for them, and then they issue the orders to their Operation Clean-up teams.'

The Officers returned, and Brady was glad of the chance to change the subject. 'I've got something else for you and yours.' He opened the rear doors of his ceramic, cream-coloured Sattva Systems™ FusionCar™ - he had once attempted to decorate it, to stamp it with his own identity, but it had a NanoCoat™ which repelled this, just like it repelled the dirt from the Highways - it even had a field which prevented even insects coming into contact with the vehicle as he travelled. Brady began unloading hundreds of items of clothing into the trailers the old cops had brought over. 'I know the Greens are a bit short on style, but these are either nearly new or cleaned.'

The Judge said, 'I don't think we have anything of value to trade with you.'

'I'm giving them to you, Judge.'

'Please, let's dispense with the formalities. I don't mind if you call me Audre. I stopped being a Judge a long time ago.'

Brady smiled, 'Ok, Audre.' He continued, 'To tell you the truth, I've more than enough to trade with other Trad towns. I can afford to let some come your way. That's if you want them…'

'Yes. We are desperately short of clothing.'

'I know that. You'd be surprised at the offers I get from the womenfolk from my other Trad districts.' He joked. 'Brady Mahone has become quite the Mister Loverman.' He knew the humour was inappropriate but at least it warded off the feelings of soppiness, that he was always on the verge of, here.

She laughed at his bluntness of language. 'Actually, Brady, that wouldn't shock me in the slightest.' She ran her hands over the garments. They were well made and practical. 'I'm guessing these are made from recycled materials.'

Brady laughed, 'Not my area of expertise, I'm afraid. All I know is they won't be making any more.' He noticed that the Judge looked a little shabby in her long black coat that covered multiple sartorial sins. He looked down to see she was wearing sneakers, and just above he could make out the bottoms of a pair of grey sweatpants.

She spotted him looking her up and down but chose to ignore this. She had long since passed worrying about her looks. She said, 'And why's that?'

'They are wearing, what they call, YellowSuits™. The NanoTech™ means they can change their appearance in an instant. All they need is their Suits™ from now on. Apparently, they are saving the planet by running down the manufacturing of clothing.'

'Whatever next?'

Brady didn't understand rhetorical or redundant questions, 'I'm hearing rumours about GreenSuits™ being the next big thing. They are supposed to recycle the human waste within the bodies. The NanoTech™ breaks it down to something the size of a pill.' He laughed loudly, 'They will only need to use the shitter about once a month.'

Audre tried to grasp the impact of this latest monstrous idea, 'Why is this important to them?'

'They are recycling water within them. They will barely feel the need to take a piss. It is to reduce the need for water - y'know, one of the most precious resources blahdy-blah.'

'My God. They are not planning to cut off our freshwater supplies, are they? That was one of the few things we are grateful for.'

Brady could see the alarm in her eyes and hastily searched his recollections of half-remembered conversations in his quest to find some reassurances for her, 'Ah yes, they didn't want the untreated water spilling out onto the earth from the Trad areas. Also, they don't want human diseases to spread into other animals.' He added, 'I remember them joking about reverse pandemics, y'know transmittable viruses spreading from Trads to animals.'

She spat out, 'It's disgusting the way they talk about us. Have they forgotten that we are human beings as well?'

'I don't know, Judge. They said the Trads were killing the Earth for profit, and you lot were going to take them down to hell with you. I don't think you've - I don't mean you, personally - have the right to take the moral high ground here. Sorry, Audre.' As she shook her head, he could see she was trying to control her rage. He added, 'Anyway, the good news is, is that I don't think they are going to cut off your water. It's not in their interests. It will be the Greens who will be cutting down their own consumption.'

Long seconds passed by while Judge Audre Jefferson returned to her usual calm and rational state. She said, finally, 'I'm not angry with you, Brady. I think my frustration was getting the better of me. You've been very kind, and I don't mean with just the clothing. It will do my mental health a world of good to get stuck into the substantial puzzle you have set me within these documents.'

'You're welcome, Audre.'

Audre called her officers over, 'Gary, could you take the clothes to the Town Hall.' He nodded and began to load his hand-drawn trailer. She said, 'And Norbert, I would be grateful if you could take the legal papers to my home.' She smiled softly, as the two old men struggled to get the trailers to move. To Brady, they looked like twins, or brothers born not too far apart. They both looked in reasonable shape - for older white dudes - and both were white guys with short white hair, which gave them a military bearing. *Old soldiers who've seen better days.*

'I'll need some time to organise and read the documents. When were you next planning to visit?'

He joked, 'Brady Mahone is a very busy businessman. Would two weeks from today be good for you? Same place, same time?'

She smiled, 'That would suit me just fine, Brady Mahone.'

She watched as he got in his now empty FusionCar™ and sped away in the direction of the Mahone Ranch. She sat at the bus stop, deep in thought, while she waited for Officer Norbert, as she warmly referred to him, to return from delivering the papers to her home, and then to push her back in the wheelchair.

12.HOME FROM HOME

Officer Norbert wouldn't leave until he was satisfied that Judge Jefferson had everything she needed. He cleared the large dining room table. She recalled the days when twenty people would be seated around it for one of her famous Thanksgiving dinners. He moved all the chairs to the room's sides to give her as much wheelchair access, as possible. She stood up using her two sticks and began to organise the piles of documentation with his help.

She knew Los Banos had inadequate administration procedures. Their Judge had a reputation of taking the police at their word, and if you were white, you'd get a limited hearing, but if you were black, you would go straight to jail. This meant there was little requirement to be scrupulous in record keeping. She tried to make sense of indexing. It wasn't always clear, but it gave her a framework to start with. If in doubt, then the papers would be placed into date order across the table. Even the dating of documents wasn't always completed.

She eyed with suspicion, the number of redacted passages in the FBI and CIA notes, but even more so, the notes from the Boulder Creek departmental files.

They completed the stacking of documents just before darkness fell. The lack of daylight ruled her world in a town which hadn't had a power supply for sixteen years. She didn't mind. She was tired and needed sleep. She told Officer Norbert to go home and thanked him for his help. She went to the living room to her bed - it had been many years since she had been upstairs, and there were times when she lay in the near silence that she was sure she could hear dripping water after a period of rain.

She noticed that he had left her a jug of water and a glass next to her bedside. He had left before she had time to thank him for yet another gesture of kindness from the old man.

She looked at the jug of clean water. We are so close to utter annihilation.

She struggled, as she did every night, to get undressed and into her nightgown, but it was a matter of self-respect for her. She lay in bed and thought of her strange relationship with Brady Mahone.

He always had a childlike view on life. That's why I had to lock him up on every occasion he appeared before me. He never understood the world as a place for mutual respect. In his mind, the world boiled down to the basest of reasoning. I want, and therefore I'm going to have. The fact that it doesn't belong to me, or whether the item had sentimental value to his victim, none of this mattered. It was there, he saw it, so he took it.

I need my sleep. I don't want to think about it now. Why do I always think about these things at night?

She tossed and turned, even though this caused her pain. *I couldn't with good conscience put Brady Mahone back into society. He would never change his ways. In fairness, I can't recall him ever promising to do that. He just stood there and took his punishment on the chin.*

She thought about what the prison system had done to him. He had been kind - now. Had she mis-judged him all along? She remembered reading the prison reports if Brady Mahone was being assessed for parole or early release due to prison over-crowding.

He behaved in prison in precisely the same way as on the outside. He was institutionalised. *I wonder if he ever cared that much whether he was in jail or not.*

From the old days, Judge Jefferson would have agreed with any psychiatric report that suggested that Brady Mahone displayed psychopathic or sociopathic tendencies. *Has he changed in this new world order? Is it possible for sociopaths to change?* She weighed him up on the scales of justice which had been entrusted to Judge Audre Jefferson.

I've witnessed him murder, in cold blood, Manuel Fargo - he decapitated him without any hint of emotion. He'd also exploited every Trad area on the Western Seaboard. However, those were genuine tears he shed for Yuan, and although he tried to hide it as if a sense of giving was a sign of weakness, it was a knowing act of kindness.

She cursed that she couldn't slip off into sleep. Her sleep brought her relief from pain. *I'm sure my brain is supposed to work for my wellbeing, so why won't it let me get the rest I dearly need. I have work to do in the morning.* Even this thought kept her awake, as she hadn't had legal work to attend to in many years. She was highly regarded in disseminating the most complex of cases. She deduced that now she was becoming excited and the rush of cortisol and adrenaline pumping through her body would make sleep impossible, now - at least until she could regain an element of calm. She was annoyed at the lack of power in her home. In the past, she would have risen and worked through the night. Whereas now, all she had was the frustration of a racing mind defending against the forces of slumber.

She tried to pretend to herself that she was giving up the fight to sleep. *If I tell my mind that resting with my eyes closed will suffice, maybe then I would go to sleep by accident.* In reply to her plan, her restless mind jumped back to her analysis of Brady Mahone. Why is he so important? He must be important, or is he just lucky? Is it in his nature? Is it the way he was raised? She refused to open her eyes to look at the clock, as she knew the added stress of clock watching through the night wouldn't help. In the long minutes of obstinacy, she thought she was winning the battle with time, but she succumbed to temptation. Her eyes opened, she peeked at her trusty old alarm clock - she couldn't remember the last time she set the alarm. The clock leered at her like demon's eyes in the dark, its red luminous hands announced balefully it was 1:42.

She thought of Archie Mahone.

Archie Mahone and his wife were outsiders. He was a conspiracy theorist and a survivalist. She remembered them becoming foster parents for the first and only time, to the child, in the form of Brady Mahone. She recalled that it was strange that they should ever be considered as worthy of such responsibility. She remembered how it was sanctioned by the authorities in Boulder Creek. She made a mental note to look for any references to Child Services in Boulder Creek. She never ignored her unconscious mind pointing her in the right direction when working on a case. Even if her brain was her sleep enemy, she knew it was her friend when seeking out patterns.

She blinked as if she was taking a photo of her mind from behind her eyes. Brady Mahone, Archie Mahone and Boulder Creek Child Services.

Many of her contemporaries warned against pre-judging investigations, but she always disagreed. She went into the casework with an open mind and she constructed frames of references to propel her thoughts onto. She considered the FBI and CIA involvement. She deduced that the FBI saw an internal threat. *It's unlikely to be drug related, I don't feel its presence here.* Brady intimated at fraud and corruption, but did the FBI consider this a terrorist plot? She thought about this further. With hindsight this is obvious, but did they suspect this prior to the Green Revolution? She then added the international factor because of the CIA files dwelling in the Los Banos files. They had paper copies in their offices when the Internet was used for virtually everything, in those days.

She added Los Banos, FBI and CIA to her frame of reference.

Judge Audre Jefferson awoke to the Californian sunlight streaming through her windows. She wondered what the time had been when she had actually fallen asleep. She remembered glancing at her clock at 1:42am, it now displayed 8:05am through the spread of the mechanical hands on the face of the clock.

She painfully tried to stretch out her stiff joints and got out of bed. She grabbed her Zimmer frame, which was useful in the first hour until she loosened up a little. She went to the sink and washed, before setting herself a bowl of cut-up fruit and a glass of water. She dressed in her tracksuit and old sneakers, which didn't need lacing-up. She looked wistfully at the staircase. *I would have loved to have got dressed for a day's work at the office, but any of my old work clothes are up those damned stairs.* For a moment, she wondered if she could crawl up the stairs to explore the contents of her abandoned wardrobe, but then thought better of it. The damp has probably got to them after all these years. She then considered her thin body. *They probably wouldn't fit me, anyway. I must have been at least forty pounds heavier back then. Still, I might have been able to make do with my old white silk blouses. Oh well, beggars can't be choosers.*

She looked around the decaying and damp remains of her home. It made her think of her own past. She remembered the day when Sattva Systems™ moved into West McFarland. They had done a deal with the California Governor to instil state-of-the-art FusionEnergy™ power, in a drive to make California the capital of the energy-saving world. It was part of their New Green Deal for the Planet. She thought about how proud California was of Silicon Valley leading the world out of the climate change crisis. It wasn't until much later, when it was found that FusionEnergy™ wasn't compatible with seemingly anything to do with the Internet - or so they said - whether via, Broadband, Fibre-optics, Bluetooth or even Wi-Fi. She considered the war of words and lawsuits with the rest of the big tech in Silicon Valley. She had a small part to play in these. She loved her old home in West McFarland, but there, she didn't have a viable Internet connection, so, she had no choice but to relocate to East McFarland into this home. She had flashbacks to the mocking dinner party conversations where East McFarland's booming house prices compared so favourably to those on the Westside. Once it was clear that West McFarland would never have a working Internet, the house prices plummeted, and distressed sellers sold their homes for a pittance, while there was still a chance of recouping anything.

At that point the Green Hippies moved in and slowly took over the whole of the Westside. She remembered the lawsuits from embittered ex-residents, and then the class actions from across the United States of America. Sattva Systems™ settled out-of-court on such favourable terms that speculators were second-guessing which districts would be next for the Sattva Systems™ makeovers. Then the Green Communities spread across the world. Sattva Systems™ had a trillion-dollar cash pile, and it dominated the global travel industry - but if they wanted to waste their own money, then whose business was that for anyone interfere with them.

Sattva Systems™, FusionEnergy™ and Internet Disruption were added to the budding climbing frame of Judge Audre Jefferson's mind.

She went to her wheelchair and rolled herself to the head of the table, to begin her investigation at the lowest numerical reference numbers, and those files that didn't have them - the earliest dates. *This will take a long time, but it sure feels good to be working my legal mind again.*

13.BLINDED BY THE LIGHT

Brady drove up and down the California Highways, collecting his Green Credits and collecting orders for his self-titled company, the BMEE Group. It made him feel like a bigshot when he introduced himself to new Green districts as the Brady Mahone Entertainment Enterprises' proud owner. His primary reason for his travels was to keep having the excuse to see if he could bump into Rhea Laidlaw again.

He didn't have many customers in San Martin, partly down to the Bear's hellfire preaching. He had warned them of the terrible consequences awaiting anybody who gave in to the temptation of feeling nostalgia for the old world. But Brady had a couple of weeks to kill before he was due to meet with Judge Jefferson again.

The first time he visited, he spent another evening with the Bear. Tyrone had tried to get him interested in astronomy but only succeeded in boring Brady. Tyrone probably should have guessed that stories about the constellations and their connections to Greek mythology wouldn't be a subject to stir Brady's juices. When he asked around about Rhea, the Bear's daughter teased him about being sweet on her. Brady struggled to hide his annoyance and embarrassment. The Bear put him out of his misery by informing him that Rhea was away on business in Boulder Creek.

He made another journey to San Martin a few days later, but this time the Beardon family weren't there. With only the townsfolk to ask, Brady, cut a suspicious figure, as some thought he was the Devil come to tempt them while their Disciple, Rhea, and their preacher, Samuel Beardon the Third were all out of town.

His inquiries only gleaned that Rhea was still in Boulder Creek - and that this was not an unusual occurrence. He was also informed that the Beardon family were staying over in Elk Grove. This was a source of news which caused a mixture of excitement and pride to the natives of San Martin. Whereas to Brady, this was a source of consternation, as this was the largest district he had heard of, which was abandoned by the Trads. He sensed this was the beginning of a new phase earmarking the demise of the Traditional Cultures.

He still had a few days to kill, so he made a final attempt to meet Rhea Laidlaw. He was worried about him getting a reputation of a lovelorn waster or worse, a stalker.

As he pulled up to the Beardon home, Tyrone excitedly came out to greet him. 'Hiya, Brady. Big things are happening in the astronomy world.'

Brady shrugged, 'Is Samuel home?'

'No. He's still in Oakdale with Alicia. It's a huge undertaking clearing a place of that size.'

'Why aren't you with them?' Brady stared at the gangly, black youth with his thick-lensed glasses.

'It's my holiday. I'm heading down to Encinitas. Actually, I'm heading off in the next hour.'

Brady looked at the tortoiseshell glasses perched on Tyrone's nose and guessed he must be short-sighted and couldn't have a problem with his more extended vision.

He said, as nonchalantly as possible, 'I have business to conduct with Rhea. I don't suppose you've seen her around, have you?'

'No. Sorry. She's always hot footing it to some big meeting or another. I can tell her you were looking for her if you want me to?'

I'm sure she's all too aware that I've already done that. I know when I've had the brush-off. 'No. It's no biggie. I'll take my business elsewhere.'

Tyrone shrugged. He couldn't wait to get on his way. 'Hey. If you're at a loose end, why don't you come and join me? It's going to be a spectacular sight.'

'Nah. It's ok. Thanks, anyway, but I'm not as into all that stargazing as you are. I'm a basic kinda guy, y'know?'

Tyrone laughed, 'But you'll love this. It's the biggest vehicle crash in the history of mankind. That's why I had to have this week off as a holiday.'

Tyrone had successfully tweaked Brady's interest. 'What kind of crash?'

'I meet up with other keen astronomers, and I've made friends who used to work for the government at the Palomar Observatory in San Diego County. It used to be the biggest telescope in the world…' Tyrone saw Brady's eyes glaze and he knew he was losing him, 'Anyway, the mASSIVE™ International Space Station (mISS) is going to crash into the Pacific Ocean tomorrow night, by my friend's calculations, and the best place to see this, is from the coastline in Encinitas.' Tyrone leapt in the air with excitement but was amazed that Brady still seemed unmoved. Tyrone shook his head and smiled ruefully, 'It's four-hundred and twenty thousand kilograms of metal, which will fall out of the sky and crash and burn in the Pacific.'

Brady whistled and said, 'Wow. Awesome.'

Tyrone couldn't contain his excitement, and Brady couldn't remember ever feeling like this boy did, not even before a heist. 'Ok. I'll tell you no lie. I'd love to see that.' Tyrone held up his hand, and Brady gave it a lame High-Five. He added, 'I tell you what I'll do. I'll drive us both, there and back, as a way of repaying your family's hospitality.' *When I come back here, I'll be driving Tyrone back home, and it will give me one last chance to see if I can get to see that Rhea chick again. And she'll see I've done my good deed by Tyrone.*

Brady hadn't been as far south as Encinitas before, and he figured it would be a seven-hour drive if he avoided the most troubled towns - he had Tyrone's mental wellbeing to think about, if not his physical safety because some of those places had been plunged into depravity by violence and crime. He also needed to plan in some comfort breaks and time to get something to eat and drink. 'I've got stops to make on the way, but I only need about an hour in each. I'm owed Greenbacks.'

'No problem. Do you mind if I ask how much you make?'

'What's your pay-check?'

Tyrone answered proudly, 'Twenty-five Green Credits per week.'

Brady took out his Distor™ and handed it to Tyrone. The luminous green figures displayed the total of 912,435 Green Credits. Tyrone said, 'That's amazing. You'll soon be the first Green Credit millionaire I've ever heard of - well, except for Bodhi Sattva, I suppose.'

Brady said, 'I'm going to get me one of those private FusionPlanes™ when I get me a million. Then I'm going expand - big time.'

Tyrone passed the Distor™ back to Brady, but not before taking one last admiring look at the number. He might never see a Distor™ this fully loaded ever again.

Brady asked, 'Is Encinitas a big town?'

Tyrone said, 'Yes, it's about Elk Grove's size, at a guess, but it's split down the middle, either side of Highway 5. There's a massive Trad area on the East-side, but fortunately, the West-side, the all-important coastal section is a thriving Green community.'

Brady pictured his own hometown of McFarland being split into two by Highway 99. He looked at Tyrone and tried to sound enthusiastic, 'Looks like we're going on a road trip.' He added, 'Get your sh…stuff together and let's hit the Highway.'

They travelled smoothly down the near deserted Highways. Brady stopped at various towns en-route to Encinitas and continued to add to the total of the Green Credits recorded in his Distor™. Tyrone chatted excitedly, and Brady had switched off listening to him, and only occasionally responded with a nod, or the odd, 'Hell, yeah.' If he picked up on words concerning the spectacular crash.

Brady was partially attentive when Tyrone discussed the tricks which could be done with NanoShells™, he spoke excitedly of Emergency Protocols and the protection of secret sites - for the health and safety of its Green citizens, of course. He said it was for mental health reasons that most NanoShells™ were clear.

'I can see a hint of green in them, out of the corner of my eye.' Brady said, while still concentrating on his driving.

Tyrone said, 'That's interesting. I can't, and I don't recall anybody else saying that, either.'

'A day or so after the Revolution, I saw the Green goo rolling down the Highway. And when you had your Orange™ and Yellow™ ceremonies, I saw the Shells™ turn briefly to those colours.'

'Are you sure?'

'Positive.'

'Cool.' He was thoughtful for a while as he tried to figure this new information out with the mind of a budding scientist. 'Anyway, there are other super-cool things they could do with these Shells™ if they needed to.'

'Like what?'

'They can be set to any level of opacity.'

'What's that? You'll have to speak English to me.'

Tyrone laughed apologetically, 'It's how much you can see through them from either the inside or the outside. It can go to all levels of blurry until you reach a point where you can't see through it at all.'

'So, you could hide a whole town?'

'Yes, even a city.'

'Why would you bother to hide a town or city from the Trads, if they can't get in, anyhows?'

'It's covering all eventualities. If we had visitors from space...'

Brady laughed, 'Now, you sound just like my Foster Daddy with his talk about UFOs and conspiracy theories. Next, you'll be telling me there's an Area 51.'

'There is. I think.'

'There you go. I knew it.'

Tyrone smiled, 'I gotta admit it. I do love all that stuff.'

'You should watch some of my entertainments. I got all kinds of things my customers love - y'know, movies about space travel and aliens.'

'It does sound like fun, but Uncle Sam would go up the wall if I did that. It's a kind of commandment of his.'

'It's up to you. I don't want to go against the Bear's wishes, but if ever you did fancy it, just let me know, and I'll give you a few free samples. I don't watch that shit, but my Rep in West McFarland, Vance - well, he swears by it.'

'Thanks, Brady.'

'What else do these NanoShells™ do, apart from repelling alien invaders - who don't exist - talk about paranoid.'

Tyrone didn't want to irritate Brady with a discussion of the probability theory on the existence of extra-terrestrial beings. 'The NanoShells™ can be set to mirror-mode. I'm not entirely sure why, but I have it on good authority...'

Brady drifted away from listening to Tyrone's theories. He thought about Nano-Shell™ mirrors for a short while before he drifted into a reverie about his Foster Daddy, and he wished he was with them now, as he would have loved to have discussed his theories with this inquisitive and knowledgeable man-child.

He left the Highway and headed down the coastal roads for the last few miles. He didn't know how the Trad section of Encinitas was organised, and he didn't want to find out as it was outside of his usual territory. Tyrone slept through the last few hours of his epic road trip with Brady Mahone, as he was saving himself for the long night ahead. Brady drove through the West-side of Encinitas until he found a high vantage point atop a cliff with stunning views over the Pacific Ocean. He let Tyrone continue his sleep as he left the car and retraced his steps. *They might not know of Brady Mahone in these parts, and as a stranger in a strange land, it's always good to plan for a quick getaway.* He walked along the clifftop road, examining the directional signs and committing them to memory.

Tyrone was stretching outside the car and admiring the view. He saw Brady and said, 'This will be perfect. I'm expecting a few people, in the know, to begin the watch from around midnight, as the International Space Station's re-entry will become visible from the west. At first, it will be a speck of light, like a star, but over the following hours, it will grow and grow, until it crashes into the ocean about fifty miles away.'

'When will that happen?'

'About an hour before dawn. Which is brilliant, as it will still be just about dark, and that will make it look so much more spectacular.'

Brady laughed, 'Cool. Can't wait.' He said, 'Don't know about you? But I'm hungry. Let's say we eat?'

'Yes. It's a good idea. We'll need to keep our strength up.'

'You speak for yourself, sonny boy.' Brady mockingly showed off his biceps and put his fists up, playfully, as if preparing for a boxing match. 'Brady Mahone never has to worry about his strength.' He laughed, 'Let's go. My treat.'

As Brady wandered around the Green Community, he made mental notes about its size, population, and potential customer base, should he return in the future. In the café, with Tyrone, he chatted with the waitress who attended their table. She informed him that the Trad community was a well-administered town run by the old and respected Mayor, in conjunction with, the local church leaders. She spoke of other family members who were Trads and hinted that she occasionally communicated with them. Brady was surprised at how the Disciple who ran this community seemed to rule in a more relaxed and informal manner to the others he'd observed. He didn't seem to be a stickler for the rules.

After Brady and Tyrone finished eating and using the all-important bathroom facilities, Brady flirted with the waitress. 'I may visit here again someday soon, if that's ok with you, honey.'

She said, 'You'll always find a warm welcome waiting for you in Encinitas.' She smiled coyly.

'Hey, sweetheart, what's your name?'

'Why I'm Lilith.' She teased, 'Now don't get it in your that handsome head of yours to go calling me Lily. Otherwise, you and I might not be friends.' She smiled, and Brady liked that old familiar Californian smile full of gleaming white teeth, and soft red lips. She said, 'And what's your name? You ain't round from these parts.'
He took her hand quickly and kissed it, 'I'm Brady. Brady Mahone, and honey, I ain't from this world, never mind round here.'

Tyrone returned and attempted to join in the conversation. He interrupted absent-mindedly, 'He's a Trad.'

Brady looked at him sharply, and Tyrone looked away, embarrassed. Tyrone spent his spare time on his science files rather than checking out the rules of engagement in pulling a short-term partner.

She said, 'You are one special man. I ain't ever heard of a Trad being able to come in here - not on the West-side.'

He said, 'I could show you one or two of my magic tricks. What time do you finish?'

'I'm on a double shift. I don't finish until 6am. I gotta save hard for my Yellow-Suit™.'

'You mean you ain't got one, yet?'

She looked away and bit her lip, 'I got into a spot of bother with this boy, and they fined me, which means I have to make up my Green Credits. You do know what they are, you being a Trad 'n'all.'

He joked, 'I'm just going to get something out of my pocket, that will amaze ya, baby.'

'I'm sure you will, hun.' She teased.

He pulled out his Distor™ and showed her the amount. She said, 'Wow! That's really something. How did you get all those credits?'

'Well, Lilith.' He smiled, broadly, 'I sells entertainment products to the trendier end of the Green market.'

She faked a look of concern, and playfully raised a finger as if she were about to admonish him, 'The Preacher here, warns innocent young girls such as my good self, to resist the Devil and his wares, and that I should not allow myself to be led into temptation.'

He said, 'If I was the Devil. Could I lead you into temptation after your shift? I'm going to be just over yonder, near the cliffs at 6am. You might be just in time for my big show.'

She giggled, 'I'll be there, it's a date.' She looked around to check if her boss was watching. She wasn't, so she leant in and kissed him on the cheek. She whispered into his ear, 'And what do you do for an encore?'

'I'll bring fire from the skies, and hell on Earth for you girl.' He could tell that neither Lilith nor the other locals seemed to have a clue about crashing space stations. In the old days, everybody would have known about it, and there would have been advertisements everywhere. He chuckled, as he thought about this brilliant prank, he could pull on her. 'Will that be enough to satisfy a girl like you?'

'That's for me to know - and you to find out. I'll see you later - Brady Mahone.' She saw her boss watching, and she rushed over to pour coffees at the far end of the café.

Brady waved to her as he left, and she blew him a kiss. It took his mind off Rhea.

He also could tell that Encinitas could be an excellent place to do business. *Hell, I might even employ her as a rep for the world-famous Brady Mahone Entertainment Enterprises.* He chuckled as he and Tyrone headed back to the Hearse.

Brady found a spot of grass on the cliff edge and kicked off his shoes and made himself comfortable. He took out a couple of rolled-up sleeping bags and handed one to Tyrone. 'It ain't for sleeping. You can use it to rest your head on.'

'Thanks, Brady.'

While Tyrone chatted amiably about the stars and planets which were emerging in the darkening skies. Brady's mind wandered back to the last time he was on a clifftop overlooking the Pacific. He didn't look where Tyrone was pointing, he had his head resting on his sleeping bag, and he was happy to watch the stars appearing above him, and he had no desire to learn what they were called. He drew in deep breaths of the salty air and thought about the hot-tub, cigar and brandy he enjoyed with Bodhi's mother and old Hollywood starlet, Libby Kane. He chose not to reflect on all the heavy stuff around the whole Kane dynasty thing, all he wanted to do was think about how it felt to be on a luxury holiday. He enjoyed this feeling of calm and tranquillity. He whispered, 'This was a great idea, Tyrone. Thanks, man.'

Tyrone surged with pride, 'My absolute pleasure.' *My work here is done.*

The two stargazers barely said in word in the next contented hour. The only movement was when Tyrone went to retrieve his binoculars from the Hearse. Tonight, was a night for a sweeping vision of the horizon, and not for training his field of view on one distant object in a tiny part of the sky. Gradually, a thin crowd of people began to gather in small groups along the coastline. Brady said, 'In the old days of social media and the Internet, this place would have been packed out by now. I suppose it's just down to word of mouth with you Greens, and I'm guessing the Trads are doing basic stuff like barely surviving.' He laughed at his own insightful comment, but Tyrone was exploring the whole sky before the arrival of the star of the show.

Brady scanned the clifftop for potential threats but saw nothing but family groups and the Green Community demographics' geekier end.

I hope they don't think I'm a geek.

He also looked over the cliff edge to the beach parties held around the fires on the beach. He guessed the Greens still had the ability to make fire - even if the NanoFireRetardants™ had cut it out for the Trads. They didn't use it often, maybe it was a special occasion. *That looks more like my idea of fun.*

He figured he still had a bit of time to get a bit of shut eye. He was also getting cold, so he retrieved his Poacher's trench coat and lay back down on the ground with his head resting on the rolled-up sleeping bag. *Doesn't matter if I nod off. I'm sure that Tyrone won't let me miss it.*

Tyrone glanced over at Brady but noticed he had his eyes closed. Within a few seconds, Brady was snoring loudly. A young boy from a neighbouring family giggled at the snoring man who was missing out on all the fun. Tyrone prayed that Brady wouldn't wake up to witness anybody making fun of the legendary Brady Mahone.

A short while later, he tapped Brady on the shoulder. 'I caught my first glimpse of the Space Station. Do you want to see?'

Brady would have been happy to remain in the hot tub of his mind, but sleepily replied, 'Yeah, sure.' He took the binoculars. Before he put them to his eyes, he turned in a circle and then stopped. He was facing in land. 'I can see it without them. It's to the right of the Moon.'

Tyrone didn't want to embarrass Brady, but he needed him to look in the right direction. 'Normally, that would be the most spectacular feature - that's Venus ascending.'

'What does that mean?'

'The Sun rises in the East. That means it ascends. As it's June 6th, 2100, then on this day, Venus ascends into the sky just before the Sun. It does look radiant. We are lucky to have clear skies this morning.'

Brady could do without the poetic rhetoric. 'Ok, just point me in the right direction.'

Tyrone steered Brady around, and Brady tried to concentrate. Tyrone pointed and said, 'You see that bright star?'

'Yep.'

'Look down a little from there, and you'll see a box shape.'

'I got it.'

'Well, that is the torso of Hercules - another legendary strong man like yourself.' He joked. 'Train your binoculars on where the heart of Hercules would be, and you should be able to make out a bright star-like object with a hazy tail behind it.'

Brady shouted, 'I see it.' He added, 'It ain't moving, though.'
Tyrone smiled, 'In space terms, it's driving up to the doorway of our house. But in our way of measuring things, it's about eighteen thousand miles away.'

'Oh.'

Tyrone continued, 'However, it's travelling at about fifteen thousand miles per hour.'

'Wow, that's real fast, so that means...'

Tyrone wanted to say splash-down, but he knew this softer term wouldn't excite Brady. 'That means in just over an hour, a hurtling, gigantic piece of space junk will crash into the Pacific. It's a once in a lifetime show.' Tyrone and Brady took turns with the binoculars until it became clearly visible to the naked eye. They both watched it grow in the night sky with a sense of awe and wonder. Brady keenly enjoyed the sense of anticipation as he imagined this inter-galactic mash-up.

Then it seemed to snowball. Tyrone suddenly became anxious. 'I don't like the look of this. The trajectory is all wrong.' He went to run away, but Brady caught hold of him. Tyrone screamed, 'I think it's coming straight for us.'

Brady scoffed, 'We've got a NanoShell™ protecting us. I've seen how strong these things are. Stay with me and be a man.'

Lilith had just finished her shift at the Ocean View Café, she scanned the cliff-top and saw Brady, she watched in a mixture of horror and awe, as the skinny black guy with glasses put his arms over his head in fear, while Brady Mahone stretched out extravagantly in a Christ-like pose, summoning…

Neither man had any time to escape anyway. Tyrone flinched and hunched up into a ball, while Brady raised his arms to greet the astral traveller, and he whooped and hollered as the International Space Station crashed and burned right in front of him. The hot metal and flames erupted as the NanoShell™ rose into the sky to meet it. 'Oh man, this is some show…woohoo!' He heard large explosions and crashing sounds coming from behind him. He whirled to see the International Space Station's main body cut a wrecking swathe through East Encinitas. He stopped cheering as he heard the screams and panic of the Trad families who lived there. He also heard the sounds of excited laughter coming from the beaches below him. *I woulda done the same, but they can't see what I see.*

Lilith watched Brady laughing maniacally, and she ran away from him as fast as she could.

Tyrone unwound his body and began to take in the devastation of the Trad side of East Encinitas, but then his attention turned to his primary concern. He checked the westside and saw that it was intact and the NanoShell™ had held firm against its crucial stress test. He felt an immense sense of pride in the technology of his Green saviours. And then he felt the Earth tremble. 'Brady, did you feel that?'

He hoped Brady hadn't noticed, so he could give in to denial, but Brady said, firmly. 'Yes.'

'It could be the crash, maybe a wave in the ground which only just reached us?'

I don't survive by waiting and seeing. 'It might have triggered a quake.' Brady retrieved his sleeping bag and headed to the car. He pushed through the frozen crowd as they seemed to still be in shock and didn't know how to react. 'Get your ass in the car, now.' He shouted to get Tyrone to move, 'If there's an earthquake, then the Highways might be hit.' Tyrone was rooted to the spot. Brady wondered if this was a defensive reflex of the Red NanoSuits™. He shouted into Tyrone's face like a Drill Sergeant from the Hell Division. 'Get your fucking skinny arse in the car fucking now - that's if you want to see your family again.'

Tyrone stared at Brady and then appeared to awake from his nightmare. 'Yes, sir, I mean, Yes…'

Brady was already running to the car, and Tyrone ran fast to catch up with him. He jumped into the Hearse next to Brady, and Brady expertly reversed the car and spun it around at high speed to face inland and began to drive through the unharmed streets of West Encinitas. He had to drive carefully to avoid the families, who had been awoken, and had headed outdoors to investigate what was going on. Brady flung his arms extravagantly to encourage them out of his way. 'Move it Grandma…Out of the fucking way, cunt face…Thanks for fucking nothing you slow-assed, no good, son of a whore…'

241

He turned into a major road heading East and then he saw a sight that he would never forget. The ground shook violently, and a massive crack in the road began to open. It was already a few feet wide when Brady decided to leap over the void in the Hearse. He put his foot to the floor and drove fearlessly at the gaping hole and flew across it. The car landed heavily on the other side, and something was caught in the wheelrim. He could hear and feel it. He got out of the FusionCar™, and he used his strength to unbend the material of the body of the Hearse with his bare hands. Tyrone panicked and jumped out of the Hearse to go to Brady.

The Earth heaved, and they both fell. They looked up to see a house crash into the hole the Earthquake had created, and a whole family was swept away into the void as they tried to dive out of the way of their collapsing home and the trees in their front garden followed. Tyrone screamed, 'Brady, we have to help them.' Tyrone wobbled as the hole became a cavernous void behind them. Tyrone saw one of the family, on a ledge, hundreds of feet below him. 'Brady, they can survive any fall in a RedSuit™, but they'll need help to get them back to safety. Otherwise, they'll starve down there.'

Brady said, 'Fuck 'em. We ain't got time for this shit.'

'But Brady, there were children down there.' He shouted to try and be heard above the roar of the continued quake and buildings' crashing.

'No. I'm a Trad, and I've witnessed thousands of the dead and the dying. Hell, you just see them as rubbish to decompose and be rid of. Fuck you. Time to learn what it feels like on this side of the track. Now get back in the Hearse, or I'll leave you here. Go be a hero, if that's what you want, but Brady Mahone is outta here.' He stared balefully at Tyrone. 'Last chance, what's it gonna be, boy?'

Tyrone got into the Hearse and slammed the door in the act of useless defiance. It wasn't going to hurt Brady's feelings. He was utterly focussed on his escape route. The timing of the banging of the car confused both passengers for a split second as a blinding white flash, and a vast mushroom cloud erupted in the distance. The wave swept across the land in front of them, it hit East Encinitas and then crashed against the NanoShell™. The Earthquake still rumbled and tore up the ground, but Brady sensed it was temporarily losing its power. He stared at the mushroom cloud, he struggled to get his words out, 'What the fuck was that?'

Tyrone couldn't reply for a few seconds, but then said, 'The FusionPlant™ has been destroyed.' He watched and didn't believe his eyes. He saw Trads running into the West-side of Encinitas. 'The Shell™ has failed.'

Brady said, 'Are we going to die of radiation sickness? Isn't that what happens - when one of those things blow? If you don't get turned into a burned-out shadow, then you die of radiation poisoning?'

Brady asking a science question seemed to bring Tyrone out of his spell. 'No. That used to happen with Fission-powered nuclear reactors. This is Fusion, it will have radiation, but not as much. We have to get out of here.' As he said it, the Earthquake stopped, almost as quickly as it started. It made the town seem eerily quiet, except for the Trads who were looting the shops and houses of the spoilt brats of the Green Community of Encinitas. Tyrone added, 'Your FusionCar™ has a sensitivity setting.'

Brady sneered, 'Oh, how delightful, my good man.'

Tyrone grimaced, 'It means as you drive it will assist you by scanning the front of the vehicle for animals and insects.' He knew this information wouldn't be of interest to Brady, so he added before Brady could retort, 'It will also self-steer around obstacles and holes if it senses that you've not noticed them. It might help in getting us safely out of here.'

Brady visibly calmed, 'That will be useful.' He asked, 'What's likely to happen next?'

'There will certainly be many substantial aftershocks to follow - mini-earthquakes.'

'Do you know when? You know, in the next few minutes, or hours?'

'I really don't know, but they could appear at any time over the next few weeks.'

They continued to drive slowly through Encinitas on Brady's escape *out of Dodge*. As the word spread about the riches on offer on the West-side they saw more and more desperate Trads running to join them before all the good stuff was taken. All the while, Brady was checking his mirrors for the sight of the mushroom cloud, as if he were adding it to a collection of his more precious memories.

They had many obstacles, holes and rifts in the roads to navigate, but they finally found Highway 5. Brady said, 'What about that other thing, y'know, the mushroom cloud?'

'I know you're worried about your Trad friends, but they'll have to fend for themselves. It's a strict policy on non-intervention. We get disqualified if we give in to the temptation to help them.'

I ain't getting into a discussion. I ain't no politician. 'What about the Greens? Do their NanoSuits™ still work? Y'know after the big-ass nuclear explosion?'

'Yes. They are powered by the individual wearer's energy. Individual vehicles, like this, run off their own power source. Those guys will have to find a new home, but other communities will be duty bound to accommodate them. It's the law.'

Brady laughed, 'There's gonna be some pretty crowded places along here. It always causes troubles when the immigrants invade.'

Tyrone said sniffily, 'I don't think we see things through the same lens as the Trads.'

'If you say so.' Brady had a thought, 'Say, kid, could you do me a favour? I'd do it myself, but I'm driving.'

'Sure. What do you want me to do?'

'I want you to write down all that happened back there in Encinitas. Under your seat, you'll find my Order Book. There's a pen and some spare paper in the back. It'll give you something to do. It's a long drive back.' He added, 'I don't care if you write the stuff you think makes me look bad. I don't care. It ain't for me. I know what happened.'

Tyrone said, 'You're not a bad person. I'm not saying I agree with you, but I do hear you.'

Tyrone had a pattern of stopping to think for a while, then writing furiously, then stopping again, then followed by more writing. For Brady, this meant Tyrone wasn't talking, and he enjoyed having a little quiet time. Occasionally, they came across some huge rifts in the Highway, which meant a detour to find another way around them, but mostly, he drove for miles with his thoughts, keeping him otherwise occupied. He wondered how fast the news of this event would travel. There was no Internet. No TV. He hadn't even seen a newspaper at even a local level. All communications seemed to be word of mouth or at the big town meetings. He guessed that a disaster like this would shake the faith in Bodhi Sattva and Sattva Systems™ at the very least. He asked, almost absent-mindedly, 'Y'know you said those people who fell down the crack in the Earth would starve?'

'Yes.'

'Would they die of thirst as well?'

'At the moment. Yes'

'What do you mean? At the moment?'

'The new GreenSuits™ will extend the recycling of water and food exponentially in the body. You could even survive under water for days. It will help dramatically in Operation Clean-Up of the Oceans.'

He had a sudden recollection of the Bear's sermon. *Still, at least I know these fucks aren't indestructible. And their power supply can be got at. Although, I ain't got the power to cause no earthquakes.* He chuckled, but when he thought of his friend, the Bear, he smiled. *The Greens have been a profitable business for Brady Mahone. I'd be cutting off my nose to spite my face if I hurt them real bad.* He laughed, and Tyrone looked up from his writing assignment but decided Brady was laughing to himself. Brady had a vision of drowning Siddha. *I know he hates me, but one day I'm gonna drown him like a cat in a bag.*

Brady pulled the Hearse over into the bus stop outside East McFarland on Highway 99. He said to Tyrone, 'Hey, I'll have those notes you been writing, now.'
Tyrone straightened his papers out and put some last-minute page numbers on them. He passed the pages over to him. Brady examined Tyrone's notes, and it reminded him of the sort of writing which the loser geeks used to do on the few occasions Brady actually attended school. He joked, 'I hope you're not waiting for me to grade them.'

'Only if you give me an A. Otherwise, I'd rather not know.' Tyrone laughed.

'I'm sure my friend the Professor, would have given you an A - but he's dead now.' He smiled, but Tyrone could detect the hurt Brady felt with this memory.

Brady strode out of the car and unclipped the timetable holder and packed the bundle of papers tightly behind the Perspex cover. He double-checked to ensure they were held securely before returning to Tyrone and the Hearse.

He drove away from McFarland, but after rounding the bend after a couple of minutes, he slowed the car down to check out what the Green Work Crew was working on. Tyrone knew instantly, but he didn't say anything. Brady rode past, slowly and watched them spraying a mound of approximately twenty former East McFarland residents.

244

14.THE FALL-OUT

Cain and Siddha were having a meal in their West McFarland Green Community home when they got the call on their Sattva Systems™ Satellite phone asking them to head over to Boulder Creek to meet up with Bodhi. They had felt an Earth tremor earlier in the evening, and they wondered if something had happened.

For Cain, the request had not been particularly unusual over the last few years, now that he had become the Western Seaboard Regional Disciple, but for Siddha, this was a rare honour. He said, 'I know I pushed it too hard with Bodhi on my last meeting, but you know how much I dislike and mistrust that Brady Mahone.'

Cain smiled as he headed out to the small FusionPlane™ with his oldest friend and comrade Siddha. 'Bodhi wasn't angry with you. I've never seen him lose his temper. I think it was that you weren't telling him anything that he didn't already know.' He added, 'I keep him informed of all I can find out about Brady, for good or ill.'

They clambered into the ceramic, cream-coloured machine with the Sattva Systems™ logo in moss green embossed into the side. The plane lifted off vertically and soundlessly - except for the discreet sonic boom.

Soon they were flying above Highway 99 en-route to Boulder Creek. The aircraft tracked the Highway route as flights outside the road framework, were not allowed, yet. Siddha asked, 'Why have I received the order to attend?'

Cain laughed, 'I've never thought of Bodhi as the kind of guy who issues orders.' He added, 'I've always been asked, and I give my time freely. Some people refuse to talk to him, and Bodhi doesn't hold grudges or dish out penalties or disciplinary action.'

'Who would refuse to deal with Bodhi?' Siddha said, disbelievingly.

'He frequently has heated discussions with his scientists and engineers. *They* have heated discussions, but Bodhi simply listens, agrees, disagrees, or agrees to disagree, his colleagues are the ones who let their tempers get the better of them. Suffice to say, a course of action is always settled upon. As long as the work feeds into the hundred-year plan, then that is what matters most to Bodhi.'

'Does that explain the frequent delays to the upgrades to the NanoSuits™?'

'Yes. You see, with your situation, you don't give him any new insights. Therefore, he doesn't need to see you again. It's not personal, and it's not a snub. However, with regards to his scientists and engineers, they always have new developments and progress in bringing to him.'

'What about those who don't want to talk to him?'

Cain smiled, 'Then Bodhi will talk with their colleagues and assistants instead.'

Siddha thought for a moment, 'Then I wonder why he wants me to visit him tonight?'

It didn't take long to reach Boulder Creek, but they found themselves in a queue of traffic. They watched as the FusionPlanes™ dropped down into the Sattva Fusion-

Plane™ Park. Cain said, 'It looks like we are not the only visitors.'

The queue moved slowly in front of them, while other planes lined up behind them. After a few minutes, Cain brought the FusionPlane™ into land.

Sissy Garcia came out to greet them, 'Hello Cain. Welcome Siddha. Bodhi is waiting for you.' She was heavily pregnant. Pregnancy was becoming a rare occurrence as it was an expensive undertaking, as a parent had to demonstrate a commitment to the planet before bringing into the world another human life. Green credits earned - offset the resources a new life would consume until they were old enough to contribute themselves. She stretched out a slender arm to guide the way.

Siddha looked around at the other planes coming into land, 'Just us two. I thought we were going to be a part of a gathering.'

Sissy smiled, 'No. He wants to speak with you two alone. I'll be sitting in to take notes.' *Although, I'll no doubt have to intervene when Bodhi strays onto his weaker areas.* She thought.

'We're not in any trouble, are we?' Siddha still struggled with the concept that he was talking to the Governor of California, even though that was many years ago.

Sissy laughed warmly, 'Not at all, my friend.' She added, 'If you would care to follow me, then I'll take you to him.'

They passed through the Main Hall, and they both looked up at the giant hanging banner displaying the thirteen promises, written in the hand of the revered Green Warrior - Glenarvon Cole. Cain and Siddha followed dutifully until they came to a small drab office, furnished only with a functional desk. A couple of stackable chairs were out, in readiness for them. Siddha looked around and spotted a couple of stacks of chairs in the corner of the room. Sissy dragged down another chair for herself and readied herself with a notebook and pen. 'Bodhi won't be long. He hates keeping people waiting, but it's been a busy evening.'

Siddha looked at the austere desk, covered with a clear screen - there were a couple of document files, the top one was labelled, Nano-properties of Enzyme Replication and Self Replication. Cain whispered, 'He doesn't believe in ostentation or material exhibitions to demonstrate ego. In the old world, he used to be ridiculed for it. He used to say that it was his job to save the planet and not plunder Her for his own gain. I loved him for it.'

Siddha noted that Bodhi's chair was just the same as his own.

Bodhi glided in. He was dressed in a simple grey tracksuit with grey sneakers with no logos. He was tall and athletically built, he was slightly bronzed, and his bald head reflected the overhead lighting. He looked at them with his friendly brown eyes and reached out to shake their hands. He shook hands with them both in a firm but friendly manner. 'Hello, Cain, and to you, Siddha, my friend, I hope you are keeping well.'

He sat down opposite them. "Have you heard the news from this morning, coming out of Southern California?' He put in a Black File into the side of his desk, and a map of California appeared. He zoomed in to the Encinitas area, while he awaited the reply from his guests. The delay in their response suggested to him that they didn't know.

246

Siddha and Cain looked at each other, Cain said, 'No. What's happened?'

'There has been a series of disasters in Southern California, centred on the Encinitas area. Before I go any further, I want you to hear me. My top scientists have confirmed that these are utterly explainable. They are not a supernatural event. Do you understand?'

Siddha said, 'I think so.' He shuffled and re-examined his chosen appearance, as he suddenly felt as if he looked too much like a businessman in his black suit and open necked white silk shirt. He believed that not adopting a tie would make him look a little informal, but not too much. In Cain's company, he was used to Cain only ever wearing his white robe and bare feet - even when he adopted the Yellow™, he only changed from a cloth robe to the *appearance* of a cloth robe. The Yellow™ was wasted on Cain. But now, in the presence of the most important person in the world, as far as siddha was concerned, he looked at the simple grey tracksuit and sneakers, and he felt pretentious. He started the changes from his feet, as Bodhi couldn't see him below the desk's level. He changed to sandals. He then switched to khaki-coloured slacks, and when Bodhi glanced away from him to look at Cain, Siddha adjusted the sleeves on his white shirt to short from long, and he lost the collars to a grandad-collar. He wondered if he should echo the Polynesian skin colour of Bodhi, from his own brown skin, but thought this would be a step too far, but he did add stubble to his clean-shaven Asian visage. He was lost for a moment in his self-study and appreciation and realised he wasn't concentrating on what was being said.

Bodhi took a breath and said, 'The International Space Station came to the end of its life cycle and fell to Earth as predicted. It should have landed fifty miles into the Pacific, but for some unknown reason its trajectory altered by a fraction of a degree and crash-landed in Encinitas.'

Cain said, 'That's awful.'

Bodhi raised his hand, slowly, 'That's not all, my friend. There's much more. Our scientists believe this triggered the much overdue Earthquake event on the San Andreas Fault, which, in turn, ruptured the foundations of the Rancho Santa Fe FusionPlant™.' He paused, 'It exploded, and took out the NanoShell™ protecting West Encinitas. We have a mass evacuation of Greens heading north because the southern escape routes are severely damaged. And we have the neighbouring Trad population looting West Encinitas.'

'How many have died?'

Bodhi looked at Sissy, who sat behind his guests - but deliberately in his eye-line - diligently making notes. She looked at him and smiled as if to reassure him that he was doing the right thing. Bodhi looked away for a moment and said sombrely, 'Many thousands of people from the Traditional Cultures have sadly perished, and several hundred of our Green Community members have been reported missing.'

'And the FusionReactor™ site? Surely, that's a huge problem?'

Bodhi said softly, 'The FusionReactors™ are not nearly as dangerous as the old fission reactors. Safety, as well as clean energy, were the reasons we adopted them. However, the debris will be highly radioactive for a considerable period. We have teams on the ground and a fleet of HeavyLoaders™ heading to the Plant. We can contain this, but the area will not be used again for housing. We will decontaminate it, and re-wild it ahead of schedule.'

Siddha was suitably honoured to be involved in this inner sanctum at Sattva Systems™, but he couldn't figure out why he had been invited. He listened intently, as he didn't feel qualified enough to comment upon anything that the great Bodhi Sattva uttered.

Cain looked at Bodhi with his crystal green eyes and said, 'With you, the situation is in good hands. What is it that we can help you with?'

'We have a problem with our friend, Brady Mahone.'

Siddha spat out, 'He's no friend of mine. I think he should have been killed off...'

This is NanoRespect™, a trademark of Sattva Systems™. Your stress levels indicate a threat of violence has been detected. Please refrain. This is your first warning. The welfare of our consumers is our highest priority.

Bodhi smiled gently. It was the action most likely to have a calming effect on Siddha. 'Do accept my apologies, my friend. The Security Protocols™ devices around me are far more sensitive than you have in your home communities. This isn't to protect me from others - it's to protect me from myself. I cannot impose rules on our people if I cannot live up to them.' He watched Siddha's chest rise and fall more slowly. He continued, 'I have been known to have had some heated discussions with my team, and I need to stay calm. Otherwise, I would make hasty decisions which would have a detrimental effect on my project. I hope you understand.'

Siddha said, 'I do. I still wish to apologise. I've never understood why we have pussy-footed around Brady Mahone.'

Bodhi smiled, 'He is an important part of my plan, and he must be protected. If I told you that I need you to trust me and that there is a bigger picture here - would you do that? Could you bring yourself to trust my judgement, even if I told you that Brady Mahone needed a friend now, and you are the most qualified to do this, for me?'

Siddha shuffled, 'If this is a test of my loyalty to you, then of course. I will do as you ask of me, freely.'

Cain glanced at Siddha with a look that informed him that he hadn't understood what was happening. Bodhi watched the interaction between the two friends while he waited for the inevitable follow-up question. It was a question even he would struggle to answer, as it was so outlandish that he hadn't considered a situation like this cropping up.

Siddha tried to resist uttering the two words that undermine his desire for demonstrating his unquestioning fealty to Bodhi Sattva. He looked at Cain, hoping that he would intervene, and save him from this dilemma, but Cain was deep in thought. Finally, Siddha uttered, 'But why?'

Bodhi's shoulders sagged, and he breathed out a deep sigh, 'The fall-out of the physical effects of the disaster are relatively straight-forward. I'm a scientist at heart.' He laughed, 'Is that a contradiction of terms?' Sissy laughed, Cain and Siddha looked around and smiled, they had forgotten she was there. They didn't want to laugh in case it wasn't a rhetorical question. Bodhi continued, 'We seem to have a spiritual fall-out which could cause our plan even more harm, in the long run.'

Cain said in an almost priestly manner, 'What is it that troubles you?' His crystal green eyes shone like those of a saint, 'Please, unburden yourself.'

Bodhi said, 'The word is spreading that Brady Mahone is some sort of anti-Christ figure who will destroy the Greens and their shelters.'

Siddha breathed slowly, deliberately, trying not to invoke the Security Protocols™. 'He is not indestructible, he is a man, a Trad. He could easily be made to…go away.' He added, 'I know we do not harm any sentient creatures, not even Trads, but we are intelligent people, we could come up with something between us.' He looked up, half-expecting to be smothered in SecurityFilm™ for his words, but nothing happened. He let out a loud sigh of relief.

Bodhi rubbed his big hands over his bald pate, extinguishing the LED reflections for a moment and then they reappeared like stars from behind the clouds. 'He is part of my plans. I need him - alive. I need you to break the spell of the myth surrounding him while keeping the man, intact.'

Siddha, unconsciously brought his hand to his face as he tried to understand, but he couldn't, 'I will do whatever is in my power to help, but I know this man will come back to haunt you? I hate to question your judgment, but you do see that - don't you?'

'Yes. Siddha. I see, and I want it to happen. It is the order of things to come. It is part of a chemical reaction which must occur to complete the project. The situation which has evolved around the Encinitas incident and Brady's role in it, is adding too much of the Brady Mahone compound to the mix, he has become too potent, and you have to bring him back to the levels I require.'

'Ok. So, Brady Mahone needs to be pulled down a peg or two?'

Cain sensed that Bodhi was becoming frustrated with Siddha. He was close to Bodhi and knew that when Bodhi used scientific analogies to get his point across, it was time to change approach. He knew Bodhi would prefer to discuss facts. 'Could you tell us what happened in connection with Brady Mahone? This will aid us in our planning on how to neutralise these unwanted side-effects.'

Bodhi looked visibly relieved to be asked to report and not to engage in needless wordplay, 'We have the facts on what happened. The International Space Station fell to Earth, as expected, by the people who still study astronomical events. However, it landed a few seconds early, and the trajectory took it into the path of Encinitas, instead of safely crashing about fifty miles off the coast and into the Pacific Ocean - it really should have been hundreds of miles…' He put up his hand to deter any questions, 'Brady Mahone was there, and he told a woman who worked in the Ocean View Café, that he would bring fire from the skies and hell on Earth for the Greens. She wasn't sure, but it was something like that. He told her to come and see for herself at 6am. She said that when she did, she saw him adopt a Christ-like pose and summoned the fire to him, and he laughed as he destroyed Encinitas and the Nano-Shells™ with his power of command. I needn't tell you the significance of the date and time.'

Cain whispered, 'Six, six, six.'

'It is a coincidence. My engineers think it might be a sick joke by the engineers at NASA or even the astronauts left stranded after our Revolution. They all died long ago. It might even be the lack of maintenance on the Station, which caused the change of dates and trajectory over time. The outcome is that the faith in the communities has been dented by the gossip, suggesting that Satan, in the form of Brady Mahone, is coming to destroy the Green Communities as a revenge for the delinquent Trads.'

Siddha thought. *It could be true. I could believe that. I've seen through Brady Mahone. He's a Trad, but one who can infiltrate the Greens. He leads our people into temptation, but now he has shown his true face and his malevolent power.*

'I want you to tell the people that he is no threat.'

Siddha was lost in his thoughts and didn't hear this properly. 'I'm sorry, what did you say?'

Bodhi repeated, 'I want you to tell the communities, that you will visit, on my behalf, that Brady Mahone is your friend, that you trust him, and that he is no threat to anybody. I want them to continue to trade with him, exactly as before.'

You ask too much. He is the Devil confirmed, and you want me to befriend him, and become his apologist?

'And you Cain, my friend. I want you to accompany Siddha and tell of the peaceful future to come. The hard work will come to an end, and then there will be years of rest and harmony to follow. They only need to keep their faith in me, to follow the rules, and not to be led into temptation. Maybe, you could take Lizzie along with you. Many know that she shared some time with Brady.'

Cain said, 'Lizzie hates Brady. Everybody knows that. She still hasn't forgiven me.'

'That's exactly why she is perfectly placed to persuade them that Brady is a simple man.'

Siddha growled inside. *Lizzie has shared the Devil's bed. Whore.* He remembered to bring down his stress levels. He concentrated on his breathing and his heart rate.

'I will reward you all for this act of faith in my judgment.' Bodhi turned to Siddha and looked at him as if he could see his thoughts transcribed upon his face. 'This is the test of a lifetime, for you, my friend. Do you have faith in me, over your doubts about Brady?'

He wanted to believe, but he knew he would struggle with his allotted task, but he still said, 'Yes. My faith is with you.'

Cain said, 'If you don't mind me challenging your approach, but I would handle the whole situation, differently.'

'I don't understand.'

'There's a humanitarian crisis here, first and foremost. We must handle this with utmost urgency. The rumour-mill can be contained at the same time. Can I demonstrate?'

Bodhi looked over at Sissy, who nodded vigorously. He said to Cain, 'What would you do?'

Cain moved over to Bodhi's side of the desk and Siddha came over to his side. Cain looked over at Sissy, but said to Bodhi, 'We haven't had anything like this to deal with in years. As an ex-Governor of California, Sissy should be involved. I know I am the Regional Disciple, but here the Division of Labour applies. I could do with her invaluable input.'

Bodhi looked at Sissy, sheepishly, but she roared with laughter. 'Oh Bodhi, human resources is never going to be your strong suit. Stick with what your most qualified for like ecology and biology and leave this to us. You know I love you, but don't tell my partner I said that.' She laughed again. She looked over at Cain, 'What did you have in mind?'

'Where are the evacuees?'

She focussed on the map, 'There's a huge rift across Highway 5 that opened up, swallowing the Batiquitos Lagoon that's forced them to move on foot, eastwards.'

He wanted Bodhi to stay involved. 'Bodhi? I don't know how far the effects of the FusionPlant™ explosion will stretch for. Do you know?'

'The effects will dissipate quickly. Why?'

'Ramona to the east, is a Trad town that's near to its official abandonment threshold. If we displace the remaining Trads, then instead of re-wilding Ramona, we could turn it to a Green Community for the displaced Greens from West Encinitas.'

Bodhi said firmly, 'It's against our plan. We have a plan for a reason. I promised all abandoned land to Her.'

Cain paused, partly to stay calm. 'The displaced are heading north, into Brady Mahone's territory. It could cause disruption to the Green Communities on these routes if they are ordered to make room in the already crowded properties. It wasn't what we promised the people.'

Sissy intervened, 'Bodhi, he's right. We serve Her, but we have a duty to look after our citizens.'

'I do look after them. Right at this very moment, I am working night and day on a project to give every one of our people, who were with us at the dawn of the Revolution, the chance to live a healthy life to a minimum age of one-hundred years.'

Sissy put her arm around Bodhi's shoulder, and her long auburn hair touched his face, she said softly, 'There's not much point in living to one-hundred if you live in a crowded home and in poverty.'

Cain had never seen Bodhi sulk before, and this certainly wasn't what Siddha expected to see. Finally, Bodhi said, 'Ok. Do what you have to do. I just hope She will forgive me.'

Cain said, 'It will need a lot of resources.'

Sissy saved Bodhi from having to answer, 'Whatever you need.'

'We'll need to clear Ramona of the remaining Trads. Then we'll need a fleet of HeavyLoaders™ to ferry the evacuees to Ramona. Once there, we'd have to incentivise them to make a new Green Community from scratch, from the FusionPower™ supplies through to the erection of NanoShells™.'

Sissy added, 'And we'll need to send in food and check the water supplies aren't contaminated. Leave it to me. You'll have everything you need.'

Siddha looked on impressed at seeing his old friend at work, in a way he hadn't seen before.

Cain sought to appease Bodhi, even though he didn't consider it particularly important in the current crisis, but it was to Bodhi. *Who am I to question Bodhi after all he has done for us? He has always known the way.* 'There are bound to be a few who made it out quickly, especially if they had access to FusionVehicles™, who may have made it to other Green Communities to the north - and we'll get to them. However, if we can keep the citizens of West Encinitas together, we could talk to them en masse. I could address them in a town meeting and try to put a lid on this Brady Mahone nonsense. It makes logistical sense.'

Sissy said, 'Cain's right.'

'Before this, I had Brady exactly where I needed him…' Bodhi breathed in deeply before uttering, 'Ok.' He stood up and left. They guessed he was heading to the factory floor as his grey tracksuit turned into the Sattva Systems™ cream overalls.

Sissy said, 'Good work, Cain. In the old days, we often ran through Earthquake and other disaster scenarios, but you came to grips with the problem. I would have been proud to have you on my team.'

Cain smiled and partially bowed. Siddha intervened, 'But what about the Brady situation? I hate the idea of becoming his apologist and making excuses for him.'

Sissy smiled, 'I've lost count of the times when I have doubted Bodhi's plans, especially before the Green Revolution. I used to lay in my bed, thinking I had gone completely insane, but he was always right. Always. Do not lose your faith in Bodhi. Don't let this Brady Mahone Alpha-Trad male disrupt you.'

15. BAITING THE BEAR

Brady wanted to drop Tyrone off and then head home after the long trip, but Tyrone insisted on him staying for dinner. He had a fantastic story to tell and wanted Brady there to back him up on the facts.

As Tyrone opened the door, the noisy house, full of people, all fell silent at the sight of Brady coming in alongside Tyrone.

Samuel Beardon the Third stormed over and yelled defiantly into the face of Brady, 'I should smite you down where you stand, Satan.' He raised his fist and went to strike Brady, but the Security Protocols™ smothered him and froze him into place. Brady looked at the snarling features of the Bear in utter bewilderment.

Alicia came over to them and threw her arms around Tyrone, 'Thank God, you're safe. We thought you'd been killed?'

'If it wasn't for Brady, I might still be there. He saved me.' Tyrone looked at the frozen figure of the Bear, and said, 'Can he still hear us?'

Brady said, 'Yes. I've been done over by that goo before. He'll be fine. He'll just have to wait for someone to release him.' The other residents left their meals half-eaten and retreated to their rooms. An old lady held a silver cross out, pointing it at Brady as she walked backwards up the stairs as if she was protecting those ahead of her. She looked at the cross quizzically, as if it wasn't working when it should have done. 'Have you not seen this stuff before?' Brady said, pointing at the Security-Film™ encasing the Bear, and levitating him just above the ground.

Alicia said warily, taking a step back from him, 'Of course, we know what it is. It's just never had to be used here, before.'

Tyrone said to Brady, 'I'm starving. What about you?' He said impatiently, as if his Uncle Sam was spoiling his fun, but at the same time, knowing he was utterly safe from harm.

'Sure.' Brady looked at the Bear, and joked, 'I don't suppose he'll be giving us one of his specials.' He laughed alone.

Alicia whispered to Tyrone, 'Daddy was in Boulder Creek when the news broke about the Earthquake. He was doing a sermon with the workers when one of the scientists rushed in and told them all. They are saying that Brady made it happen.'

Tyrone roared with laughter, he looked at Brady, and then at Alicia and laughed so much that he began to cry. 'Oh, that is so funny.' He continued laughing. 'Oh my. Brady made it happen! The scientist said…and he calls himself a scientist!' Tears rolled down his face as he looked at Brady. 'Hey man, it's all your fault. You made the International Space Station crash land - all on your own.'

The laughter infected Brady, and he laughed with him, 'I sure did. It must be these super-powers I have.' He looked at the Bear still wrapped up in SecurityFilm™ and said, 'Looks like I got you with my super-power, my friend.' He uttered a ghostly noise and waved his hands like a magician at the Bear. He put his arms around Tyrone and said, 'I've had a blast, today. Now, where's that food you promised.'

Alicia intervened, 'I'll get it. You two sit down.' She welcomed the excuse to remove herself from the madness playing out before her eyes. She knew her Father would want her to throw him out, but Tyrone treated him like a best buddy - and Tyrone, her geeky cousin, hadn't had a proper friend in the whole of his life. She could hear the good-natured banter from the kitchen as she prepared a simple but hearty meal for them.

She then heard the sound of raised voices coming from Shako's room, the old woman seemed to be imploring her son, Tauri, not to do...she couldn't make out exactly what. She knew the stories about Brady would alarm her family, as they used to be devout followers of the Native American Church. She wasn't an expert, but she knew they believed that Jesus and the Great Spirit were one and the same - she'd never asked about the Devil. Alicia heard a crash from Shako's living quarters, and then her pan of vegetables boiled over. 'Shit, shit.' She turned the pan down but heard Tauri's footsteps racing down the stairs. She ran out of the kitchen to see the tall Tauri brandishing the family's large ceremonial cross and waving it in the direction of Brady.

Brady raised his bulk from out of the chair. He heard Shako calling for help from an upstairs window. Brady walked up to Tauri, he was a big guy but wasn't known as a fighter, Brady feinted to his left, and as Tauri flinched, Brady effortlessly took the cross from him. 'You're a lucky lad, that you found me in one of my better moods, and in the company of friends. Now, be a good boy and go back to your room, stay out of my way, and I promise, I'll leave after dinner.' Tauri stood aghast. Brady examined the cross, in the manner of the unofficial jewellery expert he was - in another life. 'English hallmarks. Very old, probably brought across with the Missionaries. I'm guessing this used to be in a church at some point.' He ran his fingers over it, 'Solid silver - very nice.' He added, 'In the old days, I would have kept this, but it has no value to me in this world. I tell you what. I'll keep it with me for safe keeping.' He kissed the cross and then put it on the table. 'We wouldn't want anyone to get hurt with this - would we?'

Brady barked, 'Answer me, boy.'

Tauri stuttered, 'N - No.'

'Then scram and let me eat in peace.'

Brady, Tyrone and Alicia ate in relative silence, punctuated with a smattering of small-talk and pleasantries. Brady wanted to make the point that he wasn't going to be ejected by a Green stranger. If Tyrone, Alicia or the Bear had asked him to leave. He would have departed with little fuss. Tyrone had invited him, and he felt duty-bound to stay.

After about an hour, Rhea arrived. Brady smiled, 'Hey, how are you? It's great to see you. Did anyone tell you that I'd tried to contact you?'

Rhea ignored him. She went to the suspended figure of the Reverend Samuel Beardon the Third and released him from the Security Protocols™. He thanked her, 'God bless you.' He looked at Brady. 'It's time you left. Don't ever come back. You are not welcome here.' He looked to the heavens, 'Please, Lord, help us remove this demon from our home. Out Brady, out.'

'Oh, come on, man. Have you lost your mind? It's me, Brady, your friend. I haven't…'

Rhea said coldly, 'You heard what the man said. You are barred from entering the Green Community of San Martin. I imagine you'll struggle to find a welcome anywhere, now that your true face has been revealed.'

Tyrone said, 'I thought it was the young who are warned against taking drugs. What are you on, lady?'

The Bear said, 'Tyrone. Enough. You don't know what we're dealing with.' Alicia put her arm around him and said, 'He's right.'

Shako and the rest of her family assembled on the stairs to witness; and offered the support they dearly wished wouldn't be required.

Brady took an apple from the table and took a bite. 'Ok.' He headed out the door, crunching at his apple. Before he left, he threw the half-eaten apple back into the room. He looked at each of them in turn and said, 'See ya around - losers.' He slammed the door behind him with enough force to make the house shudder.

16. ALONE TIME

Brady took the drive east for a while across small roads and dirt tracks. He used to believe he had a sixth sense for when the cops were onto him. Later, when they had put him behind bars - again. He would conclude that his sixth sense was unreliable. Here he was again, staying away from the main roads as he tried to digest what had occurred to him in San Martin. He was sorry to leave them all behind. He'd never got particularly close to Alicia, but he thought the Bear could have been a long-term friend and ally. *Hell, I even began to like the stringy dweeb, Tyrone. He was alright.*

He couldn't understand why the reaction of Rhea hurt him. *That was cold, man.* Brady had never met a woman who he wanted to belong to before. He had mates and male acquaintances he'd treated as pseudo-brothers before; at times he would have laid down his life for them - especially if it had been them or the cops. Brady thought on this more as he drove deep into the night. He remembered female associates who were close to him, but they were accomplices. Rhea had made an impression that he didn't recognise.

He thought back to the last time he felt anything like this, and all he could come back to, was when he had a puppy-dog crush on Analise in the second grade. *Yes, that's it, it kinda hurt but felt good, all at the same time. Fuck, this broad has really got to old Brady Mahone.*

After driving aimlessly for a while, with a series of switchbacks, in case he was followed - he wasn't, and deep down, he knew it. He finally picked up Highway 99 and headed south to go home. He had come out near Madera, north of Fresno.

He drove over to the Green Community area, but soon, wished he hadn't. They had lookouts trying to spot anybody matching the description of Brady Mahone. As he approached, the townsfolk gathered around the hastily erected roadblock. Many were holding out crosses while still in their nightclothes, they looked like they were freezing cold, even though he knew deep down they weren't, but they soon warmed up when Brady got out of the Hearse and approached on foot. At first, a lone voice shouted, 'Out, Brady out!'

Charming. I haven't even visited here before.

Other folks were emboldened to join in, and the chanting drew to a climax of screaming voices. He could see the hatred in the eyes of people who confronted him. With religious fervour and the safety in numbers of a congregation, they continued the call and response of *Out, Brady out! Out, Brady out!*

Brady tried to summon up a semblance of defiance, but he struggled with a weak smile before heading back to the Hearse.

Brady found similar receptions waiting for him when he left Highway 99 to venture to Hanford. He admitted that it hurt to see his regular customers and even his Brady Mahone Entertainment Enterprises Rep in the crowd.

It happened again in Visalia. And if that didn't ram the *Brady Mahone isn't welcome* message home, then the hastily erected burning cross in Delano did. Usually, the sight of the burning cross falling over and causing amateurish panic among the Green mob would have made Brady laugh, but it had all been too much for him, and by now, all he wanted to do was head back home to the comfort of his ranch.

He stopped off at the East McFarland bus stop to check for any messages. He noted that Tyrone's essay on the exploits of Brady Mahone in Encinitas had gone. He now wondered if that was another mistake. He was almost relieved to find a note from Judge Jefferson accusing him of withholding evidence.

Hi Brady

I hope you're keeping well and staying out of trouble. □

This made Brady laugh wryly.

Thank you for the documents. In my old days as a District Attorney, this is what I would have called a career defining case. I am grateful to you, for giving me something substantial to think about.

However, there are clearly documents missing from the evidence trail. Without these, I cannot give you a meaningful account of what fully transpired.

Maybe, we should postpone our meeting until August 9th? This would allow me to continue to interrogate the trail of evidence you have already provided.

If, by some miracle, you do have, or come across, more paperwork from your Los Banos haul, then please leave it here. I'll have people checking this location, every evening until then.

Until then, I hope business continues thrive for you.

Love Audre x

He reread it. It sounded friendly, even if it was a bit legal-like in places. Also, Judge Jefferson signing off, *love Audre*. He smiled. *That doesn't sound like she's got it in for me like the Greens have. I suppose she only knows what I tell them. I don't even know what Tyrone wrote her.*

Brady parked up at the Mahone Ranch. It was early morning. He watched with annoyance as Mary-Lou called for Amie to get indoors at the sight of Brady's return. Amie looked sheepishly in the direction of Brady before running back to the Lopez Ranch.

He forced himself to make breakfast. He remembered how easy it was to fall into the blues and do nothing when he first went to Juvey. He had to keep on moving. He washed up and then sat on the porch to give thought to his predicament. He sipped at his hot black coffee. *I ain't got no friends, no customers or no business. Hell, I ain't even got a girlfriend or nuthin'.* He unconsciously felt for his Distor™. *I got me a ton of Greenbacks, but not enough for a FusionPlane™ to set me up somewhere new.*

He watched the Lopez's working away on their chores. I don't want to hang around here any longer than necessary with them no-good pieces of ungrateful shits.

Brady brooded, and as his coffee cooled, he drained the cup and then poured himself another. He returned to his rocking chair. He remembered something his

Foster Daddy used to say. *Worrying is like a rocking chair. You can rock all day and get nowhere.* He looked over in the direction of Archie Mahone's grave. *Why didja have to do all those terrible things you did, Pops?* He watched Lucian stoop to tend his crops, and then stand awkwardly as he tried to loosen off his backache. It struck Brady how quickly he was ageing. He never noticed the time flying by when he was in the company of the ageless Greens. *One thing I do seem to have is time.*

He wandered back inside his home. He went from room to room, picking up trinkets and refreshing his memory of times long gone. He found an old family photo album that his Foster Moms used to keep. He flipped through it. The pictures of himself as a child brought back happy memories. There were many photos of a cheeky young Brady Mahone playing in trees, or swinging on a rope and jumping into rivers. He looked full of action and full of life. His Foster Pops always had that mischievous smile and that lame habit of still trying to discreetly put two-fingers up just as his Foster Moms was about to take the photo. He recalled her always trying to trick Archie as she wanted to avoid him doing this. The occasional shot of his Foster Moms made her look as if she was trying to hide her torment and sadness behind a forced smile, but maybe that was the way Brady viewed them now with the benefit of hindsight.

His day was filled with moments like this. Early, he went to bed, because he was bored; and had run out of things to do. His dreams were filled with people screaming at him, *out, Brady out* like someone was performing an exorcism on him as he slept.

The next few days were very much the same. He had forgotten about Archie Mahone's old bunker, so he headed down there, for a change of pace. He looked at the useless old tech and he smiled at all those old conspiracy theories about Deep Cons, Deep State and every other crackpot story under the Sun. They seemed like strangely innocent days, now. He saw the fading newspaper cuttings hung up on the bunker walls, with UFO photos. *You really were convinced that one day we would be invaded by aliens, weren't you Pops.*

He looked closely at another wall of press cuttings. There was the Loch Ness monster from Scotland, Big Foot from the Rockies, Sasquatch from Canada - or were they the same? Brady couldn't recall what his Pops' thoughts were on this topic. He then examined the Yeti photo purporting to be a sighting from the summit of Mount Everest. Next to these, were all the wildlife drawings Brady did as a kid. He traced the progress of the blossoming talent he had, from the stick figures as a child to the highly detailed pictures of his adolescence. They brought back powerful memories. It was almost as if he were right back in the moment of sharing precious time in the recreation of the miracle of God's creatures. He pulled down a sketch of the Kangaroo rat. He had been so into drawing and learning about rare species of animals in California that his Foster Pops had driven him all the way down to San Bernardino and stayed there for three days until Brady finally found his Kangaroo rat. *He did that for me, all that trouble so I could draw a fucking rat. I never did thank you for that - you just did it to make me happy - and more likely to keep me out of trouble.*

He clutched the drawing to his heart and whispered, 'Thanks, Pops.' He blinked, in the bright sunshine, as he left Archie Mahone's bunker. He packed his Hearse for a long road trip and grabbed a supply of sketchbooks, pencils and charcoals. *I'm gonna find me another of those Kangaroo rats.*

17.JUDGE JEFFERSON

It was a Sunday in East McFarland, which meant Judge Jefferson attended church. A horse and trap picked her up. She greeted her friend, 'Hello, Officer Norbert.'

'Good morning, Judge. You haven't forgotten my official title is Officer Stillman?'

'I haven't forgotten, Norbert, but we are long past the old formalities.'

He smiled, 'Are you comfortable enough for the full Sunday tour first?'

'Yes. Thank you.'

They set off in the horse and trap, which Officer Norbert had cleaned and polished as usual and set off around the perimeter of East McFarland. Based on the information Brady Mahone had passed on to the late Professor Chu in those first few weeks after the GreenRevs Revolution back in '84, the Professor was quick to spot the danger of GreenShell™ encroachment - as he had christened it. He carried out experiments using abandoned properties on the town's outskirts and deduced that if a green area was left unattended for more than precisely seven days, then the GreenShell™ would reclaim the land. Sometimes, he noted, that just a garden would be reclaimed. He began the daily checks to ensure any dead were removed and replaced quickly with the living.

In conjunction with Judge Audre Jefferson, he developed a systematic plan to ensure that the perimeter's must always be occupied - even if that required the townsfolk to relocate there from the properties in the central areas.

Sixteen years on, the town was populated in a doughnut shape, with the few hundred residents living on the outer edges of their territory, and the central areas deserted.

It was a particularly delightful Californian summer's day, and although everybody in any of the Trad areas hated to admit it, the climate had undoubtedly improved, markedly. She occasionally stopped to talk to her people if she spotted them in the garden. The youngest person in the town was sixteen, there were no more small children. Most of the population was elderly in appearance, if not in the number of years, as the living conditions they had endured had prematurely aged them. Still, they were grateful that they lived in the sunny climes of California. At church, on Sundays, they always counted their blessings. She often wondered how those who lived in harsher climates might have survived. She reasoned that they didn't.

Officer Norbert pulled up the horse and trap at regular intervals, to give a people the chance to stroke his horse, Palladino, and also for them to talk to Judge Jefferson, at the same time. She was a beloved and respected figure in the town, but her fading health caused much consternation, as she was the towns talisman, and they felt sure that the town's fate would be sealed with her demise.

It made her dwell on what had happened in all those other lost areas of the Traditional Cultures, and she guessed that the death knell for such places probably rang out loud and clear, when their chosen leaders died. She didn't want to think about what happened in the more dystopian and violent places - sometimes ignorance was bliss.

After a couple of hours of travelling around the outskirts of the town, they pulled up in front of the church. Officer Norbert helped Audre out of the carriage and supported her as she struggled into church on her two sticks. She never let her pain become evident to her people, as she loved to sing the hymns loudly, and to the amusement of her fellow townsfolk, she would shout Amen if the priest made a significantly positive statement. This was something he always bore in mind when constructing his Sunday sermon.

After the church service was done for another week. Officer Norbert and Judge Jefferson would ride to the southern edges to the bus stop, to check if there had been any further messages from Brady Mahone. She had given thought about ending his banishment, but even after sixteen years, his brutal violence could not be forgotten or forgiven by her fellow citizens. He scared them, and his return into the heart of East McFarland would be treated as an ill omen by them.

She had read the latest letter he had left, which was written in an unknown hand. It was well-written, and she wondered how Brady had befriended someone with obvious high intelligence. From the description of the events in Encinitas, including Brady's showing off to a waitress, she feared that his knuckle-headed attempts at showing-off might come back to haunt him - but that was Brady all over.

They used the Sundays to visit the bus stop because the horse and trap could carry anything left there. She was not to be disappointed on this day. Brady had left two boxes of documentation. Officer Norbert Stillman dutifully loaded them next to Judge Jefferson and then started on the return trip to her home.

She opened the lid and examined the index numbers on the folders. They were the numbers she had hoped to find. She was excited. She knew she had the missing piece to her complex puzzle - all she needed to do now was to fit them into the right places. Brady had given her a sense of personal fulfilment to supplement and allow her to conduct her civic duty.

She said, 'It won't help us, other than give us the satisfaction of how and why it happened. Brady has done as I had requested.'

Over the sound of the clip-clopping of hooves, Officer Norbert said, 'I'm pleased for you. I've seen a pick-up in your wellbeing since you've been working on this project of yours.'

'When I'm done, I'll tell you everything I've found in here - just in case anything happens to me.'

'Nothing will happen to you, Judge. You'll go down with the ship.'

She laughed, 'I'm not sure that analogy of yours brings me comfort Officer Norbert.'

He laughed, 'Words have never been a strong suit of mine.'
They pulled up in the driveway of Judge Jefferson's home. He brought in the boxes and listened carefully as she instructed him precisely where to put each document wallet. He followed her instructions to the number as well as the letter. He helped her into her wheelchair. She didn't notice him drift away for a few moments as she was engrossed in her latest addition to her greatest investigation.

Officer Norbert, without asking, washed and put away her most recent collection of dirty dishes. He cleaned her kitchen and then made her some lunch with black coffee. He laid it out on a table away from her precious piles of documentation. She looked up, and she had a tear in her eye when she spotted his acts of kindness. Before she could even thank him, he raised his hand and said, 'It's the least I can do, after all, you've done for us.' He left quickly, he was old-school, he didn't want to discuss his emotions.

18.WHERE IS HE?

Cain was summoned to Sattva Systems™ HQ. Sissy and Siddha remained in Ramona to continue to assist with the relocation of the West Encinitas refugees. They had all worked long and hard to make the mission a success, but it had taken a couple of weeks longer than expected, as they hit snags, which needed to be fixed. Still, it was a huge undertaking, and they felt proud of their achievements.

Bodhi greeted Cain at the Main Entrance. He was dressed in a business-like manner - black pinstripe suit, white silk-shirt and tie - which hadn't happened before when he had met with him. Cain felt intimidated and under-dressed for the occasion, but his white-robe and bare feet was his trademark appearance, and it kept him grounded. He felt overpowered by Bodhi.

Bodhi reached out his hand to shake Cain's, and there was the clanking of large metal jewellery on his wrist. He shook Cain's hand hard and held it for a few seconds longer than necessary. 'So, how's it going in Ramona.'

'We had a few problems. The NanoShell™ wouldn't activate, the water supply needed additional treatments but overall…'

'Good. Good.' He added sharply, 'What about Brady Mahone?'

'The work required in Ramona held us up, but we are…'

'You haven't done the one thing that I asked you to do. It was important to me, but not to you, so that's ok?'

'No. It wasn't like that.'

Bodhi moved out of the main entrance, without warning, and Cain had to rush to keep up with him. Bodhi didn't look to see if Cain was with him. He talked as if it didn't matter. 'Decades, I worked on all this, for the likes of you.' He walked on, and Cain hurried after him. 'You gave me wish-lists for a world of change.'

'It wasn't just me…'

'Can you pour your fortunes into this? Could you invent that? Could you borrow trillions of dollars on the back of your good name to finance this? Bodhi, could you make our dreams come true? And all I asked in return was that everybody completed their tasks to a high standard.' He brought his hand up to his face and brought his thumb and forefinger close together to symbolise something tiny, 'But when I asked for one little job to be done with a sense of priority. A tiny task which meant something to me and my overall plans. You decided that you had more important things to do.'

'No. No, I didn't…'

'Then, where is he?'

Cain's shoulders sagged in utter defeat and shame, 'I don't know. Nobody does.'

Bodhi strode on. He didn't dismiss Cain, but neither did he talk to him. He chatted amiably with his engineers. Cain knew the jokes and good-humoured remarks he was having with them were aimed, pointedly at Cain. Bodhi picked an engineer at random. 'If you decided to leave one part, any part, out of this machine, what would you expect to happen, eventually?'

'It would malfunction, which would create additional costs and over-runs - or it would break down and become a useless piece of junk.'

'But you're a professional, and you wouldn't dream of doing anything so neglectful.'

The engineer looked at Bodhi in the off chance that he may be in trouble, but he knew he was the best in his field and knew this couldn't be the case. 'Never in a million years - that would be a low-class way of working.'

Bodhi patted the engineer on the shoulder. 'You are a credit to Sattva Systems™, and I hope you realise how highly I value your work and your commitment.'

Bodhi moved on, and Cain spotted the look of pride in the engineer's face as he trailed after Bodhi.

They walked for an hour until they reached the Research and Development area in the next part of the industrial complex. He walked into the central laboratory. Some of the technicians stopped working and gathered around Bodhi and Cain.

Bodhi introduced Cain, 'This is Cain. He is the Regional Disciple for the Western Seaboard. I wish to demonstrate the high-quality standards you work towards.' He smiled, 'I have a question to the chemists amongst you. If you were to withdraw the tiniest amount of a chemical compound out of one of our completed experiments, what would happen to that experiment?'

One of the technicians in a cream-coloured lab coat emblazoned with a moss-green Sattva Systems™ logo answered, 'You would have a different result, and you would have begun a completely different experiment. You would effectively be starting over.' She looked at him with reverence.

'So, you wouldn't do that?'

She shook her head, 'Not until it was authorised. We are a part of a complex structure of experimentation and manufacturing.'

He smiled, but then asked the gathering, 'I'd like to ask one of you who works in NanoTech™. If you were to remove or replace a single molecule from one of your Nanostructures, would it matter?'

A young man at the back shouted, 'Of course it would! You would destabilise the whole structure, and then there would be no telling how disastrous the outcome might be.'

Bodhi said, 'Thank you for your passion. I'm lucky to have such brilliant people working for our noble cause. I'm deeply proud of you all.' He added, gently, 'Now, don't let me keep you from your work.'

They wore proud smiles as they disbanded and returned to their benches.

A voice called out, 'Oi, Bodhi. Who the fuck gave you permission to bring civilians into my Research area? Wait, don't tell me, I can figure it out, because it wasn't me, and I'm the only one who gives permission. Am I right?' The woman came out from the shadows, she was dressed head to toe in black leather.

'I was trying to…'

'You don't try anything in my space. Surely, I don't have to explain.'

Bodhi was quietened but didn't seem offended. 'I apologise. It won't happen again.' He ushered Cain forward. 'Before we leave, I just want to introduce our Regional Disciple, Cain.' Cain shook hands with the woman who appeared as eastern European in origin. 'Cain, this is Professor Pinar Dogan, the most important person in the world.'

Pinar said with little humour. 'Fuck you, pay me.'

Cain at first thought that Bodhi was being humble, but the fierce look that Pinar gave Bodhi suggested that he might be telling the truth. 'And what do you do, here?'

'Everything. Nano and enzyme research and development. From the NanoShells™, NanoSuits™ to the outer coatings of the LeviathanLifters™. I integrate the work of the FusionPower™ engineers into the Green Infrastructure. As well as our friend's here little vanity projects. Bodhi's Project X.'

Cain had no idea what Project X was, indeed, he had never heard of a Leviathan-Lifter™. He asked timidly. 'Are you Green?'

'Of course, I fucking am. Do you think I would develop all this…'? She gestured grandly, '…and not take a taste myself?' She added, 'As long as I am paid for what my efforts are worth, then we are all hunky dory here. Right Bodhi?'

'Naturally.'

'Great. Then we're done here. Now, you can fuck off.' Pinar turned on her heels of her knee-length leather boots and strode away. She issued orders to return to work and to stop gaping at Bodhi.

Bodhi continued to lead Cain around his industrial complexes. Cain knew he must have appeared diminished by his encounter with Professor Dogan, and this explained why he carried on in the same vein as prior to this confrontation. Cain remained respectful and suitably shamed as Bodhi occasionally stopped and asked questions about the importance of adhering to detailed instructions in their work to his HeavyFusionLorry™ drivers, his Repairs and Maintenance team, his Trainers and Educators, and even the cleaners. In this instance, he even spoke to them while they were cleaning the toilets. Every time, he left his workers feeling uplifted, and Cain knew they would go home to their families and talk of the day that Bodhi Sattva had personally thanked them for the brilliance of their work.

Cain felt Bodhi was being heavy-handed in the way he was forcing his message onto him. They walked and walked, and Bodhi never tired of stopping and talking a worker who had a role which hadn't been previously covered. Cain began to zone out of his punishment. Cain remembered how he felt when he received that very first phone call from Bodhi Sattva when he was still just the new Disciple of West

McFarland. He also recalled, that even sixteen years ago, at the beginning of the new Green world, all that Bodhi wanted to discuss, was the stranger who had appeared in their town called Brady Mahone. He also reflected; that Brady Mahone had a disproportionate amount of his allotted discussion time with Bodhi in all the time he had known him.

He struggled with his thoughts, trying to consider the subject of Brady Mahone in ever more abstract ways. Brady was a Trad who could travel freely in any Green Zone, he hadn't heard of any other example. Ok, he looked a little like Bodhi, but Cain remembered doing his homework on Xavier Kane or Bodhi, as he became subsequently known, in the days of the Internet. Bodhi had an extended family, scattered across the globe, and a few went Green, but most were Trads - not surprising considering that John Kane's wealth had trickled down to them, and being Green was not an attractive proposition.

Cain knew he had to be careful with his next thoughts. *Why didn't he have him captured or killed? Even Brady couldn't escape the Security Protocols™.* The next question was the opposite. *Why is he keeping him alive? What purpose does Brady Mahone have? I don't think even Brady Mahone has a purpose for his own life, never mind a reason to serve Bodhi.* When he thought harder on this, he realised that Brady had never shown any interest in Bodhi until Libby Kane invited him to her home.

Mercifully, for Cain, they arrived back at the Main Hall. Bodhi stood, in silence, gazing at the banner of the demands written in Glenarvon Cole's scrawl.

The end to capitalism. End materialism. The most destructive ideology against nature.
Equal rights and opportunity for all citizens.
An end to all weaponry, so that our people can live in harmony with nature without being threatened.
To protect all Green spaces across the globe and bring an end to the exploitation of the land.
To protect all living creatures. Stop the killing.
End intensive farming.
Reduce the population of the planet by peaceful means and self-selection.
Improve education, with a more prominent focus on ecology, environmental sciences and ethics.
To repair the damage brought on by the Industrial and Technological Revolutions.
To bring an era of peace, harmony and tranquillity to those that help to save the planet.

Bodhi then pointed to the three requests outside of the top ten primary goals.

End hate thoughts and crimes, including gender identity and discrimination.
Remove all traces of Imperialism and Colonialism.
Improve mental health by establishing kinder societies.

Bodhi said, 'This isn't about me. I hadn't considered the last three items on my list; because they don't directly impact Mother Nature. However, I did recognise the impact of these for the betterment of Human Nature. This caused a massive upheaval in our plans and timelines, but nonetheless, I am still working on this, sixteen years later, out of respect, for the people who made it happen with their dedication and bravery. People like Glenarvon Cole - I can't tell you enough how much I respect that man.'

He looked into Cain's crystal green eyes, 'I made a promise. I will move Heaven and Earth to keep my promise. What would help me complete every task on that list is for people to keep theirs.' Before Cain could reply, he added, 'You will find and rehabilitate Brady Mahone for me. You will give it the highest priority because it is important to me?'

Cain said softly, 'I will.'

'You promise?'

'Yes. I promise.'

Bodhi didn't answer, but his appearance changed back into his comfortable grey tracksuit with sneakers devoid of logos. He walked away with a lightness in his step.

19.REHABILITATION

Cain flew back to Ramona. He would have preferred a direct order from Bodhi because he could tell Sissy and Siddha what to do. However, when he thought long and hard about his day with Bodhi, he realised that he didn't have a single good reason for persuading them to leave Ramona and embark on the Rehabilitation of Brady Mahone tour with him. Bodhi had signalled his desire for what he wanted to happen next but left him, without a compelling reason to persuade his colleagues other than to implore them to follow him on blind faith.

He considered doing this alone but knew that with Sissy being part of the inner sanctum of the Sattva Systems™ elite, coupled with the fact that some of the older members of the Green communities would remember her being the ex-Governor of California then he needed her. He also knew that bringing along Siddha, whose distrust and dislike of Brady had spread far and wide, would, or should, give him enough firepower to calm and reset attitudes against Brady.

But first, he had to persuade Sissy and Siddha, to abandon their current project, which even in his own opinion, he considered far more critical.

As he arrived in Ramona, he was consoled by the positive development that the NanoShell™ was working.

Before he could approach the subject of leaving and taking Siddha and Sissy with him, he knew he had to fulfil his leadership duties to the new Green Community of Ramona. As he went around the community giving praise to all those who worked so hard to make it happen, it made him relate to Bodhi's methods. He began to wonder whether Bodhi was sincere in his thanks to his loyal team or whether it didn't matter at all because his reason for doing it was primarily to get him to do his bidding.

And here am I, doing just the same, praising people for their hard work, but all I'm really doing is a perfunctory duty to enable me to steal key people from the project.

Before leaving Ramona, he arranged for a Town Meeting. There were thousands of refugees from Encinitas who believed that Brady Mahone was the Devil incarnate, and he had to begin the process of Brady's rehabilitation here.

He found Siddha and Sissy together, they were discussing the quality of the water supply with a technician. They acknowledged Cain's arrival but continued their consultations until they were satisfied. Siddha went with the technician to the next filtration system, while Sissy went to join Cain. 'How did it go with Bodhi?'

'Not good. I've never seen him so angry and disappointed.'

She smiled consolingly, she moved her hand to her stomach, 'They are kicking.'

'Is it twins?'

'No. I'm educating myself for the next upgrade in NanoSuits™, by the time this little one becomes a teenager we should have the BlueSuits™. This will enable gender fluidity, both mentally and physically. My little one will live in a different world to the one we grew up in. I want them to be fully immersed in it. It will be beautiful.'

Her optimism warmed him. He needed a vision of the future to remind him why they were here. 'Just because we won the revolution, it doesn't mean we have to stop evolving.'

She rubbed her stomach, unconsciously, 'Now. What has Bodhi been up to this time? He can be a little irascible if he's not getting his own way. The inclusion of the BlueSuit™ development caused massive disruption in his one-hundred-year plan, but he came around, eventually.'

Cain's crystal green eyes sparkled as they caught the orange light of the setting sun. 'He didn't seem at all concerned about the work we were doing here in Ramona. He was fixated on our lack of progress with the Brady Mahone situation. He believes I failed him.'

'What makes you think that? What did he say?'

'He didn't say anything precisely. He just made me tag along as he used many clumsy analogies about missing pieces of puzzles, missing elements in compounds, and lots of other examples. He made me feel like an incompetent fool, one who was letting the team down. They were professionals, and I was not.'

Sissy smiled, 'He can do that to you. I've been on the receiving end of that treatment - it's not nice.' She added, 'What you have to remember is that he has flaws of his own. This is why he needs us. He can't do this alone.'

'What kind of flaws?'

'He struggles with art and literature, for instance. He cannot appreciate art, and he converses like a scientist…industrialist…same ballpark.'

'I can see why he needs his engineers and scientists, but what use am I to him?'

Sissy laughed, 'Oh my dear Cain. He really has got to you?' She rubbed her stomach again, 'They are active, they must want to join us. Don't worry, little one, you'll soon be with us, and then I can't wait to introduce you to Uncle Cain.' She returned her gaze back to Cain, 'You have a spiritual bearing which plays well in your Communities. You are also a natural communicator. Trust me, he needs you. Have you ever wondered why he makes so few public appearances?'

'No. Not really. I just thought he was too busy.'

'He is busy, but that's not it. He knows he doesn't come across well to audiences. He struggles with empathy. He needs his Disciples to do that part of the heavy lifting for him. You persuade the people to do the work. I mean, look what we have done between us, here, in Ramona. We have evacuated thousands of refugees, reconnected power and water supplies, and have erected NanoShells™ in record time to keep them safe. Without our communications and planning skills, this couldn't have been made possible.'

Cain smiled and said, 'I'm in need of a hug.'

Sissy laughed and said, 'Come here. You can hug the baby as well - if you can get your arms around me.'

He hugged her tightly, and let his head rest on her shoulders, he didn't want his tears to show. After a minute, he pulled himself away from her soothing arms and said, 'I need your help. I can't, for the life of me, figure out why he is so fixated on Brady Mahone.' He reminded himself of just how close Sissy and Bodhi were, and he wondered if he had made a mistake in questioning Bodhi's judgment to her, of all people. *I'm committed to this path, it's too late to turn back now.*

He wasn't immediately reassured as she took long seconds before answering him. Finally, she seemed to reach a decision, or maybe it was a conclusion. 'What are your thoughts on the subject?'

She's answered a question with a question. Is she interrogating me? Trying to find out if I know, but using her to confirm my suspicions? I've come this far, maybe it's time to find out whether honesty really is the best policy.

'I'm ashamed to admit that my thoughts have spanned all the sins of the humanity of the old world when I have considered the apparent link between Bodhi and Brady Mahone. I'll refine that by adding that I've considered the links between Xavier Kane and Brady Mahone. I've had doubts relating to cronyism, nepotism, conspiracies, criminality - it's even given me doubts about everything we've achieved.'

She smiled, 'I think we need a coffee, and I need a sit-down.'

They wandered into the refreshed town centre of Ramona and went into a refurbished café called New Start New Day Café.' They ordered coffee, Cain's was black, whereas Sissy's was white with lots of sugar, 'I'm hoping I'll stop craving this after they are born.'

Cain said, 'I'm sorry if I have gone too far and put you in an uncomfortable position. If you don't want to discuss Bodhi's intentions, then I would fully understand. I shouldn't doubt him, not after everything he has done for us all.'

She stirred her coffee. 'I don't know why Brady is important to Bodhi. I really don't. All I can say is that Bodhi rarely turns out to be wrong. You know my history. I was a radical Democrat who won the state of California, only because I had the support and considerable financial backing of Sattva Systems™.'

He said, 'I'm sure you had something to do with becoming the Governor of California.'

She stared out of the window, she waved at the passers-by who recognised her. 'In the arrogance of my youth, I certainly thought so. But with the benefit of hindsight, I realise I wouldn't have stood a chance without Bodhi. He needed me. He needed my oratory back then - I've become less confident with age, and he needed my good looks; appearance was always over-valued in the old world. He needed all of these things because he didn't possess these skills. There were so many times back then where I doubted him. I was a firebrand of a politician, and I would argue fiercely with him, and at first, I defied him. But I learned that if I enabled him, then wonderful things followed. We made a difference in the effects of climate change in California. I recognised in him the greatness he could achieve for his people and the potential for what he could do to the whole planet. All I had to do was believe in him. He never disappointed me. We owe him our loyalty.'

Cain looked crestfallen, 'I'm sorry. You are right.'

269

She took a drink of her sweet coffee, 'Having said that. I am troubled by Brady Mahone. He brings nothing of value to our future plans. We are not supposed to indulge in nostalgia for the old world, and yet, Bodhi encourages him to sell his entertainment wares to our people.'

'They are security controlled.'

'Yes, the Security Protocols™ do not permit illegal stimulants. Therefore, his customers have learned not to become over-stimulated by any scenes of sex, violence or hatred. Otherwise, they risk being Filmed. I'm sure his bestselling lines are all Middle-of-the-Road and relatively harmless titles.'

'Why let them have them at all?'

'Maybe, for Bodhi, they are an important element in his chemical compound. He will have his reasons.'

Cain said, 'Ok. Why doesn't he sell and distribute these items via Sattva Systems™? He could do a better job than Brady Mahone and his tin-pot amateurish operation. And why make Brady a rich man in the process?'

She said, 'The only thing I can think of is that nobody has ever been perfect. The human spirit has always hankered after the forbidden fruit. Maybe Bodhi considers this a harmless outlet - a satisfying of a human need.'

'But I don't need it.'

'That's why you are a Regional Disciple.'

They finished their coffee and strolled through the new town to be re-christened Green Ramona at tomorrow night's ceremony. It was getting dark, and Sissy looked tired. Cain said, 'You need your rest.'

She said, 'Have you decided what you need from me, specifically?'

'I need your help to convince the people here in Ramona to alter their view of Brady Mahone. Then I need you to help me to convince Siddha - that will probably be even harder.' He laughed. 'Then I need you both to travel with me to visit all the Green Communities to rinse and repeat.' He looked at her, 'Although, I think your baby might have other plans.'

'I don't think we'll be able complete the whole tour.'

Cain took her hand, 'This is why I must get Siddha on board.'

She smiled, 'I'll sleep on it. I want to help because Bodhi wants this to be sorted. Whatever his reasoning.'

20.HIGHWAYS OF THE SUN

Cain was awoken by Sissy in his hostel room. She said, 'I want to let you know what I've decided.'

He sat up in his basic bed. She smiled, 'I'll deal with Siddha, alone. You can be too close to somebody, and I think his concern for your wellbeing will cloud his judgment. His instincts will be to protect you from Brady, and his influencing on you.' He nodded sleepily, she continued, 'I am more detached. I have the power of office as being so close to Bodhi. I will make him come around. It's what I used to do.'

'Are you sure you don't need me? I don't want to be seen to be shirking my responsibilities - not after yesterday's events.'

'No. You concentrate on your speech for this evening and trust me to do what I'm good at. I need to return to the HQ with everything back on track for Bodhi. I won't let Siddha become a problem.' She smiled and put a soft hand on Cain's naked shoulder, 'Mingle with the town's folk, talk about the settling in process and be upbeat and reassuring, but don't bring up the Brady situation.'

'But what if they mention Brady?'

'Then be calm and treat it as a storm in a teacup. You must reiterate how the future plans are unaltered - if you need to - talk about the Suits™ in development.' She kissed him on the forehead and left. He noticed she had made her appearance change on the way out of the room to a style she would have adopted when she used to be the Governor of California. He knew she wouldn't fail.

A few days later, after successfully calming the residents of Green Ramona, and setting them stretching targets to complete the town's refurbishment. The three high-ranking representatives of Sattva Systems™, and the personal envoys of Bodhi Sattva; set off in their four-seater FusionPlane™ to speed through as many locations as possible across the Western Seaboard of the United States of America.

Cain hadn't understood the power the three of them possessed as they landed in any of the Green Communities. Cain was always aware of his spiritual charisma, but it was only now that he recognised that his gifts had been used almost exclusively to deliver good news. In this environment of distrust and fear, Sissy shone. She exuded power and confidence, she did the one thing Cain couldn't do, she gave them the impression that she was a formidable force to be reckoned with by any threat to their Community. The biggest persuader came when Siddha spoke. He had always been the biggest sceptic of Brady Mahone's activities, but when he said of his change of heart, and that it was, in his honest opinion, that they should go about their business, the same as before, then the townsfolk were relieved. It seemed, all they needed was for someone in authority to tell them that everything was going to be alright, there was nothing to worry about, and the future was bright.

The most significant problem area they encountered was when they landed in Santa Clarita. There had been an outbreak of religious revivalism which had infected the key players in the town. As they landed, they saw burning crosses and bonfires with effigies, which they deduced were of Brady Mahone.

A flustered Disciple came to greet them as they left the FusionPlane™. He had adopted the appearance of a man going to a banquet in a tuxedo, with a red silk sash, mistakenly thinking that Garcia must mean she had pride in Mexican traditions. 'I'm so sorry you have to see us like this, but I cannot convince them. They think that it's the apocalypse and that without a sign of the second coming of Christ to save us, then we will be punished for the way we have treated the Trads. We have treated them terribly - haven't we? We deserve our damnation - don't we?'

Sissy smiled, nonplussed, 'This is Cain, the Regional Disciple of the Western Seaboard, this is Siddha the Disciple of the Green Community of West McFarland, and I am Genesis Garcia...'

'Of course. Please forgive my outburst - and my manners. I'm Oleg Faustbender. The Disciple of the Green Community of Santa Clarita.' He thrust out his hand sharply. She shook it firmly, in a business-like manner. 'Please, call me Sissy.' She added, 'You've lost control of the situation.'

He looked at her sheepishly, 'You don't understand the strength of feeling here.'

The breeze changed direction, and smoke engulfed them. She coughed, and instinctively felt down to her unborn child with her hand, 'For pity's sake, douse those fires.'

'But...'

'Do it. That's an order.'

Oleg looked around nervously before he summoned enough courage to call over a couple of the welcoming committee to him. He argued with them in heated whispers before Sissy intervened, she barked, 'I am here on the authority of Bodhi Sattva to sort out this mess of a town. Now, put out those damned fires.' She added, 'We are very busy, we are trying cram in as many Green Community visits as we can. As you can probably tell from my condition...' She coughed and choked on the fumes.

Cain intervened, 'Take us to the heart of the trouble, and hopefully we will find a place for Sissy to sit down. Have you got any transportation on hand?'

'Yes. Of course.' He clicked his fingers and pointed, and a young woman who looked like she could be his daughter boarded a FusionCoach™ and brought it over to his VIPs.

As they boarded the coach, Sissy was still choking. Oleg ordered, 'Turn on the filtration systems.' As the air became fresher, Sissy began to regain her breath. She said, 'The baby hasn't got any Suit™ protection, so I have to reduce my Orange™ protection to enable unfiltered air into the blood. It's an anomaly which the team are working on. It's a rare vulnerability which only affects pregnant women.'

Siddha handed her a glass of water. She drank, more out of the need to clean her throat than to quench her thirst. She said, 'Where are the ringleaders?'

'The Christ Lutheran Church. It's only a short journey.'

When they pulled up outside the church, the crowds of demonstrators were fervently waving placards either praising Jesus or denouncing Satan. Some had bible passages on them. Sissy thought the marketing skills for these were abysmal, as you couldn't read and decipher the messages quickly, therefore what was the point of going to the trouble to make them and wave them in front of people's faces.

She left the coach, fearlessly. Oleg followed. She looked at the unimpressive build-ing, which called itself a church. It was grey, with ungainly and angular slabs which made the design look more suitable to a split-level oven than a place of worship. The church was packed with an audience of whirling dervishes being whipped up into a frenzy by a loud preacher.

Oleg pleaded for quiet as Siddha followed them in. Siddha walked to the pulpit and forcefully removed the microphone from the Preacher. He said, 'Is this how you greet your representatives of Bodhi Sattva? Now be quiet. We have come, to halt these unfounded stories about Brady Mahone, with all the authority of Sattva Systems™, and the ability to impose any appropriate sanctions. This includes withdrawing your Green Community status, which means Santa Clarita would return to Traditional Culture restrictions.' He looked around the room, where a semblance of calm had returned, but the suspicions of the crowd were still apparent. 'You are behaving like Trads, maybe that's what you really want?'

The audience was then stunned into silence, not by Siddha's appeal for calm, but at the sight of Cain moving noiselessly through the crowd in his white robe and walking on bare feet with his crystal green eyes set into a distant gaze. Then a scream of pain was heard as Sissy went into labour.
He went to her, and a crowd gathered. Cain said calmly, 'Is the baby on its way?'

Sissy was breathless, she moaned then tried to bring her breathing under control. 'I believe so. This is my third child, but they are early.'

She moaned loudly, and this removed any doubt. Cain said, 'Tell me what to do. I know you have reduced OrangeSuit™ protection…'

Sissy looked at Cain, 'It will reduce the pain, and produce the correct levels of hormones - it will even monitor and produce the correct rate of dilation changes. All I need from you is to bring my child into the light. It won't be long now.'

The congregation around Cain and Sissy gasped at her choice of words, the Chi-nese whispers spread like a shock wave through the church and out into the streets, 'It won't be long until a child brings us back to the light.' Siddha gently urged the crowd around them to give them more room and ushered anyone, among them, to bring whatever they thought might be needed. Siddha wanted them to feel useful, a spirit of helpfulness had a calming effect on Santa Clarita's townsfolk.

People rushed off to find blankets, sheets and jugs of water, while the Preacher went to retrieve his bottle of Holy Water.

Sissy let out short screams of pain, and each time she looked at Cain, figuring that he needed more reassuring than she did. She smiled, 'Don't worry, Cain. This is normal. I need you to be in the moment with me.' He held her hand. Her clothing dissolved away from her body until she was naked. Cain didn't know if this was her doing, or whether she had lost control of her YellowSuit™, there were so few babies born since the introduction of the Green Parent cost of child commitment. She panted and said, 'It's time.'

The baby's head appeared, and Cain moved to help deliver it. An elderly woman appeared at his side to assist him. When the baby was born, Cain brought the child close to him, his robe was stained, but he didn't allow the self-cleaning of the Yellow™ to operate. The stained robe held significance to him, he felt honoured to be a part of Sissy's moment of joy. The old woman cut the umbilical cord and handed the baby to Sissy and then attended to Sissy, making sure she was physically and spiritually sound, and just as crucial to Sissy - comfortable. The baby cried for a short-while until it was brought against the comforting warmth of Sissy's skin.

The word spread through the crowd that the new-born member of the Green Community of Santa Clarita was a boy.

After a few minutes, Sissy passed the child to Cain, 'Please, display my child to the crowd.' He looked at her oddly. She whispered, 'Trust me.'

He took hold of the child and held it high above his head, and the crowd cheered. The Preacher came forward and said to Sissy. 'I wish to introduce the child to our Green Community. It is our hope that you will give the child its name in our sacred home and complete the formalities in the New Green tradition.'

She said, 'I will.' She stood up, and she became fully clothed in her cream-coloured Sattva Systems™ business suit. She looked immaculate. Nobody would have known it had only been a few short minutes before that she had given birth. All of her Nano-Suits™ were now fully-functioning.

The Preacher asked formally, 'What are the names and occupations of the people in this arrangement of bringing a new child into the GreenWorld?'

She thundered, 'I am Genesis Garcia. Marketing Director of Sattva Systems™. Although many of you remember me more for my old job as the Governor of California. Until the moment of the New Green Day of the Revolution.'

There was nervous laughter, and the Preacher smiled and nodded his encouragement for her to continue.

Sissy said, 'My partner in the arrangement of the child's development is Annabelle Mason. Xe will be the homemaker to them and our other two children.' She looked across at a young man writing the information into a leather-bound ledger, which she knew would be displayed like a holy relic in this church.

The Preacher said, 'And what are the sexual preferences of those in the arrangement?'

She said, 'We are both Asexual. We chose not to be led into temptation.' There was a murmuring in the congregation as this was unusual, but not utterly unheard of. It was a choice among the most pious of the Green cause.

'And who is the seed, planted in Her ground?'

She could smell the incense, and she looked around the room, which was rammed full of people, as more people tried to squeeze into the church to witness this historic moment first-hand. She spoke softly but clearly, 'The Father is unknown. It was chosen by Bodhi Sattva himself, and he stated that it could be his own, but we should never know this truth so that all people of the New Green World should treat the child as if he was the Father.'

The scribe gave a puzzled look at the Preacher, who shrugged and then indicated that he should write what he saw fit. The Preacher looked at Sissy and said, 'I wish to use the Holy Water upon the child's head as you name him. This isn't a Green custom but would be an honour, and a confirmation of the truth that dwells within the soul of the child. Do you consent?'

'Of course. As long as it is noted that my baby is them, not him, xe will be brought up as gender fluid as that will be the future way of all children born from now.'

A look of consternation crossed his face, but he was dealing with the wishes of Bodhi Sattva and Genesis Garcia. She added, 'The old ways are the Trad ways. We have promised to abandon the Traditional Cultures. If anybody considers this to be abhorrent to them, they can always choose to regress and live among the Trads. The Security Protocols™ are to be enhanced to prevent Gender hate and discrimination.'

She waited until the expected uproar reached a crescendo and then quietened quickly, as the realisation hit the congregation that they could be Filmed at any moment. The Preacher took a moment to understand that he was free to practice his religious freedoms, but he couldn't rebel against the people who had promised and were delivering Heaven on Earth. He unconsciously gripped his bottle of Holy Water, and then he relaxed, he didn't want the religious significance of his breaking of the bottle - not here, not today. He completed his service, 'And what is the given name of the child?' He added, to prove that he had listened and received her message, loud and clear, 'What are they to be called?'

She said, loudly and proudly, 'Century…Brady…Garcia.'

He looked at her, astonished, he declared, 'In the name of the Father, the Son and the Holy Ghost. In the presence of the Green Community of Santa Clarita, I name this child, Century…B…Brady…Garcia. So, help me, God.' He put the sign of the cross in Holy Water on the baby's forehead. The child gurgled and smiled as the water touched his brow. Cain moved in close to Sissy, his robe was pure white, once more. He looked at Sissy, she smiled and turned to her child and gazed into his brown eyes. Cain looked at Siddha and nodded, he then looked into the congregation and smiled warmly, as he scanned the audience with his crystal green eyes, and he caught the gaze of as many as he could.

Cain then moved slowly forward, and the congregation parted before him. He led Siddha, Sissy and Century out of the Christ Lutheran Church and back to the haven of their FusionCoach™, where Oleg the Disciple and his daughter were waiting to take them back to the FusionPlane™ to fly Cain and Siddha onto their next problem district and to take Sissy back to Boulder Creek to deliver the baby into the arms of Annabelle.

Sissy, still holding her child, looked Oleg up and down and said, 'I've done my bit. Sort the Brady Mahone situation out. Do you understand?'

He nodded, but his daughter stepped in and said, 'Don't worry. It will be done - I'll spread the word, far and wide.'

21.SURROUNDED

Brady had been no more than half-a day's drive from home in the three weeks he'd been in San Bernardino, but he had lost his desire to return to his more familiar stomping ground.

He had sketched every new creature he came across from weird insects and lizards to bobcats and Mountain lions to the Black bears. Even as he was running low on supplies, he had a senseless superstitious rule - to increase the stakes - that he wouldn't allow himself to return home until he found his Kangaroo rat. In a twisted logic, Brady felt that fate had brought him his lousy luck - ignoring the scientific fact that it was the International Space Station - and therefore the discovery of the Kangaroo rat would be the fate that would signal his next move.

He considered his dislike of rats in an urban setting as he recalled them crawling over the dying girl in Los Banos. There were few creatures which made Brady's skin crawl. *It's probably because the lowest of the low in the criminal world are rats. Maybe, that's why they make my skin crawl.* Kangaroo rats weren't in the same ballpark as the urban rats in Brady's world. They were a rare and exotic breed, and a treasure to be discovered.

He hadn't showered in his time in the desert, and his clothes were dusty, and Brady had grown an unkempt and bushy black beard. The dust in his clothes added to his camouflage, but he guessed his stink of three weeks of not washing probably countered this. *It's like being in solitary without the walls.*

He went to his Hearse and checked on his dwindling water supply. *This is gonna make a good contest between me and the rat.* He ate some stale bread and cheese, partly out of a desire to stave off the hunger pains, and partly act as penance for his stupidity in getting himself into this mess. He picked up his Distor™ on his regular check to ensure his Greenbacks were still registered. He had an increasing paranoia that the Greens would empty his account. He had never considered before that his wealth wasn't backed up by any laws that he knew. His money was still there.

He went back to the day of the Revolution when his fifty-thousand dollars of life savings had been wiped out by the GreenRevs. *They stole from me back then - and they could do it again.* He laughed at the rhyme and thought it would make a great slogan against those Green bastards.

He flicked through his latest sketches. He had enjoyed exploring in the dark, under the glittering stars. *At least, I didn't have Tyrone trying to tell me all their names.* He found snakes he liked to draw, the Sidewinder, Western Diamondback, and Tiger Rattlesnakes. They reminded him of the time he spent down here all those many years ago with his Foster Daddy. Archie Mahone had been telling the young Brady about the scaredy-cat city-slickers and their tall tales about Rattlesnakes chasing them through the desert and all the way back to their cars. Archie took him on night-walks to find the Rattlesnakes, and he recalled being told to always treat them with respect, and they could kill a man if you didn't take care, but let's go and see if they really dare chase a man.

They found a dozen Rattlesnakes over the next couple of nights, but not one chased them. They went out of their way to back off from these encroaching humans.

He walked alone this time and relived those times. The humans may have changed their behaviours, but the snakes acted the same as they ever did.

He thought he caught a glimpse of a Kangaroo rat last night, but not clearly enough to complete his quest. It was about a half-mile east of the Hearse. He thought he would check the area out again, tonight. He felt confident he would track down his quarry.

Another week had gone by, and he was out of water, but he packed up his car in readiness for his journey home. He had his drawing. He had won his wager. Brady's anger at his treatment hadn't subsided. His mind rang out with the screams from the crowds. *Out, Brady out!* He hadn't made the mental leap into the patterns of his life, where anger always led him into trouble.

He wanted action.

It had been sixteen years since he had last been through Castaic. He knew that the Cesare crime gang would take control with an iron grip. He could have taken the same route back as he came - on Route 58, but he wanted to go via Highway 5. He always knew Castaic would end up being run like a prison, with Vincent Cesare as the Warden with his family as the Prison Guards. Brady had had enough of prison back then, and he wanted out of the survival of the fittest deal he had known in Ridgecrest Supermax.

He set off in a dark mood. Somebody was going to pay, someone was going to satisfy his need for vengeance, his need for violence. As he made rapid progress along the virtually deserted Highway, all he thought about was his preparedness to fight.

Before he reached the outskirts of Castaic, he pulled into a layby. He grabbed his Poacher's coat and double-checked that his blades were still in the right pockets, for convenience and speed. He took out his sharpening tool and ground them until their razor-sharp edges shone in the sparkling fall sunshine.

He quietened his mind to sharpen his wits. When he was at action readiness, he pulled onto the Highway, and a few minutes later, he turned off into Castaic. He cruised toward the town centre, but unlike in a previous life when he would have cruised for girls, this time he was cruising for victims. The first thing he noticed was that the main road into Castaic was protected by a NanoShell™. Hungry looking youths were throwing bricks at him as he went by them, but they bounced off the Shell™, harmlessly. It reminded him of when the Hodgson boys were throwing rocks at the NanoShell™ around the New Road around West McFarland. He also remembered brutally dispatching the same Hodgson boys. *That Cain fella couldn't handle watching a good old boy dishing out a little instant justice.* He considered jumping out the Hearse and confronting these scrawny looking youths but changed his mind. *They ain't too much of a challenge and would probably just run off down an alley. Brady Mahone needs a worthy opponent.* He gave them the finger but cruised on.

The sight of the town's neglect soon began to dampen his enthusiasm. There was garbage piled up everywhere. He stopped his car and looked out, and the place seemed deserted. He'd explored places in this state, hundreds of times before, as he went scavenging for entertainments for his business. He wasn't even sure if he had a business anymore, so he wasn't planning to search too thoroughly for new finds, today.

He turned down a side road, and even Brady was shocked at what he saw. Hanged bodies were dangling from old shop signs, and a couple of dead bodies hung from meat-hooks. There were men, women and children. He examined one a little closer, and he saw a cardboard sign, which was hung around the neck of a young boy with coarse string, it stated. *Death for those that disobey. Vincent Cesare.* Although the street was silent, except for the sounds of birdcall, and rats scurrying. He felt as if he was being watched. He instinctively turned back. He wanted a fight, but this felt like a lair. He strode back purposefully, but then an old man, being pushed by a younger man who looked skeletal, as if he was on the brink of starvation, pulled out in front of him. There was something in the movement's arrogance, which suggested that the old man was still the boss around here. Brady knew that others would be coming up from behind.

It looks like I've found my fight.

The old man said, 'I know you. You look familiar. I don't recall the name.'

'Brady. Brady Mahone. I used to have a Green bike and a trailer.'

The old man thought for a while. 'I remember. You gave me advice on how to run this place without guns.' He added, 'You've aged remarkably well, my friend.'

He looked at the old man, whose sharp glances suggested an agile mind at odds with his fragile body. 'You're Vincent Cesare. I was in Ridgecrest with one or two of your extended family.' He added, 'You seem to have everything under your control. Please accept my congratulations.' The odd formality even surprised Brady, as that was always how he felt he should address the more dangerous members of the Mob.

Vincent nodded, but Brady also spotted a glance away which suggested a signal. Brady put both hands through his black hair, as an unconcerned demonstration that he was unarmed, but then casually put his hands in his Poacher's coat pocket. The old man said, 'Unfortunately for you. Strangers aren't allowed in my town, especially those with their eyes on a potential takeover. I know what you're doing. You've let me do the heavy lifting, while I whipped this place into shape, and then you think you can just stroll in and take it from me. Do you think I'm helpless?'

'I don't want this poxy town, but I know you won't believe me, and I don't care. Do what ya gotta do.'

He heard footsteps behind him, and he saw two men approaching. In another life, they looked like they might have been hard men. He tried to imagine their large and emaciated frames padded out with muscle like they would have been in their prime. They had knives in both hands. They swung at him, but Brady evaded them expertly. They were not agile, and they were frailer than they looked. He knew they wouldn't be much of a contest for Brady Mahone in his prime. He was just beginning to lose interest, when he spotted people at the windows, watching the spectacle. They looked weak from malnutrition and fearful. He looked at the dead bodies hanging only a few feet above the pavement.

The two old gangsters prodded and probed with their knives but missed hitting Brady by long inches. Brady looked in their faces, and it reminded him of the look that one or two of the death row prisoners had in their eyes on the days leading up to their executions. It was a look that said, *let's just get this over with.*

278

He sensed they wanted him to attack, and to allow them to die in combat, rather than the shame of fading away in starvation.

Brady toyed with them, he circled them around to keep his eyes on Vincent and his tall, skinny companion. *I also know the look of a sneak and a runner.* Brady almost felt he was too kind to his attackers by giving them the chance to die with respect, as they were most likely responsible for the dead bodies lined up along the pavements. He let them have one final lunge to see if they could even land a scratch on him - they couldn't. And that's when Brady moved in for the kill, the first he plunged his blade into his heart and then hooked the knife viciously upward to fatally wound him. He knew the second would attack while the blade was momentarily stuck in the chest, so he swung his other arm around with the blade held out to catch the second attacker in the stomach, then with his released hand he slit his throat. In an instant, he threw a knife at tremendous speed, and it plunged into the head of the tall, skinny accomplice before he could even contemplate running away. Vincent tried feebly to back up his wheelchair, but his helper's body was in the way.

Brady shouted to the watchers, 'Are there any more, Cesares?'

Feeble voices from the surrounding buildings replied, 'No.' One voice attempted to shout, 'Only Vincent Cesare.'

Brady marched on Vincent Cesare menacingly. He stood over him and whispered, 'Not anymore.' He stabbed him in the heart, twice, and then watched him die. He smiled before retrieving his other blade from the skinny sneak.

He took one last look at the ruins of Castaic and assessed that the population would soon be at a point where the Greens would move in and relocate the remaining Trads, and then people like Samuel Beardon the Third, Alicia and Tyrone would come along and dispose of the dead bodies. He walked back to his Hearse. He ignored the cries of one or two of the survivors to stay and help them. They recognised the hope of having somebody as healthy as Brady to save them. But Brady had bigger fish to fry, and his thoughts were turning to the biggest fish of all - Bodhi Sattva.

22.MOUNTING EVIDENCE

Brady brooded and planned. He chose not to stop off and check what the current state of play was with the Green Towns and their views on Brady Mahone. He felt as if he was in the zone and making big decisions about his future. *I feel like I could live forever at this rate, but what's the point if I didn't have anything to do?*

He was in auto-pilot mode as he headed back to McFarland. He was aware of his poor personal hygiene. *I stink real bad.* He laughed alone as the car moved serenely on the near-deserted Highway - even after all these years he still couldn't get used to that - *It's another good reason not to visit anyone. I don't want people to think that Brady Mahone has let himself go.* He decided that the first thing on his embryonic to-do list was to shower, shave and maybe use his Foster Daddy's hair-clippers and trim his hair. He remembered that he had missed an appointment to meet Judge Jefferson a while back. *It's not the same as when I used to meet Professor Chu - I used to look forward to that. He was good to me. He made me feel real good about myself.*

He stopped off at the East McFarland bus stop and left a brief note. There wasn't an apology. *She just gotta accept that sometimes Brady Mahone is busy, y'know, indisposed.* He was proud of this latest addition to his vocabulary.

Hi Judge

Castaic won't be long until it turns Green.

I'll be here tomorrow at 6pm - if ya wants to see me.

Brady.

He went home. Even though he was hungry and thirsty, Brady cleaned himself thoroughly, first. Then he made himself a big meal and drank heavily. Brady gave a lot of thought into what he wanted out of life, especially if he planned to stick around for the long term. He wandered onto the porch. He looked outside, and he saw the Lopez family, in the near distance. He then caught a hint of green at the extremes of his vision. He didn't need to check it out. He had been away for more than seven days, the GreenShell™ had enveloped itself over the Mahone Ranch. He thought of himself as a kind of honorary Green, he wasn't concerned about his home being visited by Operation Clean-up teams. He was emotionally troubled by the thought that the Lopez family couldn't visit his house, barn or bunker ever again. He wondered if they had noticed yet. The idea brought him down, but he needed to plan. He shook his head vigorously, trying to eject the negativity away. *Fuck 'em. I've done my bit for them.* He considered that he was lying to himself. Lucian had saved his life.

He headed back inside and poured a hot black coffee in the vain attempt to sober up. It took a while before the anger subsided about how the Lopez family had dishonoured him, unfairly. He began to feel more positive as he became distracted by his mind adding to his plans for the future. He knew he was entering a dream-like state when his background thoughts over the last few weeks had completed their tasks and were about to present him with their conclusions. *What do I want? What would make Brady Mahone happy and contented again?* His inner-mind responded, *So, you have been happy at some point in your life - do you admit it?'* He knocked back a large whiskey. *I hate to admit it, but the happiest I ever felt was after the Revolution. I was kinda legit most of the time. I felt respected and needed. I provided, and people listened to me. And I really liked being rich in this world - that felt real good.* He had his roadmap out of the blues, he just had to confirm his route. He had to identify his destination, his mode of transport, and what he was going to do when he got there. He needed purpose and reason, the things that kept Brady Mahone moving forward. He considered this with a positive mental attitude - a problem-solving catchphrase for Brady Mahone. He never knew where this came from, he felt as if it had always been there - something he was born with.

I want my business back...I want to expand my business...I want to sleep with that Rhea. She's my kinda woman, and she's kinda cute for a Green. Brady put on some music he liked from the forties. It was a stripped-down industrial metal. It was tough, and *not that electronic synthesiser crap* - as he described it, Brady thought that was music for wimps. *I want to see Boulder Creek. I want to find where that Bodhi Sattva hangs out. Maybe Brady Mahone could show him a thing or two to shake that smug bastard up.*

He went to the jewellery box in his bedroom. He picked up the Sattva Systems™ ring he had found from his haul at Libby Kane's home. It was part of Bodhi Sattva's secret stash. He had it affixed to a chain and he hung it around his neck. It was the first time he had done that for more than a decade. Ten years gone. He then picked up the Tiberius Black File. *If I find him, this could really fuck him up, or the people around him.*

He wanted to let this thought sink in, so he went for a walk around his grounds in the fresh night air. He looked at his Distor™. *I really want to get to a million Greenbacks. I want to be a Greenback millionaire.* He stroked his Hearse. *It sure is the most boring car design ever, but it's been real reliable. I love you, honey.* He was drunk, and yet he had hit the sweet spot in his drinking where he felt high on positivity. Brady knowing precisely what he wanted and needed, seemed to clear the fog of loneliness. He then laughed as he looked at his Hearse again. *I want me one of those FusionPlanes™. I'm gonna get me my own private jet.*

It took him most of the next day to get over his hangover, but Brady felt it was worth it. He deemed it a price worth paying to blast the negative thoughts and self-pity he had been harbouring over the last few weeks. In keeping with this newfound self-worth, he decided to dress up smartly to meet with Judge Jefferson this evening. He also filled up his car with more discarded clothing from the Greens, which he had stored in his barn.

He took the short trip in his Hearse and arrived simultaneously as Judge Audre Jefferson and another man. She had arrived in the horse and carriage. As Brady pulled up in his Hearse, Audre was being helped out of the carriage. She said, 'Hello Brady. This is Norbert, he is my friend and is a tremendous help to me.' Brady stuck out his hand, and Norbert shook it firmly. Brady noted the strength and assumed Norbert worked out to keep fit. He also noticed his frayed suit was clean and pressed, and his worn-out shoes were still polished. Brady could smell soap. *He smells of discipline.* Brady looked into the deep blue eyes of Officer Norbert Stillman, and he didn't catch a glimpse of fear or concern. He quickly helped Officer Norbert fill-up the carriage with the donated clothes, before getting down to business with the Judge.

Norbert helped Audre to the seat in the bus shelter. He then retrieved a binder from the carriage and Audre took it from him and placed it on her lap. Brady moved to sit alongside her. She said, 'I'm pleased you could make it today. I've completed putting my case together against Sattva Systems™ and the State of California.' She laughed, 'Not that it means anything, but it's always good to know the truth, and history needs it recorded, even if history may only live on in the mind of Brady Mahone.' She looked at him kindly, 'Brady Mahone, for reasons I still cannot fathom, history as chosen you to bear witness to what happened here. Soon, you will be the only man alive, who knows the truth about how this all came to pass.'

'I'm nothing special. I'm just a guy who puts one foot in front of the other and keeps moving forward.'

She removed her wrinkled black hand from the binder she was clutching and rubbed Brady's cheek, 'You are still so young, and you have many years of life ahead of you. Who can tell how far you will travel in that time, taking your one step at a time - and forever moving forwards? You could go a long way, Mr Mahone.' She slowly moved her hand away from his face and returned it to the binder. 'I could have returned all the files you gave me, but I wasn't sure you would turn up today. In this binder, I have summarised my findings down to a couple of hundred pages. I have resisted the urge to use the legalese, which was so prevalent in my profession. I would be happy to tell you the potted headlines - that's if you have the time to listen?'

'Yes. It would be useful to know about these people. I have plans to meet with this Bodhi Sattva one day. You could say I've got a business proposition to put to him.'

'If you ever did meet him, then I would strongly advise you to listen carefully, especially if he gives you his word on a deal.'

Brady looked at her, he trusted her judgment, 'What do you mean?'

'He gave his word on so many business transactions before the crash. What he said and delivered was the literal truth. He didn't lie, he didn't renege on his promises, but he knew what was going to happen, and he made his words snake around this omission.'

Brady thought deeply before asking, 'If he said he would give me a million dollars, would I end up having it?'

'If that was all he said, then yes - that would be his word. But if he gave a million dollars for a service, or for the completion of a task, or a business deal, then don't be surprised if he has made you do something with entirely unforeseen consequences. You will then re-examine his words and see the plan was there all along.' She watched Brady cup his chin with his hand as if trying to work out this puzzle. She added, 'The problem for you is that this was the way he dealt with what we now call the Trads - I think colloquially he would have been called a double-dealing-four-flusher.' Brady laughed at hearing Audre using this term. She looked at him as if she were trying to find a definitive answer from his appearance. She noticed some scratches and abrasions on Brady which were healing over from his recent exertions in Castaic. She said, 'However, with his Green friends, he gave these people his word, and he delivered unto them precisely what he promised, and in the spirit of which it was promised - of this I am sure. Of vital importance to you Brady, is that if you ever do meet, or confront this man, is knowing how he views you. Would Bodhi Sattva believe he is dealing with Brady Mahone the Trad, or Brady Mahone the Green? Who are you, Brady Mahone?'

Brady Mahone roared with laughter, 'It sounds like a joke we used to make about the prison shrinks after the tell me about your childhood, we would ask - Who am I? What am I? What am I doing here? Then I would say - Twenty years with time off for good behaviour.'

Audre was disappointed with Brady's attitude. It reminded her of the man she used to pass sentence on, and maybe he hadn't evolved as much as she had hoped. He saw this and knew he had regressed to an older version of himself - like an old dialect returning after years away from home. He said, 'Sorry, Judge. I hear you. I'm a Trad who got lucky - is all.'

'Then be careful, his promises will have hidden depths and ulterior motives.'

He nodded, but Audre smiled. She said, 'Now you must let me tell you what I have discovered. This would have been the case of a lifetime, and I would have loved to have discussed it with all my old friends and colleagues. This case would have had me making press conferences, TV appearances. And I would undoubtedly have been promoted. However, you are my only audience, and I can't wait to tell you.'

Brady smiled, 'For once in my life, Judge - I can't wait to hear you hand down your verdict.'

She licked her lips and unclenched her stiff fingers around the binder and passed it to Brady. She said, 'Sattva Systems™ had a global reach, but I will tell you about what happened in California. But what happened here was replicated across the planet, the only thing that made California special was its links to Silicon Valley.'

'Ok.'

'I won't go into all the technical stuff about Nano-technology's research and development, Intense Renewable Energy and FusionPower™.'

'Thanks. I don't fancy going back to science class.'

'If ever you did want to know, there's a chapter on it in the binder.' She looked at Norbert, who was feeding the horse with a couple of apples. 'The major felonies revolved around the corruption of key politicians. Here it was the Governor of California. He bankrolled her campaigns. She used to be an influencer on social media. Do you remember those?'

Officer Norbert interrupted them, 'I'll just take a ride to the pasture to let him have some grass.' She nodded, and he rode away.

Brady said, 'Vaguely. Not really my bag. They used to have millions of followers who would be obsessed with taking pictures of themselves all the time.'

'Close enough. Anyway, Genesis Garcia had over one-hundred million followers who admired her radical Democrat credentials and her fire-brand rhetoric when it came to the environment. Her ideals matched those of the Kane family. To cut a long story short, she paved the way for Sattva Systems™ to raise billions of dollars, and she ensured the passage of everything they desired to expand the company. She was the Governor of California, but she hated what big business and big tech had done to the planet, she even despised those of her own constituents who disrespected the environment, so she effectively went to work for Sattva Systems™.' She knew she had to deliver this information in bitesize chunks as she knew Brady's attention would drift. 'Were you a Republican or a Democrat back then?'

'Neither. They both sent Brady Mahone to jail. What about you, Judge?'

'I was a Republican. I believed in law and order.'

'That kinda makes sense. I get it so far. A corrupt politician with a funny name is in the pocket of the Mob.'

'Yes, in essence. The information you supplied had transcripts of secret emails, invoices demonstrating corruption and fraudulent transactions - that kind of thing.'

Brady said, 'It's good to know, but it don't help me much.'

'I know. But it's important to me that I passed this knowledge on before I leave this world. I couldn't countenance this dying with me. I have told the folks here in East McFarland, but I think we both know that our time here ain't long.' She said this like an old blues musician was uttering it.

Brady nodded. 'I got it, Judge.' He tapped his temple, 'It's in here.' He then tapped the binder, 'And here.'

She said, 'I do have another investigation here, which I have most of the answers for. And that concerns the disappearance and death of John Kane.'

Brady braced himself, for an uncomfortable few minutes ahead. He wasn't guilty in this upcoming interrogation, but he was withholding evidence. He listened as she added the inevitable comments, 'However, I am missing a few facts which would help me tie-up some loose ends. I have to admit, that it's a bit of a mystery as to why these key players in an international conspiracy all ended up here in McFarland at one time or another.' She smiled, but only received a smile in return, it was less defensive than a no comment to the Judge.

She said, 'Let me tell you how far I got into this investigation. First of all, John Kane's name has been redacted from every single document. However, his is the only name that fits the situations and timelines from the volume of evidence. I am certain that we have the clues to his disappearance and murder.' She took a deep breath. 'John Kane left his Boulder Creek Headquarters on February 14, 2050, at 9:30 am. He told his PA that he was going to visit his ex-wife, Libby Kane in Malibu. Libby was adamant that no visit was arranged, and she had an alibi which checked out. She was a suspect because she had been left out of his will. She kept her home, but she believed her prenup had entitled her to a quarter of Sattva Systems™ wealth…'

Brady thought of her home and daydreamed about extorting that from Bodhi Sattva, while Audre continued to present her findings, Brady added the Malibu home to his wish-list, he wanted Bodhi to have to give him something which he was personally attached to. *It would make a great retirement pad, and eventually, it could be my pension.* He was then shaken out of his pleasant reverie.

'…The last sighting of John Kane was in McFarland. He never made it further south than that. You were probably too young to remember, but the FBI combed the area around here for weeks after his disappearance.'

Brady smiled. *Pops was a paranoid conspiracy theorist he would have buried him real deep.* He said insolently, 'True dat.' But this was a clue to Judge Jefferson that she was on the right path. She knew Brady knew more than he was letting on.

She said, 'There are detailed maps of Sattva Systems™ HQ in Boulder Creek and McFarland and the surrounding lands, as these were the places the FBI carried out their most intensive searches.'

'The Boulder Creek maps could come in handy.' He asked, 'Are the maps in here?' He tapped the binder.

'Yes.' She continued, 'This is the point where the prime suspect in John Kane's murder makes an appearance. He was the rather grandly titled, Samuel Beardon the Second. Have you heard of this man?'

'No. Why should I have?'

She knew he was lying because it was too much of a coincidence that the notes, he had left for her, detailing the events in Encinitas were signed by Tyrone Beardon, and they were written in a highly educated hand. 'No reason. Only asking.'

Brady tried to ask as if he was only making polite conversation, 'What's the deal with this Beardon guy?'

'The Beardon family had close ties to John Kane and his son, Xavier. John Kane covered the costs of his education. Samuel Beardon the Second received his Doctorate in the Effects of Climate Change. He was a passionate follower of John Kane and a key member of the Sattva Systems™ hierarchy.'

Brady laughed, 'Doesn't sound like a killer to me?'

'I agree, except for Samuel Beardon the Second having a major falling out with John Kane and his son Xavier.'

'What about?'

'Samuel Beardon the Second had evidence from fellow professors in his field - people he respected, who claimed that the work Sattva Systems™ had already done with Intense Renewable Energies and FusionPower™ in the millions of New Green communities across the planet had already done enough to improve the effects of climate change on the planet.'

Brady's interest in this development was piqued, he knew this was crucial to what followed. He focussed intensely on Audre. 'There wasn't the need for the Revolution. All of this was unnecessary - and he knew that. I'm betting he told them, but they didn't want to change their plans. Next, he would threaten them, maybe expose the story to the press - his Father was an Internet Preacher for Sattva Systems™, he would have access to millions...'

She had his interest, and she needed to work with this. 'That's about the gist of it. Samuel Beardon the Second had been caught on CCTV in McFarland on the morning of John Kane's disappearance. He was refused bail by Judge Pilkington in Boulder Creek and remanded - how can I put this politely, Judge Pilkington had a one-eyed view on dealing with black men accused of murdering a white man of high standing in the community.'

Brady said thoughtfully, 'Xavier Kane or Bodhi Sattva as we now knew him, still had a problem. He needed to shut this guy up - he knew too much - so he had him killed. Bodhi seizes control of the company, Samuel Beardon the Second gets pinned for his Father's murder, and the Revolution continues as planned.'

Judge Audre Jefferson laughed and said, 'Fancy a job as an investigator?'

'Detective Inspector Brady Mahone, at your service, Ma'am.' He laughed heartily as he mockingly bowed to her. 'I'm well qualified. I have a unique insight into the criminal mind. These guys are just criminals with more cash - is all.'

She nodded and smiled softly, 'Brady. I'm going to make a leap here. I have no evidence other than my gut tells me that you are at the heart of this. I don't know why, or how, but McFarland is a small, inconsequential town in many respects, and yet we have one of the most talked about murder mysteries happen on our doorstep, and then we have you, a local man from the same small town who seems to link all the pieces together.'

'If this all happened in 2050, then I was only seven or eight-years-old at the time.'

'I know. I have no jurisdiction over you. I am no threat to you, whatsoever. If you told me the whole truth, I could do nothing with it. Uttering the truth is powerful, it has the power to wash the past shames away. I just want to hear the truth to go to my grave understanding how this all came to pass. I might be able to still help and advise you.'

Brady didn't want to snitch on anybody. It was a code embedded into his psyche. It went against his sense of honour. 'I don't know, Judge. It's a lot to ask.'

She deduced that even as an uncontrollable wild eight-year-old, Brady could not have murdered a man. He wouldn't be struggling with his conscience if he had evidence on an old resident of McFarland. It had to have something to do with his parents. With her next piece of evidence, it would lead to his Foster Father, Archie Mahone.

'In that binder, is where the CIA's interest comes in. John Kane's name is judiciously redacted throughout, but they believed he was involved - no - an international human trafficking operation leader. They abducted children from across the globe. They deliberately selected as many child variants of race, sex and creed as possible. They made fortunes on the back of sex trafficking, but even more worryingly than that, the CIA believed that John Kane and Sattva Systems™ were carrying out NanoTech™ experiments on them, and when these were concluded, they worked on the most efficient means to dispose of the bodies, using enzymes and NanoTechnology™ hybrids.'

Brady pulled both hands up to cover his face. 'What the fuck? This is totally fucked-up.' He said, 'John Kane was the leader of a paedophile ring. My Foster Daddy was a member. It was called All Friends Together.'

'That corroborates the evidence you hold. That was the name of the Californian Chapter - as they liked to call themselves.'

He nodded slightly, 'John Kane came for me. He wanted me.' He stopped before stating, 'My Pops never laid a finger on me. He was always good to me. He loved me - that was why he killed John Kane. He wouldn't let him take me away. I've seen what my Pops could do to a child, it's utterly disgusting, but he never did that to me. You do, believe me, your honour?'

'I believe you, Brady Mahone.' She hugged him weakly, but with as much tenderness as she could muster. 'The Beardon family have made contact with you.' It was not a question.

'Yes. Samuel Beardon the Third, his daughter Alicia and his nephew, Tyrone. They are good people, like you - not like me.'

'I'm guessing he has been investigating the death of his Father, for the last fifty years. You have the answers he needs. If you could bring yourself to tell him what you have told me, then you would prove yourself to be a very good man indeed. If I had the power of a priest, I would absolve you - I truly would, for such an unselfish act.'

Brady thought about the futility of protecting the past, and the potential healing he had to give in the here and now. 'If he will ever want to see me again - then I'll do it. At the moment he thinks I'm some kinda devil or something.'

She smiled, 'I ain't a priest, but I am a Judge, and I'm going to give myself the power to pardon you for all your past crimes and misdemeanours - though they are many.' They both laughed, and Brady felt the burden lift from him. She joked, 'And if anyone wants to argue with my judgment. You tell them to come and discuss my decision with Judge Audre Jefferson of McFarland.'

He turned to go as he heard the clip-clopping of horse's hooves as Officer Norbert was returning. She shouted, 'I'll make it more official than my word. I'll have it typed up on official letter-headed stationery - I still have some supplies left. That way you can show them. It will be in the usual place behind the timetable.'

23.BIDING TIME

Brady spent the next few weeks carrying out some maintenance on his home during the day and reading the binder which Judge Jefferson had given him in the afternoons, and then in the evenings, he would drink moonshine. He made it the way his Pops had taught him, he wanted to keep his last few alcohol bottles for special occasions.

He used his evening times to reflect upon the information he had disseminated earlier in the day. He only read a couple of pages at a time. Judge Jefferson had written out her findings in a dumbed-down way for Brady, but at times it still wasn't dumb enough. In fairness to Brady, the deals' descriptions were convoluted, no matter how much they were simplified.

The items in the binder which Brady gravitated back to repeatedly were the highly detailed maps and photographs of the Sattva Systems™ complex and the surrounding area of Boulder Creek. He knew he was preparing for a confrontation with Bodhi Sattva, it felt like his destiny. Any future battles with any part of the Green organisation would be played out with words and not actions. He tried to visualise the layout of the complex, but he reminded himself that this information could be up to twenty to thirty years out of date, maybe even longer when it came to the John Kane part of the investigation.

Sometimes, he would be aware of the Lopez family going about their business. He would strain to try and hear parts of their conversation, but even the slightest breeze seemed to blow their words away like smoke. They didn't look over in Brady's direction, and he felt that this was forced, as he was convinced, they were doing this deliberately to snub him.

He thought back to his big showdown with Lizzie, where he had outsmarted a teacher. He was focussed that day - he was also angry. This focussed anger was something he needed to feel if he was going to teach Bodhi Sattva a lesson. *They under-estimate Brady Mahone at their peril.*

He had often wondered about the differences between the crime bosses he came upon inside prison, and their foot-soldiers. The soldiers were always afraid of losing violent battles, whereas the bosses were forever afraid of being outplayed. Having information that they didn't have - was a potent weapon. He knew it was vital that he knuckled down to his homework assignment before heading off to Boulder Creek. He also was aware that he needed to put his words and revelations in the correct order, so he began working on his delivery like a best man preparing a speech at a wedding.

He had photographs in the binder of the critical figures of the investigation, he looked hard at the last known portrait of John Kane and imagined his Pops garrotting him with a cheese wire. He had seen him before, of course, but there he was dressed in a Roman Emperor's robe, and his face was covered in make-up - he wondered if John Kane was jealous of his wife's acting career. He looked at the cute looking Governor of California, Genesis Garcia. Brady had paid so little attention to politics back then that he hadn't been aware of her at all. Then he examined the photograph of Xavier Kane, the portrait photo was all fresh-faced and gleaming white teeth and a bald head. He still looked young. A more distant shot showed him to be athletically built, a near perfect human specimen.

At night, the vision of Bodhi Sattva filled his dreams. Bodhi perched on a golden throne peering down at Brady with contempt as Brady stumbled to get his words out in the right order, while John Kane, Genesis Garcia, Libby Skye and thousands of others laughed at the stupid, Brady Mahone who foolishly thought he could outsmart these giants of the liberal elite.

His days began to blend together with his routine of maintenance, reading, thinking and dreaming.

Then, on one rainy evening, he heard raised voices from the Lopez Ranch. This time he couldn't make out the words because of the pattering of raindrops, but he could tell that this was one unholy row. He thought he could make out the sound of Amie crying, and Lucian and Mary-Lou shouting at each other, and even the sound of smashing crockery.

It then went quiet again, and he thought nothing of it, as he returned to his thoughts on the latest couple of pages of evidence he had analysed earlier in the day. It was a gruesome report on the discovery of many dead children in Pakistan. It was stamped, Top Secret - CIA. There were redacted passages where the names were obscured, but Judge Jefferson had pencilled in John Kane and other characters he hadn't heard of before, but John Kane's name was mentioned the most and was obviously the key player in the investigation. They had pictures attached with areas circled where they indicated puncture wounds, needle marks and cut-away skin rectangles. Some children had had their eyes surgically removed, and all of them had been sexually assaulted.

Even though Brady had heard the paedophile stories in his time in jail from his fellow inmates, this information still appalled him. Judge Jefferson had written a note for Brady:

These children were used as Guinea Pigs to develop their NanoSuits™. They used examples from all races to ensure they worked in all areas of the world. The FBI and the CIA were investigating child sex slave trafficking. They identified the link with John Kane, but they had no idea about the real purpose behind these child abductions.

Brady Mahone had no illusions about his own base nature, but this was beyond him. He would rather die himself than do this to a child and save his own skin. He thought back to when he set those children free from Small Hand Don, he remembered Angelique's kiss on his cheek and recalled her smile of gratitude. *I know I'm a bad guy, but these so-called pillars of society are worse than me. Always remember that when you are dealing with them.* He repeated it as if it was essential to remember precisely who he was dealing with and what they were capable of. *I ain't the bad guy here - they are.*

He then saw the Lopez family walking over toward him and his Ranch. Lucian was almost dragging Amie along with him, with Mary-Lou on the other side of him. They stopped at the edge of the NanoShell™ which now enveloped the Mahone ranch. This kept the Lopez family of Trads away from his home.

Lucian cried out, 'Brady. We need to talk, man.'

Brady downed his moonshine and looked out balefully at his neighbours. He was at least grateful to be shaken out of his reverie on child abuse. He pulled his big frame up slowly out of his rocking chair and stood to his full height as if to use his body language to remind them they were dealing with a man of strength and power.

He paced slowly toward them and beyond the NanoShell™ to confront them. 'You might need to talk, but I couldn't care less if I never had to deal with you and your collection of ingrates for the rest of my life.'

Amie was cowering behind Lucian, but he pulled her forward, forcefully. She still had tears in her eyes, and she looked down at the floor, as she tried to keep from making eye contact with Brady. Lucian said, 'Tell him.'

Amie said quietly, 'I'm sorry.'

Brady laughed, 'Hey bitch. I can't hear you.'

Mary-Lou said, 'She's just a girl, Brady. You've no idea what it's like to be brought up in this world. She has no friends of her own age - and never will.'

'I do believe you called me a pervert. You never even gave me a chance to hear my side of the story. I've moved heaven and earth for you and yours, and you treat me like scum. Do you think I don't hurt none?'

Amie's cry sounded like an outburst from the depths of her soul, 'I'm sorry. I'm sorry. I am ashamed and embarrassed about what I did that night.' She lowered her voice and said again, 'I'm so sorry.' She burst into tears, and Mary-Lou moved to comfort her daughter. Mary-Lou said, 'For what it's worth, Brady, I'm sorry too.'

Brady didn't know what else to say or do other than a nod in acknowledgement. He turned to Lucian, 'I'm surprised at you, of all people, Lucky. All those times in prison where you complained that you were jailed for a crime you didn't commit. Remember? How they shoulda investigated properly and all that shit. And then, here you are, accusing Brady Mahone of molesting your daughter, well, her daughter, technically.' He pointed at Mary-Lou. 'You never once defended me. You just up and took her word against mine. How long have we known each other, man? How could you think I would do that? You don't think that Brady Mahone can't get a bit of girlie action on his own when I'm on the road? You think I'd resort to taking advantage of a young girl who I considered as family? I would have done anything I could to help her. I would have got her anything - if it was available. I treated her like a daughter of my own.'

Brady's shoulders slumped. Lucian said, 'I know that. You are right. After everything you have done for us, we shouldn't have treated you that way. It was wrong.'

Brady recalled how Lucian had saved his life in Ridgecrest but was damned if he was going to bring that up, now. He wasn't going to water down their act of contrition by offsetting their shame, with this memory. 'Ok. Apology accepted.'

Mary-Lou said, 'What happens now?'

'I can't get rid of the Shell™, so you won't be able to come over no more - and you won't be able to use the barn. Not that that matters anyway as my business has dried up.'

She said, 'How did the Shell™ get here?'

'I left the building unoccupied for more than seven days, so it considered the Mahone Ranch to be deserted. I think if it was anybody but me living here, you would have seen the Operation Clean-Up crews come over and spray it into oblivion with their Green goo.'

'Anybody but you?'

'Yep. For good or ill, I seem to have become an honorary Green.'

'Well, if we can't come to you, then you'll have to come to us. If you want to, of course.'

Brady felt relieved that one area of his life had returned to normal, and he had missed having friends. 'I suppose so.'

24. REUNITED

Brady made frequent trips over to the Lopez Ranch over the next few days. He brought over clothes and supplies and regaled them with his latest travels. He spoke with enthusiasm about his time in Encinitas, and the crashing of the International Space Station, and how he timed it to perfection to greet the crash to show off to a local waitress - he had forgotten her name by now. They listened politely to this, believing that Brady had probably over-egged this particular story.

As they were tucking into an evening meal in the Lopez home, he told them about the Judge giving him his pardon, and proudly showed off his letter-headed paper - signed Judge Audre Jefferson of McFarland.

Lucian said, 'I don't understand why she would do that. Surely, you are an escaped felon on the run - just like me.'

Brady sighed, this was one story he needed to keep quiet, as the power was in its secrecy. 'That was a long time ago, and in the meantime, I've been giving them a lot of information - it didn't seem particularly earth shattering to me, but the clever people, like Professor Chu, put it to good use to protect the East McFarland Trads. Also, recently, I have been donating lots of clothes to them, the Greens are dumping them as they don't need them anymore. It looks like the good old boy, Brady Mahone has been doing his bit for charity.' He laughed, 'What's the word for one of those rich dudes that gives stuff to the poor.'

Mary-Lou answered, 'A philanthropist. Judge Jefferson clearly believes you are a reformed character. She's giving you her blessing in the hope that you will stand up and fly right.'

Brady laughed, again, 'She's betting on the wrong horse with that one.'

Amie searched for the voice within her. She hadn't said a word since her night of shame and apologies. She had to say something while there was a subject in the conversation which interested her, greatly. She feared either Mary-Lou or Lucian would take the conversation spinning away from her. She took two deep breaths. Her Moms looked at her with concern, and mouthed, are you ok? Amie with an effort blurted out before the words could be sucked back in on the next breath, 'Why don't the Green people need their clothes, anymore?'

For a moment she felt stupid and pathetic as no one answered immediately, but then Brady looked into her eyes. 'What do you know about NanoSuits™?'

'Nothing.' She looked down at the remnants of her dinner. 'I know which movies, TV shows and music the teenagers in the Green communities like, but that's about all.' She added with an apology, 'Not that I'm not grateful for that, I love to hear the sales reports. It kinda connects me to the outside world.'

Brady smiled as softly as he could, in a spirit of reconciliation, 'I could tell you all about the NanoSuits™ they wear - providing, of course, that Lucky and Mary-Lou don't mind me having to take over the dinner conversation with a lot of stuff they already know.'

Mary-Lou grabbed Brady's hand and smiled warmly, 'That would be nice, Brady.' She lied, 'I never really understood it really, so it would be good to have a recap.' Lucian knew what Brady was doing in trying to reassimilate Amie back into the group. He smiled his gratitude at Brady.

Brady tried to put his thoughts in order, and the process of storytelling recalled the time he spent with the Beardons - and the shark story which still haunted Brady. 'It started with the Green Revolution back in '84, when you were a babe in your Mom's arms. There was a company called Sattva Systems™, and they developed all kinds of technology in their quest to save the environment and the planet from extinction.' He smiled, 'They sure do like to sound like the good guys - but they ain't, believe me.' He continued, 'Then they developed this Nano-technology making it impossible to hurt someone who wore this Suit™. This is where the Green Revolutionaries or the GreenRevs joined forces with Sattva Systems™ to bring down capitalism - the old way of running things. They planned this way back in 2050 when the governments rescinded some climate change accord or something like that.'

Lucian said, 'Hey, man. I didn't know that.' Amie looked at him sheepishly, it had taken an effort to get Brady to discuss anything with her. She didn't want the conversation to move onto the politics of way back when. She wanted to know how the other kids lived. He said, 'Sorry. I didn't mean to interrupt.'

Brady said, 'Anyways, those indestructible NanoSuits™ were called RedSuits™. At the 2085 New Year's Day ceremony, Cain passed on the RedSuits™ to the whole of West McFarland.'

Amie said, quietly, 'What was that like?'

He pulled out his Distor™, 'Cain, the Disciple, had one of these, fully loaded with NanoBots™, and the whole community held hands, and it kinda got passed on from one to another.'

Mary-Lou said, 'I've seen this Cain. He looked like a vision of Christ, our Lord.'

Brady didn't feel it was appropriate to give his feelings on Cain at this point. Why spoil a good story with the truth? 'Since then, every few years or so, they keep adding layers, or upgrades or some sh-, stuff like that. They had the OrangeSuits™ next. This put NanoBots™ inside them to cure any known illnesses, it means they don't suffer from cancer, pandemics, or even coughs and colds anymore. And this is where we come in - the last Suits™ they upgraded to was Yellow™. With these they can conjure up imaginary clothing, at least that how it appears to me, maybe it's real - who knows. This means they can dress any way they like, whenever they want. They can change clothes in an instant - just like that.' He sprang his fingers open as if he were completing a magician's trick.'

Amie's eyes widened, 'That sounds amazing. I can see why people would want that.' She added, 'Would you buy one of these NanoSuits™?'

'I sure could afford to, but my Pops...'

Mary-Lou said, 'It's ok.'

'My Pops was always into his conspiracies. He wasn't always on the money, but he had his moments. Anyway, he warned me about being tempted by governments offering bribes, he said, "Son, that's how they get you." I never really understood, but it felt right. I didn't fully get it, but I think he was cautioning me to wait until the big picture emerged. So, I've resisted the urge to fully join them.'

The more I see of their big picture, the more certain I will never want to be one of them. Any organisation that makes Brady Mahone feel he is on the righteous side is an organisation that nobody should join.

'Will there be any more NanoSuits™, or is that it?'

'Personally, I think they are gonna keep on coming. I've heard that the Green-Suits™ will reduce the Green's need for water. It will cut down on sewage, apparently.'

The Lopez family laughed, Amie giggled and said, 'What does that mean?'

Brady roared with laughter, 'It means they will pee and poop less.' They all laughed and shook their heads in disbelief.

Lucian said, 'Does that mean you'll be making a roaring trade selling discarded toilets next?' He laughed at his own joke until he was crying, he spluttered, 'I apologise for using toilet humour at the dinner table.' They all laughed and laughed.

25. THE STOPOVER

Brady didn't know what reception awaited him in the Green Communities. He hadn't visited one since he was ordered to leave San Martin many weeks ago. He knew Boulder Creek was only about a half-day drive from his East McFarland Ranch, but he wanted to see if the situation had changed. He decided to try San Martin again, as it wasn't too far out of his way. He felt like letting fate decide if Samuel Beardon the Third should ever get a shot at the truth of what happened to his Father. However, if it came to pass that Brady should meet up with the Bear again, then it was up to Brady Mahone as to how much, and what version of the truth, the Bear would receive.

He chose to take the longer route to San Martin. He had become a little bored of forever travelling along either Highway 99 or Highway 5. He headed west to Paso Robles and then north through Salinas. He had become accustomed to fleets of HeavyLoader™ FusionPlanes™ flying overhead in formation, noiselessly, usually consisting of between ten to twenty at a time. Brady never ceased to enjoy the sight of these flypasts. They had become a frequent sight since more of the Trad communities were emptying, thus prompting Operation Clean-Ups to begin their tasks. As he journeyed closer to the coast, he saw a sight which may have appalled others, but Brady thought was totally out of sight. Hugging the California coastline, there was a fleet of hundreds of HeavyLoaders™ in strict formation. Brady had never seen so many FusionPlanes™ flying together before. They were flying low and heading steadily southwards. *Somewhere real big must have fallen.* He pulled over for an hour as he watched this magnificent procession fly by. He felt the thrill of the subsonic booms as they reached him, and he chewed on his sandwiches and drank coffee from his thermos and tried to picture being in the city where these vehicles would be spraying their Green goo.

He didn't leave his chosen spot until the formation drifted into small specks on the horizon. Even as he headed up to Salinas, he still couldn't resist trying to spot them in his mirror, they reminded him of a murmuration of starlings he'd watched when he was in Terra Linda - it was an event which happened more often since the Green Revolution.

By the time he reached San Martin, Brady was feeling peaceful. He had enjoyed the show of power the Greens had put on for him, and he felt vindicated that he had chosen the relatively scenic route here. He entered the small town with a sense of trepidation, but he needn't have worried - the townsfolk treated him as any other benign visitor. They tipped hats or smiled their good afternoons - almost over-eagerly. He then wondered if he was entering into a trap. He maintained a high level of preparedness, but nothing transpired.

He pulled up, in his Hearse, outside the Beardon's home. Tyrone came out to greet him, 'Brady! I've missed you - come in. Come in.'

Brady was taken aback when the old woman - who on his last visit here was brandishing her bared teeth and a silver cross at him - came over and hugged him and begged for him to accept her apology. He did, and then she made her excuses to leave Brady and the Beardon family in peace.

The Bear came out of the kitchen and hugged Brady and slapped him on the back a couple of times. Brady always respected the physical strength of Samuel Beardon the Third. 'You must stay for dinner.' Brady thought the smell of roasted vegetables and onions smelt real good, and the Bear could see he was tempted.

'I'm on my way to Boulder Creek. I just thought I'd drop by, to see how…'

'It was all a misunderstanding, once Cain, Siddha and even Genesis had explained everything…'

Tyrone interrupted, 'And me. I stuck up for you Brady. I told them you were just showing off is all. I explained that you didn't cause the International Space Station to destroy Encinitas…'

'Is that what they thought? Cool.'

The Bear said, 'We can talk about it over dinner. What do you say?' He added, 'I've got an appointment at Sattva Systems™ tomorrow. I could drive you.'

'You know people there?' he said deceptively.

'I've told you before, my friend, the Beardons and the Kanes go way back.'

'Ok, it will be good to catch up.'

The Bear returned to the kitchen. Brady decided to steer the conversation to what he wanted to talk about before Tyrone could assault him with his science-talk. 'What's the deal with the HeavyLoader™ fleet?'

'Uncle Sam is in the know. He says the guys at Sattva are all excited because San Diego has fallen. It's the biggest one yet in this part of the world.'

'I keep forgetting it's not just happening in California. The world is too big a thing to get my head around.'

Tyrone smiled. He didn't want to state that he viewed the planet to be a mere speck of cosmic dust in the universe. 'San Diego is going to take years to clean up, but we are only sixteen years into the hundred-year plan, so, we have got time on our side.'

'Why, one-hundred-years?'

'It's part of the promise Bodhi made to the GreenRevs. Uncle Sam says they have a thirteen-point pledge hanging up in the foyer of Sattva Systems™. The teams are pulling out all the stops to keep it on schedule. They are a great bunch of hard-working people, and the scientists are the cream of the crop. I would love to work in their laboratories one day.'

Brady nodded, 'How long would it take to clean up Los Angeles if that ever fell?'

'It's inevitable that all the cities will fall. They will probably all go at about the same time. That's why they are building a fleet of millions of HeavyLoaders™ around the globe. There will be loads of employment opportunities. You'd make a great HeavyLoader™ pilot.'

Brady was swept along with this daydream. 'That would be cool. But I'm a businessman, not a truck driver - or a pilot.' He smiled at the thought of flying within that massive formation. He'd love to see a sight like that up there in the clouds with them. He thought, I'm definitely gonna get me my private jet. He said, 'Why will all these areas collapse at the same time?'

'The Trads are dying out. Even for the babies born at the dawn of the Revolution - their life expectancy is likely to be no more than seventy - and seventy years would still leave another thirty years to clean up the last lingering towns and cities.'

Brady noted how matter-of-factly Tyrone discussed the topic of millions of human beings dying. He knew him to be a sweet soul at heart. He didn't think he was brain-washed in any way; it was just a part of his everyday life and upbringing. He remembered how he watched the news about wars, pandemics and famines - it was just news - nothing to get emotional about. 'I suppose you're right. How does the building of millions of HeavyLoaders™ tie-in with protecting the environment?'

'Sometimes you have to harm the planet to save the planet. That's how Bodhi Sattva rationalises it - he's right.'

The Bear came in with dinner, and they sat and ate and caught up on things which had happened in their lives since the last time they met. The Bear led the conversation and steered them away from controversial topics, as he wanted to create an atmosphere of informality. After the meal was done, Brady volunteered and insisted that he do the dishes - alone. As he was washing and drying the Beardon's crockery, he thought about Rhea. *My-oh-my that girl has really gotten to you Brady Mahone - and you thought you were above falling for anyone.*

When he had finished; and returned to the living room, he noticed that Tyrone had gone. He heard the sounds of the other families in other parts of the large house. The Bear said, 'I've got some home-made wine, would you care to join me?'

'Sure.' Brady sat down in an armchair, he felt the strange dry warmth of the FusionPowered™ central heating, which was a preferred choice of the Green Communities - he missed the subtle smell and warmth of the gas fires from the old days. 'Where's Tyrone?'

The Bear poured them both glasses of white wine, 'It's been the first clear night in a few days, and he wanted to catch some winter stars.'

Brady knew he was lying. The Bear wants to talk. He drank from his glass of wine and nodded his appreciation. 'It was never an accident that we met in Los Banos, was it?'

'No, my friend. But I'm glad we did.' He drained his glass and poured another for himself and topped up Brady's glass. 'I have been investigating my Father's murder for longer than I care to remember, and the trail always went cold in McFarland. And then there was this guy, a Trad who could enter into Green Communities, and he just happens to come from McFarland.'

'You are not the only person who has come to that conclusion. Would you believe me if I said that I don't know why it happened to be me?'

'I know you well enough to take you at your word, Brady Mahone.'

It was Brady's turn to drain the glass, and the Bear grabbed another bottle. He uncorked it and poured them both another drink in a spirit of camaraderie. The Bear raised his glass and said, 'I think you could put me out of misery. From the depths of my soul, I believe you know more than you are letting on.'

Brady avoided the imploring eyes of the Bear. He thought of Bodhi Sattva and his priority goals for his desired confrontation. He then returned his gaze to the Bear, and knew he had the sweet taste of anticipation, he knew that spike of adrenalin would be eating him up with dark pleasure. He deliberately paused, he wanted to savour this moment, the moment before the revelation. 'Your Father, Samuel Beardon the Second didn't murder John Kane. It was my Father - my Foster Daddy, Archie Mahone. John Kane was coming to reclaim me for his own needs. My Pops garrotted him with a cheese wire and buried him. He did it because he loved me. I was seven or eight-years-old, and he treated me like I was his real son.'

Even though he knew deep down Brady would give him his answer, Samuel Beardon the Third was stunned into silence. Brady watched his mind turning over all the pieces of a thousand scenarios he had ever considered and trying to fit them into the frame of facts Brady had presented him. Brady continued to drink; the hazy effects of the alcohol danced with his sense of relief. He wondered if he would be of any further use to the Bear now that he had given him what he had wanted. He thought, *It could be useful for me to find out what he knows about this - or what he doesn't know.* He asked the Bear, 'Is that what you expected?'

'No. Not at all.' He added, guiltily, 'There were times when I dishonoured my Father's name that I considered that he may have actually done it - that the authorities got it right, and he was guilty of murder. I knew in my heart he wasn't capable, but still…help me, God.' He took another drink, and Brady noticed tears forming in the Bear's eyes. He watched as the Bear discreetly tried to brush them away. The Bear said, 'I knew my Father had some major ideological differences with John Kane at the time of his disappearance. I thought it possible that they may have had an altercation which went badly wrong…'

'Did you find out what these differences of opinion were?'

'No. I was too young, and my Mother - God rest her soul - told me that everything my Father worked on was top secret. He worked in the inner sanctum with John Kane and his son, Xavier - Bodhi, now, of course. I did find out that my Father was responsible for the establishment of Green Communities across the world. I am deeply proud of him for that incredible achievement. Did you know he created the Green Communities?'

'No.' Brady lied.

The Bear stood. 'If you allow me to drive you to Boulder Creek in the morning, then we can discuss this further if you wish. I know this must be difficult for you…'

'That's fine by me.'

'I need to be alone with my thoughts and my God for a while.' He left, and Brady watched him slowly climb the stairs to his bedroom. *Looks like Brady is doing a bit of sofa surfing tonight - but not before I've finished off this wine.*

They set off early the following morning. Brady wasn't happy as he had had an uncomfortable night and he was trying to shake off the effects of his hangover. *At least I don't have to do the driving.* He soon realised why they had set off early. 'Hey, man. Why are we dawdling? These FusionCars™ can go faster than forty, y'know.'

The Bear laughed, 'This is a safe speed. I can do without the stress of racing against Father Time.'

'Aw, come on. We can step up to seventy, or even eighty on here, it's a Highway with no traffic on it.' *I wish I had driven now.*

The Bear said, 'Brother, time is on our side, and as my Grandfather always used to preach - 'tis better to be late in this world, than early in the next.'

'You're all wrapped up in your NanoSuits™. So, there's no chance of that, even if we did crash.'

'Then let's just say I'm showing consideration for my passenger. You are my precious cargo, my friend.'

Brady sulked as the miles drifted by. His head was throbbing, and even another fly-past of HeavyLoaders™ couldn't cheer him up. The Bear barely acknowledged the sight, he kept his eyes fixed firmly on the road. Brady had noticed that they had dropped the speed to thirty-five, he shook his head and closed his eyes, he couldn't bring himself to look at the speedometer anymore - it was aggravating him.

He then felt the car judder. He opened his eyes and realised that he must have fallen asleep. They were now on a small road surrounded by a forest. The car was heading straight into the trees. Brady was alarmed and yelled, 'Watch out! You're heading for the trees you stupid fucker!'

The Bear roared with laughter and headed straight for the trees - and through them - as if they weren't even there. 'It's a NanoShell™ illusion, my friend.'

'What the actual fuck.'

'The road leads other travellers away from the Sattva Systems™ HQ - not that there is anything to hide. It's for the health and safety of our people. We are taking the visitor entrance. The main entrance has all the industrial vehicles coming and going.'

Brady breathed out a huge sigh of relief. 'Don't do that to me, man. You'll give Brady Mahone a heart attack - and I don't want my heart to attack me.'

The Bear laughed, 'I confess to being somewhat mischievous, brother.'

'Ok. You got me.'

'We have arrived in plenty of time. Is there anything you'd particularly like to see while we have time?'

'I only wants to meet this Bodhi Sattva.'

'I can arrange that for later - don't you trouble yourself. This is a big place, are you sure you don't want to see more of it. Who knows? This might be your last chance.'

Brady thought about this offer, 'I would really love to see the insides of one of them HeavyLoader™ FusionPlanes™.'

'You got it. Leave it to your guide for the day - Samuel Beardon the Third at your service.'

They drove on for another thirty minutes when they came upon a vehicle park which seemed to stretch out to the horizon. They were at the top of a hillside, and then the Bear steered the FusionCar™ carefully down the twisted track to the FusionPlane™ park. They moved slowly passed the fleet of smaller FusionPlanes™. Brady dreamed of flying one of these out of here before the day was done. Brady said, 'Y'know, my favourite thing of all from the old days, was going to the Monster Truck rallies - boy Truckasaurus was really something.' They moved past hundreds of vehicles that all appeared to be modified for some very specific uses. The Bear tried to explain, but the science eluded Brady's attention. They then came to the section which contained thousands of parked up HeavyLoaders™. The Bear saw somebody he knew who would accommodate Brady's curiosity. The Bear parked up and urged Brady to join him. Brady expected to be assaulted by the smell of fumes, oil and grease. He was disappointed to only take in the fresh cool air.

The Bear shook the black woman, by the hand. Brady looked all around him, while the Bear exchanged pleasantries with this woman called Marjorie. They talked about family, and he heard her mention Alicia and Tyrone. All the time he was awestruck by the immensity of these vehicles. He remembered comparing them to the jumbo jets from way back when and assessed that these giants might be at least five times larger.

The Bear called out, 'Brady, come and meet Marjorie. She's a Fleet Driving Instructor.' He joked, 'She took heed of my safe driving habits.' Marjorie laughed, but Brady only smiled, ruefully.

She moved toward Brady, 'Pleased to make your acquaintance, Brady. Samuel tells me you'd like a tour?'

'Yes. Sure. That would be cool.'

He followed as she led them around the back of the first vehicle. It had a huge cargo hold. 'This is obviously for transporting plant and equipment.' It was empty and looked like the open mouth of the most gigantic beast on the planet. He also noticed that it was immaculately clean.

She showed him around others which transported goods, animals, people and chemicals. After a couple of hours, Brady was tiring of looking in the backs of these industrial leviathans. She then showed him one which she nicknamed the Sprayer. 'These are used to decompose man-made structures of the old world. They spray enzymes and NanoReplicators™. There is no cargo hold on this one. Instead, there are a dozen skin layers with different formulas for eroding, concrete, steel, glass - you get the picture. The spray hits the buildings, it is attracted to its allocated material, and then it replicates and breaks everything down to a molecular structure which Mother Earth could re-use to foster the growth of vegetation.'

Brady reminisced when one of these vehicles flew over the Mahone Ranch and caused Mary-Lou's miscarriage with their sterilising goo. Marjorie continued, 'There is an exception, and that is with road compounds. We want to protect the road infrastructure, so, when they hit ground level and recognise the compounds used in road building, it actually forms a protective layer.' She added, 'Would you like to see inside the cockpit - get a driver's eyes view?'

'Yes. Absolutely.' Brady grinned like an excited schoolboy.

He followed her into the cockpit, and he was amazed at how small it was and how simple the controls were. He had expected to see a thousand blinking electronic lights and an array of instrumentation.

She said, 'We maximise all our vehicles' storage area to reduce the number of flights required. They are exceptionally energy efficient and virtually emission free, but still, Her resources shouldn't be wasted.' She ushered Brady to sit in the pilot's seat.

He loved it. He looked out through the windscreen and felt like he was flying without leaving the ground. It didn't feel that different from being inside his Hearse, apart from when he pulled back the steering wheel, and he imagined lifting off. He also saw a pull-handle into the floor.

She said, 'Vertical take-off and landing. Here, I'll show you.' The HeavyLoader™ levitated, 'I'll take us on a five-minute trip, I want to show you something which will blow your socks off.'

Brady liked her down to earth way of talking. She flew the giant for a few minutes and then it became obvious what she wanted to show him. It appeared to be the skeletal remains of the largest dinosaur that had ever roamed the planet. She said, 'It will take another five years to construct, it's the size of fifty HeavyLoaders™ combined. It's called the LeviathanLifter™.'

Brady was awestruck as she glided the HeavyLoader™ over the mechanical monster. Then Marjorie guided her vehicle back to its original parking spot and listened happily as Brady reeled off the entire list of superlatives in his limited vocabulary.

After a few minutes, she climbed out of the cockpit, and he could hear the Bear thanking her for her time and hospitality. He stayed a few moments longer and savoured his last few moments before re-joining the Bear.

When he stepped out, she said, 'There are one hundred and twenty HeavyLoaders™ due to take off. We can stay and watch if you want?'

'Sure thing.' Brady grinned like an excitable child.

She ushered him around the next corner that looked out onto a vast expanse of land. She heard something in her earpiece, and then she turned to Brady and said, 'They are ready.'

He watched them simultaneously rise in almost silence and then he was hit by a sub-sonic boom which winded him. Marjorie said, 'You haven't got a NanoSuit™ - how unique. If I'd have known I would have warned you.'

'Don't worry about me none. That was like the best gig ever - it was one helluva rush.'

As the HeavyLoaders™ continued their ascent, there were more sub-sonic booms, and Brady roared his appreciation, 'Yeah - YEAH - Woohoo - Alright!' He turned to Marjorie and added for good measure, 'You rock!' The HeavyLoaders™ turned in unison, and the whole fleet flew as one over Brady's head as they headed south to help with the Operation Clean-Up of San Diego.

Once the last of the HeavyLoaders™ had left the Fleet Park, the Bear said, 'I've asked Marjorie to arrange a meeting for you and Bodhi. It's my way of re-paying you for the truth you gave me. I didn't want to see you trying to force your way in - it wouldn't do much for my good name and reputation.'

Brady surprised himself by feeling nervous, it wasn't a feeling he was used to. 'Thanks, man.'

They got into the car and headed to the main entrance. The Bear said, 'It'll take a little while to get there. We are at the rear of the HQ. We'll pass a couple of the industrial complexes on the way.'

Brady said, 'Last night, you said that Cain, Siddha and…' He feigned not recalling her name.

'Genesis Garcia.'

'Yeah, that's it. You said they were going around telling people not to treat me unkind.'

'They were, indeed, brother. Genesis is very close to Bodhi.'

'You mean…'

'No. Not like that, my friend.'

'I can just about get my head around Cain, helping me out. He has that whole fixer vibe about him, but Siddha, well, he hates me.'

'That's impossible. Hatred is not allowed. Nor is humiliation, stress, violence, or even the threat of violence. While we are on the subject, exploitation, hate crimes and discrimination are forbidden. Otherwise, the Security Protocols™ come into force. You saw what happened to me when I lost my temper with you on your last visit.'

'Yeah. That happened to me when I tried to steal an apple, or not pay for a plastic bag, I can hardly remember now.'

'I had forgotten. Of course, crime is forbidden. When you talk to Bodhi, you will have to keep your wits about you, the Security Protocols™ are even more sensitive here.'

'Why is that?'

'Bodhi sets himself very high standards. He practices what he preaches. Also, he believes his key staff should set an example to others. Siddha doesn't hate you. He probably just doesn't trust you. You can't blame him; nobody knows what the deal is with you. Even I struggle to comprehend your role.'

Brady laughed, 'Me too. All I want is to make some Greenbacks and grab a few of what counts for luxuries in this God-forsaken place.'

26. THE NEW DEAL

Brady and the Bear strolled into the foyer of the Sattva Systems™ HQ. They both gazed at the thirteen-point banner. It listed the pledges which Sattva Systems™ was sworn to complete, in kind, for the members of the GreenRevs.

As they turned, they saw Glenarvon Cole smiling broadly. Brady thought he was being challenged by the dirty-looking action man with the bearing of a marine who'd just come straight out of combat. He looked vaguely familiar.

Brady said, 'What's the deal with him?' He nodded in the direction of Glen.

'If we had a national hero, then that would be him. He's the leader of the Green Revolutionaries - Glenarvon Cole. He was an extraordinarily brave man. He was one of the first to wear the RedSuits™ in a confrontational situation. He was like a test pilot. He ensured, personally, that the Suits™ would combat any threat. Where he went - others followed. He had faith and purpose.'

I remember. He was the guy with Rhea on the TV.

Sissy came out to greet them. 'Hello, and welcome. How are you doing, Samuel?' They hugged. She examined Brady. 'And you must be the famous Brady Mahone. Your reputation precedes you. I'm Genesis Garcia, but I insist you call me Sissy.'

She went to hug him, which he might have taken as a flirtatious move, in less stressful circumstances, but here he felt like it was more akin to a potential body search. He held out his hand before she became too close, and he shook her hand firmly, as he would with any other politician. He smiled without warmth, and he fixed her eyes with his. He didn't reply. The atmosphere was awkward, which suited Brady just fine. He had to use his physical presence to ward off regular inmates, but he had to keep them guessing with the mob bosses. *The moment they figure you out is the moment they got you. You can't let them have leverage over you.*

She said to the Bear, 'Maybe you would like to make yourself comfortable in the canteen - a few of your friends are in there, taking a well-deserved break.'

The Bear turned to Brady, 'You'll be ok. Bodhi is a good man, and he'll treat you with respect.'

Sissy laughed, with a hint of falsehood, 'Of course he will. Bodhi is so looking forward to meeting Brady. Since the very first day he has followed his progress closely.' She turned to Brady and said, 'Bodhi is your biggest fan.' She then added with a hint of contempt, 'Lord knows why.' She smiled at the Bear, who smiled in return and headed off to the canteen, but she noticed he went to sit on his own. Brady could smell the unappetising odours of cabbage and coffee in the air. She said, 'If you would care to follow me.'

He followed dutifully, but silently. He assumed if he said anything at all, it would be dissected and used later. He practised his breathing and held onto his calm, almost bored state he had achieved in the desert. He also recalled the many fights he had got into in jail. If he had a particularly tough opponent, then the most dangerous moments had appeared at the point when he thought he was winning. The cold-blooded psychos used to let him think they were weaker than they actually were. They did that to get him to be over-confident, to lower his guard, and then they would strike.

As they paced down the long corridors with cream-coloured walls, he also recalled the gang tactics where the largest aggressor would grab his attention while the small one crept up from behind. He focused on these scenarios while watching out for these same tactics in a battle of words. He knew he was utterly incapable of taking any Green on in a fight, they were invulnerable to physical assault, but the events in Encinitas had taught him that they could become afraid of him, psychologically. All he had to do was to make Bodhi convinced that he was a threat that couldn't be neutralised, easily.

He summarised his learnings into a mantra. *Be calm. Stay detached. Beware the feeling that you're winning. Watch your back.* As he heard the clicking of her heels, and the sound of his sneakers in a counter-rhythm, ricocheting off the walls, - he repeated his mantra, over and over again. *Be calm. Stay detached. Beware the feeling that you're winning. Watch your back.* His sneakers were a reclaimed pair from one of the Green Communities. His jeans and greying white T-shirt were recycled garments, but his poacher's trench coat had been regularly waxed and glinted under the lights. His hands were kept in the coat pocket but inside his fingers tapped unconsciously in a nervous rhythm and a state of heightened readiness.

She came to a nondescript door that looked like hundreds of others they had passed along the way. She knocked three times and didn't wait for a reply.

It wasn't the palatial palace with a golden throne which Brady had expected. It was a small, drab office space, decked out in the company colours. Behind the desk was Bodhi Sattva, in a grey tracksuit and grey, unmarked trainers. Under the LED lights, his bald head looked like one of Tyrone's star globes, with little constellations forming patterns on Bodhi's dome. He greeted Brady and stuck out his hand in a show of informality. Brady shook it with a firm grip and looked down on the desk and was pleased to see it was equipped to show Black Files.

Brady sat in the functionally designed chair. He leaned back and rested his right foot on his left knee.

Bodhi sat upright as if he was monitoring the position of the vertebrae in his spine. Bodhi folded his arms. Brady took this as a sign of respect.

Bodhi said, 'I've been following your progress for sixteen years. I'm delighted to finally have the chance to get to know you.'

'Only sixteen years. I thought you'd been interested in my development for longer than that.' He watched Bodhi's eyes. He thought he detected puzzlement.

'No. I am known for being scrupulous about honesty. The first time I became aware of your presence was when you breached the NanoShell™ security in West McFarland. At first, I believed it might be teething troubles, but it was something to do with you, and not the Shells™. From that moment on, you piqued my curiosity. Cain regularly reported on your activities, and from then on, I had many others keeping an eye on your progress.'

'Private Investigators - that kind of thing?' He noticed the absence of niceties like being offered coffee or alcohol. *Straight down to business.*

'What a quaint term - very evocative of the old days. I'll admit an oversight on my part. The Internet would have been useful for looking into your background, but we destroyed that with our NanoBots™. It took decades for them to spread and replicate, undetected, but the Internet was the pillar that held their world together, by then. But whereas in the Bible it was Samson, a strong man who laid the temple low, here we had the smallest mechanisms on Earth to wreak havoc and end the chaos of the Traditional Cultures.'

He thought, *don't be fooled, Brady. The fight has already started, that's a feint to the left.* 'I had guessed. All the stuff about viruses and solar flares was a contingency plan. If your Revolution had failed, it would buy you time, rather than have the Trads call for your head.'

'Ancient history, now - clean water under the bridge.' He placed both his hands palm down on the desk. 'You've been very busy. You've built up a sizeable business from scratch. I commend you for your hard work and dedication. However, it is not an enterprise I can officially condone, but it is one I will choose to overlook.' He looked up, and Brady thought he could detect an air of eagerness. It reminded him of the look his fellow criminals made when it was time to divi-up the spoils.

Brady looked around the cream-coloured walls of the cheaply designed office. 'Tell me first, what's the deal with the cream and green everywhere?'

'It's branding with an anti-marketing message. The Era of Exploitation is over. The Trads ravaged the world in its endless greed for more resources. Humanity battled each other literally and metaphorically in the constant craving for things. They were addicted to materialism.' He added, 'The drug of materialism has been eradicated, and we have no desire to start it up again. We are ending ownership, gradually. Your product is relatively harmless, and it helps us monitor whether our communities are completely clean - so to speak. I do insist that my Disciples refrain from sampling your products.'

Brady felt edgy, he had to get this right. He knew he shouldn't use the word blackmail - he didn't want to invoke their Security Protocols™. He also had to avoid threatening or even humiliating Bodhi. He pulled out a Black File from his pocket, and he handed it to Bodhi. 'I have brought you something to look at. It's educational, even though it comes in the form of entertainment.'

Bodhi looked at the Black File quizzically. 'I cannot accept your gift, however well-intentioned.'

'It is something you would want to see - to have the opportunity to stop others viewing it. I could give it to you freely.'

'I still could not permit myself to receive it.' Brady could see he was rattled.

'What if I played it, on your screen, and you just happened to catch a glimpse of it over my shoulder? Trust me, you do need to see this. It's vital for the continuation of your business, and for your reputation.'

'You are trying to tempt me, Mr Mahone. Is it really that important?'

'I believe it is.' Brady sensed he was asking Bodhi a question he couldn't respond to. Brady stood up and placed the Black File into the slot at the side of the screen, without waiting for permission. The screen lit up, and the child pornographic movie played out on the screen with Bodhi Sattva's Father, John Kane, in the leading actor role as Emperor Tiberius. When Bodhi looked away at the wall, without comment, Brady ejected the File and pocketed it away. He returned to his seat. *I feel kinda dirty doing that. Maybe extortion is not my thing, after all.*

Brady was still on high alert, he forced himself to speak softly, 'You know I have copies. I know your rules and the risk of being SecurityFilmed™. When I distribute my entertainments, this movie has been disguised. My customers will open them up, unwittingly. They will not open them up, knowingly, otherwise, that would be an act of choosing to humiliate you. I can stop these spreading through the Green Communities - for a finder's fee. You could count yourself fortunate that I found them before somebody less willing to trade did.'

Bodhi pulled open a drawer and selected a spray and a cloth. He sprayed the screen and rubbed it until it gleamed under the LEDs.

'What is your finder's fee?'

Brady licked his lips. *Be calm. Stay detached. Beware the feeling that you're winning. Watch your back.* 'A FusionPlane™ of my own - not a rental. One million Green Credits - and Libby's house in Malibu.' He felt the need to clarify, 'I will be the sole owner of that property and its surrounding lands.'

Bodhi smiled, 'How long have you lived alongside the Green Communities?'

'Sixteen years. Since Day One of the Revolution.'

'And in that time, have you ever heard anybody discuss me in terms of hatred, fear or untrustworthiness?'

I'm not going to tell him about all the stuff in the Los Banos records. He thought. 'No. You seem loved and respected by your people. The Trads have a differing point of view.'

'Your Trad side is showing.'

'I'm a Trad. I don't have a side.'

'You could have just asked me for what you wanted. I would have given it to you. Why do you assume that I don't want you to be happy? Instead, you just assumed that you would have to find a way to extract it from me by exploiting my feelings. We are a kind people. We have the Security Protocols™ not to impose our will, but to protect people's feelings. That's all.'

Be calm. Stay detached. Beware the feeling that you're winning. Watch your back. Brady sensed he was off-balance. He knew Bodhi would be smart. You knew it would come to this. He controlled his breathing, before he said, 'Can I still have what I asked for? Will you give them to me freely?'

Bodhi said, barely louder than a whisper, 'I am saddened that you see me as your enemy. I have watched you develop your business, you made friends and acquaintances in every Green Community you have visited. And when I heard that these Communities had turned their backs on you, out of misplaced fear and hatred, it was me who made it the highest priority to make them change their minds and see you, as I see you, as someone who should be cared for, not shunned.' He added, 'I sent out Cain, Siddha and Sissy to repair your reputation. Sissy even gave your name to her newly born son - Century Brady Garcia. I ask you, does that sound like the act of your foe? Or does that sound like the act of a friend?'

Brady squirmed, he struggled to get one word out, 'Friend.'

'Here's what I think. What you have asked me for is too little. You are thinking like a small-time businessman and not an international tycoon. That's understandable, you haven't had my training or upbringing. Thinking globally is my default outlook. Would you like to make notes of my offer? I know you don't trust me; you'll think I'm trying to trick you or hide something in the small print.'

'I don't need to take notes. Let's hear it.' He forced a smile.

'What's your company called?'

'Brady Mahone Entertainment Enterprises.'

'Ok. I'm outlining here, I'd need to bring R&D, manufacturing and finance in on this. I would set up a manufacturing plant to scale up your business. You can explain to my field team how you recruit, sell, distribute and monitor customer feedback, so they can replicate your methods in every country in the world - we would need storage space to keep inventory…'

Is this one of those corporate takeover kind of deals?

'…and then we come to the kind of money you would expect to make.'

'Would it still be my company?'

'Of course. It would have to be. My focus would be the planet - if I appeared to diversify it would look like I've changed course. The hundred-year plan to save the planet is sacred to me.'

'Thanks. The company is my baby.'

'Are you ready to hear my rough projections?'

'Sure.'

'What do you currently make?' Brady took out his Distor™, and Bodhi looked at it. He didn't appear shocked at the Green Credits reading in excess of nine-hundred thousand. 'Let's keep the calculations simple - nine-hundred thousand over fifteen years is sixty-thousand Green Credits per year - very good. Let's multiply that by approximately two-hundred countries that will give us twelve million per year.'

The numbers were becoming mind-blowing to Brady, it reminded him of when Tyrone was trying to convert light-years to miles. Brady zoned out then, but here they were talking big bucks.

Bodhi continued with his off-the-cuff profit and loss account, 'If you lived for the next fifty years, which looking at you, is more than possible, then that would amount to six hundred million Green Credits during your lifetime. Now, there would be start-up costs, and I would have to make a small profit. Otherwise, my accounts department might think I have lost my senses - so, let's strip out one hundred million

- this would be deducted at a much later date - this would still leave Brady Mahone Entertainment Enterprises with a clear profit of five hundred million Greenbacks, as I think you call them, or a half a billion Green Credits.' He put his hand up to prevent Brady from answering, 'Now, for the downside. It would take at least a couple of years to set up the factories; and complete their training in the field for the district teams. However, while you wait for this income to come on stream, I will give you what you have asked for, today. I will give you freely, your one million Green Credits, my Mother's home in Malibu, and I'll have Marjorie give you a FusionPlane™ of your own.'

Brady was stunned, 'I don't know what to say. Thank you. That's amazing.'

Bodhi looked at Brady with a strange mixture of triumph and sympathy. 'I'll have the Security Protocols™ set up, to my satisfaction, to ensure you will destroy these Tiberius Files - and hopefully, in a spirit of mutual respect and friendship, we will never discuss them again.'

Brady reached out his hand.

27.THE BEAR'S DILEMMA

Sissy went over to the Bear's table in the canteen. She had known him for more years than she cared to remember, and she could see he was distressed. She sat opposite him at the cream-coloured table and sat on her moss-green moulded chair. He didn't acknowledge her immediately, he just stared into his coffee cup.

'What's the matter, Samuel?' Sissy said.

'Brady confessed something to me - something significant. Now, I don't know what he is talking to Bodhi about, and I don't want to cause any trouble, but I fear that if I don't speak up - I will regret it in the future.'

She smiled and put her slender hand upon his, 'I don't wish to pry, but who does this information concern?'

'Me, Brady and our respective Fathers.' He kept back the murder of Bodhi's Father.

'But you obviously think that Bodhi might be unwittingly involved; otherwise, you wouldn't be so worried.'

He shrugged, 'If I'm wrong then I will have betrayed a deep confidence of Brady's. It was something he shared when it would have been easier to keep to himself.'

Sissy tried to guess at what this might be, but she couldn't put the clues together. Her political instincts warned her not to let it go. 'I think you should share with me. I know more about Bodhi than you. I could advise you. I want to help.'

The Bear sighed and rubbed his chin with his big right hand, 'You know how everybody believed that my Father, Samuel Beardon the Second, had probably killed John Kane?' He added, 'Well, Brady has informed me that this wasn't true.'

'And how would Brady Mahone know that?'

'Because his Foster Father, Archie Mahone, confessed to murdering John Kane and disposing of his body.'

Sissy's eyes stared back at him, at first in disbelief, and then in shock at the revelation. 'But why on Earth did he do that?'

'Brady told me, that John Kane had visited the Mahone Ranch in McFarland to enact some claim he had over his foster child, Brady Mahone.'

She said, 'And you think he's going to use this information in some way to hurt Bodhi?'

'I don't know. Maybe. But if I'm wrong…'

'You've got to tell him. It could be vital. Come with me. Now!' She got up immediately and almost dragged Samuel up and out of his seat. She sprinted ahead, and Samuel struggled to keep up. They raced through hundreds of yards of corridors until finally, they came to Bodhi's office. She burst in without knocking, and shouted, 'Stop.' Just as Bodhi was about to shake hands on his deal with Brady. 'I'm sorry, Bodhi. Something urgent has come to my attention, and I think you must hear it first.'

Brady withdrew his hand. *Be calm. Stay detached. Beware the feeling that you're winning. Watch your back.* He watched as the Bear came in behind her, he was out of breath and looked on the verge of a panic attack. *Watch your back.*

They waited for a few moments for the Bear to get his breath back.

Bodhi then asked, 'What is it, Samuel?'

The Bear looked across at Brady, and said, 'I'm sorry, brother. I have to speak the truth.'

Brady was careful to hide his true feelings, 'That's alright. Say whatcha gotta say.' He didn't smile.

The Bear took a deep breath. 'Brady's Foster Father killed your Father.'

Bodhi looked at all of them in turn. He grimaced, but then nodded his thanks to Sissy, but then turned to face Brady. 'Is this true?'

'Yes. My Foster Daddy confessed to me on the same day that he took his own life. He was a part of that thing we were talking about earlier.' He assumed Bodhi knew he was being deliberately vague about the Tiberius File. 'Your Father came to take me away from my Foster Daddy - I was about eight years old - nobody knew when I was born, precisely. My Foster Daddy, Archie Mahone, believed he was saving me, so he garrotted your Daddy with a cheese wire and buried him, way deep in the forest.'
Bodhi stood up, paced the room. He disseminated the events and worked out the timelines. 'How old are you now?'

'About fifty-eight.' Even though Brady knew Bodhi was RedSuit™ protected, he still assessed his height and build as if he was preparing for a physical battle - it was a deeply ingrained habit. He estimated he was a similar height and build to himself.

'So, your Foster Father killed mine, sometime in 2050.'

'Yeah. That sounds about right.'

He continued his pacing, and then stopped and said, 'Thank you. All of you. This has been a day of revelations. I'm going to need time to let it all sink in.'

Brady said, 'Does this affect our deal?'

'No, Brady. It doesn't affect our deal.'

Brady smiled. *Beware the feeling that you're winning.* 'Is it too late to ask for one more thing? It's a minor one, but it would mean a lot to me.'

Bodhi said, wearily. He knew Trads were greedy, but Brady was in a different league. 'What do you want?'

'I have three friends; they are almost family. I want them to be taken in by the Greens.'

Bodhi barked, 'Out of the question. We cannot have Greens mixing with Trads. It would make them feel guilty and erode confidence in all we've done. There can be no interaction.'

Samuel intervened. He sensed an opportunity for redemption if he could liaise in this matter. He didn't know about the overwhelming generosity that Bodhi had already shown to Brady. 'Do you owe them, brother?'

'Lucky is my best friend. He saved my life in Ridgecrest. He was falsely convicted. He is a better man than I. He is married to Mary-Lou, and he took in her daughter, Amie. He is an innocent victim in all this madness.'

Sissy said, 'Madness? What did you think the world was like before?'

Bodhi also felt obliged to Samuel for his intervention. Bodhi looked to Sissy, but she shook her head. He said, 'You don't know what you are asking for. I cannot do this.'
Brady raised his arms and placed his hands behind his head. He pulled a chain from over his head and the ring dangled in front of Bodhi. It swayed as if Brady was hypnotising him. The outer diamonds sparkled in the LED lights and inset was a letter S made up of emeralds laid out in the same font as Sattva Systems™. 'I could make a trade. It fell out of a coat your Mother gave me.'

Bodhi stared at the ring. 'I can't do it, Brady.'

Brady laughed, 'It was worth a try. Here, you can have it. You've been more than fair. This doesn't belong to me, really. It must have sentimental value to you. I want you to take it back.'

'I accept the spirit in which you freely offer it to me. I receive the offer of its return in a spirit of friendship and trust.' Bodhi struggled to find a warm smile to give to Brady. His memories flooded him with images of his Father, and the day he had given him the ring, for his thirtieth birthday. The same day they broke ground on the Sattva Systems™ new headquarters. They had a glittering ball, held at Libby's Malibu home, with political big-hitters and Hollywood stars, and then they all held Xavier Kane in their rapt attention, as John Kane placed the ring on his son's finger, and promised the assembled guests a brighter, greener future. They clapped and cheered and had no idea whatsoever that they were cheering on their own destruction. He came to his senses and said, 'I will allow your friend to be reassimilated to Green. I won't trade. I will give it freely. Don't push me any further on the subject. You can keep the ring. It was given to me by my Father. I know you understand why I don't wish to regard it for any longer than necessary.'

Sissy gave Bodhi a puzzled look but saved her questions for when they were alone.

Brady put the ring back over his neck. He was satisfied that he had repaid his debt to Lucian.

Bodhi swiftly moved into business mode. 'Hand me your Distor™.'

Brady took it out of his poacher's coat and placed it in the hand of Bodhi. Bodhi tapped on his screen, and the right-hand-side of his desk slot glowed green, and a Green File emerged, encouraging Bodhi to use his thumb and index finger to retrieve it. He took it out and placed it into Brady's Distor™, the display informed Brady that he was now the proud owner of 1,912,442 Green File Credits.

Bodhi said, 'The Security Protocols™ will secure *My Word* in respect of the following. Brady Mahone is now the owner of my Mother's property in Malibu. Brady Mahone will be allocated a FusionPlane™ for his private and exclusive use, in perpetuity.' He said, more informally, 'These things I have freely given you from today. The expansion of your business will go into the planning stages with immediate effect. As my friend, you will be welcome to visit me here at any time to check on its progress. If ever you need to see me, ask for Genesis, and she will arrange it.' He smiled. He was determined to take any signs of animosity away from the meeting before Brady left. 'She is my marketing guru, have you put any thought into your logo - something that could be recognised the world over.'

Sissy knew Bodhi well enough to spot when he needed her to flatter a problematic client. She wanted to object, but she recalled how upset Bodhi was when they disregarded his request to make Brady a top priority after the Encinitas disaster. It was apparently still vital to him that Brady becomes a central part of his future plans. She said, 'Brady Mahone Entertainment Enterprises is fine, but it needs a snappier variation. Its initials would be a good starting point, so BMEE might work.' She looked at Brady, 'Are there any symbols you are fond of? Something which represents you and your business identity?'

He pulled out his notebook and cloth pack of pencils and charcoals. He put it on Bodhi's screen, and they gathered around. The others looked around at each other as Brady flicked through his highly detailed and skilled sketches of animals, birds, insects, plants and lizards. He stopped at his drawing of a Kangaroo rat. 'This little creature took me weeks to find.' He said, proudly.

Sissy looked but wasn't impressed by its potential to become a logo. 'Are there any other creatures? This is a little bit too fluffy to represent the Brady Mahone I see before me.'

He shuffled forward a couple of pages to the Diamondback rattlesnake. 'What about this?'

She asked, 'What were you thinking about when you drew it in such exquisite detail?'

'I was thinking about how afraid people were of it, and how it had the potential to kill a man, but always chooses not to - if approached in the right way.'

Sissy was impressed, and for the first time, caught a glimpse of why this man could be fascinating to Bodhi. 'I feel it. This is better. I see a column of the letters BMEE with the snake curling through the letters.'

Brady turned his sketchbook diagonally to make the snake appear to be standing on its tail and then drew the BMEE letters around, and through the Diamondback's body. It gave the impression that the rattlesnake was moving through them. Sissy said, 'I love it. Can I borrow your pencil?'

'Sure. Knock yourself out.'

She surrounded Brady's sketch with a shield.

He said, 'It looks like an old Porsche badge. That's really cool.'

'Then, this will be your brand.'

Bodhi and The Bear took turns in looking at it, approvingly. Bodhi said, 'I need to prepare myself for my next meeting. Samuel, if you could take Brady with you - go and see Marjorie and organise his FusionPlane™ - I know they are easy to operate but get her to train Brady before he flies solo.'

'Yes, Bodhi.' He smiled at Brady, and they left together.

Bodhi said to Sissy, 'I want you to put together a team to plan the launch of BMEE - as we will call it from now on. I want it given a high priority. I want it fully functional inside ten years.'

'Leave it to me.'

'As for Brady's friend to become a Green - ensure that there can be no contact with his former family. I've thought about it. I want it to become Samuel's responsibility to take in his friend in San Martin - faraway from McFarland. He will have to explain it to Brady. I don't want to see Brady again until that part of my deal is sorted. I can do without any more emotional stress.'

'I'll bring Cain in on the handover details. He needs to know what's happening in his region.'

28. VISIONS OF ANGELS

Brady was flying all over the State of California showing off his FusionPlane™ like a kid with a new toy. On a brief stopover at his Ranch, he gave Lucian the news of his chance of a new life in San Martin - as an honorary Green - just like Brady Mahone. He talked so excitedly of all the fun they could have together that Lucian could hardly get a word in. He left Lucian with the instructions to start planning for the future before heading off to his new home in Malibu.

Hunter, Libby's old servant, was still there, with his staff, who maintained the building. He had been briefed on Brady's ownership and did everything he could to help Brady settle in comfortably. He had Bodhi's old clothes and possessions Nano-Cleaned™ and NanoRepaired™, and he arranged for a suite to be kitted out for his friend Lucian Lopez.

Every Rep who worked for Brady received a visit from Brady to see him in his private jet - as he preferred to call it - and all of them were told of a big future ahead of them, as he showed them the sketch of the new BMEE logo. He didn't mention Sattva System's™ involvement at all. It was part of the deal, and it became a superstition in Brady's mind, that if he let slip about Sattva Systems™, then his empire might disappear.

He spent Christmas alone. *He didn't want to be a part of the emotionally charged atmosphere it was likely to be at the Lopez Ranch. Lucky would have told them.*
He concluded, it would be like a marriage break-up kinda deal, and I know there will be lots of tears because that's what girls do. Who am I kidding? Lucky will be crying as well, and I don't want to see that.

Hunter put the traditional Christmas decorations up, and Brady ate heartily and drank well, alone. *Is ok. Next Christmas will be a blast.*

On Boxing Day, he visited West McFarland to meet with Cain, ahead of the handover. He made a point to vertically land outside the home of Siddha, Lizzie and Cain. It landed, noiselessly, but he knew they would have been made aware of his presence by the soft sub-sonic boom. He alighted his FusionPlane™ and glanced up at the upstairs window to see Lizzie - until she closed the curtains.

Cain came out to meet him. Brady was dressed like an international playboy from a distant age. 'Hi, Cain. All set?'

'I'll pick him up, in an hour. He has to travel with me to receive the previous versions of the NanoShells™ in Boulder Creek. Then I'll take him over to San Martin where he will reside with the Beardons and come under Samuel's mentorship.'

'Great. I'll see you later.'

It was then a virtual hop, skip, and a jump for Brady to land at the bus stop outside East McFarland and place his note behind the timetable holder, informing Judge Jefferson that San Diego was in Operation Clean-Up and was turning Green. He knew this news would alarm her, but they had always wanted the unvarnished truth from him, regarding developments in the outside Trad world.

He was busy, but the action made him feel exhilarated. He hopped over in his private jet and landed next to his barn. He saw Lucian waving to him from beyond the

NanoShell™. Brady yelled, 'I'm busy, man. I'll catch you after I've showered. Big night tonight, buddy.'

He went inside, undressed quickly, showered, shaved. He dressed in one of Xavier Kane's old business suits and a silk shirt and tie. He put on his highly polished black shoes, and then he put on the Sattva Ring of diamonds and emeralds. He had never felt guilty owning it, after all, it was a gift from Libby - sort of - but now he had Bodhi's blessing, he felt like it truly belonged to him. He enjoyed wearing it, it had a manly weight to it, making him feel wealthy and successful.

He then went out to be with the Lopez family.
I'm gonna do the handover of Lucky to Cain. And then I'm going to duck out of the fall-out with Mary-Lou and Amie. I can't be doing with that kinda comedown.

Brady strolled over to beyond the NanoShell™ which enveloped the Mahone Ranch and onto the Lopez land. He had deliberately left only a few minutes to spare before Cain was due to take Lucian to his new and better life. Lucian raced up to greet him as soon as Brady had crossed the Green boundary which separated them. 'Hey, Brady! I can't do it. I can't go. I can't leave Mary-Lou.' Mary-Lou and Amie stood far enough away to hear, but not so close as to antagonise Brady. This was a delicate negotiation between the two best friends.

Brady blurted out, 'Of course you can. You'll both be dead and gone within ten years. I mean, look at you, man. You're ageing real bad. Just make the fucking decision and be a man. We can have some great times together.'

'No. Brady, I won't leave Mary-Lou. I'm not leaving her alone.'

'She won't be alone. She'll have Amie.' *They deserve each other.*

Lucian said, 'About that. We want Amie to go and live out the rest of her life with the Greens. It's not her idea, of course. She wants to stay and look after us.'

'I didn't do all this - for her. I did it for you. I'm paying you back for saving my life. I don't owe her anything. You do see that - don't you?'

'I do. I appreciate that more than you'll ever know. You've always been a good friend to me - the best. But I couldn't live with the guilt. However long, my life would be pointless if I knew I was the sort of person that could just let the loves of my life die, while I had fun. That sounds like what the Greens have done to millions of people like me. I don't want to befriend people who could do that to others. The Trads have been dying out in their billions, while they play with their Suits™, getting dressed up and partying…'

Brady didn't want to take up a position of trying to defend the Greens policies and lifestyle choices. 'You would be with me. I'm a Trad…'

'Are you?'

Brady didn't have an immediate answer.

Lucian said, 'You're right when you say that me and Mary-Lou might have ten years left, at the most. After that, Amie would have decades of loneliness. She would have nobody to talk to. We fear what she would do to herself. She's not made for being alone.' He choked up.

Cain emerged within an aura of spectral white light. Brady saw the look of astonishment in the faces of Amie and Mary-Lou. He turned to see Cain padding along the ground with his bare feet and glowing white robe.

He reached out a hand to Brady, but Brady refused to shake it. Cain said, 'I've come to take Lucian Lopez to be a part of our Green Community.'

Brady said, 'You see. You have to go. I've done the deal for you, not anybody else to go.'
Lucian said to Cain, 'I want Amie to go in my place. Can you do that?'

Cain looked at Brady, and said, 'Sissy believed this would happen. When we discussed it with Bodhi, she said that you didn't understand loving families and that you would see the situation through the prism of your own needs. Therefore, Bodhi made an accommodation for this situation.'

Brady barked, 'But it was the fucking deal.' He turned to Lucian and said, 'Sorry, man. I'm doing this for your own good - you'll thank me for it in time.'

Lucian looked to Cain for help, Cain said, 'I was informed that Bodhi's deal was that one of your friends could be assimilated.'

Brady hastily replayed the events of the conversation in his mind. *He did say that. I mentioned Lucian to the Bear, but not to Bodhi.* He petulantly considered stating that Amie was not a friend of Brady Mahone, like a lawyer searching through the small print to renege on a deal, but then shrugged his shoulders as if he were throwing off the emotional weight of caring for them, anymore.

'Fine. Do what you want - see if I care.'

Lucian went over to Mary-Lou and Amie, and they all hugged and cried together, as a family connected by grief and hope. They walked, holding hands over to Cain like parents would walk a bride down the aisle. Lucian to Amie's left, and her Moms, Mary-Lou on her right.

Cain held out his arms to greet them, his white robe was luminescent, and his crystal green eyes sparkled. 'Come child. You have so many new friends to meet.' She took his hand and walked off into the darkness with him. She occasionally looked back and tried to smile from within her tears. Lucian and Mary-Lou waved her goodbye until they disappeared from view.

Billy Big Paws rushed past Lucian and Mary-Lou to join Amie. She stroked him and he padded along after her obediently.

Brady shouted spitefully. 'They won't let you keep the dog. I'm just saying'

Lucian looked at Brady, but Brady turned on his heels and went to his Fusion-Plane™. He took off and headed to Malibu, to live in his new home. He had no plans to return.

THE END.

2142

The Revealing Science

Book Three of the Green Deal Quartet

By

Jim Lowe

1.TWENTY-SECOND-CENTURY MAN

Brady Mahone stared out over the Pacific Ocean from a balcony of his luxurious Malibu home, which had been his pride and joy for the last forty-two years. The sun sparkled off the water on this chilly and bright January morning. He had a fleet of FusionCars™, FusionCoaches™, and FusionPlanes™ ready for use in his extensive grounds.

He wished he'd known his exact birth date.

It didn't usually bother him - the not knowing - but this would have been a good year to celebrate. He thought he'd been born and then abandoned in the early part of 2042. As it was now early January in 2142, he would have had a party to commemorate his hundred years on the planet.

He had hardly aged in the past sixty years. He was a Trad, and he should barely be able to walk. However, apart from a trace of grey streaking his black hair, he was a picture of health and physical power.

He had explored many parts of the world in his FusionPlane™. Occasionally, he had taken large groups of friends overseas with him, in his FusionPassengerJet™, he didn't mind his guests partying in their dull - to Brady - Green ways. He liked the thrill of flying his private jets. He sometimes thought back to the dividing days, pre-and post-Revolution and wondered whether the human race had progressed at all. When there used to be the Internet, people were obsessed with their appearance and looks to their friends in photographs. Now, the same vanity existed, but it was in the form of changing their appearance instantly. Ever since they developed the Yellow-Suits™ at the dawn of the Twenty-Second Century, and then with the advent of the BlueSuits™ a dozen or so years ago, they could now even change sex, or be no sex at all. Admittedly, it took an hour or two, but it caused Brady much consternation. He was a Trad and lived by his Trad values.

He moved away from his balcony and went for his morning shower. Hunter prepared his warm bath towels and robe for when he finished. He'd never really known how to describe Hunter's role. He was still generously paid by Sattva Systems™; therefore, he wasn't Brady's servant, and he behaved like an old-fashioned butler. He was probably quite the fashion accessory back in the days of his pre-Revolution role, as he attended to Libby Skye, the Hollywood starlet's every whim.

If he was good enough for her, why shouldn't he be good enough for Brady Mahone? After all, I am probably the richest man in the world after Bodhi, of course.

Brady's staff had his breakfast prepared for him as soon as he was ready. They kept watch to make sure the timing of their delivery was seamless and immaculate.

Who'd have thought I would have gone from being an ex-con on the run from Ridgecrest Supermax to this. I earned it, though. I worked hard and played the system.

Anytime he thought back to his prison days, he thought about his old friend, Lucky. He always regretted not returning to the Lopez Ranch to see them again after Lucian had betrayed him by staying with Mary-Lou. He was informed too late to have them buried and arrange a funeral for them. The Greens sprayed their decomposing Green goo over their dead bodies until they seeped back into the Earth - just like billions of other dead Trads. Later, he felt the pangs of guilt that the old Hodgson Ranch, had unmarked graves for the undeserving Hodgsons - the graves that Lucian had dug for them.

He had arranged for other Greens from West McFarland to look after his home. He couldn't bring himself to let his Foster Daddy's house fall into disrepair. It had been fifty-eight years since Archie Mahone had taken his own life, and yet to Brady, it felt like only a fraction of that time elapsed. Such was the glacial rate of ageing among the Green population. It gave the impression of time standing still.

He had witnessed some Greens die of natural causes. With their indestructible RedSuits™, coupled with the upgrade that followed - the NanoHealing™ of the OrangeSuits™, he thought they had the potential to live forever. *Libby died at one-hundred and fourteen.* Cain felt the need to explain to Brady that the promise, except for unforeseen circumstances and accidents, to the Green Communities, when the OrangeSuits™ were launched, was that anybody born before the Green Revolution of 2084 should live to at least one-hundred-years of age. He also forecasted that many could live well beyond that age. The most significant advantage from a Green living to one-hundred and a Trad would be the quality of life - and death. They would be healthy, active and feel decades younger than they would in the equivalent Trad years, but then, when they died, their bodies would give up at a time they were sleeping - there would be no fear and minor pain.

That wasn't the case for Judge Audre Jefferson of East McFarland. On the last day, he had left the message for them, behind the timetable at the abandoned bus shelter on the outskirts of town. He was informed of her death. Officer Norbert had said that she died peacefully in her sleep, but Brady knew a liar when he saw one. She had been racked in pain with her crippling rheumatoid arthritis, and he could all too easily imagine the agony of her last moments on Earth.

I'm a Trad, but my body acts like a Green, even though I've never been tempted to have their NanoSuits™. He remembered his Pops' words that he used to say to him when he discussed his crazy alien invasion conspiracy theories. *They'll come with out of this world gifts, and you'll want them, but it's all about mind control, boy. The moment you give in to temptation - that's how they get ya, son.*

After Judge Jefferson had died and before East McFarland was laid to waste in Brady's words or re-wilded in the Green's version of events - he had the Los Banos files relocated back to his old home at the Mahone Ranch.

He guessed that Cain, Lizzie, Siddha, and who knows, maybe even Genesis Garcia and Bodhi himself, might have gone through them. He didn't care. He had destroyed the Tiberius Files, as per his agreement, with which he had attempted? Succeeded? In blackmailing Bodhi Sattva. If they had found evidence within them that would cause them discomfort, then so be it. By letting them have the opportunity to view it, then this made Brady Mahone appear transparent and honest. They would be cautious about removing evidence if it made it clear which part of the history of conspiracy and fraud they were worried about. And in any case, if they should destroy it all, accidentally on purpose with a spillage of Green goo - then he still had the two hundred plus pages of the summary of their crimes in the binder that Judge Audre Jefferson had made especially for Brady. She had written it in as simple terms as possible to suit his truncated educational development, and he had this in his possession at his Malibu home.

He had an extensive wardrobe to choose from, but he still liked to dress simply in his white T-shirt, blue jeans and black sneakers. One of the most important he had Hunter do for him every few months was to keep his antique trench-length Poacher's coat maintained. Hunter somehow managed to get hold of some textile repairing NanoFixant™ to make it like new when it was almost worn out. He wondered if he had reached out to Bodhi and his team. *Bodhi will do almost anything to keep me happy - I love that guy!*

After breakfast, Brady flicked through the pages of an antique coffee-table book called the Times Atlas of the World. It was a book from the late twentieth century, and it had maps of the world from how it used to be. He had become bored with the old city breaks. It was fun for a while to go and see things like the Eiffel Tower toppled over and rusted, and then on a further visit a decade later, seeing it covered in vegetation, but now you needed a GreenGuide with local knowledge to find where these structures used to be. It was nice to see the local species of wildlife that had returned to their old habitats. Brady liked animals and even plant-life, but now he hankered after the big species.

Brady perused his books on African animals and botany. He slowly made a list of animals and birds he'd like to draw. He considered who he'd like to take with him on safari. He had friends all over the world. Whenever Brady visited, he was greeted like a VIP, as he was the owner of BMEE, Brady Mahone Entertainment Enterprises. He would ostensibly be there to check up on the business, but it was primarily for leisure and pleasure with Brady. He usually travelled with free samples of the latest discoveries of ancient TV, movies and Trad music. He liked the professionalism of the look of the Black Files, which were manufactured by Sattva Systems™. Not that his customers knew that. As far as they were concerned, Brady Mahone was an entrepreneur whose net worth was over five-hundred-million Green Credits - this in a Green world where the hardest workers, and therefore the wealthiest of a Green Community might only have ten to twenty thousand Green Credits to their name.

He decided that he would take the four sales competition winners for this year with him. Last year, the prize was a month in China, and all four winners were women. Brady smiled as he reflected on the fun, he had with them. He hadn't been supplied with the data for the best performing BMEE Reps from the Western States of America in 2141 yet.

He made a few calls on his Satt™ to confirm the results and inform the lucky winners. He told them to get them in place for the coming Saturday, and he would personally pick them up in his FusionCoach™ from their homes. He wanted to make a big show in their respective Green Districts - and then jet them over to Africa for a month-long safari.

2.FREQUENT FLYER

He landed his FusionPlane™ in open ground in Green Cape Town. His USA Rep, Steve Dorsey had called ahead on his Satt™ to ensure a greeting party would welcome him. Brady was one of the few people in the world who would be considered like the celebrities and Hollywood stars from the old days. He was undoubtedly one of the few who would be allowed to be treated this way in the New Green World.

The proverbial red-carpet treatment would only be given to Continental Disciples, but they would usually eschew it on the grounds of equality of all its Green Citizens. Brady had no such qualms. He enjoyed the attention and believed he had earned their respect. In a world of the equally rich - and similarly poor, he was a super-rich entertainment mogul. His only concession to his magisterial status was that he liked to do the flying.

He alighted the plane to be welcomed by the Northern South African Regional Disciple, Lubanzi Khumalo. He was black, but he surrounded by people of a variety of races. Lubanzi opened his arms wide and embraced Brady warmly. 'Our people have wondered when you would visit our great Green Communities. It is so good to finally meet you. Come, I will introduce you to some of our most dedicated Green workers.'

Brady shook hands and shared pleasantries with a few dozen Green South Africans. He also introduced them to his four Reps - one of them gave Brady his free samples suitcase. Brady noted that there was a FusionCar™ and a couple of FusionCoaches™ waiting. Lubanzi said, 'You can travel with me in the FusionCar™ and work on a potential itinerary - if that's ok with you?'

'Yeah, sure.'

'I'm sure you would like to do a bit of sight-seeing while you are here. We have a rich history to discover.'
Brady approved of the way Lubanzi drove - he was quick and didn't wait for the FusionCoaches™ to keep up. He hated going anywhere at a crawl. 'I'm not big into history, and haven't your old buildings fully decayed, yet?'

'Not completely, my friend. There are still remnants of Cape Town City Hall, a new hill has formed around it, or maybe you'd care to see the Union Buildings in Pretoria, they both have historical links with Nelson Mandela.'

'Who's that?'

Lubanzi tried to hide his dismay, 'He was the greatest man in South African history.'

'When?' Brady always seemed to have to go through this with foreign dignitaries.

'From the mid to late twentieth century.'

'I'm supposed to know about a guy who lived nearly two-hundred years ago. Anyway, aren't we supposed to be looking to the future, y'know, the planet, in your case, and business opportunities in mine?'

Lubanzi didn't have an immediate answer, so he continued to focus on the road ahead of him. Brady looked out of the window. He had expected to see a desert landscape and not the verdant greens of vibrant grassland and tall trees in the distance. Lubanzi tried another approach - he was talking to a businessman. Therefore, he had to sell his idea. He didn't want his District Disciples to see that he wasn't getting along with one of the most important visitors in post-Revolution history. He said, 'How about the Palace of the Lost City. It's in Sun City.' He neglected to mention that it was only a grandly named hotel.

Brady nodded to signify his interest had been piqued. He liked the idea of lost cities - it sounded adventurous. Lubanzi continued now he felt a sense of encouragement, 'It used to be a palatial property fit for a queen…'

Used to be. My home is like that - it was built for the Queen of Sattva.

'…Most of the grounds and property has, of course, been re-wilded. However, it overlooks the stunning Pilanesburg Green Game Reserve. You could go on safari there with our Sun City District Disciple - she's an expert on the wildlife and fauna of the area.'

Brady said, 'Like what, precisely.'

'Lions and leopards…'

'That's more like it. What else have you got?'

'My friend, you have to see the Cape buffalo, elephants and rhinoceros.'

Brady laughed, 'Yes! I'd love to see all of those.'

Lubanzi may have been dismayed by Brady's lack of history knowledge, but his enthusiasm for nature enhanced his Green credentials. 'Since the Green Revolution, these species have thrived and can be seen in an abundance. You are going to see the giant herds. They are among the most spectacular sights you could see anywhere in the world.'

Brady said, 'I would be truly grateful if you could organise that for my competition winners and me. I can meet the people over the next couple of days, y'know, to do my duty and all that, and then we could do the Safari.'

'Leave it to me. Sattva Systems™ wants you to enjoy your stay.'

As they pulled up into Green Cape Town, the streets were lined with Greens of all ages. Brady said, 'We'll get out here. I'll work the crowd.'

Brady got out of the car, and the crowd cheered him. His Polynesian skin shimmered like bronze in the sparkling sunlight. He put on his designer sunglasses which had once belonged to Xavier Kane, and he had his NanoRepaired™ white T-shirt, jeans and sneakers. All Brady's garments had to be renewed by Sattva Systems™ for him, as there hadn't been a textile industry since the turn of the century. He knew it was always good PR for Brady Mahone's Entertainment Enterprises for him, personally, to concentrate on giving out his free samples of Kid's TV shows from history to the children - it also worked like a charm on the females in the crowd. He didn't have to get lucky. By now, luck didn't have anything to do with his well-rehearsed pickup routines.

He gave out his free samples to the children and his middle-of-the-road wares to the adults - anything too stimulating would attract the Security Protocols™ machines, which would effectively cling-film anybody who became over-excited. It didn't matter to Brady what the content was, as long as they sold and kept his fortune accumulating.

Brady hardly noticed the Security Protocols™ machines anymore, even though his friends would report that they could usually spot them around Brady if they caught a glimpse of them out of the corners of their eyes. They theorised that now the Green communities had lived with them for the best part of sixty years they were hardly required anymore. On the other hand, Brady believed they were instructed to follow him, as they had got him out of several tricky situations over the years. He had the feeling that his welfare was a high priority to Bodhi Sattva and the rest of his Sattva Systems™ Disciples. He never fully trusted Bodhi Sattva, even though Bodhi could not have been more honest and caring with him over their frequent and regular meetings. He dwelt on his relationship as he went into autopilot with the crowd. In every place he visited outside his native Californian home, this was a routine job. Apart from the profits, the only thing that made this worthwhile, was the hunt for an accommodating woman.

He worked the crowd, and he felt the silky caress of a young and beautiful black woman. She had casually touched his hand as she selected her free sample. He handed her a Hollywood movie from the 2040s. He gave her the Black File with the movie title in tiny writing on one side, and on the reverse the BMEE logo with the Diamondback rattlesnake threading through the yellow blocked letters. He looked up into her brown eyes with his own. She said, 'Your skin is so soft for a hundred-year-old Trad.'

'What did you expect? A doddering old man?' He staggered around mockingly, she laughed - as did the crowd around her. 'Maybe later, you might allow me the pleasure of checking if your skin is as soft as mine. I would like to explore what lies behind that NanoSuit™ of yours.'

She smiled as Lubanzi whispered to Brady and then nodded to her. Brady's work here was done. He had arranged his evening's entertainment.

The only thing that put a dampener on his ardour was never knowing exactly which sex his conquests were, originally. It didn't matter to the selected Green, but it still irked Brady. Most of his sleeping partners were savvy enough to lie to him and profess they were born female, as Brady was a Trad who gave off primitive alpha-male signals. He had wondered whether the Disciples had been briefed ahead of his visits because the potentially confusing relationship issues had become more infrequent in recent years.

The following morning, another woman knocked at his host's door and, informed him that she was the Sun City Regional Disciple, and she was going to be his guide for his time in Sun City. Brady was in his underwear. 'Ok. Give us a moment.'

She smiled, 'Don't worry. I'll wait while you make yourself ready. It's going to be a busy schedule.'

He stepped back inside his temporary partner's home. He showered, dressed, grabbed a coffee and kissed his sleepy partner goodbye. She was exhausted. He then ventured out into another bright sunshiny day. His host was waiting for Brady in her FusionCar™. He had long since lost the disappointment that every FusionCar™, in every country, looked precisely the same - they were all cream-coloured ceramic vehicles adorned with the same moss-green Sattva Systems™ logos. *These Greens have no imagination.*

Brady jumped into the car like an excitable child waiting to go to the seaside. He looked at her and thought she looked more Asian than South African. *But what do I know?* He introduced himself unnecessarily, 'Hi. I'm Brady. Brady Mahone.'

'Hello, Brady. I'm Precious.'

'I'm sure you are.'

She laughed politely at the joke she had heard about a thousand times. She lied, 'I'm the Regional Disciple of Green Sun City. This is going to be a very long jour-ney.' She added, 'You can pop your case of entertainment samples in the back.'

'How long is the ride?'

'It's about fifteen hours by FusionCar™, and that's with no stops. So, we'll split the trip over two days. I've got plenty of supplies. I do hope we get along as we will only have each other for company, and these FusionCars™ are at best, cosy, shall we say.'

He wasn't sure if she was flirting with him, even though he knew Disciples weren't allowed or chose to abstain from the pleasures of Brady Mahone. He always suspect-ed the Disciples as playing him as a fool, even though he had made countless Green friends across the globe. The Disciples still had an air of superiority toward him. They didn't do this overtly, as their Security Protocols™ regarding others' humiliation wouldn't allow it. However, he suspected them of disrespecting him and his busi-ness achievements. He believed they were just subtle about how they did it. He said, 'Couldn't we take a FusionPlane™? We could get there in no time.'

'Normally, we would. However, we are staying at the Pilanesburg Green Game Reserve, and the sub-sonic booms of the FusionPlanes™ disturb them. That's why we have a no-fly zone over it.'

'What would have happened if I had flown over it?'

'Are you aware of the reflection shield around your FusionPlanes™, which pushes birds and insects away from your path?'

'Yes. Some clever shit. And it keeps my windshield clean.'

'Well, it's a similar system from the grounds of the Protected Species Reserves. They push out a repelling signal which would have gently forced your FusionPlane™ around the no-fly zone.'

Brady accepted her explanation. 'Couldn't we have all travelled by FusionCoach™ with my colleagues?' *It might have been more fun.*

'I have to make a detour over to Prieska. I'm having a few problems with the Dis-trict Disciple there.'

'What does that matter to me?'

'Bodhi wants to test him, and you seem to be the source of Disciple Pastor Jacob's ire.' She laughed. 'You are not in any danger Mr Mahone, and this is a business opportunity for you. He has had a Security Protocols™ infringement, but now he seems to think he can circumvent the Sattva Systems™ rules by outsmarting them.'

'I've never met this Pastor Jacob. Why should I be bothered?'

'If he chooses to boycott your products, then that is fine. What is against our rules is that if he punishes and humiliates others for wanting to buy them. They have been quietly sanctioned by Sattva Systems™ - the Disciples have all been informed. Their instructions are to let your Reps do their job while they turn a blind eye to this semi-legitimate operation.'

'It's fully legit.'

'I know. Sattva Systems™ wishes to protect its brand and the clarity of its goals. In the old days, this would have called a side-hustle.'

Brady thought about it for a moment, 'You mean, like, if I had a regular job, but I was earning an extra bit of cash on the side?'

'Precisely.'

'I suppose I could take offence if I was a sensitive soul - which I'm not.'

Precious laughed again at another of Brady's unnecessary attempts at humour. She said, 'But you could always console yourself by gazing at the huge numbers on your Distor™.'

Brady said, 'When we get to Prieska, what do you want me to do?'

'The same as what you always do. You are a visiting celebrity, a wealthy man, with a highly successful business. Meet the people, hand out your samples, charm the local females…' She smiled knowingly.

'I can do that. Then what?'

'I will observe Pastor Jacob and be ready to take the necessary steps should the Security Protocols™ be invoked. It needs a Disciple of a higher level of authority to deal with the transgressions of a District Disciple.'

As the FusionCar™ sped along the open road and the landscape barely seemed to change over endless miles, Brady caught up on some sleep. One of the very few signs that Brady was getting older was that he did need an extra nap from time to time.

As they approached the outskirts of Prieska, Brady felt like it was a home from home. Precious had mentioned the Orange River - they had plenty of oranges in California - and Prieska looked about the same size as McFarland.

Precious joked, 'So, you're back in the land of the living?'

'Yeah, sorry about that.'

'The Trads who used to live here used to speak Afrikaans or Xhosa, but all the Green Communities around the world were taught American English.'

'I had picked that up. All part of the One World, One Nature, One Humanity thing.'

She said, 'All of us are equal under the Sun.'

As they drove into the town centre, they saw the first of the demonstrations, they were shouting *Out, Brady Out*. It reminded him of the trouble he had after the International Space Centre crash in Encinitas. *I've said it before, and I'll say it again. These Greens have no imagination. Why do I get the blame for everything?* He said, 'I have seen demos before. I'm ok with that - not everyone is into old movies.'

'I know, but Bodhi is keen to show his friendship, and it hurts him to hear of people treating you in such a hostile manner. He wants to make it right, but of course, nobody will be harmed. He just expects better from his appointed Disciples.'

Precious looked around at Brady to check if he was ok. She slowed the car but drove into the protesters. The repelling field around the FusionCar™ seemed to gently push them aside. Even the most determined, who lay down in front of the FusionCar™, were brushed aside like an old-fashioned road-sweeper vehicle.

When they had passed the demonstration and headed into the town centre, these Prieska residents' attitude altered markedly. They cheered enthusiastically as if to make up for the disrespect he had encountered earlier. He grabbed his bag of free entertainment samples. Just as he was about to leave the FusionCar™ she grabbed his arm lightly, 'They have plenty of South African entertainments - they are hungry for the products you have brought with you from the States.'

Brady got out of the car and waved to all parts of the crowd. He went through his well-practised routine of greeting the children, and like a bronzed God, he chatted to them before giving them their gift. He worked harder for these customers, as they had demonstrated the love for his products in the face of hostility from their neighbours. He even went through his routine of selecting another female companion for later. He would have preferred a fellow male to conclude the arrangements, but Precious seemed to know what was expected of her, and she completed her task diligently.

He then spotted hundreds of other demonstrators who had trapped Brady and his supporters in a pincer movement. One of the demonstrators placed a wooden box in Main Street's centre, and an old black man with white hair and beard was raised by his followers and placed on the box.

District Disciple, Pastor Jacob, raised his hands to the heavens. With a surprisingly loud and deep voice, he said, 'The Devil's Spawn is sent to walk among us. He is sent to lead us into temptation. Look how he steals your children's souls.'

The crowd responded with chants of Out, Brady out. Out, Brady out!'

'He will lead us all into eternal damnation. I have received the Word of God. He has named this demon to me, and I shall share his name to all of you who are gathered before me. I implore you, as your Disciple, you must destroy the Devil's Spawn.' He retrieved a silver cross from his jacket and held it out - he pointed it at Brady. 'I name you, Brady Mahone, as the Devil's Spawn.'

As he said this, he was doused in SecurityFilm™. He was motionless upon his box, his frozen contorted face trapped in a moment he couldn't escape, with his silver cross held out before him, in an accusation aimed at Brady Mahone.

Brady said, 'Always with the silver crosses? Do they think I'm superstitious or something?' A few of the crowd around him began to laugh. They laughed louder when he joked, 'At least in America, they once accused me of being the actual Devil. It seems that in South Africa, I've been demoted to the Devil's Spawn. How humiliating.'

The Security Protocol™ stated in amplified words to reach all parts of the crowd:

This is NanoRespect™, a trademark of Sattva Systems™. An act of humiliation has been detected on another human being. This was the third and final warning. The welfare of our consumers is our highest priority. Please inform the Regional District Disciple to remove District Disciple Pastor Jacob from his role, with immediate effect. Thank you for using Sattva Systems™. Together, we save the world.

Precious approached the SecurityFilm™ enveloping Pastor Jacob, and as she touched it, he was transported at high speed until he disappeared over the horizon. She took his place on the box. 'Sattva Systems™ does not condone such unkind treatment. Pastor Jacob's motivations were cruel and without foundation. He will not be harmed. He will be re-educated and placed in another district far from here. The Security Protocols™ will be tightened until order is restored. Bodhi Sattva will appoint a new District Delegate in due course. Thank you.' She alighted the box and headed back to Brady's side as if he needed her protection.

There were shouts from a few of Pastor Jacob's supporters, but the Security Protocols™ moved in swiftly and Filmed them. They hung like flies trapped in a spider's web.

Brady said, 'It said it was his third offence.'

'Yes. I was disingenuous. I knew he wouldn't be able to resist. I used your presence in our country to make a stand against the dissenting Disciples. The word will spread, and others will be deterred.'

'Is this something you are doing alone, or are you working under orders?'

'I wouldn't call it that. This is what Sattva Systems™ needs us all to do. Disciples are supposed to be the paragons of discipline. They should act with a higher purpose. The rest of the Green population can have a little more freedom, but we Disciples are better than that - we have the great responsibility of leaders.'

Brady shrugged, 'I suppose so.'

She smiled, 'Anyway, Mr Bigshot Brady Mahone, Disciples like Pastor Jacob are bad for business. You wouldn't want that, would you?'

3.MSORO MONTY AND THE BWANA DEVIL

There were thousands of Greens who claimed they were personal friends with the legendary Brady Mahone. They told their stories at dinner parties or as bedtime stories to their children, about their conversations with him and how he had confided in them. The meetings with Brady were predominantly true, although grossly exaggerated.

Brady knew that his Reps on safari with him would feast on this time in his company - a winner's safari with Brady Mahone - one of the world's richest men and one of the oldest surviving Trads. The truth would be less fascinating. Brady spent much of the safari in his own company. He wandered off to find an interesting creature to sketch. It wasn't all about the Big Game. He wanted to study everything which lived in this land, except for his fellow travellers. Even if Brady remained reasonably polite with his guests and guides, after all, they were here to be rewarded and recognised for the sales performances, he still had a way with his body language to get them to leave him alone. Usually, this materialised in his *I'm not really listening* pose.

He had been fascinated by a purplish pink plant which his guide had said was particularly rare. He had her write it down for him in his sketchbook - he didn't want to misspell it. She had written, *Bottelborsel, Eckion's Bottlebrush*. He then stopped speaking. His whole focus was on the structure and texture of the plant. She soon got the message to leave him in peace, even though she had wanted to flirt with him while alone with a celebrity. At other times he added other plant drawings to his collection over the following weeks. These included Ericaceae, Berzelia Rubra, and a personal favourite, Rock Brachysphon or Sissies. He loved the pink and yellow rock flowers, and he felt the name was subversive, and he made a mental note to show this to Sissy the next time he visited the Sattva Systems™ HQ.

Of course, Brady took great delight in capturing the promised Cape Buffalo, elephants and rhinoceros - but he loved the surprises of the animal kingdom, the sort of animals who don't appear in the Tour Guide's headlines. He had heard of an aardvark but not an aardwolf. He took enormous pleasure in capturing this in his sketchbook. He collected images of the ground pangolin, the African wild dog, and his most favourite of all, the brown hyena. He felt it had character.

He enjoyed his routine of heading out at dawn before most of his entourage were awake. By the end of the day, he was ready for the small talk of the dinner party conversation. He usually steered the conversation to the animals and plants which had caught his eye during the day. His love of the animals, especially the lesser revered ones such as the insects and reptiles, endeared Brady to his Guides - all of whom were original members of the GreenRevs and were responsible for laying the foundations for the Green NanoShells™ in the decades leading up to the Revolution.

In recent days Brady had the strange sensation he was being stalked. He monitored his group's movements and only felt secure if he could account for the whereabouts of all of them. They just had a couple of days remaining, and the lions and leopards had been elusive so far. The decision was taken for them all to travel together in a FusionCoach™ to track down the last elusive creatures on Brady's wish list.

Brady insisted that he sat up front with Precious so that he could ask the driver, Khumalo, questions about the landscape and wildlife as they travelled serenely across the high, flat plateaus, the tree-dotted plains, or the bushveld as Khumalo called it, and then into the highveld, the rolling grasslands, where they would camp, and hopefully spot the Big cats coming out to hunt at night. Precious informed Brady that the lions preferred the richer, grassier soils and higher rainfall, as this gave them more animals to prey on.

As the honoured guest, Brady was allowed to avoid helping set up camp, but he knew it would look good to invoke the Division of Labour directive and help out. He always thought of Rhea and their washing of the Beardon's dishes together when he did this. Brady worked hard and volunteered with the heavy lifting - manual labour always made Brady feel more honest.

Brady took a few minutes out of his work to revise the top-line details of his competition winners. *Trust them to be all men this time - last year, I had four female winners, and that was great, but this time all I have is a bunch of Sci-fi geeks.* He flicked to the back of his sketchbook and tried to memorise the information, so he would look like he was interested in them over this evening's meal. He had done this before but had forgotten them again. *All these Green geeks are boring, and they all talk like Tyrone, with their jibber-jabber about light years and inter-galactic space travel.* For the third time on his trip, he stared at the information on the paper - written in pencil, so he could erase this information when he returned to his Malibu home. He laughed when he noticed that he hadn't erased the female winners of earlier sales competitions on the previous page.

Asher. Twin Falls, Idaho. White, skinny, black hair and whiny voice. Likes nature documentaries.
Theodore. Provo. Utah. Looks like a Viking. Beard with jewellery. White hair. Blue eyes. Likes talking about robots.
Atticus. Coolidge. Arizona. Black. Always wears a black leather beret. Uses long words all the time. Speaks Klingon?
Oliver. Eureka. California. Black. Dresses like me. Over competitive with the others. Annoying.

Once they were done. They all dined together. Brady ate heartily as he had worked up an enormous appetite. He punctuated his conversations with, 'That's why you're a winner, Oliver…Oh, you are way cleverer than me…You'll have to dumb it down so I can understand, Atticus…I've seen that up close and personal in the wild, Asher…If they could invent a robot to do that then that, would be brilliant, Theodore…'

He delighted his guests and cemented his reputation with the group when he volunteered to do the washing up on his own. There were dishes from a dozen people. His competition winner's felt shamed into offering to assist him, but Brady insisted, and it wasn't as though they put up much of a fight. It was the last thing Brady wanted - he'd much rather work and have some relative peace. However, Precious was politically savvy enough to spot this opportunity to help Brady - as a high-ranking Regional Disciple, she knew it would play well with her fellow Greens. So, she didn't contemplate refusing to help, no matter how much Brady protested.

Like Rhea before her, Precious used the reasoning of RedSuit™ protection for doing the washing while Brady dried. There wasn't a lot of kitchen space, so Brady stacked up the pots and pans as he dried them. He would sort it out later where to store them.

Precious chatted as they worked together, 'You sketch well, my friend.' He took this address as a sign that he had won her over. She said, 'How many sketchbooks do you possess?'

329

'I've filled hundreds over the years. There is a library in my Malibu home. I keep them all neatly arranged on the bookshelves.' He laughed, 'I had to throw out a lot of old books to make room for them.'

She smiled ruefully, 'Do you look at them, often?'

'Yeah. They bring back many...' He tried to find the right word - he knew it wasn't *happy,* 'peaceful memories.' He added, 'Nature doesn't judge me - only other people do that.'

Precious thought this was profound. However, she didn't believe that Brady intended to give her this impression. 'Where did you get hold of your sketchbooks? We don't fell trees for frivolous uses. I'm curious as to how you obtained them.'

Brady laughed, 'Most of them I robbed from the Trad areas. While I was hunting for entertainment products in the good old days, when Brady Mahone Entertainment Enterprises was just me, Lucky and Mary-Lou, if I came across an abandoned art shop or an upmarket gift retailer, then I would grab some books and art materials, and pop them onto my GreenBicycle and trailer.' He said, absentmindedly, 'God, I miss those days.'

She continued to wash the dishes efficiently. She asked, 'When did you learn to draw like that? Was it a natural ability, or was it a practised skill?'

'I'm not sure what you mean. I just draw, is all.'

'But when did you start drawing?'

'When I was first in Juvey. In the early days, it's quite exciting, y'know, when there's lots of threats and fighting, but after that, well, it all starts to get a bit dull. That's when Brady Mahone picks up some scraps of paper and a pencil and just draws what he sees.'

He was the only person she had ever met who talked about themselves in the third person. She wondered if it was a characteristic of the Trads before the Revolution. 'What did you see?'

'Birds in the Exercise Yard, or cockroaches and flies in the cells. It didn't matter none to me. It helped to pass the time. Sometimes, there would be a wildlife book in the Prison Library which I would borrow and copy out the animals - and then there were botany books...'

'Did you draw anything else?'

'Like what?'

'I don't know - maybe people or landscapes.'

'No. they don't appeal to me.'

They heard excited chatter coming from the others. Khumalo went into the kitchen, 'Our trackers say there are lions nearby.'

Precious said, 'We'll finish up here and join you in a few minutes. You go on ahead and take our guests with you.'

Brady and Precious left the camp and could see the rest of the group a few hundred yards ahead. It was dusk, but not yet fully dark, and he could smell the soil, grass and the nearby trees. His senses were heightened by the anticipation of the hunt. The guides ahead had switched on their FusionTorches™, and this prompted Precious to take her own out. Brady heard the sound of animals scurrying away from them as they crept onwards. He wondered whether this land had always been this full of life and whether the old Climate Change fears would have destroyed this area - and everything that lived in it - eventually.

The group in the distance halted, and Precious quietly urged Brady to do the same. He complied because he felt strangely uneasy. His mind flashed back to the time when Lucky had saved his life in Ridgecrest when the danger was behind him.

Brady heard a rumbling roar of a colossal beast, followed by another. The roars were coming from behind him. The first lion was a vision of teeth and claws, it was about to plunge them into him when it froze, and then a second male lion came in at him from his right and leapt at him and again froze. Both animals were frozen in mid-leap, with their mouths wide open at the point they were going to feast on the flesh of Brady Mahone. They were Filmed by the Security Protocols™.

Khumalo rushed over from the group in front, with the others following closely behind. The Guides still had the foresight to keep watch if there were other dangers to be wary of. When Khumalo reached Precious and Brady, he checked that Brady was unharmed. He then stared and studied the lions. 'Brady, my friend. If there was ever any doubt that you were a Pure Trad, then we have the proof right here.'

Brady didn't question the use of the term *Pure Trad*. He had considered it many times, as he grew older but looked forever young, while most of the Trad population aged rapidly. He backed away instinctively from the lions and moved next to Khumalo - he would never admit that it was a sign of a need for comfort and protection. He considered why the Security Protocols™ saved him. He wondered if they would have appeared in the past if he hadn't the skillset to escape a threat himself. He looked at the pair of lions and knew he wouldn't have stood a chance. In a moment of clarity brought on by a near-death experience, he felt sure that he led the wrong life. His life was becoming self-centred and worthless.

He took a deep breath to release his anxiety. He didn't care - for the first time he could remember, whether people could sense his vulnerability. He placed his hand on Khumalo's shoulder, 'What do you mean? What proof?'

Khumalo's eyes widened as if he had disrespected Brady. 'I didn't mean...'

Brady smiled kindly and squeezed Khumalo's shoulder, 'This is important to me. You, my friend, can answer one of the biggest puzzles in my life. I would be truly grateful if you could share with me your insights. Please speak candidly and without fear.'

Khumalo looked at Precious, and she nodded her consent and reassurance. He said, 'These are two of the most fearsome man-eating lions in this area. They have feasted on hundreds of Trads in their time. They have a craving for human flesh.'

Brady looked over both of them. He examined the teeth and their gaping mouths. He looked with wonderment at the wild hunger in their eyes.

Khumalo continued, 'All of the Trads in this land are dead. They haven't picked up the scent of a Trad in years, but they picked up on the scent of you, my friend.' He knew he hadn't fully conveyed his message.

Brady said, 'Just tell me.'

'If you were Green, or even *partially* Green, they would not have smelled you. Our NanoSuits™ make us no more attractive to feast upon than a robot would. The NanoSuits™ emit no scent. Whereas you may have alerted them to your presence from miles away. Only a Trad could tempt Msoro Monty and Bwana Devil - that is what the local villagers used to christen them - to come after you, and only you.'

He moved around the lions, 'See this?' He pointed at a jagged fang. 'This is the broken tooth of Bwana Devil. He got this name when a villager tried to bash his head with a brick.' He wandered around the second lion, 'And these are the wounds on his side where he was once caught on a razor-wire fence.' He looked Brady up and down. 'If you had any further doubts, and they were planning to attack the group, then consider why they would attack the one man who looked the biggest and strongest among us. Lions would select and hunt out the weakest.'

Brady said, 'Thank you. I believe you. What's going to happen to them now?'

'When you are out of harm's way, they will be released. We do not harm Her creatures.'

Brady thought for a moment and then said, 'Could you leave them like this for a couple of hours?' Precious was about to object, but Brady held up his hand to stop her. 'I've been hung up in this SecurityFilm™ for hours before. It didn't harm me none. In fact, I felt better than ever afterwards. I only want to draw them. It's important to me. I need to remember this day.'

Precious nodded. He retrieved his sketchbook and handed it over to Khumalo at two open, blank pages, 'Could you write down their names for me, just here…' He pointed to the top right-hand corners of the pages. 'I don't write so good, and I want the spellings to be correct.'

4. THE WRONG SUIT

It took longer than expected to return to his Malibu home, as Asher-Twin Falls-Idaho had begged for the chance to be flown over the Antarctic to witness the undeniable good the Greens had done for the climate. Asher-Twin Falls-Idaho waxed lyrically about the replenishment of the Polar Icecaps. All Brady could discern were endless blank white landscapes. The only relief came in the few moments they spotted a colony of Penguins which stretched for miles, but even this sight was quickly obscured by clouds followed by a ferocious blizzard which lasted for hours.

He wanted to spend some time alone in his Malibu home, to consider his new-found certainty that he was indeed a Pure Trad. He had to head north at some point, as he needed to check-in with Bodhi. He was owed a considerable sum in Green Credits from his business since he hadn't seen Bodhi in over a year to collect his profits. Brady then decided he would visit Cupertino, as these were some of the last Trads on Earth still living in a sizeable community. He felt a need to be with other Trads before they became extinct.

After a couple of days of decompression after his South Africa holiday, he took his FusionPlane™ and flew to Boulder Creek to meet up with his friends at Sattva Systems™. When he arrived, he noticed that the atmosphere was downbeat. He had never seen the people like this before. Sissy came out to greet him. 'Hello, Brady. Long time, no see.'

'I've been busy, and I've just spent the last month in South Africa. What's going on? Nobody will tell me.'

She attempted a comforting smile but failed, 'Bodhi is ill.'

'What's wrong with him?'

She sensed the workers were listening in, such was the desire for new information. She ushered Brady to walk with her and get out of earshot. 'With hindsight, it was a basic error.' Brady didn't respond. He wanted to encourage her to talk. 'Bodhi has always been the test subject for the new NanoSuits™. I know a lot of people don't believe that, but it's true.' Almost as if she was talking to herself, she said, 'I don't know why people ever doubt him. He has always been truthful with them.' Brady walked alongside her but still retained his silence a little longer. 'The Suit™ in development was to give people enhanced senses to improve the experience in studying nature - now that Mother Nature is close to being fully restored to her pristine beauty.'

Brady said, 'I don't understand.'

'In the coming decade, all traces of the Traditional Cultures will be eradicated and their old lands fully re-wilded.'

'Yeah. I know that.'

'We are going to give our Green communities enhanced vision, smell, taste, touch and hearing to fully appreciate this new era of Natural Beauty.'

'Ok. But what's this got to do with Bodhi's illness?'

'First, I have to tell you about the IndigoSuit™. This was going to drastically reduce the need for sleep. This was to allow everybody to study our nocturnal wildlife - remember our people would have improved senses - and, of course, people would have more time awake to make the most of their lives.'

They reached the Main Entrance. Sissy involuntarily looked up at the banner with the thirteen Green Commandments while Brady took in the odour of boiled cabbage and coffee from the nearby canteen. *I wouldn't want an enhanced sense of smell of that.* He was glad to move away from this area and start down the long, sterile corridors with their cream-coloured walls. She said, 'We had the plan the wrong way round. It was stupid. You see, with the advanced touch and hearing, Bodhi hasn't been able to sleep in months. He is suffering from sleep deprivation and nightmarish headaches. I think he might die.'

For some reason, Brady had never considered that Bodhi could die. Nobody seemed to age - not even himself. If this was a shock to Brady, then God only knows how his devout followers would take this news. 'I don't sleep much. Are you sure it's that bad?'

'Sleep has always been a mystery. I mean, why are we designed to waste so much of our precious time sleeping?'

'That's what I think. Having said that, I seem to be needing more sleep than I used to. I put that down to getting older.' He wanted an explanation but dreaded a boring scientific lesson. 'How can losing sleep kill Bodhi?'

She wanted to avoid discussing the sleep process as neuropathways being cleansed. 'Imagine the gutters around your old Ranch are full of dirt, but the weather is stormy. You want to clear them out, but you have to wait until the storms passed.'

'Ok.'

'This is the same with sleep. While you are awake, your brain is the storm - there is so much going on. Therefore, you have to wait until you are asleep, for the brain to clear the clogged-up gutters in your mind.'

'Why do you think I don't need as much sleep as other people?'

This was a potential rabbit-hole, so Sissy made a best guess, in as simple a form as possible, to keep Brady with her. She didn't want to suggest that Brady didn't have as much activity in the brain as other people, 'Maybe, you work harder and faster than others at cleaning out your gutters.'

Brady laughed. He could believe that. He said, 'So, you're telling me that Bodhi's brain is so clogged up that it could wreck his house.'

Sissy smiled. She had reached him. 'Yes, Brady. That's it - in a nutshell.'

They reached Bodhi's office. She knocked on the door almost inaudibly. Bodhi answered, 'Who is it?'

'It's Sissy. I have Brady with me. You said you wanted to see him when he re-turned.' She said in a voice barely louder than a whisper.

'Thank you. Send him in.'

Sissy said to Brady, 'Talk to him as quietly as you can.' She added, 'Treat him like he has the worst hangover you could possibly imagine.'

'Got it.' Brady strode into Bodhi's sparse office. He shook Bodhi's hand, and he noticed the shocking weakness in Bodhi's grip and then sat opposite him.

Bodhi uttered, 'I've wanted to see you. I've been such a fool.' He was in his almost perennial uniform of grey tracksuit and sneakers, just as Brady had his preferred look of jeans and a white T-shirt. It seemed that all the choice in the world was no longer worth the effort.

'Are you going to be ok?' He noticed how even the act of thinking about a simple response looked like it had the power to rob Bodhi of the last remnants of his energy.

'I don't know. I'm in unknown territory. They are going to try to unpick the... Suit™ from me. It's fused at a molecular level with the other colours - each Suit™ builds on the foundation of the older - it could take years, and with no guarantee of success.'

'And if it doesn't work?' He had forgotten to lower his voice.

Bodhi grimaced, 'Then I will die.'

'I'm not being funny, but why didn't you do the experiments on somebody else, first? Surely, you are too important to take all the risks on yourself.' Brady said softly.

Bodhi smiled, 'That was my Father's way of doing things, remember?'

Brady was confused. He understood Bodhi's meaning, but the timeline didn't fit. 'Tell me if I'm getting this all wrong - but I blackmailed you with what your Pop's did with those kids - but you already knew about it?'

'You didn't blackmail me. I chose to work with you.'

'Whatever. You knew John Kane was abusing children and then carrying out experiments on them.'

'Yes. He experimented on me. He raised me in isolation. Everything he did to me was utterly normal, in my mind. I had no idea what your idea of a normal life was. He wanted me to be perfect. He immersed me in every part of Kane Industries until he damaged me.'

'How did he damage you?'

'I was forty-two, we were in the final stages of developing the Infrared™ primers to apply on the human body, to enable them to take the NanoSuits™. He told me my genetic design was the key to making it work - I was the fruit of all those appalling experiments.'

'And then what?'

'It worked - at first.' He winced at the pain in his head. 'Everything was going fine. I was the first person to receive the RedSuit™- that worked perfectly, except there was a small part of my brain which had been fused with the Infrared™ NanoBots™ primer. It first became apparent that I had memory issues - not memory loss, but errors with my powers of recall from when I was a young child. You have to take into account that I was constantly tested and assessed daily from as early as I could remember.'

Brady remembered to keep his voice low, and this made him appear to be sympathetic, 'That doesn't sound so bad to me.'

'It did to my Father. He needed a perfect test subject. He had raised me to be his perfect son and heir. In his eyes, I was brain damaged. I was no longer perfect.' Bodhi continued, 'He wasn't uncaring. He promised that I could be fixed - he said he had a plan…' Bodhi grimaced and added, 'He hated humanity. He thought mankind had wilfully wrecked the planet and caused untold damage to the environment. When he disappeared, I vowed to continue his work, but I didn't hate all of humanity like he did - there were a lot of people who cared as much as I did about the health of our planet…' He clutched his head as if he were in agony. He screamed quietly in pain as if his own voice would make it worse. Brady rushed to his side and held him. 'Hey. You'll be ok. There's a lot of clever people working to save you. They love you and want to see you recover. I want that.' He felt shudders of pain from Bodhi's body as if he was caught in an internal storm. He continued to hold him for many minutes until he sensed that the storm had receded. 'Are you ok? Can I get you anything?'

'No. I'm fine. I won't lie to you - the pain is unbearable at times. Thank you for your kindness.' He shuffled upright in his seat as if he had to demonstrate that he was feeling better.

Brady said, 'I'm guessing they can't give you something to help you sleep?'

'No. The OrangeSuit™ should work.' He stood up and then promptly toppled over like a felled tree. He was writhing on the floor. Brady went out of the door and yelled at the top of his voice down the empty corridor. 'I need someone. Now! It's Bodhi - he's having some kind of seizure. Where the fuck is everybody!'

This is NanoSecurityFilm™, a trademark of Sattva Systems™. You are emitting signs of stress which are above-permitted levels in these Headquarters. Please return to the required calm state. Take deep breaths and exhale slowly until you have achieved the desired reduction of stress. Have yourself a wonderful Green Day and thank you for saving Mother Earth.

Brady couldn't understand why the Security Protocols™ gave him grief about his stress levels and not save their supreme leader. He was trying to figure out how he could yell for help while staying calm enough to keep the Security Protocols™ off his case - when he saw Sissy strolling calmly up the corridor. He said sharply, hoping his voice would travel to her, 'Bodhi is having a seizure. He is in agony. Get help, for fuck's sake.'

Sissy stopped. She turned and ran away.

He hoped she had got the message, but if she wasn't going to do anything, then that wasn't his fault if Bodhi died. He went back inside to tend to Bodhi. He was still shaking violently. Brady looked for something for Bodhi to bite down on, as the look of agonising pain on his face suggested to him that this might help. He also thought he might be struggling to breathe. He took out his Distor™ - it was the right shape and size, but then he thought better of it. *What if I lose all my money if he breaks it?*

336

He had his leather sketchbook in the back of his jeans, the one he had used on his South Africa trip. It was pushed down the back of his jeans in the same way he used to put a pistol in the old Trad days. He used brute strength to prise open Bodhi's jaws, and then he slipped the leather notebook into the mouth, and Bodhi's jaws clamped down on the book with the power of a vice. Brady picked him up and propped Bodhi up in the corner of his office.

Brady said, 'You can do this, man. Breathe. Come on, breathe, God damn you. Follow my lead.' He grabbed Bodhi's face and forced him to look at him. 'Breathe in…Breathe out…Breathe in…Breathe out…' Brady saw signs of air coming in and out around the sides of Bodhi's mouth. Bodhi's teeth had bitten through the leathery skin of his notebook. Brady continued, 'Breathe in…Breathe out…' Bodhi nodded almost imperceptibly, but it was enough to encourage Brady that he was doing the right thing, 'Breathe in…Breathe out…'

From behind him, Brady heard Sissy enter the room with workers and a trolley which looked like it was carrying a coffin in Brady's eyes. She shouted, 'What have you done to him?'

'Nothing. You stupid c…' He stopped. 'Apart from saving his fucking life. But hey, it shows what you really think of me…thanks for nothing.'

Bodhi couldn't speak through his pain, but he made an effort to raise a hand and held it against Brady's face as if it was the only thing he could do to express his gratitude. Sissy said, 'I'm sorry.' She turned to her support team, 'Get him inside…be careful!'

They picked him up. Brady saw that they would attempt to open Bodhi's jaw to remove the sketchbook, 'Leave it. It's helping him to breathe.' Sissy nodded.

Brady asked, 'What's that?'

'It's a sensory deprivation chamber. It will buy time while our NanoEngineers™ figure out their next move.'

'If only you hadn't got rid of all the hospitals.'

She didn't want to explain how hospitals were redundant with the advent of Orang-eSuits™, and that old-fashioned medicines and surgical procedures were useless in curing a NanoReplicant™ malfunction.

Brady said, 'Can you fix him?'

'I don't know. I hope so. I don't know how we will continue without him. It doesn't bear thinking about.'

'Do you mind if I pop in from time to time - to see how he's getting on?'

'Of course.'

Brady and Sissy followed the team, transporting Bodhi back to the Main Entrance. She issued instructions, and they headed to the Research and Development area of the massive industrial complex. She stayed behind with Brady. 'Where are you going next, anywhere exotic?'

'Not now. Not until I find out what's happening to my unofficial business partner.'

'That reminds me. Pass me your Distor™.' She added, 'That's why I wasn't with you earlier - Bodhi wanted me to organise your payment.'

Brady said, 'It's ok. It can wait. It's not as though I'm short on funds.'

'No. I insist. If Bodhi asks me to do something, then I do it. I've learned, over the years, that he doesn't like jobs being left undone. Anyway, you've earned it.'

He passed her his Distor™. She completed the payment. She said, 'Another two-hundred and thirty-three thousand Green credits have been transferred.'

Brady said, 'Thank you.' It was a lot of Green Credits, but now his tally may as well have been in telephone numbers. He only got excited when his total clicked over a numeric milestone.

5. APPLES AND PEARS

Brady laughed at the people waving to him as he came into land at the centre of the old mASSIVE™ Park. He never thought he would be pleased to see a crowd of more than a thousand centenarians. He felt guilty at the thought that he used to call these people the *Cupertino Clowns*. Nowadays, of all the places in all the world, this was where he had the most fun. Of course, Brady was one-hundred years old, but he looked like a cool forty-something in Trad years. In fairness, most people who still lived at mASSIVE™ Park looked about seventy in old money. Some of them looked like very healthy seventy-year-olds.

They seemed to have found a way to grow and manufacture Euphoric Nootropics, which had become the Park's leading source of nutrition. In the early post-Revolution days, they attempted to restore power and connections to the outside world, but soon realised the futility of their actions, once they had tried and failed to break through the NanoShells™, which were primarily for protecting Green spaces, but also had the side effect of trapping Trads into their own areas. The circular structure of mASSIVE™ Park became a natural boundary once the rest of Cupertino turned Green.

The residents of mASSIVE™ Park - or *The Park* as it became shortened, especially as there wasn't a business called mASSIVE™ - or anything else for that matter - soon gave up on enhancing people's addiction to digital entertainment products and instead started to improve their own life experiences by continuing long-running experiments with brain food and juices instead. It benefitted the community in having something to research to pass the time. Also, they had to do this without a power supply, so they went back to basics of using whatever they could find to mix and match foodstuffs and out of date medicinal compounds to come up with something which would make their lives more bearable. In the end, they not only found new ways to achieve euphoric states of mind, but they also discovered that it improved cognitive thought and extended their lifespans.

Brady got out of his plane and went over to his chosen best buddy in this crazy community. 'Hi, El Duque.'

The old white man with the flamboyant Afro of white hair greeted Brady with a beaming gap-toothed grin. His blue eyes sparkled in the Californian sunshine, 'Crazy-man-crazy, hey Brady buddy, have you come to stay awhile.'

'Sure. I'm in need of some rest and recreation. I hope you got some of the good stuff.'

'We got your favourite. In fact, we re-christened it in your honour. It's now called the Brady Bomb. It used to be called the Brahmi Bomb, but this is a much more fun name.' They walked together through the Park, and they repeatedly stopped as they chatted with many of the elderly revellers. Not everyone was pleased to see Brady, some didn't trust him, but the rest seemed happy due to the Nootropics they were taking, apart from when the old resentments came to the surface. 'I still can't believe they sabotaged our power; this place was totally powered by renewables. I thought that was what the fucking Greens wanted.'

Brady said, 'Sattva Systems™ eliminated all competition. You lot were mining for rare metals all over the world. they were never going to forgive you for that.'

'I suppose.' He smiled beatifically, 'We were the lucky ones, at least we had the best Trad area on the planet. We have excellent living spaces, trees, and the Gardening Barn where we can cultivate the *Good Stuff*.' He nudged Brady, 'Hey, we're even protected from one of your personal earthquakes.'

'Talking of which, I need my own personal earthquake. Things have gotten weird for old Brady Mahone. I'm in need of the Bomb.'

'All in good time, my friend.' He slapped Brady on the back and then laughed loudly.

Brady asked, 'Have you lost any more people since I was last here?'

'Yes, sadly. Frieda was one of them.'

'That's a shame - I really liked her - she was funny.'

'I know, man. We are down to the last one-hundred and three Park residents. We have a large area to cover, but walking is keeping our daily exercise routines going. I hate the thought of the Greens taking over this place.' Brady knew this place well as they walked around the Ring through its wide hallway. They went up some stairs until they came to El Duque's room.

The whole campus still appeared futuristic to Brady, even though it was older than he was by about twenty years. There wasn't a flat piece of glass anywhere. Brady wondered not only how they made all this curved glass but also how it was strong enough to have survived unbroken after one-hundred and twenty years. In the early post-Green Revolution years, the trapped workers, who became residents, used to crowd the circular windows which looked out over Cupertino. They watched in horror as the HeavyLoaders™ circled the Park. However, they took Brady's knowledge and ensured that no area within the Ring remained unoccupied for more than seven days. They also took his advice on dealing with the dead and left the bodies at the Ring's outer edges for the Operation Clean-Up teams to deal with.

Despite everything that had happened globally, the Park residents still had enormous pride in this building that had once been their workspace but now had become their home. Like Judge Jefferson before, the mASSIVE™ residents craved news from the outside world, and Brady's friendship with El Duque meant that he became Brady's default liaison officer.

Brady slumped onto one of the oversized blue beanbags while El Duque brought over a large glass bowl. He said, 'I've got the Brady Bombs, but before we partake, tell me stories from the *Outer World*.' He placed the bowl on the ground carefully and flopped back onto a neighbouring brown beanbag - it used to be green, but it had been dyed with orange - green had become a superstitiously bad colour and interfered with the residents' chi.

Brady looked at the glass bowl hungrily. He smiled broadly, 'Things have been getting seriously weird lately. I think I'm going through some kinda old-life-crisis.'

'Like what, brother.'

'How about that I found out for certain that I'm a Trad, and not a Trad infected by Green goo, courtesy of a couple of man-eating lions.'

'Did they eat you, man?' El Duque laughed at his own joke.

'No. But they sure wanted too.' They both laughed. Brady added, 'I was on safari in South Africa - as you do - and apparently, the Greens don't give off any scent in their NanoSuits™, so the Greens were invisible to them. However, they could smell a Brady brunch from miles away.'

'How do you feel about that?'

'I feel better, y'know, like I've still got roots.'

'The big question is - whose side are you on? The Groovy Trads or the Stinking Greens?'

'The only side I'm on is what works for Brady Mahone. It's the only thing I'm sure about.' He looked sideways at the bowl of Brady Bombs but knew he still had to give to receive. 'I only thought about it later, but I think I had an opportunity to kill Bodhi Sattva.'

El Duque leaned back on his beanbag until he was almost horizontal. He appeared to be watching an imaginary projection on the ceiling. 'I thought the Greens were invulnerable.'

'They do all their NanoSuit™ trials on Bodhi first. That's the way they structure their organisation. I've thought about it a lot lately. If any other Green had a Suit that was more powerful than all the others, they could be a threat. It's a bit like being in a gang where only one person owns a gun.'

'So, how did you, a mere Trad, have the chance to kill the leader of the Greens?'

'Let me ask you something first?'

'Go on.' El Duque said dreamily.

'Do you consider that the Greens killed the Trads?'

'Yes. Of course. Seven billion souls and counting.'

Brady tried to refine his question, 'Ok, I get where you're coming from, but they made life difficult, and some people died before their time, but they didn't actually murder anybody.'

'Semantics, my friend. To deliberately neglect; and withhold vital requirements for living; and plunge people overnight into abject poverty; is another form of ethnic cleansing in my book.'

Brady wasn't arguing with El Duque, but he tried to clarify his own position on this issue. 'It wasn't ethnic cleansing. It wasn't racist.'

'Not in the old world's context, I grant you. But in the new world, the Greens ethnically cleansed the Traditional Cultures.'

Brady scratched his head, 'What if they thought it was all in a good cause?'

341

'All oppressors think they are on the side of righteousness and against wickedness or sin. Even if they don't personally think like that and have other more selfish goals, they certainly ensure that their followers receive this point of view loudly and clearly.'

Brady thought deeply on the Greens, who knew the best. He considered Bodhi the most. Bodhi Sattva had always told the truth, as far as Brady, or anyone else for that matter, was concerned. He had probably helped to make Brady one of the wealthiest people in the Green world. He struggled to find any reason to dislike him. He then thought of Cain - he was kind and caring. He was less sure about Sissy and Siddha, but they had helped out Brady when he needed it. He thought of others like his Reps - they were loyal and worked the system like any other criminals on-the-make would do, in the old or the new world. He remembered Lizzie, the schoolteacher in West McFarland, she certainly didn't like Brady, but then he recalled how he treated her and concluded that she couldn't be blamed for feeling that way about him.

He hadn't noticed that he had fallen silent for a few minutes. Even though the subject he was discussing with El Duque was particularly dark, he felt at ease here, almost as if he had entered a meditation centre. He said, 'If a man was dying, and I could help him to survive, but I chose not to, would I have been done for murder, y'know, in the old days of courts and stuff?'

'If it wasn't pre-meditated, then I suppose it wouldn't be homicide - maybe manslaughter…'

Brady said, 'I guess that if I was a soldier, and it was an enemy on the battlefield, then that would be ok - I think, but I couldn't do that to a friend, could I?'

'Is this what happened with you and Bodhi?'

'Yes.'

'What caused this?'

'Something went badly wrong with the latest NanoSuit™ he was given. It was killing him, but I think I saved him. I can't be sure I did, but I certainly didn't let him die. What does it say about me?'

'I would have viewed him as the evilest man alive and helped him on his way to hell. Whereas you saw him as a friend and let him continue his genocide.' He saw the look of discomfort on Brady's face, 'I don't blame you, my friend. You have been of benefit to our residents. At least, you have proved you care for others - this means you are not one of those psychopaths. You have discovered that you are a Trad and a human being with a soul. I would consider that a win in your battle for self-worth and discovery.' He sat up straight and reached for his bowl of Psychedelic Nootropics. Brady took a handful. He planned to be out of this world for the next couple of days.

6. A HANDFUL OF SOIL

Brady felt as if the life he was leading wasn't his own. For the first forty-two years, he lived as a criminal in the old world. He knew it was far from ideal, but at least it was considered comparatively normal with the rest of the world's population. Everybody lived within the same rules - even if Brady Mahone broke most of them - he was aware that they existed and for what purpose. He knew the law was to prevent people like Brady from hurting others and stealing their property. It wasn't complex. Therefore, he understood. There were other similarities between his old life and that of others. From the poorest to the wealthiest in society, most people had a family. Brady knew his family was considered dysfunctional. He was fostered, but they still became mothers and fathers and looked after him as best as possible, even after becoming an adult. His Pops still looked out for him even when he was a convicted felon, and his Moms had passed away.

He considered what he had learned about Bodhi in the days when they shared the same old world. Bodhi, or Xavier as he was back then, was at the pinnacle of high society, with his glamorous Hollywood actress for a mother and a fantastically wealthy Father in the industrialist, John Kane. It all seemed so different from Brady's upbringing, and yet, arguably, Xavier's roots were just as twisted as his own.

Now the world was divided, and he didn't belong to either side. As the effects of ageing on the Trad side and the Green's youth-preserving side effects invaded his thoughts, he felt like an outsider. He had nobody who experienced life like he did. He started to wonder if this is what loneliness was. *Is this why I didn't want Bodhi to die? I think he is the only person who understands. Maybe he is lonely too.*

If he had spent forty-two years in the old world, then he had now survived for fifty-eight years in the New Green World. He had exploited every opportunity to amass his fortune as part of the New Deal. He considered that the two richest people on the planet were Brady Mahone and Bodhi Sattva. Yet, he still felt frustrated and unsatisfied. He considered the Ring at mASSIVE™ Park as he was on his comedown from the huge intake of Brady Bombs which had left him conscious but zonked out for the last two days. He saw it through his Pop's eyes and his conspiracy theories of aliens from another planet landing their spaceship called mASSIVE™ Park to fool the human inhabitants of Cupertino. He was high on imagining it land and the Greens emerging in a spectacular light show, but then he had a Brady Bomb vision, which was far less spectacular but no less profound. He envisioned the Ring as a doughnut. It had substance on the outside but was empty in the middle.

Brady emerged from the funk of his comedown with this thought. *I'm a somebody on the outside, but I feel like I'm nothing in the middle. I have everything and nothing. I have power and wealth, but with no-one to rule and no-one to share it with. Soon there will be no Trads left, and the Greens don't love Brady Mahone. Sure, I have friends, acquaintances, and work colleagues, but I'm one-hundred-years old - even I won't live forever.*

He thought of Bodhi. He wondered if he was already dead - the residents of mASSIVE™ park would never know unless Brady told them. He considered the potential death of Bodhi and who would take over. *Sissy would be an obvious choice, but then again, so would Cain. I suppose one of those Continental Disciples would make a claim.* He chuckled. *Maybe there would be a Green Civil War, and I bet that Glenarvon Cole would be the head of one army.* He stopped laughing when he imagined Rhea marching by his side.

El Duque stood up. He had emerged from his own high at the same time as Brady. He held out a hand to help him to his feet. Brady was groggy. El Duque handed him a liquid concoction designed to bring him back to his everyday senses and optimise his brain function. Brady drained the gravy textured substance and headed over to the softly curved windows which looked out over Cupertino from the outer ring. It was a place El Duque could only look longingly at, but Brady could claim the freedom to roam at will. *I want Bodhi to live. He shows me more care, maybe even love, than all of the others combined. I can't explain it, but he wants me to live. He wants me to thrive. It's good for Brady Mahone that Bodhi Sattva survives. Of that, I'm sure.*

'How are you feeling? That's the Choline Mind Cleanser or CMC - it will work wonders.'

Brady noted a strange warmth coursing through his body and could feel the fog of his mind lifting like the mist rising off a field at the coming of the first warm rays of the morning Sun. 'Good. Real good.'

'Did you find the answers to your predicament?'

'Yes. But it's not the answer you would have wanted. Really sorry, man.'

'No worries. No point.'

Brady rubbed his black hair, which he regularly trimmed, as he never wanted to be one of those *Long-Hairs* from the old days. He knew he wanted to leave here soon. He loved getting high here, but he also liked to keep clean, and they didn't wash too often - he didn't know whether that was because of the cold water only being available to bathe in or whether it was just an old-age thing. He was old but still felt young. Whereas, these people were still old, even if they were reasonably well preserved - or pickled as Brady would occasionally joke.

Brady said as he scanned the horizon. 'You'd have thought that Bodhi would have had children.'

'It's patently obvious that the Greens don't want an excess of humans wandering about the planet, using up all Her precious resources.'

'I know, but the Greens still have children. Although they have to spend big to prove their commitment.'

El Duque considered the contradiction. 'How? Why?'

'They have to earn enough Green Credits by either working harder, or doing the dirty jobs, or taking on more responsibility. They call it offsetting.'

'I remember that. It was a short-lived thing called carbon offsetting. We used to do that - until we found a way around it, like everyone else, of course. It was bad for business, although we could never come out and say that.'

Brady said, 'And that's why they planned the Revolution. They couldn't believe anything the Trads could say about climate change. This much I've learned.'

El Duque laughed, 'I'll have to ban you from taking the Good Stuff if it's going to make you that insightful, my friend.'

Brady laughed with his friend, 'I'm sorry, man. I didn't mean...'

'That horse has bolted. Although, I concede that you have a point. But, as you were saying, it does seem surprising that Bodhi didn't have children. Maybe, he thought he was too busy, you've said before he is strung up about keeping to his so-called one-hundred-year plan.'

'Yes. He promised Glenarvon Cole, and Bodhi takes his promises very seriously.'

El Duque rubbed his chin with his right hand and shielded his eyes as the Sun burst through the clouds with his left. 'What has Bodhi Sattva promised you, my friend? What gem has he offered to the great Brady Mahone for his support?'

'I don't know. I don't think he's promised me anything but his help and support.'

'Whatever you are doing, it seems he wants you to succeed, brother.'

Brady thought about his business with a sense of pride. His products were being sold in every single territory across the globe. 'I'm succeeding in business. I'm just not sure...'

'Aha! I can feel it. Here it comes.' He looked at Brady with his beatific smile, 'This is it, spit it out.'

Brady said with the shadow of his earlier high and the restorative power of the CMC, lifting him to a warmer and gentler high, 'I'm just not sure... I'm succeeding in life.'

'Oh man, that is so spiritual. I love you, brother, let's hug.'

Usually, hugging a man would be the last thing he would want to do, but he hugged El Duque as warmly as if he was greeting a long-lost lover in his euphoric state. He hugged El Duque as he wished he could hug Rhea. El Duque whispered into Brady's ear, 'What do you need, brother?'

'I need family.'

El Duque put all his strength into hugging Brady, 'Then go and get one, my friend. It's as simple as the birds and the bees - even the Greens can't argue with that.'

7. OLD GROUND

It had been more than a decade since Brady last visited the Mahone Ranch in what was East McFarland. Today, East McFarland was mainly vegetation as the last of the most stubborn building substances made their final stand against reclamation. He had avoided the area in the early decades of the twenty-second century because it brought back too many memories, but they had faded now, and he sensed that he needed to be here to consider his next move.

He wandered around this green landscape and looked over toward West McFarland, where everyday Green life continued with barely a thought for the people who used to live here. Brady thought of Judge Audre Jefferson and Professor Yuan Chu. *It would have been real good if I coulda talked to him. He woulda set me straight.* He sat down for a while to take in the Californian spring sunshine and listened to the birdsong. *There are only pockets of the largest cities left, soon they will all look like this, and then I will be the only Trad left in the world, presuming I live that long, of course.* He smiled ruefully and then closed his eyes. It was hard for him to think of this place as the result of malice as he listened to the bird calls and smelt the meadows' fresh fragrances.

Brady stood up and strolled over to his FusionPlane™ and took the short hop into the Mahone Ranch grounds. A West McFarland native greeted him and then headed back to his home on the other side of town. It was part of an agreement with Cain that they would maintain the Mahone and Lopez Ranches whenever he was away - for a small fee paid with Brady's Green Credits. The only part of the homestead that was off-limits was in his Pops' old nuclear bunker, as this was where Brady stored his most personal belongings and the Los Banos Files, which he once loaned out to Judge Jefferson for her investigation.

He spotted that someone had been playing table tennis, but he could understand the lure of this, and guessed he would have been tempted to play down here with friends, especially if he led a life as boring as the teenage Greens. He wasn't going to raise the matter, it was too trivial to become a snitch over.

He entered the bunker first, and the smell of his Pops was still lingering in the stale air. He smiled as he looked at the racks of long-lasting foodstuffs in cans - many of the labels had begun to peel off, and some labels were on the floor. *Let's hope I don't have to play guessing games with what's in these things, Pops.* Even handling a can without a label brought back powerful memories of the old world, as he caressed the metal ridges and thought about a time when cans were mass-produced to hold food and then be transported to the four corners of the globe.

The light was blinding as he went back up the stairs, blinking in the brilliant sunshine and headed back into his old home. It struck him how small it appeared now that he had got used to staying in his Malibu home. He wandered around the place, and he allowed the memories to come back to him, unhindered and unfiltered. He wanted to feel real once more. He was pleased to see that his caretakers had left fresh food and coffee. He made coffee and a simple lunch and reflected on the times when he would listen to his Pops' stories. He allowed the full force of the guilt of how he had walked out on Lucian and Mary-Lou to sink in.

After lunch, he strolled over to the Lopez ranch. He thought back to the New Year's party they had to greet in the New Century - forty-two years ago. *That was such a fun night. It was such a shame it had to end that way.* He had never truly forgiven them for choosing Amie to take Lucian's place. *I wouldn't have been lonely if Lucky had been with me.* He wandered into Mary-Lou and Lucian's bedroom. He looked at her hairbrush and imagined her sitting on her little stool as she brushed her hair in the mirror. He went into Amie's room. It was a shrine to a Trad girls' room, a relic from a distant age. It had old pop star posters, which had to have belonged to Mary-Lou because there weren't any pop stars in Amie's time.

This made him consider what it was like to be a teenager.

He travelled back into his own teenage years and to a time of one of his infrequent attendances at High School. He was in with his *bad crowd*, and they had skipped lessons and tried to catch a glimpse of the cheerleaders undressing by removing a panel in the suspended ceiling above their changing rooms. He remembered the thrill of seeing a glimpse of a naked girl for the first time. He savoured this memory for a moment. Before understanding that girls like Amie might feel the same way for the first time in their life.

Taking a moment, he considered what he would have done in Mary-Lou and Lucian's position. It was difficult for him to imagine another point of view. He sat down on Amie's old bed. It creaked under the weight of his still considerable bulk. He imagined the promises they would have made her, to always look after her and keep her safe from harm. He had a vision of Mary-Lou kissing her daughter good night and telling her that she loved her, over and over again, day after day, year after year. He then imagined the same scenario with Lucian. He would have done precisely the same. *That was the kinda crazy guy he was.* Brady smiled as he guessed that Lucian would have read her stories at bedtime when she was little - stories about good guys saving the girl.

There's no way, after all that, that Lucky would have saved his own skin and let her die, all alone. Brady felt a jolt to the pit of his stomach as the imagined pain of this scenario hit him. He tried to hold this feeling. It hurt so good. He considered how he would have died in a hail of bullets to protect him from the cops if they were in a bust, but that was out of the heroism of being a man, a soldier, but this was utterly different. *Could I ever lay down my life for someone because I simply loved them so much? I don't know if I could.* He did realise something, though. Brady acknowledged a grudging respect for what Lucian and Mary-Lou, for that matter, had done for Amie. He knew that staying here for a few days was precisely what he needed. He felt grounded here.

8. THE WANDERER RETURNS

As the Disciple of West McFarland, the news reached Siddha that Brady had returned to the area for the first time in years. With Bodhi still in sensory deprivation, Siddha didn't like these omens. He went to meet Lizzie, after she had finished her teaching duties at the West McFarland New Green High School. In the absence of Cain, who had taken on increased responsibilities and duties in Bodhi's absence, he needed somebody, who he could trust, implicitly, to talk to. And he knew Lizzie distrusted Brady as much as he did.

'Hi, Lizzie. Have you heard?'

'It's all over the campus. The celebrity has finally returned to his hometown. Some of the kids have never met the local legend, and they know that he comes bearing gifts.'

Siddha winced, 'I could do without this.'

Lizzie said, 'There's a chance he might just be picking up a few things before flying back to Malibu.'

'I really hope so. There's something about him that just feels off. Do you get that?'

'Yes. He's bad news.' She took a deep breath, 'However...'

'I know. I know. He saved Bodhi, for the time being...'

'He may have saved us all. Although it pains me to say it.'

Siddha looked puzzled, 'What do you mean?'

'Imagine if Bodhi's illness had developed slowly. We might all have been infected with the same sickness.'

Siddha spat, 'Brady gets entirely too much credit. He would have saved Bodhi for nothing more than his own personal gain. I don't understand how a virus developed in the NanoSuit™ he was testing.'

'I agree. I know Brady, and the one word you would never choose to describe him is altruistic. He's an opportunist, a chancer, no more than that.'

Siddha said, 'We'll talk about it more over the communal meal, and then I guess we'll have to make suitable arrangements to greet our honourable guest should he decide to regale our town with his presence.'

Lizzie left the home she shared with Siddha and others and headed off to her High School. She was distracted by the thought that Brady could descend on their side of town at any moment. Typically, the introduction of the Relationship, Health, Sex, and Identity lessons for the spring term for thirteen-year-olds would be enough to keep her pupil's rapt attention, but the gossip about Brady Mahone potentially visiting could even upstage these lessons. She thought of the old days and how a movie star visit would be greeted. Not that any movie stars ever visited McFarland, even with its proximity to the old Hollywood studios.

The students were excitedly gathered in their self-allocated tribes. She heard the word Brady repeatedly fly into the air like jumping beans. She shouted sharply, 'Students, please! Take your seats.' She watched them shuffle along to their seats while some gamely tried to conclude their conversations. 'Quiet!' The students sat, and the murmuring subsided.

Brianna put her hand up, 'Is it true that Brady Mahone is going to visit? You are friends with Siddha. You'd know before anybody else.'

Lizzie's shoulders slumped. She didn't like the prospect of today's lesson as it was. She was supposed to discuss the issues with frankness and sensitivity, but she wasn't in the mood, and all this Brady chatter was making her angry. 'I don't know.'

Dermot interrupted, 'Aw, come on, Lizzie...'

'I don't know. What I do know is if any of you decide to go anywhere near the Lopez or the Mahone Ranch, then the Security Protocols™ will be invoked. Do I make myself clear?'

The class nodded despondently.

She said firmly and in an entirely different tone than she would usually use, 'Now, pay attention. Today's lesson is Relationship, Health, Sex, and Identity. This is an important part of the Green curriculum, especially in the light of the sexual freedoms introduced by the BlueSuits™.'

She sat down behind her desk like she would for any other lesson, but then she remembered that for RHSI, she was supposed to sit on the edge of the desk to appear more informal and at ease with the subject. She stood up and perched herself on the edge of the desk. This prompted some giggling at the back of the class. 'Mary-Jane.' She barked, and the giggling stopped. 'Today's lesson has important implications for the rest of your lives. I need you to be fully present. We will be discussing subjects you may find embarrassing, although some of you might already know a lot about this, especially those with more progressive parents. If you are already enlightened, please give others a chance to learn. This is a place for frank and honest discussions in a safe environment. With that in mind, the sensitivity of the Security Protocols™ in today's class have been substantially desensitised, as there is a significant risk of accidental humiliation, and we don't want you to leave today's lesson with the memory of being Filmed in front of the rest of your classmates.' She looked around the class, ensuring she made eye contact with each of her dozen pupils. 'We have rules which dictate how we behave with other Green societal members, and these rules apply to intimate relationships. Let's remind ourselves of what they are so we can establish a grounding for today's work. You don't need to raise your hands today; we will have an open discussion. What are some of the rules?'

Mary-Jane raised her hand then pulled it back down again, 'Not to humiliate any living creature.' She said, obviously repeating back Lizzie's own words.

Franklin said, 'We must never hurt anyone's feelings.'

Lizzie said, 'Yes. Good. This is especially relevant to today's lesson.'

'Violent thoughts and acts are forbidden.'

'Excellent, Dermot.' She said, 'There are others, but we'll cover these later.' She composed herself and addressed her class, 'You are one of the earliest teenagers to approach puberty with the BlueSuits™. What does this mean?'

'My parents told me that they were advised to name me with a non-binary name when I was born.' Brianna said. 'That's why I can switch between Brian, Anna or Brianna.'

'Your parents are particularly progressive' Lizzie said. 'I presume they've already informed you about sex and relationships.'

'Yes, I've come into this lesson as Brianna, my Non-binary identity, as I don't want to experience a binary view of today's lesson. I want to learn as Non-binary to enhance all my future relationships.'

'Well done, Brianna, and thank you for sharing freely.' She said, 'Xe exemplified how you should be approaching this. There are no preconceptions in how you should express xyr sexuality.'

She looked around the room, 'You should all have tried out your BlueSuits™ and changed sex at least once to learn how to use it. Has everybody done this?'

There were mutterings of yes around the room. Hadley said, 'It takes me about an hour, and it hurt a bit.'

Lizzie saw some nods of agreement, 'That's perfectly normal, and I'm here to reassure you. The developers made it as quick and as painless as possible, but with such fundamental changes to your physiological makeup, never mind the hormonal changes, this was the best they can do. However, we must look for the most positive way to deal with this. I would say that if it was too easy, then this could become a frivolous benefit, in much the same way as changing your appearance with the YellowSuits™. With the time and relatively mild discomfort, at least you will make the changes within your body with a deeper part of your mind.'

Dermot said, 'Have you changed, and if yes, have you done this very often?'

Lizzie had taken the RHSI classes hundreds of times, but it still seemed odd that she should be asked if she had ever been a biological male. 'I will tell you, but don't let my life prejudice yours. I'm not Pure Green like you. I was a Trad for my first twenty-seven years, and I was binary. Therefore, I had traditional binary sexual relationships with Trads. You will encounter this generational divide with large parts of the Green Community, but you will be the enlightened ones. It's the older generations which will have to catch up.' She added, 'For instance, there are questions which are pertinent to today's lesson. The NanoSuits™ in development require a biological switch at least once. This is a biological change, but people can be trans without changing their biological sex. Also, *changing sex* implies the more outdated term *transexual*, but trans individuals use gender expression rather than biological as a marker for their gender identity. I know this could cause concern, but the requirement is one physical change to activate the Suits™, and to future proof them, but after that you can revert back to being you.'

He pressed, 'But have you changed?'

'Yes. I had to test my BlueSuit™, the same as you, back in 2126.' She knew she had to tell the truth. She had to hope that credibility would be better than lying. 'I had lived such a long life as a straight cisgender woman that I didn't enjoy being cisgender man - it wasn't me. I've been biologically male twice and gender-neutral once.'

'How old are you? If you don't mind me asking.'

She wanted to remove herself from Dermot's gentle interrogation. She asked the class, 'Seeing as you would all prefer Math to RHSI, then I'll let you work it out. Whoever answers will have to show their workings. I was twenty-seven at the time of the Revolution. When was I born, and how old am I, now?'

They busily scratched away at their calculations when Mary-Jane raised her hand. She wasn't sure if she should, but how else could she prove she had worked it out first. 'The Revolution was in 2084, therefore deduct twenty-seven, which takes it back to 2057, then take 2057 from 2142, which leaves eighty-five - depending on which month your birthday was.'

'Well done, Mary-Jane, I'm eighty-four, or eighty-five next month. In Trad years, that would be very old indeed, but our NanoSuits™ mean I look about forty in the Trad equivalent years.'

'Were there no non-binary people before the Revolution?' Brianna asked.

'There were many, but it was difficult for them. Some used to go to extreme lengths to do what you can do within an hour of deep thought. Gender dysphoria was prevalent in the pre-Revolutionary days, but this is something that's largely been eradicated now, thankfully.' She smiled and looked into each of the faces of her pupils to check that they were both understanding, and that she hadn't offended anybody. 'They used to have surgery and hormonal treatments. Those of you not aware of Trad healthcare, this meant they were injected with needles and cut open with knives. I fought alongside many of these soldiers in the GreenRevs, and they were responsible for including the three additional promises to the Saving the Planet promises. Who can tell me what these were?'

As if he was reciting a prayer, Andrew said, 'End hate thoughts and crimes, including gender identity and discrimination. Remove all traces of Imperialism and Colonialism. Improve mental health by establishing kinder societies.'

Woody Wilson said, 'My Grandmoppa is against all this.'

Lizzie said, 'Mrs Wilson was old before the Revolution. Xe is of another generation entirely.' *I'm not going to mention that Brady saved her. I've only just got their attention away from him.* 'Xe has had to change xyrself at some point. It was a mandatory requirement to test out the BlueSuit™. Mrs Wilson shouldn't be allowed by the Security Protocols™ to challenge you on your gender decisions.'

Woody said, 'Grandmoppa Wilson doesn't challenge me. Xe tells my Moppa not to bring me over to visit xyr when I want to be Rowena. I love myself more when I am Rowena, but when I'm in my Grandmoppa's presence, she acts like I'm a stranger to xyr, but when I'm Woody, xe loves me. My Moppa thinks it will be better if I wait until my Grandmoppa has died before I fully become Rowena.' Woody started to cry but said, 'Moppa's said Grandmoppa Wilson hasn't got long to live, but I don't want xyr to die, just so that I can be happy.'

Lizzie went over and asked Woody if she could hold him. He nodded, and she hugged him tightly, 'Xe hasn't the right to emotionally blackmail you over how you want to live xyr life. I will talk to Siddha about this.'

'No. No...'

'This has to be tackled. We have to sort this out - it cannot be allowed to fester.'

Dermot interrupted, 'It's funny how the older Greens can be - no offence, Lizzie.'

'None taken. You were saying.' She knew where he would go with his story.

'My Grandmaddy was one-hundred and ten before xe began to live exclusively as a cisgender woman and not the biological male xe was born as. Xe now says it was the most wonderful moment of xyr life when xe used the BlueSuit™ for the first time. Xe said it was a dream come true and that everybody should find xemselves - their true identity.'

'Thank you, Dermot. I knew xem as Arthur, a warrior of the Revolution. I've spoken to xem many times, and I know how happy xe is now as Xarlotte.' She smiled at the memory.

This encouraged Andrew to ask, 'Did you have sex with Dermot's Grandama?'

Her instant reaction was to deny this, but she also knew that no one could be considered the property of another. They were encouraged to be open and unashamed of past relationships, and not to deny the past of those with whom they had an arrangement - however longstanding. All eyes were upon her as she paused before considering her answer. She tried to pretend she had forgotten and attempted to change the subject, 'Anyway, you can experiment on all versions of your bodies, to understand your own sexual needs and desires, but you cannot form a sexual arrangement with another until you are sixteen...'

'But Lizzie...'

'Let me finish, this is important, and the Security Protocols™ will intervene if anyone tries to exploit you through their age or position. However, this does not rule out any consensual arrangements...'

'You did have a sexual arrangement with Dermot's Grandama!' The class erupted in laughter, and as the Security Protocols™ settings were removed, for the enablement of frank discussions in an educational setting, they couldn't come to Lizzie's rescue.

Almost hoping that the laughter would drown out her reply, she said, 'Yes. We had a sexual relationship for a brief time while we were both Trads, in the months leading up to the Revolution back in '84.' She tried to change the subject. 'You can move through different genders until you settle on the one that fits your chosen identity, but in this mode, it's almost as if you become a mannequin and you can't have sexual relations until you have fully adopted this new body. You can't just change genders in one sexual session...'

Brianna asked nicely, trying to win over Lizzie, 'What was it like having sex as a Trad? Is it different?'

Marthain had stayed silent so far. But he didn't like Brianna, so he shouted, 'You want to have sex with Brady Mahone. You fancy him.'

Lizzie had lost control of her class, and it was on the point of relative anarchy for an assembly of Green pupils. She saw Brianna was blushing. She was trying to concoct a strategy to restore order when Andrew said, 'Lizzie had sex with a Trad while she was a Green - that's what my Dama told me.'

Brianna said, 'Is this true?' She looked shocked and saddened.

Lizzie knew that Brianna had a crush on the cartoonish celebrity version of the man she thought she knew as Brady Mahone. She was ashamed of her evenings with Brady and still, to this day, hadn't fully forgiven Cain for using her, to get information on the Trad intruder who had found a way through the NanoShells™. This generation would never understand the consternation Brady caused the town on that day - they had been promised safety from the Trads - and in walked Brady Mahone like he owned the place.

'Yes. It's true. I spent two nights with Brady Mahone - nearly sixty years ago.'

Dermot said, 'Is Brady a *he* or a *xe?*'

'He is a Pure Trad. He would be offended if you addressed him as xe. He has the right to identify as a straight man. Brady wouldn't recognise the term cisgender, and it could be construed as an act of humiliation by the Security Protocols™ if you used this label to identify him. Brady has the same right to self-identification as anybody. Therefore, you should address him as he, and he is a man. I wouldn't even use the term straight in his company. Remember, he comes from the dark ages of our history.'

Brianna looked wide-eyed at Lizzie. 'What was it like to have sex with Brady?'

'It was no better than ok. It was rough and one-dimensional, and I have no desire to ever repeat the experience. He was unskilled and animalistic.'
Marthain said, 'Anyway, only people who used to be Trads should have the aches for other Trads. As Pure Greens, that desire should have been bred out of us by now. We are a superior species.'

Lizzie said, 'You've gone too far, Marthain. We are a species, period. We are no better or worse than any other living creature.' She decided to use the lack of Security Protocols™ to put Marthain back in his box by using a type of old-fashioned authority she hadn't used since the days of the Green Revolution. 'Marthain, you will apologise to Brianna, myself and the rest of the class.'

He was about to speak when Lizzie barked, 'Stand up.'

Marthain stood up and said, 'I'm sorry for uttering such deeply offensive comments. It won't happen again.'

She knew she had humiliated him. She didn't like feeling this way, but she had panicked and didn't know what else to do. *I'll learn from this later; I have failed miserably today. I've let Brady Mahone get to me.*

She was just about to resume her lesson when the sound of cheering could be heard from outside, and then the cheering turned to a roar, with cries of *Brady! Brady!*

Andrew was the first, but others joined in, 'Can we go and see him? It's Brady Mahone. He hardly ever comes back to West McFarland.'

Lizzie tried to deny them, but with the pleading and the knowledge that today's lesson plan was beyond saving, she finally acquiesced.

The pupils raced out of the classroom and headed to where the cheering was emanating. When they reached the crowds, some managed to wriggle their way to the front, where excited parents pushed the pre-school children to the fore, in time for Brady to shake their little hands and to hand them their Children's Entertainment Black Files with the BMEE logo with the Diamondback rattlesnake weaving through the letters. He moved with the assurance of visiting royalty. He always concentrated on the youngsters when giving away his free samples, as he thought the adults should be able to afford their own. He considered adults asking for freebies to be moochers, except for the good-looking women.

He moved to the end of the line of young children. There weren't many left in any of the places he visited, as they were a significant investment in Green Credits which many Greens considered too high, and they had the reasonable excuse in saving the planet from another human consumer.

Brianna, Marthain and Dermot had made it to the front and received their free samples from the Great Giver - Brady Mahone. Brianna could hardly utter a word in the aura of stardom of her schoolgirl crush. Marthain had no such problem. 'Hey, Brady, great to see you, man.'

Brady could tell when a youth was trying too hard to be grown up. 'Likewise, buddy.'

Marthain smiled, 'What are you doing back in your hometown?'

All around, there was the noise of the crowd and the occasional squeals as he moved down the line. He noticed a cute woman looking at him, and he was distracted, but he answered the cocky little youth, 'I'm here on a bit of personal business.'

Dermot said and wished he hadn't afterwards, 'What kind of personal business?'

'It wouldn't be personal if I told you, would it?' He smiled, knowing full well he'd put the nosey kid back in his place.

While Brianna stared at him dreamily and Brady winked at his selected target ahead, Marthain asked, 'Who are you visiting, man?'

'I want to have a chat with Siddha and Lizzie - if that's ok with you?' He joked.

'Are you going to have sex with Lizzie again?'

Brady frowned and said, 'You got a lot of spunk, kid.'

'A lot of what?'

'Get up and go. Now, get up and be gone.'

Brianna shouted, 'Marthain, how could you? I don't believe...'

Brady left them to their burgeoning argument. He turned to notice the woman he had selected had left the crowd arm-in-arm with another woman. Brady waved to the crowd and yelled, 'That's all, folks. Great to see y'all. Now it's time for Brady Mahone to take care of business.' He waved for a few minutes until the crowd began to dwindle and drift back to wherever they came from.

He headed off toward Siddha and Lizzie's home. He knew Cain was travelling on vital business for Sattva Systems™, but he wondered whether he still resided there. *Why in hell's name would Lizzie tell some spotty kids about having sex with me. She didn't exactly give me the impression that she had feelings for me.* He was turning the corner into their street when an old, vaguely familiar face appeared. The old woman said, 'Brady Mahone. Please stop. I owe you an apology.'

Brady said sharply, fearing an insult or another verbal trap, 'I'm not looking for apologies, lady. Just business.' He stopped and looked at her a little more closely. She looked about one-hundred-years old even in Trad years, which meant she must have been old at the time of the Revolution. He still had an echo from his past that he should show some respect toward his elders. 'What can I do for you, ma'am?'

She said, 'I'm not long for this world, and I think heaven sent you to allow me the opportunity to atone.'

'You don't owe me anything. I just look after the needs of Brady Mahone is all.'

'But I do. I owe you, my life. I'm Mrs Wilson, and you saved me from those awful Hodgson boys. I treated you with utter contempt, which was appalling behaviour on my part. I offer you my deepest apologies. Please accept this, so I can go to my grave with a clear conscience.'

Brady wondered how any Green could have a clear conscience, but he remembered back to that first day post-Revolution. 'You were scared. They shouldn't have treated a lady that way. It's no problem for me.'

She looked at him as if she was imploring him to say the words that could save her soul. He said, 'Lady, I accept your apology.'

'I know I am going to die, very soon. I've had the signals from my OrangeSuit™ warning me to prepare my last wishes. I am going to die in my sleep tonight.'

Brady said graciously, 'I'm very sorry to hear that, ma'am.'

'Thank you for your old-fashioned courtesy. I only joined the Greens because I had a bit of an identity crisis after my husband left me in my fifties. We'd been married for twenty-five years...'

Here we go, all I need is an old-timer's life story, but hey, she is dying and all. That must feel real bad to know when you're going to die unless you're in one of Samuel Beardon the Third's sharks... Brady smiled at his own humorous recollections. Mrs Wilson took his smile to mean he was interested in hearing her story.

'I found friendship in the Green Community which was establishing itself in West McFarland. I was lonely, and it gave me comfort, and I became one of those old Hippies.' She sighed, 'I don't like these new-fangled days. I was more at home as a Trad. I haven't said that to anyone else but you.'

'I get where you're coming from. I don't get all this gender shape-shifting businesses. It confuses the crap outta me.'

Mrs Wilson laughed heartily as if her senses were heightened by the realisation that this might be the last laugh of her life. She said, 'I want you to attend my funeral tomorrow.'

'But I…'

'I'm having a dedication read out that praises you for helping me all those many years ago. It would make me so happy to think that you might actually be there, in person, to hear it.'

Brady knew when a lie would suffice, 'Don't you worry, none. I'll be there.'

She kissed him on the cheek, 'Thank you. I won't keep you any longer. I know you are a very busy man.'

He watched as she walked away from him and back into her home.

Brady marched along and soon let the last wishes of Mrs Wilson drift to the back of his mind. He had his own life to concentrate on, and he was on the verge of some potentially big changes in lifestyle choices. He knocked on the door but got no answer. He tried the door, but it was locked. He laughed and sat down on the doorstep, prepared to wait for Lizzie and Siddha to return home. *Fuck. Of course. The whole town is on its way home after going out to see me - the living legend Brady Mahone.*

9.RULES OF ENGAGEMENT

Siddha had left others to deal with the arrival of Brady Mahone into West McFarland. He couldn't abide the thought of dealing with Brady as a visiting dignitary, to be honoured and fawned upon like a conquering hero. In any case, there was no shortage of volunteers. Brady was the nearest thing to a celebrity in the whole world, apart from Bodhi Sattva and Glenarvon Cole. Siddha went instead to meet Lizzie from her teaching assignments, as she knew she was one of the few other people in town who would rather not have anything to do with Brady.

He spotted her leaving the West McFarland Green High School, and he could tell by the way she meandered out of the school gates with her head looking to the floor disconsolately, that she must have heard about the great man's arrival. 'Hi Lizzie, you look sad, I'm guessing you've heard that Brady is back.'

'Yes, he fucked up my first Relationship, Health, Sex and Identity lesson - the first with teenagers who have had the BlueSuits™. You can imagine how much I was looking forward to that.' She stopped, 'I'm sorry for swearing, it's been the worst day as a teacher I have ever had.'

He watched her clench her fists in frustration and began to worry that she might invoke the Security Protocols™. He put his arm around her shoulder. 'Let's take a slow walk home. I'll leave the rental here, and you can tell me all about it.'

'Ok. Let's take the long way home, via the park. I don't want to see people worshipping him.'

They strolled through the park while Siddha gave plenty of space in the conversation for Lizzie to tell him all about her awful day.

Eventually, they hit the roads that would carry them home. She said, 'You know, there is one thing I sorely miss from the old days.'

He spotted a mischievous grin that suggested that Lizzie was emerging from her funk, 'And what's that?'

'Retirement.'

He laughed, and she continued, 'If we still had the Trad world, I might have retired in my fifties, or maybe sixties at a push. And yet, here I am, eighty-four years old, and I will never retire because our health will hardly deteriorate. I could end up working forever.'

Siddha joked, 'I think we call it progress - and I'm older than you, remember?'

'I know, but you've got to admit that it sucks - on days like these.'

'Us original GreenRevs make tremendous sacrifices for the normal Greens so that they will soon live a life of leisure and appreciation of our reclaimed world.' He squeezed her shoulder as he comforted her, 'But we will be rewarded with eternal life in heaven. We only need to do our duty to see the hundred-year plan completed.'

She laughed, 'Great. Only another forty-two years of teaching to go. I'm sure it will fly by.' He laughed with her, but they stopped when they turned the corner to reach their home.

They saw Brady waiting for them on their doorstep, looking more like a tramp settling down for a warm, than visiting royalty. Brady was asleep. He had become bored at the length of the wait. The street had been deserted as the folks of West McFarland held an impromptu party at the Green Town Hall. Lizzie prodded him, half hoping he was dead. Brady stirred sleepily and said, 'Hey. Hi Guys. Sorry to doorstep you like this.'

Lizzie said dismissively, 'What do you want, Brady?'

'It's kinda personal. could we discuss it inside? Plus, I need the loo.'

She said, 'Ew, I forgot you Trads still do that. Fortunately, the toilets still work, so I suppose you'll have to come in - we don't want you urinating in the street...'

'Actually...'

'Please. Spare us the details.'

Siddha unlocked the door, and the nearest he could bring himself to a friendly greeting was, 'Come.' Siddha prepared food that was suitable for a Trad and made fruit juice drinks. It was a take-it-or-leave-it deal.

Brady came into the living quarters, he showed his hands as if he were making a joke about having washed them, and he sat down and lounged on the sofa. He had noticed his hosts sitting upright in the chairs as if they were preparing to interrogate him. Brady tucked into the vegetable dish hungrily and slurped his juice. Brady said, 'Thanks, man, that really hit the sweet spot.'

Siddha said, 'How can we be of assistance to you?'

Brady burped and put his hand to his mouth, in mock politeness, 'I need a bit of family planning advice.'

Lizzie tried not to laugh, the last thing she wanted to do was encourage this beast, but these words were so absurd that she couldn't help but laugh. And because she tried to hold it in, her laugh burst out like a seal's bark. This only made her laugh even more. She said, 'Siddha, did you spike my drink? He didn't just say what I thought he said - surely?'

Brady was laughing at Lizzie laughing. *In another time and place, I might have made a go of it with her.*

Siddha said, 'I think he did, indeed.' He turned to Brady, 'So, you are thinking of starting a family?'

'Yes.'

'And why do you feel the need to discuss it with us?'

'I've never even thought about it before, and I don't really know what the rules are. Obviously, I can't have kids with a Trad - the women still alive are decrepit and well past their childbearing sell-by dates. So, I've got to get a Green pregnant if she's going to give Brady Mahone some sons.'

Lizzie let out an exaggerated sigh. She didn't know where to begin addressing the litany of Green sins in Brady's choice of words. While she floundered, Siddha took up the discussion in the manner of a Guidance Counsellor. 'Usually, the topic of funding would come up with Greens developing an arrangement to bring another human life on the planet, but clearly, that won't be an issue for your good self.'

Brady didn't like Siddha and knew he would be condescending and patronising, but he had the required answers. He treated him like he would the Governor in Ridgecrest Supermax. 'You're right. I've got plenty of Greenbacks.'

Siddha said, 'First of all, as a Trad, you can only produce children with Greens who were once Trads.'

'Like Lizzie?'

'Yes. But you can't with someone who was born Green, that is, after 2084.'

'But aren't people like Lizzie way too old to have babies?'

Lizzie was exasperated, 'What is it with everybody having a go about my age today? I look no older than you, Brady Mahone. In fact, I'm considerably younger than you, you old fart. How old are you?'

Good to see I can still push her buttons. 'I'm exactly one hundred.'

'Well, I'm eighty-four, so put that in your pipe and smoke it.' She huffed.

Siddha said, 'In Trad terms, we age about two to three times less quickly, and with the OrangeSuits™, this means women can remain fertile to approximately one-hundred and ten years.'

'This is a bit embarrassing…God, I feel like I'm in the clap clinic. Err…how long will my…will my seed still be up to it…y'know…for getting a woman pregnant…y'know, considering my old age and all.' Brady joked feebly.

Lizzie smiled viciously. It wasn't often that anybody would see Brady Mahone in this much discomfort.

Siddha put his hands together, almost as if he was in prayer, 'With the advantages of the OrangeSuit™ and its NanoTechnology™ if a cisgender woman, or a cisgender man or any gender for that matter.' He watched Brady squirm, he almost wanted him to explode and storm out, as the prospect of any future Mahones could leave with him, but he recalled how insistent Bodhi was in giving as much help as possible to his adversary. He restated, 'If a woman chooses to become fertile, she can flood her body with hormones, release her eggs and the NanoBots™ will examine your sperm and select the most perfect examples and guide them to fertilise her eggs. If there is a lack of perfect sperm samples, the NanoBots™ will repair suitable candidates. In any case, you appear to be a fit and healthy male. I can't see that being a problem. You *appear* more Green than Trad…'

359

Brady laughed, 'That's not what the Trad-eating lions in South Africa thought.' Lizzie and Siddha looked at each other with puzzled glances. Brady said, 'That's some clever shit, I have to say.'

'It was ground-breaking technology developed by a McFarland resident at Stamford University. You probably didn't know that.' Siddha said.

Brady knew that was a dig at his lack of intellect, 'Are you talking about Professor Yuan Chu? If so, I'll have you know he was a good friend to Brady Mahone. I loved that man.'

To Lizzie, it seemed Brady Mahone's purpose in life was to destabilise her core beliefs. 'If that's true - then what did he tell you?'

'That he was part of all this Nano stuff, but Sattva Systems™ disagreed with his work, as it was about increasing and not decreasing populations. However, it looks to me that his work was ok by the Greens - as long as it didn't help any Trads.'

'Sattva Systems™ used his research to develop the Sterilisation Protocols™ by reverse engineering his work. so much for your Trad professor's work.' Lizzie snapped.

'That's not his doing if you corrupted his intentions.' *And the Professor is still helping me from beyond the grave. I'm going to have some mighty sons to deal with you Green bastards.*

Siddha tried to calm the situation, 'Let's get back to the original discussion. I'll summarise. Brady, you should be able to have children of your own. However, you need a consenting Green, who was once a Trad. If you come to the appropriate arrangement with her, then you could start a family together. What else would you like to know?'

'Can she give me sons?'

It was difficult for Siddha to use the old pronouns with Brady, after all these Green years of enlightenment, but he felt he had handled the conversation with Brady in a satisfactory manner. 'With Greens, a child can choose their own sex. Your child will be a Green, and they will be born with all the available NanoSuits™. A mother could influence the original sex of the child. Before the BlueSuits™, as part of the conception, she could alter her hormonal balance to influence the default cisgen... sex. Your chosen partner might still be able to do that with a Trad father. But remember, the child's wishes will prevail - you cannot alter this - the Security Protocols™ will not allow you to interfere.'

Brady shrugged, 'Thanks, man. I suppose I'll just have to find a workaround.'

'There is no workaround.'

10. A LATENESS OF BEING

Mrs Wilson died as planned.

Brady didn't really want to go to the funeral. He was itching to be on his way and begin implementing his plans for the expansion of the Mahone Family. He had sons to make, and he was losing valuable time. He looked outside his ranch at the pouring rain and wondered if it was going to let up at all today.

Siddha had sent over one of the Greens who looked after Brady's house during his extended absences to inform Brady that the funeral had been re-arranged from 11:00am to 6pm to give the rain a chance to ease off. He was told the cemetery was becoming waterlogged.

Aside from his impatience to get going, he pondered the meaning of death in the Green world. He had attended many funerals in the long distant past. Death wasn't an unusual occurrence in the Trad criminal fraternity. *They'd have never been able to rearrange the funerals to further on in the same day back then. Funerals had to be organised days, sometimes weeks ahead, because people were dying all the time. I suppose Greens dying is a rare event.*

Brady looked out over the view of the land from his porch. He lingered on the sight of the old Lopez Ranch. The black clouds stretched out to all parts of the horizon, and he began to think that even this evening would be cancelled. He looked at the FusionPlane™ and thought of leaving here and heading to Boulder Creek, San Martin or seeing if the Sun was out in Malibu.

He decided to stick it out in his East McFarland Ranch. *Is it even East McFarland - seeing as it doesn't exist anymore?*

Brady went back inside and lazily wandered around his old home. He occasionally stopped to make coffee or to have a bite to eat. He even whiled away the time check-ing out some of his Entertainment Files, but there wasn't much that interested him. *I'm feeling low, man.*

It had been so long that he had attended a proper funeral that he had forgotten that this is how he used to feel on days like these. He had become hardened to death. He began to calculate just how many Trads he had seen die and how many bodies had been left at roadsides wherever he went, anywhere in the world. Brady always lost track once the numbers started to approach the millions. He tried to equate the num-bers of dead bodies to the Green Credits on his Distor™. He had more than five-hun-dred-million Green Credits, but he was sure that someone said there used to be seven billion Trads and nearly a billion Greens in the world. *Oh man, that's one helluva lot of death.* He tried to rationalise it. He needed to shake off this feeling. *They just died early. Not many of them would have lived to be a hundred like me. Anyways, is not being born at all the same as dying?*

Again, he thought of getting into his FusionPlane™ and just flying away. His con-science tugged at him to stay. *I said I would stick around for her funeral. I don't owe her anything because she lived longer because of me. I don't want Siddha and Lizzie to say that Brady Mahone doesn't know the meaning of respect. I don't want those Greens to think that Brady Mahone is wary of funerals - or scared of facing down death.*

As the afternoon came around, he started to glimpse a break in the black clouds from the west. He sensed the rain was easing, and the wind direction suggested that fairer weather was approaching. He wondered if Bodhi was still in his sensory deprivation box. Of all the Greens in all the world, he was the only one he knew of, who might also die soon. *I wonder what he's thinking about in his living coffin.* He contemplated why Bodhi hadn't had children. *He coulda had a dynasty like the one I'm going to build. Who are you going to give it all to, man? After all, you can't take it with you.* He took out his Distor™ again and imagined his funeral with five mighty sons in attendance. He laughed at the thought of them scrapping over his empire. *Men should fight for what's theirs. they would each have a minimum of one-hundred million Green Credits apiece if it was shared equally.* He smiled with satisfaction and pride.

The change in the weather would allow the funeral to go ahead as planned, he guessed, so he showered and dressed. He didn't have his fancy clothes from his Malibu home, so he dressed in his usual jeans, T-shirt, and sneakers. He was conscious of his lack of black clothing. *Do Greens wear black for funerals? I'm fucked if I know.* He compensated by buttoning up his black trench-coat length Poacher's coat. He raised the collars to keep out the drizzle. He also borrowed an old black leather cowboy hat of his Pops'.

He rechecked the rain, and now it had seemed to be petering out. He didn't want to make a show of taking the FusionPlane™ or even taking a FusionCar™. *I don't want to make no poxy grand entrance at a funeral. Brady Mahone has got too much class for that.* He didn't want the townsfolk to pay much attention to him, and he tried to enter the funeral as quietly as possible. *This is Mrs Wilson's day - not mine.*

His old Green Bicycle and trailer caught his attention. It filled him with memories of the early days of his business empire before he owned a FusionCar™. *It will be like old times - good times.* He decided to travel through the lands where East McFarland used to be. The road networks were all that was left.

He rode slowly. The day seemed to deny the use of speed. He stopped at the site where the old bus stop used to be. He alighted his bike and stood in silence for a minute as he reflected on the people who used to live in East McFarland. He remembered his previous visits with Judge Jefferson, and later Officer Norbert, and then the time when the last people had died. He shuddered at the vivid recall of viewing the Operation Clean-Up teams moving in to complete their gruesome tasks of decomposing the remaining bodies. He recalled how grateful he was when Samuel Beardon the Third said that he had volunteered to lead the crew, as he knew how much this place meant to Brady.

Brady was uncomfortable about attending a Green funeral, as he still remembered the dead of East McFarland piled at the roadside, as they were running out of burial spots in East McFarland because they desperately needed the green spaces to grow food. *And now they are using green spaces in East McFarland to bury the dead from the westside. The Greens get buried with dignity while the Trads were dumped like roadkill.*

He fondly recalled his times with Professor Chu. *I loved that guy. He got buried properly, but the East McFarland Trads would never have let Brady Mahone attend his funeral, and I probably loved him more than anyone. My team hates me - but the opposition loves me - and makes me one of the richest men in the world.*

Remounting his bike, Brady headed to the ceremony. As the cemetery was on East McFarland land, he didn't have to travel through the populated westside. When he arrived, he saw the chairs laid out, and the Green Reverend Akston stood on a small makeshift stage so the attendees could all see him. Brady left his bike about a hundred yards away and strutted up towards the ceremony. He was partially relieved to see the townsfolk had switched their YellowSuits™ to all-black attire, but he still felt underdressed for the occasion.

There were notes on the chairs, with names on. He wondered if he were about to be embarrassed by looking for his name and finding out that he wasn't allocated a seat. Sensing his awkwardness, a woman came over to him, 'Hello, Brady. I'm so glad you could make it. I know you are a very busy man, but this meant a lot to my Mother. I'm Pauline Wilson.'

Brady spotted a tear in her eye and knew she was struggling to keep her grief together. 'No problem at all.'

She led him to the front row of seats, passed the wicker coffin with the dead body of Margaret Wilson wrapped and completely covered in a white biodegradable cloth. The seat on the edge of the aisle indicated that it was reserved for Woodrow, but the next seat was reserved for Brady Mahone. He sat alone. He looked at the seats to his right, and they were reserved for Lizzie and then Siddha. In front of him, a crowd of High School children comforted a girl grandly decked out in intricate black lace. They took it in turn to comfort the child called Rowena.

Lizzie came to the front and perused the seats. She spotted her name on the seat next to Brady. Lizzie barely acknowledged him as she switched her name with Siddha's and placed this reservation next to Brady. She sat two seats away but turned deliberately away, ensuring he received the message loud and clear that she didn't want to talk to him.

Siddha joined them and said with a false smile, 'So good of you to attend, Brady. I'm sure it is very much appreciated by the family.' Siddha sat next to him and assumed a sad face for the occasion.

At least I know where I stand with Lizzie.

Reverend Akston called the service to order. Brady inspected the old figure in black robes to see if he could discern whether the Reverend was male or female. It was a puzzle he couldn't decode as Reverend Akston was utterly indeterminate. The attendees took to their allotted seats, and Rowena went to sit next to Brady- who was still distracted and fascinated by the Reverend's appearance.

Brady looked Rowena up and down and said, 'Sorry, Miss. This seat is reserved for Woodrow.'

Rowena howled and burst into a torrent of tears. Lizzie jumped up. 'Brady, how could you. This is Mrs Wilson's Grandkid.'

Brady said, 'How was I to know that? It's not as if it's obvious by looking at him, her…it?'

Rowena's friends had jumped up to help their friend in need, and Brianna gave Brady a look as if she were a girlfriend of his whom he had embarrassed in the company of her friends.

Brady said, 'Hey, look, I'm sorry, ok? I can't help it if I'm not used to this shape-shifting freakery. I'm a Trad, and we had men and women...well, I suppose there were...'

Lizzie snapped, 'Enough, stop digging...' She looked at the open grave, 'Oh God...' She closed her eyes and breathed in and exhaled deeply.

Marthain felt as if he hadn't had his chance to express his feelings on the subject. He went over to Lizzie and Brady and ensured he could be heard by his classmates, 'The quicker we get rid of all the Trads with their Neanderthal ideas, and the old Greens with their outdated views, the better. You've had your time, now get out of our way and let the Pure Greens lead our lives the way they should be led.' He turned to Brady, 'The way you treated Rowena was nothing short of disgusting. Why don't you just get lost - forever.' He went back to join the throng, comforting the grieving Rowena, and clearly enjoyed receiving the congratulatory pats on the back from his friends.

Brady sat down and put his hands in his pockets. *I should have gone to Malibu.*

After a few minutes, Reverend Akston walked and whispered to those still on their feet and the High School children who had flocked around Rowena, and slowly they all returned to their allotted seats.

He went to his lectern and addressed the congregation. 'My dear Green friends. We are gathered here today to celebrate the life of Margaret Wilson. May our Great Mother take her back and give her eternal life in Heaven on Earth. Let us pray.'

Brady looked around for clues about what he should do, and it looked like an old-fashioned church service. He clasped his hands together and closed his eyes. *I don't want to cause no more fuss and bother by not playing along.*

'Our Mother.
Who art Heaven on Earth.
For what we are about to receive
May we be truly grateful
And lead us not into temptation.
Show us the way.'

The audience murmured in reply, 'Show us the way.'

He peeked to see what the others were doing, and he straightened up with them and stared straight ahead at the Reverend.

'As is customary, I will read the last thoughts of Margaret's, and as a mark of respect to the wishes of the dearly departed, the Security Protocols™ have been deactivated.

Brady smiled. *That's probably how I dodged a bullet earlier.*

"I, Margaret Wilson, lived a full life as a green Citizen. I worked to help make the world a greener place. I brought my extended family to believe fully in the ways of Sattva Systems™ and Mother Nature. However, I did yearn for the old days when things were simpler. I believed in the Ten Green Commandments but never agreed to the additional instructions, especially regarding switching genders at will - to my mind, it wasn't following Mother Nature's wishes. Sattva Systems™ is an abomination."

Noisy protests erupted, and Rowena burst into more tears. Brady laughed heartily at the Greens in chaos - he hadn't seen them behave like this since Encinitas at the turn of the century. *I can't make up my mind whether it's the free speech or the plain honest truth which is unravelling them. They ain't nearly as well-disciplined as I thought they were.* He considered whether the absence of Bodhi and his leadership role was causing this existential crisis. *It's probably just because it's a funeral. Death can have that effect on people, I suppose.* He cast his mind back, and he felt the hurt in the pit of his stomach when he discovered his Pop's dead body. *Yeah, it's tough, man.* Brady consciously reset his emotions to make himself feel sombre. He didn't want to be the one to be blamed for the ceremony falling apart. He didn't want to be viewed as a demon, he didn't like it, and it wasn't fair. *I just survive, is all.* Brady sat down before the others and held his back erect and jutted out his jaw and put his hands together in his lap.

The Reverend appealed for calm. 'Please. Please, people. This is a sacred Tenant of the Dead. Margaret is allowed to share her true feelings on her last day. However, they are her feelings. They are not our truth.'

Dermot shouted, 'She doesn't speak for us. She was a relic of the old age, and I'm glad she's dead.' The other members of his High School class jumped up and cheered him. Dermot was aglow with pride.

It was Pauline's turn to cry, and Lizzie jumped up and barked. 'Dermot, sit down and shut up. All her family are here.' Before the other pupils could respond, she shouted, 'I'll deal with the rest of you in school tomorrow.'

Brady sat perfectly still, a strange figure of calm dignity. He looked straight ahead at Reverend Akston.

The pupils sat down begrudgingly. Siddha leaned in and whispered to Lizzie, 'Who'd have thought it would come to this? Where a GreenRev is putting down a rebellion against the status quo.'

Lizzie half-joked, 'I'm starting to believe the Security Protocols™ was the best thing we ever invented.'

Calm descended upon the proceedings, and Reverend Akston was keen to move the service towards its conclusion. 'I will continue with Margaret Wilson's final words.' "I, Margaret Wilson, am satisfied with my life's work, and I love my daughters and their grandchildren so much. I'm going to miss you all, as I still miss my husband, who died long before the Green Revolution. My final wish is to make it public how much I owe Brady Mahone for saving my life. I was attacked by two ruffians before I had the benefit of the RedSuit™. He came to my aid, protected me, and made sure I was safe, yet I repaid him with ignorance and disrespect. Please convey to him my thanks and sincerest apologies for my actions. I am content to return to Her Good Nature."

Brady nodded his acknowledgement to Reverend Akston.

'As we move the coffin to the grave, we shall all sing her favourite hymn. *All things bright and beautiful.*'

There were no musical instruments, as learning music was considered a skill that recreated the history of the Trads, and reinforced stereotypes, colonialism, imperialism, and gender labels. The only music allowed was singing acapella at births and funerals. Reverend Akston mouthed three, two, one, and the congregation began to sing. Brady knew this hymn and sang along heartily. He liked all creatures, great and small. It was the one hymn that spoke to him.

The Pallbearers moved the coffin to the grave and signalled that they were ready to lower Margaret Wilson to rest. The congregation moved slowly to the graveside, the ushers leading the front rows first until all the mourners were in position. As the coffin was lowered, Pauline Wilson, her daughter, threw dirt over the wicker basket, and the dirt left its stain on the pure white cloth.

Before the coffin had moved even a mere six inches, a shadow emerged from the cloth and wicker casing. It transformed into an almost transparent version of the late Margaret Wilson.

Pauline and her child Rowena screamed at the apparition as it climbed from the coffin and glided to the mourners. Brady was appalled and fascinated. The ghostly form gazed at the mourners in turn as if looking for someone in particular. Most of the congregation stepped backwards, unsure if they should run for their lives or bear witness. The apparition moved from Pauline and then Rowena, it hesitated in front of Brady and shimmered as if it was trying to connect with him, but it gave up and then started to move in a jagged circle as if tracing a large cog on the ground. At each serrated edge, it paused as if trying to sense its pathway away from here.

Questions filled the air. *Is it a ghost? Is that what the soul looks like? Should we be scared? Is that really Mrs Wilson? Is it a demon?* Siddha shook his head and shouted to make himself heard above the din. 'Please, listen. I can explain. Do not be afraid.' All the time, like a moving part of a clock, Mrs Wilson's ghostly form moved around in a circle.

The apparition found Brady in its sights for the second time, and it had made its decision. It walked quickly over to him. It howled and then tried to fit all around and over him. He heard the voice of Mrs Wilson, she wailed, 'I have returned to my maker - I give to you my essence freely.' Brady tried to shake her off. He was disgusted by her clambering all over him. Brady felt like she was fusing her being with his - as if he could merge with her. He flung her off, and she looked at his face with the remnants of her blank stare, peering at his face as if she was trying to bring him into focus. She let out a banshee scream and howled in a high-pitched whine, 'You're not Bodhi. Where's Bodhi? Bodhi, where are you?' She swirled violently, lashing out her ghostly arms at the crowd where they fell back in a mixture of terror and abhorrence. The ghostly figure of Mrs Wilson then seemed to find a positional fix in the far distance as she gazed ahead with her dead eyes. She then marched away. She walked faster than anybody else could run. The ghost of Margaret Wilson was lifted like a leaf in a breeze and then flew away, soaring ever higher until she disappeared high into the sky.

The grey slate sky continued to drizzle on the mourners, but it had no discernible effect on the ascent of Mrs Wilson.

Siddha shouted, 'Please listen.' They listened, but nobody had dared take their eyes off Margaret Wilson, as she raced away, their eyes tracked her until they were convinced that she would not return from the heavens. 'You should never have had to see this. That isn't Margaret. That was xyr NanoSuit™. It is heading for recycling.'

He acknowledged the murmuring and worried chatter as a sign that he had their attention. 'Xyr Suit™ is programmed to return itself to Sattva Systems™. However, xyr funeral was delayed, and now you've seen what happens. I'm so sorry for the hurt and distress caused.'

Pauline Wilson cried out, 'What have you done to my Mother?' Her sister came to her side and hugged her.

'Trust me, she is fine.'

'I want to see what you've done to her.'

Out of a morbid fascination, Brady wanted to see, as well. Siddha said, 'Please, Pauline. No.'

She yelled, 'I want to see my Mother.'

Brady tried to make sense of what had happened, but he felt violated, and this feeling interfered with his thought patterns. He wondered if he had been given an opportunity to try her NanoSuit™ on, and whether he could have taken on some of its abilities. He was grateful for his instinctive reaction to throw her off him, as he might have been tempted to get one of his own, and he felt as if that would be an act of surrender - and Brady Mahone wasn't going to let the Greens make a coward of him.

Siddha signalled to the Pallbearers. They formed a human shield so the other onlookers couldn't see. The sisters moved to the graveside, and Brady went with them unnoticed and uninvited. Reverend Akston unclipped the wicker casket and then unwrapped the mud-stained white cloth and revealed the hideously deformed body of Margaret Wilson. The OrangeSuit™ which had held her body together had deserted her, and the body had suffered nearly sixty years of wear, tear, and decay in the space of a day. The pace of the ageing had left a twisted and crumpled body that had lost all fluids and cellular structure.

Pauline put her hand to her mouth in horror, wobbled and fainted. One of the pallbearers moved in to catch her fall. Brady was transfixed by the horrific sight before him, but then he caught a sudden movement out of the corner of his eye. He moved smoothly and quickly to gather up Rowena as she tried to rush past him. He held her in his strong arms, 'Oh no you don't.'

'But I have to see.'

Lizzie went over to her students as Brady was carrying Rowena in their direction. She was curious as to how Rowena had ended up in the arms of Brady Mahone.

He carried her over to her friends. He looked around at them and decided to try and explain to Brianna. 'If you care about your friend, then get her out of here.' He remembered to use her name, 'Rowena will never get over that. She has to remember Mrs Wilson as she was at her best. Can you do that? She needs all your strength and support.'

Brianna said, 'Ok. We understand.'

Brady looked back and could see the physical husk of Mrs Wilson being recovered and lowered quickly into the ground. He waited for another few seconds to ensure the girl in his arms didn't wriggle away, and then placed Rowena down with her friends.

He placed his big hand on Rowena's petite shoulder and said, 'I'm sorry for your loss.'

He walked back through the departing mourners toward Siddha. Lizzie followed him. She wanted to know what mischief he was up to now. Siddha thanked Reverend Akston, who shuffled disconsolately away.

Brady said, 'What really happened?'

Lizzie moved to Siddha's side, 'Some things don't concern you.'

'Ok. I was only trying to help. I know loads of guys at Sattva Systems™ - they seem to want to tell me everything. I'm just saying.' He added, 'If I didn't know better, I think Bodhi orders them to keep me involved.'

'I've already broken the rules.' Siddha said to Lizzie, 'I'm done for, I may as well tell him. I've got nothing left to lose.'

Brady said, 'Bodhi's my friend. If I tell him, you've helped me, that's gotta count for something.'

Siddha said, 'If I tell you, then will you answer some of our questions?'

'Fine by me.'

'The NanoSuits™ should return in a flash to Sattva Systems™.' Siddha said.

Brady rubbed his chin. 'It looked stuck.'

'Yes. It means something's wrong in Boulder Creek.'

'Bodhi's the thing that's wrong. He's ill.'

Siddha said, 'What happened with you and Bodhi?'

Lizzie wanted to ask Brady what he had done to him but thought better of it.

'He was trying out the Indigo™ and Violet™ NanoSuits™ for size, but they had been put on in the wrong order. Genesis, Sissy, whatever her name is, anyway, she said they had been stupid.' Brady laughed, 'Seems to be catching.'

Lizzie said, 'I don't understand.'

'They should have fixed the getting off to sleep first, before heightening the senses of touch and hearing. Now he hasn't been able to sleep for months, apparently.'

Lizzie said to Siddha, 'That's not what we've been told.'

Siddha looked puzzled. 'No, it's not.' They both considered this latest information. They struggled to make sense of it. 'I'm a Disciple, and I wasn't told this, and yet, Bodhi confides in you.'

'I know. Bodhi treats me like his best buddy. I'm not complaining. He's helped make Brady Mahone a very rich man.'

Lizzie said, 'And now you've paid him back. You don't owe him anything.'

'Watcha mean?'

'You saved his life.'

'Oh, that. I just want my sketchbook back. I had some real good drawings in that.'

'How did you save his life?'

Brady smiled, 'The damn fool went into some kinda seizure. I wrenched his jaw open, cos he couldn't breathe and put my sketchbook between his teeth. It kinda kept his airway clear.'

Siddha asked, 'What happened next?'

'Genesis had some orderlies pop him in a coffin thing.'

Lizzie said, 'A coffin?'

'It's one of those long words. Sensory chamber?'

Siddha said, 'Sensory Deprivation Chamber?' He muttered something which suggested he was answering his own unsaid question, 'It's impervious to Nanoparticles and prevents magnetic emissions from escaping. I always wondered what they were for…'

Lizzie spoke, and it seemed to shake Siddha from his reverie, 'There were about a dozen kept in a Panic Room…'

'That's the baby. It helps him sleep while they work on how to remove his Nano-Suits™ and put them back in the right order.' He looked at them both, 'I'm guessing they didn't tell you because it might cause you Greens to panic.'

Lizzie said, 'So, what happened with Margaret Wilson?'

'Her NanoSuit™,' Siddha took charge, 'was supposed to go to Sattva Systems™.'

'I think you've got that wrong. The animals have got it right.' Brady was pointing in the direction of where Mrs Wilson's NanoSuit™ flew after its' steep ascent.

'I'm sorry, I haven't a clue what you are talking about.'

'Homing pigeons use magnetic fields to find their way home, but beached whales have had all their systems go haywire. Mrs Wilson's homing instincts were off kilter. I think she was looking for Bodhi, not Sattva Systems™, but he's kinda off-grid, as we used to say.' He muttered as much to himself as the others, 'She was looking for family, or her Suit™ was attracted to family, and then it searched out Bodhi. It couldn't find him. Therefore, it chose the strongest magnetic field left. She headed due north but not northwest.'

Lizzie said, astonished, as much to Siddha as to Brady. 'Could that be possible?'

'Bodhi has the latest generation Suits™…' Siddha stroked his chin.

Brady interrupted, 'Obviously. If someone else had the most powerful Suits™ and abilities, then they would run the show…'

'Nobody wants anything to happen to Bodhi.'

I ain't bothered either way, as long as Brady Mahone is doing just fine.

Lizzie asked, 'So, where has Margaret gone if she can't locate Bodhi? She headed off somewhere.'

Brady said, 'Sattva Systems™ is northwest of here, but she was heading north.' He laughed as he confirmed his theory, 'She's gone to the North Pole, man. I bet there's a whole load of dancing NanoSuits™ twirling around that sucker.'

11.ALTERED STATE

The twisted image of the decrepit figure of Mrs Wilson in her grave left a deep impression on Brady's psyche. He checked over his body repeatedly, as if the face he saw looking back on him was a mirage. He always knew it was too good to be true that he could be one hundred going on forty years old. He pinched and played with his skin to check it was real. He took a razor and peeled away the surface believing he could spot a covering of Nanomaterial.

He checked his memories of Mrs Wilson. She looked virtually unchanged from 2084 to 2142. But was I looking close enough? He started to wonder whether the whole world was a magic trick, an illusion, and if he examined the movements and actions closely enough, then maybe he could pull the puzzles apart. *I don't look like this. This is what I'm shown. They've made me think I'm young when really, I'm an old fossil.*

He wandered around his old home, the Mahone Ranch. Brady still considered the place belonged to his Pops and not him. He dwelt upon all his Pop's old conspiracy theories, but now out of a belief that he had been a silly young pup and that maybe he should have listened. *How could I have not seen what Mrs Wilson really looked like? It musta been one of those mind games, whatchamacallum, power-of-suggestion kinda deals.*

He had wandered down to Archie Mahone's bunker in a trance-like state. He reflected deeply on all his meetings with Bodhi Sattva. He wondered how he could fool everybody on the planet. *Am I in a coma, Pops? Is it still 2084? Is this a sign that I am waking up?* He ran his fingers over the dusty old technological equipment. He found a sharp edge, and deliberately cut his finger. He found pain both reassuring and confusing. *Is Bodhi Sattva a figment of my imagination? Is he another version of me in my dreams?* His Pops old newspaper cuttings about UFOs and aliens living on planet Earth had long since fallen from the walls. He picked them up reverently and placed them back on Archie Mahone's old work bench. He caught another flashback of Mrs Wilson in her grave. He blinked the image away. He recalled the hundreds of women he had slept with. He even considered the whether the gender fluidity of the BlueSuits™ was his unconscious mind dealing with a potentially repressed homosexuality. He laughed at the idea of Brady Mahone having a modern possibility within his profound dilemma. *Professor Chu would be proud of me. He would say I've become enlightened. I think I spent far too long in jail with only other men for company.* He then remembered that on this journey as a passenger on his train of thought - Professor Yuan Chu didn't exist.

He went back up the stairs to the open air outside the bunker. The air was colder than usual for a Californian winter. He meandered over to the Lopez Ranch. The memory of Professor Chu worried Brady, as he highlighted the deficiencies in Brady as a man, and therefore in his potential explanation of his current circumstances. *I don't have the smarts of a professor. There's no way that I coulda made up all that shit about NanoTechnology™. It wasn't a thing I ever had an interest in.* He laughed. *But how many times did I switch off when Pops was on one of his diatribes about what the Deep Cons were going to do with all those weird science ideas - it could have still crept into my brain while I wasn't listening.*

He went into the Lopez house and slowly explored the place, picking up ornaments and putting them down again, absentmindedly. He lay down on Amie's bed and he considered all his sexual conquests. *They seemed real enough. Their skin felt young and normal like. But what if I was really sleeping with ghouls who were really like the dead body of Mrs Wilson?* He discarded his theories about comas. This all felt too real.

He was still deeply troubled. His Pops used to talk about alternate realities and multiverses, but Brady couldn't get his head around them back in the day. He tried to recall what he used to say, but it was useless. It was far too complicated. Space crafts he could handle, but astrophysics was another thing, entirely. *Note to self - don't bring up the subject with Tyrone.*

He turned over on his side on Amie's comfortable bed. Something was comforting about being in Lopez home. He felt as if he could still smell their presence. He thought about Lucian, Mary-Lou, and Amie as he drifted off to sleep.

He was disorientated when he awoke in the middle of the night. He had been asleep for as long as he could ever remember. He usually only required a few hours, but he had slept through the whole day and into the middle of the night. He got off the bed and straightened the bedclothes out of habit. He went to the Lopez kitchen and made coffee - strong and black. He went out onto the Lopez porch. He left all the lights off as the stars were sparkling against the inky black backdrop. He watched a lonely HeavyLoader™ drifting by looking like a spaceship his Pops would have dreamed about.

After the HeavyLoader™ had passed overhead, Brady sensed the restorative power of silence. He stood alone for long minutes, breathing in the cold fresh air deeply, and watching the stars and gazing at the moon. He appreciated that the world might have changed, but the night sky was beyond the reach of the influence of mankind. I am Trad, and I am real. The Greens are wasting away inside their Suits™. They are *mere shells hiding dead souls - it is they who aren't real. The I Stands for Individual. The Individual Stands. If the last real man on Earth to bear witness to what the Greens did to humanity - then let that man be Brady Mahone.*

12.TARGET ACQUIRED

Brady flew into San Martin. Usually, he would enquire if Rhea was around. She never was. He thought of her differently, now. He estimated her age to be somewhere in the region of ninety years old inside her forty-year-old skin. This was enough to dampen his ardour for her. It was enough to dampen his desire for most women, as he could no longer take them at their young-face-value.

He wanted to have the company of the most genuine person he knew. He knocked on the Beardon and miscellaneous resident's abode, and Samuel Beardon the Third greeted him warmly. Brady had long since given up on inviting the Beardons over to his Malibu home. It became embarrassing as they ran out of excuses. It was apparent that they didn't want to accept anything from him. The Bear always made it clear that Brady was welcome and could stay if he liked. Brady had no problem in receiving and was a regular visitor to the Beardon's home. He viewed them as part of his extended family. He rationalised that even his late Foster Daddy hadn't been a blood relative. He had known the Beardon family for more than four decades.

The Bear invited him in and insisted that Brady join them for dinner. There was a large gathering with Tyrone, Alicia, the Native American family consisting of Shako, the old matriarch of the family, her son Tauri, and his younger brother. There were other guests who Brady hadn't met before, and they seemed thrilled to be sharing the same table as the legendary Brady Mahone. He was polite and friendly and generally just soaked up the happy vibes. He was no longer carrying the baggage of trying to impress them, as they were only partially real to him. He spent a lot of time doing the math to figure out their actual ages and what they should really look like by now. The trickier ones were the Greens he had watched grow up as children. They generally kept the correct appearance in Trad years until they hit their mid-twenties, and then their appearance hardly changed, leaving them forever young.

He wanted to listen to their conversations at the dinner table. They talked about their days and gossiped about work colleagues while all the time staying on the right side of the Security Protocols™. Occasionally, somebody would ask Brady about his business, but he would give a nondescript answer and gently take the conversation back to his dinner table companions. It made Brady look modest and only served to endear him more to them.

Brady listened with interest when they talked about the one person who would usually be with them, but tonight was out with *xyr goyfriend*. It turned out that Amie was madly in love, and they talked in detail about the way xe and Helgarth adored each other. They joked about them both fully using the BlueSuits™ in their true gender-fluid relationship. The BlueSuits™ had been around for about fifteen years, he estimated, and he still couldn't get used to the idea.

He hadn't seen Amie for quite some time. She used to dote on him and follow him everywhere when he stayed over at the Beardons. At first, it was taken as a sign of how much she missed her old life with her Moms and Lucian, and that Brady was the last link back to those days. It was assumed that Brady was a Father figure to her until it became apparent that it was more than that. He had confided in the Bear that he hadn't been involved with her - *in that way.* He had stated that she was too young, and that he would never do such a thing to Mary-Lou and Lucian.

Once Amie had made her affection for Brady explicitly clear, he gently declined her advances and stayed away from the Beardon home for more than a year. If he wanted to discuss things with the Bear, he would engineer a chance encounter with him at the Sattva Systems™ HQ. He should have been happy for Amie that she had moved on with her life, but he was quietly annoyed by the development.

He returned to his math. Amie was about seventeen at the turn of the century. She was a babe-in-arms when Mary-Lou, her Moms had sunk an axe into old man Hodgson's skull. *That was quite something. Poor Cain didn't know where to look.* Therefore, inside that cute twenty-something skin, she was really a sixty-year-old Trad. It didn't make him feel that much better. He felt as if he had lost her to a rival, and Brady didn't like losing.

Shako was talking about the importance of family and how proud she was of her boys. Brady listened intently as he wasn't sure if that's what he wanted anymore. He wanted to be convinced before he committed. She said, 'Why would the Creator, our Lord, give us the power of creation if he didn't want us to use it?' She sipped at her fruit juice. Brady worked out that she was probably about one-hundred and thirty inside her eighty-year-old visage. *Who'd have thought that Brady boy would end up being good at math?* She looked at her sons and grandson, who sat beside her, 'Nothing I have ever done in my life can compare to the joy of having been a part of my boy's creation. I'm so proud of xem.' Brady noted how she failed and succeeded in the end with the new terminology. *She done better than I would have done. I'm not giving in to that crap. They will remain what I think they are. I ain't buying into this bullshit.*

Brady hid his cynicism behind his gentle smiles of encouragement and tacit agreement. The mood was light around the table, and he wasn't going to spoil it. Often, in company, he would be expected to offer free samples of his Music and Film Entertainments, but this gathering never wanted that from him. They made him feel relaxed, and he revelled in leaving his business at the door.

The Bear told one of his stories. Even Brady had heard of Noah and the Great Floods, but the Bear twisted it a little to contemporise it into a homily against climate change. They laughed heartily at the strange creatures he listed going into the ark, two-by-two, and Brady enthusiastically joined in by naming weird creatures of his own, especially, the recent ones he had drawn in his sketchbook, which he would enthusiastically share with the guests. Shako's grandson loved Brady's drawings.

There was much debate around what constitutes a soul. Brady didn't mention the more alarming aspects about the mystery of Mrs Wilson's recycled NanoSuit™ or Bodhi's ill-health - only he and the Bear knew about this - but he wanted their opinion on whether the soul was trapped within the Suit™. The Bear tried to convince him that the soul belonged to God and not Sattva Systems™, and he offered the unrequested confirmation that Trads also have souls that will one day return to God. The Bear was careful not to bring the Devil into the conversation, as it brought back bad feelings from a much earlier visit by Brady. The only potentially provocative comment was when the Bear seemed to suggest that God would be pleased with the work the Greens had done to repair the Earth and that He may judge the Trads differently.

Brady let Shako and Tauri do the washing up, as apparently, it was their turn under the Division of Labour directive. Brady stayed up and chatted with the Bear until everything had been tidied away and ready for another Green day. As the place was full, Brady slept on the sofa. It was plenty big enough to accommodate Brady's large frame, and the place was cosy. Brady felt he needed to be with the Greens he respected most. He needed to see first-hand their human qualities, but he still couldn't shake off the image that inside them all was a Mrs Wilson-like ghoul controlling the NanoSuits™ which enveloped them. He drifted off into an uneasy sleep.

He was awoken by the sound of laughter and two men stumbling through the front door. He looked up and saw the face of Amie looking over him. She was a manly version of herself. She said, 'Hey, Garth, this is the great Brady Mahone.' She laughed as if she was high, and Helgarth giggled uncontrollably. They kissed passionately in front of Brady, and he felt they were teasing him. He controlled himself. He remembered the Security Protocols™ worked both ways and that they would protect Brady from humiliation, whether he desired this or not.

When they finished virtually devouring each other's faces, he said, 'Hi Amie. I was told you had a new friend.'

They both laughed, but Helgarth laughed louder. Amie tried to calm down, but she was still buzzing, 'Long time no see, Brady. I was beginning to think you were avoiding me.'

Brady lied, 'No. I've just been busy. You know how it is.' He struggled to connect Amie's voice with the male figure she was inhabiting. He felt like he was in the middle of a weird dream.

She said, 'This is my goyfriend, Helgarth, sometimes xe's Helga, but today xe's Garth.'

Brady reached out his hand from under the cover on his sofa. He was naked and didn't want to get up. He might have been tempted to show a substantial amount of flesh to two women, but he was coy about doing the same while they were men. 'Pleased to meetcha.' Garth shook his hand firmly and estimated that he was about the same height and build as himself. That was the only similarity, as Helgarth appeared Scandinavian with his blond hair and blue eyes.

Amie said, 'We're off to bed. Maybe, we'll have a catch-up tomorrow if you're planning to stick around?'

Brady was quietly proud of himself for being on his best behaviour for the whole evening, and he didn't want to spoil that now by requesting that Amie return to her female form by the morning. He smiled gently and said, 'Yeah, I'm sticking around for a while, so that will be great.'

Amie gave him a kiss on the cheek. It felt like an act of provocation for Brady, but when he looked into this man's eyes, he knew that it wasn't meant that way. Amie said, 'Sweet dreams, Brady.'

'Yeah. You too.'

He watched the lovers tipsily head off up the stairs together. And after a few minutes, he heard Amie and Helgarth noisily making love in the room above him. Brady wrapped the covers over his head to muffle the noise. It reminded him of his nights in the cells at Ridgecrest Supermax.

13.THE NEXT DAY

Brady broke his fast around a noisy breakfast table. The Bear and his associated families were in good spirits on the new Green Day - as they insisted on calling every day. Afterwards, he went for a walk around the small town of San Martin. He headed for Paradise Park and then sat down next to Little Llagas Creek. This winter had been wetter and colder than usual for a Californian Winter, but today the Sun had returned with a bit of warmth within the sparkling sunshine which reflected sharply off the babbling water. Brady breathed in the fresh air and the scent from the nearby trees.

He gave thought to his plans to have a family. He knew he would have to overcome his newly uncovered thoughts about the lack of visual appeal of the Greens. He knew they were elderly people disguised as something more attractive on the outside. His first-choice woman to start a family with would have been Rhea. His heart skipped a beat when he hoped she would chance upon him here by the creek. She was never here when he was in town, and besides, she was a Disciple, and Disciples avoided having intimate relations with Brady like the plague.

He tried to dismiss her as a possibility by reminding himself that he was pining for a ninety-year-old woman. He succeeded, but only with the consequence of discarding every other potential mate.

He had thought that Amie might have been perfect. He once had overwhelming reservations about seducing Mary-Lou's daughter. He lost his chance at having a life-long, best buddy by his side to enjoy these eternal days because of Lucky's self-sacrifice for her. However, that was more than forty years ago, and his viewpoint changed. He now saw it as the next best emotional move. He considered that maybe Lucian might have approved, especially if he had named a first-born son after him. He hoped he would have been honoured. *I got my doubts about Lucian being a strong name for a son of Brady Mahone - it sounds a bit modern. I want a man's name for a boy of mine.*

His memory flashed with Amie kissing him in the guise of a man. *I gotta get over that as well. Every Green on the planet can do that shape-shifting thing. If I rule her out, then all bets are off.*

Brady shook his head as if to physically reset his brain, and he forced the image of the Amie he could desire. Even after all these years - he still felt as if he should see her like family - and not as a woman in her own right. He mulled over Amie as potential mother for his sons when he recalled how much she was in love with Helgarth. *She must have been with him for at least ten years. She ain't gonna give him up - not for me or all the Green Credits in the world.*

He considered the problem with Helgarth. He drifted off into dark fantasies about disposing of his rival, which entwined with imagining how to kill a Green. He thought about grappling him or choking him to death, and sometimes the person he was killing changed to Siddha or even Bodhi. Then he remembered the Security Protocols™ machines. *Anyways, why would I want to kill Bodhi? It's not like I'd have the smarts to take over his business, with chemical factories and all.*

A vision of Helgarth as a person who must be removed to save the nascent Mahone family emerged, and Brady dwelled darkly on how he could get rid of him forever. He wondered if Bodhi would switch off the machines if he asked him to? *Probably not.* He then remembered stories about abandoned weapons shafts that were hundreds of feet deep and located deep into the Trad lands, or maybe old deep wells. *Perhaps I could be far away from the Security Protocols™. I could come up with a pretence to get Helgarth there in my FusionPlane™ - and then I could challenge him to a fight to the death, for the hand of Amie, like one of those soppy women's bestselling dramas that make me millions of Green Credits.* He laughed loudly, which drew strange glances from an old couple strolling by the creek. He paid them no attention as he was onto something. He imagined him challenging Helgarth to a physical fight with Amie as the prize. He chuckled as he imagined a super-ripped version of himself, like a prize fighter from the olden days. He envisioned the smug face of Helgarth, as he knew he couldn't lose because he had his RedSuit™. Brady bobbed and weaved as he threw air blows at an imaginary punch bag. He was shouting, 'Come on, are you scared of a Trad? Have you never seen so much power in a man? You Greens are all cowards on the insides. Come and finish me off right now - unless you don't want Amie - is that it? Are you saying you don't really love her?'

Brady's imagination was firing. He didn't notice that his hands were clenched hard in his daydream. His dream drafted in more people, Amie was crying out to Helgarth, 'Don't do it. You don't have to prove your love to me.' Brady's mind had imported the Beardon family to witness his victory. They had to see that a Trad could defeat a Green. After he had finished his shadow boxing, Brady said to Helgarth, 'You are weak. You are a piece of low-life scum who ain't fit to shine my shoes.' He saw the anger in the *yes* of his opponent.

At first, there was a couple of strides, but then this was followed by a loping gallop, and Brady stood tall, ready to receive this battering ram of a Green. Helgarth ran at Brady but then disappeared. He had fallen into the trap that Brady had prepared for him. He was screaming as he fell down the weapons shaft. Brady roared with laughter. He remembered Tyrone's words in Encinitas when that family fell into a crack in the Earth caused by the quake. He looked at the Bear, 'I got the idea from you!' Brady squatted and lifted up a large rock and then threw it down the shaft, and then another, and another. 'I'm not having any of you attempting a rescue mission. When he's gone, he's gone.' He then walked over triumphantly and grabbed Amie by the arm, 'You're all mine, now.'

A group of teenagers noisily ran past, and it shook Brady out of his reverie. He remembered how the Security Protocols™ were with him, even in the remotest parts of South Africa. *Between the Suits™ and the Security Protocols™, they've pretty much got the threat from Brady Mahone covered. I'm gonna have to work with him and not fight them.*

He got up and shook off the dirt and soil from his jeans. He strolled back through the streets of San Martin. He considered other alternatives on his way back to the Beardon home. There was that sweet thing down in Encinitas. She was a waitress, what's-her-name? He struggled to remember as he walked a few hundred yards without noticing as he tried to tease his memory back into action. *It was like Lucy... Linda...no, it was weirder than that...Lilith, that's it. She was real cute.* And then he remembered the circumstances in which he'd fled. And how his name was blackened by those events. *I don't suppose they'd have a warm welcome for Brady Mahone in their new town. I'd better scratch Lilith from the list.*

377

Lizzie came into his mind, and Brady sensibly discarded her immediately as a non-starter.

He arrived back at the Beardon home at the same time as the other residents after they had finished going to church. The Bear let Brady into the house first, and it struck Brady that he'd never seen this house empty before, not even for a moment. He sat in the living room with the Bear while Shako hobbled around while dusting around the ornaments on the mantlepiece. Brady knew better than to ask the Bear about the subject of his sermon to the people. 'How's work?'

'Still a lot to do, brother. I'm heading down to San Francisco for the next couple of weeks, but it could be another decade before it's been completely re-wilded. I don't like discussing it on the Lord's day, but many dead are still to be cleaned-up in the city. They are going to be getting their full value of the Bear's work, to be sure.'

Brady thought about the work the Bear did when he first met him in Los Banos. He didn't envy him. 'How are they doing in the other cities?'

'New York State is completely re-wilded, I'm told it's a thing of beauty. It looks pristine…'

Shako interrupted, 'As before the white man came.'

Brady laughed, 'I'm not fully white, so I ain't taking on the white man's burden.'

Shako put her old hand on Brady's shoulder in a mark of solidarity and wandered off into the kitchen.

Lounging back on the sofa, Brady said, 'I thought all the work would be finished by now. It's been nearly sixty-years since the Revolution.'

'It's all going to plan. We never deceived ourselves about how long it would take to undo the damage that mankind had done to the planet - that's why it was always going to be a one-hundred-year plan.' The Bear smiled, 'However, within ten years, we'll start to enter the time of leisure. I'm guessing that will be particularly beneficial to your business.'

Brady knew this was excellent news, but he already had so many Green Credits he couldn't spend them in a thousand years. *It would be good for my sons if I ever have any.* 'I suppose it will be an opportunity for me to employ more staff.'

Shako came back in with coffee for the two men. They thanked her, and she left them to return to her chores. She explained, 'My way of thanking the Lord is to do menial work on a Sunday afternoon as my penance.'

Samuel Beardon the Third raised his cup, 'To Brady the Benefactor.'

Brady laughed, 'It's got a nice ring to it.' He asked, 'If I'm still around for this time of leisure for the Greens, what will it look like?'

'The working hours will shrink to next to nothing, and it will be less laborious. There will be a massive expansion in travel, as Bodhi wants all our Green people to see all we have accomplished all over the world. The planet will be healed. We will have created heaven on Earth.'

'I've heard the roads will be crowded. I'm not sure that sounds like heaven to Brady Mahone. Right now, I have the place virtually to myself. I kinda like it that way.'

The Bear laughed heartily, 'Who'd have thought that Brady the Benefactor would have to learn to share.'

Brady said, 'How's Bodhi doing?'

'It's complicated, but his engineers think they can have him back up and running again within a couple of months.'

'It sounds like they are servicing a car rather than healing a man.'

'I concur, brother.'

Brady said, 'I know everyone directly connected to the Sattva Systems™ HQ know the truth, but the rest of your Green communities seem to be in the dark.' He relayed his account at Mrs Wilson's funeral and the fact that Lizzie and even Siddha - a Disciple - were unaware of the dire nature of Bodhi's condition.

The Bear gave time for Brady's words to sink in before sharing his reply. 'It is to contain any panic. This isn't a good time for people to stop believing in the project. There is some frustration at the length of the project.' He leaned in and whispered, 'Sissy is planning for Bodhi to go on a world tour if he recovers sufficiently. He has been viewed as a recluse, but the time has come for him to demonstrate a more visible leadership role.'

Brady said grandly, 'So, he's taking me as his role-model. That's what I do. I tour the world and make sure everybody knows the Brady Mahone Entertainment Enterprises brand.'

The Bear considered a tailored sermon for Brady on the topic of pride coming before a fall, but he chose not to antagonise his friend. 'It seems Brady Mahone has much to teach the world.'

Amie and Helgarth entered the home noisily. They were both in their female forms. Amie was much smaller than Helgarth, who Amie was addressing as Helga. Brady looked at the impressive stature of Helga, who as a man had a similar physique to Brady, but now, as a woman she looked like a Viking warrior.

Amie saw Brady watching her as she was complaining, 'I still don't see why we have to work so hard. I've been slaving away on that farm for months. I used to have an easier life as a Trad.'

Helga pleaded, 'It won't be forever, another ten years…'

Amie shouted, 'I can't take another ten months…I'm sorry, I love you so much. Why can't we just be left alone to do what we want.'

The Bear stood up and hugged them both, 'Patience, my friends, heaven is waiting. There will be decades of holidays to come for all of us.'

Amie slipped out from under the Bear's large arms and ran up the stairs. Helga raced after her.

Brady said, 'I've seen this with the kids in McFarland. They don't see the world the same way as their elders.'

The Bear scratched his head, 'They didn't see the sacrifices we made, and if they didn't witness it - then they think it didn't happen. Therefore, they need strong leadership.'

'It's always been the same - all work and no play.' Brady shrugged.

14. FIELD OF PLAY

While the Bear was away on his Operation Clean-Up duties in San Francisco with his nephew, Tyrone. Alicia, his daughter, was having a well-earned vacation - she was allowed four weeks complete rest per year under the Division of Labour rules. This meant she was even spared the household chores. She took her breakfast and coffee into the living room and didn't say a word. She could see that Brady was there, staring out the window, and it was evident that he hadn't seen her come in.

She sat down and peacefully shared the space with him, unnoticed.

The rest of the house was deserted as the other occupants had all gone out to complete their Green duties. There was still a lot of saving up to do to acquire enough Green Credits to pay for the imminent IndigoSuit™, and further down the line - the VioletSuit™.

There was much bemusement among the general population as to why the properties of the Suits™ had been changed. They had been promised enhanced senses with the Indigo™ upgrade, which had caused much excitement - when it was announced at the last New Green Year celebrations. She recalled how nervous Rhea - as her Disciple - was about changing the plans at the hastily convened emergency meeting at the San Martin Green Revolutionary Hall. Now they would receive the IndigoSuit™ in two years, and it would be a sleep reduction benefit, and five years after that, the VioletSuit™ would have the senses upgrade. She told the assembled residents how the sleep function would allow them to instantly go to sleep, and they would only require three hours sleep per day, and the most significant benefit in her mind, not only would the pre-Revolution Green Community Members be able to live to one-hundred-years of age - minimum - but they would also get an extra five hours per day of high-quality living. The younger members were told that they would obtain five hours of increased leisure time per day to use on nature, especially the appreciation of nocturnal wildlife.

No matter how hard Rhea had tried to sell them the features and benefits of the sleep enhancements, it couldn't match the appeal of the Violet™. The older members of the Green Communities took the disappointment stoically, but the younger elements began to quietly vent their frustration. They hadn't fought in the Revolution - they believed in saving the planet - but they hadn't given up so much to be as invested in it as their parents. They wanted to use the higher performing senses to continue the exploration of their heightened sexuality and identity.

Brady went into people watching mode at the Beardon residence, and the people he was watching the most was Amie and Helgarth. He was watching them right now, and he observed their work in the fields. It looked back breaking and dirty. They were planting and digging.

He considered whether it tired them. He knew the OrangeSuits™ would protect the physiques. He also guessed they wouldn't need as many drinks breaks because of their GreenSuits™. He was quietly fascinated by them. *I don't know if it would physically wear them out, but I guess it would be mentally draining.* He noticed that today Amie and Helgarth were in their female states. He laughed as Amie threw soil over Helgarth, and she, in turn, chased her and held her. Some instruction must have been given as they swiftly returned to their labour.

The clink of Alicia's coffee cup, as she reached out to put the empty cup on the coffee table, shook him out of his reverie. Brady averted his gaze from the window and turned to see Alicia and her long slender black frame stretched out on the sofa. She said lazily, 'What's so funny?'

Brady ambled over to Alicia and flopped down in an armchair which faced her. 'I was just watching Amie and Helgarth together. I hadn't realised before that they were an item.'

'Could that be because you couldn't imagine your little Amie being non-binary?'

'Hey, I'm a Trad. These things take a lot of getting used to. It's not just that; I think we avoided each other for so many years.' Brady assessed that Alicia and Amie would be about the same age. He used his going-on phrase to think of the Greens after the Mrs Wilson incident, as he now mentally referred to it. Therefore, both Alicia and Amie were about sixty *going-on* twenty-five.

'Why did you avoid her? You saved her from a lonely Trad life, and then you deserted her.' She stretched, and Brady couldn't help but watch her dressing gown open a little, revealing his view of her supple legs.

Brady looked at her pretty face but still stole a last glance at her legs before he replied, 'It's complicated. I was upset and she reminded me of what I'd lost.'

'My Father was very confused about the whole situation, at first. He tried to question Amie about it.'

'What did she say?'

'That you were her hero - that she only wanted to be with you. She struggled to get used to her duties as a Green for many years - until Helgarth befriended her, and as you can tell, they are in an arrangement together and are very much in love.'

'Truth be told, I didn't care about saving Amie. I wanted to save the best buddy I ever had. I wanted to spend my whole life enjoying the fruits of my enterprise with him alongside me. Lucky saved my life, not Amie. I wanted to pay him back.'

Alicia said softly, 'He was her stepfather, and he sacrificed himself for her. Maybe she hero-worshipped the wrong guy.'

'She did.' He reminded himself that he was talking to a very mature woman and not her girlish visage. 'What happened to her? She's very different to the coy little girl I used to know.'

Alicia sat up a little as if this questioning had piqued her interest, 'Helgarth was about the same age as Amie, but far more sexually precocious, shall we say. She took her to parties; in the old days they probably would be called orgies. From then onwards, Amie became obsessed with sex. However, I'm guessing she always had that demon within her.'

Brady noted the word *demon*. It was clear that the daughter of Samuel Beardon the Third disapproved of her actions.

She continued, 'And she transformed into a totally changed being once the BlueSuits™ were launched. You've probably noted how often they change.'

Brady nodded.

'Well, it's a painful process and can take more than an hour to complete, but that pair change more than anyone else I know.' She smiled, 'Having said that, they are also the happiest people I know. So, who am I to judge?'

Alicia watched the internal gears of Brady's mind processing this information. She observed every minuscule frown and twitch at the corners of his mouth. For a moment, she found him quite fascinating, like watching a dumb beast doing something which seemed beyond their perceived intelligence.

He was still weighing up the potential breeding potential of Amie, when his eyes strayed upon Alicia's bare legs, and he began to wonder whether she could be the mother of his sons.

She had watched his eyes move from her face to her legs, and she squirmed inside as she felt him leering over her whole body. Alicia pulled together the dressing gown, which had exposed a fraction of cleavage and then covered the gap which had unwittingly exposed her legs. She didn't say anything, but the defiance in her eyes was obvious to Brady. He concluded that seducing Alicia was a non-starter. *Anyways, it would take some explaining to the Bear. I lost Lucky to a daughter; I don't want to lose the Bear as well.* He whispered, by way of a near apology, 'I'm sorry, I was miles away.'

15.THE INDECENT PROPOSAL

Brady decided to get to know Amie a little better. He was also intrigued by how she appeared to be high when she had returned home late at night with Helgarth in tow. He waited until the evening meals dishes were cleared away and the rest of the household had retired to their bedrooms. Just as Amie and Helgarth were about to head to their bedroom, he said, 'Hey, Amie?'

She turned to face him with a mixture of insolence and defiance. 'What do you want, Brady?'

She might be sixty, but she behaves like a bloody teenager. Fine, I can work with that. 'You were high the other night.'

'What's it to you?'

Helgarth joined ranks, 'Yes, what's it with you? You're not her Father.'

Brady laughed, 'Couldn't agree more. I just want a taste of the good stuff if you can get it, of course.'

The young-looking couple looked at each other and seemed to come to a decision telepathically, 'You'd have to come with us. Xe would give out extra if we brought the local celebrity along.'

'I'll be anything you want me to be.' He joked, 'Let's party.'

'Ok, but no annoying people with your old Trad fuddy-duddy ways.'

Brady roared with laughter, 'Hey, sweet-thing, nobody calls Brady Mahone a fuddy-duddy.'

Amie joked, 'Brady the fuddy-duddy-diddy-daddy, that sounds real funny.'

'Hey! Leave off with the diddy.'

They reached an old, abandoned barn at the north side of town after much shushing and hushing for fear of Brady's heavy stepping waking the townsfolk on the way. Helgarth tapped out what sounded like a secret code to Brady on the barn door, and as it swung open, a youngish looking male in a Goth trench coat adorned with silver buttons greeted Helgarth. He announced in a loud whisper, 'Hey everyone, we've only got Brady Mahone to come and visit - and partake?'

'I wouldn't have it any other way.' Brady watched the stoned and strung-out bodies on the floor. If they had noticed him, they probably thought they were dreaming. 'What's your name, man?' Brady had his hand in a pocket of his Poacher's coat.

'I'm Debrock, sometimes I'm Debs, but today I'm Rock.' He stuck out his hand, but instead of shaking it, Brady shoved a stash of Premium Files from his Entertainment Samples. 'I usually give these to the Green VIPs who move the most of my product. I don't want you to think that Brady Mahone will leave your hospitality unappreciated.'

Debrock smiled broadly at Brady and then turned to Amie and Helgarth, who looked proud that they had made Debrock so happy. They went through the stack of Black Files, with occasional outbursts of, *I didn't even know this existed...I love that.* Debrock said to all of them, 'I'm going to share with you some of my finest stash as this is a very special occasion.' He handed him a small wax ball and wondered what Brady would do with it. He knew Brady as a businessman and not as the criminal he was in the old world.

Brady put it under his tongue and carried on talking as if he wasn't concerned about when the effects would kick in. 'They used to grow a lot of this stuff - why do you use dabs? Surely, the Greens haven't got a problem with smoking Mother Nature.'

Debrock was handing out his dabs to Amie and Helgarth, and as aficionados, they knew this was the cream of the crop. They took them off him hungrily. Debrock answered Brady, 'We don't create smoke because of the Security Protocols™, but this way, we don't alert them to our presence.'

Brady had already started to giggle. When he considered giggling to be distinctly unmanly, it only made him giggle even more. His laughter was infectious, and soon Amie and Helgarth joined in. Brady said, 'So, the Security Protocols™ don't trouble you as long as your chill?'

'Yeah, man. They roam everywhere, looking to damp out fires. They used to be kept busy by the Trads trying to rekindle the NanoProtected™ vegetation, but since there are hardly any Trads, the vegetation grows free. However, they now patrol to put out the forest fires.'

Brady struggled to hold a serious conversation, 'I noticed that it wasn't long before the Trads couldn't have their barbecues.' He laughed, 'The whole of their civilisation was at stake, and they thought barbecues were the answer. Man, we were so dumb.'

Amie said, 'Yeah, we were.'

Helgarth said, 'What's a barbecue?' At which point, they all collapsed in a fit of uncontrollable laughter.

A few hours passed before Brady emerged from his industrial-strength haze. He was surprised to see that Amie and Helgarth had come around before him. He watched them stand shakily, and they headed outside, holding each other upright. He attempted to stand but raising himself to his full height felt like trying to reach the clouds. He made another attempt and finally achieved a standing position. He shuffled off to follow them. He didn't want to risk taking even one foot off the ground to walk properly. He found them sitting on the grass, propped up next to each other and gazing at the full moon. He flopped down next to them.

He said, 'Watcha thinking about?'

Amie said, 'It's always work tomorrow.'

Brady tried to think of some interesting interjections and observations, but in his fogginess, he struggled. Instead, he cut to the chase. 'I've been doing some thinking.'

Amie joked, 'Ooh, if Brady is thinking, then it must be serious.'

Brady ignored the invitation to banter, 'I've got a proposal for you…for both of you, actually, as I can see you come as a pair.'

Helgarth burst out laughing at Brady's poor choice of words, 'We certainly do!'

Brady was derailed for a moment until Amie asked, 'What proposal?'

'I've got a big ask, and I know you'll reject it out of hand, at first, but I want you to think about it carefully. I'll be asking for a lot, but Brady Mahone has got a lot to offer in return.'

Helgarth was troubled that Brady might be planning to take Amie away from her. 'You said both of us?'

'Yes. What I am willing to offer, is a life of luxury in my Malibu home. It has hot tubs, views over the Pacific Ocean and staff to cater for your every whim.' Brady let his opening gambit sink in. He looked at Amie and felt guilty and a little bit grubby. He tried not to think of Mary-Lou and Lucian.

Helgarth took up the negotiations, 'And what precisely do we have to do to be worthy of this gift or is it obvious.'

'It's like that, but not that.'

Amie said, 'I don't understand.'

This emboldened Brady to make his intentions clear. 'I want you both to have my babies - my sons.' He expected an explosion of anger and indignation but was shocked to have his request land into stunned silence.

A few moments passed, and he couldn't decipher the looks that flickered between Helgarth and Amie, but it seemed like they were processing their next move as if they were one. Helgarth spoke for them both, 'We'll let you know our answer tomorrow.'

Brady was encouraged and believed he should lay down all his conditions. He wouldn't want them to agree, only for them to pull out of the deal once the full implications were communicated to them. He shook his head as if he was trying to remove a physical cloud from around his head. 'Ok, here's the deal. I want five sons between you. I want them raised as men, not as…y'know, neither one nor another. I want them to have manly names like Bill, not William, Willie, or Liam. I know they will have to have all the NanoSuits™…' *I'm going off track here.* 'And I want you to be women in my presence. I'm a Trad and old-fashioned. What you do when I'm not there is entirely up to you. You two can be together. I don't want that kind of relationship with you - but it would be nice if we could be friends.' He smiled hopefully.

They didn't utter a word, they turned and tottered away, and they held hands as they headed back to the Beardon home without him.

Brady felt they needed space to come to a decision of this magnitude. He thought about trudging around San Martin through the day, but the place had never really captivated his imagination. He found it dull, and there wasn't much to do there. He could understand why the younger crowd passed the time through sex, drugs and the entertainment products provided by Brady Mahone's Entertainment Enterprises.

He went back into the barn. He nudged Debrock, who had not entirely returned to the real world. Debrock opened his eyes, 'Hey, man. I'm still having that crazy trip where Brady Mahone is travelling high with me.'

Brady smiled, 'It's true dat, buddy. Brady wants some more of your good stuff.'

'Sure.' He rummaged around as if locating his stash was a puzzle beyond his current level of mental acuity. He seemed to find it more by accident than design. 'Take what you need, man - plenty more where that came from.'

The old criminal emerged for a moment within Brady, and he considered taking it all until he remembered that he was probably the richest man on the planet - apart from Bodhi Sattva. He took one dab, admittedly the largest of the waxy lozenges, and placed it carefully under his tongue. His only concession to discipline was to ensure that in the next few minutes, he would focus on his next moves with Amie and Helgarth and also to consider a contingency plan if they refused his offer.

As Brady drifted away, he couldn't help but imagine that he might spend the rest of his life on his own.

16. WHAT IS LOVE?

Amie and Helgarth finished labouring in the fields of San Martin. They returned to the Beardon home and were greeted by Alicia. 'Hi goys, how was work today?'

Helgarth replied, 'Same as it ever was. Say, have you seen Brady?'

'No. I'm happy to say that my day was way more chill without him.'

'So, he hasn't been here all day?'

Alicia thought for a moment, 'I can't say I've seen him since yesterday evening.'

Amie said, 'Ok. Thanks.' She led Helgarth by the hand and upstairs to their room. She shut the door behind them. 'Do you think he's gone?'

Helgarth looked out of the upstairs window. 'I don't think so. The FusionPlane™ he arrived in is still there. However, transport isn't a problem to a man like Brady.'

Amie flopped down on the bed, 'We've missed our chance. We shouldn't have played it so coy.'

'Maybe.' She heard movement on the landing. She poked her head out of the bedroom door, she saw Shako. 'Hey, Shako, have you seen Brady today?'

The old lady said, 'No. I've been in the town today, delivering and sorting vegetables at the GreenGrocers™. The town was busy, as they were all hoping to catch a glimpse of Brady, but nobody had seen him. I'm sorry.'

'That's ok. Thanks.' She went back into the bedroom and closed the bedroom door carefully. She said in a loud whisper. 'He's not been seen all day.'

Amie said, 'We'll have to find him before it's too late. What if he's already found someone else?'

'Alicia seemed a bit off when we brought the subject of Brady up. I wonder if he's already asked her. We both know plenty of others who would agree to anything for a chance to escape all this.' Helga flopped down on the bed beside Amie. 'We'll have to find him first.'

'Let's go.' Amie jumped off the bed.

'We can't. Not yet. It's Alicia's holiday, and it's our turn to do the meals and the washing up.'

'Fuck!'

Helgarth said, 'We'll go afterwards. I think we should head back to Debrock's place - that was the last place we saw him. We'll start from there.'

Amie said, 'If he's been there all day, on Debrock's premium…'

'I know. He might have forgotten everything he said.'

After the chores were done. Amie and Helgarth rushed off to search for Brady. Fortunately, he was still in the barn. He was propped up on the floor, laughing infectiously with Debrock, like they were new best buddies. He only had one foot in this world when Amie and Helgarth entered the barn. They were trying hard to look cool. Debrock greeted them, 'Hey, madies, how y'all doing? Brady here has got the constitution of an ox.'

Brady giggled like a schoolchild, 'Yeah, I'm a real-life beast of burden.'

Debrock asked them, 'Do you want a dab?'

Helgarth answered, 'In a little while.' She had decided for both of them that they needed clear heads. 'We'd just like to have a little word in private with Brady. It's a home thing. He's not completed his Division of Labour at the Beardon home. Y'know, they've been kind enough to put him up and all…'

Debrock roared with laughter. Brady laughed in sympathy as he hadn't had enough concentration to listen to the whole of Helgarth's comments. Debrock said, 'Sure, I mean if it's a Division of Labour…' he couldn't finish his train of thought as he had been utterly derailed by laughing at his own joke.

Amie whispered to Helgarth, 'We need to get him outside. Grab some water and let me do the talking.'

'Why?'

'He'll feel more guilty with me. He still sees me as almost family.'

'Ok.'

Helgarth was stronger than Amie. She was almost as big as Brady. She lifted him up, and she placed his arm around her shoulder for support. Amie grabbed a bottle of water and opened the door, and they all headed into the twilight of San Martin.

They sat Brady up against a tree, which was far enough from the barn not to be overheard. The cooling breeze whipped around Brady, and they plied him with water. Amie talked about old times, deliberately keeping the conversations to innocent subjects. She spoke at length about Lucian and encouraged Brady to remember those days until they deduced that he had recovered enough to hold a coherent discussion.

Brady could feel his head clearing. He suddenly realised that his proposal wasn't dead. They were here and caring about his welfare. Helgarth and Amie patiently waited for Brady to bring the previous night's offer up first. He said, 'Have you made a decision? Y'know, about…'

Amie said, 'We have some questions.'

'Shoot.'

'What about our friends?'

Brady's brain was still misfiring, 'I don't want a commune. I don't go in for sharing my property like you Greens do?'

'We still want to see them.'

He said, 'Ok. I'll throw in a FusionPlane™ and a FusionCar™ of your own. You can visit them any time you like, as long as...' He added, 'I'll have to arrange Nannies and the like for when you're away, I suppose...' He drifted off, 'This family thing is more complicated than I thought...' He returned her gaze, 'Will that do?' He asked hopefully.

'The Nannies, and the other staff you've got - do they work for you?'

'No. They are employed by Sattva Systems™.'

He watched the two women look at each other. He envied this silent communication between two entwined souls. He watched them barely nod, but it was enough to know they had agreed.

She said, 'If you don't give us notice, then you might catch us in different gender forms - we can't just switch in a moment. It takes time, and it's quite painful...'

'I understand. It's not a problem.'

'We did want children, but we could never afford them. I suppose this is the next best thing.' He watched as Helgarth hugged her, and he could sense their sadness.

He said, 'How about this?' He paused for a moment, they looked at him expectantly, 'If you deliver me, my five sons, then I'll pay for you to have two children of your own. Do we have a deal?'

They both looked at each other and couldn't hide their poker faces any longer. They smiled broadly. Amie said decisively, 'Yes, Brady. We have an arrangement.'

Helgarth said, 'I have a request.'

Brady didn't like adding to a deal after it was agreed. He frowned. She said, 'We want to conceive your children in your bed, at your old ranch.'

Brady said, 'What?'

Amie blushed, but Helgarth said to her, 'I want to do this for you. I know it was always your fantasy. I want to be with you when you make it come true.'

Brady was confused. That was the worst night he could remember. He wanted to make an additional request of his own, but it was too late. He had to hope that their plans would coincide with his own. He wanted to ask them to appear as sexy as possible, not out of a desire to treat them as sex workers, but so they could distract him as much as possible, as he didn't want the image of Mrs Wilson to subdue his performance. He didn't see these Green girls the same way as he used to. He said, 'Ok. When do we do this thing?'

Amie said, 'Tomorrow night.' Neither she nor Helgarth wanted him to change his mind - or select another to take their place. A rival may be less demanding.

17.THE OLD RANCH

Brady landed his FusionPlane™ with his two passengers on the grounds of the Mahone Ranch. His Green staff maintained the Ranches and their supplies, so he knew his guests could travel lightly. As the Greens didn't need clothing, they travelled light by default.

Amie took Helgarth by the hand and spent the next few hours giving her a guided tour of the properties and detailed accounts of every memory a place or an object inspired. It was apparent to Helgarth and Brady how much she had missed the place in the last forty-two years.

He watched apprehensively as Amie took Helgarth to Archie Mahone's grave and headstone. Brady felt guilty about not burying Mary-Lou and Lucian. He had been so angry with them that he didn't even know precisely when or how they had died. He knew they had been dealt with by Operation Clean Up teams, like any other dead Trads.

He was relieved when they moved on to the following memories, and they still seemed in good spirits. He went to check up on his own home - he felt as if he had to make a good impression. He checked the bathroom - he remembered to put the toilet seat down, but then smiled when he recalled that the Greens hardly ever use these anymore - not since the GreenSuits™. He went into Archie's old room and considered what his Pops would make of his plans to start a family. He then went into his own room. He tidied around and straightened up his bed. He planned how much he should eat or drink, so as he wouldn't ruin his performance. *I need to be on top form tonight.* He felt strangely anxious, it was usually just a pleasurable way of passing the time, but tonight it was an event.

Brady wandered into the kitchen and felt that as their host, he should make the evening meal. He roasted vegetables and baked potatoes, and lured by the smell of food, Helgarth and Amie came into his home, and his dining room to join him. Brady avoided this turning into a formal occasion. He was averse to any situation which enforced him into being on his best behaviour.

As Amie continued to relay her memories, Helgarth gave Amie her undivided attention. Brady knew that she was making this night all about Amie. He wasn't convinced it was for the luxury he had promised.

Afterwards, He offered to clear up while suggesting that Amie and Helgarth could get freshened up and prepare themselves for later. Once the dining area and kitchen were clear, he took in the relative silence and let his last-minute doubts rise to the forefront of his consciousness. *My life could end up being totally different from tonight. I wonder if it will change me?.*

He showered and put on a white dressing gown and padded down the hall to his old bedroom. He heard giggling from his room. Brady was glad that he hadn't had to invite or order them to attend.

They stood before him. They had chosen their appearance as if to excite a Trad Alpha Male, and they were dressed in sheer see-through lingerie. He hadn't imagined Helgarth as the statuesque beauty as she stood by the coy Amie. He wondered if Amie was putting on an act that she thought would please him. The women kissed each other gently as if signalling that the game had commenced. He wandered over to them, and they let him undress them slowly until they were both naked. Amie slipped off Brady's dressing gown and pulled him down onto the bed. Helgarth lay behind him and watched Amie excitedly explore his body with her fingers.

Amie's fingers moved down to his manhood, and when he was hard, she slipped him inside her. Helgarth watched and didn't interfere. She wanted Amie to scratch her forty-year itch. As Amie moaned, Helgarth echoed her. She moved her body over Brady's back, he could feel her breasts on his flesh, and he could hear the moaning from under and on top of him, and then he couldn't contain his excitement any longer, and he came into Amie. Helgarth pushed from behind him to encourage him to fully spend himself.

Brady pulled himself away from Amie. He felt Helgarth reach over him as she and Amie then made love to each other, with the prostrate body of Brady no more than a fleshy barrier between them.

Long minutes passed as they continued to writhe next to him. The frustration of him lying between them, preventing their fingers from fully exploring each other, only seemed to intensify their passion for each other. In the heat of this passion, Brady slowly began to recharge himself. Amie went down on Brady to encourage his returning hardness, and when she came back up, it was her signal to Helgarth that he was ready for her.

Helgarth turned him over and sat astride him, and he held her breasts as she plunged him inside her and rode him. Amie kissed his mouth as she urgently wanted him to taste her, and then she kissed him on his chest and then moved around the back of Helga. She slipped her hand under Helgarth's buttocks and then caressed Brady's balls. She wanted Helga, and the more she could excite Brady, the quicker he would come, and then she could have Helgarth back. Brady couldn't hold back. He didn't want to. This was about making sons and not about his performing abilities. He felt that he had almost exploded his load into Helgarth.

When he was done, Helgarth removed him from within her, and then hungrily pulled Amie to her with such force and speed that Brady felt as if he was being pushed off the bed. He stood up and watched them making love to each other. They moaned and wrestled and then they moved their fingers into each other's cunts and then they paused for a moment. He felt like he was intruding on something profound. The way they looked at each other made him realise that he had never loved anybody like these two loved each other. *Nobody has ever loved Brady Mahone like that - not in a hundred years.*

He suddenly felt exhausted, and he knew he wasn't needed or wanted here. He put his dressing robe back on. As he left the room, he heard the moans turn to squeals, and he knew this would be a long night. He also knew he would find sleep hard to come by at the Mahone Ranch.

He wandered outside in just his dressing gown, looking like a ghost in the dark Californian night. His bare feet padded on the grass, and it looked soft and inviting enough to sleep on. He couldn't remember being so tired. *If it's not the sex, then maybe the weed is still having an effect.*

Brady went through the door of the old Lopez Ranch and went straight to Amie's old bedroom. He lay on her bed, he could still smell the Lopez family in this place, and he could still sense Amie's scent on her pillow.

It was warm and springlike on the following morning, and Helgarth and Amie strolled around the Ranch's grounds. They moved between the trees on the borders, holding hands and listening to the birds chirruping away happily.

Helgarth said, 'You haven't said your little catchphrase yet. You know how much I love to hear you say it.' Amie smiled teasingly. Helgarth said, 'Aw, come on.'

Amie laughed and said, 'I'm knock-kneed and knackered.' They both laughed and hugged. Amie said, 'Do you think it worked? I'm sure I can sense something.'

'We don't get many pregnancies, but I've heard that with the Orange™, you might be able to know within a day of conception - more so with default males.'

'Do you feel it?'

Helgarth closed her eyes and let her mind wander over her body, looking for signs of difference. After a few moments, she said, 'Yes. I think I do. It's like a static charge in my belly.' Amie flung her arms around Helgarth. 'It's wonderful to have you share this journey with me.'

'Is that the NanoBots™ working?' Helgarth whispered.

'I don't know. I hope so.' Amie added, 'I've heard it feels kinda strange if you switch to being a man while you're pregnant. However, your body defaults to being female at the actual birth.'

'We'll have to try that. Have you given any thought about when we should have them?'

Amie said, 'I think Brady is thinking about Trad births, which can be painful. I don't think he realises just how easy it is to carry and give birth with the Orange-Suits™. If this is the case, then I think we should have the children quickly, maybe all done in five years, then we could spend the rest of our lives enjoying the luxury of our new way of life.'

They strolled over to Amie's old home. They were arm in arm and swaying from side to side playfully. They heard loud rumbling noises from within. When they reached Amie's old bedroom, they found Brady snoring loudly. They giggled at first and then laughed when Brady caught his breath and snorted. They snook away as they didn't want to wake him.

Helgarth said, 'I'd heard about Trads snoring - that was hilarious. Did you used to snore like that?'

Amie dug Helgarth in the ribs, 'No, I did not.' She said with a mixture of play-fulness and indignation. They heard sounds of movement and guessed that they had woken him up. They headed for the kitchen and prepared to make breakfast and coffee for them all. Amie had strong memories of her Moms doing that for her and Lucian - all those years ago.

Helgarth joked, 'So, are you playing mum?' She corrected, 'Pomma.' She spotted a tear in Amie's eyes.

'I was just thinking of her.' She sobbed as she cushioned her head on Helgarth's breasts.

Brady was about to go into the kitchen when he saw the two women hugging each other and displaying signs of sadness. He took a step back to stay out of sight. He had flashbacks from the night before, and he felt a sense of guilt and shame. *What's done is done. It's too late to turn back now.*

He stood up and tried to summon up his former sense of arrogant pride and marched into the kitchen. 'Good morning, girls.' He said, deliberately refusing to use the correct gender usage. 'I trust you had a good night's sleep.' He added, knowing full well that they hadn't.

Amie tried to find her former cheerfulness, she said, 'Well, you certainly did. We could hear you snoring from outside.'

'Oh.'

Helgarth burst out laughing, and Amie joined in, laughing within her tears. It wasn't long before he had to laugh with them. He joked, 'It must be the dabs. Jesus, that was strong stuff.'

Over brunch, they talked about many things, but nobody brought up the subject of the previous night. Brady brought up the issue of future plans. 'I was thinking that I could fly you down to Malibu this afternoon.'

Amie said, 'I'd like to stay here - just for a couple of weeks.' Helgarth looked at her with her puzzled head tipped to one side. 'I haven't been here for such a long time. It's bringing back so many memories - and not all of them were bad. I loved Moms - and Lucian too.'

Brady asked, 'Are you sure?'

Amie looked at Helgarth, who nodded. Amie said, 'Yes, I need this.'

Brady said, 'No problem. I can make that work. It could give the staff plenty of time to make the place ready for your arrival.'

18.BEAST OF BURDEN

Brady brooded on whether he needed to tell anybody about his plans. He'd left it a few weeks to see if there was any need to mention it. The girls said to him that everything had worked, but he had an old-fashioned view of pregnancy and wanted to be sure. He certainly wasn't going to treat Bodhi or anybody else at Sattva Systems™ like a boss. *What I do with my life is my business.* However, when he considered that they would find out from his staff at his Malibu home, soon enough, he thought it would save a lot of hassle down the line if he told them now. *It's not like Brady Mahone has anything to hide.* He didn't make appointments to visit. He came and went to Boulder Creek as and when he pleased. He boarded his FusionPlane™ and took the short flight to the Sattva Systems™' HQ.

He was greeted by Marjorie; she was now a Fleet Captain and commanded respect within her teams for her attention to detail. She said, 'Hello, Brady. Your Fusion-Plane™ is overdue for its' service. Would you like me to get one of my crew to do this while you are visiting?'

Brady smiled warmly, 'Yeah, that'd be great.'

'I could drive you to the Main Entrance…'

'No. I'd rather walk. I'll go on my own. Anyhows, I know you'll be real busy.'

'I am, actually. Thanks, Brady. Enjoy your Green day.'

He knew she would contact the powers that be to inform them of his arrival, so he wasn't surprised to be greeted by Genesis Garcia in the lobby. She stood beneath the banner of the thirteen promises. 'Hi Sissy, how's it hanging?' He joked; he often threw in the old Trad phrases to remind them that he was proud of his heritage.

'It's been a troubling period.'

'Is Bodhi getting better?'

'The engineers are making progress. It's difficult to extract two individual Nano-layers without disrupting the other six - if you include the primer. We are dealing with exotic properties and electron behaviour within the Diamonoid Shells™. They've been studying the quantum dots and the effects of electron behaviour. They believe they have identified magnetic field signatures which means they could extract the Indigo and Violet layers through a form of levitation.'

Brady knew she was trying to belittle him; it was a thing about the Greens he detested most. He tried hard to concentrate as he grew older, as he felt a sense of duty to honour the intelligence of the Trads before they started grouping them in with the Neanderthals in their history of the human race. He said, 'So, it's like pouring a tall frosty beer and then scraping the froth of the top.'

She looked confused and then stunned, 'Yes. I suppose except it's at a molecular…'

Brady switched off until she had finished quoting from a science textbook. He said, 'So, I guess you're in charge, now.'

'No. Glenarvon Cole has returned to take the reins. Of course, he isn't an expert in Nanotechnology, but he is a figure who has the required gravitas to instil calm in a time of crisis.' They continued to walk down the nondescript corridors, which were now familiar to him after hundreds of visits over the years. She added, 'He's keen to see you. He's been waiting for your next visit.'

Brady asked the only question he wanted to ask Glenarvon Cole at this point. 'Has he got some kind of arrangement with Rhea?'

Sissy looked at him as they approached the door to Bodhi's office, 'Yes. They do have some *kind of arrangement* as you put it.'

She knocked three times on the door and waited to be invited in. This was already a change from Bodhi's open-door policy. They stepped inside, Sissy announced, 'Brady Mahone to see you. I'll be off - I've got to check on the FusionPlane™ mass production line.' She left abruptly. Brady wondered if there was an element of conflict between them. He guessed that Genesis Garcia resented his presence and his assumption of leadership.

Glenarvon Cole greeted Brady with a vice-like handshake. 'We've never properly been introduced. So good to finally meet you. I'm Glenarvon Cole, but please, call me Glen.'

'I'm Brady. Brady Mahone. Pleased to meetcha.' It irked Brady that it was obvious what Rhea would see in this guy.

Glen moved to behind Bodhi's desk, and he looked like an old-fashioned environmental activist. His hair was scraggly and matted black. He had studs in his ears and tattoos on his forearms. He plonked his heavy muddy boots on Bodhi's polished screen on the desktop. 'Please, make yourself at home.' Brady knew a fighter when he saw one. He had the bearings of a General who had risen through the ranks. He knew Glen would not be scared by Brady or of anything else, for that matter. Brady sat on his chair and leaned back - the front legs of his chair were off the ground, as Brady demonstrated his own nonchalance. Glen said, 'What brings you to Sattva Systems™?'

Brady noted the difference in dealing with Bodhi and Glen. He would have felt chilled about giving Bodhi the news of his impending fatherhood, but with Glen, he sensed he would be viewed as soft, or even worse, weak. 'You might hear about my plans to start a family from others. I just wanted to give you the news first - not that you could stop me anyway.'

'My dear Brady, congratulations. I mean it, I'm delighted for you.' He said formally. He removed his feet from Bodhi's desk and shook him firmly by the hand once more. 'If there is anything you need…'

'I might need Nannies. The girls want to be able to visit friends when my sons have been born.' He wanted no doubt about how his boys were going to be raised.

'No problem. I know Bodhi would have agreed. Consider it done.' He said out loud to himself, 'Girls…sons…' He laughed softly.

Brady said, 'I would have thought you'd hate to be stuck here, in the middle of an industrial complex.'

'You're right. This is probably the ugliest and most polluted place left on the planet, but it is a necessary evil. Would you like to get out of here?'

Brady was confused. He had only just got here. 'My FusionPlane™ is in for a service…'

'Then we'll take mine. We'll have a road trip while we get to know each other better.' He said it as if he had no doubt that Brady would agree.

'Ok. Why not.'

Glen jumped up like a hyperactive child who'd just been allowed to go out and play. Brady followed him as Glen marched on purposefully. 'I'm dying to show you my favourite place. It's in Florida.'

'Florida?'

'Yes. It's only four hours from here. I promise you; you'll love it.'

They saw Sissy at the main entrance. She said, 'You haven't forgotten that you have a meeting with the Regional Disciples at 4pm today, have you?'

Glen said as he swept past her, 'You do it. I'm going on a road trip with my new bud, Brady.'

She sounded alarmed, 'Where are you going?'

'Florida.'

'But what shall I tell them?'

He shouted back at her as he marched on with Brady in his slipstream, 'Just tell them that Glenarvon Cole said that everything is going to be hunky-dory. Stop worrying.'

Glen and Brady had already left the building before Sissy could ask him anything else.

When they climbed aboard Glen's FusionPlane™, Brady couldn't ever get used to the disappointment of how every vehicle was precisely the same as another. They even self-cleaned when not in use, which meant they didn't even have the detritus to leave a sense of the individual who owned it. They took off vertically and headed east across the USA. Glen asked Brady about his life story, as they had plenty of time to kill. Brady told him about his childhood with the Mahones. He was open and honest about his criminal past but was circumspect about how much he knew about John Kane. He guessed that Glen knew about his time with Bodhi's mother, Libby Skye, as he now owned her Malibu home. Glen listened in a non-judgemental manner. Brady wanted to dislike the guy, as he was in possession of Rhea, in Brady's mind. However, resistance was futile, Glen was charming, and he was the kind of guy who Brady respected. He might be in charge of the only game in town, but he carried himself like a rebel and an outlaw.

After a couple of hours into the journey, Glen said, 'I know you like the big machines. Marjorie told me. Look ahead. Can you see?'

Brady peered through the cockpit, and he detected what appeared to be a black smudge which was slowly growing more prominent on the horizon. 'Yeah, I see it.'

'That's a formation flight of three-hundred and thirty-three HeavyLoaders™ in nine columns spraying Dallas. I thought you might like to fly over them.'

'That would be real cool.'

'They are locked in formation. They do multiple flyovers. The sprayers have different jobs to complete. Some will concentrate on concrete, while others break down the steel and glass. There's still about a decade of spraying to do here, but eventually, it will all break down and then seep back into the ground.'

Glen guided his FusionPlane™ into a rapid climb, and then he levelled off, and they slowed down so that they were at about the same speed as the vast array of HeavyLoaders™ below them. Brady noted that Glenarvon Cole seemed to have the authority to fly at any level he chose. Brady had never been able to get this high in the upper atmosphere, and he had pushed his FusionPlanes™ and FusionPassengerJets™ to their altitudinal limits. It reinforced his view of how important Glenarvon Cole was to the Green organisation. The subsonic vibrations shook the plane, and Brady loved the sensation.

He looked down upon the swarm of gigantic cream-coloured machines and exclaimed, 'They look like giant sea turtles from up here.'

Glen said, 'I must take you over the oceans, one day. Did you know they've been entirely cleared of surface garbage?'

'No.'

'Have you ever been on a FusionSubmarine™?'

Brady turned his gaze away from the HeavyLoader™ fleet for a moment and looked in amazement at Glen. 'Of course, you would have submarines. Why hadn't I thought of that?'

'There are thousands of them at sea, right now. They've been cleaning up the ocean's bed for the past fifty years. When we have finished our work, the Earth will be in the rudest health of Her entire existence.'

Brady stared dreamily around the scene beneath him as the re-wilding of Dallas continued with its inexorable progress. Glen said, 'One day, I'd love to take you on my sub to see the glory of life under the sea. You'd love it down there.' Brady imagined the wonderful creatures he could sketch. He also remembered the sermon about the shark over the dinner table by Samuel Beardon the Third. Brady asked, 'You know about me, but I don't know much about you. What's your story?'

'We have something in common, you and I.'

'Like what?'

'We were both abandoned as babies.'

'That's not cool, man. I hope you were left in a better place than me.'

398

Glen smiled sympathetically, 'I was born in England, but I've spent most of my adult life in the States.'

'I thought I couldn't pick your accent.'

'I was left outside a touring party of artists and political activists, called the Arts Collective. I was born sometime in 2029. I was about three months old when I was abandoned.'

'Hey, so you're older than me.' Brady intervened.

Glen continued, 'Anton insisted on looking after me - nobody else wanted the responsibility. He called me Glenarvon as a joke, as he claimed I came out of nowhere - I still don't get it. He wanted to call me Glenarvon Galt, but Terri, their leader, said I should be called Cole because I had black hair. I'm just grateful that they didn't name me after a fossil fuel.'

This joke went over Brady's head, but he laughed anyway, 'Political activists - that explains a lot already.'

Glen smiled, 'You're a believer in nurture, not nature.'

'Without knowing who our true parents are, what else have we got to go on?'

'Spoken like a true scientist, my friend.'

Brady asked, 'Then what happened?'

'I was looked after by a psychotic cartoonist - I kid you not - called Anton - the goy I mentioned, earlier. He was a paranoid schizophrenic and conspiracy theorist. You could say I had an unconventional upbringing.' He laughed heartily. 'At first, like many kids, I wanted to be a vet, but then I drifted into splinter groups that took direct action against laboratories that used animal experiments. And then, I ended up leading a direct-action environmental group called the Green Account. I made the national news when I climbed into the trees in the Amazon Rainforest, and the loggers continued to cut down the tree I was in. This brought me to the attention of Samuel Beardon - or Samuel Beardon the First, as he was subsequently titled. He, in turn, led me to John Kane. He sold me his vision to repair the damage done to the world. He said he was looking for somebody as brave as me to lead a huge environmental group. He called it his New Green Deal. I loved the name. I felt the fates calling me.'

Brady could tell by the reverence with which Glen uttered John Kane's name, that he had no idea about what this monster was really like. He was taken aback that he mentioned Samuel Beardon the First as his initial contact with the organisation, but he held these thoughts in check. He already liked the guy - a lot, but he reminded himself to be cautious when dealing with the upper echelons of Sattva Systems™. Glen continued, 'And then came Bodhi Sattva and the rest is history, as they say.'

Brady said, 'Could you draw? You said you were brought up by a cartoonist.'

'No. Not at all. I was a bit of a hellraiser. I used to climb anything that didn't move, trees, building frames - it was no wonder that I ended up helping with the rigging for the Arts Collective events in my early teenage years.

Glen brought his FusionPlane™ down next to the rocket launch site on the abandoned NASA complex. The whole area was covered in verdant green vegetation, and the local wildlife scattered as they alighted the vehicle. Brady saw one giant but lonely tree in the near distance, except it didn't seem to have any branches. Glen marched forward, and it didn't even occur to Brady not to follow. After a few minutes, they stood before the bushy tower that was the size of a skyscraper.

Brady said, 'What is this place?' *Why have we come so far to see this?*

'This is Cape Canaveral. This is where they used to launch all their space rockets.' It was apparent in Glen's tone that he wasn't impressed.

'Oh. One of those space centres.' *Please don't give me a Tyrone lecture. I'm tired, and it's been a long trip. I could do without a day out at a museum*, he thought.

Glen smiled, even though it was apparent that this didn't impress Brady Mahone much. 'Come with me. I want to show you that whatever humanity has tried to do to the world, nature always comes through.' He pushed aside the vines and leaves, which opened up an entrance into an underground chamber. The sight which greeted Brady astonished him. He was standing beneath a rocket. There were three vast upturned ceramic bowls, and Brady stared up into the black void. Glen said, 'You are standing beneath the latest in the last throws of the dice of the non-Greens. This marks the betrayal of Mother Earth. If she had a relationship with man, then this was the point where she was about to be dumped.'

Brady could spot a lecture from a mile away. He picked up on an over-enthusiastic tone of voice which Tyrone used to adopt when he wanted him to be enthralled in the vastness of space. All light-years and millions of this, and billions of that. Brady was impressed enough already by the gigantic proportions of this rocket. His imagination raced with images of white flames and dripping chemicals being forced onto the point where he was standing. He imagined being enveloped in the fire and surviving everything it could throw at him. He daydreamed about being invincible and then watching it levitate away from him and then blast away into the sky.

Glen was disappointed that Brady obviously didn't want to listen to the *pay-off* of his anecdote. However, he was thrilled at the shock and awe the sight of this technological beast had inspired in him. He let Brady have time to let the picture fully imprint itself on his memory.

Brady said, 'Awesome, thanks, man.'

Glen said, 'Do you want to climb it?'

Brady had no desire to do that. He could handle heights, but only when he had to - he didn't climb for fun. 'It's not my thing.'

'I'm going to. It's what I come here for. Do you mind?'

'No. Knock yourself out.'

Glen marched out determinedly while Brady inhaled the immenseness of this place. It struck him that the colours of this subterranean world were the same as Sattva Systems™. The internal shells of the rocket boosters were the same ceramic cream, but within this place, where the vegetation had reclaimed the launchpad, everything was moss green. There was little point in checking out the other three rocket boosters, but Brady wasn't going to leave until he had taken memory snapshots of every square inch of the place. He might not have been remotely interested in astrophysics, but he would have loved to have driven this thing.

He went around and around the launchpad until he finally got bored with the place. He ventured outside, and the sunlight blinded him. He could hear a distant rustling sound. His eyes slowly adjusted. Brady covered his brow with his hand and gazed up at the rocket, which was covered in vines and vegetation. He saw birds had nested in it, and then he spotted Glen, about three-quarters of the rocket's height. He was climbing confidently toward the summit. There was something about his sure-footedness which symbolised his leadership.

With a strange sense of certainty, Brady knew that if Glenarvon Cole made a promise, he would keep it, whether to an individual or to a whole race of people.

Glen reached the summit and fearlessly stood atop it, with perfect balance and raised his hands to the sky. Brady knew what this symbolised to him. This was the moment that the Greens had conquered the Trads. The Greens were the winners, and Glenarvon Cole was its champion. Glen jumped and twisted one-hundred and eighty degrees in the air, and Brady gasped, but Glen knew the geometry of his fall as he landed on the rocket tip as it sloped away from him. He caught the first vines he fell upon and then nimbly made his way back down to Earth.

Only afterwards, Brady remembered that even if Glen had fallen, his RedSuit™ would have saved him. When Glen had completed his descent, he went over to join Brady. Glen patted Brady on the back and said, 'Have you had a good time today?'

'The best. It was awesome. Do you climb mountains and stuff?'

'I could, but I've always chosen not to for fun or sport.'

'Why not?'

'You'd think I was being deep or heavy. I can see you're not into those kinds of discussions. I wouldn't want to bore you.'

Brady was impressed that he had noted that. It always irritated him a little that Tyrone never understood this about him, which was a pity as he liked the guy. Brady was concerned that he hadn't shown enough gratitude for a terrific day out. *It won't hurt to listen and let him get it out of his system. I'll encourage him. It'll make the return trip go quicker.* Brady deduced that there was no point treating him as a potential enemy. 'No. It's cool. If we're going to be buddies…'

Glen smiled with a sense of satisfaction like a soldier would smile at successfully completing a mission. 'It's a question of mindset. I like climbing all over man-made structures. I used to love free climbing skyscrapers. However, if I climbed any of Mother Nature's mountains, I would feel dirty, as if I was expressing myself as her conqueror. She's had enough of mankind raping and exploiting Her. She deserves more respect.'

They walked back to Glen's FusionPlane™, and Brady took one long last lingering look at the Green rocket before boarding. The vehicle completed its vertical lift-off and headed back on its four-hour journey to Boulder Creek. Glen said, 'Can you remember the date of the first Green Day when the revolution was won?'

'I remember it better as my last day in the Modern Ridgecrest Supermax Penitentiary.' Brady laughed at his own joke. 'Yeah, it was the 25th of June 2084.'

'Well, that rocket was due to set off for Mars on the 26th.'

They lifted off and headed westwards. Glen said, 'Your FusionPlane™ service should be finished by the time we get back. You'll notice it is much smoother, and the FusionBattery™ should be recharged to last the next hundred years.'

There was a tone in Glen's voice that it was as if he was taking it for granted that Brady would still be around for that long. Brady dwelt on this as the miles flew by. He ensured he didn't miss the convoy of HeavyLoaders™ as they made the return flight over Dallas. He didn't want to talk because it would have interrupted his appreciation of their power and precision.

He approved of Glen's lack of neediness. He was at ease with the silence between them, and he was not living the Glenarvon Cole show. He was a working man - just doing his job. Brady finally shared an observation, 'Is it a coincidence that the place looked like it had a connection with Sattva Systems™?'

Glen returned from his focussed concentration on flightpaths. 'In what way?'

'The colours. It had a cream and green vibe to it.'

'Well spotted, my friend. No flies on you.' He laughed, 'Sattva Systems™ did a lot of work with NASA. We used them to launch our satellites for our Satts™ and SattNav™. Bodhi used NanoDiamondoidShells™ and FusionBatteries™ to ensure they would last for thousands of years, if not forever, in space. They stole our technology - they used the word, adapted.'

Brady said, 'happens all the time in business, I woulda thought.'

Glen nodded, 'It was the last straw - not that they had stolen it, but what they were going to do with it.'

Brady might not have been interested in NASA or space, but now they were on his territory. He was discussing people stealing and their rivals taking revenge. This was a mindset he was used to; this was the collective mentality of criminals and conspiracy theorists. 'Go on, you've gotta tell me now.' He laughed.

'They were using our technology to colonise Mars.'

Brady was disappointed in the answer. He was hoping it was about saving millions of dollars or somebody getting rich. 'So, what's the problem. Sounds reasonable to me.'

'I don't want to give any disrespect to you, but this starkly illustrates our different world views. You see the world and its problems through the eyes of a Trad. I see the world through Her eyes. She had given us everything, and when we had taken everything, she had to give, we run off to start a new life somewhere else, anywhere else. And then we leave her to die. I couldn't do that. We couldn't let that happen.'

'But the Earth was going to die at some time. We all gotta go sometime. We can't go worrying about it. We just gotta live while we can. That's nature, isn't it?'

Glen hadn't dealt with a Trad point of view in decades. He said bluntly, 'That's *human* nature.'

Brady shrugged, 'Maybe.' He said, 'What's done is done, I suppose.'

Glen tried to sound more conciliatory, 'We took the point of view that man had the wherewithal to put his mind to saving *this* planet, rather than looking for a new one. We have plans to extend Her life by billions of years.'

Brady said, 'But won't the fire go out on the Sun eventually. I mean, all fires do.' He added, 'My friend Tyrone says that the Sun will get bigger, but that doesn't happen to any fire I've seen. Yes, I could see how a fire would spread in a forest, but they don't have no forests in space.'

'I don't want to get into a discussion about astrophysics, but can we just assume for a moment that your friend is correct. The science leads us to the conclusion that your friend is right - the Sun will become a red giant and will engulf the Earth in about four and a half billion years time.'

'Sounds like astrophysics to me, but I suppose you've started.' Brady went into the same mode when his Pops used to go down one of his conspiracy theory rabbit holes.

'At the moment, we are clearing up the mess that man has created in the last few centuries, and we'll complete that in the next few decades.'

'I can't argue with that.' He would have argued about the death of the Trads, but he didn't want to make this conversation last a moment longer than necessary.

'Once this has been completed, we plan to build a RedShell™ around the whole planet to protect Her against extreme heat and radiation. Even if it takes a million years to research and create, we have that time. At the rate we were going, we would have been lucky to get to the end of this century. I can't think of anything worthier to fight for in the history of mankind. Surely, you can see that.'

'Yeah. If it's true.'

'It is, my friend, and you will play your part in this. You will have to be strong; you will carry the weight of the world on those broad shoulders of yours.'

19.UNSETTLED

Brady picked up his newly serviced FusionPlane™ and took off as he planned to fly down to his Malibu home to see how Helgarth and Amie were settling in. As he was flying over the vast industrial complex of Sattva Systems™, he saw a puzzling sight. He observed Glenarvon Cole striding down toward the main entrance, and then he saw Rhea emerge. He watched them approach each other, and they shook hands. There wasn't a warm embrace or a kiss between lovers, not even a peck on the cheek. They shook hands like business partners.

He dwelt on what this could mean all the way back to Malibu.

Amie could tell that Brady was distracted when he arrived in Malibu. She greeted him and said, 'We really love it here.'

'Great. I'm glad.' He strode on ahead, and Amie struggled to keep up with Brady's march.

'I know we are only six weeks, but the Orange™ would never have let it get this far on if there was a problem.'

'That's good then.'

Amie tried to sound excited, 'Before you do anything else - because I know you're a busy man. Can I just show you what we've been working on?'

'Sure.' *I'm not a relationship kinda guy, but can you have a girlfriend where you shake hands with them? Is it a Green thing? If it is, then I haven't seen it.* He asked, 'You know, if you hadn't seen Helgarth for a long time, how would you greet her?'

Amie tried to figure out if she had anything to be concerned about. She feared he might be planning to send Helgarth away. 'Xe's not going anywhere, is xe?'

'No. I'm just curious.'

Amie smiled beatifically as if she could feel the longing in her stomach for her absent lover. 'I'd fling my arms around xyr and give xem the biggest hug I could, and then I would kiss xem.'

'You wouldn't shake her hand then?'

She laughed, 'You are funny. You know that - right?' She caught up with him and grabbed him by the hand, in part to slow him down and also to lead him. They went into his enormous and luxurious home. Amie lost her bearings at one point, as she was still getting used to the layout, but she soon found the room she wanted to show him. She opened the door and said, 'Voila.'

Brady looked around the nursery. It was decorated all in blue. He wondered where they would get the paint but guessed it was something to do with a Nano-something. He saw the old toys which Libby used to keep for the children of her many guests. There were fire trucks, garages, and games with model cars and planes. 'I love it. Thank you, Amie.'

'Helgarth helped.'

'Where is she, by the way?'

'Xe's changing back to Helga. We weren't expecting you. You don't mind - do you?'

'No. That's fine.'

Amie said, 'When we've delivered your five boys. You don't have any objections to us bringing up our children as Pure Greens by any chance?'

'No. They will be yours to raise as you wish.'

Amie said needlessly but, in a manner, to flatter an alpha-Trad ego and his sense of fatherhood. 'It will be nice to think that our children will have five big brothers to watch out for them.' She knew that hers and Helgarth's children would have the RedSuits™ and the Security Protocols™ to protect them.

He smiled, 'Yes. I'll ensure they know their responsibilities to their younger…I don't know what you'd call them…brothers…sisters…siblings…'

'Sibs.'

'Hey, I nearly got it.' He laughed but then added, 'Is there any circumstance where you would shake Helga's hand if you hadn't seen her in ages?'

Amie was puzzled by Brady's obsession. She gave it a lot of thought, imagining various scenarios until she finally delivered her verdict. 'The only thing I could think of is if we had to keep it secret, or if we were ordered to…' She laughed and joked, 'on pain of death.'

Brady stuck around his Malibu home, which more and more felt like *their* Malibu home, for a few weeks. At first, their excitement was reassuring, for it made him relieved that they didn't feel that they had been used by him. But soon, their incessant baby talk bored him. He couldn't tell them to leave, so he started making business excuses to get out of there. It was a massive home he owned, but it felt like it was shrinking by the day.

He left under the guise of checking in with his Reps across the Western Seaboard. He lied, 'I need to keep the Green Credits coming in, to provide for a growing family.' He hadn't worked out that this was an arrangement that suited Amie and Helgarth perfectly.

20.TIMELINES

Brady considered taking a FusionCar™ for the trip. It appealed to him because he liked the idea of being on his own for long hours on the road. It was almost a superstitious feeling which made him change his mind and take his FusionPlane™ instead. He thought about his Pops a lot lately. He wondered if it was an age thing with seeing conspiracies everywhere. He had a strange sense that his destiny was being chosen for him. *What did he mean with that comment about carrying the weight of the world on my shoulders?*

He decided to fly over the Ridgecrest Supermax. It didn't matter that it was out of the way. *How can it be out of the way if I ain't got no particular place to go?* He wasn't overly surprised to find the Modern Ridgecrest Supermax Penitentiary didn't exist anymore. There wasn't a single trace of it left. *I suppose it was abandoned and uninhabited real quick.* He wondered if there was a clue to his sense of unease if he returned to the place where it all began for him. He then took the scenic route over the Sequoia National Park. It seemed to ease his worried mind to see a place that was the same as before the human world changed irrevocably. *How come they seem so sure that I have still got a long time to live? I ain't Green, I'm a Trad. I knows it and feels it in my bones.*

At the beginning of this impromptu field trip, he had planned to do surprise visits on half a dozen of his Reps but ended up spending the whole day in the air. By teatime, he had to decide whether to return to Malibu or head somewhere else for the evening - or maybe longer. He laughed at the irony of choosing to head to San Martin to see the Bear. *For saying I'm such a hotshot businessman, why do I think I've traded my home in Malibu for theirs in San Martin?*

The Bear greeted Brady excitedly, 'I've received wonderful news, brother.'

'What's that?'

'Bodhi is returned unto us. He is saved. He is risen.'

'Oh. I'm pleased for you. You must be relieved.'

The Bear exclaimed, 'Relieved? We are exalted.' He hugged Brady and almost dragged him inside. 'Get ready to feast, my friend. Tonight, is a celebration. We are all choosing the brightest colours to wear, we want to have fun, we are going to play games and tell stories.'

Brady felt as if he had made a mistake. He wasn't in the mood for putting on an act. He liked Bodhi, but not that much. 'Great. Do you mind if I shower first and maybe take a short nap? It's been a long day.'

He wandered off upstairs to one of the spare rooms and flopped onto the bed. He laced his fingers around the back of his head and stared at the ceiling. *Am I being railroaded? Should I have ever tried to make friends with these people?* He decided to make his excuses and leave. There was something inside him that didn't sit well with him sharing in the celebrations of the Greens when the Trad cultures were on the brink of extinction. He didn't want to stay here, and he didn't want to return to Amie and Helgarth's baby talk - even if they were his babies. He wasn't in the mood for any plans the Bear would make for visiting Bodhi.

He told the assembled partygoers that he had forgotten some vital business documents back at the Mahone Ranch and quietly left. They were in such an excited state that they didn't plead with him to stay. They could see that Brady wasn't in the mood, and it was probably better if he kept his grumpiness to himself.

Brady took off in his FusionPlane™ and pounded the dashboard with his fists in frustration. A piece of the dashboard broke and fell out. He panicked and checked that he wasn't going to crash due to him damaging the plane. After cursing himself for being so stupid, he flew his FusionPlane™ carefully back to the Mahone Ranch. He didn't let the debris of the dashboard and components distract him.

Once he had landed, he examined the damage. He wondered if it would repair itself, as that was what he had been led to believe. He could see that the navigation unit appeared to slot back readily into place, except for a different coloured piece attached to it. He kept trying to make it fit, repeatedly. He grew frustrated as he had innately believed that real men, by simply being male, should be able to fix mechanical things. He pulled the seemingly superfluous piece of technology away from the navigation unit, and as he relocated this into place, it fitted snugly, and he watched, bemused, as the dashboard began to repair itself. After ten minutes, there were no signs of damage at all.

He wanted to check that the FusionPlane™ was still operating correctly so he took off and went for a quick flight over West McFarland. The additional piece of technology that he had rested upon his knee lit up with a string of numbers that kept changing slightly. *Those are coordinates. I'm being fucking tracked.*

Brady stopped worrying about the capability of his flying machine as he was overwhelmed by a sense of paranoia. *The last time I heard of one of my buddies being tracked was back in the old days by the sneaky bastards in the FBI.* He knew that they would hide things in ever more ingenious places, so he was prepared to tear the place apart. He considered the tracker. *I'm convinced they haven't rebuilt the internet, so they musta only put these things in stuff that moves around with me.* He went back inside to think.

I'm guessing they've put tracking units in every vehicle. Marjorie always offers to service my vehicles for free - even the Green Bike. I gotta assume that every single one of them is busted.

He knew he couldn't break open the dashboards on every vehicle. *I gotta trade them. I'll have to take a loss, but it's gotta be done.* He knew that once all the vehicles were swapped, the new data his snitches would receive would inform them that he had found them. *It will be interesting to see who gives themselves away. It's gotta be Bodhi, but who else? What about Glen. He seemed keen to take me out on a day trip to do a spot of male bonding. So, that means I've got Bodhi, Glen's a maybe, but Marjorie is a definite...*

He tried to figure out how long this had been going on and why. If the Green Bike was involved, then this could go back nearly sixty years. The FusionCar™, if that was the first, would go back forty years - or was it a recent development? He started to dwell on what had happened recently. *It might not be Bodhi. What if this is something that Glenarvon Cole had done since he took the reins? He might have a different way of operating.*

He thought of the vehicles, but then his mind went back to the items he always had with him. He took off his sneakers and jeans. He pulled them apart but found nothing.

Then he reached for his Poacher's trench coat. He emptied all his many pockets. *I really don't need half this stuff I carries around with me.* He laughed. Some items he had to try hard to recall what they were, as he had picked up many things, he thought could come in handy one day - but they never did. He then examined every stitch from around the collar and the inside of the coat. He was becoming convinced that this would be the one item of clothing he would bug if he wanted to know the whereabouts of Brady Mahone. And then he found something. Around the bottom of his coat, near the inner lining, he spotted some stitching that was somewhat different to the rest. It wasn't a different colour, but it was stitched in a slightly different pattern. He grabbed a razor-sharp knife, and he carefully unpicked it. He found the tracker. It was smaller and less sophisticated than the one in his FusionPlane™, but the co-ordinates flashed their dim green numbers.

He held it up and examined it from every angle. And then he thought again about that handshake between Glenarvon Cole and Rhea Laidlaw.

21. A VISITOR FOR AMIE

Rhea landed in the Green Communal FusionPlane™ Parking Lot in Malibu. She rented a FusionCar™ to drive up to the luxurious private property on the clifftops with stunning views over the Pacific. The summer sun and the smell of saltwater on the light breeze reminded her of her holidays in California when she was a Trad. Rhea drove up to the black railed gate, which marked the entrance to the Brady Mahone residence.

She informed the guard that she had come to visit Brady Mahone. When she was told that he wasn't at home, she asked to see Amie Lopez. The guard called through to the house, and after a few minutes, the head of the serving staff came to the gate to greet and escort her to see Amie.

'I'm Hunter. Amie will be down shortly. Is there anything I can get you?'

'A coffee would be nice.' She scanned the room just as she had observed everything on the way into the building. All those years of training would never desert her. She sat on a comfortable chair, overlooking a lower level where a hot tub bubbled away, even with nobody in it. She mused on the waste of energy. Beyond this was the most spectacular views over the Pacific she had ever seen. The opulence was an assault on her senses after decades of Green living.

Amie said softly, in an almost genteel manner, 'Hello, Rhea. So very nice to see you.'

As Amie's Disciple in San Martin, Amie had been a brash woman who skirted on the very edges of what was permitted in the Green community, but she seemed to have blended seamlessly into her new wealthy surroundings. She looked elegant, even with the minor bump which displayed her pregnancy.

Rhea said, 'I'm sorry I came unannounced, but I'm looking for Brady. Do you know where he is?'

Hunter came in with Rhea's coffee. 'Amie, is there anything you would require?'

'No. Thank you. That will be all.'

Hunter turned and moved smoothly away.

Amie said, 'Brady said he had important business to attend to. He doesn't tell me where he's going. He used to in the old days when I lived with my Moms. I used to love to hear stories from the outside world, but he doesn't feel the need to tell me anything now.'

'Do you know when he will be back?'

'I haven't a clue. I'm sorry. How is everything back in San Martin? We hope to visit with the babies.' She rubbed her stomach. 'We want to stay in touch. Unfortunately, Brady won't let anyone stay here. That's why I wasn't sure if I should let you in. However, you are a Disciple, so I suppose that's different.'

Rhea looked at Amie's stomach and then back at Amie's face. She was staring dreamily out to the ocean. 'You are looking well. How is the pregnancy going?'

She smiled, 'With the OrangeSuit™, it feels like I'm getting progress reports at an almost psychic level. Everything is perfect. I'm going to have the son, which Brady demanded. He wants strong boys, and that's what he'll have.'

'And Helgarth? How is xe getting on?'

'Great. She loves it here. We've got so much time, and there is no labouring in the fields in Malibu.' A serene smile seemed to glow from her.

'Do you mind if I take a look around your wonderful home while I'm here?'

'Yes. I do mind. Brady was insistent. Any visitors, especially Bodhi, Marjorie, Glenarvon Cole or you, must not be given access, freely or otherwise. And I'm under strict instructions not to let any of you near his precious vehicles.' She didn't want to sound too unfriendly. She feared being barred from entering San Martin for refusing a request from its Disciple. 'I'm sorry, Rhea - it's not me. I'd love to show you everything, it's like a palace, but it is Brady's home, not mine. He is the king of the castle, so to speak.'

Rhea smiled. Amie had unwittingly given her a lot to consider. 'I understand. I was just being nosey. I knew Samuel and the others would want to know everything about where their friends were living and how they were settling in.'

'I would love to show you around, but...' She added, 'Brady wants to put the staff on his payroll. He doesn't want them employed by Sattva Systems™. He's been paranoid since he knew he was going to be a father. He doesn't trust anybody.'

'I'm sure he trusts you. He's known you since you were a baby.'

Amie stroked her stomach again and appeared lost in a distant reverie. 'Yes. I'm the nearest thing to family he has.' She shuffled uncomfortably as she said this. She changed the subject. 'You've travelled a long way. Would you like to stop for dinner? Hunter could get you anything you fancy. We have the most amazing chefs.'

Rhea wondered if she could find out any more information by staying for a few more hours but thought better of it. 'Thank you, but no. I have urgent business back home. You've obviously heard that Bodhi is recovering.'

'Yes. I can't wait to hear about the next Suits™. I can guess you're busy. Say hi to everyone back home for me - please.'

'I will.' Hunter appeared out of seemingly nowhere, almost as soon as she had got up out of her chair.

'If you'd like to follow me.' He said courteously.

She took one last look out at the stunning view of the Pacific and watched the cotton clouds drift lazily across the horizon, and then followed Hunter back out into the grounds and then to her rented FusionPlane™.

22. THE RING

Brady landed just outside the Park in Cupertino. Recently, as the deaths mounted among the drugged-up centenarians, some had started to show their resentment toward the phoney Trad, Brady Mahone, with his FusionPlane™ and still youthful appearance. They had begun to throw rocks at his vehicle. They knew it was useless, but one or two came up with the theory that, one time, the shields might be weaker, and a rock might make it through to its target.

At first, it amused Brady, and he thought it was good exercise for them. An ancient couple, who had taken in a couple of stray Doberman Pinchers, had taken it upon themselves to train them into guard dogs. They used to set them onto Brady but had refrained after the Security Protocols™ had frozen them in mid-attack. Joey and Joan thought the Film would harm their vicious dogs with its abominable Green materials.

He strode up to the entrance, and he saw a much bigger pile of dead bodies than usual, awaiting the Greens Operation Clean-Up crews. He grimaced when he saw the body of Joey in the gruesome pyramid of human remains.

He assessed the Trad population of Cupertino was down to its last few dozen, and the big barman in the sky seemed to have rung last orders for the survivors. It was already far more depressing here than he had ever known, which chimed with his current mood.

El Duque had seen his old drug buddy arrive and shuffled down to see him. 'Hey man, good to see you, buddy. I only wish it could have been in more auspicious circumstances.'

'What do you mean?'

'We've had a lot of deaths, man. It seems we can't live forever after all, even with the finest Nootropics known to man. Times up.'

Brady patted him on the shoulder. He was gentle as even El Duque looked like he had lost a lot of strength in the last few months. 'Let's not waste the time you got left. Shall we share some precious moments together with some Brady Bombs?'

'I'll give a stash to go. They don't work for me anymore. I think I've built up a tolerance to them. I had a real bad trip last time. I hope you don't mind, buddy.'

'No. That's fine.' He thought, *I'll get out of my head back at the Mahone Ranch instead.* He wondered that if Sattva Systems™ couldn't track him anymore, might they not stake out his usual haunts. *I'll have to find another place to get bombed out of my mind.*

Brady watched the colour drain from the face of El Duque, and he grabbed him by the arm to stop him from falling. He picked him up as if he weighed the equivalent of a feather. 'Don't you worry, none. I gotcha. I know the way from here.'

He carried the old man to their usual haunt and placed him gently on a beanbag. 'Are you ok?'

'I ain't gonna lie to you, brother. I've seen better days.' He laughed feebly. 'Go fill yourself a jar of Brady Bombs. You know where I keeps 'em.'

'Cheers, man.' Brady grabbed a jar and filled it to the brim, and then sealed the cap on tightly.

El Duque said, 'I got something to tell you.'

Brady flopped down on the beanbag next to him. 'Shoot.'

'Our old CEO, Tia Cassandra, has got loads of dirt on John Kane.'

'Thanks, Buddy, but she can't have any worse than I already got. I found a ton of stuff at the Los Banos Police Department. There were FBI files, CIA files, all kinds of stuff. I even had a Judge go through it - not that you can do anything about it now.'

El Duque laughed and coughed, 'Business back then was all about dirty tricks and cyber-espionage. I know she had lots of incriminating stuff on John Kane and Sattva Systems™, wouldn't you like to know what she's got?'

I ain't got anything better to do, and it might be good to hang out in a new place - away from prying eyes. 'I take it this Tia doesn't live here, or I woulda known about it.'

'She was away on the day of the Green Revolution at her experimental desert farm. She would have had plenty of food, and she grew the same Nootropics as we do - they were her idea - to boost creativity and precision thinking. There's a good chance that she might still be alive.'

Brady stroked his chin. He wondered if she might have more of the good stuff. 'Where can I find her.'

He expected El Duque to go hunting for an address, but it seemed imprinted on his mind. 'She was in Cima, in the Mojave National Preserve, just off the Morning Star Mine Road.' He added, 'She might have the dirt on you. She had mentioned your name, that's why I wanted to know more about you. If you were important to the corporation…' He spluttered, 'We haven't got long left. We can feel it. It's making one or two of us go a little crazy. I think if Tia is still alive, then her time might not be long.' He coughed again. 'This information ain't gonna be no use to anybody but you, now. You may as well have it.' He forced himself to stand up. Brady helped him. 'I'm going to have to let you go. I'm exhausted and need to rest.'

'Hey, man, no problem. I'll find my own way out.'

'No. I'll escort you. I want them to see that you mean us no harm.'

Brady didn't know what to make of this. He hadn't raised a hand or even his voice to the Cupertino hippies. He walked alongside El Duque. He held him up with one hand while cradling his Brady Bombs under his other arm.

As they emerged into the Californian sunshine, El Duque's legs buckled under him, and he died on the spot.

The other residents in the Ring came rushing to his aid, but it was too late. A decrepit old man shouted, 'He did it. He killed El Duque. He's stealing his Nootropics.'

As he turned around, he saw Joan throw a rock at him. He didn't duck, as he expected to be protected by the Security Protocols™, but they didn't appear. The rock glanced off his forehead with a loud thud. He yelled, 'Ow…watch it, lady, you could have someone's eye out with that.' He winced with pain. She threw another one, and it hit him again on the head. The jar of Brady Bombs fell to the floor and shattered on the rock which had just hit him. Brady was furious. He stormed over to the old woman and punched her. He killed her with one blow.

A Doberman Pincher appeared and grabbed his arm. It bit threw his Poacher's coat through to his arm, and its jaws tightened around his flesh. Brady howled in agony. He spotted the other dog coming for him, and he also saw other elderly residents collecting rocks. He guessed they weren't throwing them yet in case they hit the dogs. He whipped out his blade and stabbed the first dog quickly and repeatedly, like a prisoner attack with a shiv in jail. The dog didn't let go immediately until Brady stabbed it in the throat. As the second dog leapt at Brady, he stabbed it, underhand in the stomach, and then finished it off with a slash to its throat.

He didn't have time to dwell on the dogs as rocks flew at him from all directions. He raised his coat over his head for limited protection and ran and barged past his geriatric aggressors until he finally made the safety of his Green protected Fusion-Plane™.

23.MORNING STAR

Brady's FusionPlane™ wobbled on its vertical take-off. The old folks of the Ring around the Cupertino Park cheered heartily as if they had waited years for one act of defiance of the new world order that would strike a blow. It didn't matter that Brady called himself a Trad; to the survivors, he was a collaborator, and he had got rich on the back of their suffering. They would talk about their own mini rebellion with pride until their dying days.

Many had only put up with Brady out of respect for El Duque and his reasoning that Brady was their only source of news from the outside world. Now, they knew they didn't have long left in this world, and it could go and rot without them.

They watched on as a few gathered around the corpse of El Duque. They lifted him tenderly and moved slowly to the edge of the Park, where the Green NanoShell™ held them captive, and they placed his body onto the other bodies which had not yet been sprayed with the Green goo of their oppressors. They bowed their heads out of respect. They then moved to the older piles of the dead, in advanced stages of decomposition and bowed their heads again. Until they returned to live out the rest of their few remaining days ahead.

Brady struggled with his sense of direction. He couldn't remember the last time he felt in this much pain. He thought he was going to pass out. He caught glimpses of the jeering crowd beneath him, but his vision was swirling. He felt the blood trickling down his throbbing head, and the pain from the dog bites on his arm was excruciating. His heavy eyelids were threatening to remain permanently closed. In his daze, he called on the autopilot and gave out the only address he could focus on, the one he didn't want to forget. He called out, 'Cima, Morning Star Mine Road - anything related to a farm there or Tia Cassandra.' He wasn't sure if he had the information correct or even whether the autopilot would work, but at least he knew the FusionPlane™ wouldn't crash if it had a destination of some kind. Brady then fell into unconsciousness.

He didn't know whether he had passed out for hours or even days. He came round, and the FusionCoolers™ of the vehicle were on full blast. The windshield had darkened against the blinding light of the Sun outside. He felt the crusts of blood on his forehead, and he took off his coat and was shocked at how deep his bite wounds were on his forearm. He knew he wasn't thinking straight. *I used to heal quicker than this. My skin must be getting old.*

For the first time in years, Brady doubted that he was invincible. He dwelt depressingly on the idea that he would die soon. He understood why those Cupertino geriatrics did what they did, as that's what he would have done. He would have had his last rage against the machine rather than go quietly. *There ain't no dignity in death. It's just the final surrender of the coward.*

He alighted his FusionPlane™. It was blistering hot, and he grimaced in agony. He retrieved his Poacher's coat from the cockpit and put it on as the Sun's rays felt like burning laser beams on his arm. In the distance in front of him, he saw a FusionCar™ trundling along an empty road. He tried to figure out why the FusionPlane's™ autopilot had landed in the middle of nowhere. He rarely used the autopilot. Brady liked to drive all of his machines. He recalled Marjorie, the Sattva Systems™ Fleet Captain, telling him that they would self-land either in authorised parking lots or in the safest places in more rugged terrains.

Brady slowly turned full circle. He felt dizzy. He saw something in the hazy distance in the opposite direction of the road. He checked again. He couldn't be sure if his concussion was playing tricks with his mind. He saw a green smudge on the horizon, but it would mean heading toward the centre of the Mojave Desert and away from the safety of his FusionPlane™ and the open road.

He recalled his last instructions to the autopilot. *Morning Star Mine Road - that must be the road, and anything related to a farm owned by Tia Cassandra* - that must be the farm. In his fugue state, he was still far from making a decision. *I don't get why the autopilot didn't take me to one place or the other, and if I gave it two options, why aren't I slap bang in the middle of both of them?* The wounds on his brow were burning. Even though the desert heat was almost unbearable, some remnants of Brady's survival instincts kicked in. He went back into the cockpit again and retrieved his black cowboy hat and sunglasses. *If I get lost at night, I might freeze to death.*

He looked deep into the desert landscape once more. He put on his sunglasses and looked again for the green smudge. It was no more than a superstitious thought, but he believed that if he could see this with his sunglasses on, that would mean it wasn't a mirage. He located his goal and focused on it until he had made up his mind to head toward it.

Brady strode away. He reasoned he would have to move quickly in this environment. He had travelled no more than a hundred yards when he found the reason for his autopilot's selection for a landing spot. Brady marched straight into quicksand. *Holy fuck! Fucking Jelly Sand.* I don't want to die here - not like this. He struggled and found himself sinking quickly. He thought his heavy coat was dragging him down. He struggled to free himself from the coat, and then he watched how it seemed to float when it was laid out across the top of the quicksand. He sank further and felt that now he was not sinking but being sucked in. *What's wrong with me? You gotta calm the fuck down, Brady Mahone. Get a grip on yourself. Think your way outta this.*

He stopped panicking and raised his arms and stretched them out across the surface. At first, he felt disconcerted as he sank deeper, but then he started to swim through treacle to reach his coat. He slowly edged onto his coat, and even though it sank under the surface, it still floated enough to act as a raft. He pulled himself along to the edge of the quicksand and then pulled himself and his coat back out. He lay exhausted on the hot desert sand. He lay there until the pain in his arm flared up again.

Brady spotted his hat floating on the surface of the quicksand. He put on his coat, which was soaked in the quicksand. He wondered whether it would infect his wound, but it was still better than exposing it to the Sun. He looked around for something to reach and grab his hat. He spotted a Juniper branch. He moved exceptionally carefully toward it. He spotted another smaller area of quicksand, and he wondered if it would be impossible to get to Tia Cassandra's farm from here. He considered giving up and heading back home. *Brady Mahone giving up would be a pussy move.*

He used the Juniper branch and eventually retrieved his hat. It felt like a small victory, and he placed it on his head proudly. He chose to ignore the slimy quality of the quicksand on his forehead, seeing as he had gone to so much trouble to rescue it. He examined the Juniper branch. It was twisty and about eight feet in length. He pulled out a knife from his coat pocket and whittled it into something resembling a staff. He prodded it into the ground. He smiled and then tested it on the quicksand.

It took a few minutes of finding the right rhythm, but soon he was walking and prodding the ground and making progress toward his latest green goal. He came across many areas of quicksand. One appeared to be more than a mile across. He cursed the constant changes of direction.

As the cold of night descended, he estimated that he still had another day's walk to go before he reached the place, which may or may not be Tia Cassandra's farm. Her place was a day in front of him, and his FusionPlane™ was a day behind him. He had reached the point of no return. He no longer cared whether it would be the correct destination. It was just a challenge and a sense of pride to find that green smudge and see what it looked like up-close. He also knew he needed to treat his wounds, and green places usually had medicinal items. The Greens might still have NanoHealing™, although he hadn't seen much of that since the days of the OrangeSuits™. On the other hand, the Trads had old medicines they had to create without power or even fire.

Brady found a sheltered spot to rest. He still had to be careful of the nocturnal predators which would emerge after sundown.

The following morning, Brady was alarmed that he hadn't so much slept, as fallen unconscious, as the sun was high, and he had slept too deeply to be alert to danger. *I was lucky not to be attacked.*

He searched his pockets for his emergency rations he always kept on him, and the old bottles of water he always kept refilled. He ate and drank sparingly and then focussed on his goal for the day. It seemed further away than he recalled. He put it down to a trick of the light and that by now, it was barely casting a shadow.

His arm was throbbing as he shook the dry sand from his coat. He wanted to walk in as few clothes as possible, but he had to protect his wounds. He slipped his arm gingerly through the sleeve, put on his hat and sunglasses, grabbed his staff, and headed off purposefully toward his goal.

After numerous diversions around patches of quicksand - he pondered why there were so many - and a whole day of walking, he finally made it to the strangest looking building he had ever seen. The green smudge was an area of vegetation covered by a transparent plastic tube with a hint of ever-changing shades of green bubbling through it. It reminded him of those light shows the old rock bands used to put on, except they had better colours. It looked to Brady as if they were reacting to subtle changes of light. At the end of the tubular farm was a dome that looked like it was on the wrong planet.

Brady reached out to touch the plastic. He half expected to be able to reach through it, like he would with the NanoShells™, but the flimsy appearance didn't match the feeling of impenetrable stone that his sense of touch informed him this stuff was made of. The green psychedelic patterns spread from where his hand was a moment ago, and he moved along the outer area of the tube until he came to the main entrance of the dome. He pressed a large square button, and the door opened. He stepped inside and the door swished closed behind him. A CCTV screen flickered on, and a stern patrician voice said, 'Who is it?'

'Mahone. Brady Mahone. You don't know me, but...'

'I know you. You are the last person I am going to let in here. This is not a place for bad seeds. Goodbye.'

The screen flickered off. Brady banged on the door, which looked like an airlock for a submarine. His fists barely made more than an inadequate slapping sound on the metal. 'Fuck it, lady. I'm hurt real bad. Can't you at least fix me up?' He spotted a small camera above the blank screen. *I bet they are watching. I'm guessing they haven't had a visitor in more than half a century. I just gotta tease 'em out with something.* He removed his hat and showed his scars on his forehead to the camera. Brady then took off his coat and displayed the weeping wounds from the dog bites on his arm.

There was still no sign of life from the TV screen. He sat down and considered this place and the people or person in it. *They've still got working old tech. That means they got power.* This already felt like a miracle to Brady. He was driven as much by nostalgia as he was by his urgent need for medical attention. He wondered what else they might have inside this weird place.

For all I know, this Tia Cassandra might have been as rich as Bodhi. She was his biggest business rival. I bet she got some tech of her own that the Greens couldn't destroy. She could be an ally. Maybe we are on the same side. Is this my reason for being here? Is that why El Duque was always friendly to Brady Mahone?

Brady spread his coat out on the floor of the lobby. He made a point of exaggerating the thorough search of his pockets. He removed every item, showed it to the camera, and then placed them on the floor if she wanted to zoom in on them. When he'd finished, he spread out his hands in a gesture to signify that this was all he had.

There was no response from the TV screen.

He took off his boots. He emptied his jeans pockets, and still, this made no impression.
Brady looked over his possessions. His knives, one empty and one half-empty water bottle, a half-eaten packet of Green-produced biscuits, assorted tools, his Satt™, his wraparound cloth containing his artist's materials, and his notebooks. He recalled that one of his ways of gaining trust with the Greens was to show off his pictures. He picked up one of his books and showed his drawings to the implacable camera. He preceded to show them every page of all four notebooks, as he wondered if they might think he was a low-life journalist. He wanted to display that he hadn't any notes or codes hidden within their covers.

No response.

He took a small sip of water, as he had precious little to sustain a return trip to his FusionPlane™. He gathered up his possessions and put them back in their respective pockets, especially his knives, as he had to retrieve them at a moment's notice of any threat to his life. He stood up, put on his boots, sunglasses, hat and coat and went to leave. He pressed the square button, but the exit door was unresponsive. 'What the fuck, lady. You don't want to see me, so I'm leaving.' He pressed the button repeatedly, but it refused to open. He sat back down again. He wasn't even sure if anyone had watched him. He felt like a spider trapped under a glass.

They are afraid of me - that's why they don't want to let me in. However, they are curious. That's why they don't want me to leave - yet. Brady stroked his chin. *She said she knew me, but that's impossible if she's a Trad. But this feels like a Green place...* He shook his head. *Green places don't have old tech - remember?* He scratched his forehead and then grimaced as he had forgotten his wound. *They definitely want to*

*know about the outside world but are trying to figure out how to contain me. I ain't
going back to prison. I better keep my guard up. If she was as rich as Bodhi was, I bet
they got all kinds of tricky tech to keep me captive.*

'Hey, lady.' He shouted but then said in a more conciliatory tone. 'If you could just
give me some water and food, then I'll be on my way. I can tell when I'm not welcome.' He waited for a response, but when he received none, he continued, 'I didn't
want to come here anyhows. It was my friend El Duque who had the bright idea that
this broad Tia Cassandra would want to see old Brady Mahone.'

He was considering barging the exit when he remembered his throbbing arm and
then he thought better of the idea. 'El Duque thought we'd like to compare the dirt we
both got on Bodhi Sattva. Y'know, maybe mine is shittier than yours?'

Brady remembered the one item he hadn't shown because he had forgotten about
it as it hung under his T-shirt. He yanked the chain and pulled out the Sattva Ring,
which hung upon it. He put it up to the camera to ensure the lens could pick up the
detail.

There was still no response.

He put away his ring, but then he heard a loud gasping of air, and he watched the
airlock open. He walked inside, and the heavy metal door closed behind him. He
heard the door lock, and he was inside a tiny antechamber. He was alarmed by the
thought that he was trapped, but he tried not to show any fear. He felt the air in the
chamber change, and the sound of hissing surrounded him, and then it fell utterly silent. After about five minutes, the door in front of him opened, and two female figures
stood before him. One looked about seventy in Trad years, and the other looked about
fifty.

The older one addressed him without warmth or humour, 'I'm Tia Cassandra, and
this is my daughter, Dagny.' She didn't wait for Brady to respond. She turned on her
heels, and Dagny followed dutifully, and Brady knew that he had to follow them
accordingly.

Brady asked, 'What is this place?'

Tia marched ahead as if it wasn't her job to answer. Dagny replied, 'Mother was
going to step down as CEO of mASSIVE™ to concentrate on her project to colonise
Mars. This was a New Village simulator. The Orchard was built to re-create the conditions on Mars. Obviously, we never got the chance to achieve our dreams.'

'Glenarvon Cole put a stop to that.'

Tia looked straight in the face of Brady. She didn't say anything. She didn't need
to. Brady had got her attention.

Brady knew his ace was the knowledge he had from the outside world. He needed
to know what they knew already. 'Why do you think you're trapped here?'

Dagny seemed to have been designated to the role of communicating with visitors.
'Fifty-eight years ago, we received messages that our worldwide infrastructure had
malfunctioned. Then we saw on the last remaining news channel, Free News, that the
GreenRevs had destroyed the Internet, and Glenarvon Cole was being interviewed by
a news reporter who'd been poking around in our internal affairs. Her name was Rhea

Laidlaw, and then…nothing. We've been trapped here ever since.'

'You didn't know if your friends, family and colleagues were still alive?'

'No. The first thing we've heard was you mentioning that El Duque was still alive.'

'He died - a couple of days ago. Old age - very old age come to think of it.' Tia Cassandra headed off in a different direction without any indication. 'Your Mom's a bit of a cold fish.'

'She's has her work to do. Mother would consider this gossip.'

'Surely…'

'She'll want your life story later, but she needs to check in on the colony.'

'Isn't that a waste of time? You ain't going to Mars unless you've got a space rocket hidden around here.'

Dagny said, 'Has the space program ceased.'

'Yes. There is no Trad tech left - I would have said, anywhere until I found this place.'

'Oh, you've just robbed us of our purpose.'

'Hey, don't blame me. I'm just the…'

'I know.'

He asked, 'What's the colony.'

'We have a dozen or so volunteers who are still alive. They are simulating conditions on Mars to see if it was feasible to start a new civilisation on another planet.'

Brady wanted to avoid discussing the most boring subject on the planet - to him. The topic of *other* planets. *I suppose I have to build trust, but these people with their heads in the clouds ought to live in the real world.* 'And how's that going?'

'We were pleased with the results. They've built 3D printed domes of water ice in the farm tunnels. The horticultural area is thriving. They've adapted to life in there, and we've had children. The early decades were hard on the mental health of the volunteers, but now it's become their home.'

Brady said, 'You mean, they've been living in an igloo inside a plastic tunnel for all this time, and you haven't told them that they are wasting their lives on something that will never happen?'

'Until today, we thought it might. Anyway, it's for Mother to decide if you're lying. You might have been sent to spread disinformation.'

Brady roared with laughter, 'Pops would have loved this. The fucking scientists and business fucks are the biggest conspiracy theorists of all. You are fucking insane, completely bonkers. Lady, you are fucked. You better get used to it.'

Dagny assessed him and said calmly, 'You would say that.' She led him to a medical centre. 'Any medications we have are obviously decades past their expiry dates, but Doctor Roberts will do his best to attend to your needs. He was one of the finest medical minds in the world, that's why Mother hired him. I'm sure he'll fix you up.' She added, 'You are invited for dinner later. Mother will want your life story. She won't say much. She doesn't believe in wasting breaths.'

'And what will Brady Mahone get in return?'

'She will dissect your information and compare that with her own knowledge, and then efficiently fill in the gaps in your own knowledge. She will impart information, and you will learn. Her role in life is to instil a sense of reason, purpose and a rational view of the world around them. This is why she was so successful.'

Brady tried to work out if this was a good deal. He didn't like showing his hand on the trust of a complete stranger.

Again, she said - as if she was trying to explain something profound to the jock at the back of the class. 'You will walk out of here with the evidence you don't currently possess. It could change your life. I know what my Mother has for you. We just don't know what you have for us.'

'I don't have anything to give you hope. You have lost. The Greens have won.'

'Mother doesn't concern herself with winning and losing. If she beats a wealthy moocher, it brings her no pleasure. If she is defeated and outplayed by a superior rival, it gives her no pain - it makes her want to raise her goals and performance to a higher level. It is a reason to survive. She is indefatigable.'

'Whatever turns you on. Ok...Dagny, you got yourself a deal, but Brady Mahone has a long story to tell.'

Dagny turned away and left sharply.

Doctor Roberts asked Brady to undress and then gave Brady a sedative, which knocked him out instantly, and then he attended to his wounds and his infected arm.

Brady awoke several hours later. He felt clean to the point of being sterilised, and he was dressed in a hospital gown.

'It will take you about a week to be fully recovered. I suggest you take it easy and let the enriched oxygen levels here help to heal your wounds.'

Brady rubbed his eyes and felt groggy. 'I'm feeling hazy.'

'I'll give you something to pick you up. It will enhance your powers of recall. Would you like me to administer it?'

'Knock yourself out, Doc. I'm a hardcore advocate of the Brady Bombs. I'd be a bit of a pussy to refuse the drugs now.'

Doctor Roberts smiled. He went to his pharmacy cabinet and then to a freezer before loading up his hypodermic and injecting Brady. He didn't feel any effects at first.

But after a minute or two, he could sense his mind sharpening. He blinked his eyes open wide. 'Whoa! This is good stuff.'

'I'm glad to hear it. It's not addictive, but if you need a top-up shot in a couple of days, please make your request known to Dagny, and I will accommodate you. It's been too long since I had a new patient.'

'Cheers, Doc.'

'How old are you, Brady?'

'I'm one-hundred years old, sometime this year.'

'I've given you a thorough check-up, and I have to say you are in remarkably good condition for a man your age. In fact, you are in fine fettle for a man half your age.' He joked, 'Enjoy your meal, and eat up all your greens.'

Brady laughed, 'I will.'

Dagny escorted Brady to the dining room. He expected to have a spaceman's macrobiotic meal inside a sterile environment, but instead, he was invited into a grand room that would have befitted an aristocrat from a long-gone age. A servant pulled a chair for him to sit, and silver cutlery was laid out neatly ahead of the evening meal. He accepted the offer of white wine. He guessed these geeks produced their own.

Tia arrived in a black suit and a pearl necklace and was seated at the head of the table. It reminded him of his time with Libby Skye. Dagny dressed more casually but still smart in her black jeans and grey T-shirt.

Over dinner, Brady was questioned about his life. He began with the first days after the Green revolution but was surprised that Tia wanted to know all about his childhood and upbringing. He liked talking about his Pops. He didn't even have any qualms about talking about his criminal exploits. He boasted about many of them. He raced through the early part of his life; Tia required more information from him each time. Her manner reminded him of Judge Jefferson - the one who used to pass sentence on him, not the later version who he came to like and respect.
She surprised him when she said, 'I know all about Archie Mahone. I know what he is and who his known associates are.'

Brady responded, 'I guess you already knew about me - so why the interrogation.'

'I never assume I know everything - eliminating the unknowns leads to better decision making.'

In this game of show and tell, Brady decided to reveal the details about the murder of John Kane. He made a point of stating that he loved his Pops and that he hadn't done anything untoward to him. He also felt the need to share how he had murdered Small Hand Don and set his captive sex-trafficked children free. Tia seemed almost emotional when he spoke about the bravery of the eldest one, Angelique. He noted that Tia was doing the talking while Dagny observed.

Her servants brought out a decanter and glasses and offered them all brandy. It had been many years since Brady's alcohol stocks had run dry, so he ensured he didn't miss out on this opportunity. Brady guessed that they had moved into the next period of the game when his interrogation changed. Tia moved to an armchair without explanation, and Dagny took over. She asked about his recollections from the day of his escape from Ridgecrest Supermax.

She seemed wary. At first, he wondered if she was intimidated by her mother, but then another thought occurred to him. *She's scared of me. I keep forgetting that she's not a Green and therefore unprotected. I could kill them both in a heartbeat and have this place to myself.* He stared at her, letting her know that he held some power over these discussions. She poured herself another drink and then offered another to Brady. He accepted and then left his glass hanging before she poured in more brandy.

Like her mother, Dagny didn't allow him to race over the details. She took him back to go over the first few days post-Revolution to figure out how they succeeded in pulling off this world coup.

Brady asked, 'What did you think had happened?'

'We knew about the non-violent Green demonstrations around the world. We also knew that Sattva Systems™ had developed their body armour. We had informants that the FBI were about to arrest Bodhi Sattva and shut down his business in Boulder Creek, but then the Internet infrastructure collapsed. We saw the Free News broadcast from Wall Street, and that was it. From then onwards we don't know anything at all. We have been in complete isolation here ever since. We lived in the hope that normal life would be restored eventually. We carried on with our research, but nobody ever appeared until you showed up.'

'I don't suppose you've been outside.'

'No. We have CCTV which can see out, but that's it.'

'That's the Green NanoShells™. I'm like you, they call people like us, who are not Green, Trads as in from Traditional Cultures. I'm the only Trad I've met, anywhere in the world, who can move freely through their Shells™. I'm as much a puzzle to the Greens as anybody else.'

Tia looked across as if he had said something which carried weight with her.

Dagny said, 'We observed you taking a bizarre route to our colony. Why was that?'

'I had to find a way around the Jelly Sand. It's fu... everywhere.'

'We never used to have a problem with quicksand.'

'Well, you do now, lady.'

She tried to work out what could cause the molecular structure of the sand to change. She was a scientist and knew that quicksand could be caused by interactions with water. However, there hadn't been any unusual weather patterns in years. She asked, 'How did you find us, precisely?'

'The autopilot on the FusionPlane™ landed in the safest spot after I'd given it your location. It was two days walk away, which was a real ball-ache.'

Dagny put aside any questions about FusionPlanes™ for now. He shouldn't have been able to see them from that distance, as the colony had been designed to blend into the desert-scape. It was part of the planning restraints. 'Did you have binoculars? Could you see it when you landed?'

'Lady, you saw the state I was in. I was barely conscious when I landed. I got out, I saw the road, and then I saw a green smudge on the horizon, and I guessed it was either your place or a mirage.'

'But we don't have a green outer building.'

'You do, now. It's like one of those crazy light shows, except in a thousand shades of green.'

Brady understood what had happened just ahead of Dagny. 'The Green Nano-Shell™ is battling against whatever this place is made of. It felt like stone to me when I put my hand on it.'

Dagny said, 'You're right. Our outer shell is designed to withstand everything a harsh Martian environment can throw at it. Their Nanotechnology has been designed to work with Earth-like conditions.' She pondered on the puzzle for a few more moments, 'The conflict between the two materials is changing the molecular structure of the desert. I don't know what the implications of this mean for us…'

Tia interjected, 'Or the planet. I need to think over the causes and implications.'

Brady said, 'Fuck me. You mean this could spread?'

'It already has. The question is, how far, and at what rate?' She smiled as if she had just discovered she had won a battle in a war she had thought was over. 'That will make Bodhi sit up and take notice. He will have to work with us, after all.'

They all sat in silence for a while as they analysed this latest revelation. Brady made his excuses and went to the bathroom. He needed to think outside of the spotlight of his interrogators.

Have I got any leverage here? They need me to relay this information to Bodhi, which means they have to let me go. Bodhi's plans will go shit if this place destroys the planet over time. How long? Who cares? he's got plans forever if what Glenarvon said was true.

He washed his hands and examined his wounds in the mirror. They were showing positive signs of healing.

What does Tia want? Obviously, she wants freedom. Would she join the Greens if they offered her the chance? I'm guessing she would. She wouldn't live out her days quietly - that tough broad would want a piece of the action.

He washed his face and combed his hair with a brush which was by the sink. He took his time because he still hadn't worked out his angle.

I could sell the information for a ton of Green credits, that's what the middlemen and power brokers do, but I feel this should be worth more than that. I just can't figure out what it's worth. I might just have to wait for the right opportunity. I can use it as an ace up my sleeve for now.

When Brady went back into the dining room, he noticed his glass had been refilled and placed next to a leather armchair. Dagny sat in an armchair opposite him, and she resumed her questioning. It was as if the previous topic of the possible end of the world had been dealt with and was no longer considered a matter of interest. Brady knew they had already decided what they wanted, and now he was being mined for background information.

He reminded them, 'Hey, remember, you are supposed to tell me stuff.'

Tia said, 'All in good time.'

Dagny pressed him on his time with the Greens, the hierarchy of their communities, and she was especially interested in the NanoSuits™ and the dissolution of the Trad areas.

They talked, or more accurately, *he* talked, and they listened until the early hours of the morning. Finally, he got to the final days, and his interaction with Tia's former colleagues at mASSIVE™ Park - Tia displayed little emotion or nostalgia, apart from the mention of the death of El Duque.

Tia announced, 'I think we should retire to the bedrooms, and I shall give you what I promised in the morning.' She stood up and left, making it clear that this was not up for negotiation. Dagny showed Brady to his room. He flirted with her drunkenly and made a pass at her, but she refused his advances nimbly, and Brady flopped, fully clothed on his bed and drifted into an uncomfortable alcohol addled sleep.

Brady awoke late morning with a hangover from hell. A servant knocked on his door and wheeled in a trolley with a large breakfast for him to have in bed. It was an old-fashioned fry-up with bacon, fried eggs - sunny side up, hash browns, sausages, and baked beans. He guessed they were vegan substitutes, but they tasted just like he remembered. There was also a silver tray with matching teapot, cups, saucers, milk, sugar, and if this wasn't to his taste, there was a coffee pot and fruit juices.

He ate heartily, and it took the edge off his hangover. It was the best meal he had eaten since the old days. He took a long hot shower, and he noticed that somebody had provided a toothbrush, toothpaste, a razor, shaving gel, and even aftershave sometime in the night. These were antiques, but he appreciated the thought.

24.ORIGINS OF MAN

Dagny came for Brady and escorted him around the complex. He thanked her for the hospitality and made an effort to be on his best behaviour. She showed him the control room, which was virtually a miracle, in Brady's mind, that it still had fully functioning technology, aside from the Internet and communications with the outside world. They strolled around for more than an hour, and he smiled but zoned out of most of the conversation, as it centred around inter-planetary flights and distant habitats and atmospheres. He was disturbed when they viewed the colony simulator. 'Surely, you could have told them. Y'know, let them out for good behaviour.'

She laughed at his sarcasm, 'They are simulating the real problems they would have experienced if communication to Mars had broken down. This was the point of the experiment, to see if they could survive without us. They did, and we learned a lot in the process.'

Brady wanted to protest but knew it was futile. *Scientists would never listen to a lowlife criminal like me. If those guys want to volunteer for prison, then who am I to tell them they're wrong?*

Dagny led him to Tia's office and pulled out a chair for Brady. Tia looked at him from behind an ornate desk. She sat in an orthopaedic chair which appeared to be ergonomically designed to fit her frame precisely. Dagny sat to the side of her and took out a pad and pencil.

Tia said, 'Our colony is powered by a super-small nuclear fission reactor housed underground and requires only a small team to keep it running. It produces carbon-free...' She noticed Brady's attention wandering. Tia had spent her whole life surrounded by scientists and high-achievers, she avoided the general public as they irritated her, and now she had to use this dullard, Brady Mahone, to get a message to another high-thinker. She endeavoured to simplify, 'Brady?'

'Yeah.'

'You flew here in a FusionPlane™.'

'Yes.'
'It's powered by FusionPower™. This means it takes its energy from a Fusion Nuclear reactor.'

'That's right. One of them blew up in Encinitas at the turn of the century. Long story, I probably didn't tell you that one. Anyways...'

'Maybe later. The point is, we use Fission nuclear reactors. If this NanoShell™ succeeds in breaking down our outer defences and comes into contact with a working Fission reactor, it could be catastrophic - for the planet.'

'You know this?'

'No. From the information you have given, it would appear that they used Nano-technology to shut down all other reactors. This means they knew it would be dangerous to leave them operational. But they didn't realise that we had an operational reactor here. You have to tell them.'

'So, you'd help them for nothing. I ain't buying that.'

She shrugged and tried to think of Brady Mahone as a businessman. 'They would require my help, and for that, I would want a high price.'

Brady laughed, 'Now you're talking, let's cut to the chase. I'll pass your message on, but I'm going to get a cut of the action. I'm just saying.'

'And what will that be?'

I haven't a clue, but I'll figure something out. Brady tapped his nose, 'That's for Brady Mahone to know and you to find out.'

She looked aside in irritation at having to deal with a double-dealing middleman. 'My price would be all of these NanoSuits™ for me and my team and the re-introduction of the Mars Colony Program. Have you any idea how these NanoSuits™ could revolutionise space travel…'

'Save the lecture, lady. Just put everything down in a letter, and I'll deliver it to Bodhi, personally. What I need is food and water to take with me back to my Fusion-Plane™.'

She nodded to Dagny, 'I'll compose a letter and include supporting technical documentation.'

Brady said, 'I've done my bit. You said you had information for me.'

'I'm not known for my bedside manner, so if I tell it harshly, under the hard light of truth, then you'll just have to understand that I don't know how to sugar coat things. I deal with facts, reason, purpose, cause and effect. I'm interested in propelling humanity forwards, not in dwelling on past emotions - feelings.'

'I'm a big boy. I can take anything you can throw at me.'

'Good to know.' Tia sat upright, and her chair moved with her to embrace her new position. 'We had carried out many investigations on John Kane and Sattva Systems™ as they were our biggest industrial rivals. It was difficult to get into his private inner circle because the kinds of people he was dealing with were especially secretive and cunning. Brady nodded. He recalled how his Pops and Small Hand Don were paranoid about strangers. 'John Kane had three identical children. He didn't love any of them. He bred them for experimental purposes. You've probably gathered from your own investigations that he was a sociopath. However, he possessed a brilliant mind, and I admired his business acumen. He was indeed a worthy competitor.'

'Yeah, he was a real good old boy. If Pops hadn't have killed him, then I would have, eventually. But hey, you're saying he's a good old nonce…'

Tia stared at him as if she couldn't care less about Brady's thoughts on the situation. She waited for him to finish. Once Brady had completed his tirade and had gone silent, she continued. 'The three boys all had the same mother, but she didn't know that…'
Brady laughed at the impossibility of her story. 'Jesus, lady, you are having a laugh at Brady Mahone's expense. I'll remind you that I could break your scrawny neck in a heartbeat. Now, quit fucking around with me.' Tia gulped involuntarily, and Dagny got out of her chair in a vain attempt to protect her mother. Brady laughed, 'Do you

really think that you could stop me.' Tia pulled a gun from a drawer in her desk. Brady looked away from her as a deception while his left hand swept the gun from out of her hand. 'You aren't nearly as clever as you thought if you thought that Brady Mahone hasn't had a gun pointed at him before. I ain't scared of a gun, and the only chance you had to kill me was to shoot straightaway. One moment of doubt or hesitation, and Brady Mahone is gonna get ya.'

Tia raised her open hands and said, 'I'm telling you the truth, I'm begging you, please let me finish.'

Brady put the gun in his pocket. He guessed that if old tech worked here, then so would the gun. However, he knew the Security Protocols™ wouldn't allow it to be used on the outside. 'Alright. Say watcha gotta say.'

She said, 'We had a source from inside the FBI - she was on our payroll - and she gave us the crucial lead to Samuel Beardon the Second. He gave us the information we were looking for before he could give it to the authorities. Our source kept it from them. She was well rewarded for her silence.' She looked away as if she vividly remembered the old days. 'John Kane despised the human race. He viewed them as worse than animals - he loved animals, but that's hardly relevant here. He blamed the human race for trashing the planet, and therefore he used humans for his experimentation. He was fascinated by nature, and he believed that humans were unnatural. He conducted little side experiments to understand the effects of nurture on virtually identical embryos.'

Brady knew this was important, but he didn't like Tia, and he was suspicious of being played by her. He didn't like these kinds of stories. He huffed and slumped in his chair, but he kept his eyes focused on her in case she tried something funny again. 'It sounds like the kinda stuff Professor Chu used to talk about.'
She said nonplussed, 'That name doesn't mean anything to me. Should it?' Brady sighed; he was getting bored. She said, 'The first child he had was Xavier Kane, the person you know as Bodhi Sattva. He bred him to be perfect. From the moment he was conceived he was hot housed to be the perfect heir to Sattva Systems™. The next child was born in the UK. He was indoctrinated with extreme values from before he was born. John Kane had people bombard the foetus with socialist doctrines and then raised by left-wingers. His name was Glenarvon Cole. Brady Mahone was his third experiment.'
Brady sat bolt upright, 'Wait a minute.' He put his hands to his face. He hadn't even considered any potential threats from Tia or Dagny. He peeked at them through his fingers. Tia stared back at him implacably, but Dagny's look was one of sympathy. He lowered his hands. 'Let me get this straight. John Kane is my real Pops, and Bodhi and Glenarvon Cole are my brothers?'

Tia said matter-of-factly, 'Closer to identical triplets. And Libby Skye is the mother of all three of you.'

'Get the fuck outta here, she would have had sex with me if I'd given her half a chance. That's some seriously weird shit.'

'She didn't know you were her son. She had her eggs removed by her husband and he had them fertilised in a different time and place. The only son he wanted *nurturing* by the natural mother was Xavier.'

Brady's thoughts were racing, 'That's what you meant when you called me a bad seed.'

'It's true. That is precisely what you are.'

Dagny interrupted, 'I don't think that's fair. Brady is a victim of a mad man.'

He shouted, 'I ain't no victim.'

Tia said, 'He's the result of a remarkable experiment if you cast aside traditional ethics and morality.'

Brady said, 'So, my father chose a low-life junkie criminal to carry me in her womb, one of those surrogate kinda deals, and then what?'

'He strung her along, incentivising her and her friends to talk to you as a criminal while you were in the womb. He had a script for them to follow, as they weren't particularly bright.' She laughed at her own humour. 'This process continued until after you were born, and then your Mother, so to speak, died of a drug overdose.' She couldn't help but snigger at the imagination of her rival, 'and then he placed you with a paedophile.' She laughed.

Brady said sharply, 'Pops loved me. He didn't do anything like that to me - and if you dare to say I'm in fucking denial - I swear to God, I will not be responsible for my actions.' He banged his fist on her desk.

A few minutes of silence followed as Brady processed this information. Tia and Dagny remained silent and tried to keep calm.

Finally, Brady said, 'Why did John Kane try to find me?'

Tia said, 'I don't know. We believed, like everybody else, that Samuel Beardon the Second had him killed, but as they never found a body...' She added, 'There were strong indicators that Bodhi may have had Samuel Beardon killed in jail. Our source said he was about to talk.'

'The Bodhi I have dealt with doesn't come across as being that ruthless.'

Tia laughed, 'After all this.' She stretched out her arms. Then she softened her voice, 'It was the smart business move. It paved the way for his inheritance to be enacted. With hindsight, his Father's disappearance probably aided his own plans for the future.'

Brady sat back in his chair, 'Ok, I know my limitations when it comes to the scheming of corporate types. I want to ask some questions which you will think are stupid, but I'd appreciate it if you cut out the sarcasm.'

Dagny said, 'You've had quite a shock. Ask away, and we'll answer as best as we can - won't we, Mother?'

'Why, of course. What's uppermost on your mind?'

Brady breathed in deeply, 'Who knows what about who?'

Dagny said before Tia could produce a cutting comment about his lack of articulation. 'Break down your question into specific areas.'

Brady didn't understand her request initially, and he thought about what he really wanted and needed to know. 'Do you think Bodhi knows about me? Y'know, being his brother and all.'

Dagny took up the task of answering these relationship and emotional queries. 'I think he strongly suspects. I hope you don't mind me saying, but if I were him, I would be wondering if there were more like you in the world. Have you heard about anybody else with your ability to breach their security shells?' Tia watched on with interest.

Brady said, 'Since the revolution, there hasn't been anybody like me.'

She looked at him quizzically as she waited patiently for his next question.

'Do you think Glenarvon Cole knows about me?'

Brady noticed that she gave this question a lot of thought; it made him feel his needs were being taken seriously.

She said, 'I think he has only found out or suspected something recently. It would explain the sudden urge to take you on an old-fashioned, male-bonding trip.' She added, 'On the plus side, it feels like he wants to protect you, as opposed to removing you.' She pondered further and seemed to drift off dreamily. She sighed, 'There's a possibility that he knows more than Bodhi about you.' She considered her theory for long moments. 'On second thoughts, I'm not sure he's that clever. Bodhi may not even have figured it out…'

Tia intervened, 'Bodhi Sattva inherited his wealth, but if you investigated him as I did, you'd realise it's the people he employs that have all the talent. I tried to lure Professor Pinar Dogan away from his organisation to no avail, but it did cost Bodhi a fortune to keep her - so I still hurt him in the pocket - or so I thought at the time.' She reflected, 'Pinar and I could have achieved great things if she hadn't been so greedy.'

'How can I move through their NanoShells™?' Brady wanted to keep the topic of conversation on his needs.

'Mother has given that more thought than I? She is more technically adept than I am to answer that question.' Dagny looked reproachfully at Tia, and then back at Brady.

Tia said, 'There are several possibilities, but the most likely is that your DNA sequencing is so close to Bodhi's that you could have authorised access to anywhere and everywhere.'

'You mean like a skeleton key?'

'Yes. That analogy would suffice.'

'So, that means I am definitely a Trad and not a Green?' He looked at the two Trads before him and thought about Bodhi, Glenarvon, Rhea and the Beardons, and then of the two potential mothers of his children, and for the first time actually wondered whether being a Trad was all it was cracked up to be. He smiled to himself while he waited for the answer to arrive.

'I was fascinated by the qualities of the NanoSuits™, and I believe you when you said that you have refused them all - not that I can understand your logic.' Brady wasn't going to say it was because he believed in his Pops' conspiracy theories. Not here, in the company of Tia and Dagny Cassandra. She added, 'I also don't think you would pick them up from visiting their communities frequently. You said they had ceremonies to gain them or to have the NanoSuits™ applied?'

'Yes. Definitely.'

'You mentioned a primer, an InfraRed™ version?'

'Yes.'

'That sounds like a similar technology to the bubbles used with the Sattva Aviation company. Knowing John Kane, I wouldn't be in the least surprised if he hadn't primed the embryos or foetuses.' She continued to analyse the situation. Brady began to wonder if she was a robot, as her face was fixed like a frozen computer. 'I believe the aviation Nanotechnology bubbles were temporary, but you may have been given a permanent variant. I believe the combination of these theorems is the most probable outcome. The combination of your DNAs being identical in addition to you all having InfraRed™ primers as part of a growing foetus means the Nanotechnology believes you are one and the same.'

Dagny said, 'To come on to your identity issue, you are a Trad with a minor Green infection at a DNA level. But you are a Trad if that makes you feel any more comfortable. It would be safe to say that no Green would view you as one of them.'

Brady laughed and sighed at the same time, 'Story of my life. I never fitted in with the Blacks or the Whites, and now I don't fit in with the Greens or the Trads.' He turned to Tia, 'Could you have got this wrong?'

'Of course! It's a pure hypothesis. I have neither evidence nor proof. We would have to run a series of tests to…'

He thought about his Pops' alien conspiracies and said, 'I don't think we've got time for that.'

Dagny laughed; she may have even understood Brady's joke. She watched Brady stare out of the window and into the far distance. He looked concerned. 'What is it?'

Brady wanted to leave. He wished to get back to familiar territory. He had travelled worldwide, and yet he had never felt so isolated and alone as he did right now. He dreaded the days of walking ahead of him, while all the while having to dodge the quicksand. He answered her, 'I'm going to need binoculars or a telescope.'

'I don't understand.'

'This is a big place, and it was green against a desert background. My Fusion-Plane™ is tiny by comparison, and it is cream-coloured. I might never find it.'

Dagny sensed his anxiety and vulnerability. 'You are right. We have binoculars - you can have them, and we'll give you plenty of food and water to take with you. I'll have Doctor Roberts to give you some medicines and pills to help - if you want?'

'Yes, that'll be great - thanks.' He stood up and walked away. He didn't want anybody to see him like this.

25.TRANSPORT HUB TRAINING DAY

After four torturous days of trekking through the Mojave Desert, Brady finally located and boarded his FusionPlane™. He felt the urge to return to friendly and easy-going companions, like Amie or maybe the Beardons. But the large envelope of schematics and technical documents - complete with Tia's list of demands insisted that he should fly to Boulder Creek and visit Bodhi. He had already decided to keep his newly found discoveries and theories to himself for the time being.

The thought of families reminded him of when Mary-Lou and Lucian suffered their miscarriage shortly after the Greens took power.

At least I know I am capable of having kids. I did wonder at the time whether that Green goo had finished the Mahone line.

He realised that the children he was now producing were from the heritage of John Kane and Libby Skye. He also considered that they were going to be Green, as confirmed before he made his arrangement with Amie and Helgarth, but he didn't like the idea of his sons displaying their biological Grandfather's tendencies.

He started up his plane, and a Sattva Systems™ announcement rang out, not unlike if he had invoked the Security Protocols™.

This is a Sattva Systems™ travel announcement. All vehicles must travel via the established Highways and Road Networks. Ground Level is for pedestrians, Green Bicycles, FusionCoaches™, Fusion Lorries™ and FusionCars™. Height Levels Two through Four are for Private and Rental FusionPlanes™. Level Five is for Fusion-PassengerJets™, and Levels Six through Ten are for HeavyLoaders™ and emergency vehicles. This is to enable mass-vacational travel for all our members. Enjoy your New Green World by witnessing the fruits of your astonishing labour. This message is endorsed by Bodhi Sattva and is delivered courtesy of Sattva Systems™.

Brady said, 'What the actual, fuck!'

Another announcement in a more authoritative voice stated:

Please remove your vehicle to a designated Level or park it in an authorised space. Thank you for using Sattva Systems™ transportation. Have a nice Green day.

He slung his package of documents down on the passenger seat and took off in his FusionPlane™. The autopilot took him via the shortest route to the edge of Morning Star Mine Road, awaiting Brady's choice of direction. He went to head north, but the FusionPlane™ wouldn't let him until two other vehicles had passed.

I'm going to have to get used to fucking traffic again.

For decades Brady had become accustomed to complete and utter freedom of travel, and he hated being constricted by the rules of the road…Levels, or whatever. He couldn't remember the last time he had to wait at a junction staring at the rear end of a vehicle in front of him. It bugged him that these vehicles were being driven so slowly. He figured out that they weren't necessarily going anywhere in particular, but they were sightseeing. For Brady, seeing the meadowlands and grasslands that had re-placed Bakersfield - all except its roads and highways - had long since meant nothing to Brady, but to the New Green Tourists, they were astounding. The thing that really bugged Brady was that there were even speed limits for FusionPlanes™.

By the time he reached Boulder Creek, he was in a belligerent mood. He still had the wooden staff next to him in the plane. He thought about dumping it but then decided to keep it as a memento of his time in Cima. He changed into his heavy leather walking boots and retrieved his coat. He cast aside his sneakers. Brady was prepared for trouble - even if he had to make it happen. He patted the pocket on his Poacher's coat with the package from Tia Cassandra in it. He needn't have double-checked as it bulged the oversized compartment. The autopilot landed in a tight spot as the parking lot was nearly full.

He parked up and was frosty with Marjorie, as he suspected her of having put the trackers on his vehicles. He refused her offer to escort him to the Main Entrance. Brady strutted through the industrial areas of the Sattva Systems™ complex, darting glares at anybody who caught his eye. He didn't see any of the leading players. At the reception desk, there was a man he had dealt with before. Brady asked without waiting for the usual professional pleasantries, 'Where is everyone?'

'Hello, Brady, have you got an appoin...'

'Look fuckhead, I asked you a simple question, now cut the crap.'

'There is a Regional Disciple meeting in the Training Hall, but you can't go in there...' He said, uselessly as Brady had already marched away.

Brady opened the door to the large Training Hall. Bodhi was addressing a few hundred Regional Disciples who were seated in neat rows. He caught the eye of Cain, and if Bodhi had spotted his entrance, then he didn't show the slightest signs of alarm as he continued smoothly with his presentation. 'Over the next decade, we are re-opening the rail networks. As you were well aware, from the very first of the Operation Clean Ups, we fixed the highways and railways with NanoRepair™ and Nano-Protect™ to keep this one area of the Traditional Cultures operational. It was prudent to have a coordinated system that worked in tandem with SattNav™. The rail system will encourage environmentally friendly mass transportation to allow travel...'

Brady marched to the back of the Hall, and he saw a model town laid out across three large tables. It was an architect's dream of the New Green transportation system. There were models of houses, churches, GreenGrocers™ and down the model roads and highways, placed on pins of various lengths were miniature versions of all the green vehicles, there was even a model railway running around it, complete with cream-coloured coaches, pulled by a cream-coloured ceramic engine with a moss-green Sattva Systems™ logo on its livery. Brady watched the train move almost silently around its never-ending circular route. He then glanced up and saw Rhea take a seat behind the Green model village as if she was a meeting assistant and not part of the main group.

His mood changed instantly. He recalled the thrill of one of his few days he attended High School when he flirted with the meanest and baddest girl in class - she was a looker, and she knew it. Brady was intoxicated by this memory. He looked around and grabbed a chair and parked himself right next to Rhea. He slunk his chair back and brought his big heavy boots down on the model village, destroying a row of houses in the process. He smiled mischievously, 'Oops. Am I bad? Fancy seeing you here. Long-time no see.'

She laughed and shook out her red hair. Brady could have died a happy man, right then and there. She teased, 'I wouldn't have thought that this was your kind of thing.'

'Anything could be my thing if you were there.' She smiled coyly, and Brady was encouraged. 'What's Bodhi going on about now?'

'The changes required to adjust the hundred-year plan. He takes his promise to Glenarvon Cole super-seriously.'

Brady said, 'What I take seriously is my right to travel anywhere I want when I want. Who do I have to bribe around here to get out of these new travel restrictions?'

'You mean complete freedom to fly anywhere?'

'Yeah.'

'You could apply to become a Regional Disciple. Cain is free to roam.'

Brady laughed, 'Let's say that's not an option.'

'You could afford to buy a permit for five million Green Credits per year or a one-off payment of two-hundred million Green Credits for a lifetime permit.'

Brady brooded on this transaction, 'We'll see about that.' He asked as he needed to check his math, 'How many years is that? Y'know, I can't explain what I'm asking.'

'Forty years - if you paid it yearly.' Rhea smiled as she watched Brady's face contort as if he was literally chewing it over. She laughed as he looked at her in sheer bemusement.

Brady was on good behaviour for a few minutes, while it was clear that Rhea wanted to listen to this passage of the Bodhi lecture. He continued to address his Regional Disciples from across the globe, 'You are all aware of the difficulties I encountered with the next series of NanoSuits™. Therefore, we have had to adapt the plan. This is why I have brought forward the freedom of travel by five years. I know my illness caused much consternation among our Green Communities, and I need to restore confidence and belief. The FusionVehicles™ will be heavily discounted so that those who have saved for the Indigo™ NanoSuits™ can use these Green Credits to pay for holidays and travel around the world. The Indigo™ NanoSuits™ will now be released five years from now, and they will be sleep variant and not the higher senses. The Violet™ NanoSuits™ will be delivered by 2170...'

Rhea appeared disappointed even to Brady's unskilled emotional perception. He asked, 'What's the matter, babe?'

Rhea laughed, 'Babe! I haven't been called babe since the twenty-seventies, and that was in a biker bar.'

'Don't you miss those days? They were a lot of fun, but now, it's all so serious, and everybody is so well fucking behaved.'

'I do. I was never into the Green thing. I was what they would label a Trad, right up until the Revolution. I'm just doing what I need to survive.'

Brady said, 'Then why don't you just run off with me. Brady Mahone knows how to show a girl a good time.'

She laughed playfully, 'I bet you do, but it's a physical impossibility.'

'Why's that? I don't understand.'

She looked around the room as if she feared being seen, but the audience was held in rapt attention on Bodhi's speech, the only people facing out who could see her and Brady, at the back of the class, were those on the stage with Bodhi, and they were Genesis Garcia and Glenarvon Cole. She whispered, 'I'm dying without these Suits™. If I went with you, they would strip me of them, and then I would die. I should have been dead already. I lose the Suits™ - I lose my life.'

Images of Mrs Wilson in her grave flooded Brady's mind. But he looked into her eyes, and it didn't matter. He saw Rhea in front of him, and not whatever was contained inside her Suit™ 'Are you sure?'

'Yes. My only hope is the UltraViolet™ NanoSuit™.'

'UltraViolet™? All the Greens I know are certain that the Violet™ was the last. Nobody has mentioned this UltraViolet™.'

Rhea said, 'Regional Disciples and above know. The Disciples will be made aware during the final decade of the hundred-year plan. It's the outer edges of Nanotechnology, but Bodhi's team are convinced they can do it.'

'Why are you telling me this?'

'Because the UltraViolet™ will give its wearer virtually a thousand years of life, and I have been told I will be fully restored. Maybe you might survive until the culmination of the plan, and if you are, well, maybe we could start this conversation again, but you'd have to keep your good looks. I'm not saving myself for an old-timer, y'know.'

That's how they get ya, son. 'I can't envisage any circumstances where I would take the Green and put on their NanoSuits™, but I hope it all works out for you. You are my favourite Green; you've always known that.'

'Yes, Brady, and they know that as well.'

Bodhi was addressing his audience. '...The hundred-year period is going to be extended by six months for the general Green population. I have to do this to allow my scientists and engineers to recalibrate. The Disciples will still receive the UltraViolet™ NanoSuits™ on the day of the Centenary of the Revolution, but the rest of the population will have to wait until New Year's Eve 2184. Technically, it still fulfils the promise of a hundred years. I haven't taken the decision lightly...'

Brady stuck his hand up fiercely. It wasn't a custom that applied any longer, but Bodhi was thrown off his speech. Bodhi apologised to his assembled guests and said, 'Yes, Brady. Have you got something to contribute?'

'Hey, bro.' He laughed and teased and then said loudly - he didn't have a microphone like Bodhi, and he wanted to be heard. 'Your precious one-hundred-year plan depends on there still being a planet by then, I guess.'

Most of the audience were aware of Brady Mahone and his business, as Regional Disciples had to welcome him if he visited their part of the world. However, they also knew that Brady was an oaf, an uneducated Trad Alpha-Male. They sniggered at Brady's unwelcome intrusion into their educated and informed lesson on the future of the planet.

Bodhi said, politely, 'Of course. This is true.'

Brady said grandly, 'I have it on good authority that your NanoShit is threatening the planet's very existence. You ain't got anywhere like a hundred years left because of FusionPower™ this, attacking Fission power that. It's already turning deserts into a sea of Jelly Sand. I seen it. It's a real bastard travelling around that stuff; it's miles wide in places.' The audience was utterly confused by Brady's jumble of information. However, the more scientific minded among the Regional Disciples were alarmed at this account of Fusion, Fission and lakes of quicksand. 'What's it worth to old Brady Mahone to tell you more?'

Bodhi answered, 'What do you want that you don't already have?'

'You can make your travel restrictions for Greens, but I ain't a Green, I'm Trad, and I'm proud. I want to be exempt from this and all your other hair-brained schemes. I also want all the profits from my company, Brady Mahone Entertainment Enterprises - I'm going to have a growing family to look after.'

Bodhi thought carefully on what he had heard as some in the audience argued and disseminated the greed of the old Trad ways and how Brady embodied all the worst characteristics of the Trads. He was being accused of exploitation of the Earth's need for his own gain. Bodhi called for calm and restarted his interrogation before opening negotiations. 'Brady, I need more information. You said you have this on good authority. May I ask you, on whose authority?'

'Before you get in in your head, about rushing me and stealing my information I have removed half the documents from this.' He pulled out his package and waved it in the air.

'What is contained within there.'

'You know me, I ain't no scientist, but I'm assured you need these, she called them schematics, structural compounds and whatever. She can't solve this at her end. She says you have to work with each other. To tell you the truth, I don't think she would give a damn if you refused. She's not bothered about you Greens surviving. She only wants to complete her project.' He laughed and pointed at Glenarvon Cole, 'Sorry, man. You ain't gonna like what she wants at all.' Brady roared with laughter. He pointed at his captive audience, 'You should see your little faces. You're like a bunch of scared rabbits.'

Bodhi said, 'Who is the woman you are referring to?'

'Do we have a deal?'

'If your source is someone in who we can confirm her integrity, and if your documents confirm the severity of the threat you infer, then yes, we will have a deal. I will make you exempt from all travel restrictions; I will relinquish my stake in your business, but I will continue to provide you with the manufacturing capacity, distribution networks and the Field Teams on the ground - just as before.'

Brady said, trying to talk like one of his many defence lawyers who had represented him in the old days, 'My client has demands of her own.' He looked down on Rhea who was engrossed in Brady's power play. She was shaking her head, but she also wore a disbelieving smile.

Glenarvon Cole and Genesis Garcia formed a huddle with Bodhi on the stage, as they appeared to be attempting to come to a joint decision. Brady joked with Rhea, 'It's no biggie, saving the world and stuff, at least I know I'm just a man and not pretending to be some kinda God like the big guy on the stage. I think I just popped his bubble.'

Bodhi asked the question as if it was the final point of clarification, he required before agreeing to Brady's terms. 'Who is your client?'

'Tia Cassandra.'

There were audible gasps around the room, and Brady triumphantly gazed at Rhea, but she seemed more troubled by this than any of the other revelations he had shared.

Bodhi said, 'And what would Tia want from us in return for her help and expertise?'

'Freedom for a start.' He joked with his audience, 'Who wouldn't want a bit more freedom?' He added, 'She wants all the NanoSuits™, past, present, and future for herself and all her teams, including those working in her colony. She wants Sattva Systems™ to develop her Space Program. She was on about colonising Mars, but God knows why anyone would want to live up there.' This was the only statement that chimed with the gathering of the Greens. Brady watched Glenarvon closely. He could tell when an opponent was struggling to keep his emotions in check. Brady said, 'I don't think you have to agree that with me. You can sort that out with Tia and her daughter Dagny. Hey, maybe the best thing you could do is rescue her and then send her to Mars - it might just be cold enough for her.'

Brady walked to the front of the Training Room and handed over the documents to Bodhi. He opened them, and scanned the first few pages, and then called for some desks to be carried over and pushed together. Sissy left to gather some of the key scientists from around the Sattva Systems™ base.

'Get Pinar, and don't take any nonsense from her. 'Bodhi barked after Sissy.

Bodhi called an end to the meeting but kept some of the more technical, as opposed to spiritual and ethical Regional Disciples behind. It appeared to Brady that his work here was done, as nobody seemed to notice that he was here any longer. Rhea moved to his side, 'I'll walk with you back to your FusionPlane™. You won't see me often; they plan my movements to reduce the chances of bumping into you.'

Glen called out, 'Rhea, where are you going?'

'I'm heading back to Brady's FusionPlane™ to get the rest of the documentation. Isn't that right, Brady?'

'Yes. I don't trust anybody else. Is that ok with you, buddy?'

Glen smiled thinly, 'Sure. Just don't be too long about it.'

Brady felt as if they were being followed on the way back to his vehicle. He could read the signs within the conversation that Rhea was sticking to small talk if they could be overheard. They reached Brady's FusionPlane™. He boarded it and gave her the missing documents. 'It's a real shame that you can't leave 'em all behind and come with me.'

She didn't answer this redundant offer. She waited for some of the Regional Disciples to start up their FusionPowered™ engines, which throbbed with their sub-sonic pulses. Rhea decided that the noise would be enough to tell Brady something important.

Rhea looked around from side to side, furtively, before staring straight into Brady's brown eyes, 'I put the trackers in all of your vehicles.'

'What the fuck! Why?'

'To protect you. If you venture too far away from the Green Communities, the Security Protocols™ can't find you.' She didn't have a chance to explain, as one of the Australian Regional Disciples called out, 'Rhea, you're wanted back in the Training Room.' He shouted, 'Now,' before she could respond.

'Bye, Brady. Stay safe. You can trust Marjorie. She's with me. One of the few.' She turned and walked quickly away. Brady watched her leave until she was out of his sight.

26. THE WINNER TAKES IT ALL

Brady elevated his FusionPlane™ but was immediately stuck in traffic. Many of the Regional Disciples were stuck in a holding pattern as they waited to head off to the far-off places, they called home. *I thought these Regional Disciples were free to roam.* While he waited, uselessly, stuck a few hundred feet in the air, he took time out to look around the Sattva Systems™ complex. The HQ looked tiny compared with the rest of the industrial maze. Beyond the domes and chemical plants, he saw a FusionCar™ compound which stretched to the horizon. It was a sea of cream. He watched as the HeavyLoaders™ were loaded with vehicles to take to the Green Communities across the land.

Fuck! How long is it going to take for the traffic to fucking clear? If his Fusion-Plane™ had a horn installed, he would have blasted it in useless frustration. He wished he could open a window and yell at the plane in front of him. It would relieve his anger, even if it didn't have any effect on the traffic delays. He had elevated his FusionPlane™ to Level Four in the vain hope that this would be the fast lane, but he still only moved a few feet per minute. The sub-sonic pulses of accumulated engines at first annoyed him but then began to calm him. He ungripped the joystick and put his FusionPlane™ into autopilot.

It looks like I'm going to have to wait a while for them to put my freedom to roam deal into action. He set his paranoia free for a time to grab hold of the possibility that Bodhi had screwed him over in his deal. He wondered if they were laughing at his stupidity. *I shouldn't have handed over the rest of the documents over to Rhea. Maybe, she is one of those femmes fatale types.* He thought it over and decided that Bodhi had never, ever, reneged on a deal. *It probably takes time to organise, processing payments and passes. I'll give them a week before I complain.*

He watched a Regional Disciple in a vehicle alongside him throw his hands in the air and gave Brady *a what are you looking at?* stare. Brady roared with laughter at the sight of some good old days' signs of humanity. *It must be teething troubles, good to know that these Green fucks can't get the traffic moving on time - good luck with your FusionTrains™.*

Brady then saw a sight that always cheered him up. A fleet of HeavyLoaders™ was rising in the distance at the front of the queuing FusionPlanes™. They almost levitated, which seemed like a technological miracle to Brady - given their immense size. They advanced gently up to Levels Six through to Ten. They rose slowly enough for Brady to count them - there were forty. He loved the whopping sub-sonic booms of the HeavyLoaders™ as they glided overhead in strict formation.

His FusionPlane™ radio lit up and stated:

This is a Sattva Systems™ travel announcement. We apologise for the delay, but the meeting in the Training Room ended earlier than scheduled. The FusionCar™ Transport Fleet had priority of bookings. Please enjoy your New Green Day courtesy of Sattva Systems™.

Brady laughed as he realised that the traffic chaos was probably all his fault. He wondered if that was what the guy in the vehicle alongside him was so angry about. Brady looked over to him and shrugged and then grinned broadly. A further message rang out in his cockpit:

*This is a message from Sattva Systems™. Brady Mahone's freedom to roam appli-
cation has been approved. This will be activated in five minutes. Please indicate your
destination, and the autopilot will fly you via the fastest available route. This message
was brought to you courtesy of Sattva Systems™.*

Brady decided to leave his vehicle on autopilot mode while the switch to freedom
to roam was enacted. 'Malibu, home. Hugging the coastline.' He wanted to view the
Pacific.

His Malibu home was eerily quiet when he stepped inside. Hunter came out to
greet him. 'Welcome home, sir.'

'Yeah, thanks. Where is everybody?'

'Your arrival caused a bit of panic, your partners were in an indeterminate sexual
appearance, so they went to their rooms with other staff in attendance. They are going
to need a little time to adjust to an appearance which you deem acceptable.'

'I don't suppose we could just say women and be done with it.'

'I'm sorry, sir. I have to abide by the protocols.'

'Ok. Just get me a coffee and a light lunch.'

Hunter turned and left. Brady headed out onto the terrace to look over his personal
view of the ocean. He sat on an armchair under the canopy and tried to chill in the
warm Californian sunshine. He reflected upon all he had learned in these last few
weeks.

Hunter returned with freshly made sandwiches and coffee.

Brady said, 'Could you get my sunglasses for me?'

'Of course.'

Brady had his meal in peace. He tried to find pride in wresting control of his company, but it didn't bring him as much satisfaction as he had hoped. *It all seemed a bit
too easy.* This was always the thing about the Kanes and this house that troubled him
the most. He watched Hunter moving silently around the large neighbouring lounge,
hovering, and awaiting his master's next instructions. *He probably knows more
about what went on in this house than anybody left alive. I haven't a clue how long
he worked for Libby and John Kane, but he's probably worked longer for me now.
I wonder if his loyalty is still with Bodhi.* He thought about Hunter for a long time.
He equated him to the quiet lifers in prison, the ones who watched but never caused
any trouble. They knew all the secrets; people trusted them because they kept their
mouths shut. However, if you became friendly with them…

His sunglasses covered his eyes as he studied Hunter. He called out, 'Hunter, I'd
like you to walk with me as I want to inspect my fleet of vehicles.'

'Yes, sir.'

Brady strolled at a crawl. He wanted Hunter to relax. 'How old are you, Hunter?'

'I was born in 1972, sir.'

'So, that makes you, one-hundred and seventy - going on eighty. Wow, you must be one of the oldest Greens.'

Hunter smiled, 'There are many who are much older than me, but I have done well with the Green's help. Sir.'

Brady said, 'You don't have to call me sir while we are having an informal chat. How did you end up working for John Kane in the first place?'

'I travelled from England like so many others to find fame and fortune in Hollywood. I managed to acquire an agent on account of my British accent and good looks…' He laughed, 'Hard to imagine, now, I concede.'

Brady laughed along while he established a rapport, 'No man, I can see it…'

'Anyway, I struggled to get more than a few minor roles when my agent suggested an alternative career path. You see sir - I'm sorry, I forgot, years of habit. My agent found out that Libby Skye was looking for an old-fashioned manservant to impress her guests, and my agent put us together, so to speak. He had a man-to-man chat with me to ensure I took this offer seriously, as he didn't think I had what it took to make it in the movie industry.'

They continued their stroll past the tennis courts, Brady asked. 'So, when was this?' Brady took in exaggerated deep breaths of the salty air to reinforce his attempts to show how relaxed he was.

Hunter said, wistfully, '1997. I recall being very disappointed that my dreams were over by twenty-five, but in later life, when I watched the movies, I had a bit part in, I understood that I wasn't as talented as I thought I was. My agent was right, and I was luckier than most to find a job for life and in a beautiful location.' There was a hint of a resigned smile on Hunter's face as if he still secretly held a desire to go back to those halcyon days and have another try at being a successful actor.

Brady had a sense that Hunter hadn't been asked about his life, and Brady reproached himself for not doing this before. 'Libby was only a few years older than you back then, was there, y'know…'

'No. Nothing like that. Mr Kane had Libby well under his control. He had the staff spy on her and report back to him. She couldn't have got away with anything like that, and certainly not with me.'

There was something about the way he said this, which suggested that Hunter, a good-looking Hollywood wannabee back then, wouldn't have refused an offer from Libby. 'I'm trying to work it out. You worked for Libby for…'

'One hundred and forty-five years - if you count my service to this day. After all, this is still the same place of employment for me. You've probably noticed that you are not allowed to retire - it's immoral to expect Her to allow you to spend your years of leisure using up Her resources. We have to earn our Green Credits.' Hunter took a deep breath and let the tension leave his shoulders. 'However, we will all be rewarded for our service and patience, when the one-hundred-year plan is successfully implemented. Bodhi Sattva is a man of his word.'

'Yeah, strangely, everybody seems ok with this.'

'There are very few old animals in the wild, apart from the apex predators, it is Her way of controlling the population. I am fortunate to still have my health and a job I enjoy.' He said in the manner of a man who was very much aware that he was in the company of his employer by proxy.

Brady said, 'So, the forty-two years with me in charge is a relative blink of an eye for you.'

'That's still a long time, and I hope it continues…'

'Don't worry. This job is yours for as long as you want it.'

Hunter nodded but smiled knowingly. They walked down the steep steps toward the vehicle holding area. Brady said, 'Libby told me that John Kane indoctrinated Xavier with environmental ideas from before he was born.'

'That's not strictly true, sir.' He winced as he realised, he had slipped into his old habit. 'He had staff, teachers, professors, zealots and other assorted weirdos, teaching and reciting to Xavier from before he was born. However, I don't know where the interest in the environment came from. He was able to recite the periodic table backwards and forwards from the age of three. They taught him business strategies, math, physics, chemistry, and biology, primarily. Any interest in the environment John Kane had expressed was in the money-making potential of recyclables and renewables.' He looked away for a moment, 'I thought it was utterly disgusting the way Mr Kane treated his son. It was relentless hot housing of the worst kind.'

What the fuck did they do to me? 'And where was Libby while all this was going on?'

'She was here - moving into her new home. Mr Kane had Xavier taken away from her. She barely saw her son, and when she did, Xavier was kept under strict supervision.' At the bottom of the steps, Brady looked back up to his home, his most visceral achievement of his life. Hunter said, 'It's quite magnificent. Libby loved this house.'

When they reached Brady's vehicles, he inspected them all. He stroked his trusty old Green Bike like a child with a much-loved old toy. He moved on to his Fusion-Car™, van, lorry, coaches, his FusionPlane™, the passenger jets of assorted sizes and then onto his very own HeavyLoader™. He said, 'At some point, maybe in the next few weeks, I'm expecting a visitor.'

'Who will that be, sir?'

'She's a Fleet Captain with Sattva Systems™. She may not be attending with their authorisation, but she's doing me a personal favour.'

'I see.'

'I don't want her to come to the house. Her name is Marjorie - I don't know her surname, she's black and about so-high...' He put his hand up to just under his chin. 'She is to have access to every vehicle on the property. She can do whatever she needs to them. It's for my personal safety and security. Is that clear?'

'Perfectly, sir.'

Brady smiled, 'I think we should head back up to the house and see if the girls are ready.' As they began their walk back, Brady added, 'We'll have to do this more often. I've enjoyed our little chat.'

Hunter smiled in acknowledgement as if he was relieved to have kept his job, and Brady concluded that he had gained Hunter's trust. He believed he could be useful.

Amie and Helgarth acted as if they were delighted to see the returning master of the house, and they had returned fully to their female appearance and had used the Yellow™ to dress as Brady would have approved. They were both showing the early signs of their pregnancies. Brady wondered if they had exaggerated their shapes with the illusion of the YellowSuits™. They both hugged and kissed him as if he were a returning conqueror, even though they had no idea about what he had done or where he had been in the last few weeks. Brady played his part and informed them that he was delighted to be back. He even agreed to the evening's plans for a celebration.

Brady spent the afternoon contemplating his life. It was as if everything had taken time to sink in. The thought of having sons of his own turned to questions on how he should raise them. *I'm completely fucked up. I might not even be thinking with my own mind. If John Kane - I mean, what the fuck - do I start to think of him as Real Daddy! If he had me brainwashed into being a lowlife criminal then I am obviously not the role model for children - maybe I should let Amie and Helgarth raise 'em, but haven't they been conditioned by all this Green crap over the years? Is this the sort of thing that all new fathers think about? I wonder how I might have turned out if I had been raised like any other normal kid.*

He chuckled to himself as he gazed over the Pacific. *You've gotta admit it though, Brady Mahone has ended up being one of the wealthiest and most successful businessmen on the planet.* He watched a bank of clouds gang up on the Sun, and his mood darkened in sympathy. *Was that me that achieved that? Was it really all down to my own hard work? I had all these things just go right for me. Sure, I had the opportunities, and I exploited them, but without Bodhi, technically and biologically, I suppose, being my brother, would I have been successful at all? Would I have survived?*

John Kane entered his mind, and he was laughing at Brady Mahone, his little experiment to produce the lowest of the low. *I wonder if Bodhi and Glenarvon Cole know? Would they have the same misgivings as me? Or would they just carry on as if it meant nothing to them?*
For a moment, he even had a warm glow at believing he was part of a family. He tried to imagine what his life would have been like if he had two older brothers watching his back. Bodhi seemed knowledgeable and wise and couldn't have done more to help Brady Mahone develop his business ideas. *He had welcomed me and treated me real kind - even when I tried to blackmail him. My God, I couldn't have done what he did. I couldn't have forgiven somebody like me putting the squeeze on, never mind, go out of my way to make Brady Mahone's dreams come true. I owe him big time for that.* Brady began to feel bad about pushing Bodhi out of Brady Mahone's Entertainment Enterprises.

He considered the middle brother of the three, Glenarvon Cole. *He's a fucking legend to the Greens. He's the baddest and the bravest of the lot of them - and then he might find out that I'm his little brother. I bet he ain't too proud of that fact.* Brady sighed as he considered his unusual feelings of inadequacy.

Amie and Helgarth wandered over to him and seemed to be blooming - as the expression went - but Brady knew that with the YellowSuits™ appearances could be deceptive, and he believed he would never really know the real person inside these Suits™, ever again. *My boys are gonna be just as hidden from me.*

Amie said, 'We've been discussing the birthing arrangements…'

Here we go, I'm back for five minutes, and already we are in baby talk territory.

'…and we were wondering when you'd like your boys to be delivered. We can choose any day within a one-week window to give birth, and it's turned out great because as a Trad you might like to choose Christmas Day - we could do that if you want?'

Brady shrugged and forced a smile of interest.

'…or we could go for a New Green Year baby, that would be fantastic, and I'm sure it will be good luck.'

Brady suddenly had a vision of Libby in agony as she was being butchered by her surgeons. 'I'm not keen on either of those. Sorry.'

Amie looked crestfallen, so Helgarth said, 'What would you like, Brady?'

Brady thought about it for a moment and then said, 'I want it to be on the 30th December 2142.'

Brady watched Helgarth do some working out in her mind and then nodded to Amie. Helgarth said, as if she was thinking out loud rather than addressing Brady directly, 'New Green Year is on a Tuesday, so that would be a Sunday - that's cool. Also, it means we could birth the babies, have a day to recover on Monday and then we could party on New Green Year's eve. That would be fabulous.'

Amie said, 'With the Orange™, we are able to recover in just over an hour - so, I've been told.'

Helgarth said, 'Brady Mahone, you are going to be one proud Daddy. We agree. That sounds like a wonderful day to bring two new Green boys into our wonderful world.'

They both hugged him. He said, 'Thank you. I'm thinking of leaving their upbringing to you, as long as they have a masculine attitude to life. I don't feel like I'm the best of role models for them. Would that work for you?'

Amie protested with an absence of vigour, 'You'll be a great Pops, Brady.'

'Thanks. It's nice of you to say that, but you two will do a better job than me.'

27. IN SEARCH OF SPACE

'There is a lot to consider with this plan.' Bodhi said, as Genesis Garcia, Glenarvon Cole and Marjorie, or Fusion Fleet Captain Hampton - huddled around the layout of Tia Cassandra's Mission to Mars Colony. Tia had provided plenty of detail for the outsiders to use and fulfil their deal or complete a rescue mission, depending on whose point of view you looked at the potential catastrophe.

Glen said, 'I'm going to state the obvious, for the record. There are hardly any Trads left anywhere in the world. I know we have our mantra, but we could ignore the deal and let them die, or even just kill them - and then we could return to our one-hundred-year plan. It would save a lot of time and effort, and the risks could be drastically reduced.'

Bodhi glanced at him and said dismissively, 'We will not harm another creature. We are not giving away the moral high ground, especially to Tia Cassandra. History will judge us on our actions in this world. I am the holder of that history, and I will not be damned by decisions on life and death. People live and die by their choices and self-selection, not by our decisions on their behalf.' He watched Glen's face twist in a mixture of anger and shame. Bodhi added, 'Anyway, we made a deal, I know, it sounds like the old days…'

Glen breathed out heavily, 'Ok, I get it. I don't want to start up the space program for her - she's a right-wing zealot, and I think she's extracted a heavy price from us.'

Bodhi said, 'Do you think she's rational, intelligent and cunning?'

'Yes.'

'Tia Cassandra has the potential to spot tricks and traps. I wouldn't want to jeopardise the planet just to get one over a business rival.'

'Ok. How are we going to do this?' Glen wanted to take himself out of the firing line of Bodhi's intense gaze.

Bodhi said, 'We have so many conflicting problems. They are Trad, and they can't leave to receive the NanoSuits™. The pools for the *intense giving of Suits™* are here in Boulder Creek. We could use the less powerful Distors™ as in the New Year Ceremonies, but they are more diffuse and need weeks of rest between each coloured layer, instead of hours with the pools.'
Marjorie added, 'We also have the issue with the quicksand and the landing of the FusionVehicles™ - they could hover in a standing pattern for about eighteen hours, but that's pushing it.'

Bodhi summarised, 'The pools are in the wrong place, there isn't a place to land the vehicles, and we only have an eighteen-hour window of opportunity.'

Marjorie said, 'If I was in Tia's shoes, I would want Brady to act as a go-between. They must have a rapport, as Brady needn't have come here. One thing's for sure, and please don't take this the wrong way, Bodhi - but she isn't going to trust you as far as she can throw you.'

Bodhi brushed his hand over his bald head, 'God only knows how much more he'll want in payment for his further assistance.'

28.DREAM JOB

Hunter knocked on the door of Brady's unofficial study. Brady had found a quiet hidey-hole in his palatial home. 'You have a visitor, sir.'

'Who is it?'

'Fusion Fleet Captain Hampton.'

'Never heard of him. What does he look like?'

Hunter adapted his language to fit in with Brady's version of normality, whereas as with the Greens, and especially with Amie and Helgarth, he would have to have challenged Brady's binary notation. 'It's a woman, sir. She's black and from the Sattva Systems™ HQ in Boulder Creek. She's travelled a long way to see you, and she wants you to know that it's important.'

'Ah, Marjorie, you should have said that in the first place.'

'Sorry, sir. Shall I bring her here?'

'Yes. Yes, and offer her food, drink or anything else she wants.'

Hunter left, and Brady went to his en suite to use the bathroom and freshen up. He smiled broadly when Marjorie arrived. 'Whey hey! So, now you can see where the legendary Brady Mahone lives.'

Marjorie lived with seven others in an ecologically and environmentally friendly home, but she wasn't going to challenge Brady on his opulent way of life. She needed to keep him sweet. 'You've done exceptionally well for yourself, especially when you consider that you are a Trad in a Green world.' She sat down in a luxurious armchair which was probably a design classic back in the old days. Marjorie lay back and appeared to enjoy taking time out to relax. She noted Brady mirrored her relaxation. 'I have some work to do here, but I want to do it with your full knowledge.'

'What's that?'

'I need to replace the trackers on all your vehicles for your…'

'Protection. Yes, I know. That's ok.'

'I also need to place them on your everyday items - your favourite shoes, jeans and coat, maybe even in your artist's notebooks and materials. I have to plan for all eventualities.' She apologised, 'I know this is a huge intrusion on your privacy.'

'It's ok. Rhea said I could trust you, so that's good enough for me. Anyways, at least you are being upfront about it, not like they did in the old Internet days, eh?'

She nodded and smiled. 'There's something else.'

'Go on.'

'You are going to be approached by Bodhi or possibly Glenarvon Cole with a request to help them deal with Tia Cassandra. Rhea wants you to give it freely.'

'Does she now.'

Marjorie wasn't sure how he had taken this. His face was unreadable at first until finally, he grinned from ear to ear, 'Brady Mahone, secret agent, now that sounds like fun. Sure thing, count me in. Will it be exciting?'

'I'll ensure you'll be at the heart of the action. I promise.'

Brady slumped back in his chair and chuckled and said to himself, 'Brady Mahone - secret agent, and the Brady gets the girl...' He didn't realise he had said the last bit out loud. 'How do you know Rhea?'

'We were friends before the Revolution. We go way back.'

'How come she wasn't a natural Green like you?'

'We had disagreements about just about everything. However, we laughed at all the same things.' She looked away dreamily, 'We used to have the best times.' She added, 'We met through my husband, Michael. He was in the military when I met him. I was in the Air Force.'

'Is he still around?'

'No, he was an Alpha-male Trad not unlike you. I went through a radical environmental phase which made me Green enough to qualify to be here now. I left the Air Force to become a test pilot for the experimental FusionPlanes™. When the Green shutters came down, we were separated forever. I was in Boulder Creek, and he was in Saudi Arabia...'

'I'm sorry.' He wanted to know more about Rhea, 'And you and Rhea, how did that work out?'

She smiled. She knew he was eager for information about her, 'She drifted from job to job.' She laughed, 'She had only just got that job as a TV reporter for the low budget Green News Channel. It had a really crappy name, what was it? Ah, yes, Free News.' She laughed again. 'Rhea said that it only used to have about ten thousand regular viewers until that day when it was the only channel left standing.' She laughed even more loudly, 'She's hilarious. She says that only she could have landed the highest ratings ever and then be out of a job!' She then looked at her watch. 'I'm sorry, Brady. I've got to get on with my task. It's more difficult than it looks fitting the trackers into the NanoSecured™ dashboards - and I need the utmost concentration.'

'Sure. I get it. When do I get to do my secret agent thing?'

She smiled, 'It will in about fifteen weeks from today. We have a schedule of works. Does that work for you? I know you travel a lot...'

'Not a problem.' He added playfully, 'I'll keep a space in my diary. Brady Mahone has accepted his mission.'

29.ANY COLOUR YOU LIKE - AS LONG AS IT'S GREEN

While the teams in Boulder Creek were frantically formulating plans and analysing test results, and while Tia Cassandra and her staff were pulling together their findings from their fifty-year experiment on the feasibility of Martian Colonies, Brady Mahone rested. He took an occasional interest in the ongoing pregnancies of Amie and Helgarth. He took swims in the pools, and he walked along the shore, alone. His thoughts revolved around Bodhi at the centre of his universe, with Glenarvon Cole and himself as the nearest planets to the Sun. Even though he didn't like the old Tyrone talks of the Solar System, some of it had sunk into Brady's brain - maybe it had been all the talk about Mars which had made him see the world this way. He thought of all the other people he knew from Amie, Helgarth, Genesis Garcia, Marjorie, all his Sales Reps for Brady Mahone Entertainment Enterprises. He considered Cain, Siddha and Lizzie. He wondered how the Beardon family fitted in with all of this, but most of all, he thought about Rhea.

He had asked Hunter to remind him when his fifteen weeks of waiting were up, as he no longer trusted himself to remember, especially as all his days were rolling from one sunshiny summer day in Malibu into the next. He had not arranged for any overseas trips, as there was little pressure on him to drum up more business. Bodhi's manufacturing network and sales teams had added to his fortune - considerably and effortlessly. The only job he could think of doing, which was his alone, was to head up to Boulder Creek one day to collect his next millions of Green Credits and have them installed on his Distor™, freely. He was in no rush.

Finally, the fifteen weeks were up, and Marjorie turned up at his Malibu home to curtail Brady Mahone's semi-retirement. He often felt sorry for the old Greens like Hunter, who had to keep working, but having tried to relax, forever, he decided it didn't suit him. The lazy days sapped his restless energy, but it also felt like his life force was ebbing away from him.

'Hi Brady, are you ready? We have to move quickly.'

Brady was sleepy and groggy. He hadn't done anything particularly physical for at least three months. 'Yeah, just give me a minute. I need to freshen up.'

She watched him move lazily to the bathroom, and then she glanced at her watch. A few minutes later, he returned. She noticed he was not as sharp as before. He dressed slowly. She hid her irritation. He took an eternity to decide whether to put on sneakers or his heavy boots. He chose the boots, and he huffed as he tied up the laces.

He smiled tiredly, 'Ready when you are.'

She marched off, and Brady couldn't keep up with her. At first, he was blowing. She stopped to give him a chance to catch up, and then they walked together, slowly. When they reached his fleet of vehicles, she said, 'I'll fly in front, and you follow. I would suggest that we lock formations, so your FusionPlane™ takes its lead from mine. It will give you a chance to acclimatise.'

'Yeah, sounds like a plan.'

When they landed in Boulder Creek, Marjorie parked their synchronised vehicles in two allocated spaces right next to the Main Entrance of Sattva Systems™. These were usually reserved for emergency use only and watched over by the Security Protocols™.

Fuck. These guys must be in a hurry.

Sissy raced over to them. 'Great. You made it. Hi Brady. The convoy is ready to go…' She looked at her watch, 'in ninety-three minutes. We've got plenty of time. The FusionPassengerJet™ is ready to take us - if you'd care to follow me.'

They moved through the Main Hall and headed to the rear exit of the Sattva Systems™ HQ. Marjorie and Sissy were in animated discussions about logistics and scientific theorems. Brady rubbed his tired eyes and struggled to keep up with his quick marching companions. When Sissy flung open the manual door to the rear exit, the sun nearly blinded Brady. He took out his sunglasses from his Poacher's coat pocket, like a drunk with a hangover. His restored sight established that they were boarding the FusionPassengerJet™. When on board, he saw most of the top team of the Greens were already there, including many scientists he had only met briefly with in the past. He noted how Bodhi was seated humbly between two engineers in the centre rows. He never needed the security of self to demand special requirements. Brady recalled how sparse and dull Bodhi's office was.

Marjorie led Brady to a reserved seat at the front of the plane for herself and Brady. She said, 'I thought you'd appreciate the extra legroom.' She teased him playfully, 'If you are a really good boy, then I've got a big surprise for you, Brady Mahone.'

He felt like she injected his brain with energy as his fogginess started to lift from him. He didn't say anything. He wanted the window seat, but that was taken, and he was seated near the aisle. She saw him trying to peek through the window. Marjorie whispered to the man next to her, and he drew the curtain.

I suppose secret agents have to get used to secrets.

He said, 'So, this is it, then - the big rescue mission.'

'What is it, Brady? Don't you like surprises?'

'The only surprises I likes are the ones I give. When people have surprised Brady Mahone in the past, it's usually been the law.'

She laughed, 'Have you ever heard the phrase, *if the mountain will not come to Mohammed, Mohammed will go to the mountain?*'

'I like the way you talk. It kinda reminds me of the old days - yeah, sure, I heard of that.'

'Well, unlike your good self, Tia and her mates can't travel to the Green Community area of Boulder Creek.'

Brady smiled, 'You're spoiling it now - you mean Sattva Systems™ HQ.'

'Whatever. Anyway, they can't come to us, so we are carrying the five operational NanoPools™ to them. They are each the size of a football field.'

Brady tried to imagine the wires and attachments required to lift something of that size and weight. He had visions of old aircraft and helicopters pouring water on the forest fires that used to rage all the time back in the old days. 'Wow, that's gonna be real tricky, I guess.'

Marjorie nudged her elbow into his across the arm of the passenger seat and said playfully, 'Yeah, real goddamn tricky.'

He saw the passenger peek through the FusionPassengerJet™ window. He watched him gasp and then mouth the word *whoa!'* Brady demanded, 'Hey, man. Open the curtain, I wanna see.' The man who looked like a Japanese tourist looked to Marjorie, and Marjorie shook her head in disappointment and then nodded her approval. The man pulled back the curtain, and Brady leaned over both of them to get a better look. He was awestruck at the sight before him. It was the largest machine he had ever seen, he used to watch the History of Mega-machines on the old TVs, and he had never seen anything like this. 'Fuck me, it's huge!'

Marjorie said, 'That was going to be my surprise, but I guess you took a crafty look at the presents under the Christmas tree.'

Brady couldn't utter a word, and his brain couldn't look at this monster and talk at the same time. His conscious mind was laid to waste as the machine was probably larger than fifty HeavyLoaders™ combined. It was circular. He thought he could make out concentric circles in the subtle changes of shadowing across its cream-coloured ceramic body. The only indication of a front part of the craft, was the Sattva Systems™ logo on one part of the circle. On the top of the vessel in the giant centre circle was a massive arrow which seemed to levitate within a flattened glass globe - it was moss-green with a gold tip at the point. He tried to communicate his awe, 'It's fucking...y'know...'

The Japanese tourist-looking guy stepped into the verbal breach, 'It's fucking awesome.'

Brady, who didn't seem to notice he had clambered all over Marjorie, clasped the man's shoulder and shook him in celebration. 'Too right, buddy. Awesome.'

They laughed, and when Marjorie saw the other passengers watching them with Brady sprawled all over her, she had a fit of the giggles, which infected Brady and the Japanese tourist. The FusionPassengerJet™ began to circle away from the giant machine, and Brady calmed down and returned to his seat. 'What was that?'

Marjorie said, 'You saw the inner structure decades ago, but that was just the first circle. It's had another five circles surrounding it since then. It's the Prototype LeviathanLifter™ it's only had one test flight, and that was my job.'

'You flew that thing?'

'Yes, I tested it to its limits. If it had any flaws, then fifty years of manufacturing would have gone up in smoke. Spoiler alert - it worked like a dream. In hovering mode, it uses the Earth's magnetic core to stabilise itself.'

'And what's the deal with the arrow? It looks like a hunter's compass.'

Marjorie said, 'That's it - in a nutshell. You set the compass, and when you lift off, it will align itself with your chosen destination. It indicates to SattNav™ when it's in motion, and all other traffic is pushed out of its way. It moves comparatively slowly, and it takes an eternity to bring to a halt.' She added, 'When we are up and running, you can sit with me. I might even let you have a go on the controls. They are intuitive.'

'Oh, wow.'

'That was my surprise. I thought you had enough Green Credits. I thought this would be a better way to reward you for your help.'

He faced her and grinned broadly.

The PassengerFusionJet™ dropped slowly onto its slot, and the Great and the Good of the Greens alighted the vehicle - as did Brady Mahone. The sub-sonic throbs hit him immediately, and he counted sixteen HeavyLoaders™ landing in columns of four on each side of the LeviathanLifter™ in squadrons of eight. Marjorie said without waiting for Brady to ask - she knew he wanted to know everything. *If they had taught him all about big machines at school, then who knows how Brady might have turned out - he might have ended up working for me.* 'It's only its second flight. The Heavy-Loaders™ will lock in-formation to give it extra stability.'

'Does it need it?'

'No. But it's a safety precaution. However, I've got the most important Greens on the planet in my care, and the NanoPools™ are three-quarters full of NanoMaterial™, which can't be mixed. It's not gaseous or liquid, it's viscous, but it will roll if the LeviathanLifter™ becomes unbalanced. It's risky but doing nothing about the situation in Cima carried a catastrophic threat.'

He gazed upward at the giant mechanical monster, but Marjorie urged him up the cream-coloured steps into the belly of the beast. The size of its innards made Brady feel like he was walking into a small village. The central area had the five NanoPools™ in the sequence of the Suits™ the Greens had given out over the decades since the Revolution. Marjorie rushed off to the front of the vehicle. There appeared to be no designated cockpit. She headed toward the one Sattva Systems™ logo, which he guessed mirrored the position of the one on the outside of the creamy ceramic shell. She put in a cream-coloured earbud, which other members of the crew had. He watched them take up their positions around the circumference. He counted thirty-six co-pilots - and they were all equidistant from each other. They pressed switches, and all ran checks - he could see it was at her initiation.

The Sun burst through the clouds, and the windows around the whole ship all darkened at different levels, dependent upon the amount of light hitting them. He spun around, gathering in a panoramic view of the world outside this vessel. He looked up, dizzily to the enormous glass dome above his head, and he stared up at the clouds. They looked like they would if he had put his sunglasses on. He watched the underside of the magic arrow as if it was in suspended animation. The golden spearhead glittered in the sunlight. *If I could die right here - I'd die a happy man.*

His neck began to hurt from looking upwards for too long. He strolled around the belly of the beast, and for a fleeting moment, felt a twinge of fear, or maybe it was apprehension as he recalled the Bear's Great White shark story. He flung out his arms as an unconscious reaction to the sense of being trapped.

He moved through the crowd of dignitaries who were like a pack of businessmen at a sales conference. Some glanced in Brady's direction, but their body language, even to a virtually illiterate reader at this level of subtlety, suggested that nobody wanted to speak with the Trad, Brady Mahone - not even Sissy, Glenarvon or Bodhi. He passed the last of the hangers-on until he was alone by the NanoPools™. He remembered the people who lived in Tia Cassandra's colony in their spacesuits. He wondered if they were all-American Trad astronauts, whether they would choose to be Green, and if they did, would that entice him to join them?

That's how they get you, son?

The Red NanoPool™ was supposed to be transparent, he had always been told, and yet, he was convinced he could see the colours of the NanoShells™ alter whenever a Green Community held one of their ceremonies, to upgrade the NanoSuits™. He didn't need anybody to tell him what he could or couldn't see with his own two eyes. This NanoPool™ was a reddish haze. He took a closer look, and he could just about make out the changing depths. They looked shallow at both ends but much deeper in the middle. He recalled playing with a thermometer he had smashed in a mindless act of vandalism when he was a kid. He remembered playing with the mercury which spilt from it, and this red goo appeared to have a similar texture except that he could see right through this weird stuff. He strolled past the Orange™, Yellow™, Green™ and Blue™ NanoPools™ until a hidden Tannoy announced that it was time to take their seats in preparation for vertical take-off. A young woman came over to Brady and escorted him to a seat at the front adjacent to Marjorie.

Brady was impressed with the relaxed professionalism of Fleet Captain Marjorie Hampton. She smiled as if she were only taking an old Honda Civic to the supermarket. Brady felt a surge of adrenaline race through him. He couldn't remember ever being this excited - not even in a fight to the death - that was taking care of business, whereas this was the ultimate thrill. He smiled at the *Fasten Your Safety Belts* announcement as this seemed quaintly old school.

The massive sub-sonic wave hit him like the opening blast of bass guitar chords at a heavy metal concert, and he did now, what he would have done then, he whooped and hollered at the top of his voice. The rest of the passengers didn't have the time or the inclination to warn Brady that he might be impeding the concentration of the pilot crew and their captain right beside him. Brady hollered his way through the entire take-off. He felt the throb coming up through the base of his swivel chair. He spun around and, for a moment, looked at the apprehensive passengers, but he was far more interested in the two blocks of eight HeavyLoaders™ on either side of the LeviathanLifter™. He wondered what their fabulous view of this machine looked like from their vantage point. He watched the co-pilots at work, and he noticed that they were having to apply considerable pressure on the joysticks and lifting gears. He had taken it for granted that only a light touch would be required for such futuristic technology - in his mind. He didn't want to think like Tyrone and all his space travel crap, but he wondered whether this monster would be better suited to zero gravity. He recalled the mention of magnetic fields and gravitational pull and wondered if this was why it took a small degree of physicality to lift off. He turned to see Marjorie, and he noticed beads of perspiration on her forehead, even if her body language to the passengers behind her suggested all was calm, and she was in complete control. He looked down at the ground, and he was sure that it was moving up in tandem with the LeviathanLifter™. It appeared to be bulging. I *wonder what it would do to the Jelly Sand.*

He soon sensed that the whole convoy was edging forward in strict formation. Over many minutes the convoy began to increase speed. He was surprised to find that they only moved as high as Level Ten on the Highway network. He believed they would fly at a much greater altitude. He ignored the Safety Belt warning and got out of his chair. He wanted to see the view from the rear of the vehicle. He heard a loud and resounding thump, and he saw the land slump back into position. He didn't doubt that these clever Greens had done their calculations, but he wondered what their risk assessments on potential earthquakes concluded. He saw one of the pilots on P18 struggling with his lifting gear. 'Hey, man. You look like you're struggling with that. Do you need a hand?'

The youngish looking man was listening intently to instructions that presumably came from Marjorie. He turned to Brady, 'The Power Assistance on my lifting gear is malfunctioning. I need to level up by 0.0025 degrees, but I can't overshoot.'

Brady watched him straining and then said, 'Here, let me help.' The co-pilot looked at the six-foot-six and eighteen stone bulk of Brady and thought it wasn't as bad an idea as it sounded. He let Brady take up the strain while he concentrated on his joystick and monitored his instruments while listening to his Captain on his earbud. *I can see why the little guy is struggling. It's fighting like a bastard to nosedive.* Brady put all of his brute force into keeping the lifting gear from its desire to plunge back to the floor.

The co-pilot said, 'If we can get it to perfectly level, then I can apply the automatic lock, at least until we can check out what's gone wrong.'

Brady said, 'What do you want me to do?' He added, 'What's your name, son?'

'It's Leroy.' He ignored Brady's improper binary assignation because he knew who Brady was - like everybody else on the ship. 'I need it to pull up another 0.0011 degrees.' He needed something that Brady could measure that would make sense. 'The lifting gear needs to come up another inch and a quarter.'

'Got it.' Brady moved into a squatting position like he used to do in the gym at Ridgecrest Supermax. He got a good grip on the lifting gear, and he put all of his might into moving the lifting gear a fraction of an inch at a time. His face reddened, and he bared his teeth as he put all of his strength into completing his task. The lifting gear made slow progress upward until Brady felt a loud click from under the floor.

Leroy shouted, 'It's locked.' He said into a tiny microphone that Brady couldn't see. 'Automatic lock secured, Captain.' He turned to Brady and said, 'Thank you.'

'You're welcome.' Brady watched a small team head down a hatch, presumably on Marjorie's orders to investigate the problem. He added, 'Probably looked harder than it was. It was just a short workout. I'm feeling real good now. Brady Mahone is ready for anything.'

As the LeviathanLifter™ moved serenely onwards on its journey to Cima and the Mojave Desert, Brady soon relaxed into the journey once his initial euphoria had subsided. He even felt a little embarrassed about his lack of cool in front of these bigshot Greens. *I probably shouldn't have cheered the lift-off -still, at least I got up and did something when Leroy obviously needed help. These Green bigshot fucks just sat on their backsides and watched him struggle.*

He slumped back on his cream-coloured swivel chair and parked his heavy boots on the panelling. He noted that Marjorie neither noticed nor cared about Brady's posture, as she quietly concentrated on the instrument panels in front of her. She occasionally issued calm instructions…*Level up 0.03 degrees P27…Angle down 0.0012 degrees P3.* Brady looked around to note the movements of her team and deduced that the P stood for Pilot or maybe Position, and she was positioned at P0. Marjorie said, 'Thanks for your assistance, Brady. Maybe you should be a permanent member of the crew.'

Brady laughed, 'Hey, I'm way too busy for that.'

She laughed with him, 'Ok. You can be an honorary crew member.'

'Yeah. I'd like that.'

30.CIMA

The convoy crawled over the final miles approaching Cima. Brady had watched Marjorie slowing the LeviathanLifter™ from more than twenty miles away. The Sun was behind them, and the immense vessel and her accompanying Heavy-Loaders™ cast a massive shadow in front of them over the town of Cima and then across the desert sands. Brady wondered what the townsfolk were thinking as he watched them leaving their homes to view this procession. He guessed some may have welcomed a moment's relief from the blistering sun, while others would have been troubled by the giant crafts. *I woulda thought it was real cool.* As they headed to Tia Cassandra's experimental Martian Colony, he looked over the area he had walked across a few months earlier, and he could see from up here why he found it so difficult. The LeviathanLifter™ caused the quicksand to move in waves like an ocean made of sand. He recognised the large lake of quicksand - which was more than a mile wide - that had caused him so much consternation. He couldn't be sure with his measurements, but he was convinced that it was even more prominent now.

They finally reached the Colony, and the LeviathanLifter™ held its position about a mile short of it and about the same height above it. Brady couldn't understand why it didn't position itself directly overhead. Suddenly, he was aware of intense activity occurring around him. After the leisurely pace to reach here, everybody acted as if there wasn't another moment to lose. Scientists rushed to the NanoPools™, and Bodhi, Sissy, Cain and Glenarvon Cole came over to Brady. Bodhi said, 'You'll have to lead the way. Tia doesn't trust us. However, you need to impress on her the need to move quickly.'

'Ok. Let's move.'

A hatchway opened behind some guard rails near the NanoPools™. He watched Bodhi check his transparent Red Distor™. Brady instinctively headed to the hatch. At first, Brady was alarmed at the view of the mile-high drop to the desert beneath him, but then he saw the NanoSteps™ being rapidly constructed; they edged downward, changing from clear to moss green as they grew down to the floor. Sissy said, 'You don't have to wait for them to reach the entrance to the Colony. When the steps turn Green, then they are safe to walk down.

Brady stepped out gingerly but then quicker as he gained confidence in his footing. He watched the steps being rapidly constructed in front of him. The steps then dug into the sand as if they were searching for an anchor point. Brady approached the entrance, and he knew this time that they would be waiting, as they should have seen them coming from fifty miles away. The airlock was already fully opened as if they had initiated whatever procedures they needed to do beforehand - to save precious time. Brady assumed this meant that they were worried about what was happening to them. He guessed this would alleviate the need for complex negotiations if their minds were focused on emergency evacuation mode.

Tia and Dagny greeted him. He knew their rivalry with Bodhi would mean they wouldn't show panic. It was almost a criminal code to Brady. He said, 'We don't have much time. This is Bodhi...' He said, 'Let's just assume you know everybody. We don't have time for niceties...'

Bodhi said, 'Hello Tia, I wish we were meeting in more auspicious circumstances. How many people do you have?'

'Have we got a deal?'

'Yes. Now, how many of you are there?'

'Myself, my daughter, Dagny.' Dagny shook hands with all of their rescuers. Tia continued, 'Thirty-eight workers, scientists, engineers and technicians. We also have seventy colony astronauts and volunteers. They are still in the spacesuits; it is too risky to take them off. They are extremely weak, and the Earth's gravity is dangerous to them.'

Bodhi thought about the situation. He said, 'I need to give you all the InfraRed™ Primer to enable you to leave this facility. They need to place flesh on flesh to receive it. Otherwise, we cannot save them.'

Dagny whispered to Tia for a few moments. Tia replied, 'We can remove the gloves while the rest of their bodies remained sealed.'

'Good. On your plans you have a large training room - can you assemble everybody there. I will do the bare minimum of our ceremony to make everybody Green.'

Tia said to Brady, 'Are you going Green?'

'No.'

'Why not?'

'I don't fancy it. I'm Trad, and I'm proud.' Due to the urgency of the situation, he added, 'Can't say I've ever seen anybody having any side effects or nothing nasty like that.'

Tia nodded to Dagny, who rushed off to gather her crew. Tia said, 'This way, please.'

They all followed Tia to the Training Room. Dagny was arranging the group so that the astronauts and colony volunteers were propped up by the Colony workers. Bodhi headed to the front of the room and announced, 'This is a simple procedure. You will not have any of the benefits of the Green Nanotechnology until you are processed in the NanoPools™ on our LeviathanLifter™ vessel, which is awaiting you outside this facility.' He tried to use the language of the scientists as he was aware of their presence in particular here. He wasn't addressing his devout followers here. 'This ceremony…procedure is a NanoCoating™ which will allow the NanoSuits™ to take the GreenSuits™ which will give you protection for your skin, and enormous health benefits. Primarily, it will allow you to leave this facility. I'm sorry, such is the urgency of the situation, I cannot answer your questions - this is a matter of trust…'

Tia said, 'This is an order. Follow the instructions.'

Bodhi smiled sincerely, 'Everybody must be connected flesh on flesh, ideally by holding hands with a person next to you. When everybody is physically connected, I will complete the chain, and this thing…' He held up his Distor™, 'it's called an InfraRed™ Distor™ will apply you with NanoCoating™.' He looked up and said, 'Cain, Sissy, can you make sure everybody is connected.' There was a shuffling of people for a couple of minutes.

Sissy said, 'We are ready.'

Bodhi wasted no time. He completed the chain with Cain and Sissy at his side, and Brady saw the room glow in an almost invisible red mist. He wondered if he was the only one in the room who could see it. The shimmering disappeared, and Brady felt the ground beneath him heave upwards and then collapse back down again. Brady shouted, 'We gotta get outta here - now!'

Tia shouted over Brady's alarm, 'You will leave in an orderly manner. This isn't a time for stampedes.'

They moved at a quick march out to the entrance. Tia stopped for a second to take in the fact that this was the first time in nearly sixty years that she had left this facility. She saw the grotesque green psychedelic patterns dancing across the outer shell of the buildings. Then she saw the steps leading up to the largest machine she had ever seen. The steps headed a mile into the air and into the belly of the LeviathanLifter™. She said to Bodhi behind her, 'Many of the older astronauts are going to be too weak to do the climb.'

Bodhi said, 'My team will help. We won't leave anybody behind.'

She ordered, 'Those in the support roles - select an astronaut or Colony volunteer to aid up the steps.' She went to one and encouraged him to put his arm around her shoulder - and they began their ascent.

One astronaut was already struggling with the gravity. Brady lifted him up and carried him in his arms like a baby. He was lighter than a child, even though he was as tall as Brady. 'Come on, man. Not long to go. Hang on in there.' Brady went on past them all on the stairs. They knew he wasn't being impolite. They assumed he would come back and help the others. Once clear of the pack, Brady picked up the pace and streaked ahead of them. He talked as he ran, hoping it would keep his patient conscious. 'What's your name, buddy?'

The astronaut knew what Brady was doing, and he complied, 'Commander Rocky Fitzpatrick.'

Brady tried to humour him, 'I like it. That's a man's name.' Brady laughed, 'Are you in charge around here?'

'I was the lead on the experiment. I had to get through the difficult first few years. You could say I was the test pilot for the Colony.'

'Well, you get yourself fixed in the NanoPools™ and what say I get you meeting with the pilot of this thing.'

'That would be good.' He said weakly, 'What's your name, soldier?' Brady liked being considered a soldier. 'I'm Mahone. Brady Mahone.'

When he reached the top of the stairway, he didn't go inside. He handed over the astronaut cradled in his arms and headed back down the stairs. He bounded down the steps two at a time and selected his next patient, judged by who was most in need.

On his third trip, Tia collapsed. Everybody had underestimated how old she was in Trad years. Brady picked her up like a rag doll. The woman she was helping lay gasping on the floor, and one of the crew, who Brady had relieved of rescue duty earlier helped her up.

Once they were all inside the LeviathanLifter™, a co-pilot handed an earbud to Brady. He put it in, and he heard Fleet Captain Marjorie Hampton. 'Well done, Brady. If nobody else says it - I will - I'm proud of you. That was outstanding work.'

He said, 'Thanks. Just doing what anybody else would have done.' He wasn't even sure if this thing had a microphone.

'If you say so. Keep your earbud on, we are in unchartered territory, and I may need you. Is that ok?'

'No problem. I think we need to move sharpish; I think the ground was moving under that Colony thing.'

Marjorie didn't answer him directly. She put out an order. 'Drill positions.' He watched people move purposefully to all parts of the giant circular ship. He watched the Colony residents being helped with putting seatbelts on. 'Unlock formation.' He watched the HeavyLoader™ convoy break from their holding patterns. 'Commence Operation Clean-Up.' The HeavyLoaders™ broke free of the apron strings of the LeviathanLifter™ and Brady watched their hoses release, and they appeared to have received their fire at will orders as they sprayed the Colony. 'HeavyLoaders™ one through eight, target the Colony and HeavyLoaders™ nine through sixteen target the position of the underground Nuclear Fission plant.' Brady watched them in awe as they deluged the facility and the surrounding desert in Green goo. 'We are setting course back to HQ. Good job, goys.'

Brady watched the giant arrow above him turn slowly but smoothly through one hundred and eighty degrees. He was the only one who wasn't strapped into a seat. He wouldn't have complied anyway - he wanted to see it all. He refrained from cheering this time. The presence of Tia seemed to have a fearsome headmistress effect on his behaviour. He was transfixed by the HeavyLoaders™ at work, and he was conscious that he had to alter his position slightly. With nothing in his eye line on the desert horizon, he might not have believed he was moving at all, but the Colony gave away the LeviathanLifter's™ change of direction.

He then saw a giant sinkhole appear in the desert sands next to Colony, and then the sands poured into it like water. It didn't feel planned to Brady's untrained eyes. He felt the LeviathanLifter™ tilt slightly, and he didn't think that was a good sign either. He was relieved, even if he couldn't explain why, that the vessel he was on was making progress away from the scene of desert madness. A vast rumbling sound from under the desert emerged, there was a blinding white flash, followed by the most enormous explosion he had ever heard, the automatic sun shields tried to cope with the flash, but they plunged the LeviathanLifter™ into temporary darkness, and there were screams of panic echoing around the cavernous unit. The light returned, and then Brady saw the HeavyLoaders™ being obliterated by the shockwaves from the explosion. It was like a nuclear domino effect. The closest HeavyLoader™ to the blast exploded, sending its Nanoparticles at incredible speeds, ripping through all the other HeavyLoaders™ in the convoy.

There were screams from the people inside the vast industrial circle and howls of anguish as the seemingly impossible happened. The Green's machines and their loved ones who worked in them had been killed. Many of the co-pilots and workers on this craft worked in a close-knit community with the HeavyLoader™ crews. Fleet Captain Marjorie Hampton's colleagues wouldn't have been on those ships if it wasn't for their secondment to help with the rare deployment of the LeviathanLifter™.

Sissy was distraught, 'Bodhi, no! How could this have happened? The RedSuits™ should have been able to withstand nuclear attacks. They should have survived this.'

Bodhi said uncertainly, trying to work it out himself. 'The Nanotechnology has worked against us. It repels all forces, except it wouldn't repel the Nanobots propelled at light speed against its own kind.' He sounded panicked for once in his life as he begged Sissy, 'Brady must never know about the details. You have to convince him that it was just the nuclear blast which destroyed them.' He shook her out of her shock, 'Did you hear me? Do you understand?'

'Yes. Yes.' She said shakily.

Even Brady could guess what had happened when he saw the mushroom cloud. He'd seen a nuclear explosion before, but this looked dirtier, somehow. There were green flames all over the windscreens of the craft. Marjorie called on his earbud. 'Brady, I'm going to need you. Come to P0.' He raced over to Marjorie.

He could see small holes appearing in the shell of the LeviathanLifter™ near P2 - and then he saw the shockwave destroy the town of Cima. The buildings collapsed as if they were made of balsa wood. Fires started up instantaneously. The co-pilot in P2 had a heart attack and died on the spot. Marjorie said, 'He's died of shock. Even the Orange™ can't cope with that. I need you to take over. The HeavyLoader™ debris is made up of our own materials, its velocity from the blast has given it the energy required to inflict damage on the hull. I need you to take his position and then be ready for my instructions.'

Brady unbuckled the co-pilot and unceremoniously dumped his body on the ground. Brady pushed the dead Greens body over to cover some of the holes, he didn't know if this would have any effect in blocking the radiation, but it couldn't hurt, from Brady's point of view. If the guy's NanoSuit™ was still active, then he was merely stuffing the cracks with NanoArmour™.

He jumped into the seat. He heard Marjorie addressing the crew on his earbud. 'We are going to ascend to forty-thousand feet. It's never been done before with the LeviathanLifter™. We haven't the speed to outrun the danger. Radiation will seep through the breaches in the hull. We are going to ascend out of harm's way. We need to stay as level as possible, as the contents of the NanoPools™ will add to the danger, as I'm informed the raw materials have never been mixed before. We do not want to conduct that kind of experiment in these unusual conditions. Await my command to begin ascending. Over.'

Brady looked at the small holes in the hull and wondered if he would die of radiation sickness. Would he have to receive the Suits™ to survive? *That's how they get you, son.* Marjorie could see Brady's fixation on the holes and wondered whether he might be in shock at the sight of the Green Town of Cima being destroyed. 'Brady. Brady...' He looked at her, 'I need you on top form. I need you to keep your position steady and level. Can the great Brady Mahone do that for me?' She said again, 'Brady, can you do that?'

'Yeah. Sure thing.'

She announced over the Tannoy, 'Please stay seated and remain calm. We are going to ascend to forty-thousand feet for a smoother journey back to the HQ. NanoPool™ processing for the residents of the Colony will be delayed by approximately one hour.' She knew Bodhi would understand that this was a code for emergency procedure as the LeviathanLifter™ shouldn't be attempting to reach that altitude. It had specifically been designed as a low-level workhorse.

He looked at Sissy and Cain to indicate that he understood Marjorie's signal.

Brady tried to keep his concentration on the controls, but it wasn't easy as he gravitated upwards and watched the mushroom cloud billowing outwards above him and the scenes of the devastation below. He also oversaw the light glowing through the holes in the machine. Then he saw Marjorie looking over to him past the co-pilot at P1, and he knew he had a job to do. He focused on his instruments, and it seemed to calm his worried mind.

Tia moved next to Bodhi without being invited. 'What's the plan for my Space Program to colonise Mars?'

'I'm intertwining your wishes into my hundred-year plan.'

'What does that mean? Remember, this is all new to me.'

He smiled and said softly, 'Please forgive me. Today has been shocking for all of us.'

'Cut the politician crap. I want the information to rebuild my plans. I know how to make it work up there after fifty years of research and development, but you have the technology to improve on my plans.'

He kept his composure, 'By 2184, the Earth will be restored to full health, and then we will begin with our plans for the next billion years...'

'Really.' She sneered.

'Yes. We will provide you with our FusionPower™, Nanotechnology and our Biotechnology for your missions. Within five years, you could commence with your space flights to Mars - that will be up to you. However, the last mission I will authorise will be on 1st December 2184, as I will not have space travel from Earth beyond that date. This is your deadline.'

'You never mentioned deadlines in our deal.'

'Neither did you.' He smiled, 'You've been planning for this for decades, and you have a further forty-two years to complete your dream, and with the NanoSuits™ which I will provide, you could complete this task, and if you wish, live on Mars for a thousand years. I didn't mention that in the deal either.'

'No. You didn't. It's a very generous package. I accept your offer.' She shook his hand in the old-fashioned business way of sealing a deal. Bodhi said, 'I give it to you freely, as you have self-selected your future.'

She was perplexed by his choice of words but was content with the completion of her negotiations. Bodhi watched her body language expertly as she relayed the contents of the deal to Dagny. He could tell that Tia Cassandra was satisfied and energised - he wasn't sure that Dagny was quite as enthusiastic.

After an hour had elapsed, and the mushroom cloud of the atomic explosion was far behind them, Marjorie brought the LeviathanLifter™ down to Level Ten and put the giant machine on autopilot as it moved serenely onward to Boulder Creek.

Brady got up and stretched his legs. He found concentrating on one task for long periods of time tiring. He had tired of helping to fly the LeviathanLifter™. He soon understood the reasoning for the autopilot mode, as work crews came out with tanks on their backs, not unlike the ones that Samuel Beardon used in Los Banos where he first met him. They sprayed around the holes in the hull with their NanoFixant™ and NanoRepair™, and within seconds, he saw the edges blur and begin to fill in the holes.

He wandered over to the NanoPools™ to watch the shortened ceremonies commence. He checked himself over for wounds or rashes, but he couldn't detect any damage, so he shrugged off his fears and resisted the temptation to enter the NanoPools™ himself.

Unlike the ceremony in the Tia Cassandra's colony where Bodhi conducted it, Sissy took over the instructions. He watched Tia clearly explain to Dagny who Sissy was - or maybe, who she used to be. Sissy didn't look as comfortable with her public speaking as she should have done with all her experience. She summoned the scientists, engineers and workers, to be the first to take the Red™. She then said, 'Tia, Dagny, we will do you as well. We will do the astronauts last, as they will have to be quick due to their frailty. If they've listened and watched your example, we will then speed them through - after they've received the Orange™ then they may recover quickly. Although I can't be certain, I don't know what shape they are in until they remove their spacesuits.'

Tia and Dagny joined the others. Tia shook her head as if she were being asked to join a religious ceremony.

Sissy said, 'Unfortunately, you will all have to strip naked. The NanoSuits™ have to make contact with every part of your flesh.'

Brady smirked but didn't say anything. *This will be interesting.*

Tia marched to the front and stripped instantly. She showed no signs of embarrassment. She was making a show about leading by example.

Brady perused the old woman's body. *Then again, maybe not.*

Sissy continued, 'You need to go through the showers, then walk slowly through the Red NanoPool™. It is shallow, and then it will be above your heads, but you have nothing to fear, it's not liquid, you will not drown, then when you emerge at the far end of the pool, walk back to the beginning and repeat the procedure, including the showering, through the other colours.' Sissy realised that many of them hadn't been informed by Tia or Dagny what the colours meant. 'The Red™ gives you a hardened shell on your skin's surface, which protects you from external injuries. The Orange™ instils Nanobots to monitor and deal with harmful cells within the body, which improves your health and life expectancy. The Yellow™ does away with the need for textiles, as you can appear in any way you wish to others. The Green™ recycles food and water within your bodies, reducing the strain on sewage systems.'

Tia intervened and addressed her teams, 'Think what all this could do on Mars. I instruct you to complete this process.'

Sissy said, 'The Blue™ will give you the ability to be the gender you want to be, and you have the ability to move through the genders anytime you choose.'

This was the first time there was a look of confusion, or maybe consternation on the faces of the Colony's crew. Tia was about to comment, but Brady got there first, 'Hey, it's not compulsory to be a...'

Sissy corrected him, 'It is compulsory for at least one occasion, as it has to be activated to enable future developments. The Blue™ is the last one our people have taken.' She saw the uncertainty, she added, 'If you take the Blue™, then the next one, which will be released within the next decade, will be Indigo™, which will allow you to sleep instantly at your initiation, and you will only need three hours per day to complete its neuropathways cleansing, and you will only feel utterly refreshed, this will give you twenty-one hours of highly focused wakefulness. And finally, the Violet™ will enable you to have enhanced senses, improved sight, hearing, smell, touch and even taste - but you have to take the Blue™ to enable you to have these...'

There was a moment of communal reflection, but then Tia moved purposefully to the showers. Dagny followed her example, and soon the rest of the Colony formed an orderly queue. The twenty astronauts and civilian volunteers hung back and remained seated in their spacesuits while they acclimatised to the new gravity levels on the outside of the Colony.

Brady sat next to Commander Rocky Fitzpatrick. 'Hey, back in the old days, you astronauts were like all American heroes. Do you mind if I just call you Rocky?'

'Sure, son.' He replied from inside his space helmet. 'I'm getting the impression these people don't have a space program of their own.'

'No. they don't believe in abandoning the planet.'

'Is that how they see it? Do they not want to explore further, seek out new worlds, and find the origins for life on Earth?'
Brady thought he had made a mistake. He sensed that this could be another of those science-y space talk kinds of deals. 'Take it from me - they are not interested.' He changed the subject, 'What are you looking forward to, y'know, when you get out of your suit?'

Commander Fitzpatrick was momentarily distracted as he observed the team making serene progress through the NanoPools™. 'Sorry, I'm feeling a little light-headed. It's the change of environment. What did you say?'

'What are you looking forward to, now that you're back in the real world?'

'I know it's not healthy, but I'm looking forward to eating a huge steak meal, washed down with cold beer.'

Brady said, 'Good luck with that. You've got more chance of that on Mars. The Greens put a stop to that as soon as they took over, and the Trads didn't have any electric or gas - hell, they couldn't even get a fire going once the Greens doused everything in Nano goo, whatever.'

Rocky asked, 'What are Trads?'

'You are looking at one of the last surviving ones. All the others were left to die.'

'What? How many?'

Brady said, 'I don't know precisely, I mean it's big numbers, but they were talking about seven or eight billion - it's definitely billions because sometimes I get it mixed up with millions.' Brady looked at the blank expression on Rocky's face, and it reminded him of the old days because Rocky's face looked like a computer whose screen had frozen. 'Anyhows, apparently there is just less than a billion Greens left on the planet - I mean, that's still a lot, isn't it?'

'All dead, in half a century...eight billion dead.'

Brady said darkly, 'That would be one helluva funeral bill. In case you're wondering, they dissolved the dead with their goo, just like they did with everything the Trads made or owned.'

'You mean the cities, the artwork and the cultural artefacts from ancient civilisations?' He added, 'Surely not?'

'I've travelled all over the world, and unless it's left standing in a Green area, where the stuff would have been recycled or repurposed, then yes, you'd struggle to know that the Trads ever existed.' He added cheerfully, 'Hey, did you know that Brady Mahone has his own FusionPlane™ - in fact, I've gotta whole fleet of vehicles, I gotta Fusion…'

Commander Rocky Fitzpatrick zoned out of Brady's endless list of features and benefits of every vehicle in his fleet, from his Green Bike to his very own Heavy-Loader™. He watched the last of his colleagues take the Blue™. He struggled to take in the enormity of the knowledge which Brady had imparted.

Sissy came over to rescue the frail Commander from Brady's enthusiasm. A team of assistants followed her; Brady noted that there were twenty - one for each of the astronauts. Rocky said to Sissy, 'I know you.'

'Back in your day, I was Genesis Garcia - The Governor of California.'

'That's it. I met you at one of those tiresome functions they used to make us attend, to drum up support for NASA. That's why I went to work for Tia - I couldn't stand that nonsense.'
Sissy picked up on his angry tone with her, and she looked at Brady with suspicion. Brady said, 'What are you looking at me like that for?' He stood up and walked over to the NanoPools™. 'I'll be around if you need me.'

Rocky said to Sissy as he watched Brady march away. 'He's not one of yours - I take it.'

'No. He's an Alpha-male Trad.' She said this as if she was describing a Silverback gorilla rather than a fellow human being. She helped him out of his spacesuit, and her team followed her lead with the others. She said, 'I'm told you are the leader.'
He looked at her, and he felt like he had been time-travelling, as he felt weak and ancient, while she looked as if she hadn't aged a day. 'Yes.'

'Then I'll help you to the front, to encourage the others.'

Brady stood at the front with Tia and Dagny. They were coming to terms with the shape-shifting appearance of the YellowSuits™. Tia settled on something suitably severe, which she would describe as business-like, while Dagny flirted with more colour until her Mother stared her down. She chose something more sober. Dagny said, 'Commander Fitzpatrick is going to lead them. He's looking very frail.'

Tia said, 'He's determined. He knows this is the rational thing to do.'

Brady was aghast as he watched the emaciated astronauts emerge out of the space-suits and line up near the showers. They reminded him of the war documentaries his Pops used to watch, where the Jews used to line up to enter the gas chambers in the concentration camp. He felt as though his Foster Daddy was haunting him. *That'll be us one day. Trust me, boy. That's what the powers that be will do to us if we don't remain vigilant and fight back...* The image of Mrs Wilson compounded his horror. He shouted, 'What the fuck did you do to these people. You're a fucking monster.'

Bodhi came over to calm Brady down. 'What is it, Brady? What troubles you?'

'Look at them. These were all American heroes. The TV used to tell us all the time that there ain't no bigger heroes than the astronauts - fucking heroes, man, and this is how we treat them.'

Tia said calmly, 'I didn't do anything to them. They volunteered. They self-selected themselves for future research, for the good of mankind, and for life on Earth. Mars could be the new Ark...'

Bodhi said, 'Brady, she's right, not about the Ark, we should save the Earth, not abandon Her. However, nobody forced them to choose this life, they knew the rules, and they knew what they signed up for. It was self-selection, and Tia Cassandra is not responsible. These are the scientific decisions we make for the betterment of the planet we rely on.' Commander Fitzpatrick's legs buckled, and Sissy worked to keep him upright. Bodhi said, 'Listen to me, Brady, if we don't hurry, then Commander...'

'It's Rocky.' Brady interrupted.

'...then Rocky will die. The NanoPools™ will save him, and in time, restore him to full health. You want that, don't you?'

'Sure.' He took Rocky from Sissy. 'Those showers don't have no goo, do they? It's just water?'

She said, 'Yes.'

'I'll take him as far as the showers and wash him down. He's a man, a hero. He don't need a woman with him. It ain't respectable.'

Sissy had a thousand arguments and objections to Brady's assumptions, but she let them pass on the grounds of expediency.

Brady washed Rocky but in a very man's man and masculine way, like a wounded soldier on the battlefield. Rocky said, 'If there's anything I could ever do for you in the future...'

'There is. Get back to full fitness, and if you are ever sending them big-ass rockets into the sky, I want an invite. I wanna see one of them mega-machines fly.'

31.COMING HOME TO SEE YOU

Brady had many reasons to make this year's Holiday celebration one to remember. This was his one-hundredth Thanksgiving and Christmas and his last as a man without responsibility, now that his first two sons would be born just five days afterwards. He reflected that this year had been one of the strangest he had ever lived, and he even included the year of the Green Revolution in that list. *I spent half of that year in Ridgecrest Supermax and the rest trying to get by - albeit under a new government. That was pretty fucking normal for Brady Mahone.*

In the last few decades, he had almost become Green by default. He had become accustomed to fitting in with them and only visiting the Trad areas for a change of scenery. He recalled the lions in South Africa who had confirmed his Trad identity - in his mind. He looked at his sketches of them while he was lazing in the main living area.

Hunter and his other staff were working hard on decorating the Tree with items from Libby Skye's extensive collection of baubles and tinsel. She had various colour themes for different years, so there was enough to decorate twenty giant Christmas Trees. It struck him that this must be a strange job for him to have allocated to a bunch of dyed-in-the-wool Greens.

He smiled as he watched them work, carefully and precisely. If he wasn't the last Trad on Earth quite yet, he was undoubtedly the last one to celebrate the Holidays quite so lavishly. The Holidays had never been that important to him in the past, but now, he felt as if he had a hero's responsibility to keep the flame alive - not out of respect for Christianity - but out of respect for the Trads that had died along the way.

Amie wandered into the room. She looked like her baby could be born any minute, never mind in a few weeks. 'The Christmas Tree is up too early. It should be on the fourth Sunday before Advent - that's what Moms always used to say - y'know, just after Thanksgiving.'

'I don't know all about those fancy dates. I just wanted to see it up now. Having said that, it does explain the funny look old Hunter gave me when I gave him the order.' Brady laughed at the recollection. He looked at Amie's stomach. 'How's everything with my boy, any problems? Are you worried?'

'That's such a Trad attitude. It will be perfect, nothing ever goes wrong with Green births, and your boy will inherit all the NanoSuits™ from me, from Red™ to Blue™.'

At the mention of Amie's Moms - Mary-Lou - he realised that Amie had been a Trad for the first sixteen Christmases of her life. 'Do you ever think of your Moms and Lucky much?'

'Of course, but maybe less so as the time passes - being Green for so long kind of erases the memories. I don't think the NanoSuits™ have nostalgia inbuilt into them.' She laughed as if she thought this was a funny thing to say. She looked wistfully at Brady, 'I have to say, that here, with the Christmas Tree and all, it does bring it back, it's the smell of the Pine and the tinsel…'

Brady said, 'I miss them all. I miss those days.'

Amie tried to dispel the melancholy. The place was happier when Brady was in a good mood. 'Me and Helgarth were wondering if we could invite some old friends from San Martin over.'

'Are you sure it wouldn't annoy them? Seeing you living in the lap of luxury?' He then thought of the Disciple of San Martin, Rhea Laidlaw, 'Do you think Rhea would want to come?'

Amie was nonplussed, 'No. Xe's away over that period. Urgent business overseas, she told the Community.'

'Oh. I don't think the Beardons would come.' *I bet he still celebrates Christmas, even if it's on the quiet.*

'Definitely not. None of the older Greens would visit a Trad home. No, I was thinking about our younger friends, the ones who'll be up for a good party.'

Brady mused over the plan for a few moments, 'Will your mate Debrock be one of them?'

Amie chuckled, 'Xe's top of the guest list.'

'Go on, then. Get Hunter to organise everything. I don't want you two overdoing it.' He added, 'Let me know the numbers, and I'll take them there and back in the FusionPassengerJet™. It needs a bit of a run-out.'

Amie kissed Brady on the cheek and flung her arms around him. Brady felt the baby kick as she pressed against his body. 'Thanks, Brady. It's going to be the best Christmas ever.'

Maybe it was the onset of becoming a Father which made him quite so reflective. *I wonder how many years I've got left; it's so hard to tell. In the old days, I might have been lucky to reach eighty - and that was if I didn't get killed in a shoot-out.* He assessed his condition, and he felt much as he did when he was in his late thirties. *I'm strong and racked. I feel better than before the Green Revolution, never mind since they took over. I look like one hundred going on forty-something.*

The days drifted by. He had so many days like these - days of routine and lazing around. There had been years in his life where he couldn't recall them because nothing of note had occurred to pin the year in his mind. He lived for the times when something, anything happened but those years were few and far between. He thought about this year just gone. *This had been a vintage year for old Brady Mahone, I saw man-eating lions, and I rode the LeviathanLifter™ - yeah, and a kick-ass nuclear explosion.*

He smiled to himself as he tried to snapshot the memories. He concentrated on the year 2142 as if this was a pivotal year for him. His thoughts turned to his future sons; he pressed the date into his mind once more. *2142 is the year of my firstborn sons.*

His thoughts returned to his original musings. *How many years have I got? How old will my sons be when I die? Will I have any memorable years to look forward to, or will I just drift through the days?* He smiled. *I need to get back into my hobbies.* He knew this was one decision he had made; he wasn't planning on being a full-time Daddy.

He picked up some of his favourite coffee-table books and made a neat stack of them so he could refer to the spines and began to leaf through them. He had a pen and paper at hand to make a note of his selections. Through the world atlas, he jotted down countries and territories he still hadn't visited. He ruled out the Arctic, Antarctic, and the Sahara Desert. *I'd need one of those RedSuits™ for those places - pity, as I'd love to have seen a Polar bear up close.* Brady then perused his wildlife and botany books from Libby Skye's stash. He noted many animals that he hadn't yet seen, and he did the same with his botany tomes. *I don't know how long I've got, but let's be optimistic and make this a fifty-plus year hobby.* He deliberately avoided plans to increase the market penetration of his Brady Mahone Entertainment Enterprises, as this didn't excite him as much as it used to do. He dwelled on it, but he knew that one day he would give it away to his sons, and he had more Green Credits than he knew how to spend. *Maybe my boys will have the hunger to take it to the next level, but in the meantime, I'll just keep it ticking over.*

By the time he flew his FusionPlane™ to San Martin to pick up the twenty-seven friends and revellers of Amie and Helgarth, he was glad of having something to do. He had decided to hang about the place for the first two or three months after his boys were born, and then after that, he would become enough of a pain that Amie and Helgarth would want to see the back of him. Little babies and kids held little interest for Brady - even if they were his own.

The Christmas was a veritable feast for the thirty people around the table, and the party afterwards went on for days, with the help of the good stuff courtesy of Debrock. Brady ensured he was exceptionally well compensated for his generous offerings.

When it was time for Amie and Helgarth to give birth to his sons on 30 December 2142, Brady was stoned out of his mind. It seemed a blur as they gave birth effortlessly and then presented the boys to him. Amie had insisted that they would be surrounded by friends at the birth, and all her friends were high as well. The naming ceremony and the Green Administrator did his duty in front of his stoned audience. Amie and Helgarth kissed passionately to augment their sense of achievement. The onlookers were too chill to object when Brady answered the Administrator's questions with provocative anti-Green responses. 'I want them identified as boys, men, male, masculine...Amie's child is to be called Bill, not William, Liam, Wills, Will, Willie or any other variation. His name is Bill, Bill Mahone.'

Brady liked that name as it reminded him of the very first Green, he met, who came across as a straight-ahead guy who just did his day job on Highway 99.

The gathering laughed at the tiny binary mind of the Alpha-Trad gorilla, but it was his party, and his goys could cry if they wanted to when they grew older. As for Helgarth's child, Brady answered the Green Administrator. 'The boy is to be named Rock, but I can live with the nickname of Rocky, that sounds manly to me, Rock Mahone, or Rocky Mahone.'

Debrock laughed his stoned laugh and said, 'That's funny, man, really funny. Bill.' He joked and said in a mock manly voice, 'Hey, Brady, Didja name the other one after me, y'know, Rock, Deb-Rock?'

Brady waved his hand dismissively as Debrock had another dab and giggled away incessantly. Brady wanted to laugh and leave the formalities behind, but deep down, he knew this was a moment he should cherish. He looked at the mothers of his children and smiled and mouthed a *thank you* to them both.

After the administrative duties were complete, Brady took Bill first, and then Rock, and held his naked sons high above his head, in turn, as his declaration to the future. His sons would rule his self-selected role as the greatest Trad left alive, and they were duly anointed to be the kings in waiting of his business empire.

THE END.

2184

Twenty-Second-Century Man

Book Four of the Green Deal Quartet

By

Jim Lowe

1: THE ONE HUNDRED YEAR PLAN

The one good thing to come out of the Green's family planning is I only have one birthday to remember, and it covers all seven of the kids. Brady laughed at his own inner joke.

Brady looked around the dining table on 30 December 2183. It was Tuesday, and Thursday was the start of the New Green Year, the year which promised the fruition of Bodhi Sattva's one-hundred-year plan. His eldest sons, Bill and Rocky, were both forty-one going-on twenty-five in Brady's conversion method for the difference in actual Green years to old Trad year equivalence. Therefore, his next two sons, Wilder and Troy, were thirty-nine going-on twenty-five, and the youngest, Hawk, was thirty-six going-on twenty-five. All Pure Green children - those born post-Revolution, aged as they would have done as Trads until they reached twenty-five. From then, they barely aged even over the decades.

Amie and Helgarth had put up with a few years of Brady calling their own children: *things, its* and other derogatory labels. As Mothers to his five sons and as per their agreement with him to keep his sons' masculinity uninfluenced by the Greens non-binary way of living, they had tried until they couldn't have their children brutalised any longer. Brady begrudgingly called the goys and eventually even called them by their real names Lucy-Ian - Amie named xem after her stepfather Lucian - and Raelynn. They were allowed two children of their own, and Brady didn't want any more children in the home, and he funded the Green cost of having children. In the last twenty years, the cost of bringing children into the world to consume Her resources had risen considerably. If they could have had one more, then it would have been Amie's turn to name her and Helgarth's child, and she would have called her goy Mary-Louis, after her Moms; maybe she should have done this with their first baby, but xe looked like Lucian, irrespective of the lack of a direct bloodline.

Brady looked at Lucy-Ian, who was indeterminate in appearance - he had no say in how Amie and Helgarth raised their own - he kept his bargain with them. Raelynn was dressed in her ever-present Goth gear, complete with black hair with white lightning streaks. They were both thirty going-on twenty-five. Lucy-Ian had a Hodgson boy look, which Brady never uttered - as no good would be done by bringing his old hoodlum neighbours' lineage into a discussion. He could see something in the eyes which might have made Amie think of Lucian, his late best friend. He referred to Raelynn as her, as a concession to his Trad ideals. Brady wouldn't countenance using xe as a pronoun. He also viewed Lucy-Ian as female to distinguish between Amie and Helgarth's daughters and his own sons.

His boys looked like variations of Brady - a point which made him proud. They were all above six feet tall, and his iron rule that they had to work out in the gym for a minimum of an hour a day had built them up. He ignored all protestations that they could have any appearance they desired courtesy of the YellowSuits™ and explained that the Greens were weaklings inside their shells. The vision of Mrs Wilson in her grave and Rhea Laidlaw's words about dying inside still haunted him. He needed the reassurance that beneath their NanoSuits™, they were as healthy as Trad athletes.

The only variations in their natural state were that Amie's children by him, Bill, Wilder and Hawk, had black hair and brown eyes. Whereas Helgarth's Scandinavian looks gave Rocky and Troy her blonde hair but they still had Brady's brown eyes, and all of them had his Polynesian colouring.

And as for Brady, he was well aware that he was at an impossible age of one-hundred and forty-one years old. He guessed that his birthday was probably on January 1st. He used to think of this as John Kane's sick joke, as he went to great lengths to have Xavier Kane the first child to be born in the Millennium. He dwelled on the thought of Xavier Kane or Bodhi Sattva as he rebranded himself, and Brady wondered if he knew or guessed that Brady was his clone. Glenarvon Cole, his other cloned brother, who may or may not know the truth about the relationship between the three of them, like Brady, didn't know precisely when he was born. It's gotta be the same. That's the way that sick fuck thinks. Brady didn't think it was the same thing at all, that he should have seven children in his home, five of his own, all celebrating the same birthday. *That's just convenience - is all.*

There was a roar of laughter around the dinner table as Troy delivered the punchline to his anecdote. Brady smiled broadly, even though he hadn't been listening. Hunter, his old servant, brought Brady his dessert. Brady played with it while he drifted away. His family had got used to this and put it down to his old age. He let them think that - it was easier, but he knew he still felt as good as he was in his Trad forties - which meant he felt like the same person he was when he was still in Ridgecrest Supermax on the eve of the Revolution, almost a hundred years ago.

Brady loved the way his boys looked. They were big and robust and unmistakably out of Brady Mahone's stock. He also bred into them the ethics of competition and winning at all costs, but something about them unnerved him. They had sharp and cunning minds, which was to be welcomed, but it was in business - again, something he could put down to something they inherited from Brady Mahone. After all, with business booming under the stewardship and drive of his sons, he was indisputably the richest man in the world outside of Boulder Creek and Sattva Systems™. He should have been reassured as this business was named after him, named by him, Brady Mahone Entertainment Enterprises. However, it was the way they did business which troubled him. His sons were ruthless winners, but in a corporate way, sometimes they even sounded a bit scientific to Brady's ears, and one thing Brady wasn't - was a scientist.

He disliked the science of Sattva Systems™ with their Nano-everythings, and he disliked Tia Cassandra and the way she treated her crew. Sending her on the last mission to Mars later in the year was the best place for her. Tyrone Beardon, the Bear's nephew once, informed him that Mars was a hostile and freezing desert, and he remembered the delightful laughter from his buddy when Brady said *I can see why she loves it so much.'*

The memory of Tyrone's laughter merged and then was subsumed by the laughter around the table, and then the word his mind was reaching for emerged, it was summoned by the laughter of his sons. It had a timbre and a tone that could only be described as corporate.

Is this what I'm on this planet for?

Brady didn't dismiss this question, and he had every right to be concerned. His biological father was a monster. Bodhi and Glenarvon hadn't had children. The John Kane line would come to an end if it was left up to them. Whereas with the man's man Brady Mahone, he would have five Grandchildren ready to rule the world. Brady thought of himself as merely a racehorse put out to stud.

He listened to the heated business discussions around the table. He watched the servants taking away the dishes and cleaning up around the family. Amie and Helgarth excused themselves from the table. *That reminds me, I must get Amie to trim my hair tomorrow. It reminds me of when Mary-Lou used to cut my hair.* He recalled the last time she did it when she showed him the first flecks of grey growing under his black hair. It also reminded him of the 2160s, where he tried growing his hair long and experimenting with all kinds of beards and moustaches. *What is it about the 60s decades which makes men want to be long hairs? The 1960s, 2060s and then 2160s, always with the fucking 60s.*

He had gone through a phase of wondering whether he was losing concentration because he was getting old, but then he decided this was bullshit. It was just a case that the conversation was getting boring - just like math at school.

Brady's sons carried on debating and planning and were no longer paying attention to Brady at the head of the dining table. Wilder had taken up the theme. He kept thumping the table to make his point. 'Glenarvon stated clearly that there would be 26.5 million Disciples and devout followers by no later than June next year. Therefore, out of a worldwide population of 900 million, that still leaves us a potential new customer reach of 18.5 million. That's a helluva lot of Green Credits still left on the table.'

Troy said, 'Hang on a minute. How do you work that out?'

Wilder shook his head in disgust at having to spell it out, 'We currently have a market penetration of the global BMEE brand of 95%, which is great, don't get me wrong. However, the likelihood of selling to the Green zealots is zero, so that is 2.94% of the population we will never reach.'

Bill joined in, 'And why's that. We can sell to anybody; they might take a little more persuasion...'

'No chance. Glenarvon has got them under pain of death or something...'

Hawk said, 'Or on a promise...' Rocky laughed loudly. He loved his youngest brother. Brady laughed along with them.

Wilder continued with his analysis. 'Assuming, there are 5% of potential customers still to exploit, but 2.94% are out of reach, for now...' He conceded. 'Then that means there are 2.06% of winnables. In customer numbers, this converts to 18.5 million potential new customers to reach. There are five of us, so I propose that we agree to sell to a further 3.7 million each.'

The boys quietened for a moment, and Brady observed them, even though Wilder had nearly lost him with his numbers. Rocky said, 'I can easily get more than that out of my Asian base. We have been booming with Traditional Chinese music, and the fashionable Indian Greens can't be seen without their cache of Bollywood movies.'

Hawk said, 'Oceania has a much smaller population...'

Rocky smiled, 'How many can you do?'

'About 1.2 million at a pinch.'

Rocky said to the group, 'Put me down for Hawk's shortfall. It's the least a brother can do.' He slapped Hawk on the back.

Bill said, 'If Wilder puts forward what he can do with Africa, and Troy does the same with Europe, then I'll take up the rest with the Americas.' He pronounced, 'The home of Brady Mahone's Entertainment Enterprises.' They raised their glasses to Brady. He had an image in his mind that he would struggle to shake off - were they raising a glass to him, or were they raising their glasses to the Grandfather, John Kane? Not that he had ever told them about John Kane. He said to them that Archie

Mahone was their Grandfather after finally convincing Amie to back his story.

Wilder added, 'I'll meet my 3.7 million targets in Africa before June. What do you say, boys?'

They all shouted, 'Hell yes!' and banged their big fists on the table repeatedly. Brady was making a note in his sketchbook of the targets his sons had agreed.

Brady looked at his boys with dismay, he loved his boys and was satisfied with Amie's and Helgarth's efforts in raising them in his own image, but they still seemed a bit too Green for his liking. He thumped the table to grab their attention. Amie had just walked in, and it made her jump. She looked at Brady and gave him a look which asked if it was really necessary to do that. Brady announced to his boys, 'I'm going to add a little competition to the mix. The first one to hit their sales targets will receive their own private FusionPassengerJet™ from me.'

Hawk smiled for a split second - aware that his target now appeared easy before the yelling erupted…*I would never have agreed…It's a fucking fix…you're bound to win it now, you little…*

Brady laughed as he got out of his chair and headed out of the room and on to his study. He added, 'You can't start until January 2nd. That's a rule. After that, you can win by any means possible which the Security Protocols™ will allow.' Amie grabbed him by the arm and said, 'Why did you do that?'

'Don't worry, I've got a more pleasant surprise for them on my best-guess-birthday. I just want them to feel like a Trad. That's what they would have done in the old days. It will make men of them.' He kissed her on the cheek and grinned before walking away.

Brady went to his study and flicked through the books where he had marked off all the plants and animals he had ever seen. There was still many more to find. *I need a break from my hobbies and so I might complete a little bit of life admin this year.* His fingers stroked over a glossy photo of a Polar bear. *This is an excellent year to plan for the future, especially as the Greens come to the end of their hundred-year plan. You never know, maybe after they've completed their work, I might share my thoughts with Bodhi and Glenarvon Cole. I wonder if they've guessed that we are all brothers?* He carried on examining the one creature he couldn't see up close. *Y'know, I don't think they do. They woulda said something by now.*

2: ONE HUNDRED AND FORTY-TWO, NOT OUT.

The New Green Year's Eve party was lavish but spoiled by the acrimonious atmosphere between the brothers. Brady watched on with pleasure as he spotted clandestine meetings between pairs of his sons. He was transported back to his old prison days when prisoners would try and suss each other out, forging alliances, and working out what the other was planning, and all the time thinking where the double-crosses were in the agreements.

One thing which still united the boys was the Green influence on everybody in the world. When the obsession with the FusionPassengerJet™ competition subsided briefly, then all talk turned to the last of the Green's NanoSuits™ upgrades. Sattva Systems™ had kept it sworn to secrecy from anybody outside the Disciples' circle. There was talk that the Security Protocols™ had been set to silence them if they merely *thought* about spilling the secret. And if the Security Protocols™ detected this, then they would be ejected from the Disciple-hood.

The only pieces of information which had been released from Sattva Systems™ HQ was that it was to be called UltraViolet™ and that it would be released in two phases, the first for the Disciples on the 25 June 2184 - the Centenary of the Green Revolution, and the rest would receive the UltraViolet™ on the 31 December 2184, just in time to fulfil the Bodhi Sattva promise for the end of the hundred-year plan to save the planet.

Brady laughed as his boys bickered at the realisation that many of their potential customers would now have a decision to make. If they chose to spend their Green Credits on Brady Mahone's Entertainment products before June, would they risk missing out on the UltraViolet™ upgrade - as nobody knew exactly how much the UltraViolet™ would cost? There was the possibility that the payments would be due in June, even though there was a delay in receiving the upgrades for the ordinary Greens.

Bill approached Brady, and the others were not going to be outmanoeuvred, so the remaining sons hurried to follow him before he could steal an advantage. Bill looked around his gathering of brothers and then asked Brady, 'What would you do?'

'About what?'

'Come on, Pops. I know you've been watching and listening to us all night.'

'So, it's noisy in here. I can't hear everything, not over the noise of Amie, Helgarth and Debrock's crowd of hangers-on. What's the problem?'

'If the Greens who haven't bought our products before are waiting for the UltraViolet™ upgrade, then why would they risk missing out on the upgrade to start using our product now? I mean, I would get the UltraViolet™ first and then think about the upsides of our product offering.'

Brady looked at his sons, 'What's the deal with this UltraViolet™?'

'We don't know. Nobody does. Well. The Disciples and the Devout know, but they aren't telling.'

'There's your way in.' Brady looked at his bemused sons' faces. He was disappointed at their lack of perception of the art of deception. 'If they won't say, then you can make up anything you want. They can't deny it, or that could give their game away.' He watched them think out the opportunities, but he could see they were struggling.

He knew they could only think of the exciting possibilities of the UltraViolet™. 'Make it not worth waiting for. The UltraViolet™ is a boring upgrade…' He thought on it for a second, 'Remember the InfraRed™, it was nothing more than a primer, it didn't do anything interesting, it was an undercoat. Well, make the UltraViolet™ as boring as that. To get around the Security Protocols™, just suggest that it is nothing more than a gloss finish, a topcoat, nothing special…of ceremonial use only.'

Bill smiled, 'That could work…it really could, thanks, Pops.'

Brady said, 'I know you boys are mad at me right now, but at my pretend-birthday party tomorrow, I've got something to share that I know you'll like. Now, get back to your competition and may the best man win.' He grinned mischievously and watched them re-join the party. He was proud of his boys.

The following day he watched his sons pack as they were treating his competition with the utmost urgency. He walked down to the Mahone Fleet Parking Lot in his extensive Malibu grounds and saw his boys loading up, ready for departure at the earliest possible point. He wondered if he should have let those with the longest distances to travel have a head start if seemingly, every minute counted, but he wasn't going to change the rules now. He smiled as he considered that he would have his Malibu home back to himself for the next few months. As his USA leader, he had told Bill that he would have to live elsewhere for the duration in case the others thought he would use his Pop's counsel for an unfair advantage.

He took a birthday walk down to the bottom of the Malibu cliff, where his home was perched upon. It was a glorious Californian day, with azure skies, wispy clouds and the bright yellow sun casting its sparkling rays across the Pacific. It was breezy and cold, but this refreshed him. He walked along the shoreline for a couple of peaceful hours before returning to the home.

Hunter had some lunch prepared for him. Hunter said, 'I wanted to book a holiday for the end of June, sir.'

'I'm guessing you are one of these Devout Greens, and you want the time off to get your UltraVioletSuit™.'

'Yes, sir.'

'Tell me something. You were a wannabee Hollywood actor before you worked for Libby Skye. How come you've never shown an interest in my entertainment products. I woulda thought they would have been right up your street.'

'I saw, very early on, that John Kane and his son, Xavier, were sticklers for rules. I would never break them lightly. I suppose that's what they could see in me when I joined their employ.'

Brady said, 'I suppose so. How old are you, now?'

'I confess, I lose track.' Brady watched Hunter working it out in his mind. Hunter said, 'Two-hundred and twelve, sir.'

'Two hundred and twelve going-on ninety. Amazing. Don't you worry about dying in service? Do you ever wonder if you've wasted your life?'

'No, sir. Not on either point.'

Brady ate up his lunch and went over to the main lounge to check how Amie and

Helgarth were getting on with their preparations for his maybe, one hundred and forty-second birthday party. The dining table was already laid out, hours before the actual evening dinner. Helgarth had rounded up some of Debrock's friends to assist - well, those that weren't already stoned out of their minds. They were fixing up banners, and giant numbers had been found in Libby Skye's stores of unrecyclable plastic partyware from a long-gone age. One thing about taking over the house and contents of a rich Hollywood actresses' home was, if you needed something, you could probably find it somewhere in this sprawling palace.

The giant gold numbers of one, four and two were being pinned up and checked for the straightness of their positioning, while Helgarth was issuing instructions of… *down a bit…an inch lower on the left-hand side…*

Brady went to see Amie. He had noticed her frustration in recent weeks that she and Helgarth had to maintain their female appearance while he was there. 'I'm going on a bit of a road trip for the next few weeks, maybe longer. I don't plan on going too far because if I turned up on another continent, the boys would think I'm influencing the competition…'

Amie had already zoned out, as she couldn't wait to inform Helgarth so that they could both relax into being who they wanted to be. She nodded along, distractedly.

Brady continued, '…I might even stay at the Mahone Ranch in McFarland for a while. I'm feeling a bit nostalgic for the old days. Anyway, I want to ask you a favour.'

Amie returned from her daydream. 'Yes, anything. What can I do for you, Brady?'

'I'm going to do a little speech tonight, but it's got some numbers and math stuff in it, and you know I'm not good with that kinda thing.'

'Ok.'

'I know you are good with that. I don't just want you to help me write it. I'd like you to speak out the bit with the numbers. Could you do that?'

'I'd be happy to. I could hardly refuse you, it being your birthday and all. I'll go and fetch a pen and some paper, and we'll work on it together.'

At the evening celebrations, he noticed his sons were quieter than usual. *The private FusionPassengerJet™ incentive has really got my boys focused.* He thought. Brady was hardly the life and soul of his party, as he now wished he hadn't planned a speech. *Brady Mahone ain't afraid of anything…except speaking in public, it seems… gotta get a grip here.* Fortunately, the rest of his stoned attendees were making a lot of noise to make up for the ordinarily loud guest of honour and his usually raucous sons - their infectious giggling providing a surreal backdrop to the birthday party celebrations.

He knew the Christmas, New Year, and Brady's birthday celebrations usually disrupted the routine of the resident Greens at the Malibu home. The IndigoSuits™ meant that non-Disciples were advised to sleep from 11pm to 2am. While the Disciples slept from 2am to 5am. Brady chuckled to himself. *The kids are going to be up way past their bedtime.* He shuffled in his chair and played with his food as he thought about his speech. Unlike the competition, he wanted this to land in a positive way. He wanted his boys to understand the need to protect himself and the company. He looked over his notes, and he spotted Amie doing the same. *She looks as nervous as I feel. At least we won't need microphones now that they've got super-hearing and super-everything-else for that matter.*

Amie left her seat and went over to Brady. She whispered, 'Are you ready?'

'I think so.'

'You've got nothing to worry about. You are thinking like a Trad, whereas we are Green.' She kissed him on the cheek, and he noticed the curious looks on the diners who were spread across five large tables in the grand room. He took this as his cue to make a start. He tapped the glass containing the non-alcoholic fruit cocktail, which had been christened a Bradysnapp for the special occasion.

'Thank you for celebrating my one-hundred and forty-second birthday with me.'

The boys shouted, 'Happy birthday, Pops.'

Brady was glad of the interruption, he smiled, as he took these moments to compose himself, 'I'm a Trad. I've already lived well past my allocated Trad years, and yet, here I still am.' His audience laughed along, like any other family with an elderly relative giving a speech. 'I don't know how many years I have left, but I have to make contingency plans for, y'know, death and all.'

Bill shouted, 'You ain't gonna die, Pops - and anybody who says you are is gonna have me to deal with.' There was laughter as Brady nodded in Bill's direction and grinned.

'I know you boys weren't happy with my competition idea, but I want you to keep the Trad values alive. It troubles me that you follow the leaders so blindly. It's dangerous to behave too predictably...' *That's how they get ya, son.* His audience listened to him with the good grace to acknowledge that it was Brady's party, and he could preach if he wanted to. 'Anyway, I didn't want to die and risk that the Brady Mahone Entertainment Enterprises would be lost to Sattva Systems™, and more specifically left for Bodhi Sattva and Glenarvon Cole to do with as they wished.'

Troy said, 'What claim would they have on your company, Pops?'

'It's complicated. That's why I'm doing something about it now. Later in the year, I'm going to sit down with Bodhi and make a Last Will and Testament. Now, I know you might not know what that is, as you Greens don't pass on material possessions and assets after death, but I'm a Trad, and I'm going to leave my worldly goods to the family. They owe me that much.'

Raelynn was stoned and looked out of step with the other guests; as she was in a gender-neutral state but dressed in a high camp Gothic outfit, she stood up shakily, and Amie looked across at Helgarth as if priming her to intervene if necessary. She said, 'If we inherit this place...' She spun around dreamily with her arms open wide as if she was a flight attendant from the underworld. 'Then we wouldn't be allowed to live in this place all alone. We would have to fill the rooms with other Greens. This means all our friends could live here. That would be so cool.'

Lucy-Ian and Raelynn's friends let out stoned cheers and giggles. Debrock shouted, 'We love you, Raelynn.' Helgarth gestured for Raelynn to sit and be quiet. Raelynn flopped on her dining chair.

Brady wasn't going to be flustered or derailed, 'When I'm dead and gone, that will be the least of my worries.' He grinned at Raelynn and then at Helgarth to indicate that no harm was done. He continued, 'I've drawn up a proposal, which will come into effect from my next birthday. I want you to honour my wishes and not challenge the details.' He looked at each one of his sons intently and in turn - and then he looked at Amie, Helgarth, and their children, Lucy-Ian and Raelynn. 'Now, you know

I'm not too hot with math, and so I'm going to hand over to Amie to give you the details.'

Brady sat down as Amie stood up next to him. Her shaky hands held her crib sheet. She said nervously and quietly. Brady could hear her as he was beside her. But he knew the rest of the room would be utilising their VioletSuits™ to listen to her. 'From January 1, 2085, Brady Mahone Entertainment Enterprises will be split as follows...' She took a moment to ensure she got her figures right. '...Brady will retain 51% of the company. His five sons, Bill, Rocky, Wilder, Troy and Hawk, will each be given an 8% stake, and Lucy-Ian and Raelynn will receive a stake of 4.5%.' She waited for them to grasp the implications of Brady's decision. She continued, 'Brady's has 2.1 billion Green Credits, which means each son's stake is a gift to the value of 168 million Green Credits and Raelynn and Lucy-Ian's share is be valued at 94.5 million Green Credits.' She looked over at Helgarth, who already knew the contents of her speech.

Brady said, 'This takes place at the turn of next year. I also want Amie to tell you what will happen with my 51% should anything happens to me.'

Amy said, 'In the event of Brady's death, the boys share would rise to 16% each, and Raelynn and Lucy-Ian's would rise to 10%.'

Brady said, 'As for the Malibu home and all the contents and vehicles, I am giving these to Amie and Helgarth. I want this to be their home, to do with as they see fit.' He looked over at Raelynn and then at Helgarth and Amie, as he hadn't told them of this plan.

'Thanks, Pops. Will Bodhi allow this?' Bill said.

'He made an exception for his Mother in leaving Libby Skye this place after the Revolution. I don't think he would risk being called out as a hypocrite if he refused me the same courtesy. I know you see him as some kinda God or guru, but he is just a businessman in my eyes. He will make the deal. I know he doesn't want me as an enemy. I can tell by the lengths he goes to keep me as a friend.'

Helgarth came over to Brady and kissed him on the cheek and held both his hands. 'Thank you for the gift of this home and thank you for your generosity to our children.'

3: BOULDER CREEK RENDEZVOUS

B rady had a sort out in his Pop's old bunker. The tinned food was over a century old and taking up a lot of space on the racks, and he had come to the decision that if the world came to such a state that he would have to rely on this, then he'd rather not bother. He'd called over a couple of Greens from McFarland to give him a hand on emptying the bunker of surplus tins and other perishables from the Trad days. It felt good for his body to be doing some hard physical labour and good for his mind to be organising the space. He dwelled on the fact that even he called the town simply McFarland again, now that there was no trace at all left that they'd ever been an East McFarland.

He kept Archie's old tech. It gave the place a feeling of a private museum to Brady - not that Brady ever visited museums even when such sites were found in nearly every town. He scrubbed, cleaned, and swept the whole bunker, and he had left the doors wide open to encourage the fresh Californian air to come and visit the old place - it seemed to be afraid of being trapped down here forever. He took time out to watch the billowing dust roll up the steps as if it had the power to defy gravity. He thought the thousands of dust particles glinting against the sunlight up the concrete steps looked *real pretty.*

As he sat on the bottom step with his Thermos of coffee - he didn't want the temptation of the homestead luring him to stay and stop working - he looked around at Archie's newspaper cuttings on the wall, and he desperately wanted to tell him everything that had happened. *Pops would have been amazed and would have wallowed in the horror of it all. He would have abhorred the domination of the Liberal-Lefties.* Brady spied a cutting of a UFO and laughed. *Pops would rather have had the alien overlords than this lot.*

Brady screwed his plastic cup back on his old Thermos flask and muttered, 'This ain't gonna buy the baby a new bonnet.' He had prepared the racking to store documents and evidence. He looked at the assorted pile of dozens of boxes of different shapes and sizes. Some of these were his own stash, but most were the ones he'd retrieved from East McFarland after Judge Audre Jefferson had died but before the final throes of the Operation Clean-Up of East McFarland. He took rolls of industrial shrink-wrap and covered the boxes thoroughly but left Judge Jefferson's neat filing labels showing through. He picked them up one-by-one and placed them on the racks. As he went, he kept re-sorting them if he spotted a sequence of numbers and dates. He found the whole experience therapeutic, even if he had no apparent use for these any longer. He seemed to find the same thrill as a child involved in the burial of a time capsule.

After his work was done, he inspected his Los Banos Police Department filing system, and grinned broadly. He traced his fingers across the plastic wrapping. *They were right - this stuff will last for a thousand years - that's a good thing, isn't it?*

Brady left the bunker, and for a minute, he considered sealing it up and camouflaging the entrance, but he couldn't see the point. *The Greens have known about Pops' bunker all this time and the stuff we kept down there. If they'd have wanted to do anything about it, they woulda done it by now. Maybe it's a stealing deal which the Security Protocols™ would get involved in.*

Over his well-earned lunch, Brady perused his ad-hoc Last Will and Testament, which Amie had drawn up for him. He also checked over the divestment of his business interests to his family. Amie has done a fine job of these. I don't want to get bamboozled by all those nu*mbers and percentages - not in front of Bodhi and his cronies.* He laughed. *Hell, the older I get, the more I'm starting to sound like my old man.*

Brady got a taste for tidying and cleaning, and for the next few weeks, he cleared out every room of unloved junk, not only in the Mahone Ranch but also the Lopez Ranch. He only kept the items that brought back strong emotional memories, everything else he dealt with ruthlessly. It helped him think; each tidied room seemed to lead to a tidied section of his mind. He imagined his sons flying to all parts of the world, pushing and consulting with their reps - his reps - and strategizing on how they could win the FusionPassengerJet™. *Wilder is the numbers guy, but my money would be on Troy winning - he really understands the Asian market. I'll have to think of a good idea for the presentation ceremony.* Finally, he reached a point where every room in both ranches was cleaned and tidied.

He considered taking a FusionCar™ up to Boulder Creek for a moment, but the roads were always full of Green Tourists. *Shame, I woulda liked that. I miss those times when the roads were always empty, and nobody but me could afford something like my old Hearse. It seems like everyone owns a piece of the Brady Highway these days.* He boarded his FusionPlane™ with its cream-coloured livery and its moss-green Sattva Systems™ logo and flew to Boulder Creek. Brady was probably the only person on the planet who didn't ever need to make an appointment to see Bodhi Sattva.

When he arrived, he had his usual chat with Marjorie - Fleet Captain Marjorie Hampton - about HeavyLoaders™ and LeviathanLifters™ and since the 2150s, the Cassandra rocket launches to Mars. He never tired of attending the frequent lift-offs from the Cape Cassandra FusionPads™ in Florida. Marjorie said, 'This is the last year for the rocket launches, Brady. I know you'll miss them.'

'Yeah, I know. My buddy Tyrone would love to be a part of that. He's had his head in the clouds from the first moment I met him.'

'There's still a chance - but he has to enrol in the last call for volunteers by May at the latest. They will have the UltraViolet™ before anybody else, seeing as they will be moving to another planet.'

'What is this UltraViolet™?'

'I'm not at liberty to say, other than that it will be incredibly beneficial for them in their hostile new environment.'

'Fair enough. Anyway, there is no way on Earth that Samuel would let him go.'

'Is that a pun there, Brady?' She nudged him playfully, and Brady laughed when he realised what he had just said. She added - because she didn't want to appear to ex-clude Brady from the HQ's plans, 'Most of the equipment is on Mars and assembled. The FusionSpaceShuttles™ are returning the astronauts over the coming months for them to get the new and final NanoSuits™ - by mid-June, the last ever transports will leave Earth, and they will never be allowed to return.'

Brady said, 'Not even if they get ill?'

'No. It's the Green Deal with Tia Cassandra. The rocket launches and the Earth's resources have been allowed to be plundered within Bodhi and Glen's one-hundred-year plan; beyond that, it is all about preserving Mother Earth. There are no more compromises to be made.'

Brady was worried for a moment. 'What about any deals I have made or will make with Bodhi?'

'You will always be an exceptional case. He will always honour his deals with you. In fairness, he has with Tia Cassandra. She accepted the deal with her eyes open, Tia has not been fooled.' She added, 'Anyway, Tia will make it work - she drove a hard bargain.' She thought about Brady's question a little deeper and then offered him her best advice. 'Everything will be different from 1st January 2185, more than you can ever imagine. They are even changing the units of time for the next phase of Green Science Discovery. With that in mind, I would make sure you have your personal dealings laid down before then. It's getting hectic around here as we are closing in on the end-of-year deadline.'

Brady felt like he was back in his old criminal underworld dealings, 'He can't claim he was busy, and he forgot...'

'No, he wouldn't do that. His word and his integrity are beyond reproach. I'm just saying if you've got business to be concluded with Bodhi, Glenarvon and Sissy - then do it, soon.' Marjorie walked and talked with her old friend, Brady, as she went with him to the main entrance. Sissy and a man - to Brady's eyes in a gender-neutral Green world - met them both. Marjorie said, 'I'll leave you with Sissy and Century. I know you haven't met before, but Century has the same middle name as you.' Marjorie smiled and headed back to her work.

Brady shook Century's hand. 'Really, how come?'Sissy said, 'Long story, maybe later. Anyway, Century Brady Garcia wanted to meet his namesake, and seeing as I spoil my children...'

'Mops, I'm eighty-four...'

Brady said, 'Eighty-four going-on twenty-five - I'm Brady, Brady Mahone, pleased to meetcha.'

Century shook his hand with a firm grip, 'Likewise, and an honour.' He added before Sissy could interrupt, 'Love your products, man. They are so cool.'

'Now, Century, I believe you have work to attend to.' Sissy said.

Century turned on his heels and strode away. Brady said, 'I want to see Bodhi. I might need you around because you handle the administration stuff, y'know paper-work - I know it's not his strong point...'

Sissy laughed, 'Paperwork, such a quaint term.' She added, 'Not many people criti-cise Bodhi's talents or lack of them, but when you're right - you're right.' She walked with Brady to Bodhi's drab office.

Bodhi was in a quiet discussion with Glenarvon Cole. They looked up at Brady, and the office fell silent for a brief moment as they all faced each other. Brady thought he had wandered into a delicate moment of negotiations between Bodhi and Glenarvon, but Brady wasn't interested in the future planning of the Greens. He gestured to indicate the office space, with its Sattva cream-coloured walls and joked by way of breaking the ice, 'I think I woulda got myself something a little swankier by now.'

Glen smiled and reached out a hand. Brady gripped it firmly. Glen said, 'Good to see you, man. How have you been keeping?'

'Is all good, man. I'm glad you're here as well, as I need to discuss some private business, y'know, put my affairs in order.'

'Pull up a chair.'

Brady grabbed a chair from the stack against the wall and put it down for Sissy, almost as a statement of his out-of-date Trad values. He then pulled one over for himself. He pulled out his paper notes written in Amie's neat handwriting.

Bodhi smiled a warm smile, 'We are at your disposal, my friend. What is it you wish to discuss?'

'You are all Green, and you don't seem to worry about dying anytime soon. However, I am a Trad, and I gotta go sometime. I'm already well past my sell-by date.' He laughed at his own joke. 'Anyways, even I can work out that you, Bodhi, are one-hundred and eighty-four years old, Glen is in his hundred and sixties, and as for Sissy…' Again, Brady teased, 'But you must never ask a lady her age…' Brady laughed while Sissy, Bodhi and Glen humoured him. Brady continued, 'Bearing in mind I'm very old for a Trad, I am making some changes to the structure of Brady Mahone Entertainment Enterprises before you start your roll-out of UltraViolet™, so, I'm thinking of May this year.'

Sissy said, puzzled, 'Ok.'

'I've made a Last Will and Testament that I want to come into force from 1st January 2185.'

She said, 'Why not straightaway?'

'Because I don't want any small print clauses to surprise me with the end of your one-hundred-year plan. It's spooking me, maybe it's my criminal background, but I want your word that my wishes will be taken into account after that date.' He watched Bodhi and Glen glance at each other. He handed his papers to Bodhi. Glen, and Sissy leaned in to read them alongside him.

Bodhi said, 'You are the only person left on the planet who is allowed to pass on property to another after death. You are the exception - as you are the only Trad left alive. You are a non-Green. I will give you my word that your property will remain in your family's hands from 2185 and in perpetuity.'

'Is that the same as forever?'

'Yes.'

Brady was troubled with the mention of the word family. His puzzled head tipped to his right, and he grimaced. Glen said, 'What troubles you, friend? Something's off, I can tell.'

Brady stood up and paced the room before he returned to his seat. He looked from Glen to Bodhi and back again. 'By family, you mean the people named in these documents. It doesn't mean anybody who isn't named who comes out of the woodwork to make a claim on my company - does it?' He suddenly felt as if he was in the biggest poker game of his life, as he studied every minor twitch in their expressions, but they revealed little. Bodhi and Glen looked at Brady as if this subject meant a lot to him, but they had more urgent business to attend to. Bodhi and Glen gave each other a bewildered glance, and then they both looked to Sissy for a hint of revelation.

Sissy said, 'A Green can't become pregnant with you without an arrangement in place. There aren't any little Brady Mahones scampering around the planet waiting to stake a claim on your wealth.' She laughed, and then Bodhi and Glen laughed along with her as if she had reached the heart of Brady's dilemma. He still peered closely into their facial features, looking for signs of deception, but he couldn't detect any. The only thing he picked up on was Bodhi's grip on his Will.

Bodhi said, 'If Sissy doesn't mind, she could travel down to my Mother's old home in Malibu and carry out the group Distor™ Distribution for you.'

Sissy said, 'My pleasure.'

At first, he thought there was a clue in Bodhi choosing to refer to the Malibu home as *his mother's* old home. It sounded like the sort of thing an enemy would say to Brady's ears, but with the emphasis on *my* Mother and not even the hint of the more accurate *our* Mother. Brady concluded that even if Bodhi had given this thought at some point in his long life, then he had long since discarded it as a possibility. Glen showed no signs at all, of knowing. *All I am to them is a Trad curiosity. If the Greens had museums, then they would probably stuff me and display me as an exhibit when I'm gone. King Brady, the last Trad that walked the Earth - only ten Greenbacks for a look-see.*

4: SCIENCE FICTION MOVIES

The Greens seemed to retain their adolescence and young adulthood throughout their entire lives if they were young enough at the Green Revolution or born since that time. Tyrone was no exception. He greeted Brady's arrival at his home in San Martin like Brady was a conquering hero. 'Hey, Brady. I'm so glad you could make it.'

'Wouldn't miss it for the world, kid. It looks like you got me slumming it, again.'

'You know, Uncle Sam. Ever since that Space Station incident and the trouble you ran into, he won't let you take me anywhere. That's why we are flying with Sattva Systems™ - still, the PassengerFusionJets™ are all the same…'

'Except that, I have to sit next to a load of spaced-out Greens.' He laughed. He teased Tyrone, 'Why do you still wear those glasses? One, you can use the Yellow™ to imitate them, and two, I thought you are all supposed to have enhanced sight, now that you've had the VioletSuits™ and all.'

Tyrone slipped into a character he had seen on one of the old movies, 'Hey, it's my thing, my brand, and they are tortoiseshell…'

'Whatever.' Brady reached into his pocket and pulled out a dozen entertainment files. 'I'm out of selling action at the moment, I've got my boys in a competition with each other, and I can't take sides - but here is that series from the 2060s you asked me to keep an eye out for. They are unofficial recordings as the series was streamed at the time, but the quality's ok.'

Tyrone grabbed them off him, 'Wow!' He flicked through them all, examining the tiny writing under the BMEE logos with the Diamondback rattlesnake weaving through the letters. '25th Century Ezekiel Rovers - this is now a cult classic for all of us space geeks. Thanks, Brady.'

Brady mocked, 'Anything to keep a brother happy.'

'I cannot wait to watch these when I come back.' He looked at his watch. 'We better get going; otherwise, we'll miss the FusionCoach™ to the FusionPort™.'

'I guess this will be the last FusionSpaceShuttle™ launch you'll get to see.'

Tyrone sighed, 'Yeah, this is the only holiday I can get, which coincides with a launch day. It's a shame because there are only three more left after this, and then that will be it, forever. It seems such a shame to me.'

'So, you didn't manage to get the Bear to change his mind and let you volunteer to be an astronaut then?'

'You know what he's like. He pulled in a favour from Bodhi and blocked me. Uncle Sam's a nobody - just a sprayer, and yet he seems to have a hold over the Big Man.'

Brady said, 'The History of the Beardons and the Kanes go back a long way. That's loyalty for you.'

When they reached the FusionPort™, Brady expected to be annoyed by the hustle and bustle of the other Green passengers, especially as they all adopted weird space or Martian alien appearances, but he had to admit he immensely enjoyed being just another tourist. If anybody recognised Brady Mahone in the flesh, they put it down to a Green adopting an appearance of Brady Mahone, as he was the Trad who brought Science Fiction Movies and TV series back to the Green space freaks. Towards the rear of the FusionPassengerJet™, he spotted a carbon copy of himself. *This is fucked up but kinda funny.*

He sat next to Tyrone, and for the next few hours, he let Tyrone babble away about today's launch and what a hostile planet Mars was compared to Earth. Brady didn't mind, some of this seeped into his brain, but mostly, he just liked being in the company of an old and cheerful friend. Brady let the hours drift by, he looked out of the window to watch the banks of white clouds below him, and as the FusionPassengerJet's™ only sound was the sub-sonic hum of its engine, then he could close his eyes at times and listen into the conversations around him. In the old days, he would have hated these geeks dressing up and going to their conventions, but now, the very reminder of those old Trad days was intoxicating. His fellow passengers were giving their critiques of all the Science Fiction shows and movies they had ever seen and pulled them to pieces if they missed out on out crucial scientific details or made the crime of not predicting the future from the long-distance run-around of the past. He smiled as what they were actually doing was disseminating the cultural impact of Brady Mahone and his exclusive Entertainment Enterprises. *I made this happen, me, Brady Mahone. If it wasn't for me, they would have died of boredom in this dull Green world. If there was a God in Heaven, then he must be real proud of Brady Mahone. I have brought happiness and entertainment to the people.*

After the FusionPassengerJet™ had vertically landed, they boarded the Fusion-Coach™ to take the hour-long drive to Cape Cassandra. There seemed to be a competition to see who could catch the first glimpse of the FusionSpaceShuttle™ ready to leave this Earth from its FusionPad™ on its last logistical trip to send machinery to Mars. The return trip would bring Mars' construction workers back to receive the UltraViolet™. Tyrone scoffed at the crawling progress of the old space missions of the past, and how the months had turned to days with Sattva Systems'™ development of zero-gravity FusionBoosters™.

The FusionCoach™ pulled up within a few hundred yards from the launch pad. Brady said, 'I'm a Trad, and the heat of the blast could kill me. I'm heading back about half a mile.' He looked up at the giant tipped up spacecraft, and it still staggered him how it was about four times bigger than the vine-wrapped rocket at Cape Canaveral. He recalled Glenarvon Cole scampering up to the top of that rocket like a kid playing hooky from school. He smiled at the recollection. He cocked his head and wondered how they secured the equipment, as they were tipped up at the moment, and presumably, they would level up later. He shrugged. *They probably got some Nanostraps or Nano-Blu-Tack knowing those Green fuckers.*

Tyrone said, 'I'll go with you. I keep forgetting, you always seem like a Green to me.'

Brady laughed and put a big hand on Tyrone's skinny shoulder. 'Wash that mouth out, boy.' Tyrone laughed as well, but Brady added, 'You stay up front with your buddies. It must be one helluva rush up there.'

Tyrone didn't protest, 'The heat and the sub-sonic boom is stupendous…thanks, Brady.'

'No problem, kid. I still get a heavy dose of it from my vantage point. Now shoo, I don't want you to miss it.' Brady watched Tyrone rush to join his friends. They were all old in Trad terms, but for these Greens, it seemed they remained like children for the whole of their lives. He headed back to a nearby hill. He had attended many of these launches over the last few decades, but usually, he travelled alone, in his own FusionPlane™ and rarely had the opportunity came along to travel with Tyrone, either because of lining up Tyrone's vacations or the objections from Samuel Beardon the Third. *It seems that these Forever Children have Forever Parents and Forever Family.* Brady thought of his own family and how they were all frozen in their shells, which made them appear and act like they were in their early twenties. It seems *I'm going to be their Forever Daddy.* He liked that idea.

He had an hour to wait for the launch, and he studied the panoramic views of virtual nothingness all around him. It was almost a desert. He figured it was chosen because of the damage a sub-sonic boom could do to any buildings within miles of here. He thought of the natural habitat and what the sub-sonic booms could do to the creatures that lived here. He knew this was why Bodhi and Glen would have been so coy about surrendering to Tia Cassandra's demands. He also knew that this is why they had put a time limit on the Space Program. He agreed with them. As much as Brady loved the big machines, he loved the animals more.

Brady heard the distant cheers of Tyrone and his buddies drift in the air, and he guessed that the launch sequence had begun. He hoped the ascent would go without a hitch, but when the rescue of Tia Cassandra's people in Cima had brought death and destruction to so many Greens that day, all these events now had a sense of jeopardy that wasn't there before when he used to believe that the RedSuits™ made them indestructible. They were difficult to kill, but not impossible. This knowledge added frisson to the excitement of this day.

He lay down as he knew the shock wave would knock him off his feet from bitter experience. Under his prostrate body and with his head peeking over the hill, he felt the first tremors under him, which indicated that the FusionCells™ had been activated. The vibrations in the ground made his skin tingle all over. He then experienced the massive waves of the opening sub-sonic pulses, force pressure waves over his head. He watched the crowd leap up and down, and some were sent flying backwards by the sub-sonic boom - this was a game they played like teenagers on a theme park ride. The sub-sonic boom zoomed the hill and lifted Brady up a couple of feet above the ground before dumping him unceremoniously back down. He was winded but exhilarated by this immense power. He then watched the FusionSpaceShuttle™ leave the ground slowly and then, with each new sub-sonic pulse, climb ever faster into the skies. It shone like the Sun as it soared out of the atmosphere and into the heavens and onto Mars.

He laughed loudly to himself as he watched the bodies of the sprawled Green geeks pick themselves up from wherever the sonic booms had dumped them. They were pointing and laughing at each other. It brought back powerful memories of being a hyper-active and thrill-seeking teenager. He loved Tyrone. Some of the best days he had ever had, had been with this skinny nephew of Samuel Beardon the Third, aka the Bear - his oldest and dearest friend since Lucian had departed this world. He noticed that the Greens were returning to the FusionCoach™, but Tyrone hadn't joined them. Brady strolled over to Tyrone, and he was looking around in the dirt.

Brady said, 'What's the matter, kid?'

'I've lost my glasses.' He looked up, and Brady noticed they were gone. Tyrone added, 'Man, that was one helluva blast - the best ever.'

'Sure was. It all went without a hitch as far as I could tell.' He looked at Tyrone, 'Can't you just make up some glasses, y'know, with the Yellow™ and all?'

'They are my lucky glasses. It's a superstitious thing.'

'You and all your science talk, and now you've got superstitions.'

Tyrone shrugged, 'I know, it's stupid, but...'

Brady remembered how superstitious his fellow criminals were. His buddy got shot to death on the last jewellery heist he committed - the one that got him sent to Ridgecrest. He had lost his lucky chain that very day, and the stories in Ridgecrest often revolved around being caught because of a superstitious error of judgment. 'No problem. I'll be your extra pair of eyes.' They both scrambled around in the dirt, but it was difficult because the sub-sonic booms had rearranged the ground.

Minutes passed by until the FusionCoach™ driver had told them they had to leave or else they would miss the connecting flight. Brady asked for help but couldn't convince him to look for a pair of Trad spectacles without them even having lenses in, as Tyrone hadn't needed the lenses since receiving the Violet™. The driver gave them the ultimatum of two more minutes, and after that, he would be gone. Brady expanded the search and frantically rubbed away the ground, and then he saw a glint of brown from a few yards away. He pushed away from the mound of dirt, and the frame emerged. 'I got it. I found them.'

Tyrone shouted, 'Yay! Brady, you rock. Thank you so much.'

The driver yelled, 'It's now or never, boys.'

They both raced to the FusionCoach™. Some of the passengers cheered ironically, while others gave them dirty looks. Brady glared back at them, and Tyrone barely noticed as he was cleaning the dust and dirt from his lucky glasses.

5: CRIMES AND MISDEMEANOURS

It was night-time in San Martin when Tyrone and Brady arrived at the Beardon home. Most of the occupants had already gone to bed as they had Green work in the morning - even the now ancient old woman Shako. The Bear heard his nephew and Brady arrive and made his way downstairs to greet them. 'I trust you had a good time.'

'It was the best, Uncle Sam. I hope you didn't mind me bringing Brady home. It's been a long day, and I thought he could camp down here for the night.'

The Bear slapped Brady on the back, 'Of course. How are you keeping, brother?'

Brady smiled, 'I'm good. I've been organising things for the future, and I gave the ranches a real good sorting out.'

'That all sounds positive. It reminds me of something my Grandfather, the mighty fine Samuel Beardon, used to say. I tidied my room today - it made me think - should I tidy my mind today - Mmm, I'll think about it.' The Bear laughed as he watched Brady figure it out.

'Very funny. Do you people ever talk straight, or is it all riddles with you guys?'

The Bear moved next to Tyrone and put a big protective arm around him. He said to them both, 'I'll fix you up some supper. Would you like a fruit juice or a coffee to go with it?'

Tyrone interrupted, 'I'll do it, Uncle Sam.'

'Now, now, boy. It's the Division of Labour, and you are on vacation. You are not allowed to work this week - now sit down, and I'll bring it over.'

Tyrone sat down, and Brady noticed that he appeared tired. Brady said, 'You lot go to sleep between 11pm, and 2am with your Suits™, so you get your beauty sleep if you want?'

Tyrone yawned, 'Is a good idea. Thanks, Brady.' He headed to the stairs and then to bed.

The Bear said, 'My sleep shift isn't until 2am.'

Brady said, 'This Division of Labour malarkey doesn't apply to me, so let me give you a hand, old friend.' He followed the Bear into the kitchen. Brady made the coffee and chopped up a few vegetables. The Bear seemed hungry as he insisted on making a fruit cocktail for a late-night feast.

They sat down to eat, and they caught up on recent events and old times. Brady asked, 'How come you sleep at different times to everyone else - you're not a Disciple - even though you should be, in my opinion, you are ten times the man that Siddha is.'

'I'm classed as Devout. I'm not hungry for another man's respect and titles. The knowledge that the Lord loves me is all the affirmation I need.' The Bear changed the subject. 'What are your plans, brother?'

'I don't know, I think it's what they call a transitional phase. My business kinda runs itself, which is why I'm gradually handing it over to my boys to run. My mind is planning for the end, y'know, I ain't gonna live forever, but my body is still in real good shape, and I don't think I'm losing my mind unless you're hinting with that tidying my mind story, I never can tell with your twisty fables. Remember that shark story of yours when we first met?'

'That was just taking your theme and running with it, just a little scary old tale, is all.'

Brady laughed, 'You can't half tell 'em - it freaked me out for years.'

The Bear gave Brady's comment a lot of thought. He wanted to make his old friend feel better, 'I think I may have tapped into something inside you. In your old life, your worst fear was probably being locked up forever.'

I don't have no fears, and once behind bars, it just became another home from home for me, albeit the accommodation was lousier. 'Yeah, that's probably it.'

A Satt™ rang out. Brady headed to his coat pocket, not expecting it to be his, as he hardly ever switched it on. In his criminal Trad days pre-Revolution, he knew the Feds loved mobiles for tracking the movements of people like him, and the habit had remained for a Century since. *Maybe I'm as paranoid as Pops after all.* The Bear struggled to locate the ringing Satt™ as well until he found it buried in a drawer with old materials which were waiting to be recycled one day - for these useless bits and bobs that day may never come. The Bear answered clumsily as he was out of practice at using this ancient FusionPowered™ tech. 'Hi, who is this...Oh...yes, he is...' He looked across at Brady, 'It's Sissy, she says she's up to her eyes in work, but she could do your business redistribution ceremony tomorrow...' He held out the Satt™, 'Do you want to talk to her?'

'Yeah, go on then.'

Sissy asked, 'Is that you, Brady?'

'Yes. Tomorrow is too short notice. I'd have to contact my boys, and they are spread over the world. It's Tuesday today, is there any chance we could do it on Saturday?'

There was silence. Brady then heard a muffled conversation on the other end of the line, which he interpreted that she was checking or rearranging her schedule. 'It's my fault...I should have thought...yes...Saturday...evening. Would that work for you?'

'I can do that.' *I've bought me some thinking time. I still don't trust these fuckers.*

'This is a complex ceremony for us, as it's something we need to mock-up as a one-off...just for you. It would help if we had some senior Greens at the Distor™ Distribution Ceremony to act as conduits...it's the only way we can get it to work.'

'How come?'

'It's the power required to overcome a Trad such as yourself in the chain. You are a potential circuit-breaker. If you don't want to convert to Green which would make this a simple procedure...'

'No. It's ok, I get it. Who have you got in mind?'

'There would be myself, and Glen and Cain have volunteered...I thought Samuel would come along, as I know you trust him...'

Brady thought for a moment, and he looked at the Bear. Brady said, 'Hey, old buddy, I need your help.'

The Bear smiled warmly, 'How could I refuse a brother? What can I do for you?'

'I need you to come over to my home in Malibu for a distribution ceremony... maybe we could travel down together. I know my place is a bit fancy pants for your liking...'

'I'd love to. I've always been curious to see the Brady palace.' The Bear spoke the words, but Brady was doubtful that he meant them.

Brady said to Sissy, who was waiting patiently on her Satt™. 'Yeah, the Bear will be there. I'll see you Saturday evening.'

He hung up the Satt™ and hugged the Bear, 'Thanks, man - much appreciated. I've got some calls to make.'

The Bear went to do the washing-up while Brady called his sons. He knew they would pick up, as he knew his number would flash on the screen. He made so few calls in his life that he knew it would be deemed to be urgent.

After a while he glanced at his watch, he saw that it was 2am. He thought it strange that the Bear was already most likely fast-asleep in his bed while Tyrone emerged looking wide awake. Alicia was with him, and she made Tyrone his breakfast as he was still on vacation, and this was her Division of Labour obligation to him - a reward and a show of respect for his Green work he completed through the rest of the year.

Alicia said, 'Hi, Brady. Do you want some breakfast?'

Brady laughed, 'I've only just had supper.' He added, 'Hey Kids...' He said to the youngsters in their hundreds - but going on thirty. 'The Bear is coming over to my place in Malibu this weekend - do ya wanna come along?'

Alicia said, 'Normally, I'd love to, but I'm working.'

'Fair enough.'

Tyrone said, 'Absolutely. I can't wait.'

'Great. We'll head over on Thursday. We'll make a long weekend of it. I'm sure the Bear won't mind you riding along, seeing as he will be your chaperone and all. It's about time you saw the place, and it will give me a chance to return the hospitality.'

'It will be nice to see Amie and Helgarth again - it's been too long.'

6: THE YEARS BETWEEN US

The fight down to Malibu was a pleasant affair with Tyrone and the Bear treating it as if Brady was taking them on vacation. There was a lot of light-hearted ribbing of the Bear for behaving like a scaredy-cat as he grumbled about Brady flying his FusionPlane™ too fast. Brady ignored him as he swooped, banked, and pushed the FusionPlane™ to its limit. Tyrone loved it and kept talking of the top speeds of FusionRockets™. By the end of the flight, the Bear played up his role of the cautious back seat driver because it made Tyrone laugh.

Tyrone was still laughing loudly as he alighted the FusionPlane™ until he was stopped in his tracks by a vision that appeared before him. It wasn't the sight of Brady's mansion on the clifftops or the array of every kind of FusionVehicle™ in Brady's parking lot, and it wasn't even the sweeping vistas of the Pacific. It was the floating figure in the ethereal Gothic form of Raelynn. She drifted toward the new arrivals as if she was in a dream. For no apparent reason, she even twirled as if this was completely normal. She approached Brady and kissed him on the cheek. 'Hi, Brady.' She turned very slowly to take in Brady's guests, 'Hi, Brady's friends.' To Tyrone, it appeared that she even smiled in slow motion.

Brady said to Raelynn, 'These are probably the two best friends I have in the world.' The Bear smiled broadly. Brady continued, 'This is the Bear, as I call him, but his real name is Samuel Beardon the Third. I met him way back, not long after the Green's took over the world…'

Raelynn held out a soft hand, and the Bear shook it as if it might break if he held it too firmly. 'Any friend of Brady's is a friend of mine.'

Brady said, 'And this is Tyrone, his nephew, we've had some great times together…'

Raelynn kissed him on the cheek, and her face brushed his lens-less spectacles. 'You are real. I love Trad accessories. Maybe we could have some great times together.' She pulled slowly away from him, and her quiet laugh had a timeless quality to it.

If the attraction was evident to Tyrone and Raelynn, then for the moment, it bypassed Brady as he completed the formalities. 'Raelynn is Helgarth and Amie's kid.'

Tyrone said, 'Helgarth and Amie are your Moppas?'

Raelynn giggled, 'I prefer Maddies - don't you think that is so much funnier?'

'I do now.' Tyrone chuckled.

It was then that he noticed the spark between them, and he suggested, 'Raelynn?'

She took her eyes away from the lanky visitor from San Martin, 'Yes.'

'Perhaps you could give Tyrone the grand tour while I look after the Bear?'

'Love too.' She grabbed Tyrone's hand. 'Come with me.'

Brady and the Bear watched bewildered by the speed and the turn of events. Raelynn seemed to infect Tyrone with her Gothic slowness as they drifted off like ghosts toward the shoreline. He had expected her to give him a guided tour of the Brady Mahone residence, first. Brady said, 'That was weird. You don't think…'

'Yes, I do. I think your Raelynn has made quite an impression on Tyrone.'

'She's not my Raelynn, but yeah.' He strode off up to the clifftops to his Malibu home, and the Bear followed. Brady said, 'You don't think we should be concerned, do you?'

The Bear laughed, 'She sounds like she's yours.'

Brady laughed, 'No. No, I suppose I do kinda sound responsible for her. I love her like one of my own, but there must be an eighty-year age difference, even if it looks like about five, or maybe ten, on the surface.'

'You have a point, my friend, but nothing could happen that both sides weren't comfortable with. The Security Protocols™ would intervene at the first signs of exploitation, but you know that...'

'Yeah. I suppose it's the Trad side of me that thinks it ain't right.' He added, 'It's the taking of people at face value. If they look thirty, then they are thirty, even though my mind is always trying to work out how old everybody really is, even myself. I mean, I should be dead and long gone by now, and yet, here I still am.'

'Don't question the Lord's blessing, brother. If he gives, then it must be for His reason.'

Brady was careful not to brag about his home as he knew it wouldn't impress his friend. He described every room and facility as if he was taking his friend on a tour of John Kane and Libby Skye's old home, and he was given it as part of a deal with Xavier Kane, aka Bodhi Sattva. For his part, the Bear knew what Brady was doing and appreciated the effort of Brady to be humble, as he knew this wasn't Brady's usual style. The exception to Brady's rule was to show the Bear to the best Guest room in the place, and he ensured he had staff on hand to look after the Bear's every need.

Over the next few days, it became apparent to everyone that Raelynn and Tyrone had become inseparable. There had been no point in showing Tyrone to his guest room as Raelynn had insisted that he was sharing her room.

One by one, his sons returned from their far-off lands. Even Bill, as the North America Director, had to travel from Vancouver. And then, on Saturday evening, the delegation from the Sattva Systems™ HQ arrived, without fanfare.

Brady had gathered his family and his staff to greet them. The formality of the situation was unusual for Brady, but he believed the occasion and his intentions warranted it. He announced, 'I know you will know my guests, but maybe you've not had the opportunity to meet them.' He cleared his throat, 'This is Genesis Garcia - she used to be the Governor of California in the old days...I'm sorry, I don't know the name of your role for Sattva Systems™...'

Sissy smiled, 'I'm the Marketing Disciple and Chief Advisor to Bodhi Sattva. It's a pleasure to meet you.' She shook the hands of everybody.

Brady said, 'This is Cain. Since the first day after the Green Revolution, I've known him as he was the Disciple of my hometown of McFarland back then. Now he is the Regional Disciple of the Western Seaboard of the USA.' Cain seemed to entrance the gathering as he gazed at each one with his crystal green eyes. 'And this is Glenarvon Cole, the leader of the GreenRevs.'

Brady was shocked to see his sons break ranks and reach out hands for shaking and hugging him. Hawk shouted, 'You are a fucking hero, man.' Bill said, 'A true legend.'

Glen looked at Brady apologetically.

Brady looked at his three guests from Boulder Creek and said, 'Hunter will show you to your rooms. It will give you time to freshen up, and we've got some food and drink as a buffet in an hour. It will give you a chance to meet my family and make any arrangements you need for the ceremony - if that's ok with you?'

'That's great.' Sissy said 'Thank you, Brady.'

Brady watched in bemusement as Hunter came over, and Sissy hugged him, 'My dear Hunter, it's been so long, how are you?' Cain and even Glen treated Hunter as a long-lost friend. *I really should have got to know Hunter better - the sly old fox.* Sissy hooked arms with Hunter as the group headed towards the stairs.

At the buffet, Brady was strangely quiet, while others mingled agreeably. Amie and Helgarth chatted with the Bear while smiling together at the sight of the two love birds Tyrone and Raelynn. Brady had taken the precaution of having Debrock and his stoner friends have their fun at the other end of the building. It seemed as if Helgarth and Amie had arranged that they didn't need to do Green work anymore. He guessed that their exceptional circumstances would be paid for out of their share of his business. He could have got angry about that, but he was reassured by a certain Trad-ness in their thinking - plenty of his old criminal buddies would have partied their proceeds of crime away.

He was more perturbed by the hero-worship his own sons were bestowing on Glenarvon Cole. *I dread to think what they'd be like if they realised that he was their biological uncle.* It gave him comfort that he was the only one who knew this secret, for now. It gave him a sense of leverage and power. When his boys did come over and chat with their Pops, one-by-one, they all had similar stories to tell. These included how they were going to win the competition for the FusionPassengerJet™ because they were miles ahead of their targets, and also, Brady's idea of rubbishing the potential benefits of the UltraVioletSuits™ was a stroke of marketing genius.

Sissy and Cain worked closely together as they pulled out various Distors™ and primed them for use. He also noticed them rehearsing their lines and consulting his notes. He put his hand to his pocket to seek the reassurance that he had his own Distor™ on him. He took it out and wondered if, after today, he would ever bring the figure back to the 2.1 billion Green credits he had now. He wondered what had possessed him to make him want to give nearly a half of all these away within an hour from now. *I'll still have more than a billion Green credits, and like they say, I can't take them with me when I'm gone.* He urged himself to remember that his primary reason for giving them away was to ensure that the Greens didn't take them or put them out of reach of his kin.

Glen came over and spoke to Brady. He seemed warm and trustworthy, but Brady thought of him as a warrior just as his sons did. 'This is a big day for you. You've achieved so much - you must be very proud.'

'Yeah, I suppose. It just seems the right thing to do. I'm getting older - even if I don't feel it, and I need to think about other's futures and not just my own.' Brady didn't want to talk about personal and family stuff with Glen. He viewed Glen as a man first, and not a Green, possibly influenced that Brady knew he was his cloned brother, or maybe that's the same as a real brother. 'Enough about me. What have you been up to lately?'

'I've overseen the project to select 24,642,756 Disciples and the Devout as part of my one-hundred-year part of the Green Deal.'

Glen watched Brady's puzzled frown with amusement. Brady said, 'That's a lot of people…and why that number?'

'I had help. It was like an old pyramid scheme, I recruit three, who each recruit three, which means I've now recruited twelve - three and nine.'

'That still doesn't explain that number.' *What have I got myself into now? This is going to be worse than Tyrone and his long numbers.*

Glen said, 'It's something which means more to Bodhi than me. Apparently, John Kane had a thing about the number three. He always liked to have a number divisible by three or nine in it somewhere whenever he conducted a scientific project. However, Bodhi wanted one Devout or Disciple for every square mile of hospitable land on Earth. This was so that all of Mother Earth could be monitored and looked after. The number 24,642,756 is the number of square miles, and it is a number divisible by nine and three.'

'You lot are fucking insane - you know that - don't you?' Brady looked to the heavens.

Glen roared with laughter and slapped Brady on the back. Brady could see that his sons were impressed by Glen's camaraderie with their Pops. He smiled at this show of respect. He then saw Sissy gesture to Glen to prepare. Glen got the boys to remove the table and chairs to the edges of the room to leave space for the participants to form a large circle.

Cain announced, 'We are ready for the Division of Brady Mahone's Entertainment Enterprises. Glenarvon Cole will show you to your positions.'

He went over to Brady first. 'Follow me, man.' He led Brady to the top of the circle. The huge window framed the sun setting over the ocean in a blaze of reds, oranges, and pinks. He placed Bill to his left and then skipped a place. He took a smiling Wilder next. Next, he approached Samuel Beardon the Third. Cain clasped hands with him and then encouraged him to take up the next slot. Then it was Hawk's turn, and then at the bottom of the circle, he smiled as he persuaded Raelynn to leave Tyrone's side and take her place. She floated dreamily onto her spot, and the skies fire seemed to light up her Goth features. Next to Raelynn, he placed Lucy-Ian, and the two goys giggled like schoolchildren sitting next to each other in class. Cain moved without prompting to stand next to Lucy-Ian as Glen led Troy into position. Like Cain, Sissy moved to her spot and then, as the circle was nearly complete, Rocky was placed at Brady's right-hand side.

Glen retrieved the slightly larger translucent moss green Distors™ and handed these to Samuel Beardon the Third, Cain, Sissy, and then retained the last one for himself. Glen made one final check - before moving into his position between Bill and Wilder.

As he passed Brady on the way anti-clockwise around the circle to his slot, Brady grabbed him by the arm. He hissed, 'Hey, tell me I'm not about to get screwed over here.'

Glen put a hand on Brady's shoulder, 'Everything is being done to respect your wishes - I promise.'

Sissy waited until Glenarvon Cole signalled that he was ready. She announced, 'Welcome to the ceremony to complete the Division of Brady Mahone's Entertainment Enterprises as per the wishes of Brady Mahone, and with the authority of Sattva Systems™ and the Word of Bodhi Sattva. Please hold out your Distors™.' They all held out their Distors™. 'Brady, if you set yours to freely give...' She then named his family going clockwise from Brady. 'And Rocky, Troy, Lucy-Ian, Raelynn, Hawk, Wilder and Bill, please set your Distors™ to freely receive.' They set themselves in a relaxed pose. 'Cain, could you please check the status of these Distors™ before we continue.'

Cain glided around the room in his white robe like a butterfly settling on each flower. When he returned to his position, he said, 'They are ready to give and receive.'

Sissy called Amie into the room, and she came in with Helgarth. 'Amie, could you confirm the distribution details as laid out in the documents and verify that these are the figures Brady Mahone gave you.'

'Yes, they are correct.'

Brady began to worry that Amie could double-cross him and change the amounts, but he reasoned that the Security Protocols™ could kick in, and then he realised that she wasn't in the circle and didn't have her own Distor™ in the game.

Sissy's Distor™ opened, and she tapped in instructions, and this took a few minutes. Then she said to Amie, 'Amie, please confirm that the figures and instructions set in the Master Distor™ are the same as the written notes you gave unto me.'

Amie said in the direction of Brady and then looked around the rest of the participants, 'The details are correct and fulfil the wishes and intentions of Brady Mahone.'

Brady wondered why they didn't check them with him, but numbers weren't his strong suit, and it was probably better to leave this to the experts. He equated this to letting his Defence Lawyers do the talking in the old days - not that that stopped him going to jail anyway.

Sissy said, 'Cain, Glen and Samuel Beardon the Third, please activate the Distor-Boosters™ in your possession.' They all switched on their Distors™ and muttered, 'May the additional energy and information pass through me freely.'

She looked around the circle, 'We are nearly ready. I will be the last to complete the chain. I want you all to extend your hands and reach and hold onto the Distor™ next to you.' The circle complied. Brady was unexpectedly nervous, and he retreated into his mind to imagine drawing a seagull he could hear screeching outside. It was his go-to method to stay calm.

Then Sissy connected with Rocky to her right and Troy to her left and chanted, 'Let the Division of Brady Mahone's Entertainment Enterprises commence.' Brady noticed the room's walls turn Green, and then he spotted a Green glow around every person in the circle. He observed that the glow came from the Distors™. He looked down on himself, and he was reassured that he wasn't emanating Green, and he then spotted that Amie and Helgarth were not touched by the Green glow.

The process took about a minute, but it felt much longer than that to Brady. Then Sissy announced, 'The first part of the process is completed. Now, if I could ask Amie and Helgarth to join the circle, either side of Brady. The rest of you may have to spread out a little, and you can let go of your Distors™ for a moment.'

Amie moved into Brady's right while Helgarth moved to his left. Cain came over to check the status of their Distors™. He nodded his approval to Sissy. Brady looked at the other family members who were reviewing the newly replenished Green credits within their Distor™ displays, and they were delighted. The only exception was Raelynn, who didn't check at all. She looked as if she was on another planet, or maybe in another room, her room with Tyrone. Brady thought this made her look cool, and he admired her for that.

Sissy called for quiet and calm as the mutterings had increased as the realisation that they were independently wealthy sunk in. She said, 'Now we come onto the matter of the Last Will and Testament of Brady Mahone in the style pertaining to the Traditional Culture of said, Brady Mahone. Amie has already confirmed the details. However, I must point out to you all that it is Brady's wish that this comes into effect on the day after the Green's one-hundred-year plan has been completed, which at this moment means January 1st, 2085.' She joked, 'So, you better take good care of him until then.'

His sons laughed. Brady smiled. *Just like the old days when I made a deal with my fellow criminals, it's a half now, and half on completion kinda deal.*

Sissy said, 'Just as before - if you could reach out and hold the Distor™ of the person next to you…' She waited, and then when she was satisfied, she continued, 'Let the Last Will and Testament of Brady Mahone be enacted with the authority of Sattva Systems™ and the Word of Bodhi Sattva.' As before, everybody glowed Green, including Amie and Helgarth this time, but again Brady was unaffected. Again, it seemed to take a minute to complete, but it seemed a little quicker this time to Brady.

When it was over, they all released their Distors™, and the circle broke. Brady shouted, 'Let's party.' And as if this was a cue, Brady's servants and Debrock and his hangers-on came into the room. Non-binary and non-stereotype music, or Green Tunes as they were lamely called, blared out - the reintroduction of music had been considered safe, and a concession to the disgruntled young Green protestors which had sprung up in recent times. The Security Protocols™ monitored it for signs of binary, race, colonialism, imperialism, and most important of all, Trad influences. Of course, Trad music had been widely distributed courtesy of Brady Mahone Entertainment Enterprises, but he had the Green elite to consider at this party.

Debrock handed out his dabs to anyone who wanted them, oblivious to the upper echelons of Sattva Systems™ being present in the room.

Brady quietly checked his Distor™ which glowed green with the figure of 1,421,237,285 Green credits, it was still a telephone number to him, but he knew it was slightly more than he had expected. He guessed that Sissy had included his latest earnings in the figure - and he knew his boys had produced a record surge in orders. He was a little disappointed that this string of numbers didn't commence with a 2, but he also felt a sense of relief that the ceremonies were over and that he was a big enough man to give so much away to his family.

7: HUNTED

While his guests partied, Brady sought out Hunter. He found him in his own room with Sissy, Glen and Cain. Even though this was Brady's home, they still appeared shocked when Brady knocked at the door and strode in. Brady said, 'I want to talk with Hunter alone.' There were no idle pleasantries. 'You can continue your little catch-up later. This won't take long.'

Sissy placed a hand on Hunter's and said softly and just beyond Brady's range, one of the benefits of the Violet™ was the acuteness of his hearing. 'Have no fear. I have your back.' She looked at Brady, 'Of course. We shall join the others at your celebration. You have provided generously, and we are grateful.' Glen and Cain stood up to join Sissy, but as they left the room, Glen hung back, 'I'm going to listen in, and I'll report back later.'

Cain asked, 'What concerns you, friend?'

'I don't want any surprises now that we are so close to completing the hundred-year plan. I've got the Disciples and the Devout. Bodhi has been UltraViolet™ for five years with no side effects. The only person who may not fulfil the promise is Brady. I want to put my mind at ease.'

'He has behaved predictably for the most part - within the erratic parameters of a Trad.'

Sissy said, 'Ok, Glen. Just don't get caught listening in. We don't want to arouse his suspicions needlessly.'

Glen said, 'They are talking. I need to listen now. I can handle this.'

Sissy and Cain headed off as Glen listened in at the crack of the door, which he had left slightly ajar.

Brady wasn't a skilled interrogator, and Hunter had already spotted that this conversation was heading for a trawl of information, as Brady always began with discussions about his extreme old age. Brady then started to probe further, 'Who employed you? I don't think it was Libby. I think you are much higher up in this Green infrastructure than you are letting on.'

'John Kane employed me, sir.'

The one thing that annoyed Brady about his extended length of years in this world was that working out dates started to feel like complex math. 'He employed you to win the trust of Libby and spy on her.'

'I loved and respected Libby. She was an immensely talented actor, but yes, I reported back on her, just as I have reported back to Bodhi on you. In my defence, sir, you have always known that you were not my employer.'

'And the rest of the staff?'

'Yes. I am their Disciple in this tiny Green Community. They report to me, and then I report back to Sattva Systems™ - often it is to Bodhi, personally.' Hunter sat up straight and with almost regal dignity, and for the first time, he viewed Hunter as a figure of power and authority and not as a humble servant. Hunter continued, 'You cannot fire me or my team. You do not have the authority. I am a Disciple, and this is my area of responsibility. I am the Disciple of this area of Green Malibu land, even if your home no longer existed. My duty is here.'

Brady put his hand to his face to conceal his concern. He then removed his hand to reveal his brown eyes, which studied his potential adversary. He left his hand still covering his mouth. He shook his head and then shrugged and put both hands on the arms of the chair. He said, 'Well played. I didn't have a clue.' He laughed, 'What a brilliant con, you got me.'

Glen smiled at the door but was troubled.

Hunter said, 'I haven't been unhappy working here. You have been a pleasure to work with, and I am happy to continue in this role.'

'Apparently, I don't have a say in it, but yes, that's fine by me. I won't treat you any differently. I mean, I won't get nasty or play games with you. I'll just treat you as if you've got a job to do. However, it's gonna be real hard to see you as the old Hunter.'

Hunter nodded an acknowledgement.

'Ok, I'm gonna take a moment here. I don't know what to ask you as you've taken me by surprise - not many people do that to Brady Mahone.' He looked into Hunter's eyes, 'There is more to learn from you, of that, I'm damned sure.'

Hunter flinched.

Brady struggled to find the right question to open his interrogation. He drifted back to a century ago. It was apparent now that he was tricked into visiting Libby Skye. The person who made that first approach was Hunter. 'Was it Libby who asked to see me? Or was it Bodhi? Y'know, when you first approached me.'

'Bodhi ordered Libby to entertain you, but it was Cain who relayed the order to me to locate and bring you to her.' He looked away as if saddened by the memory. 'He asked too much of her...'

'The bit where she gave me access to her stuff. Yeah, I remember, she tricked me. No, wait a minute, it was you who tricked me. I'm still bloody annoyed about that.' He then realised he had taken everything in the end, but he didn't like the thought of being outplayed.

'That wasn't me, precisely. Libby issued me an order, and I was duty-bound to obey. I begged forgiveness from Bodhi, and he granted it.'

'But he didn't forgive Libby. I'm guessing that she should have lived as long as you. What happened? Was she allowed to die like a Trad for behaving like a Trad?'

Hunter said after a short pause, 'She self-selected her path. She knew what she had to do but couldn't comply. Her Suits™ were allowed to degrade at her natural Trad rate.'

'I don't understand these weird terms you Greens use. I'm guessing she was allowed to die like any other - one-hundred and fourteen-year-old.'

'Technically speaking.'

Brady scoffed, 'That's real cold, man - and I'm a killer!' He said, 'What we have here is that the great Bodhi Sattva failed to protect his Mother. In fact, he wilfully neglected her.' Glen winced and shook his head.

Hunter said, 'I suppose you could choose to put it like that.'

Brady asked, 'Could you do that to your mother?'

'My Mother was a Trad who died eighteen months after the Green Revolution, as did the rest of my family. They never listened when I tried to get them to go Green. They treated me like a crackpot conspiracy theorist. They only have themselves to blame.'

Brady shook his head in disbelief. 'Why did Bodhi forgive you? It appears to me that you were as guilty as she was. You could have ignored her instructions.'

'He forgave me because I gave away the most precious item in my possession. When Xavier changed his name to Bodhi and to eschew all the trappings of material success to embark on a journey to save the planet, he gave to me...'

Brady pulled out the Sattva Ring, which hung on a chain around his neck. The emeralds and diamonds sparkled.

'...Yes. By giving you that ring, in place of Libby's most precious items, I had proven my worth to Bodhi.'

'Do you want it back?'

'No. Never. You are welcome to it. I give it to you freely and make no claim to it.'

Brady looked at the Sattva ring and then put it back inside his T-shirt. 'So, we've established that you did the leg work to get me to see Libby. You cheated me, you let Libby die...'

'I object. She brought it upon herself If I had intervened...'

'Ok. I'll let it pass. What else have you done?'

'Just reports. Comings and goings, life events, new acquisitions...'

'Tell me something which will make me believe you.'

'Like what, sir?'

Brady was getting frustrated. He knew he should be asking more searching questions than this, 'I don't know. Is there anybody who came to visit me, who rang alarm bells with your superiors - or whatever you call them?'

'Fleet Captain Marjorie Hampton. She visited you in an unauthorised capacity.'

Brady shrugged, 'She didn't tell me anything. She just wanted to make sure I stayed safe. That's what your job is - isn't it?'

'Yes, sir.'

'Drop the sir, shit. I don't want to hear you do that anymore. Is that clear?'

'Yes.'

'Good.' Brady went back through the years, his business, this home and his fortune - he struggled to articulate his concerns, 'Did I achieve all this?' He gestured all around him, 'Or was it given to me to keep me happy, for some purpose or other?'

Hunter smiled, 'This is all your own work. You are solely responsible for the success of the Brady Mahone Entertainment Enterprises. It was your idea before Bodhi was even aware of your presence and ability to traverse between the Trad and Green world. You own this, and now your family has its share of the burden.'

Brady folded his arms and nodded with pride. 'What skills did my predecessors have when they built their businesses? Y'know Kane Industries™, Sattva Systems™.'

Hunter looked to one side as if searching a long-misplaced memory. 'Mr Kane's head was in the right place, but he had no humanity. He was cold and ruthless. His one redeeming feature was that he made his money from Green technology.'

Brady said, 'He was an utter bastard as far as I can tell. If he'd have been in Ridgecrest Supermax, where he belonged, I would have torn him limb from limb for what he did. He was in a different league from the nonces I've had to live and survive alongside.'

Glen was puzzled as this wasn't the picture he had when he had dealings with John Kane. He had been his partner and environmental mentor. He had funded all of his projects in his war to save the planet from climate change disaster.

Brady said, 'What about Bodhi?'

'Bodhi is a saint, a prophet and a saviour. He was raised to be like John Kane, but he found compassion for all living creatures from somewhere. He has sacrificed so much personal pleasure for the evolution of mankind. He believes in a race that will always put the welfare of the planet first. He has watched over you, Brady Mahone. Your welfare is of deep concern to him. A man can sow seeds in the field, but he needs a beast to plough the field.'

'I ain't no man's beast. Is that all I am to you, a beast?' Brady jumped up angrily.

Hunter drew himself up to face his interrogator. He showed no fear. 'No. You have immense qualities of your own. You inspire doubt like no other living creature. You are the Temptation we must avoid. You carry death with you to every corner of the Earth. You are Corruption. You are the Corrupter, the Deceiver and Death-Bringer...'

Glen knocked on the door and marched in. 'Hi guys, everybody is wondering where the guest of honour is.' He flashed a look at Hunter and ordered, 'Could you check everybody is happy in the main hall? That's if Brady agrees.' He looked at Brady, 'Is that ok with you?' He added, 'Are you feeling ok, man? You look tired.'

'No. I'm fine.' Brady physically and mentally shook himself out of his trance. He began to wonder if Hunter had actually said those things about him. He looked at Glen, whose smiling face reassured him enough for him to say, 'It's been a stressful day. Maybe I need to let my hair down.'

Glen rubbed Brady's head hard, 'There's not much to let down on there. Come on, let's party. Show me what a good time looks like at Chateau Mahone.'

Brady responded meekly to the challenge, 'Yeah, sure. Have you had some of Debrock's dib-dabs?'

Glen usually refused Nature's highs on the grounds of keeping his senses alert, but this felt like a potential emergency. 'I haven't touched the stuff in decades. It will go straight to my head, and you'll think I'm such a lame-ass - but if you promise not to laugh at me...'

Brady said, 'Just, shut the fuck up, brother.' Still, Glenarvon Cole showed no response to this teasing statement. Brady yelled as if he had rediscovered his masculinity in the company of a fellow soldier, 'Come on. Let's get wrecked.'

8: GRAND DESIGNS

Tyrone nudged Brady awake. 'Hey, Brady, you said you'd give us a lift back to San Martin. You also said that Raelynn could come with me.'

Brady rubbed his eyes and tried to orientate himself. He was in his bedroom at his Malibu home. 'What day is it?'

'It's Sunday. I'm back at work tomorrow. Raelynn wants to stay at my house for a week or so. Uncle Sam says it's ok.' Tyrone smiled.

'You're God knows how old, and you still need the Bear's permission?'

'I don't mind. It's a respect thing. You'd like your boys to be like that, wouldn't you?'

Brady shuffled around in bed without escaping the warm pull of his blankets, 'What do you mean?'

'Still wanting to hear their Father's advice, even if they are a hundred years old.'

Brady grunted, 'No.' But then he thought about it from his muddled stoned haze. 'Yeah, I suppose so. I wouldn't want them to ignore me - that's for sure.' His head cleared for a moment, 'Where is the Bear?'

Tyrone smiled, 'He headed back to Sattva Systems™ with Glenarvon Cole, Genesis Garcia and Cain. He said to tell you that he had a lovely time, and he thanks you for your generous hospitality.'

Brady stretched. Tyrone smelled the body odour wafting in the air, and it took him back to the time before the RedSuits™ when everybody used to smell like this. Brady said, 'Was the Bear being sarcastic?'

'I don't think so. We were all laughing our heads off at you and Glenarvon Cole. You were like a comedy double act, with all those funny Trad stories. You were brilliant with all your convict tales. Raelynn thought you were so cool.'

Brady slapped his forehead as if he were kick-starting his memory cells. 'Fuck, I don't remember a God-damn thing. It sounds really embarrassing.'

Tyrone said, 'No. It wasn't. Your boys lapped it up, and Amie was sweet when you and she told stories about what it was like for you on the Mahone Ranch. Cain was getting quite emotional as it brought a lot of memories of those old days for him.'

Fuck, Debrock's stuff must have been the bomb. I don't remember anything at all. The last thing I remember was Hunter going all-out biblical on me. I musta pushed him too hard.

Brady sat up in bed - this was his first achievement of the day. 'Where is everybody else?'

'Your boys were up early and in the gym, but now they've all headed off to win some competition you set them. They didn't want to disturb you.'

'Why? What time is it?'

'10:30. That's why I didn't want to leave it any longer.'

'And the others?'

'Lucy-Ian, Amie, Helgarth, Debrock and xyr friends are still on the beach. They've been out there since Sunup.' He had a faraway smile, 'Raelynn is waiting for me.'

Brady asked, 'Have you seen Hunter?'

'Yes. He's outside in the corridor.'

'Hunter!' Brady shouted.

Hunter came in, 'How can I help you, sir?'

'I'm gonna have a quick wash and get changed. I won't be having breakfast; I'll eat on the way.' He looked at Hunter for a reaction, but he was acting the same as he had for the last eighty-four years in Brady's employ. 'Can you get the kitchen staff to knock-up a hamper for three? I'll need it within thirty minutes.'

'Certainly, sir.' He turned away sharply.

Brady thought he had said that he didn't want to be addressed as sir anymore, but he wasn't sure. 'If you give me a few minutes to get freshened up, then I'll meet you at my FusionPlane™. Tell Raelynn I'll take you on a scenic route and make a day of it. She doesn't get out enough. I'm thinking of flying over the Grand Canyon. Does that work for you?'

'Absolutely, I can't wait to tell Raelynn.' Tyrone beamed.

'Off you go, then.'

Brady showered and dressed in his favourite NanoProtected™ jeans, a white T-shirt and a pair of Xavier's old designer sneakers. He put on his sunglasses even while still inside, as he knew when he left the building, he wouldn't be able to cope with the Californian sunshine in his present hazy state.

He relayed messages to the staff to let them know that Raelynn was with him today, and then she would be stopping over in San Martin for the foreseeable future. Helgarth would worry about her more than Amie.

In the distance, he saw Tyrone and Raelynn kissing, but they stopped when they saw Brady approaching the FusionPlane™. Raelynn raced up to greet Brady extravagantly, she leapt into him, and he caught her, and she hugged him. 'You are the best, Brady Mahone. I love you so much.'

'I love you too, honey. Now, let me give you the guided tour.'

They got in the FusionPlane™, and as soon as Brady completed the vertical lift-off, he set the SattNav™ to go to San Martin but with several diversions. He wasn't feeling fully functional to fly manually, so he put the FusionPlane™ on autopilot. He was ravenously hungry, and his staff had already left a considerable picnic hamper for him and his guests. He opened it up, 'Let's take a look-see shall we.' He pulled out sandwiches and a thermos of coffee for himself, 'Watcha waiting for - tuck in.'

Brady slowly began to feel like his old self. He looked out of the window, 'Hey Raelynn, that's San Francisco below. It used to have buildings called skyscrapers - they were called that because they were so tall, they touched the sky - and there were loads of them.' Brady laughed as he realised, he wasn't going to the most eloquent of tour guides.

Raelynn played along good-naturedly, she might have adopted the image of a Goth, but she had no idea of the mannerisms and the eternal disdain needed to complement this appearance. 'You mean the buildings were as high as we are now?'

'Sure thing, hun. And all those grids you can see were the Highways. I mean, some of the vegetation looks ok, but I'm not so sure about the brown and dust holes.'

Tyrone said, 'Some of the most heavily polluted and damaged areas are taking longer than expected to recover. They may be permanently scarred. Of course, the world is just going back to its natural state. Not all the land was beautiful, even in the beginning.'

After a short while, Brady said, 'Wow, look at that, the Golden Gate Bridge. Except it's Green - I shoulda guessed.' He laughed. 'Hey, Tyrone, of all the old Trad structures, why do they leave these standing.'

'It's as you'd guess - some infrastructure is useful - even we have to travel conveniently.'

Raelynn said dreamily, 'I would have loved to have seen it in gold.'

Brady said, 'It was always more of a red to me, except when it was lit up at night, then it kinda had a golden glow about it.'

Tyrone said, 'It's called the Green Gate Bridge now. It's turned that colour because it's been NanoProtected™.'

Brady had the FusionPlane™ head over in the direction of Phoenix. He didn't want the journey to be solely over forests and wildernesses before getting to the Grand Canyon. He wanted Raelynn to have a variation of landscapes to take in on the Brady tour.They flew in peace for a while. Tyrone and Raelynn murmured together while Brady tried to recover his lost memories from the night before. The last thing he recalled with any clarity was Hunter taking on the role of a preacher in much the same way as the Bear would do. He tried to square up how the people of God, and not just the Christians - it was the same with all the spiritual types he had met - could be on the side of the Greens. They had stood meekly aside as churches and temples of every faith had been dissolved into nothing. They didn't even seem to want to build Green communities in the same areas of the most significant buildings. It didn't make any sense to him.

He waited for a pause in the conversation between Raelynn and Tyrone to ask his question. 'Hey, Tyrone, you know me, I don't like to talk about things that get heavy and all - and you being all into the science stuff - can I ask your opinion on a few things?'

'Sure, what do you want to know?'

'I don't want a lot of technical detail - I can't cope with that.' He knew he had to get to the point, 'You're kinda neutral on all the religious aspect of this Green thing, that's why I want to see how it all fits together…I know I ain't putting this too well. I don't want to ask your Uncle Sam as he's biased, and plus once you get him started, he don't stop.'

'Ok. I'm an atheist. I don't believe in religion, I'm not even particularly spiritual, but I know how it works because I've had Uncle Sam preaching it to me my whole life. You ask me anything, Brady. I will give you the best answer I can, but it is my personal view - the Greens don't have a position on this. They are predominantly ecologists, environmentalists and all the other scientific branches which emanate from these studies.'

Brady was reassured. He could tell that Tyrone was taking his request seriously, and he didn't feel threatened by humiliation if he asked a stupid question. He noticed Raelynn watch over the both of them as if this subject pricked her interest. Brady said, 'Why doesn't the Bear get angry when he sees all these churches destroyed. Why doesn't he fight to keep them open?'

'Remember these are my personal opinions. Uncle Sam would never agree with my theories. The more spiritual Greens have conflated Saving the Planet with doing God's will. Bodhi has rationalised it as organised religion is capitalism with spiritual marketing. They were treasure hoarders and held vast lands at their disposal for thousands of years. They let people suffer instead of selling off their treasures to help them. Obviously, the Trad believers hated this idea, but those who were Green and who understood the imminent danger of runaway climate change were stuck between two opposing world views.'

'I kinda get that, but surely once the Greens had won, then you'd think they'd change their minds and ask to keep the temples for themselves. I know I would.' *But then again, I'm a criminal who wouldn't trouble myself over renegotiating a deal.*

'Who would you ask?'

Because the question was short, Brady suspected it was a trick question, 'Bodhi, I suppose.'

Tyrone looked down at the forests and then looked back up into the clouds. 'The Greens have different factions, with different mindsets but one common goal - to save the Earth. People like me study and follow the science. Others just want to work for the greater good. They used to be the volunteers and the activists in the old days. People like Uncle Sam and religious and spiritual people across the globe have many things in common in their teachings - if you apply a little lateral thinking in some cases.'

'Like what?'

'There is usually a catastrophe foretold, some kind of cataclysmic event, an end-of-days kind of deal, and this is accompanied by a saviour, a prophet of some kind, or a second coming, a son of God. If you turn away from him, you are doomed for all eternity, but if you follow, then you can be saved and live out your days in paradise, heaven, a rapture, or maybe even a Heaven on Earth.'

'Are you telling me that Bodhi thinks he is the next Jesus Christ?'

'Not exactly. Bodhi doesn't come out and say that. I don't think he is even religious. I believe he is a scientist and a businessman. However, all of the ingredients of the prophecies are there for people like my Uncle Sam to believe. He believes that Bodhi is the Second Coming of Christ.' Tyrone joked, 'And people like my Uncle Sam like structures and strict rules - all religious followers do. He follows the rules - if churches have to go - then so be it.'

Tyrone rewound the subject as he didn't like where this was going, and he needed time to think about the inevitable follow-up question. He looked to Raelynn for help, but she was mentally and metaphorically in the clouds. Tyrone chose an action story to divert Brady's attention. He smiled as he realised this was a tactic his Uncle Sam had used on him many times before. He said, 'One of the most ferocious battles took place in the early days when the GreenShells™ encircled the Vatican City. The Trads protecting it threw everything they had in attempting to fight off the Greens. They threw rocks, gathered swords which they believed carried the power of God within them to slash uselessly at the Shells™. They even used blood sacrifices to try and lift the perceived curses. This went on for months after the Revolution until they decided to place people around the perimeter to stop the encroachment for as long as they could.'

Brady said, 'They did something like that at mASSIVE™ Park in Cupertino.'

Tyrone laughed, 'That was a time when science nearly became a religion for many.' He added, 'But, eventually, they died out. But here's the thing - many of the Christian Greens wanted to preserve the City, and particularly the treasures in the St Peter's Basilica and masterpieces of art like the Sistine Chapel, but they were denied.'

Brady hadn't heard of any of these things but let it pass. He asked, 'Why?'

'Because it held the power of nostalgia, and it held the power of the Trads in its wonders. This could tempt people to go back to the old ways. Only the roads of the Vatican City remain. Everything else is gone. The same can be said of the Pyramids, the ancient buildings of Greece…I do remember there was a discussion about whether the Great Wall of China was infrastructure or nostalgia, but at the end, that went as well.'

Raelynn may have just been thinking over how to help Tyrone because she chose this moment to intervene. 'Brady. You know when you said you couldn't remember anything from last night because of your dab blackout?'

Brady looked at her. She was smiling softly, 'Yes.'

'Do you remember seeing me when you were in Libby's room?'

'No. What was I doing in there?'

'You were with Glenarvon Cole. You kept going on about how beautiful this movie poster was.' She added, 'You and Glen were having your big male bonding moment.' She paused and gazed into his face, 'You really don't remember, do you?'

Brady searched for something to remind him. He had a split-second flashback of Glen putting his arms around him and consoling him. 'Was I being soppy?' He changed his wording, 'I mean, being stupid stoned?'

'I thought it was nice. Anyway, you both left when you saw me. You went off giggling together.' She added, 'What was it about that poster, that you wanted to show it off to Glenarvon Cole? I wouldn't have thought it was his thing.'

It was the most beautiful item I have ever seen, and I've stolen some fantastic jewellery in my time. She was my real Moms, and she never even knew I existed. She was Glenarvon Cole's Moms. How would our lives had turned out if she had known the truth?

Brady felt a surge of strong emotions. He didn't speak for a moment out of fear that his voice would crack. He looked out of the window and spotted the remains of Phoenix coming into view. He nodded in the general direction of Phoenix, hoping Tyrone would pick up the reins of the appointed Tour Guide.

Tyrone looked ahead and understood, 'Raelynn, look, that's Phoenix, Arizona.'

They looked out at the vast gridlines which marked out the blocks. There were dozens of FusionCars™ on the virtually deserted roads. They looked like cream-coloured ceramic boxes using the road network to head out of the city, as there were no buildings left to visit. To Brady, it looked like an old arcade game from up here. While Tyrone and Raelynn held hands and watched Phoenix drift slowly by, beneath them. Brady took a deep swig of water and brought his emotions back under control.

Once they were clear of Phoenix, the autopilot headed north to the Grand Canyon. The conversation returned to the small talk between tourists and fellow travellers. Brady struggled to assimilate the events of last night with the troubling theories of Tyrone. The one thing that gave him comfort was the genuine affection that Tyrone demonstrated towards him - he had always been a friend to Brady Mahone. He thought, *if I was that bad, surely the Beardons would have avoided me like the plague.*

The sense of awe as they flew over the Grand Canyon restored Brady's spirits. He felt like they had entered a neutral zone. The Grand Canyon was just as magnificent now as it was in the time of the Trads. The Greens couldn't take the credit for this. Brady took the FusionPlane™ out of autopilot and swooped and explored the area from as many viewpoints as he could. He had never seen Raelynn look so happy as she raced through every superlative in her vocabulary. Tyrone being right next to her, completed her perfect day. Brady resolved not to spoil this with his heavy talk.

Once he had had his fun manually flying the FusionPlane™, he set it back to autopilot but on a course to circle the Grand Canyon while they all indulged in their picnic in the sky.

9: HOME FROM HOME

Brady needed company. He had thought about heading off to Boulder Creek after the Distor™ Distribution Ceremony had been completed, as he wanted to collect his latest instalments of Green Credits from the proceeds of his business, but even though his math work was limited, he concluded that he had already been paid. He had changed his mind, not only after his confrontational interview with Hunter but also because he was embarrassed by his stoned behaviour in the evening. He believed they would look down on him, and he couldn't face Glenarvon Cole in case he started to get over-friendly.

He decided that if Boulder Creek was temporarily off-limits, then maybe the Bear would let him stay awhile in San Martin. He knew the Bear would forgive him his transgressions, and he always felt at home in the Beardon homestead. It was the kind of family feeling he could never recreate in his own Malibu home - he thought of Malibu as being more of a party palace than a home, not just because Debrock and his friends had taken up semi-permanent residence there, but Amie and Helgarth seemed to be on a never-ending mid-life crisis since Lucy-Ian and Raelynn were born. He saw Raelynn in a whole new light since she had found Tyrone, and he felt that the Beardon influence might be good for her.

The Bear greeted them all with his customary warmth when he landed his FusionPlane™ and the Beardon home, and he had no objections at all in putting up his old friend. He surprised Brady with his relaxed attitude when Tyrone insisted that Raelynn should share his room. Samuel Beardon the Third seemed as delighted as everybody else in seeing the joy these two had found in each other.

Brady handed over the remains of the picnic hamper, as it had been supplied with enough food for ten instead of the intended three. The gift was received graciously and in the spirit of recycling and reducing food waste.

Once everybody had settled in, Brady and the Bear took a stroll together into the centre of San Martin. Brady soon understood the warmth of the welcome the Bear had offered to Raelynn. He said, 'She is a Godsend. Tyrone only had eyes for enrolling as a volunteer to colonise Mars. I had to pull in a favour from Sissy to stop his application, but now Raelynn has come onto the scene. I believe he will finally put all that nonsense behind him. What do you think?'

'They've definitely fallen for each other. I wouldn't be surprised if they want to enter one of those arrangements you have. How would you feel about that?'

They strolled past the park where a bandstand was being decked out for the Centenary Celebrations - even though these were still a few months away. The Bear said, 'I would be happy for them.'

Brady smiled, 'Raelynn is not technically my family, but she has Green Credits of her own now. She has her independence - she can come and go as she pleases.'

'You are correct, my friend. Raelynn is Pure Green, and if she gives freely, it will be accepted in that spirit.'

People came over to the Bear to offer their congratulations, 'You must be so proud…you'll have to tell us what it's like…you've earned the right…I'm so happy for you…pass on my congratulations to Alicia…'

Brady said, 'What's that all about?'

'I have been chosen as one of the Devout and the Disciples to receive the UltraViolet™ in June, on the Centenary of the Green Revolution - so has Alicia...'

Brady said, 'But not Tyrone?'

'No, Not yet. I think his application to the Mars project has confused things.'

'Why is that?'

'If he were accepted into that, then he would get the UltraViolet™ first. I think he's been missed off the Devout List because he was on the astronaut's list. I'm sure Sissy will sort it out.'

Still, more of the townsfolk of San Martin came up to congratulate their preacher, Samuel Beardon the Third, 'Well done...What is the UltraViolet™, I'm dying to know...Will you let us into the secret?'

The Bear responded to them with a mixture of thanks, accompanied by warm smiles, 'You know it's forbidden to share with you, if I was of that mindset, I wouldn't be one of the Devout, now, would I?' He laughed loudly.

Brady said, 'I've been doing a lot of thinking lately.'

'That will be because of all the chatter about the Centenary celebrations, my friend. It has a different resonance for you, as you are considering a lost way of life, whereas we are honouring all we have achieved.' He put his arm on Brady's shoulder. 'Naturally, it should cause you to reflect, and with your Last Will and Testament, you have started the difficult process of considering your mortality. You are thinking about a time beyond your death.'

Brady sighed, 'Yeah, you're right. Lately, I've been considering all the people I have known who have died, and what they left behind. I don't want to be all self-important like, but many of these people only live on in my memories. I feel that when I die I'm kinda killing them all over again, as if I'm taking their spirits with me.' Brady laughed, trying to disguise his fear, 'Trouble is, I don't think they are going to like the place where Brady Mahone is going.' He pointed at the ground, and the Bear understood that this was a gesture that he wasn't going to be moving heavenwards. Brady said, 'Can I ask you a personal question, and I don't want it to sound offensive...'

'Ask away, my friend.'

'Underneath that Suit™ of yours, are you whole? Are you a young shell over an ancient body?' He was thinking about Rhea, but he didn't want to discuss her. It wasn't that he didn't want to appear stalker-ish. He sensed that he might put her under a threat he couldn't perceive. He had a similar instinct about Fleet Captain Marjorie Hampton. He knew their clandestine operations were to protect him, he assumed, but also, he sensed that the Bear and the rest of the Boulder Creek crew hadn't authorised their operation.

'I am older than I appear, but with each new Suit™, I am repaired and renewed. Without these, I would have died many years earlier.'

'And if you know you are dying between Suits™, then there's nothing you can do about it?'

'The Orange™ informs you of precisely how long you have left so that you can make your arrangements to die.' He added, 'I don't wish to be controversial, brother, but the Trads couldn't have risked that. An old Trad knowing he had only a couple of weeks left to live, might have harmed others - to settle old scores. We have the

Security Protocols™ and the RedSuits™, one Green cannot harm another, even if they wanted to.'

As much as he loved the Bear, he had the paranoia of a criminal to hold back this information. He chose a different person to explore his theory. 'Bodhi's Mother, Libby Skye, died at one-hundred and fourteen years old. At the time, I thought that was ancient, but now, that was young for a Green - wouldn't you agree?'

The Bear was puzzled. He hadn't expected Brady to discuss Bodhi Sattva's Mother. 'I believe the promise was that we would all live, in good health, until a minimum age of one-hundred.'

'Whatever - but Bodhi had cheated these rules with Libby because she was his Mother. I know Cain would have told you this at the time.'

'Yes. I remember. You are skilled in the art of spreading doubt. Where are you going with this?' He looked troubled. He barely acknowledged another batch of congratulatory comments and pats on the back from his well-wishers.

'I think Bodhi let her die instead of helping her to live. He has form. You could say he has a history of neglect. It was well within Bodhi's power to save his own Mother, but he chose to let her die.' *She was my Mother*. 'What kind of a man could do that? I know I couldn't have done that to my Foster Moms, never mind my real Moms. And yet here he is, the great Bodhi Sattva, putting himself out there like some kinda Second Coming of Christ while he makes me out to be the other guy. I don't get it, and I certainly ain't loving it.'

The Bear hustled Brady into a side street. 'You can't go around suggesting things like that. You aren't looking at the bigger picture.'

'Sounds like the sort of thing that Bodhi would say.'

'We all have choices. Libby Skye self-selected...' The Bear looked fearful. He looked down as if he half-expected the ground to open up beneath him.

'Are you saying she chose to die? She looked full of life and had every intention of living life to the full the last time I saw her. I'm just saying, man - I knows what I sees.'

'We are creating heaven on Earth...'

Brady barked, 'You're changing the subject. Bodhi withdrew his support; he killed his own Mother for your bigger picture. You even suspect that he had your own Father killed, the great Samuel Beardon the Second...'

'Please, don't mock my Father.'

'But you do suspect...'

The Bear broke down and fell to his knees, 'Yes. Yes, I fear that he ordered my Father's death to keep the Green Deal alive. I admit it.'

'So, why am I the bad guy in all this? As far as I can tell, I've been good to you. I helped you uncover the truth about your family. You do remember how much that used to eat you up. It troubled you bad enough for you to befriend me, who you considered to be some kinda Trad demon - or worse.'

'Because it was ordained. It was prophesied. You are the beast of burden.'

'Prophesised by Bodhi - that's what you're saying. He killed your Father, his own Mother and yet you let him because you think he's a God.'

'A Son of God.'

'Well, I ain't as well versed in the Bible as you are, and I can't tell you none of your fancy stories, but I know enough to know that Jesus didn't kill Mary…' He added, 'He's just a man, more like a Godfather, who will stop at nothing to get what he wants. Just because you agree with his desires doesn't change a thing in my book.'

The Bear pleaded, 'Stop it…stop it, please. What do you want from me?'

Brady smiled and lifted the Bear up. Samuel Beardon the Third was the same height and build as Brady, but he seemed somehow diminished. Brady said, 'It would be kinda nice for you to stop treating me as the enemy. I don't think I've done anything to deserve this disrespect from you. Am I really that bad?'

The Bear searched Brady's face for signs of who he really was. He couldn't discover anything which dispelled the thought that Brady was a friend. 'No, not wholly.'

Brady laughed, 'A ringing endorsement. I suppose beggars can't be choosers. Let me ask another - is Bodhi really that good?'

The Bear smiled thinly, 'No. Not wholly.'

'There you go. That wasn't so difficult, was it?' Brady added, 'Let me reiterate, y'know, get my facts straight. I know you like your truth, well, so do I - it can be a powerful thing to have on your side, wouldn't you agree?'

'Yes. Always.'

'So, I have your agreement in my assessment of the facts. Hey, that sounds like something Judge Jefferson would say…' Brady laughed, '…That Bodhi Sattva killed Libby Skye and Samuel Beardon the Second…I'm being kind here by not mentioning the billions of Trads because they don't count to you…and Samuel Beardon the Third swears to Almighty God that this is the truth - the whole truth…'

'Yes, Brady. So, help me, God.'

10: LAST CALLS

Fleet Captain Marjorie Hampton was surrounded by HeavyLoaders™, and the multiple sub-sonic booms merged into a permanent loud hum. Rhea Laidlaw parked her FusionCar™ and walked over to meet her. She said, 'You needed to see me? It sounded urgent.'

'I'm off the Devout list. What about you?'

Rhea was puzzled, 'I'm still on it - the Disciple list - but I don't know what they're planning. Do you?'

'No. I think they know about me. I've made a decision.'

'What are you going to do?'

'I've applied for the Mars mission. I'm going to see Bodhi, but I wanted you to know.'

Rhea checked to see if anybody was watching before hugging Marjorie. A Heavy-Loader™ from across the vast parking lot ascended vertically into the sky. They waited for it to speed away and scanned the parking lot for prying eyes. Rhea said, 'What's your reasoning?'

'It's a sense. I always worry when companies secretly compile lists. If anybody asks, they always offer reassurances and tell you how valuable you are to the organisation, but deep down, you know that if you are not on the right list, then your time is up.' A technician in cream-coloured Sattva Systems™ overalls came over to Marjorie with documentation. She signed it and thanked him. She was careful to make sure he was out of earshot before continuing. 'My best workers are receiving the UltraViolet™ in the June celebrations. I've made discreet checks - they all believe I'm on it, I've said nothing to change this assumption.'

'What's your plan?'

'There are three missions to Mars left before the operation ceases. I plan to be on the next one. I'm hoping Bodhi allows me to leave because of all the work I've done for the Greens over the years.' She added, 'It will be instructive to see how he handles my request.'

Rhea said, 'I'm going to miss you, but you know I have to stay...'

'Of course, you do, especially after all this time...'

'How are you going to cope - up there?' She pointed at the sky. Marjorie stood almost to attention, 'The UltraViolet™ is a fantastic addition to an astronaut's armoury, as the final upgrade will prevent degradation - and my engineering and flight knowledge is desperately needed, especially as we will be in a low-gravity environment.'

Rhea looked into the brown eyes of her old friend, 'But there's not much up there, and it's beyond freezing cold...'

'My husband died in a desert in Iraq courtesy of the Green Revolution, he had uncovered significant intel as part of his mission for the CIA, but it was too late. I will go to a desert of my own - just the temperature will be different, and I will build a new world, seeing as I failed to protect the Traditional Cultures in this one.' She looked away briefly.

Rhea said, 'They had a clandestine department based within the Los Banos Police Department Headquarters. I know it reached there, but like you say, it was too late. I searched the place, but the Greens had taken everything. We can't do anything about it now. Ever since I've wondered if they knew we were part of the investigation into Sattva Systems™ - if they did, then we must be the enemies you keep closer.'

'I didn't think they did know until recently,' Marjorie said. 'They are onto me, which is why I'm out of here. I can almost hear the cutting of ties everywhere. They are planning something huge for the end of the hundred-year plan. I know it.'

Rhea shrugged, 'We can't arrest or prosecute. All we can do is keep the flame of truth, freedom and liberty alive - no matter what it takes.'

Marjorie said, 'I'm smuggling communications devices onboard.'

'There are plenty of devices already on Mars - aren't there?'

Marjorie looked all around her again, 'When I was in Glenarvon's inner sanctum, I was privy to his plans. The communication systems between the Mars Colony and us are set to degrade on January 2, 2185. He wants them to be cut adrift and forgotten about - forever. I might be able to squeeze another few days of comms out of them until they track these down.' She passed over a SpaceSatt™ to Rhea. 'Keep it safe. Don't let anyone know you've got it.'

Rhea pocketed it away expertly.

Marjorie said, 'What are you planning to do next?'

'What I always do, double deal and be everybody's go-to girl for discreet information.'

Marjorie laughed, 'Who'd have thought that a child TV star would end up being a spy.'

'Daddy was in Homeland Security. Most of his people were watching the extreme right, but then the CIA informed him of a radical left plot. It seemed crazy, but Daddy took it seriously enough to recruit me into the FBI - the days of pure nepotism - I know.'

'But they would have known who you were. You were all over social media.'

'That's why it worked. I put out lots of posts on environmental issues, and then I applied for a job on their news channel. It was a disastrous career move in media, but I loved being a special agent. My brief was to gather information and if I could identify the leadership. Fuck me if I didn't do exactly that, except it was on the day of their victory speech, which as we know was too late.'

Marjorie said, 'Must be the knowledge that I'm planning to leave which is making me all nostalgic for the old days. I'll never forget your final TV appearance - you got Glenarvon Cole to show himself for the first and last time...'

'Don't forget the guy who shouted, "We did it, Bodhi." I hope my Daddy got to see that.'

Marjorie hugged her and then stepped back. They were friends, but she didn't want her body language to give them away. Rhea said, 'So, here's my next moves. I need to flush out whether they know about me. You're right. I think your cover has been busted. I'm going to confirm that you can't be trusted, and my recommendation is to let you go to Mars.'

'Ok. That should build trust.'

'Bodhi has me spying on Tia Cassandra, but you know I'm doing the same for her. I will ask her to accept your application - you will be a fabulous addition. I will also inform her that you are a part of my team. She trusts me as she helped me find out about the inner workings of Sattva Systems™ back in the day. I shared what I found so that she could have an advantage over her rival - but that didn't pan out. We totally under-estimated Bodhi Sattva and Glenarvon Cole.'

Marjorie said, 'They had Genesis Garcia covering their backs. It's handy when you've got the Governor of California and, by default Silicon Valley in your back pocket. Oh, and we mustn't forget Cain, the Head of Deep Mind and Siddha at the Treasury…'

'…And other well-placed Greens across the world. I'm sure Tia will want to know everything. She will love having you working alongside her. You'll get along with Dagny - she's an engineering and logistical genius if she ever gets from out of the shadow of her legendary Mother.' Rhea added, 'It would help me if you are challenged by any of those people, that you feel betrayed by me. It will reinforce my cover.' She saw a couple of technicians approaching. 'Gotta go. You be safe up there. I'll always be thinking of you.'Rhea looked behind her at Fleet Captain Marjorie Hampton and then strode on to the Main Entrance of Sattva Systems™ HQ to find Bodhi. In the cafeteria at his reserved table - one of the few trappings of success he allowed himself - she found him.

Bodhi said, 'Hello, Rhea. Would you care to join me for dinner?'

Rhea put on a winning smile, 'I'd love to.' A staffer came over in a cream-coloured Sattva Systems™ overall. Rhea said, 'I'll have the same as Bodhi.' She looked at his meal. He was eating the same evening meal as he always did. It stopped him from wasting mental energy, and a surfeit of choices was an irritating trait of the capitalists. The same reasoning was why he had a table reserved in the same spot in the Sattva Systems™ Cafeteria. He had tempeh bacon with sauteed mushrooms, avocado and wilted arugula for breakfast. At lunch, he ate whole-grain pasta with lentil meatballs and a side salad. And the meal he had this evening with Rhea consisted of cauliflower and chickpea tacos with guacamole and pico de gallo. She said, 'Have you ever been tempted to have a place of your own?'

He smiled as their food was delivered and thanked the member of staff. 'Not at all. This is my home, and all of my family are here.' Rhea knew that what he meant was not family but colleagues. She also knew that he slept in a basic sleeping pod, and he washed in the communal showers. He looked up from his meal, 'The naughtiest things I do are my little conversations with you. What news is there from the outside world?'

'Fleet Captain Marjorie Hampton has applied for the Mars Mission, as have thirty-seven of your employees.' She handed him over the list she had written. He perused it between mouthfuls of food - he might have the same meals, but he still appeared to enjoy them.

He smiled, and his eyes widened occasionally. 'There are many that I might have suspected, but there are one or two which have surprised me. Thank you, this is excellent work.'

'Does Marjorie shock you?'

'No. She visited Brady Mahone's private residence without our knowledge or permission. She is protecting him in some way, or maybe passing on information.'

Rhea laughed, 'I think it's the former. Brady wouldn't know what to do with the kind of technical information which Marjorie deals with.'

'When did she switch allegiances - in your opinion?'

Rhea pretended to think about it, 'I think it was the Colony rescue mission and the destruction of Cima back in '42. Many Greens lost their faith when they discovered that their loved ones were killed.' She added more positively, 'Also, it's the pull of the new. Your project is coming to its conclusion, but Mars is a whole new beginning for mankind.'

Bodhi took a swig from his black vegan coffee. 'Were you tempted to join them?'

'No. I'm a home bird, a proper little bird of paradise.'

Bodhi laughed at the paradise reference. 'Do you think I should let them go?'

Rhea took back the list and re-examined it, 'There is a helluva lot of experience and expertise here. I can see how these people could be invaluable to Tia. However, they've done their bit for you, and you'll never see them again...' This was her test to see if Bodhi would confirm or deny Glenarvon's plan to cut off their comms.

'Yes. The easiest way for me to think about the future is not to have to consider the past. I will never see them again because this will enable me to not have to think about them again.'

Rhea considered the flaw in this logic - she would never see her Daddy again, but she would never forget him. 'I think you should let them leave because they have self-selected to do so.'

'You are right.' He smiled. 'Tia Cassandra has returned for her UltraViolet™ ceremony. Are you going to visit her?'

'Yes. I'm heading to Florida in the morning.'

'I want to know about any contingency plans she has if it all goes horribly wrong up there. I don't want any surprise visitors in the future. I've got the next thousand-year plan to consider.'

Rhea drained her black coffee. 'Don't worry. She trusts me, and she loves bragging about all her achievements.' She stood up and left. She walked past the thirteen-point pledge in the Main Hall and studied every point on it. *It's funny how something that big just gets ignored. It's true - familiarity does breed contempt.* Glenarvon Cole had written it. Bodhi Sattva had endorsed it, and Genesis Garcia had marketed it for Green public consumption.

The end to capitalism. End materialism. The most destructive ideology against nature.

Equal rights and opportunity for all citizens.

An end to all weaponry so that our people can live in harmony with nature without being threatened.

To protect all Green spaces across the globe and bring an end to the exploitation of the land.

The Green Deal Quartet

To protect all living creatures. Stop the killing.

End intensive farming.

Reduce the population of the planet by peaceful means and self-selection.

Improve education, with a more prominent focus on ecology, environmental sciences, and ethics.

To repair the damage brought on by the Industrial and Technological Revolutions.

To bring an era of peace, harmony, and tranquillity to those that help to save the planet.

And finally, to the three requests outside of the top ten primary goals. The goals of the GreenRevs, the army that changed the world:

End hate thoughts and crimes, including gender identity and discrimination.

Remove all traces of Imperialism and Colonialism.

Improve mental health by establishing kinder societies.

Rhea uttered, 'It doesn't say by how many.'

11: CAPE CASSANDRA

Rhea picked up her Rental FusionPlane™ - as a Disciple, she could have had one of her own, but she knew Bodhi would appreciate her refusal of ownership. She stopped off at San Martin to complete her Disciple administrative duties. As she flew over the Beardon house, she slowed down. She noticed Brady Mahone's Fusion-Plane™ parked up nearby. *I will have to be careful not to bump into him - far too risky.* She noted that Tyrone was passionately kissing a girl. She circled and watched as he pulled away from her embrace and headed off to work. She recognised Raelynn.

She set the FusionPlane™ next to her Disciple's office, and she soon was quickly surrounded by well-wishers on her being approved of being an early adopter of the UltraVioletSuits™. The people were hungry for news and gossip, and it made her feel like an old-fashioned politician when she didn't give them an ounce of new infor-mation. She maintained a cheery persona before heading for the relative calm of her office.

These people are so needy.

Once at her desk, she went through her notices. There were the usual vacation applications and arrangement proposals. But because she hadn't been around for a while, there were many of them. She read them through, plotted them on her charts, entered them into diaries and authorised them with her Green Stamper.

Rhea then opened the old recycled safe - it was the original safe - but anything which continued to be of use in the post-Trad environment was re-assigned as re-cycled. She took out the San Martin Devout Approvals. All the usual suspects were there, including Samuel Beardon the Third and his daughter Alicia, but where was Tyrone? She picked up the applications for the Cassandra Mission. She knew Tyrone was a likely candidate. She went through the few names - it wasn't a popular choice as to why a Green would forego Heaven on Earth and trade it for hell on another planet? She thought sadly of Marjorie - who sensed that she might not be left with a choice by the end of the year.

She found Tyrone's name, and it had been marked - *rejected*. His was the only refusal, and in the comments column, it had the initials SB. She guessed that Sam-uel Beardon had pulled some strings. She didn't understand the strong influence he had with Bodhi. She had uncovered information on Samuel Beardon the First and Second, but he seemed to be a humble labourer in the Green scheme of things. She then looked at the long list of the rest of the population of San Martin, which ran into several thousand. She found Tyrone on this list. She didn't understand the potential consequences of this, but deep within her gut, she felt that this was bad news. She sensed they were up to something. She didn't like the secrecy of the chosen, and one or two of the inner sanctums around Bodhi seemed delighted with Brady's sons spreading the word that the UltraViolet™ was nothing special. They were excited by the prospect of the UltraViolet™, which was at odds with the Mahone Boys' theories. She pondered on this dichotomy.

Rhea looked at her watch and decided that she would think about this while she travelled to Florida.

She waited her turn to leave the Sattva Systems™ FusionPassengerJet™ on arrival at Cape Cassandra. The plane was full of Green tourists, as today was the largest payload ever transported into space. Many of these Green tourists were Sonic Boom Surfers here for the most giant wave in history. Tia Cassandra had been allowed to take whatever she could to Mars - as long as she had completed this before the end of the year. Therefore, she was going to exploit this to its limits.

It was a way of working which suited Bodhi. He wasn't interested in possessions or even the intellectual talent. He was only concerned with keeping to his own one-hundred-year plan - everything else was an interruption or a distraction. He had used this tactic in the significant dealings leading up to the Revolution - his rivals couldn't believe the generosity of this gentle man. He also used this in lesser events, as in the Christmas offerings to Brady Mahone by his Mother, Libby Skye - except that she had tried to cheat Brady. It was the ultimate sin in Bodhi's eyes - she behaved like a Trad would when given the same instructions.

Tia didn't greet many people in person, she usually far too busy, but she made an exception for Rhea. 'Welcome, Special Agent Rhea Laidlaw. What news do you have from the other side of the tracks?' Tia said this as in the phrase as if she had precisely chosen it. Rhea always liked the precision of this giant of old tech.

Rhea hugged her and smiled, 'Who'd have thought it would have come to this when we thought we had Sattva Systems™ on the ropes almost a hundred years ago.'

Tia said, 'At least we are still alive and still have skin in the game. He is my rival - not my enemy. I don't mind being beaten by the better opponent. I'll just have to do better in the next game.' She paused, 'What's he planning?'

'He's going to cut you all adrift. There will certainly be no comms, and I suspect the infrastructure of your space missions will be dismantled. He wants you to be gone - and stay gone.'

'I'm not surprised. I was the last person he wanted to see again from the old days. If it wasn't for the fact his self-replicating nanobots and enzymes were threatening the whole planet by attacking my space materials, he would have left us there in the desert. I understand his rationale.' She looked at Rhea and smiled, 'What's his end date?'

'No later than the New Year, maybe even before the Centenary celebrations on 25 June. - sorry.'

'Walk with me. I want you to see this.'

Rhea had seen rockets before, but none the size of this. 'Are you sure it can even get off the ground?'

Tia said, 'I have to say I admire his technology. If we had joined forces, there's no telling what we could have achieved in the old world. The NanoSuits™ have transformed our astronaut's experience on the planet - all we need to do is provide oxygen - and even that in far smaller quantities than we could ever have envisaged. It's a shame he doesn't want to stay in touch because we have already developed their FusionPowered™ SpaceSatts™ with our Super-Fast-Data Laser delivery system. The time-lapse in comms has been reduced from minutes to seconds.'

'I'm planning to keep in touch - until they discover the comms link.' She paused before asking, 'I want you to do me a favour.'

'Go on.'

'I want you to take Fleet Captain Marjorie Hampton with you. She will be useful to your project, and she was my Military Intelligence source from the old days.'

'Agreed. I never turn my back on talent.'

'And I want to have a couple of reserve slots for last-minute applications. There will be little time for you to vet them. I need you to trust me. If you see my personal authorisation...'

'I can do that.'

Rhea always liked the decisiveness of Tia - time was a resource too precious to waste - a feature she had in common with Bodhi. 'I have some better news.'

Tia laughed, 'I'm always in the market for good news from our celebrity reporter. What is it?'

'Take whatever you can. When he said there was nothing off the table, he meant it. I've known him long enough to know that his word is of utmost importance to him and his followers. He will not trick you. If anybody tries to cheat you - they will be punished - not you.'

Tia laughed, 'It's gone to his head - I've seen it before with some of the old tech moguls - he's got himself a fluffy little God complex.'

Rhea thought that maybe Tia could be accused at the time, especially as she was designing a whole planet in her own image. She looked at the enormous FusionSpaceShuttle™, which was about six times larger than any flown before. Even though this was technically Tia's mission, the livery was still in the Sattva Systems™ cream with a giant Sattva S in moss green. It seemed that even if Bodhi Sattva had no interest in Mars, he was still going to leave his brand on the planet. Rhea knew the NanoRepair™ coatings wouldn't allow it to be redesigned at a later date. The Ceramic outer shell of the vehicle glistened dully against the storm clouds in the Florida sky. She said, 'What have you got in there?'

Tia laughed, 'I thought you'd never ask. I have a complete FusionTrain™ engine. I'm pushing the FusionRockets™ to the limits.' She explained, 'In the lower atmosphere and rocky terrain, a railroad network will be immensely useful. What's more, there are no inhabitants on Mars, which means no planning permission, neighbourhood protests and no need to bribe corrupt politicians. The only limits will be our imagination.'

'Aren't you concerned that the rocket launch might fail - y'know, explode under the strain.'

'Of course. It will be a massive setback. However, I believe in my heroes. If anybody can make it work, then Commander Rocky Fitzpatrick can do it.' She stood with her arms folded proudly. She had the demeanour of a woman who assumed success until failure made her reassess. 'I know we are probably too close. What do you think?'

Rhea sensed her consternation and remembered that Tia had little experience of NanoSuits™. She said, 'Imagine your feet reach hundreds of feet into the ground. This will give you the stability of rock. Don't be alarmed if you see some of the tourists literally flying past you - they will rest on the surface until the shockwave blasts them away - the Green tourists call it Sonic Boom Surfing.' She watched Tia concentrate as the countdown began. 'Are you ready?'

'Yes. I'm ready.' She smiled at Rhea and then turned her head to take in her view of the launch. The first small shock waves of the primer sub-sonic booms pulsed past them. The Green tourists wobbled and cheered. Tia looked down at the ground and looked impressed. Then a massive boom rumbled and whooshed, and crowds of whooping and hollering Green tourists were flung far and wide. Tia watched them land heavily and even crashed onto jagged rocks, but not one was in the slightest bit injured. She assessed this usefulness on the Martian surface.

The giant rocket seemed to barely leave the ground. For a moment, it seemed as likely that it would fall as rise. Another massive sub-sonic blast ripped across the land, and the Green tourists had quickly got to their feet again in time to ride the next wave. Rhea laughed at the antics of the tourists, but Tia's attention had turned to the fate of the lift-off. The rocket rose glacially, but it was now heading in the right direction, and then the final sub-sonic surge, the loudest there had ever been or would ever be heard on Earth. The rocket surged upwards at breakneck speed. She knew the NanoStructure™ would survive the outward trajectory through the Earth's atmosphere and beyond into space. Tia cheered and shouted, 'Dagny, we did it.'

Tia said, 'I can't wait to turbo-charge the Martian Project. We are the new pioneers.'

'I imagine there are going to be huge challenges...'

'I know. It's going to be marvellous - we are going to be pushed to the limits of human endurance, but also, we will continuously learn and achieve. What are these Greens going to do with their Heaven on Earth?'

Rhea laughed, 'Enjoy it. I think that's it.'

Tia said, 'I would have little use for these Green drones with their low-level labour and idle dreams. Give me the strivers and the heroes - they are welcome to the leftovers.' She looked at Rhea, 'I know you have much to do down here, but there is a place for you if you want to join us.'

Rhea stroked her chin and gave the offer serious thought. 'We need to keep our spirit flickering on Earth. We don't deserve to be forgotten - I won't let it happen.'

Tia clasped Rhea's shoulders and said, 'Good for you.'

12: THE WINNER IS.

Brady's sons had returned from far and wide to hear the results of the competition. As they landed at their Malibu home, they couldn't have failed to see the gleaming PassengerFusionJet™ in pride of place in the Mahone Vehicle Parking Lot. Soon, one of his sons would take ownership of it.

Amie had received the sales figures from Hunter, who no longer felt the need to hide his close association with Bodhi. In the start-up years of his business, sales figures were as simple as how many Files had Brady sold, but handing over the reins to the accountants at Sattva Systems™ meant there were spreadsheets and weighting allowances on many different types of sales - from freebies to pre-orders and series commitments. If he let Amie do the analysis, she could at least deal with the queries if one of his boys decided to challenge his decision. Brady thought of Mary-Lou and her cataloguing ideas at the beginning of his business journey and how Amie must have inherited her analytical mind.

Soon the Malibu home was full of noise and laughter as the back-slapping sons greeted each other and tried to suss out who was the most likely winner. They were welcomed lovingly by their Maddies Amie and Helgarth, and Brady's staffers dealt efficiently with their whims. They had guessed that the competition announcement would take place in the evening, but Brady always kept his boys on their toes, and the winner would be announced at the buffet. He wanted this to be an informal and fun affair and not sitting around a table as a bunch of businessmen at a meeting.

He called his boys together, along with Amie, Helgarth and Lucy-Ian. He felt the loss of Raelynn not being here - she had become a favourite to him in recent times, but she was happily ensconced in San Martin with Tyrone, and the thought of the two lovebirds added to his sense of joy of today. He had taken the precaution of taking Bill to one side - as he was the eldest - and asked him to ensure that the result was final and that when it was announced, he wanted the others to accept this graciously and cheer the winner whole-heartedly. He confirmed that he didn't know who'd won, and as a carrot, he put out the prospect of new competitions if this one was a success. Bill understood, and Brady watched him work the room.

Amie tapped a cut-crystal glass repeatedly with a silver spoon to bring the room to order. She handed Brady an envelope like an old-fashioned award ceremony. Brady thought that Libby Skye, his Mother, and the previous owner of this home, would have approved. He strode to the head of the gathering and said, 'You've all done remarkably well - many of you smashed your targets. You rock, boys.' They cheered Brady and each other. 'The reason we are doing this early, today, is because the winner is going to fly us to a place in their territory. I have five of my favourite Reps on standby to greet us, and when I have announced the winner, I will Satt™ them, and we'll head straight over.' Brady deliberately took his time and built up the tension like a game show host from the old days. 'When we get there, I will do a meet and greet and hand out a few free samples while you enjoy yourselves. You've earned a break.' He looked around his hushed audience. Amie looked out of the window as she had noticed each of Brady's sons had searched her facial expressions for clues. Lucy-Ian and Helgarth joined her, and each held her hand. Brady announced loudly, 'And the winner is…Troy with 4.3 million accredited sales.'

The boys cheered. If they had reservations, then they didn't show it, as they knew they had the chance of winning many other competitions to come. Troy walked up to Brady and received his congratulatory hug from his Pops. Brady shouted, 'Get your bags packed, we are going to the Green Quartiere Aurelio in Rome, Italy. My old friend Marco will ensure we are well looked after. Now let's put Troy's new Fusion-PassengerJet™ through its paces. I'll have the staff bring your things.'

As Troy wandered back to his brothers - clutching his envelope - Bill had planned a surprise from the others. The four boys rushed Troy and lifted him high in the air and carried him like pallbearers all the way through the grounds of their Malibu home and all the way to the steps leading up to his private jet. Troy welcomed everyone on board and thanked his Pops again as he was the last one passenger. To Brady, this recalled some of the old stag parties he used to go to when one of his criminal buddies used to fall for the idea of going straight and settling down - it never used to last long, but the stag parties were fun. None of the girls was accompanying them to Rome.

Brady sat at the rear of the FusionPassengerJet™ and took a back seat in the raucous conversations the boys were having. He didn't know why he felt disappointed in their sales tactics. Brady had always given free samples to the children to win over hearts and minds and then homed in on one woman to sleep with later in the day - it felt like a reward for his good works. *I'm not going to do this tomorrow. I need to set the boys a good example.* His sons were telling ever more grotesque stories about orgies, but even more concerning to Brady was the crossing over the gender lines to greedily exploit every pleasure conceivable from these days and nights of debauchery. They shamelessly told of only targeting the attractive Greens for free samples, and that giving out free samples to the elderly or the young, was just a complete waste of product. He noticed that Troy didn't pilot the vehicle long as these conversations enamoured him more than his new toy.

The boys were still in high spirits by the time they landed at Green Quartiere Aurelio. Brady told them to go and settle in while he dealt with Marco. He knew they were already planning to re-enact the roles of the ancient Roman Emperors. He thought uncomfortably of John Kane playing Emperor Tiberius in his sickening movie production. He also thought of Archie, his Foster Pops, and this both sickened and saddened him. He shook himself out of his reverie. *There's no point in doing all this for my boys just to end up being the party-pooper. I just gotta let them have their fun.*

Marco greeted him. 'Hello, my old friend, Brady. It's been many years - much too long.'

'Hi, Marco. How's it hanging?'

'It's good. Very good. Your boy Troy - he works very hard to win. I like him.'

Brady said, 'I'm pleased to hear that.'

Marco ushered Brady to his FusionCar™, 'Come, come. We have a lot planned for tomorrow. You honour us with bringing all of your sons, but you reward us mostly with your own visitation.'

Brady said, 'I want to choose a place to give away lots of free samples, but I don't want to cause any bad feelings.'

'You can trust me. What is it you request?'

'There's a funny named place, or rather there used to be - it's called St Peter's Basil…'

'St Peter's Basilica, yes, yes…why?'

'I'm still a Trad, and someone told me a story once, about that was where some of

520

the fiercest battles against the Greens took place - you don't have to tell anybody why I chose it…'

Marco looked at him from his position as the driver before returning his eyes to the road. 'It's only been a hundred years, friend, they will know - but don't you concern yourself, I will arrange it for you. Is there anything else I can do for you?'

'Yes. I want lots of children to be present. Let it be known that I am only giving away kids' samples tomorrow.'

Marco looked troubled but didn't say anything further on the subject of children. Instead, he asked, 'Do you need a companion for this evening?'

Brady smiled, 'Normally, that would be a given, but tonight I want to set a good example for my boys.'

'Good for you. I'd better not let you know what Troy has planned for his brothers then - it might make your hair go curly.' Marco laughed. 'What are you going to do instead?'

'I'm going to walk the area and get a feel for the place.'

'There's not a lot to see that you couldn't see everywhere else in Italy. It is but meadow and vineyard. There are no traces of trad existence any longer - sorry, my friend.'

Brady nodded, but he wasn't going to amend his plans. 'If you could drive me there and maybe give me an hour to myself and then pick me up later - that would be cool.'

They drove in relative silence to the site where St Peter's Square used to be, and Marco dropped Brady off in this deserted space. The Greens didn't visit the area in case they were being viewed as overtly nostalgic. This was strictly forbidden, whereas Brady's Entertainment products were a more furtive pastime and therefore seemed to be semi-permitted or overlooked if not overtly allowed. Brady had little knowledge of this almost sacred space. He had no more insight into the Catholic Church's hierarchy as he would on Islam or Buddhism - but he did understand that the old Trads used to put a lot of store in special places - even if it was sports arenas in many of his criminal buddies' instances. He wouldn't have realised that he was now standing on the same ground as where the Pope would give his Papal addresses to the faithful. Brady might have added a religious dimension to his sudden state of deep thinking about his journey to here and his current circumstances if he had.

He ambled through the old grounds of St Peter's Basilica, and he thought of all the treasures which had dissolved and seeped back into the ground. He equated it to losing his Malibu home with its own artworks on the wall - bought with John Kane's wealth and Libby Skye's taste and considered this a waste. He would never have been able to comprehend the drop in the ocean of his own art collection compared to the hundreds of thousands of priceless treasures housed here. Now there was nothing but long grass and weeds.

Hunter was the one person who shook Brady out of his one-hundred-year dream state. His accusations of Deceiver and Corrupter felt like a religious key driven through his flesh and unlocking his heart. It felt like a spiritual assault. He could have batted off and rationalised any physical assault on him, but he had a deep sense of injustice about Hunter's tirade. Brady continued his walk and headed to where he thought the first GreenShell™ had been erected within days of the Green Revolution. He imagined being a pious Trad being confronted by this almost supernatural force.

Tyrone's story came back to him vividly. He imagined all the holy people using the power of prayer to destroy this invisible Green wall. And the ordinary folk would have pounded at it with their fists or clawed at it with their fingernails. His Pops would have been convinced this was an alien invasion and he would have told everybody around him how he was right all along. *Pops woulda liked that.* Others would have claimed that this was the End of Days. *They woulda been damn right about that.*

Brady guessed the breakthrough moment would have come when somebody in the crowd decided that the most Holy of relics should be looted and used against this implacable enemy.

Brady was lost in this adventure - he was the hero, fighting off the defenders of the treasure to get his hands on holy swords, daggers and spears, and Brady would be victorious and head back to the Vatican City walls with his weapons. Priests and nuns would gather around Brady, putting their most heartfelt prayers into the holy armaments which Brady retrieved. And Brady would raise them high and plunge them into the GreenShell™ and destroy them and bring down the walls. Except…he knew what would have really happened.

He would have stabbed and flung them at the wall as uselessly as the Hodgson Boys throwing their rocks at Mrs Wilson's car. He wondered what he might have done next. *I wouldn't have slumped to my knees; that would be admitting defeat - and Brady ain't no loser. I woulda held my head up and walked right outta there. I woulda left the others to their crying and wailing.*

A crow flew past and cawed at Brady. He shouted, 'Shut the fuck up.' He usually loved animals and birds, but he irrationally felt that this bird was taunting him. It had also lost him his train of thought. *I'm guessing Bodhi only gets interrupted by doves, but me, let's just say I know when I'm being set up.* He was a criminal, he was always paranoid about being played, but Brady's paranoia had only increased since he involved Bodhi and his team in the making of his will. The doubts gnawed at him. He used his quiet time to think deeply about what they had in store for him. As he wandered back to St Peter's Square, he was ever more convinced that the end of Bodhi's one-hundred-year plan could only bring him bad news for his business. He was sure he had signed his life away, but he couldn't figure out how and why. He was late for his rendezvous with Marco, but that didn't trouble Brady. He knew Marco would wait all night for him to return if required. Brady was troubled, angry even, but he only had one strategy in his armoury, and that was to play it cool.

The following morning, Brady returned to St Peter's Square, but this time in a FusionCoach™ driven by Marco, and his five sons were fellow passengers. Brady looked at the wrecked visages of his boys and joked, 'It appears that none of you had your Green beauty sleep last night.'

Troy said blearily, 'We had to celebrate, Pops.'

'Yeah, whatever. I don't need the gory details. Just pay attention and watch the master at work.'

As they pulled up into the spot where the St Peter's Square used to be, Brady was dismayed at the paltry size of the crowd. There appeared to be no more than forty children accompanied by their parents. Brady growled, 'What's this, Marco? Are you trying to show me up in front of my boys?'

'No. Honestly. It was your request to bring only children. There aren't many kids. They cost so much money to raise - it's the temporary hyper-inflationary Green credit increases - only the exceptionally hard-working and dedicated can afford to raise children. Some of these people have travelled for hours…'

'Ok. I get it.' Brady shouted to the boys. 'I asked for only kids to attend, y'know the children are our future and all that crap. Is it the same everywhere? Y'know, hardly any kids?'

They all nodded and uttered, 'Yeah.'

Bill added. 'That's why none of us is in a hurry to give you Grandkids, Pops - they cost a fucking fortune.'

Brady shook his head. 'Ok. Forget that for now. I just want you to know that this is why we've got a small crowd.'

Troy said, assuming he had to in this situation as technically the host, 'No problem, Pops. Everybody here knows how much your customers love you.'

They all traipsed out of the FusionCoach™ and whatever the sons had been taking last night weakened them so much that they seemed withered by the sunlight. Brady smiled ruefully as he watched his boys stagger behind him. The small crowd cheered as loudly as they could to make Brady feel welcomed. They also put on a show of gratitude for the products, hopefully, rare and sought after, that he might shower upon their children. Brady played to the crowd. He picked up the youngest ones and talked to them just like the old days when kids used to traipse along to see Santa Claus in his grotto. Brady smiled, as he would have been shoplifting while everybody was distracted.

He gave them fistfuls of children's entertainment products, as he had brought along enough to satisfy a much larger gathering. Some parents proudly proclaimed that these were the first BMEE products in their child's lives, and it meant so much to them that the great Brady Mahone had given them to their young ones personally.

It touched Brady when one young girl he picked up and flung into the air before catching her safely squealed with delight and said, 'Thank you for my lovely present. I love you, Brady Mahone.'

He answered, 'I love you too, sweetheart. What's your name, little one?'

'My name is Sofia.'

'That's such a pretty name for a beautiful little girl.' He looked at the parents but said to Sofia, 'Do you want your Moms and Pops to pick you some more from my samples' case?'

'What's Moms and Pops?'

Sofia's parents looked with consternation, fearing that Brady might be offended. Brady smiled, 'What do you call them?' He pointed at her parents.

'They are my Mappas.'

Brady laughed, 'Why, of course, they are. Silly old Brady.'

'Silly old Brady.' Sofia teased. Her parents laughed with relief as they picked through his sample case and picked out the most popular entertainment products for Green Italian children.

13: THE SERMON AND DISCOVERY

Samuel Beardon the Third was working on his final sermon before his own private UltraViolet™ ceremony. Across the globe, just over 26.5 million others would take part on Friday, 25 June 2184 - it was nicknamed Green Friday - but he was chosen to represent one of the thirteen commandments at Bodhi Sattva's personal invitation. It was both an honour and a curse because the twelve knew - and only the twelve - why the thirteenth was missing.

His sermon was on the gratitude for the life of good health which God had given them.

Alicia came into his room at the Beardon home. 'Dinner will be ready soon - it's one of Shako's traditional recipes.'

'Thank you, daughter. I shall be along shortly. The Good Lord provides for us all.'

'I'm guessing that's the theme for your sermon. You always talk about the theme before the day. I guess it's your way of mentally getting into the role.'

'I suppose it is - and for His guidance may he make me eternally grateful.' He laughed to indicate he was joking with her. He stood up and went downstairs with Alicia. He wasn't surprised to hear that Tyrone and Raelynn had taken a packed lunch out with them. They only seemed to want to be exclusively in each other's company.

The lunch was a pleasant affair, as everybody speculated on what the unique functions of the UltraViolet™ might be. Samuel knew but was sworn to secrecy. He wasn't going to throw away one hundred years of work and servitude now. All around the table had qualified for the early adoption of the UltraVioletSuit™, and he hoped the administrative error would soon be straightened out for Tyrone. He was saddened that Raelynn would be missing out, he had grown to like her, but hopefully, this relationship would run itself out in due course - six months is a long time in new love.

Many of the guesses of what the new Suit™ could do were wide of the mark, which made the Bear laugh at inappropriate moments. However, some came very close and fearful he might give the game away, he laughed at these also, but then he double-checked the expressions of his fellow diners to ensure he had kept the secret secure. He also listened sadly, but not outwardly so, to stories of the other San Martin residents' frustration at having to wait until the New Year to receive theirs. This had never happened before, but it was put down to Bodhi being ill all those years ago, and that this had pushed the final date back by these crucial six months.

Then there was the bitter talk among some of the residents that Brady's son, Bill Mahone, had been going around, telling anybody who would listen that the Ultra-VioletSuits™ were a load of horseshit and wouldn't do anything but add a slightly protective gloss on everything. And being Bill Mahone, who was in the know, and he had all the previous Suits™ himself, this seemed plausible. There was much talk of him doing brisk business for the Brady Mahone Entertainment Enterprises. They also speculated on why Bill Mahone hadn't stayed for very long in San Martin until Alicia gave the definitive answer, 'Debrock and his cronies have taken their stash of weed to Malibu.'

This was before Samuel Beardon the Third was informed that Brady Mahone had taken all his hoodlum sons to visit the Vatican City, of all places. He was deeply affronted by this knowledge, but like everything else in this last year of the hundred-year plan, he had to treat it as a test of his faith in God and in his chosen one, Bodhi Sattva. He resolved to ride out the bumpy road of his emotional highway. He knew for sure that more tests would follow and that the Lord would test Samuel Beardon the Third to his limits. He was also confident that he would have the fortitude to succeed.

After the dining table had been cleared, Samuel returned to his room to complete his sermon. He had to finish it quickly as his Disciple Rhea Laidlaw needed to check it, even if this meant delivering it to her at night. She was busy and had many meetings to attend in the next few days meaning she would miss the sermon. There was too much at stake to let Samuel stray from the message either in words or tone. Before he left, he got down on his knees and prayed for God to give him strength. He went to check on Tyrone, he went into his room, but there was no sign of either Tyrone or Raelynn.

Samuel Beardon meandered through the quiet streets of San Martin and breathed in the fresh night air. He remembered the old days of smog, frequent forest fires and other climate catastrophes, and these recollections restored his faith. He was in a relaxed frame of mind when Rhea greeted him. She was still in her office working through her backlog of administrative duties.

'Hello, Samuel. How are you holding up?'

'I cannot lie to you - it's difficult. At the dawn of the Green Revolution, I had to harden my mind to the Traditional Cultures - and I did, with the help of Almighty God. But I found that easier to do because the planet was at risk by letting them survive and multiply. However, I'm struggling to grasp the reasoning behind this.'

Rhea nodded and looked at him sadly. 'It seems to me that the only things you have are your belief in Bodhi Sattva and the science…'

'I've always been a man of faith.'

'Ok. Has Bodhi ever not told the truth or broken his word?'

Samuel thought about his Father and Grandfather, he also thought about John Kane, and then he thought about Brady Mahone and how he unravelled the dark truths connecting them all. There had been times, long ago when he wondered if Bodhi could have had his Father killed in prison, but then he gave in to the reasoning that one person isn't worth more than the planet itself, and his Father, Samuel Beardon the Second, might have stopped the Revolution happening. But this still didn't sit right with his other version of Bodhi in his mind that he was the Son of God. It also seemed queer that the person who revealed this truth was a criminal in the form of Brady Mahone.

Rhea watched the struggle play out in Samuel's face. She said, 'If you didn't agree with the plan, and you wanted to stop it, would anybody listen?'

'Bodhi has spoken. It will be done. With or without a mere NanoSprayer™ called Samuel. I would leave a daughter without her Father.'

'Traditional Cultures with their armies and weapons couldn't stop the GreenRevs. Have you found a way to defeat them - a chink in their NanoArmour™?'

'No. Of course not. I am a humble servant of God.'

'What would your God want you to do?'

Samuel smiled, 'Ah, my friend. Now you've got to the heart of my problem. I do not know His plan. I believe I have been chosen, but in believing this, I feel utterly selfish.'

She took his sermon from him and read it through. 'This is fine. Consider it authorised.' She added, cryptically, 'If your mind troubles you, then maybe your mind can't be trusted. I would suggest that when the time comes to choose a side, then I suggest you follow your heart instead.' She pulled out another ledger and returned to her work. 'I'll see you at the UltraViolet™ ceremony. You have a good night, Samuel Beardon the Third.'

Samuel traipsed back home worrying about having revealed his doubts to one of Bodhi Sattva's most trusted advisers but also, considered whether she had shared with him her own reservations. He pondered on how she would have reacted if he had proposed an alternative course of action.

When he entered his home, the place was quiet. All its residence, Shako and her family, and his daughter Alicia had gone to bed, ready to get their three hours sleep. He didn't want to disturb anybody, so he crept quietly up the stairs to his bedroom. He heard laughter coming from Tyrone's room. It didn't sound like the kind of laughter between an intimate couple. It sounded like something from long ago - it sounded like they were watching TV. He listened with his ear pressed against the door. He could make out muffled sounds and then something that sounded like an explosion. It wasn't noisy because the volume was low. Samuel knew that they would turn this off if he knocked on the door, so he took a deep breath and marched in.

He saw the two lovers sitting entwined in an embrace and the unmistakeable flashing images on the Sattva Systems™ computer screen. 'What is the meaning of this? How could you?' He sobbed, 'Why? After everything I have ever said.'

Tyrone said, 'You can't just barge into my room like this. I deserve some privacy.'

Raelynn said, 'We aren't doing anything wrong.'

Samuel looked at one of the scattered entertainment Files. He examined it, but was careful not to touch it. The snake was the first thing to catch his eye, as it was captured twisting through the capital yellow letters on the black background. The letters were BMEE. Samuel knew what this File was, but it took a moment to work out what they stood for, and then he remembered. *Brady Mahone Entertainment Enterprises.* He pointed at Raelynn, 'You did this. I should have banished you the moment you got your claws into my nephew.'

Raelynn said disbelievingly, 'Me! I didn't even like old Science Fiction TV shows until...'

Tyrone interrupted, 'They're mine. I've had them for years, and all my science friends love them. Brady offered, and I took him up on it. Xe has given me some great titles over the years - because xe is my best friend.' Samuel was sobbing like a baby. Tyrone continued, 'It's no big deal. There's no point behaving this hysterically over us watching a TV programme together.'

Samuel took a deep breath. 'You're right. There is no point - now.' He marched out and slammed the door behind him. Alicia came out of her room to see what was happening, and others popped their heads around the bedroom doors. 'What's happened, Daddy?'

'Tyrone has been dealing with Brady and buying his entertainment products from him.' He heard crying, and he saw Shako shaking her head with tears streaming down her lined Native American face.

Alicia was stunned. 'It's Bodhi's fault. He should never have made you stay so close to Brady.'

Samuel Beardon the Third held his daughter, 'No. It's my doing. I should have let the past die with the rest of the Trads. If I hadn't been so obsessed with the death of my Father, I would never have had any dealings with Brady Mahone.'

14: HAZY DAYS OF SUMMER

Whenever the ceremonies took place to launch a new instalment of a GreenSuit™, it became something akin to a superstitious ritual for Brady to base himself at the Mahone Ranch. There had been seven at various intervals in the last hundred years, and this year was supposed to be the eighth, and intriguingly, the final upgrade.

In the past, he had always detected the colour of the upgrade within the Shells™ surrounding the Green areas. But now everywhere was Green, the sky adopted the glow. The new colouring only lasted a few hours, and Brady sometimes thought he was the only one who could see it.

Intuitively, he believed the existence of the Trads was dissolved and buried in the ground, but the NanoShells™ were recycled into the atmosphere as if they were protecting the skies from intruders. This was the kind of conspiracy theory his Pops would have loved, but now it might have a grain of truth in it, especially as there was life on another planet now that Tia Cassandra and her pioneers had colonised Mars.

He recalled how strange it was on the last two ceremonies when the night sky turned a hazy blue and then to violet, respectively. It was as if day and night had been temporarily fused. He was curious to see the effect when they conducted their ceremonies for the UltraViolet™.

Brady had done his reconnaissance of McFarland, and although there were a few lucky ones who were to receive the UltraViolet™ early, he was surprised to learn that Lizzie, Siddha and Cain had been specially selected to receive theirs at a separate ceremony in Boulder Creek. Brady knew in his gut that this had meaning, and his criminal paranoia made him sure that they were plotting against him. Even when Siddha pretended to be his friend, he never fell for it, and Lizzie never hid her contempt for him. However, Cain had a persona that made him hard to dislike - it still didn't mean that he trusted him.

While walking around the grounds of the Mahone Ranch, seeking out the best viewing spot, he searched out his memories from a century ago to see if the ceremony was held in June that year. He remembered escaping Ridgecrest with his buddy, Lucian. He also recalled that it was a day or so before the GreenShell™ appeared in McFarland - the Shell™ which cut the town of McFarland in half, either side of Highway 99. It didn't matter now, but he deduced that this was when the Green townsfolk were at their most vulnerable. They were without their NanoShells™ for a couple of days, and they were without their RedSuits™ for six whole months. *No wonder they were so scared of me.* These recollections confirmed what he was thinking - that tonight was the first midsummer ceremony and that all the others took place on their New Green Year Day.

The barn caught his eye, and with the excitement of youth belying his one-hundred and forty-two years, he scrambled up on the sloping roof and lay back and gazed into the heavens. It was late, but the Sun hadn't long set. He checked his FusionWatch™ and its luminous green display lit up with the information that it was the 25 June 2184 and 23:45. He thought it was mildly amusing that it was 2345. Brady thought that it was good planning to make it a Saturday. He liked the idea that this was a weekend.

Tyrone always came into his mind when he looked at the night sky, and he had a few moments to kill before the McFarland ceremony commenced. Tyrone had been waxing lyrical on something called a triple conjunction, so he thought he would try and find it. He recalled him saying something about Saturn and its rings - Brady recalled this more from the mention of rings because of his old business of jewellery heists. The one he did remember clearly was the red glow of Mars as this was more interesting now that he knew that people were living on that tiny dot in space, the third one he couldn't remember, but Tyrone had said that it was like the Star of Bethlehem that the three kings followed to the birth of Jesus, and even Brady could recall that old Christmas Carol. After scanning the heavens, he found the three bright dots in the unpolluted night sky - he found them mildly interesting but nowhere near as spectacular a sight as Tyrone had made them out to be. He looked at his watch again, just as the display flicked over to 23:59. He cast his gaze to the skies above McFarland.

Nothing happened at first. He kept his gaze fixed. For the briefest moment, everything went black, and then the whole sky appeared transparent and clear. It was the most remarkable sight he had seen in years. The sky was as clear as day, but the moon, stars and the planets were still visible. It wasn't just over McFarland. The effect stretched to all horizons. As far as Brady was concerned, this may have lacked the pyrotechnics of a Fourth of July firework display from the old days, but it was nonetheless a fantastic show of power.

Brady watched the skies for about twenty minutes until the transparent effect began to fade, and streaks of the inky black skies started to seep back through. For a moment, he wondered when the Greens were going to get their sleep tonight - it was way past their bedtimes.

He clambered back off the roof, got in his FusionCar™ and headed off to the celebrations. Their ceremonies bored him just like church services used to do, but he was in the mood to party, and maybe, he could find out what was so special about these new UltraVioletSuits™.

McFarland wasn't the party palace he imagined when he got there. He wandered through the crowds, and yes, there was a lot of Greens commenting on the transparent skies - which confirmed that he wasn't unique in observing this phenomenon - but many were quietly grumbling about favouritism, nepotism, and cronyism. It struck him that there didn't seem to be any Security Protocols™ interfering with the discussion. He had learned over the years what he could get away with saying, but some of the remarks he picked up on were being left unchallenged. There were gripes about the older generation and their constant droning on about the Green Revolution and how apparently bad everything was before. The so-called Pure Greens - those born post-Revolution however, had never experienced living in the world of the Traditional Cultures, and they were grumbling about how that way of life sounded like a lot more fun than working every day in the fields.

Already Brady was struck by how nobody was paying any attention to him. It seemed that Brady Mahone and his entertainment products were way down on their lists of priorities. I don't blame 'em. They wouldn't have been enough for me when I was younger. I woulda wanted to party, drink, have a good time and even do a bit of hellraising. I wasn't the kinda guy to stay stuck in my room watching a movie. What did Bodhi expect to happen? No wonder the kids are getting into sex and dabs - they are the nearest things that pass for living in this boring Green world.

He listened in, discreetly to the raised voices of the younger Green generation. They questioned the idea of Heaven on Earth and how Bodhi's idea of heaven was for them to live forever in their place of work - it was still work, even if the bosses called it heaven. One of them shouted, challenging the Security Protocols™, 'I'd rather be free than to work my fingers to the bone for your fucking heaven, Bodhi fucking

Sattva!' This drew gasps and laughter from his friends but frowns and mutterings of disgust from the older Greens.

One of the original GreenRevs came over to challenge him. 'There would be no Earth, never mind Heaven on Earth if it wasn't for the bravery and sacrifice of our fighters.'

He was cut down with a simple, 'Fuck off.'

As he walked away, Brady laughed at the altercation. He listened to other conversations, and not all were quite so negative, but there was still a palpable sense of distrust. Many were speculating on the meaning behind all this. He wondered if the lack of Cain, Siddha and Lizzie's presence had sparked the unrest, but then his thoughts turned closer to home, and this attitude wasn't as unusual as it appeared.

He thought of Debrock and his large gang of hangers-on, high on dabs, and they came from one of the most pious Green spaces on Earth, San Martin, with the Bear as its preacher - even Tyrone would rather spend all his time with Raelynn, who he had helped raise, than with Samuel and Alicia. For a moment he laughed at the thought of Bodhi's project unravelling, but this was quickly replaced with a feeling he hadn't had for precisely one hundred years to the day.

Brady vividly recalled the Modern Ridgecrest Supermax Penitentiary, the memories of the smells of sweat and defeat, and the moment everybody thought that Guard Askew had loosened his grip by allowing everybody into the Communal Area to have the gift - the little luxury - of watching TV. He replayed the carnage which followed and the piles of dead inmates. He had that same sense of overwhelming caution now as he did then.

Bodhi doesn't lose his grip; this is deliberate.

Brady needed information.

He searched the crowds for the most likely of the recipients of the UltraViolet™. Brady spotted Rowena, or was it Woodrow, Mrs Wilson's Grand-whatever. Her YellowSuit™ had a female appearance, 'Hey, Rowena. Have you had the UltraViolet™?'

She looked at him suspiciously, 'Yes.'

'Does it do any new fancy tricks? Y'know like make you invisible or something like that...'

'I'm curious about your logic. What made you think of that?'

'It kinda made the sky disappear.'

She laughed, 'That actually makes sense - but no. The UltraViolet™ doesn't do tricks, as you quaintly put it.'

'It does something, though...' He wanted to see if she would give anything away without her realising, as it was evident that she was going to state precisely what the new qualities of the Suit™ were. 'Does it make you feel any different?'

Her hands slid down her body as if it was a pertinent question, 'No. I am the same as I was before.' She giggled at him as if she was teasing him.

'Nothing special then...'

'No. Same old me - same new me.' She added, 'I can't tell you more. Maybe, there's nothing to add. There's only one way to find out, and that's to try it yourself. But we both know that will never happen.' She strode away arrogantly. But as she did, Brady kept an eye on her, and she joined a group who Brady suspected were fellow recipients of the UltraViolet™ - they were the goody-two-shoes brigade of McFarland, and they all seemed like the cheerleaders and the jocks from his old high school days - and he despised those who thought they were so special - so God-damned cool.

Beyond the self-selected special ones, he saw a familiar face dart away - he was obviously steering clear of him. Brady shouted, 'Hey, Vance!' *After all these years, you'd think the little creep would not be so fucking afraid of me. He's the one with all the fucking NanoArmour™,* he thought.

Vance pretended that he had only just seen Brady. 'Hey, Brady. Good to see you.' He lied.

'Can we talk somewhere quiet?'

'Sure thing.' He led Brady to a wooded area behind the New Green Town Hall, and the dry twigs crunched under Brady's boots. He made them both stop for a moment as he listened carefully for eavesdroppers. 'There's nobody here, Brady. Remember I've got enhanced hearing, I could hear someone breathing from fifty yards away - all I can pick up on are nocturnal mammals.'

'Have the Security Protocols™ stopped working?'

'No. But they've had their sensitivity settings widened. Now almost anything is allowed except murder or any kind of physical assault.'

'Why?'

Vance shrugged, 'Dunno, maybe a fault…'

'I don't believe that.' Vance looked away. His fingers were scratching on his thighs, and Brady knew he was hiding something. 'Look. I want information is all. Tell me what you know - or think you know. I'm not bothered if it makes me look bad…'Vance sighed, 'There's been a lot of weird shit happening. It's kind of freaking everybody out.'

'When did it start?'

'I'd say from the beginning of this year.'

Brady shrugged, 'Probably just this hundred-year thing of Bodhi's…'

'It is.' Vance took a moment. He breathed in and out deeply a couple of times. 'Normally, we know years in advance what's happening with any Suit™ developments, but this year it's all been surrounded in secrecy. There's a sense that something bad will happen - some are even saying that we will be treated like the Trads.' Something in the way he said this relayed a sense of dread which he had never seen in a Green before.

'Welcome to my world.' Brady joked. He looked at Vance. 'Tell me.'

'I saw you watching the crowd of goys, which Rowena joined. They are the Devout of McFarland. Every Green town has them.'

'What makes them Devout?'

'They are the true believers in the Green Ideals of Sattva Systems™. They are the hardest workers…'

'Ok. Kinda makes sense to me. You've done well out of me when you've pulled in good sales figures. So, Bodhi looks after his high performers. Good for him.'

Vance flinched. 'There's something else they have in common, but it might just be a coincidence…'

'I don't believe in coincidences.'

'They are the only people who won't buy your entertainment products.'

Brady shrugged, 'No skin off my nose. Brady Mahone is doing well enough without 'em. It's their loss if you ask me.'

Vance said with false bravado. 'Too right, man. Fuck 'em. That's what I say.'

This didn't reassure Brady. Instead, it made him distrust Vance even more. 'What is everybody else saying about this? I heard them talking - they ain't happy.'

'It's who is happy which is freaking me out.'

'Who?'

'Siddha.'

'I don't get it. What's he got to do with this?'

'He's, my Disciple.'

'Yeah, whatever. So, what's making Siddha smile.'

'Your son, Bill.'

Brady was perplexed, 'You got me there. What's Bill got to do with this?'

'I don't want to speak out of turn, with Bill being…'

'For fucks sake, Vance, just tell me everything you know, then the quicker you can back to your geeky friends. If you annoy me, I'll tell you, ok?'

Vance said dejectedly. 'Bill came over, pushing us hard to shift your product. Siddha made a beeline to talk to him, but instead of dissuading him, he thought it was… funny. He encouraged him - that has never, ever happened before. He played Bill like a fiddle, and Bill was dancing to Siddha's tune…'

'I said to tell me - not to turn it into a fairy story. So, Siddha wanted more people to experience the superior products of the Brady Mahone Entertainment Enterprises.'

'Yes. Exactly. It felt like his goals were the same as yours. Which would be fine if it wasn't for the fact that you know, as well as I do, that he despises you.'

'What did Bill make of all this?'

'To tell you the truth, Brady, he was more concerned with the orgy his more grateful customers had laid on for him. He couldn't give a fuck about Siddha - but I know you do.'

'What else is there? What do your friends make of all this? I bet they've all got their conspiracy theories.'

'I'm sorry, Brady. I've spoken to the other Reps I know in the other areas, and they have similar ideas to me.'

'Go on.'

'I think there's something really fucking special about the UltraVioletSuits™, but there aren't enough to go around - that's why the Devout and the Disciples are being so secretive and smug about it. But worse than that is the theory about the selection process and what it means.' He shrugged, 'Do I have to spell it out, Brady?'

Brady nodded. 'Say it.'

'They've used you to select which ones are going to live longer and which ones are going to be left to die. By self-selecting to use the services of Brady Mahone Entertainment Enterprises, we have chosen to forego a life-extending or life-enhancing upgrade. We have given in to the temptation of nostalgia for the Traditional Cultures, we have allowed ourselves to be corrupted, and you are the Tempter, the Deceiver, and the Corrupter. I don't believe that, of course, it's just the word on the streets.' Vance added belatedly, 'I'm sorry, man.'

'It's ok. Don't worry. I can't get my head around the implications of what you've just told me. I'm gonna have to let it sink in.'

15: THIS IS YOUR CAPTAIN SPEAKING

A couple of days came and went at the Mahone Ranch as Brady considered his next move. He had been on an emotional roller-coaster, but now he was calm. He trawled his mind for the best people to approach to find out exactly what was being planned. He even considered asking Bodhi outright what his plan was, but he knew he would get half-truths and platitudes from him. If he could, he would have loved to have consulted with Rhea, but she was expert at evading him. He went through the list of all the people he was close to or had a decent working relationship with, and he selected a suitable candidate to start his investigations.

He tried to work out what the play was. Brady focused on what he had to lose - it seemed like the most logical place to start. He had his business and his Green credits - his first thought had been a heist, or maybe Sattva Systems™ would have a more generous word for it - like a corporate takeover. This made sense to Brady. Wouldn't it be a good ploy to ruin his reputation with his customer base, thereby making his business worthless, and then buying it up on the cheap, with the wonderful Bodhi declaring that Brady Mahone Business Enterprises was now in good hands now that the discredited Brady Mahone had been removed. He deduced that a name change for the business would quickly follow.

Having considered this carefully, he was still uneasy about the threats to the existence of the ordinary Greens - it seemed heavy-handed, and he was sure there were other ways of discrediting him without causing this amount of discontent within the Green ranks.

He knew the Greens were spoilt brats and that they would bitch and moan if they weren't getting their new toys before the other kids. *Why didn't Bodhi just give the Suits™ to everybody at the same time? They coulda all had it now, or they coulda all had it in the New Year. Surely, they've got enough of this Nano-stuff to go around.*

This was the key to unlocking his decision on who to approach. One friendly face in Boulder Creek might have the inside track on Sattva Systems™ plans…

Before setting down his FusionPlane™ at the Sattva Systems™ HQ, he circled the grounds until he caught a glimpse of his target. He was reassured that she was in one of the most heavily industrialised areas on the outskirts of the complex. He hadn't been here often in this part as it was full of heavy machinery and chemical plants. He usually headed to the transportation areas to see the big machines, unless he wanted to talk with Bodhi, in which case he went to the HQ, which was miles away from here. He watched Fleet Captain Marjorie Hampton chatting to fellow colleagues, and she appeared to be issuing instructions. Then she sat down for a moment, and that was when Brady decided to land his FusionPlane™ in the nearest open space to her.

She was alarmed to see a FusionPlane™ in the Sattva Systems™ Chemical Zone, as this was a non-existent event. Usually, only FusionCars™ would be allowed to travel, slowly, through here. She watched Brady climb out, and she was concerned about why he was here. It was apparent he had sought her out.

'Hi, Brady. So, you've heard the news then. Have you come to say goodbye?'

'Are you leaving?'

'You could say that.' She laughed. 'I'm not on the list because I collaborated with you. Your friend Hunter gave me up.'

'Hey, I'm sorry to hear that. I didn't mean to cause you no trouble.'

'It's not your fault. It was my decision.'

'Where are you gonna go? You could stay at mine if you want? You could treat it as a vacation…'

'You really don't know. I'm on the penultimate mission to Mars. It was one way to get my UltraViolet™, and it will be a new challenge for me. I don't think spending my life doing a census on wildflowers was really going to do it for me.' He had a puzzled look on his face. 'What is it, Brady?'

'It's happened before, but this time it feels like the Greens want me out of the way for good.'

'What makes you say that?'

He decided to state it is as a fact and not a theory. He wanted to test her reaction. 'They've selected the people who won't receive the UltraViolet™ yet, by using my entertainment products as a kind of bad news lottery ticket.'

Marjorie said, 'That's correct. Bodhi would state that they were self-selected. However, you will be the one who tempted them to stray from the path set out before them. That will be your legacy as the Trad who survived.'

Brady pulled out his Sattva ring hanging from a chain around his neck. 'It's not just my products, is it? It's any gift. I tried to give this back to Bodhi - y'know, just trying to be nice, and he looked scared. He knew even then what he was planning to do.'

'When was this?'

'Near the end of the last century. I'm sure of it.' As he put away his ring, he muttered, 'Fucking Hunter was the same when I offered it to him.'

Marjorie was troubled. 'That doesn't fit with Bodhi's rhetoric. He's explaining the delay away as to do with his illness in '42, that and a shortage of Nanomaterials…'

'And they are calling me the Deceiver or whatever…' Brady laughed sarcastically. He looked at Marjorie, and he could tell that he had escalated the possibilities in her mind. 'You never used my stuff.'

She laughed, 'I helped to protect you - that was far worse.'

'What happens next?'

Marjorie looked around her to see if anybody was watching. Even with the enhanced senses of the VioletSuits™, it was unlikely they could hear within this industrial white-noise. 'Me - I get to escape by working for Tia Cassandra on her Martian Colony. As for you, I think they are planning for you to take the blame for the shortened life expectancy of close to nine-hundred million Greens. These will include your family and colleagues in your business.'

'I don't want to bleat about it - but does that seem fair to you?'

'No. It's not. It's like blaming a mailman for delivering bad news. However, have you heard of the saying about the victors writing the history?'

'Can't say I have.'

Marjorie shook her head. 'Never mind.' She looked around again. 'I'm going to introduce you to someone. She's Bodhi's biggest embarrassment. He keeps her well-hidden.'

'Sounds cool. Will she know more?'

'Undoubtedly. She happens to be the richest person on the planet.'

'Richer than me?'

'By a proverbial mile. Once you get used to her - you'll like her. She's more like you than a Green.' She added, 'You can't go to her. It's too dangerous - health and safety and all that. I'll bring her to you. I might be gone awhile - she'll take some persuading. Do you mind waiting here?'

'No. I've got a packed lunch in the FusionPlane™.'

Marjorie rushed off as Brady took his seat back in the cockpit.

He liked noise, but he was glad to have a rest from the din outside. He ate his lunch, drank his black coffee from his thermos, and waited patiently for about an hour before Marjorie turned up with a woman whose skin was a couple of shades of bronze darker than his own. He alighted his FusionPlane™ in his jeans, white T-shirt with his trusty Poacher's coat - he was always prepared for the worst when meeting new influential Greens. His heavy boots endowed him with a military bearing as he strode out to meet them.

Marjorie introduced her guest. 'Brady. This is Professor Pinar Dogan. Xe is the brains behind our Nanotechnological and Enzyme research. Without xyr, Bodhi couldn't have achieved anything.' She joked, 'Don't let xyr gruff demeanour fool you - if there's one genius left in this world, then you are looking at xyr.'

If Pinar was flattered by her introduction, she didn't show it. 'Hi, Brady. Pleased to meetcha. Heard a lot about you - none of it good.' She laughed so loudly it took Brady aback.

'You're not from around here.'

'I'm from everywhere. I've got hundreds of the finest properties in the world. Wherever there was a Trad dictator or monarchy, I've brought their homes.' She laughed, 'But to answer your question, my family were Turkish - my emphasis on were - they are long dead, but I was raised in England. I went to Cambridge and then to Stanford.'

Brady was intimidated by her intellect. He said cautiously, 'I once knew a professor from Stanford University. He was a real nice dude.'

She looked at him inquisitively as she had never been informed of this connection. 'Who was that?'

'Professor Yuan Chu. He lived in East McFarland. He told me he worked on Nano-technology to help families have kids.'

'NanoIVF™?'

'Yeah, something like that.'

'I think I remember him. Yes, I do, a long time ago. He left…'

'…That's right. He had his funding taken away; I think.'

'Yes. Yes, I do recall. You're right, nice guy. Where is he, now?'

'Long dead. He was a Trad.'

'I'm sorry to hear that - genuinely.' She changed the subject; she had no use for melancholy. 'As an undoubted genius, shall I share with you my four words that govern all of my dealings with the esteemed Bodhi Sattva?'

Brady dreaded a technical answer but seeing as it was only four words. 'Sure. Shoot.'

'Fuck you - pay me.'

Brady roared with laughter, utterly unconcerned if anybody was spying on them, and Pinar seemed to love it that someone finally got her humour. She looked Brady up and down in a predatory way. He had become hardened to the potential attraction of the female-looking Greens. He didn't like the thought of what was lurking underneath their NanoSuits™. There was a time when she might have been his type. This was the same time when anybody could have been Brady Mahone's type. She was slender and wearing skin-tight black leather trousers with knee-high matching boots, and her hair made her look more Japanese than Turkish.

'What do you wanna know, Brady?' She stroked his cheek with her black nails. 'Ask me something difficult - I don't want it to be too easy. I like a challenge.' He knew this was an opening play in a seductive game, but he wasn't enamoured about her taking control. Thinking of Mrs Wilson's distorted and mummified body in her grave dampened his ardour. 'I saw this weird sight once - at a funeral. Yes, Mrs Wilson. It was running late, and there was this thing that looked like a NanoSuit™ of the dead woman, except the NanoSuit™ looked like it was kind of alive, and it was trying to find a place to go. What was the deal with that?'

Pinar said, 'Every effort is made to recycle everything manufactured at Sattva Systems™. Xe had no further use for the Suit™ so, it returned here to Boulder Creek.'

'Nah, I don't believe that.'

'I wouldn't give you incorrect information. It's not in my make-up.'

'She was heading in the wrong direction.'

'When was this?'

'Way back. Maybe '42 - the time when Bodhi got sick.'

'You should have said. Mrs Wilson's Suit™ would have been disorientated.'

Brady scratched the black stubble, streaked with grey on his head. 'What's that got to do with Bodhi?'

She laughed, 'These are interesting questions. Go, Brady. I thought you'd be asking me how you could blow this place up.'

'Would you tell me if I asked?'

'I'd tell you the truth. It can't be done. You really don't know me if you'd think I'd leave a chink for a grubby Trad terrorist to exploit. Fact is, even I couldn't destroy it. Everything is protected by high-grade DiamonoidShells™ and within the treated ceramic structures are impenetrable layers which even Nanoparticles fired at incredible speeds couldn't penetrate.'

'I've seen your vehicles being destroyed. Seen it with my own eyes at Cima.'

'The HeavyLoaders™ were exceptionally close to a *fission* nuclear blast, and the

LeviathanLifter™ survived.' She paused, 'Yes, that was the only time in a hundred years - you're right - well spotted. However, there aren't any fission reactors left, so that threat has gone…'

'You're the genius. I bet you could build one.' Brady joked.

'Me, Tia and Dagny Cassandra could. But that's not going to happen.'

They strolled through the industrial grounds until they reached a quieter spot that overlooked the hills and forests. Brady said, 'So, that's it then. This will still be here thousands of years from now.'

'There were plans to dismantle it - in the early days, but there is more to do. The work never stops when Bodhi's gotta world to save.'

'Save from what?'

'Extra-terrestrial life, the red-giant Sun, comets, meteors, black holes…'

'I heard of the other spacey things from my friend Tyrone, but what's a black hole. All holes are black, ain't they?'

Pinar laughed. She never expected to be explaining black holes to somebody like Brady. 'I'll keep it simple. It's a place where everything is pulled into a tiny space, and it builds up a massive amount of energy. Imagine squeezing the size of the Earth into a penny.'

'No point. That's impossible.'

She shook her head. 'Think of something you could squeeze and let go which could return to its original shape.'

'You mean, like a sponge ball.'

'Yes. That will do. Tell me what is happening to the ball in your hand.'

Brady imagined picking up a yellow sponge ball and squeezing it in his fist. 'I'm tightening my grip, and the ball is screwed up to next to nothing.'

'And when you open your hand?'

'It springs right back to normal.'

'Imagine the Earth is a sponge ball squeezed by a God into a penny, and then he lets the penny spring back to the size of the whole planet. I know you'll say this can't be done, but it can, because the Earth is mainly empty space, and atoms are incredibly tiny.'

Brady couldn't figure this out. Rocks were big and not empty space. 'Are they smaller than your Nano things?'

At this, Pinar knew not to open the discussion on quantum electrodynamics. She didn't want to witness Brady's head exploding. She laughed at this image. 'You could say that.'

Brady continued to scratch his head. He wondered whether it might have been simpler to make a pass at her, but he thought of Marjorie, and she had guided him to Pinar for a reason. 'I kinda get it. I just don't know why people bother with that stuff. I can't even remember how we got on this subject…'

'…You were asking about what happened to an old lady…'

'Yes. Mrs Wilson.'

'She was trying to return to Bodhi as part of the recycling of her NanoSuits™.'

'Bodhi and not Boulder Creek? What's Mrs Wilson got to do with Bodhi?'

'Nothing. Nothing at all.'

'You lost me.'

'It's a classic case of quantity over quality.' Pinar said. 'She was supposed to find the magnetic position of Bodhi's homing beacon.'

'Like a homing pigeon.'

'Yes. Homing in on Bodhi's genetic code - and becoming another layer of Bodhi, where her memories would be accessible to him. The only problem for your poor Mrs Wilson was that Bodhi was in a Nano Sensory Deprivation Chamber - which is impenetrable to Nano-particles and repels magnetic fields.'

Brady laughed, 'I said she'd end up dancing around the North Pole.'

Pinar corrected, 'Magnetic North. She had quite the detour.'

'How many of these dead layers has Bodhi had?' Brady muttered, 'It all seems a bit creepy if you ask me.'

'A few thousand to date.'

'Don't they get heavy to wear - all those extra Suits™?'

'They are made of Nanoparticles; they are virtually weightless. After a few minutes, they become assimilated into Bodhi's body structure.' Pinar added, 'It's still too many…'

'Why?'

'Would you want to carry around with you the thoughts of thousands of Mrs Wilsons? I, for one, couldn't think of anything more boring. All the Greens are so dull…'

'Amen to that.'

'If I were to have the choice, I'd rather choose somebody with complimentary or even superior skills to my own, like Tia Cassandra - she's brilliant with comms technology. Like I said - quantity over quality - but he won't listen to me.'

'I'm listening.' Brady wasn't sure if he was learning.

She looked at him as if he was a puzzle to solve. 'He can be stopped, but not by force.'

'Go on.'

'He can be ousted as leader. Thirteen commandments, with thirteen representatives, mostly based in the Californian home of Sattva Systems™. A majority vote could ensure that every Green would receive the UltraViolet™.' Pinar said this in a way that suggested to Brady that he would have to do something to make this happen. 'There is no shortage of UltraViolet™. Bodhi doesn't want to threaten the world with the future over-population of humans. He'd rather let the population dwindle…'

'Like he did with the Trads.'

'We did. We voted twelve to zero to save the planet - but this is different.'

'Because it's Greens…'

'Because the planet is already saved. How much would you pay out of your fortune to give your sons a further thousand years - maybe thousands more?'

Brady had an incentive he could use as motivation, 'What would I have to do?'

'Persuade six of the thirteen to vote against Bodhi and for the distribution of the UltraViolet™ to all Greens.'

'Who's on this list? Presumably. I know them?'

'Most of them. I'll tell you the ones you won't be able to turn. They include Bodhi, obviously. Precious in South Africa - she's not enamoured with you. And Hunter - you've burned your bridges there, I'm afraid.' She added, 'Oh, and Bridgett Tarnita in Sweden, she would never go against Brady.'

'I'm not into politicking and votes and all that shit. It's not me.'

'Just hear me out. You have two votes in the bag already. This means you only have to turn four more people.'

'Who have I got?' Brady said insolently.

Pinar laughed, 'You got me. I'm a cross in the box.' She added before she could be insulted by Brady's rejection, 'And you've got Rhea.'

'Rhea? How? Why?'

'You've got to be very careful with this information. You could put her at risk. Marjorie has already been uncovered and replaced…'

'Ok, I get it.'

'Rhea is a Trad in Green clothing - you might say. She has been investigating Sattva Systems™ since before the Revolution. She has followed your progress with interest throughout. She had your back covered…and she likes you.' Pinar shrugged.

Brady said, 'So, you think me, and Rhea might…'

'Maybe, who knows, stranger things have happened.' She smiled knowingly.

'Who are the others?'

'Glenarvon Cole, Genesis Garcia. They will be difficult, but Sissy's kid Century is not on the UltraViolet™ list. Then you've got the McFarland trio of Cain, Lizzie and Siddha.'

'Fuck. They ain't gonna listen to me.'

'Cain is not wholly behind Bodhi on this.' She winked. 'And then there's Samuel Beardon the Third.'

'Ok. I make that twelve. Where's the casting vote.'

Her shoulders slumped, 'It's you. But you have to take the Green…'

That's how they get ya, son. Brady was as paranoid as his Pops about agreeing to wear their NanoSuits™. He was proud of being a Trad, even more so of being the last Trad on Earth. He wore that title like a badge of honour or like a medal worn with pride as a great war survivor. He felt like he had worn the Green for a moment, and he didn't like that slimy sensation coming back to him as if he had experienced it only yesterday.

It was the talk of Mrs Wilson which had triggered this feeling; when her ghostly apparition had tried to envelop him in her own NanoSuit™, it felt like he was being raped at a spiritual level. It was a feeling he never wanted to experience again. Brady would rather die. However, he had a duty to prolong the life of his sons, and if that meant going against his principles or going through some personal hell, then he would do it. There was always Rhea at the end of it, maybe waiting for him after all. Brady assessed the situation cautiously. There was no harm in agreeing here. It would buy him time to consider other options. 'Ok. I hear ya. I can't have long left in this world. I've had a good innings as a Trad, and maybe going Green is the way forward for Brady Mahone. You got yourself a deal. I'll get on it.'

She stuck out her hand, and Brady shook it, but he childishly kept his other hand behind his back with his fingers crossed in a ludicrous attempt to nix the deal.

Brady walked away back to his FusionPlane™, and Professor Pinar Dogan strode back toward her laboratory. After a few hundred yards, a figure emerged from the shadows in an old-fashioned hoody. He said, 'Is it done?'

Pinar waited until Brady's FusionPlane™ had disappeared over the huge cream-coloured chemical vats with their giant Sattva Systems™ moss green logos. She barked, 'Fuck you, pay me.'

'All in good time. When the job is completed. What did you say to him?'

Pinar looked around suspecting a trap, 'That he has to contact the twelve people on your list and persuade them to vote against you. If he fails, then his sons' life-spans will be considerably shorter.'

'And what will you say to the others?'

'That the traitor Marjorie Hampton tricked me into meeting Brady Mahone, and he wanted to find out how to destroy Sattva Systems™. He was seeking vengeance for the Trads, and he wanted to ruin our Centenary Celebrations. I played along and showed him some explosive devices and where to plant them. I took him to the FusionPower™ distribution network.'

Bodhi stepped out, and his face was revealed from under his hoody, 'And what possible hold over you did he have to persuade you to help him?'

'He offered me five-hundred million Green Credits, as he had heard I'd been complaining about my work being under-valued.'

'And what now?'

'Everybody is to report back developments to you and not take matters into their own hands. If they feel more comfortable in humouring Brady as opposed to confronting him, then you will understand.'

Bodhi moved in and hugged Pinar, 'Thank you, my friend.'

16: FAMILY BUSINESS

Even before his FusionPlane™ had completed its vertical lift-off manoeuvre, Brady had decided to enlist help in this election process. He knew the Greens didn't rate his intellectual prowess. They always made him feel like a dumb animal, a beast of burden, to who they would throw a treat if he let them pat him. *Something doesn't smell right with that Pinar chick. It reeks of an undercover op. I ain't too old to remember how they go down. Acting all friendly, trying to imitate your jive. I smell a rat.*

After setting his SattNav™ to head back to Malibu, he took out his Satt™ and stretched his legs and rested them with his boots on the cockpit dashboard. He called each of his sons who had scattered in the wind to all parts of the globe. He told each of them to come home urgently as he needed their help. Brady didn't do small talk on the phone, and he ran roughshod over all requests and excuses. He reminded them of his generosity and the fact that he never asked much from them in return.

A couple of days elapsed before his boys had all returned from their faraway places of business, leisure, and pleasure. After breakfast, Brady instructed them to pay attention. 'I'm going to tell you a lot of stuff - personal stuff. You are going to need this to understand what's at stake.' He growled, 'I'm fully aware that I might be being played, but for the time being, I want you to do as I tells ya. Do you follow me?'

Bill usually took up the role of answering for the group. 'Yes, Pops. What's happening?'

'You've all heard of this UltraViolet™, and presumably, by now, you've been told about the link between our products and the selection criteria to receive or not receive it.' Bill looked around his brothers, they had all talked about it, but he wanted their approval to speak freely. 'We've all taken a lot of flak for it. Especially from the late converts who, probably fairly, feel aggrieved to have missed out on the first batch of UltraViolet™ upgrades. Still, it's only a few months to wait.'

Brady said, 'I'm hearing it's never. They are going to let you die out naturally.'

Troy interrupted, 'Like they did with the Trads?' The others gasped at the possibility.

'Most of the Trads didn't make it past fifty. You've got until you are a hundred, I believe - that's still a lifetime in my book. But still…' Brady was relieved that none of his sons panicked. He was proud that they were taking the news like men.

Wilder was the numbers man. He said, 'With the maximum life expectancy driven down to one hundred coupled with the massively escalating costs of raising your own children, then within about three hundred years there will be hardly any Pure Greens left. If the UltraViolet™ leads to a minimum one-thousand-year life span, then they will be the only ones left. The nine-hundred-million population today becomes just twenty-six-million by the year 2500.'

Brady added to Wilder's math, 'One human for every one square mile of hospitable land, a friend of mine said that - something like that.'

Rocky said, 'Wow, Pops - where on Earth did you pick up a detail like that?'

'I can't remember exactly. I think it was when I was in Florida with Glenarvon Cole, back in the 40s.'

'That's an eternity ago.'

'Yeah, a hundred years in the making.'

Wilder had been distracted by his own theories, 'I bet it's 2500, it's a nice round number, I can see those smug UltraViolet™ bastards' New Year celebrations, now. Can't you?'

Troy thumped the table, and the boys spat out their curses.

Bill said, 'You've never been afraid of death. Have you Pops?'

'Life's too short.' Brady joked, and it diffused the tension.

Hawk spoke up, he usually stayed quiet as the youngest, but he picked up on the worried frown on the brow of his Pops. 'That's not all that's troubling you, is it Pops?'

'No, son. It's not. I think they got something real special planned for me. You see, they always play this game where they spin things to make 'em look good - real nice and friendly like. What they don't do - is take responsibility for all the bad shit that goes down.'

He looked around and saw the puzzled looks on his boys' faces. This was why he had to tell them everything. They were a jumble of labels to him, Green, Pure Green, indoctrinated Green, and he had to shake them out of their Green dreams. 'Some stuff you've heard before from me, and some stuff you ain't, but it's gonna add con-text-like, you get me.'

Bill said, 'Sure, Pops.'

Brady wasn't keen on Bill's patronising tone, but he pressed on regardless. 'You all know that that I blame the Greens for the deaths of billions of Trads. They say that the Trads chose or self-selected themselves for their lives outside the GreenShells™, but I think they kinda neglected them to death.' He was aware that he sounded like his own Pops when he grandstanded about his latest conspiracy theories. 'Anyways, this means they have form in my book. They've done it before, and they are doing it again - only difference this time is they are doing it to their own kind.'

Rocky said, 'This means it's a Green-on-Green assault. This has nothing to do with you Pops because your Trad…' He added to reassure his Pops, 'and proud.'

'Except, they are going to make it all about me. That's what it means to be a Trad - I am here to take the blame. I'm sure they've kept me alive for this reason. There's no way I should still be alive and this healthy - I mean, look at me. In a fair fight without your NanoSuits™, I could still whoop your asses.' The boys laughed and joshed with him with mock bravado. 'They are going to rig this so that by using my entertain-ment products, they broke their rules, their commandments, and the only person left to blame - after they have absolved themselves of any responsibility - is me, for all time.'

He looked around the table. Bill said, 'We've sold them the stuff. They'll blame us. I don't mind being accountable.'

'But it's my name on the product. It's my baby. When the Devout and the Disciples talk about the Pure Greens' loved ones, they lost in years to come. It will be followed with, "If only Brady Mahone, the filthy Trad, hadn't been around - if he had rotted in that prison where he belonged, then our friends and family would still be here today." I'm gonna have my say if they give me a half-a-chance.' He peered into each of his son's eyes, 'I don't care about what happens to me. I'll lay down my life in a heartbeat to protect my family. If it comes to that, then I'll do it and don't stand in my way.'

The boys didn't want to contemplate this scenario. Bill said, 'We've still got time, Pops. Let's not waste it on worst-case scenarios. What's the plan?'

'I'm gonna bring you up to speed with the family history. Follow me.' He led them through the many rooms of his Malibu home. He spotted Hunter lurking with the pretext of offering his services. Brady abruptly told him to take the day off and not to hang around on the grounds. Hunter nodded and left them alone. Brady paused before changing direction and going back on themselves. The boys looked at each other with furtive gestures, which questioned Brady's sanity. He took them to Libby Skye's old bedroom. He gazed at the poster of Libby Skye in the movie, *The Virgin.* She was in gossamer white and looked like an angel. The words praised her magical performance. 'This is your Grandmother.'

Wilder said, 'Not Edie Mahone.'

'No. She was my Foster Moms.'

'Wait a minute…'

'Your Grandfather was John Kane - Bodhi Sattva's Father, or Xavier Kane as he was known back then.'

Wilder said, 'Fuck me, Pops. There's a lot of implications here.'

'Yeah, there is. Bodhi is your uncle, as is Glenarvon Cole…' He raised his hand to stop the outbursts. If they were anything like him, Brady Mahone, ex-con, they would be already onto how they could exploit this. Brady needed to put a lid on this. 'I don't think they know, or if they do, then that's part of their plan. The point is that they don't know that I know. Therefore, I'm ordering you not to say anything. This is my ace up my sleeve, and it will become worthless if they know I have something to play. I'll tell you more, but first, give me your word - on my life, not yours - because that's what you'll be giving to Bodhi if you betray me…'

Bill shouted, 'It will never come to that, you have my word, and I will do anything to help.' The others agreed.

Brady looked at the poster of Libby Skye, 'Take a moment, boys, to get to know your Grandmother - my biological Moms. This is the poster that made John Kane obsessed with her. This is where it all started.'

After a minute of revered silence, Wilder said, 'I just thought all these pictures and photos were artworks from the previous owners. I never knew…'

'…Neither did I. Tia Cassandra mocked me with this revelation, but it kinda made some sense.'

'Why did they not raise you? They had plenty of resources.'

Brady wasn't going to share anything about Archie Mahone's disgrace. He'd hoped that Amie hadn't spoken of it. He felt that if he told the whole disgusting truth about John Kane, he could be tainted by association - it was a time to reveal family secrets, but not all of them. 'John Kane - your Grandfather was a cold-hearted scientist, industrialist and business bastard. He brutalised Libby to have Bodhi born on the stroke of the Millennium, and he indoctrinated Bodhi with all his knowledge and values. He had stolen Libby's eggs for some kinda social experiment shit. Bodhi was born on the Millennium, and twenty-one years, later he had Glenarvon Cole engineered and indoctrinated with socialism and radical environmentalism...'

'Why?'

'Because he could. He wanted to see how his perfect specimens would turn out if they were raised in different circumstances. I suppose at some level, my biological Pops saw me as a perfect specimen unless he was keeping me to harvest my organs or something...'

Hawk moved in and hugged his Pops awkwardly, and then stepped back. He knew he shouldn't show sentimentalism in front of his Pops, 'What did that bastard do to you, Pops?' He'd sworn to consistently demonstrate his masculinity.

Brady glanced away and took a deep breath and then blurted out what he hadn't told another living soul. 'Tia Cassandra told me that John Kane paid a junkie to give birth to me but with some strings...' He was angry and ashamed and knew this would make him sound like a victim. 'He had all kinds of criminal lowlife talking to me while I was still in my surrogate Mom's womb about every kinda lying, cheating and crimes...they even had fucking scripts...' He held up his hand to put a halt to interruptions. He wanted to share - a feeling he rarely had. 'Even after I was born, this went on for years, until my surrogate Moms died of an overdose. He placed me as a four-year-old with Archie and Edie Mahone. Now, I don't want to speak ill of them, but even that was deliberate, Edie was an alcoholic who had given up on life and never really liked me, and Archie, my Foster Daddy, was a crook...' Brady half-lied, 'dabbling in all kinda illegal shit. Then things didn't go quite to plan...'

Hawk urged Brady to continue, 'It's ok, Pops.'

'Archie changed because of me. He loved me and treated me like I was his own. I musta been hell to raise, I was always in trouble, but he was always on my side, no matter what I did. Don't get me wrong, boys, he was a real bad character, but he was the only one who coulda handled me. That's why when John Kane came to reclaim me a few years later when I was eight...Archie murdered him...to keep me safe.' Brady let out a huge breath as if he had given testimony in his own defence with his sons as the jury. 'I am not a good guy. I've robbed and murdered all my life - not in self-defence but out of pure self-interest. That's who your Pops is...'

'You've always been good to us, Pops.' Bill said.

Brady paused. He felt the urge to say to his boys something he could never have countenanced before. However, he had told them about the impact on his life from his biological father's manipulations, and he realised he might have been committing the same crime. Brady's embarrassment was evident to his sons as he looked away before returning his gaze upon his beloved sons. 'I've done you wrong. I shouldn't have tried to make you live your lives in my image. It's your life. You live it how you want to be. You don't have to be...y'know...'

Troy could see his Pops struggle, 'Cisgender male. You are giving us permission to choose who we want to be.'

Brady uttered, 'Yes. That's what I mean.' Brady wanted to feel relief, but instead, he wanted to flee before any of his boys said something emotional or sentimental. All he needed was an excuse.

Wilder said, 'You don't think you're Green, do you, Pops? I mean, I bet John Kane did other stuff to you while you were still in the test tube. It makes sense, y'know, perfect specimens, a bit a gene-splicing, altered sequencing, InfraRedPrimers™, it would explain…'

'I'm a fucking Trad.' Brady yelled. 'I don't care if I am fucking being ignorant. I know they call me; I hear them laughing…Alpha-Male Trad or Trad Alpha-Male… whatever…they say I'm a fucking Silverback gorilla in human form. I'm not a Green, and I will never take their Green goo. Pops was right. He always said they would get me in the end, lure me in with promises, make out that I was some kinda hero. I don't want that Green shit in me. I am Trad. End of.' He looked around at his sons, he couldn't give a damn if they were Green, and he had hurt their feelings. 'Follow me, and I'll show you. I can prove I'm Trad and it ain't the word of some fucking deceitful human. God knows I can't trust anybody. Everybody's got it in for that old fool, Brady Mahone.'

After a moment's shock at their Pop's outburst, Brady stormed away, and the boys quickly caught up with him. Bill punched Wilder in the arm. Wilder said, 'What? What did I say? It was only a question of logic…'

'Well, think before you use it on Pops in future. Got it.'

Brady dug out his old sketchbooks. He quickly located the one with Bodhi's teeth marks in its leathery hide. He opened the page to reveal his drawings of the two man-eating lions. 'These are Msoro Monty and Bwana Devil. While the fucking Greens left the Trads in South Africa to their own devices, these two maneaters feasted on hundreds of Trads over many years. They never attacked Greens because the NanoSuits™ they were wearing emitted no living scent, this meant the lions, or any other predators didn't view them as animals or food.' He put it a different way to ensure they understood the significance of this information. 'The NanoSuits™ gave off no scent, and they would no more try and eat a Green as they would a vehicle. The Greens were like robots to them, but not me - oh no - they followed Brady Mahone for days before they attacked. I was Trad meat to them. No politics or ideals at play, I was meat, and this is what they looked like just as they attacked me.'

Bill traced his fingers over the teeth and claws. 'How did you escape, Pops?'

'They were doused in Film from the Security Protocols™. I asked for them to be left in situ while I sketched them. After I had finished and was led to a place of safety, they released them. Of course, they cared for the lions' welfare, but they were unconcerned if there were any more Trads to feed on out there. Still, it's interesting to think that the Greens were protecting me. I was clearly wanted more alive than dead.' He turned sharply to Wilder, 'What do you think now, boy? Is that enough evidence for ya?'

No matter what Wilder actually believed, he gave the answer which Brady craved. 'You're a Trad. Absolutely, Pops.'

Brady gathered his boys close around him as if he feared that somebody might be listening. 'They tried to make me believe that I can sway some kinda vote at the end of the year. Personally, I think it's bullshit, but I'll play along. You know my version of events but keep it to yourself. Instead, I want you to make it look like they got old

Brady Mahone fooled.'

Rocky said, 'What do you need?'

'First of all, forget the business for a few weeks.'

'Not difficult. We are hardly welcome now.'

Brady stroked his stubble on his head. 'That could be a way in. There are influential Greens I'm supposed to win over. Go and throw yourself on their mercy and beg for help to get the business up and running again. They won't help. It don't matter, none. Just be seen talking to them, and make it look to others like you're being all secretive.'

'Ok. Why?'

'To buy me time. I'll do the same with a couple on the list who they would think I could influence.'

'Who are they, Pops?' Bill asked.

'There's Bodhi. I'll take him.' Brady laughed, 'Not to ask him to vote against himself, of course. I'll ask for marketing ideas, and this will draw Genesis Garcia in.' He added, 'Professor Pinar Dogan is the one who's playing me. She's the top broad of Sattva Systems™ manufacturing plant. The other one I'll take is Samuel Beardon the Third, seeing as he's my oldest *friend.*'

He looked around his sons. He was working this out on the fly. 'Troy?'

'Yes, Pops?'

'Do you know Bridgett Tarnita? She's from Sweden.'

Troy laughed. 'Yeah, there isn't a person in the whole world who hates you as much as she does.' The others joined in the laughter.

Brady smiled, 'Very funny. Just do your best to have some kinda meeting with her. Act like we're beaten if you have to.'

'And Wilder?'

'Yes, Pops?'

Brady gave his sketchbook containing his man-eating lions to him. 'Precious is a bigwig Green in South Africa. Use this as a way-in if you have to.' Wilder nodded vigorously, trying to win back his Pops trust.

He looked at Bill. 'I want you to take the old McFarland trio.' Brady laughed at the recall of an old nursery rhyme that sounded like this. 'Lizzie and Siddha will be unfriendly, but Cain will be oh-so-nice. Don't be fooled. I mighta taken them myself, but they know me too well.'

'As for you, Rocky, I'm giving you the hardest ones to track down.'

'I can do it, Pops. Just name them.'

'I want you to locate Glenarvon Cole and Rhea Laidlaw. She might, just might be on our side, but still don't reveal our hand. It might be useful if she looks surprised if we find an opportunity to make a decisive mood.'

'Why might she be on your side?'

'She and Fleet Captain Marjorie Hampton have made it their mission to keep me alive. I'll leave it at that.'

Hawk said, 'Is that who I've got to find? She's the only one left by my reckoning.'

Brady laughed, 'Not unless you follow her to Mars.' He said, 'She's been exposed as a traitor, I believe - for helping me. No, the person I want you to get close to doesn't need to be found, but he is probably Bodhi's closest confidant, and he works here. He is very slippery. Maybe use Debrock and his buddies to spread a little disinformation.'

'I'm lost, Pops. Who are we talking about?'

'Hunter.'

17: VEGETABLE MAN

A highly unusual sight greeted Brady as he drove his FusionCar™ on Highway 99 to San Martin. He had already felt a tinge of nostalgia for the old days, as he elected to take the FusionCar™ and not the FusionPlane™ for his journey. He had been chilled about the traffic - it took him back to a time before the Greens. However, it was a shame that all the vehicles were identical, with their ceramic appearance and cream-coloured livery all featuring the moss green Sattva Systems™ logos.

There were banners along the side of the Highway and even crudely built billboards. *We refuse to be treated as second-class citizens. UltraViolet™ is a right, not a gift. No man can play God, not even Bodhi Sattva. No UltraViolet™ - No Work!* The fact that they were written in gaudy colours and not the standard Sattva Systems™ moss green seemed rebellious.

Brady turned off the Highway and soon found the demonstrations blocking his way. The crowds of the younger Greens - if you could call under sixties young - chanted: *What do we want? UltraViolet™ - When do we want it? Now!*

He braced himself for trouble, but they cheered as he went past. *Hey, Brady! Stick it to Bodhi...He don't care about us...Make him change his mind, man...We know he wants us to blame you, we're not stupid...He's not my God...Not in my name...It's so fucking unfair...*

Brady occasionally shouted back an encouraging reply. *I'm sure we can sort it out...He's trying to frame me...I ain't gonna stand for it...He's gonna regret messing with Brady Mahone...Can I count on your support?*

Hell, Yes!

The crowd slowly parted to let Brady through. He drove through the centre of San Martin when he saw Samuel Beardon the Third being pelted with produce. Of course, they couldn't harm him within his NanoSuits™ - the flying fruits and vegetables bounced off him harmlessly, but Brady knew this would psychologically damage his old friend.

Brady judged the direction of flight of these squishy projectiles and alighted his FusionCar™ and stayed out of harm's way. He called to the crowd with mock authority, 'It's ok. I'll deal with him.' The demonstrators did not seem appeased. 'I'll persuade him to talk to the big man, and I'm sure we can get you the UltraViolet™.'

His hundreds of onlookers muttered among themselves. 'You know I'm a Trad, and I'm not interested in NanoSuits™, but I have five sons who have missed out - just like you. I'm gonna get justice for my boys, and I'm gonna get justice for you all!' He bellowed, and the crowd cheered.

'Get in the car, man.' He said softly to the Bear. Samuel jumped in the passenger side while Brady moved the car slowly away. 'What's going on? Where are the Security Protocols™ when you need 'em?'

The Bear - this indestructible big man in Brady's eyes, crumbled before him. Tears gushed from him, and he sobbed like a baby. Brady said, 'It's ok, man. I'm here. You know I'll try and help my oldest friend.' The Bear seemed to struggle to catch his breath. He spluttered, 'It's all gone wrong, and it's all my fault.'

Brady drove on, letting the Bear calm down, and he pulled up to the Beardon home.

As they entered, he asked, 'What's happened? I can't believe it's just the demonstrators.'

He took a lung full of air and let it out slowly. 'I should blame you.'

'Blame me for what?'

'Tyrone. If he hadn't used your entertainment products, he would have been ok. He would have received the UltraViolet™ like Alicia and I.'

'Hey, man. I got broad shoulders. I can carry the weight. But I have to say in my defence that I never got Tyrone started on my products. He always talked about his scientist friends in Boulder Creek and San Diego and how they were really into Science Fiction films. They got him started. After that, when he used to ask me for rare stuff, I gave it to him, freely, as a friend. I never made the first move. Ask Alicia. She will tell you that Brady Mahone never tried to sell her anything.'

The Bear slumped on the chair. Brady made a tactical retreat to allow his explanation to sink in. He went to the kitchen and made them both coffees. The home was quiet, and he guessed that the others were working. None of the other residents had shown any interest in his product, and he assumed they had all received UltraViolet™.

He handed his friend a coffee. The Bear said as if he was in a dream, 'Forgive me, God. I know not what I have done. I shouldn't have interfered with your plan.' Brady gulped his coffee and let the Bear continue his rambling speech. 'I have sinned. I have let the pride of ownership distract me. I should never have let the feeling of being the chosen one - allow me to take the UltraViolet™ ahead of my flock…'

'I gather this UltraViolet™ can give you another thousand years of life at least.' Brady said, interrupting his old friend's self-pitying monologue in Brady's opinion. 'I've had to give it some thought because of my boys, but truthfully, if they get a hundred years, then they've done well - we both would have sold our souls for a hundred years of life and in good health - don't you think?' Brady smiled broadly, but the Bear wasn't taking the bait. Brady continued, 'Though I understand the greed for life, it's only natural, and if I can secure it for my sons, then I'll move heaven and Earth to get it. However, I think another thousand years in your boring Green world sounds more like hell to me.' He teased the Bear, 'Don't you think, old man?'

Samuel Beardon the Third slumped in his chair and looked petulantly out of the window like a sulking schoolboy.

'Hey, man. Yell at me if it makes you feel better.' Brady said. 'It helps to get it out of your system, y'know, get all the bad stuff out in the open…'

'It's my fault. I interfered. If I'd have let him make his own decisions as a man, and not the boy I treated him as, then he would already have the UltraViolet™, but I had to meddle like an old fool, and I have cost him his life.'

'You're gonna have to tell me more, man.'

'Tyrone had applied to join the space mission to Mars…'

'No surprise there. He loves all that space stuff.'

The Bear shook his head. 'If only I had taken it as simply as that. What would you have said if it was one of your boys?'

'I would have been proud. Maybe, they coulda turned out like that Commander

Rocky Fitzpatrick - he's a real all-American hero. I coulda lived with that.'

'Wouldn't you have missed them?'

'Sure. I woulda had to change my plans to accommodate them, like. But they would be forging their own path in life - that's a good thing in Brady Mahone's book.'

The Bear shook his head, 'Well, I pulled in a favour from Genesis Garcia, and she delivered. She pulled Tyrone from the list of applicants and used an underlying health issue as justification for Dagny Cassandra.' He banged his fist on the coffee table. 'What's maddening is that her child, Century Brady Garcia, made the same mistake as Tyrone, and she put him on the ticket reserved for Tyrone.'

Brady grimaced, 'Ouch, man. Who'd have thought that politicians would be corrupt, eh?'

'I think she knew long before I asked her. I think she and Bodhi are in cahoots in all this. I don't trust them anymore.'

'You've lost your faith in your so-called Son of God?'

The Bear declined to answer.

'What's the deal with the whole colonising Mars thing?' Brady leaned in and smiled, trying to encourage his friend to talk.

'They've been sending FusionSpaceShuttles™ to and from Mars every few days for decades. The deal was that the mission from Earth has to close a month before the New Year.'

'Boy. They musta have a lot of people and equipment up there by now.'

'Tyrone told me they had nearly twenty-thousand people on Mars.'

'I suppose they've had forty years or so to do it.'

'That's not all. This will interest you.'

Even if it didn't, Brady had decided to feign interest as the topic seemed to be unlocking Samuel's defences. 'Go on. Rock my world.' He laughed.

'Tia Cassandra has fifty Trads with her. They call themselves the Originals, not Trads.'

'Whoa! You mean I'm not the only one left. Wow! Now that is a mind fuck. Brady Mahone, a true Original. Hey, it's got a nice ring to it. How come?'

The Bear shook his head and chuckled. Brady's humour made it easier for him to continue his explanation. 'Her experiment in the desert was to see if they could build a human colony on Mars. Some of the original volunteers wanted to keep the experiment pure. The older ones died out, but not before they had Trad children of their own. They were proud of their roots and refused the Green when it was offered on the LeviathanLifter™ when they escaped the Ruin of Cima.'

'But the rest of them are Green, aren't they?'

'Yes. Even Tia and Dagny. Tia wasn't going to pass up the opportunity to exploit the scientific breakthroughs. All the others are UltraViolet™, but they have pledged to keep the Trads, the Originals, alive.'

Brady said sourly, 'More than the Greens did down here.'

'Yes. I concede the truth in what you say, brother.' He added, 'Tia Cassandra, with the help of the exodus of Sattva Systems™ technicians, have developed a Nano-SpaceSuit™ for the Martian Trads. This gives them the Green benefits, but it can be removed when they have recovered or been repaired from injury. Tia's reasoning is that it is a logical development of their technological journey, and therefore the Trads can be at ease in using it.' He added, 'Would you use such a Suit™?'

That's how they get ya, son. Brady thought deeply about this fundamental question. 'I've never regretted refusing the Green. I can't see me changing my mind, now.'

'You see me as tempting you…'

Brady roared with laughter, 'I get accused of that all the fucking time. Welcome to my world, brother.'

18: THE LAST MISSION TO MARS

Rhea had completed her regular catch-up meeting with Bodhi. She had shared and acquired secrets to Bodhi's satisfaction. As she left the main entrance, she headed to the transport area to meet Fleet Captain Marjorie Hampton on her final day in that role. She joined the party onboard a parked FusionPassengerJet™. This was a commonplace occurrence over the years, wishing a fond farewell to workers and technicians at Sattva Systems™, as more and more of them joined the brain drain to Mars.

They used Bodhi's own words and the keeping of his promises to justify his actions. From the outset, he had proclaimed his disgust for this industrial monster and pledged that Sattva Systems™ was to be returned to nature once the one-hundred-year plan was completed.

The exodus of talent alarmed Genesis Garcia, who tried to beg and bribe people to change their minds, but with the recent debacle over the allocation of the Ultra-Violet™ - they didn't trust her. And Bodhi had remained silent on the subject. Thus, Marjorie was not unhappy about being effectively fired and labelled a traitor by the inner sanctum of the Sattva Systems™ hierarchy. The closer this final day came, the more she was delighted to be leaving Bodhi, Genesis and even Glenarvon Cole more than thirty million miles behind.

Bodhi had always claimed to have loved and respected all his considerable workforce, but although they happily received every development of the GreenSuits™, from InfraRed™ to Violet™, they were industrialists, chemical engineers, and factory workers. They took pride in their work, but they still felt more Trad than their more fragile-at-heart Devout Greens. They assessed their positions and potential upcoming redundancies, the quality of life - or lack of it on Mars, and then threw into consideration of the guaranteed UltraViolet™ and the potential of a further thousand years of life - courtesy of the deal Tia Cassandra agreed with Bodhi, and they aligned their future to hers.

Rhea boarded the FusionPassengerJet™, and she was greeted warmly by the partygoers. They would be leaving as part of the wrap-up crew just before the New Year celebrations, which were only a couple of months away. They would be mothballing the launchpad and taking the final industrial components with them, but today was the last mission for taking civilians to Mars.

Marjorie threw her arms around her comrade and acted as if she was drunk on one of the technician's concoctions, but this was an act. She needed to be sharp. She whispered for Rhea to go to the cockpit with her, where they could talk more discreetly. 'I managed to persuade Sissy to let me use the rental FusionPassengerJet™ to travel to Cape Cassandra as a kind of goodwill leaving present. I told her I wanted to fly myself and a few friends down there to see me off. But obviously, I'm planning to leave alone.'

'I've wrapped up the details from my end. That's all I'm going to say.'

'Understood. I'll meet you there.'

Marjorie watched Rhea walk away from the party and head to her own rental FusionPlane™, and she was almost superstitious about not making her next move until she had watched Rhea take-off and fly away, unhindered.

She headed back to the party, which was petering out on the FusionPassengerJet™. She thought she would bring it to an end by utilising a small closing speech. 'My friends, and colleagues for more than one-hundred-years in some cases. I just want to thank you all, so much, for being here and giving me all your best wishes. The Green ride was brilliant while it lasted, but I think we can all sense that the wheels are falling off the FusionCars™…'

They laughed politely at her joke.

'I know I'll see some of you again on Mars at the end of the year. But for those of you that are remaining to be a part of Bodhi's project, for I truly believe it is now all about him, and not us, I would like to make one small request. I would like you to please try and stop him from destroying the launch and landing pads. I know we are supposed to be gone forever, but I'm sure that one day, myself and your other good friends up there would like to know we would be welcome to come and visit you one day…in the distant or not-so-distant future. Thank you.'

Her colleagues and friends gave her warm applause. They came up one by one to give her goodbye hugs and slowly drifted back to their work duties.

Marjorie headed back to the cockpit. She was alone in the vehicle but still felt the need to be in the cocoon of the cockpit while she sobbed gently. She then sent the FusionPassengerJet™ into a vertical lift-off and flew from the Sattva Systems™ Parking Lot for the last time.

She headed to the outskirts of San Martin. She landed her vehicle on open ground a couple of miles away from the nearest building. She waited until darkness fell. She turned on her VioletSuit™, as the increased sensory perception was disorientating if used over long periods. To Marjorie's technical reasoning, it would have the same issues as if her windscreens were made from magnifying glass. She heard the nocturnal creatures busily searching for food. She was surprised at how many rabbits appeared in the quiet stillness of the open ground. At about 1:30am, she saw her guests approaching upon Green Rental Bikes. They pulled up about fifty yards away from her and then placed the Green Bikes carefully on the damp grass. The rabbits scurried back into hiding.

They approached Marjorie cautiously, looking all around them with their heightened senses as if they were paranoid about being watched or followed. They also tried to breathe as slowly and calmly as possible in case it attracted the Security Protocols™ to them. Marjorie put a finger to her lips and gestured for them to follow her on board. She placed them in their seats, headed back to the cockpit and set the autopilot to Cape Cassandra.

It was 1:55am before she dared to speak to them. She crept out of the cockpit and sat close to her passengers. She whispered, 'Hi. Is there anything that I should worry about?'

Tyrone answered, 'We did everything you said. Every night for the last two weeks, we have refused to go to bed at the normal Greens' time of 11:00pm. And we always took our rebellious Green Bike ride at 1am.'

Raelynn joked quietly, 'They thought we were acting like naughty children in refusing to go to sleep at bedtime.' She placed her hand on Tyrone's arm.

Marjorie looked at them and considered there was a time in the old days when a lanky, bespectacled, black man would look seriously out of place with a ghostly white Goth, but in these times, they could adopt any look they wanted, and many just found a look that suited how they felt and stuck with it like a comfort blanket. She asked,

'What did you do with regards to Samuel?'

Tyrone answered, 'I left him a note in his Bible because he looks at it every morning when he wakes up. I informed him that we had gone to Brady's home in Malibu, and that he must head down there, alone, as this would be the only way he could see us for the last time. I added that our lives were at stake if he told anybody about this, even Alicia.' He looked through the window and at the stars as if this was one part of the plan he disagreed with.

Marjorie looked at her watch. 'This was the safest time to help you escape. I want you to use your sleep period now, as it will guarantee your vital signs will remain normal.'

Tyrone and Raelynn used their chosen sleep phrases in their minds which triggered their sleep as surely as any anaesthetic.

19: SURPRISE GUESTS

Brady woke up, showered, and shaved just as he would have done on any other autumnal day. He had nothing planned. Despising Hunter took too much effort, so he became comfortable with just instructing him with his wishes. Today, he fancied a vegan cooked breakfast. He would have liked a traditional cooked breakfast, but there hadn't been any meat products since he had eaten his way through Archie Mahone's apocalypse supplies in his bunker decades ago. Still, he had to admit that some of it didn't taste too bad at all.

He put on his swimming trunks as he fancied a dip in one of the many swimming pools later. He pulled a white dressing gown around him and slipped his feet into comfy white slippers and meandered down to a massive balcony with an infinity pool merging into the Pacific Ocean in the distance.

Hunter had laid out his breakfast table, and a steaming cup of black coffee was already poured. Shortly afterwards, his breakfast arrived, and he ate it hungrily. He listened to the waves crashing on the shore, and as thoughts of problems in the Green world emerged, he dismissed them, as today he wanted to rest and enjoy his peace and the trappings of his success. He let his breakfast meal go down for about half an hour before he climbed into the pool. He swam the short lengths repeatedly and leisurely for a while until he rested his elbows on the edge of the infinity pool and gazed into the blue sky streaked with white clouds.

After an hour in the pool, he spied a FusionPlane™ coming into land in his Vehicle Lot. He wasn't expecting visitors, and more to the point, he wasn't in the mood for them. He called Hunter. 'If it's nobody I'm friends with, then I'm not at home. I'm not expecting any visitors today.'

'Yes, sir.' Hunter headed off to the Vehicle Lot to intercept Brady's uninvited guest.

The rogue visitor was Samuel Beardon the Third. Since his first visit here - at the reading of Brady's will, he had been made aware that Hunter was a Disciple and that as part of his role was to spy and report back on Brady's activities. Samuel wasn't sure whose side he was on here. He thought of Tyrone's secrecy and decided to throw his lot in with Bardy Mahone on this issue.

Samuel Beardon the Third prepared himself for battle. He pushed his shoulders up and stood straight and strong and marched away from his rental FusionPlane™. Within a few minutes, Hunter blocked his path. 'I'm sorry, but Brady Mahone is not at home. If you'd care to leave a message…'

'I want to speak to him in person.'

'Then if you'd care to make an appointment.'

'I need to see him, now.'

'I don't know where he is. Now, please leave.'

'But…'

Hunter commanded as a Disciple to a Devout. 'You will leave.'

Samuel marched disconsolately back to his rental FusionPlane™ and considered his options. As he boarded the vehicle, he noticed Hunter talking to the Vehicle Technicians, and he was sure that he would be instructing them not to let Samuel go near the house.

He pulled out his Satt™ and dialled up Brady's number. He let it ring and ring, but there was no answer.

Hawk had been chatting with Debrock and his friends inside the house but needed to use the bathroom. A rare occurrence with GreenSuits™, but one of the dabs side effects was that it sometimes made users want to urinate, even if they didn't. He heard a Satt™ ringing for ages. It was coming from his Pops' bedroom. He was about to check it out, but it stopped. He went to his room down the hall and made his futile attempt to pee in the toilet in his en-suite bathroom. He couldn't go.

He staggered lazily back to Debrock's room when he heard the Satt™ ringing again. This time he wondered whether one of his brothers was trying to reach Pops. He picked it up, 'Hello...'

'Brady. Is that you?'

'No. It's Hawk. Pops is in the pool.'

'Could you get him for me?'

'I don't think so. He's all wet, y'know.' There was a short silence.

'Ok.' The Bear added as calmly as he could. 'Is there any way you could take this Satt™ to him? It could be a matter of life and death.'

'Err. I suppose so. Who is this?'

'Samuel Beardon the Third.' When he received no confirmation of recognition, he added, 'I was at your party. When your Daddy left you his share of the business.' The Bear let out a huge sigh. He knew he had to resort to the lowest common denominator, 'I was the big black guy who talked a lot about the Bible.'

'Ah. Yes. I remember you, man. Why didn't you say?'

'Could you do me one more thing?'

'Sure. Shoot.'

'I'm kinda hiding from Hunter, so as a favour to me, could you not let him see you give your Daddy this Satt™ - or any of his staff for that matter.'

'Definitely. Pops doesn't trust Hunter as far as he could throw him. You leave it to Hawk.'

The line was quiet apart from the padding of Hawk's feet on the shiny hard floors. After a while, Samuel Beardon the Third picked up the sound of water and the more distant sounds of the Pacific. But then the sound went muffled. He heard Hawk shout. 'Hey, Hunter. You can fuck off for the day and take the staff with you. I'll look after Pops - we'll have us one of those Father and Sons' days. Do you dig?'

'Yes. Certainly, sir.'

There was a further period of silence, and then the muffled sound turned back into the sound of swimming pools and distant waves. 'Hey, Pops. You gotta call. It sounds real important, and he says that Hunter mustn't know about it. Now, I know you gotta a beef with him, so...' There was the sound of splashing water on tiles, and Samuel guessed that Brady had got out of the pool.

'Who is it?'

Hawk had forgotten the name, 'The black dude from the party with all the church stuff.'

There was the sound of the Satt™ being passed over. 'Good boy, son. You've done well.'

'Cheers, Pops.'

Samuel heard Hawk padding away, and he knew the silence was part of Brady's cautious approach to being caught unawares. Brady spoke first, 'Hey, brother. You use the Satt™ about as often as I do, which is barely ever. It must be important.'

'I got a note that I had to visit you.'

'I didn't send you a note…'

'It was from Tyrone. He left it for me to find in my Bible.'

'I'm real confused, man. I've got no idea what you're talking about.'

'It said I had to come and see you here in Malibu, in person. That it was the last chance, I'd ever get to see Tyrone and Raelynn…'

'What's Raelynn gotta do with this?'

'I wasn't even allowed to tell Alicia.'

'I don't know, man. This sounds fishy to me. Are you setting me up? I know how this goes down. We used to compare notes in prison, y'know. The authorities would always pull this scheme where they'd panic ya and make you rush out without thinking…'

'I'm sitting in a rental FusionPlane™, and Hunter has told your technicians that I'm not allowed to leave the vehicle. They are watching me now, waiting until I take off. I'm not going to do that until I know what's happening with Tyrone and Raelynn.'

There was silence for a few seconds. 'Ok. I'll come to you, but if this is a trap, I swear…'

'It's not a trap. I swear by Almighty God.'

It wasn't Almighty God who troubled Brady. It was Bodhi Sattva. 'I'm not coming down in my dressing gown. I want to be prepared. Give me a few minutes while I get changed. I'll come to you.' He cut the Satt™ off to ensure that the Bear understood that his decision was final.

Brady got changed into all his *Trouble Man* gear as he had come to christen it. He had his NanoRepaired™ jeans, boots and white T-shirt, and his trusty Poacher's coat. He even made sure he had his favourite shades on. He made his way to the Vehicle Lot the long way around. He chose to avoid any lingering staff and technicians, and after about thirty minutes, he crept up to the rear of the Vehicle Lot. He decided not to order the technicians away, as he didn't want any gossip reported back to Hunter. He patiently waited until there was a gap in the informal patrols, and he threw some dirt at the windscreen of the Bear's rental FusionPlane™. The NanoShell™ would protect the FusionPlane™, but he hoped the Bear would look where the flying dirt came from. After a couple more attempts, Brady got the the Bear's attention, and he signalled with walking fingers to let him sneak onto the FusionPlane™.

The Bear left the cockpit and crept to the back of the vehicle, where there weren't any windows. He had his Bible with him. He handed Brady the note from inside the Bible as if this somehow gave it more credibility. Brady read it and handed it back to his friend.

Brady said, 'It's definitely Tyrone's handwriting. I'd recognise it a mile off.'

'But you don't know any more about this?'

'No.'

The Bear scratched his head, and he had the look of utter bewilderment. 'Why would he want me to travel all the way down here to meet you and then not tell you about it?'

Brady considered the possibilities, 'He clearly felt the need to keep it secret - even from Alicia. He intended for me to know about it, but he couldn't get the message through. Sounds like he's in trouble if you ask me.' Brady took off his sunglasses and hung them off the neck of his T-shirt. 'Where would he go if he felt the need to hide? Where would he feel safe?'

The Bear wanted to reassure Brady that this wasn't the old Trad world and that all Greens were safe, but the secrecy of Tyrone's actions made a lie of this assumption. He discounted anywhere in San Martin. He then traced a route from San Martin to Malibu in his mind and extended it southwards. 'He has friends in San Diego. They are astronomers at the Palomar Observatory.'

'Yeah. I've heard him mention that. It's one of the few places that your Green friends didn't dissolve with your goo.'

'We have Green reasons for studying astronomy.' The Bear said, trying not to sound too defensive.

'What are we waiting for? Let's go - seems like as good a place as any to make a start.'

The Bear crept forward and looked out of his cockpit window and waved good-bye, sarcastically, to the watching technician. The technician didn't know that Brady was on board, and the Bear wanted him to think that he'd given up on seeing him. He set the coordinates to the Palomar Observatory, and he put the FusionPlane™ on autopilot and auto-landing. He guessed there would be plenty of places to land in an old scientific research centre, but he was still wary of trusting himself to fly and land in the mountains.

This was the Bear's rental FusionPlane™, and the autopilot settings flew the vehicle about as slowly as he did. Brady used the autopilot when he was tired or busy, but usually, he liked to fly as fast as he could. He sighed and tried not to get frustrated at the slow pace.

The journey to the Palomar Observatory was a relative hop, skip, and a jump from Malibu, and they were at the old National Park inside half an hour. Brady had his face glued to the window as he reeled off the types of trees he spotted. As a Green, the Bear was embarrassed to lack in the knowledge and appreciation of the vegetation that Brady demonstrated.

Brady reeled off names and an occasional whistle as he spotted a particularly impressive species. 'Oh wow…you gotta see this…look at the size of that baby…I'm sure that's a Bigcone…been here for more than five-hundred years…Incense Cedar…

Douglas Fir…Ponderosa Pine…' They soon reached the scrublands high up in the mountains which were traversed with the grey, NanoProtected™ roads.

When they left the FusionPlane™, Brady took in huge gulps of the fresh mountain air. Samuel Beardon the Third hid his frustration with Brady, as he seemed to be treating the situation as no more than a day trip.

Brady strode on ahead and went into the vast entrance hall of the observatory. It amused and troubled him to see that the signs advertising guided tours and an events calendar from 2084 still were on show - as if these had become museum pieces in the intervening hundred years. He yelled, and his voice echoed in this immaculately clean hallway. 'Hey! Service!' He laughed. 'Has anybody seen my friend Tyrone Beardon?'

He thought he heard echoing footsteps, so he stood still and went quiet. The footsteps were heading this way, and then a young man appeared, and Brady thought he looked like his old buddy Lucian in his younger days. He assumed he was probably one hundred years plus - going on twenty-five. Brady said, 'Hey, buddy. I'm looking for a good friend of mine. He seems to have gone missing. His name is Tyrone Beardon. He usually appears as a black, skinny…tall kid, kinda geeky, wears these tortoiseshell glasses…'

'I know you. You're Brady Mahone. Have you got any rare Science Fiction product?'

Brady dug around in one of his big pockets in his Poacher's coat. He always had sample products on him. He pulled out a big handful of Files. 'I ain't sorted them out into categories, but if there's anything here that takes your fancy…' He asked, 'What's yer name, kid?'

'Destin. My male form is Dustin, and my female is Destiny.' He rooted around in Brady's big hands, and he took about half a dozen rare samples. He seemed absorbed in one of them.

Brady said, 'Are you the only one here?'

'Yes. I'm the day shift.'

'Funny, I thought there'd be lots of workers, y'know, scientists and shit.'

'They've taken up other positions on the Mars colony. They're building observatories up there.'

'That's cool. Anyhows, have you seen my good buddy, Tyrone?'

Destin looked suspiciously at the Bear. 'Who's this?'

The Bear said, 'I'm his uncle, Samuel Beardon the Third.'

'Ah. Yes. Of course, you are.' Destin looked around and then back into the face of the Bear. 'Tyrone was right. You have a real problem with letting go, don't you, old man?'

'I don't know what you mean. What has Tyrone been saying? I've loved him like a son…'

'…But he's not your son, is he?'

'Look. Destin. I just want to find out where he is. I think he's in danger.'

Destin laughed, 'The only danger Tyrone is in is from you interfering with his life.

This is why we are so pissed off with the Old Greens. You won your Revolution and built the life that you want, but you don't listen to what we want. In fact, we reject your way of life. What possessed you to think that all we would ever want to do is work in fields and document the local wildlife for the whole of our lives. At least Brady here was bringing us Entertainment Files to fire our imaginations and show us that there are more exciting ways of leading our lives, but what do we get? I'll tell you what you Green Fossils did next. You punished us by depriving us of the UltraViolet™ - God forbid if we want to enjoy ourselves, and then, you try and pin the blame on Brady Mahone. Well, fuck you, we are not so easily fooled.'

Brady said, 'What was Tyrone's beef with Samuel? I've known him a long old time, and he never had a bad word to say about his uncle...'

'Your friend here used his influence with his cronies in Boulder Creek, maybe even with the man, fucking Bodhi Sattva, to pull favours to stop Tyrone's application to go to Mars. It's what Tyrone wanted to do, he had dreamed of something like this for all his life, but this old Green fucker decided for him. Like I said, the Old Greens want us to live their lives - they don't want us to live out our own.'

Brady turned to the Bear, 'Is this true? Did you ask Bodhi to block his application?'

The Bear sighed. 'Yes. I asked Genesis Garcia to arrange it. She put her own son in his place. The one she named after you...'

'I know the one. Real good customer...'

The Bear said to Destin, 'It's true. I did it in his best interests...' Destin shrugged and shook his head at this confirmation that Tyrone's possessive uncle still hadn't got the message. 'But Tyrone left me this note.' He took out the note from inside his Bible, and he passed it to Destin.

Destin read the note and looked up at the two huge men towering over him. 'It looks convincing, but I just need to check with a sample of his handwriting. I'll be back in a minute.'

He marched off with Tyrone's note in his hand and went to the elevators. Brady and the Bear watched the elevator numbers light up as the carriage reached each new level. Then there was a minute's pause followed by the sound of the elevator being shut down.

Brady and the Bear looked at each other. Then Destin's voice came over the Tannoy system. 'Tyrone is my best friend, and I will never betray him. You'll never find me - I know this complex. Fuck Bodhi. Fuck Sattva Systems™ and fuck you!'

20: HUNGER IN A TIME OF PLENTY

Of all the times Rhea didn't want to be called in for a meeting with Bodhi Sattva, it was now. This would throw her timings out, and she cut a frustrated figure as she marched down the corridors toward Bodhi Sattva's spartan office. An image flashed in her mind how this office was like something the Stasi of the old East German Republic would have looked. She smiled at the realisation that she still had a keen sense of the history of the old trad days.

She looked at her watch. Rhea worked out that she had already lost an hour by diverting to Boulder Creek. She hoped Bodhi wouldn't keep her for too long. She knocked on his office door three times and decisively marched in.

Bodhi smiled beatifically, 'My dear Rhea. Thank you for seeing me at such short notice.'

Rhea wasn't sure if the use of the term dear was appropriate, but she couldn't care less about trivialities at this point. 'No problem. What did you want to see me about?'

'I'm keen to understand what Brady Mahone has been up to.'

'Why now?'

'He hasn't been in to collect his Green Credits from his business for quite some time. This is almost unheard of for him. Brady likes his money, and he doesn't usually like to leave it in our care for a moment longer than necessary.'

She resisted the urge to defend Brady, as she knew that there had been numerous times before when he had left his money in Bodhi's trust, especially when he was busy touring the world, establishing new markets. She assumed he was testing her, so she determined that the strategy to adopt was to give him the answers he wanted. 'Brady has scattered his sons to the four corners of the globe to meet up with key Disciples.'

'For what purpose?'

'To influence or plot against you, I assume.'

Bodhi stroked his chin. 'And you know this for a fact?'

'No. But maybe you could check it out - if I gave you the names of the Disciples and the Devout, they have been seeking out...' Bodhi slid a blank piece of paper across his desktop screen which covered his desk, and he selected a pen from an office tidy made from recyclable materials. Without delay, Rhea wrote down the names:

Troy - Bridgett Tarnita

Wilder - Precious

Bill - Cain, Lizzie, and Siddha

Rocky - Glenarvon and Rhea

Hawk - Hunter

Brady - Samuel Beardon the Third, Professor Pinar Dogan, Genesis Garcia, and Bodhi Sattva.

She passed the note nonchalantly over to Bodhi. As he perused the names, he smiled and then laughed as he came to the last name. He quickly returned to a more concerned demeanour. 'The protests emanating from our younger Green communities are troubling. What are your thoughts?'

'They didn't have to put their lives on the line and make the sacrifices that you and the GreenRevs did.'

'But not you?'

'No. I worked for Free News, the Greens' TV Station, but I came to the party late - you could say. I wasn't a GreenRev.'

'What do you think I should do?'

Rhea said without hesitation. 'Give your word that the UltraViolet™ will be given to all at the New Green Year festivities.'

'Is it so wrong of me, that I want them to feel that they have won it, rather than that I just gave it to them - like I have with everything before?'

Rhea shrugged, 'If they win this - what's to say what they will try and win next?'

Bodhi left the question unanswered, he paused for a moment as if it had been considered, but then he changed the subject subtly. 'What do the Disciples and the Devout feel about these protestors?'

'They consider them to be lacking in moral fortitude and generally ungrateful. The Disciples and the Devout have followed every rule to further repair the thousands of years of damage caused by the Trad industries. They were not going to put their reputations at risk by falling to the temptation of the Trad ways - and they certainly weren't going to partake in anything that an old Trad like Brady Mahone was offering them.'

'Have you used any of his entertainment products?'

She thought she detected within his question that he was already confident that he knew the answer. 'No. Never.'

He tapped the paper with the list of names. 'Is there any possibility that anybody here could fall under Brady's spell?'

'None whatsoever.' Rhea knew from her interrogation training to answer decisively.

Bodhi brushed his bald head as if he was sweeping back some imaginary hair. 'I want you to stay out of Rocky Mahone's orbit. I'm sending you to Sweden to contact Bridgett. Ensure she's aware of Troy Mahone's mission.'

Fuck! Please, not now. She thought. 'Sure. When would you like me to go?'

'Sometime in the next couple of days. That will be fine.'

Thank God for that. 'Consider it done. I'll report back on Troy's movements while I'm at it.'

As Rhea left the room, she checked her watch. She knew she was probably already too late. She hurried along the corridors but not so quickly as to attract unnecessary attention. She raced past the Main Entrance - glancing briefly at the one-hundred-year-old banner with the thirteen promises written with Glenarvon Cole's scrawl. She was stressed as it seemed to take forever to pass all the cream-coloured buildings and giant vats to reach the Vehicle Lot.

She located a spare rental FusionPlane™ and was further frustrated when she had to await clearance before she could leave at the back of a queue headed by the other Disciple's privately owned vehicles. As she lifted off, she rapidly headed toward Malibu, hoping she could catch them in time.

She checked the tracking of Brady Mahone's FusionPlane™, FusionPassengerJet™ and his FusionCar™. She breathed a sigh of relief as they were all still in Brady's Parking Lot.

When she touched down at Brady's Malibu home, she was greeted by a technician. 'Hello. How can I help you?'

'I've come to visit, Brady Mahone.'

'Is he expecting you?'

'No. But he will want to see me.'

The technician sneered. 'I'm sure he would, normally. But I'm afraid, Mr Mahone is not currently in residence.'

'Can you call the house? Maybe you could get Hunter to see me?'

'Hunter's services have been dispensed with for the day. He won't be reporting back for duty until tomorrow.'

'Ok. Who is in charge?'

'That would be Hawk.'

'Well, call him, then.'

'Who shall I say is calling?'

Rhea worked in the shadows of the Green hierarchy. Many knew her as a Disciple close to Bodhi, but this person obviously didn't recognise her. She knew that somebody, probably Hunter, had informed Sattva Systems™ of Marjorie's impromptu visit, so she felt she should adopt a fake identity. She considered which names to choose from, where it could gain Hawk's attention but not raise suspicions among Brady's staff.

'Angela Skye.'

'Of course.' He marched away, presumably to discuss this visitor out of earshot.

After a couple of minutes, he returned. 'Hawk will receive you in the main lounge. I'm sure you know the way?'

She didn't, but she wasn't going to let him know that. 'Yes. Thank you.'

Rhea followed the trail to the house, and she came across Debrock on the grounds. He said, stoned, as usual, 'Hey, Rhea. Am I dreaming this? It is you, isn't it?'

'Hello, Debrock. Don't worry. I'm not here to take you home to San Martin. I'm looking for the main lounge. I'm here to see Hawk. You couldn't do me a favour and take me there - could you?'

'Sure thing. You follow me.'

Rhea was conscious of wasting precious time, but stoned Debrock only had one pace - and that was dead slow. They seemed to meander meaninglessly for long minutes until they finally reached the main hall. Hawk didn't say anything as he looked at his uninvited guest. His Pops' paranoia was ingrained in him. He said to Debrock, 'Thanks, man. Hey, I tell you what. Why don't you and your friends use the hot tubs? Pops is away on business, and I'm the only son left, so you have my permission.'

Debrock cheered lazily, 'Yay! That'd be sweet.' He zigzagged away as if he was dancing to an imaginary song.

Hawk said, 'I presume you are the Angela Skye I was waiting for. Funny, I did think that Pops had never mentioned any relatives of Libby.'

'I'm Rhea Laidlaw. Disciple of San Martin...'

'...Close friend of Bodhi and his cronies.'

She had to be careful not to blow her cover or do anything that could arouse suspicions with Bodhi back in Boulder Creek. She already knew she could locate Brady with the tracking device in his coat. 'I really wanted to see Brady. I suppose I should have made an appointment.'

'Pops isn't here. I don't know where he is. I'm sorry.'

'When did he leave?'

'About an hour or so ago?'

'And he's not due back anytime soon?'

'I honestly don't know. I'm sorry you've had a wasted journey and all...'

'It's no problem. It's not that important. I was just asked while I was in the neighbourhood to drop in and let Brady know that he has a lot of Green Credits to pick up in Boulder Creek, but I'm sure he's aware of that already. Anyway, I better be going. I've got a lot of other errands to complete. Would you be so kind as to walk me back to my FusionPlane™? I don't want to get lost. I wouldn't want you thinking the worst of me if I ended up being somewhere I shouldn't.'

'Yeah. No problem.'

As they walked, Rhea was conscious that she needed to find out more, but she had to take it slowly, as she knew Brady's sons were fiercely loyal to him. 'Hawk...you're the youngest, aren't you?'

'Yeah, that's right.'

'And was your Moppa Amie or Helgarth?'

'Amie is my Maddy.'

'Does she ever talk about the days when she was a Trad living at the same ranch as Brady?'

'Sometimes. But she tries not to in front of Helgarth - xe really loves xyr.'

The Parking Lot came into view, 'Brady loves his fleet. I'm surprised he didn't use one of his own private vehicles.'

Hawk carried out the inventory of his Pops' fleet in his mind. She was right. They were all still here. 'Yeah…He musta gone off in that black dude's FusionPlane™.'

Rhea knew that there was a time before the Yellow™ that any remotely racist utterings would have been challenged by the Security Protocols™, but now that anybody could choose any identity, it ceased to become an issue, and the Security Protocols™ sensitivity settings were so broad that it wasn't clear whether this remark could trigger them. All of which was beside the point to Rhea as she had her information.

21: OUT OF TIME

Brady banged his fist on the elevator door a few times. He couldn't bring forth much more in the way of anger and frustration as deep down, it was futile. The Palomar Observatory complex was massive, and Destin would know the place intimately. There was no point in searching for him as they would just be wasting time.

He turned to the Bear, 'Any more ideas? I don't know where he hangs out.'

The Bear went over to the gift shop, which now looked like the tackiest museum in the world, with plastic telescopes, mugs decorated with planets, and Palomar Observatory T-shirts wrapped in plastic. The Bear picked up a map from the bookshop which covered the South-western states. He opened it out and examined it.

Brady was distracted by the T-shirts, and he decided to buy one as a souvenir. He didn't care that it now cost a lot of Green Credits as it was technically an antique. Shortage of Green Credits was not an issue for Brady, so he took out his Distor™ and placed it in the Green Self-Service Receptacle and gave his two-hundred and fifty Green Credits freely.

Welcome to NanoPay™ at the Green Palomar Observatory. NanoPay™ is part of Sattva Systems™ Green Finance Initiative. All proceeds will go to saving Mother Earth. Your custom is important to us. Have a nice Green Day.

Brady had spent the equivalent of two weeks wages of the average Green worker for his T-shirt. He sniffed around his armpit. It was ok, he had showered and bathed this morning, but he was looking for an excuse to put his new T-shirt on. He looked around - out of ancient habits when undressing in a gift shop would be considered bad form. He realised there was only the Bear here, and he didn't count. So, he took off his Poacher's coat and stripped off his trusty white T-shirt and put on his black *I've been to the Palomar Observatory...* on the front, and on the rear of the T-shirt with stars and galaxies pictured within the black cotton it stated for all to see *...and it was out of this world, man!* He looked at himself admiringly in the mirror. He held in his belly and flexed his biceps, and he was pleased with his appearance and physique. He liked this new addition to his wardrobe. Brady stuffed his old T-shirt in one of his Poacher's coat pockets and fingered the other goods on display in the gift shop. He hadn't had a hit of retail therapy lately.

The Bear looked up from his map and was frustrated at Brady's lack of urgency. 'If you've done shopping - we've still got to find Tyrone...'

'Yeah, man. Sure.' He sauntered over and checked out the map the Bear was hunched over. 'Watcha thinking?'

'He was heading south, that's for certain. Otherwise, he'd have never sent me to you. He wanted me to be this neck of the woods.'

'Yeah. Makes sense.'

The Bear circled an area of the map with his chunky forefinger. 'He's got to be south of Malibu.'

Brady moved in closer, 'I've obviously had dealings in all these parts.'

'Any places in particular which mean anything to you and Tyrone?'

'Well, yeah. But I ain't going there?'

'Where?'

'Encinitas. Y'know, where the International Space Station crashed at the turn of the century.'

The Bear was excited. He knew that Brady was onto something. 'Yes. Yes. That's it.'

'It might be, but I can't go there.'

'Why not?'

'Maybe you'd be alright, what with your UltraVioletSuit™ and all. But that place might still be contaminated with all that radiation shit. I ain't taking a risk like that on one of your wild goose chases.'

'I hear you, brother. Can we just check it out by air? It's not far from here. We could do a quick flyover…there's nothing else there…he should be easy to spot…a FusionPlane™ or FusionCar™ should stick out like a sore thumb…'

Brady nodded, 'Ok. I know we are in your rental but promise me you won't land. I mean it…'

'I promise. You have my word.'

They walked back to the FusionPlane™. Brady dumped his Poacher's coat on the rear seat. He put his shades back on while the Bear set the autopilot to fly to Encinitas. Brady quipped, 'Hey, man. I thought we are in a hurry. You do know you can fly faster…'

'Better to be late in this world than early in the next…'

'Yeah, yeah. But I still hate being late.'

They were both quiet as the FusionPlane™ reached the airspace above Encinitas as they scanned the ground from their windows. If there had ever been a nuclear explosion around here, then Mother Nature had done an excellent job of hiding it. They were travelling in Level Two, the lowest level to the ground and usually used by the slowest rental FusionPlane™ pilots. Brady only ever flew at the higher and faster levels, those being Level Four for the quickest FusionPlanes™ or occasionally in Level Five if he took his FusionPassengerJet™ for a spin. They circled slowly over the remnants of Encinitas without spotting anything like another vehicle and certainly nothing resembling Tyrone and Raelynn.

Brady spotted another FusionPlane™ coming in rapidly, two Levels above them. It flew past them. He watched it as it descended, decelerated, and then crept up behind them. 'Hey, man. We're being followed.'

'Who by?'

'I can't see. I don't know.' He was more alarmed when the trailing FusionPlane™ was manoeuvring to overtake them. 'I thought you guys didn't have cops anymore?'

'We don't. The Security Protocols™ replaced them.'

'Well, this sure feels like a cop stop to me.'

The trailing FusionPlane™ pulled up alongside, and they were both shocked to see

Rhea frantically waving to grab their attention. The Bear said, 'She's attached to us in convoy mode.'

Rhea disappeared from the cockpit for a moment and then returned, and she held up cards to the window:

Follow me quickly.

Very little time.

I'm taking you to Tyrone and Raelynn.

Hurry.

Brady shouted, 'Move over, old man. We ain't got time for Granny driving.' He could see Rhea racing away, and he was up for the chase.

The Bear wanted to object, but Brady had already started to slide over from the passenger side. He struggled to move his considerable bulk around the driver's seat. Brady wasted no time taking over the controls and showed little concerns for the Bear's feelings on the matter, 'I'll demonstrate that this baby is built for speed, not comfort, old buddy.' He laughed heartily as he switched to manual flight mode and upped the FusionPlane™ rapidly to Level Four and pushed the vehicle to its' speed limits to try and catch up with Rhea, who was already in the distance.

He struggled but finally squeezed himself around Brady and eventually settled into the passenger seat. 'Why didn't she call me? I've got my Satt™.'

'Same reason Tyrone left you cryptic notes. She doesn't want to be traced or over-heard.'

'Where are we heading?'

'East. I don't know much else. You keep an eye on the ground and the display screens. I'm concentrating on keeping up with her. I think we may have to do some nifty driving when we fly over any major Green areas.'

'Why do you say that?' The Bear struggled to disguise his concern.

'I know you Greens aren't supposed to be nostalgic, but it sure ain't no coincidence to me that every time it's the Holidays, every Level gets packed.' He added to empha-sise his point, 'I don't think it's only the Brady Mahone entertainment products they keep secret from the powers that be - is all I'm saying.'

The Bear couldn't answer. The speed terrified him, and he gripped the sides of his seat as if his life depended on it.

Brady joked, 'Hey, you're the guy with the protective Suits™ on. It's me that should be worried if we crash. Stop being such a pussy.' He added, not too reassur-ingly, 'If we did crash. Do you really think holding onto the chair would do much good? Y'know, in the circumstances?'

'I know. I never did like flying. If God had meant us to be in the skies, he would have given us wings.'

Brady ignored the platitudes. 'Where are we now?' I'm catching Rhea, but she's changing her flightpath slightly…'

'New Green Tucson.'

'Ok. This will be fun.' Brady could see the traffic building ahead, but he also saw that Rhea was dodging and weaving through it without slowing down. 'Jeez, she's one helluva racy lady.' He swooped past any vehicle that wasn't flying at maximum speed, which was every other vehicle on Level Four. The one thing that Brady was grateful for was the innate politeness of the Greens on the road. The Trads in his day would have given him hell and every type of derogatory gesture known to mankind by now. He moved as close as he could to keep on the straightest route, trusting the shield around every Green vehicle to prevent collisions - not just with other travellers but also the flying insects and birds. The traffic eventually thinned out again as they headed over more open land.

The speed of travel didn't stop, but now Brady had Rhea closer to him. The lack of nearby vehicles as reference points made it feel to the Bear as if they had slowed a little. Brady said, 'If we pass over El Paso and then head in the direction of Houston, then I think I can make a pretty good guess on where she's heading for. However, it's gonna be a long flight.'

'The Bear looked away and then at Brady, 'Where?'

'Florida. Cape Cassandra. I think they've got a one-way ticket to Mars.' Brady said, 'Do ya think she's trying to stop them?'

'No. I think she wants us both to have the opportunity to wave them goodbye.'

'Oh. Ok. You mean, Raelynn...'

'Yes. Both of them.'

Samuel Beardon the Third and Brady were both quiet as they considered their options and potential next moves. The likely destination hurt Samuel as he realised, he was losing Tyrone forever, but he also was grateful to Rhea for this second chance to make it right with him. He asked his God to give him the strength he needed to tell him goodbye and to do it with good grace.

Brady, too, was more emotional about losing Raelynn than he ever would admit to another man. He never wanted daughters, but he liked Helgarth's baby girl a lot. He liked her otherworldliness. *Well, she sure is going to be otherworldly now. I ain't gonna blub. I'll have to use some man-up spray as this is gonna be tough for old Brady Mahone.* He was grateful for the distraction of the excuse of rapid flying and overtaking over Green El Paso, but he was also saddened at another piece of evidence confirming his theory. Rhea began to stretch her lead over him in her FusionPlane™, and Brady put it down to his concentration being negatively affected.

The Bear stared disconsolately out of the window and replied to Brady's questions and cajoling with grunts and curt phrases until Brady knew to leave him be. He occasionally heard the Bear praying for strength and forgiveness in hushed tones.

They came upon a massive amount of air traffic over Houston. Brady cursed and gestured angrily. 'Fucking Greens! If I had my own FusionPlane™ and not your rental piece of shit, I coulda headed to Cape Cassandra like the crow flies. But no - life's never that fucking simple. You have to restrict the air traffic within imaginary columns above the road network. Fucking dickwads. If we fucking miss them because of these bastard cheating Greens going home for the Holidays...' He gestured angrily and shouted uselessly as he slowly passed a woman pilot with a kid next to her. 'Hey, lady. Only Trads are allowed to celebrate the Holidays, and you murdered the fucking lot of them. Yeah, so go back home.' She looked across at Brady, and this only encouraged him, 'I wish you fucking Greens had died and not the fucking Trads. You hypocritical fuckers make me sick...yeah, I'm talking to you, bitch.'

She turned her head away, and Brady could tell she had instructed the kid to look the other way. He turned to see the Bear glaring at him. Brady let out a deep breath and shrugged, 'I told ya, didn't I? This is Holiday traffic…ok, ok, I shouldn't have let it get me so mad…'

He felt his FusionPlane™ tug, and a warning came on his screen:

Hand over controls to Disciple remote capture. Y/N?

He didn't feel he had a choice. The traffic on all Levels from One to Four had come to a standstill. He said, 'Yes.'

The FusionPlane™ seemed to move of its' own accord out to the edge of the traffic and over an imaginary hard shoulder. It then moved so close to Rhea's FusionPlane™ that it felt like it was attempting to dock with it. And then both vehicles sped away - not at maximum speed but at least at a rate quick enough to let Brady's blood pressure fall to a more natural rate.

Once through the traffic jams of Houston, the FusionPlanes™ undocked, and they raced at maximum speed and Brady knew what was happening; they could only fly at half-speed in convoy. Therefore, he knew that if they couldn't bypass the traffic quickly, then Rhea would use this tactic again. They travelled with little difficulty over Green Beaumont and New Green Lafayette but docked once more over the congested New Green Orleans. They had no problems with Green Pensacola and New Green Tallahassee, but they needed the convoy mode to make their way through the final major obstacle of Green Orlando, and then they finally arrived in the vicinity of Cape Cassandra.

22: ROCKETS AND DREAMS

The rental FusionPlanes™ docked again as they glided slowly over the Green Port of St John and onto Green Merritt Island. Brady trusted Rhea to know what to do next. He relinquished his controls to let both FusionPlanes™ land together.

Brady alighted the FusionPlane™ looking like a tourist, with his black T-shirt and shades on. The Bear followed him out, muttering complaints under his breath. Rhea said, 'Hi. You two.'

The Bear growled to Brady, 'You drive like a mad man, and you should show more respect to your fellow travellers…'

'Hey, wait a minute. They shouldn't be travelling today, not in those numbers, and you know it. You're just taking their side…'

Rhea laughed, 'You remind me of my old mum and dad, with your bickering. They were always the same, every holiday, no matter how much my mum would promise not to lecture dad on his driving, or how he would promise to take it easy on the gas…'

Brady and Samuel both looked at the ground and made some uncommunicated agreement to drop the argument on the grounds that it was making them look bad. Brady said, 'Long time, no see. Good to see you again, Rhea. I keep meaning to bump into you, but you're a hard lady to track down.'

'Good to see you too, Brady.' She kissed him lightly on the cheek. 'You wouldn't believe how much work I have to do. I think some people think that being a Disciple is a stroll in the park. Anyway, there's very little time - you'll have to follow me.'

The Bear said, 'Will I get to meet Tyrone before he goes?'

'No. I'm sorry. We are too late for that. I knew it would be a struggle with the traffic. That's why I flew at maximum speed. However, if we are lucky, we might be able to see them pass by as they board the FusionSpaceShuttle™. Come on.'

She marched away, and Brady and the Bear encouraged their stiff legs to run after her. She was waved through checkpoints as if the guards were already aware of her arrangements, and Brady knew that every minute she saved them was precious if they were to make it on time.

At the final checkpoint, Brady could hear Rhea confirming her position as Disciple of San Martin and confirming that she had escorted the close relatives of the astronauts to see them off on their journey to Mars. He watched the guards eye him suspiciously, and Brady wondered whether it would matter whether they recognised him or not. He recalled the feeling of trying to sneak on a ride that he was too small for when he was a kid. The checkpoint guard stood to one side, and Rhea waved them through. She gestured for them to join her on an escalator with no sides which rose more than a hundred feet into the air.

The Bear was less freaked out than Brady about travelling on this. Rhea said, 'It has a NanoShell™ over it for uninterrupted vision. You cannot fall or jump for that matter.' She joked. 'This Shell™ is impenetrable. It's the same when you reach the viewing platform at the top. It's protected from the sub-sonic booms of the blast-off.' She wagged her finger at them, 'So, no Sonic Boom Surfing for you boys.'

Brady found it hard to relax. He had entered their impenetrable Shells™ before when it should have been impossible for him to do so. What if the reverse could happen here? What if he could fall through it? He had a sense of vertigo, which wasn't helped by the thought that a sub-sonic boom could blow him off the platform if the structure was geared for Greens and not Trads. He was on a stairway to heaven with no means of getting off.

When the escalator let him off at the end, Brady was greeted by a bridge with no sides and far above the ground. His legs felt heavy. He wouldn't have minded revealing his fear to the Bear, but he desperately wanted to keep his masculinity intact for Rhea. He took one leaden step after another until Rhea selected the spot for them to observe from. Brady stood straight, but his body wanted to sway into the void. He reached out tentatively, and he touched the NanoShell™. He wanted to feel something, he expected it to feel squishy and filmy, but instead, it felt tough like reinforced glass or Perspex. He sighed and caught a glimpse of Rhea smiling at him.

'Hey, you Greens are used to this. Us mere Trads can still be killed easy like, y'know.'

'As if I would let anything bad happen to you, the great Brady Mahone, the Trad King of the World.' If she was playing him then it worked, as Brady stood straight and tall as if watching over an empire. It eased his mind as other Greens came up to him and greeted him as if he was a movie star being among them. These were brief encounters for the Greens on the viewing platform, as their attention was pulled back to the walkway that briefly ran parallel to their own, the walkway that would lead to the FusionSpaceShuttle™ mission to colonise Mars - a mission that used to take months had been whittled down to weeks with the advent of Sattva Systems™ FusionPower™.

And then the cheers rang out amid spontaneous clapping and the shouting of the names of loved ones. He loved the look of pride on Rhea's face. It was the look of a woman who had achieved her mission against all odds. She caught him looking at her, and she gestured him to put his eyes forward in case he missed it.

There were dozens in the procession. The astronauts didn't need space suits like he remembered from times long since passed. They had their UltraVioletSuits™, and Brady thought he could make out a misty green bubble around them. He recalled the bubbles his Pops described when he first brought him up to speed with how Sattva Systems™ had made their money in the early days. They rescued the aviation industry with their use of NanoBubbles™ for each passenger in the wake of the three pandemics of the 2020s and 2030s. He wondered if this was an extension of that to help them survive the spaceflight and thrive on Mars.

'There he is. I can see him. Tyrone. Tyrone!' The Bear jumped up and down as he desperately waved, hoping for Tyrone to see him among the crowd.

Brady bellowed across the void, 'Hey, Tyrone…Raelynn!' He saw Raelynn look over, and then she nudged Tyrone, and then he saw Brady Mahone and his Uncle Sam waving vigorously. They shouted uselessly back and forth, but their words were lost like all the others in the din. But just like all the other astronauts and the crowds which had come to see them off, the smiles and the tears were evident for all to see. Brady found it difficult to contain his emotions and was grateful for the chance to release them by playing the fool. Tyrone pointed at him. He pointed at him again and laughed and then mockingly bowed. He said something to Raelynn, which she obviously thought was hilarious, and then she looked at Brady as if she was touched by his loving gesture. It was then that he remembered the black T-shirt he was wearing proclaiming proudly: *I've been to the Palomar Observatory.* He laughed loudly enough to force back the tears. He pointed to the front of his T-shirt to leave no doubt that he got the joke. He then turned to show them the punchline: *...and it was out of this world, man!* As he turned, Rhea grabbed his hands and kissed him as if somebody had just announced that the war between the Trads and the Greens was over. She pulled away and smiled, and then she promptly turned him around before he could lose the last vital seconds of waving his loved ones away, forever.

He was giddy as he felt as if his legs would buckle under the sheer joy and sadness he felt in that moment. He watched Tyrone, and Raelynn put all their effort into one last wave goodbye, and then they slowly disappeared from view. The Bear was sobbing pools of tears, and he grabbed Brady and hugged him, and buried his head in his shoulders to hide the fact that he was crying. He felt the heat and dampness from the tears soak into his new T-shirt. He felt awkward hugging his friend. He saw many others in the viewing crowd doing precisely the same with no shame or embarrassment. He slapped the Bear on the back and then hugged his fellow giant of a friend to give the Bear and himself the comfort they needed.

After a minute, they unwound from each other awkwardly. It was then that Brady realised that Rhea had gone.

23: WITHOUT YOU

Brady let the Bear fly the FusionPlane™ back to Malibu. If he wanted to fly like a granny on weed, then that was fine by him. He looked out at the passenger window wistfully, trying to land his emotions without crashing.

He was grateful that the lift-off had gone without a hitch - and that he had been entirely safe on the viewing platform as it had been completely insulated from the sub-sonic booms. He knew it was useless, but it still didn't stop him from checking out every crowd for a glimpse of Rhea.

The FusionPlane™ made quiet if painfully slow progress westwards across the Green States of America - its given name from the New Year onwards in 2185. There were other changes planned, which Brady had no intention of adopting. It had recently been announced that the Green citizens would be adopting GreenMetricTime™ or GMT™, something which had caused consternation among the Greens, young and old alike. Sattva Systems™ believed it would simplify their calculations and computational power as they worked on the next big project - that of saving the Earth from a future cataclysmic event, with the advent of the Sun turning into a super-red giant star over the next few billions of years. They would be adopting measures of one thousand days, which meant three imperial years would become one GreenMetricYear™, which would then be split into one-hundred Green Intervals, each comprising of ten Green Days.

There were already protests about the haves and have-nots of the UltraViolet-Suits™, and to many Greens, this felt like a deliberate act of provocation from Sattva Systems™. All old mechanisms of marking time were scheduled to be replaced in the New Green Year, and the Security Protocols™ were rumoured to be set to challenge anybody using Traditional or Trad-Time, as it became more colloquially known.

Brady knew he didn't have a strong suit for math, and he couldn't get his head around one hundred Green hours, with ten Green minutes each comprising of a thousand Green seconds. He wondered if it would be easier for him to resort to the phases of the Moon if they found some way to stop his watches and clocks. He knew they would win in the end. The powers that be always did. When the metric system came in, most of the world caved into it, but America held out for as long as it could. He always used the imperial measurements, but slowly but surely, the scientists and the engineers turned to metric measurements. He knew that the Satts™ were already programmed to switch to the New Green Time on New Year's Day, and that would force people to become accustomed to it. This new development seemed to be the last straw for Brady's willingness to play in this New Green World. Maybe he was getting too long in the tooth to be a player anymore.

The blue sky gave him the impression that they were barely moving at all, and he was dismayed when he looked down to see they were passing a busy Green area and then checking the display screen to see that they had only travelled as far as Green Pensacola. Brady sighed, and the Bear barely acknowledged him.

'What do you think is going on?' Brady said, trying to break the ice.

'What do you mean, brother?'

'I dunno. The long-term plan which Bodhi is working on. Do you think he will let everybody have the UltraViolet™?'

'I think he will, eventually. If I were Bodhi, I would want the younger Pure Greens to be more grateful for what we had to go through to save the planet. They have become accustomed to the easy life.'

'What's it like, y'know, the UltraViolet™? Does it make you feel any different? I don't want to get deep and heavy, but today has kinda got to me.'

'I feel you, brother. It has had a profound effect on my soul. I thought I'd experienced all there was in life, but life has a habit of giving you something new to consider.'

'So, are you going to tell me what it's like to wear the UltraViolet™?'

The Bear fiddled nervously with the flight controls and then double-checked that he had correctly put it into autopilot. 'You know I can't divulge…'

'Ok. I get it. But surely you can talk about vague stuff, maybe even spiritual differences…' Brady felt as if he had made a mistake, in the same way as if he had asked a question about the night sky to Tyrone. He half hoped that the Bear would refuse to answer. He watched the Bear's facial movements and concluded that he wasn't going to be able to get out of this now.

'I am the same man, deep inside, that I ever was.'

'Just go along with me here. I'm not questioning your faith…' Brady bargained. 'But let's say you are 80% Nanoparticles and 20% human; does that mean that only 20% of you worships God?'

The Bear laughed, 'That was almost spoken as a man of science, my friend. When I die, I will be 0% human, but my soul will be 100% spirit, and God will welcome me to Heaven if I am well judged by him. Heaven is 0% Earth, and yet my spirit will reside there for eternity.' He was pleased that Brady didn't retort immediately. Brady put his hand on his chin and then pushed his fingers through his stubbly grey-black hair on his head and stared out of the window.

Minutes passed before Brady said, 'I think I had one of those near-death experiences, y'know.'

'You mean you nearly died? When was this, brother?'

'Not me. No, I was thinking about a time, more than forty years ago, when I attended Mrs Wilson's funeral.'

'Mrs Wilson?'

'Oh, sorry. You wouldn't know her. She was an old woman I knew in West McFarland, I mean, Green McFarland as it's known now.'

'It doesn't matter. What happened with this Mrs Wilson?' the Bear asked gently, as he assumed his role in San Martin as a preacher and spiritual guide.Brady was uncomfortable with the memory. He took a deep breath as he prepared to revisit the horror of that day. 'It was like she was two different people living inside the same body.' He paused to gather his thoughts. He wasn't sure if he understood the depths; he was about to travel. 'If I put this wrong, then I'm not trying to offend anybody - least of all you…'

'I understand. Go on.' He smiled.

'At first, I thought I saw a ghost, her ghost, everybody did, even the Greens were

screaming, but it was her NanoSuit™ rising out of the grave. Not Mrs Wilson…
it wasn't her…it was just her NanoSuit™ leaving the grave like it had a mind of its
own.'

'That must have been very scary - even for you. I've never seen this phenomenon,
but I know about the recycling. What happened next?'

'It was disorientated. It was the time when Bodhi was ill, do you remember that?'

'Absolutely. Many of my faith equated that with Jesus's walking into the wilderness.'

Brady was concerned about being side-tracked from his story and being led into
one of the Bear's Bible tales. 'Bodhi was safely tucked away in a Sensory Deprivation Chamber and wheeled away to a storage room with dozens more of them. It was
like a morgue. Anyway, Bodhi wasn't in the wilderness. He was in a stockroom in
Boulder Creek…'

'Of course. You were saying?'

'Yeah. It was weird. Mrs Wilson kept turning slowly and then stopping at intervals
as if she was tuning into something. And then she found me. I'm not explaining this
very well. Of course, Mrs Wilson didn't find me - her NanoSuit™ did. It tried to jump
me, like a drunk broad in a nightclub. It was fucking horrible.' He grimaced as he
vividly recalled the slimy substance trying to envelop him. 'I forced it off me, man. It
was horrible. I was glad to see the back of it.'

'Is that what troubles you. I assure you that if you took the Green, the feeling of
wearing the NanoSuits™ is joyous. You felt the effects of a second-hand and old
Suit™, not a new one.'

'It's not that. I wondered if she was giving me her soul.'

The Bear was astonished at this thought. 'No. It was a recycled NanoSuit™. The
soul cannot physically manifest itself…'

'Not even with the smallest of particles and the technology of the greatest minds
that ever lived?'

'No. What you saw, and what you experienced on that dreadful day, was the recycling of Nanoparticles. Nothing more.'

Brady nodded, 'I don't want to argue with you. After all, you're the expert.' He
paused, 'And it makes me feel better to tell you the truth.'

The Bear laughed warmly, 'Glad to be of service, brother.'

It wasn't the end of the matter for Brady, though. The FusionPlane™ glided serenely along, but Brady knew he had only reached third base. His mind was a whirl
of recollections from the past. He thought of his Pops and the Mahone Ranch and
the Los Banos files in his bunker. He thought wistfully of his times with Lucian,
Mary-Lou, and Amie, and he considered his unlikely friendship with Professor Yuan
Chu and Judge Audre Jefferson. He wanted to reread her two-hundred-page summary. Brady now appreciated the trouble she had taken to make it palatable for him to
digest. He also recalled his *Crime of the Century* in blackmailing Bodhi into making
him the richest man in the world. He still had those incriminating files as an insurance
policy. Maybe they could be wheeled out again and used as leverage? However, he
hated it when even criminals went back on their word. But still…He dwelled on this
pact he had with Bodhi. Bodhi had never mentioned it again. But why would he?

'Hey, man. Instead of going to Malibu, could you drop me off at my ranch in Mc-Farland?'

The Bear fiddled with the controls and checked it three times until he was reassured that he had correctly entered the details. 'Consider it done, friend.'

While Brady was thinking about Bodhi, he said almost absent-mindedly, 'Do you think Bodhi believes he has saved their souls?'

Samuel Beardon the Third took a moment to jump back on-board Brady's train of thought, 'I'm sorry. What?'

'He's recreated parts of your bodies with his Nanoparticles. I mean - you could be 80% Nano…'

'…You are the one that put a figure on it. I have no idea.' He was conscious not to have given away too much information on the UltraViolet™.

'Ok. But you've got to admit that if his scientists and engineers have made this much progress…'

'I'm sorry, Brady. But as much as I'd love to believe that Bodhi is dedicated to Christianity, he is ultimately a scientist and engineer.'

'I'd have said businessman.' Brady corrected. 'Just go with me here. Would he experiment with the idea if it didn't cost anything? I mean, it's not just the Nanoparticles he is recycling. Mrs Wilson still had the essence of Mrs Wilson, I know, I felt it.' He involuntarily squirmed. 'Bodhi wanted her to go to him. He was her light at the end of death's tunnel. And it isn't just Mrs Wilson, is it? It's every dead Green. He's collecting their discarded NanoSuits™ and their memories and feelings.' He looked into the eyes of the Bear, 'If it isn't collecting souls, then it's the next best thing.'

For the first time in his life, the Bear tried to retreat from discussing the Bible and its teachings. 'I agree with it feeling unethical, but not from a religious point of view but from Green perspective. This feels more akin to the data mining from the twenty-first century Trad tech companies. If Bodhi is at fault, and I'm not saying he is, but if he is, then he could be accused of a borderline Trad crime.' He said resolutely. 'I will question Bodhi on the ethics of this.'

Brady laughed. 'Ok. Cool. I'm on a roll now. You don't mind, do you? It's just that you seem a little aggravated, old man.'

The Bear shook his head and laughed, 'You certainly know how to make this flight go quicker. What's next from the pulpit of Brady Mahone?'

'Ok. Get this. Bodhi is always one step ahead of the rest of the world when it comes to NanoSuits™, am I right? When you were all Red™, he was Orange™ and so on?'

'This is correct, but he also stated that one day we would all be equal, and that day has come for those who now are UltraViolet™.'

'I'm not buying that. I think he is always going to stay one step ahead of you.'

The Bear chuckled. 'Bodhi has never been a cult of personality type. He lives and works simply, humbly. His whole life has been dedicated to fulfilling our wishes, not the other way around. It was the Greens who gave him the commandments, not God handing the tablets to Moses. You have him all wrong, my friend. He is a good man, and he helped bring peace and stability to the human race.' He added before Brady could retort, 'I know there are some who desire more out of life, and who are stirring up trouble, but even this, I see as Bodhi's plan, and just because I don't understand it, doesn't mean it won't turn out alright in the end. I trust him. Whenever I have doubted him, he has always come through on the big issues. My personal problems are trivial when they stand beside the goal of saving Mother Earth.'

If he thought that his summary was the last word on the subject, then Brady was about to disappoint him. 'I don't know much about this Moses dude, but I know criminals. I think he's like your Godfather of the Green Mafia...'

'Bodhi shows no desire for accumulating money.'

'Some of the gangland bosses had so much money that I doubt if they could count it. They had other motivations. It was about power and respect. They used to bang on about family, but it was more about ego. They were self-important...'

'I'm unconvinced. Bodhi can be challenged without fear of reprisals...'

Brady chewed this over and then spat out, 'I think he's handing out reprisals right now.' He asked, 'Do you think Bodhi would ever just retire? Y'know, step back and let someone else take over. I dunno, Sissy or Glen?'

'Those are questions that are above my pay grade. I wouldn't want to see that happen. Bodhi Sattva is wiser and more knowledgeable than any other candidate.'

'Ok. Yeah. Bodhi's into accumulating knowledge, wisdom...'

'Nothing wrong with that, brother.'

'I wish Professor Chu or Judge Jefferson was here. A clever Trad would help a brother out here.' Brady muttered.

He looked out of the window and was glad he had suggested going to McFarland instead of Malibu, if only because it was a change of route on this long flight home. He looked at a significant Green blot on the landscape, and his display screen indicated that they were now flying over Green Albuquerque. They were heading into the latter stages of their return journey. Brady kept his thoughts to himself for a while. Apart from when he chuckled when the screen informed them that below was the Petrified Forest. He wondered how a forest could be scared.

Brady berated himself for being grumpy company, 'Hey. Do you think Tyrone and Raelynn will be ok?'

'I can't lie. I'm really gonna miss Tyrone. Rhea helped me rectify the biggest mistake in trying to stop him from leaving.'

'If it helps, then I know that Raelynn loves him. I know it ain't been long, but it must have been a massive decision to leave behind the luxury of Malibu to go with him to another world.'

The Bear said softly, 'You didn't upset me with your questions earlier. It's good to challenge entrenched positions. Take Raelynn, for instance. It's like you were saying, the younger generation are getting bored of Green way of life, I'm not stupid, I see it. I just took it personally that Tyrone could feel like that, and as for Raelynn, I guess there's no challenge in having it all from the moment you were born. It's always been true that familiarity breeds contempt. I didn't mean...'

'I know. You aren't the sort to go scoring points off people. You've never tried to break my balls. I've always liked that about you.' He added, 'It's kinda capturing the old American pioneering spirit - heading off to a new frontier on Mars. Don'cha think?'

'Yes. I suppose it is, like the Mayflower heading to the New World.'

Brady didn't know what the Mayflower was but guessed he agreed with him. 'I know that Glenarvon Cole disagrees with this business of colonising Mars. He told me so. He thinks they are betraying this world and that Mother Earth should be restored with the resources we have, and not wasting them on messing with other pristine worlds.'

'I can empathise. Glenarvon Cole has a pure heart.'

'Yeah. He's ok. I like the guy. I know he doesn't trust me - me being a Trad and all, but I never sense that he wants to give me grief about it.' Brady recalled Glen clambering up the old, abandoned rocket in Cape Canaveral, and it made him smile. It was his sense of doing it for the fun of it and not because there was a specific reason. 'You know when we were talking about souls, and you were kinda saying that humans - or even part-humans as I was playfully accusing you UltraViolet™ Greens - you indicated that we have souls made from a kinda spirit material?'

The Bear wasn't keen on returning to this topic, but evidently, Brady was still striving to ease his mind. He wondered whether Brady was preparing for his own death. He had seen countless conversions to Christianity in the latter stages of life, especially in the pre-Revolution days. He reminded himself to view Brady Mahone as a very old man under his still youthful exterior. He took a deep breath, and reset his tone to one of a preacher, and not as a buddy to this mere mortal. 'It's a close enough analogy for the purpose of our discussion. I would have said not close enough for scientists, but they don't believe in souls.'

Brady said, 'Are all these Nanoparticles you have in your Suits™ the same size?'

'Now that is quite a question, and not one I'm really qualified in answering.' He laughed. 'However, I did receive training in my old job as a NanoSprayer, and we were told that our sprays consisted of a mixture of Nano and Microstructures. These Microstructures were far more dense and larger than the Nanoparticles, by powers of ten.'

'I don't know what that is. But basically, you say they weigh something?'

'Yes. The RedSuits™ had a tiny but barely noticeable weight, as they were made of Microstructures with an interactive NanoCoating™. The same with the Yellow™ as these had to imitate textile materials. However, the Orange™ was pure Nano as these operate within the human body. So, the short answer to your question is that our NanoSuits™ have a trace amount of weight but a high amount of density.'

Brady didn't want to ask for an explanation of density, but he thought it was interesting that the Greens wore the NanoSuits™, well, some of the Suits™, others were a part of their inner bodies. It explained how he felt as if he was being smothered by Mrs Wilson. It also made sense that the Greens called them Suits™ like they were dressed in something, even if it was lightweight. The Bear watched Brady working it all out as if he could picture the cogs in his mind turning. 'Have you ever changed weight? Y'know, the last time I weighed myself, I was about two-hundred and fifty pounds. If I had all these Suits™ of yours, would I still weigh the same?'

'You are in a strange mood, my friend.' He laughed. 'After all this time, don't tell me you would have become a Green to lose a few pounds in weight. I don't think going Green was ever sold as a new dieting fad.' They both laughed, and it broke the tension for a moment. 'The answer to your question is that we did lose a little weight. But that was mostly due to the reduction in water usage and retention due to the GreenSuits™. I think most of the other repairable parts of our bodies were replaced cell by cell.' The Bear laughed softly. 'Where are you going with this, friend? I thought you knew all of this already.'

'I've never been into the science stuff. I kinda understood at some level.' Brady laughed, 'Usually when I was having intimate relations with a Green. I knew they were solid and felt the same as the Trads I'd slept with. Sorry, man - too much information, I know, but I knew the Greens I slept with were neither more solid nor hollow than the Trads. They were the same as they ever were.' Brady added, 'I was just wondering if say the UltraViolet™ Greens weighed the same with say, 80% Nanoparticles, then would Bodhi still weigh the same if he was 100% Pure Nano. I bet that's what he'd call it, Pure Nano, just like the Greens born after the Revolution were called Pure Greens.' He muttered, 'He'd like that - Pure Nano.'

'What makes you think he's Pure Nano, as you say?'

'I figured out what drives him. Once you've done that, then it kinda makes sense where he would go next - that's if he hasn't already done it.'

'Go on.'

'It's not money, power or respect he craves. It's progress. The rest is easy.'

The Bear scratched his head. 'I don't see that…'

Brady said, 'He let all the Trads die because he had no use for them. He needed the Greens to do all the work to save the planet. But I think he's replacing you from within. You've gone through all your colours from InfraRed™ to UltraViolet™, and if it was 10% at a time, then maybe you are 90%, not 80%, Pure Nano already. There's only 10% left of you, my friend.'

24: STRIKE

The FusionPlane™ came into to land at the Mahone Ranch. After such a long journey, Brady insisted that The Bear should stay for dinner. The Bear was still deeply troubled with Brady's theories, but he didn't want to discuss it further with him. The implications were massive. Humanity was either being set up for extinction or, more benignly, it was on the verge of evolving into a new race of Pure Nano beings. He searched his teachings in the Bible and wondered if they applied to non-humans if indeed that's what they might become. He began to doubt whether he had chosen the wrong path but couldn't reconcile this with the counterargument that an ex-con without a religious bone in his body had chosen correctly.

Samuel Beardon the Third had barely ever visited the town of McFarland in his long life, and this was his first visit to the Mahone Ranch. Brady was keen to move the subject on. He had made his connections in his mind but hadn't found the philosophical crisis which his friend had. Brady had always thought the Greens, or more specifically, Bodhi Sattva was up to something. He'd thought he had busted his criminal plans and nothing much more serious than that. He was more concerned about how Brady Mahone was being used in the heist.

After they had eaten, Brady gave the Bear the tour of the property. He showed him where Amie lived and slept before she ended up in the Bear's care in San Martin. Brady talked proudly about the barn and his Green Bike, which was instrumental in the start of his business. Brady chuckled as he recalled taking the trailer by force from the bad-mouthed neighbour of Small Hand Don. He stressed to the Bear how he started without a Green Credit to his name and how he had forged his own international business. Brady even showed Samuel Beardon the Third his bunker and his collection of Los Banos police reports, all securely wrapped up in plastic. Temptingly, the two-hundred-page summary laid untouched in its plastic outer on Archie Mahone's old bench.

This overwhelming wave of nostalgia made Brady insist on retracing his movements with the Bear of that very first day after the Green Revolution back in 2084. He suggested they walk to West McFarland - now Green McFarland. The Bear agreed, and he wanted to know how the first days of the Revolution felt from Brady's point of view.

They walked for about twenty minutes, and Brady talked excitedly about protecting Mrs Wilson from the Hodgson Boys and how he fell through the GreenShell™ for the first time. As they strolled into Green McFarland, they were both taken aback by the sight that greeted them on the edge of McFarland Park. There was an open-air encampment of about a dozen young but emaciated Greens.

He saw Lizzie pleading with her pupils and ex-students. 'You must eat. You will die, and it will all be for nothing.'

A Green of indeterminate gender acted as the spokesperson for the group, 'We no longer accept the validity of your teachings. We are second-class citizens, and we are not free.'

'I'm sure Bodhi will give everybody the UltraViolet™…' Lizzie implored.

'It's no longer just about the UltraViolet™. We no longer want to work forever as slaves to Her.' He emphasised *Mother* Nature to suggest that she was a binary sexist and traitor. His cutting remark slashed at Lizzie's pleadings. 'We want to live our lives as free citizens - or not at all.' The starving Greens cheered feebly, and Brady could sense that they hadn't long to live.

Brady cheered sarcastically. 'I've been saying that along. You Greens should get out more.'

Lizzie snapped, 'You're not helping, Brady.'

'Why should I? It's your mess. I'm just surprised it took so long.' He looked over at the Bear. 'Sorry, man. I think we'll have to postpone. This situation has kinda taken the edge off.'

Lizzie said, 'Brady has never had any manners. I'm Lizzie, the Green McFarland Educator.' She shook the Bear's hand.

'I'm Samuel Beardon the Third. I'm the preacher for San Martin. You've probably gathered that I'm an old friend of Brady's.'

'Oh, you're a Green Educator, now. You used to be a teacher…' Brady quipped.

'Please. Ignore him. I think that should be a Green rule, personally.' Lizzie looked at the Bear, 'Are you one of the Devout?'

'Yes. I'm UltraViolet™.'

'We are having a gathering of the Disciples and the Devout at our Green Town Hall. We have an important update from Bodhi. You probably have the File waiting for you back home, but I thought you might like to join us?'

The Bear looked across at Brady, who said, 'I'm whacked. You do what ya gotta do, man. Ain't no skin off my nose.'

'I would like to see his latest message. It might have something which could alleviate the tensions and offer a message of hope to our young protesters.' The Bear nodded in the direction of the Green hunger strikers.

'No problem, man.' He glanced at Lizzie, 'I'm sure you don't mind dropping him off at my place to pick up his rental FusionPlane™.'

'I can do that.'

'Good. I won't wait up.' He said to the Bear. 'I'll catch up with you the next time I'm in San Martin. I won't forget today. I had a blast.' He turned and marched away before the Bear could reply.

Lizzie and Samuel ambled over to the New Green Hall. Siddha was on stage with a projector set up, ready for the viewing. He was issuing orders and micromanaging the event. Lizzie guided Samuel to a couple of free chairs at the back. About twenty people were in attendance, and many of these were the original GreenRevs, known for their bravery, devotion, and fanaticism for the Green cause. One or two others were her ex-pupils, and she was proud that they had turned their backs on temptation. She pointed discreetly toward the stage. 'That's Siddha. He's the Green McFarland Disciple. We share the same home. Have you met him before?'

'I've seen him several times at the Sattva Systems™ HQ, but I've never spoken to him at length.'

'What do you do in Boulder Creek?'

'I'm a long-time friend of Bodhi…'

'Really. Then we have an honoured guest among us.'

Siddha called for silence. He then led them in reciting the Green prayer:

Our Mother.

Who art Heaven on Earth.

For what we are about to receive

May we be truly grateful

And lead us not into temptation.

Show us the way.

Siddha signalled to one of the old GreenRevs to play the movie, as Vance was not one of the Devout, and therefore his services were dispensed with for the evening. As Siddha left the stage to take up his seat at the front and centre of the audience, the short movie began. The title credits rolled, followed by a screen with the Sattva Systems™ logo in moss green against a cream background. And then the head and shoulders of Bodhi appeared, and it was apparent that the movie was shot in his sparse office in Boulder Creek.

The audience cheered their leader's emergence on screen. Bodhi spoke softly, not in the manner of a Trad Leader of old, who may have spoken pompously in reverence at their own self-importance at addressing a global audience of more than twenty-six million Disciples and the Devout and the owners of the UltraViolet™. Bodhi's words were as quiet as if he was talking to everyone as a trusted confidant.

'My dearest friends, the bravest of the GreenRevs, my most trusted Disciples and the purest Green citizens of the Devout. I have important updates I want to share with you, and I will attempt to answer frankly some of the topics which are causing you the most concern.'

The New Green Hall was utterly silent.

'Firstly, to put today's issues into context, I want you to visualise where we came from, to illustrate just how much we have achieved.'

Movie footage shone out for fifteen minutes, with the horrors of what humanity had inflicted upon the Earth in the time of the Trads. Along with visions of toxic waste plants, dying animals, birds and plant life, there were sequences of violent storms intermingled with the laughing decadence of the wealthy elite.

Bodhi reappeared, 'You, my Green friends, have ensured, through your hard work and dedication, that Mother Earth will never suffer harm, such as you have witnessed, ever again. You should take pride in your accomplishments, and I thank you with all my heart for your sacrifices.'

There was a short pause as if he had deliberately intended to leave time for reflection.

'I now want to discuss some of our trickier issues, and I need your help.' Bodhi's bald head glittered under the harsh lighting of his office. His apparent lack of make-up endeared him to his audience, as it was the Trads who were so obsessed with their self-image. 'Many of you are wondering why we have left the Security Protocols™

on a broader tolerance setting.'

There were murmurs in the audience, indicating that he was tackling the controversial subjects.

'The research, development and investment in the UltraViolet™ program is massive. However, if I believed it would lead to a population of productive workers who were wholly committed to serving Mother Earth, I would authorise the issuing of the UltraViolet™ to all nine-hundred-million Greens on the planet, without a moment's hesitation. However, this would be a thousand-year commitment for all of us, and I wanted to be certain that I wouldn't waste Her resources. The Disciples, The Devout and my beloved GreenRevs have nothing to prove to Sattva Systems™, which is why we gave you the UltraViolet™ freely.'

The GreenRevs cheered loudly.

'I am saddened to say that early indications are that the young Pure Greens and those who have given into the temptation of the Trads have demonstrated by their actions that they think the old world had something to offer them. Remember the destruction of those days…'

He looked away from the screen in disbelief.

'The indications are that they would not work to make the world a better place, and they would rather indulge their selfish needs at the expense of others. But…' He paused for dramatic effect. 'I will give them as much time as they need. I will not force them to alter their attitude. Instead, I will leave it to you to teach, instruct, and help them to return to our Green ways. Even if it is just one person at a time, then each born again Green will be a victory. Mother Earth needs all the help she can get. I needn't remind you of the potential depletion of Her resources which would be required to keep nine-hundred-million people alive for a thousand years if they weren't going to give anything back. That is what's at stake here, and that is why they are going to have to contribute toward their thousand years of life the UltraViolet™ will offer them.'

Siddha clapped loudly, which encouraged the others in the audience to follow. Lizzie applauded enthusiastically while the Bear clapped gently, as he was troubled by this harsh approach. He was a man who helped sinners. He didn't punish or deprive them. Samuel Beardon the Third forgave them their sins and reinforced the message that God loved all his children.

Bodhi continued his Boulder Creek sermon. 'And to a matter which has troubled many of you. Some may be hearing this for the first time. If it is, and this message alarms you, please, do not worry because it is a matter that we have in hand. I am drawing your attention to a terrorist plot to disrupt our New Green Year celebrations - our Centenary of the Green Revolution…'

The Bear didn't understand this, but the raised fists of the GreenRevs at the front made it apparent that they knew.

'Brady Mahone, the self-proclaimed avenger for the Trads, has been trying to mastermind this terror plot. Let me make myself plain. I do not want to see him harmed in any way. We do not harm any living creature, even those who would do harm to us. Please let him go about his business unchallenged and unhindered.' He paused before emphasising, 'I mean it. Let him be.'

The Bear was utterly bewildered.

'Our own Head of Engineering and Nanosciences - Professor Pinar Dogan, was approached by Brady Mahone, in person, with questions about whether explosive devices in our chemical plants or, indeed, our power supply facilities could cause a catastrophic event.'

The members of this elite Green audience who didn't know of this plot against them gasped.

'He has sent his sons out across the world to ingratiate themselves with some of the most influential and knowledgeable members of our Green organisation with the express desire to gather information on our perceived weaknesses.'

He added a footnote to this, 'And Brady Mahone has been asking anybody he encounters about the weaknesses in the Sattva Systems™ working practices - he even asks about how he could destroy me. If you have had dealings with this man, then think about his questions in this context - I beg you.'

As the movie ended, Bodhi said reassuringly. 'Our facilities are safe. There is no threat to our power supplies. We have increased the sensitivity of the Security Protocols™ on Brady Mahone and his close family. You are safe, rest assured. Go to your fellow Greens and bring them back into our family. Let's look forward to our New Green Year celebrations and let us continue with our quest to make the world a better place to live. Thank you.'

The screen went blank at the end of the recording. Many of the Greens in the audience flocked around Siddha to solicit more information. Lizzie excitedly dug Samuel in the ribs. 'Fancy a walk. We could trade stories about Brady, and I'm sure Siddha would love to meet you - when he's finished up here.'

'Sure. Why not.'

They strolled back to Lizzie's home, and she spent most of the time recalling the first day when Brady Mahone appeared in West McFarland. She didn't divulge that she had slept with him. She still had an old-fashioned twinge that a preacher might disapprove of. She revelled in pulling apart Brady's business reputation by describing in detail Brady's pathetic attempts at shoplifting. She laughed as she juxtaposed this with tonight's revelation that he was being elevated to a terrorist mastermind.

Once at home, she offered Samuel a selection of fruit juices, and he chose a glass of fresh, locally produced, Californian oranges. 'So, you are unconcerned about the threat posed by Brady?' He said, between gulps of sweet, refreshing juice.

'He's a dumb Trad who got lucky in business.' Lizzie added, 'I'm reassured that Bodhi has increased the sensitivity of the Security Protocols™ on him, though.' She slumped back in an armchair, which encouraged Samuel to relax. 'How did you meet Brady?'

'I was a NanoSprayer™ in Los Banos back in 2099 when I first met him.' He wasn't going to share his reasons why he engineered this meeting. 'We got along, and my nephew took a shine to him, although Lord knows why.'

'And where's your nephew, now?'

'He had stayed with me his whole life. But now he has made a new life for himself and his partner on Mars.' He added, 'I'm going to miss him.'

'Who's his partner?'

'Raelynn. Xe's not Brady's progeny, but xe's part of Brady's extended family.'

'You and Brady have a lot of bonds. Did you know he was plotting an attack on our Green society?'

'No. It's come as quite a shock. In fact, I'm struggling to believe it. It doesn't feel like the Brady I know at all.'

She put a leg up over the arm of her comfy chair. 'So, you believe that Bodhi is mistaken? Maybe he's a little bit delusional, paranoid even...'

'Of course not. Bodhi is the epitome of reason. He's not angry. He's calm and appealing for restraint. The doubts are entirely my own. I thought I understood Brady Mahone, but I have blinkered myself to the truth. I think you could say I'm still processing...'

'Don't torture yourself. I'm an educator and believed myself to be intellectually superior to Brady, but there have been occasions when he outplayed me. I think it's the cunning of the criminal within him. You can't take your eyes off him for a second.'

Siddha came in and sat next to Lizzie. He looked at Samuel and said, 'You were a stranger at our meeting. I wondered where you had gone.'

Lizzie said, 'I thought you'd like to meet him. He's almost family with Brady Mahone and has been close to him for eighty-five years. Siddha, this is Samuel Beardon the Third, and Samuel, this is Siddha, the Disciple for Green McFarland.'

The two men shook hands. Siddha said, 'It can't be a coincidence, but I knew of a man called Samuel Beardon the Second?'

'Yes. He began the creation of the Green Communities long before the Revolution.'

'Wow. We are graced by the presence of Green royalty.'

Samuel laughed, 'I am a preacher, and before that, a mere NanoSprayer™ - but I am proud of my Father's and Grandfather's achievements.'

Lizzie intervened, 'Siddha. Samuel is a close confidant of Bodhi Sattva.'

'It's the family connection. My parents worked closely with John Kane.' Samuel smiled.

'So, you are uniquely positioned between Bodhi and Brady. Was it you that informed Bodhi of Brady Mahone's plot?'

'Not at all. This evening was the first I had heard of it.'

'I'm going to come straight out and say it - I hate Brady Mahone. He's a nasty piece of work, and I wish he could be disposed of. He's been nothing but trouble since the first day he set foot in Green McFarland. Think of all those people who are missing out on the UltraViolet™ because he tempted them into his criminal enterprise. Personally, I think Bodhi has gone soft on him...'

'I'm hoping that he is trying to forgive him. Maybe that's the preacher in me talking.'

'I do apologise. Discussions about Brady Mahone tend to bring the worst out in me. Thank heavens the Security Protocols™ have been set too broad for me. Otherwise, I'd be asking you to release me from the Security Film™ by now.'

They all laughed. Samuel asked, 'Do you mind if I asked how you came to be a Disciple?'

587

'I worked with Genesis Garcia and Bodhi in the years running up to the Green Revolution. Although, it was many years after the Revolution before I got to meet Bodhi in person.'

'I don't understand.'

'In the old world, I couldn't be seen with Bodhi because of my job. It had implications…'

'What implications?'

'I oversaw corporate finance and governance at the Treasury. It might have raised questions about my proprietary if we had been seen together.'

Samuel was puzzled at first but then remembered that Sattva Systems™ was an industrial conglomerate, albeit in a high-tech field. 'So, you corresponded with him?'

'No. I dealt with Genesis Garcia's people and rubber-stamped the trillions of dollars of loans. You must understand that I hated my work at the Treasury. I went into it, all starry-eyed until the debauchery and the decadence was utterly shocking. Then there was the cronyism and the utter disregard for the natural world. By the time I was approached by Lizzie via Cain, I was delighted to do anything I could to bring down the capitalist world.'

Lizzie said, 'I was an Ecology teacher, and I flat-shared with Cain in my student days. Cain went on to be the International Head of Deep Mind. Cain was appalled at the respect his company was receiving while using enormous amounts of the Earth's resources to mine the Earth of precious metals and consume vast amounts of energy in powering the Cloud and the Grid. I was far enough removed from anybody's contacts lists to liaise with others in the group unhindered. We set up in McFarland because it was off the radar to the other Big Tech firms but still close enough to Los Angeles to the south and Silicon Valley to the north.'

Samuel pondered this information, 'So, the Revolution began with the few and not the many.'

'The catastrophic failure of the climate summit in 2050 gave us a whole army of recruits from the highest echelons of thinkers. These people joined us secretly while leaving their political masters to entertain the doomed Trad crowds. All the hard work began from there.' Lizzie answered. 'The rest is Green history.'

'Yes. It is written. The questions remain about the future. Does it not worry you about the young ones, the hunger strikers?'

'Of course. But the Green kids don't realise the sacrifices we made when we were young. They are choosing, self-selecting to learn the hard way. We cannot be distracted by relative trivialities so close to the completion of the hundred-year plan.'

Siddha said, 'I can tell you what comes next. It will still mean we have to work. Sorry, Lizzie…' He teased. 'Would you like to know?'

Samuel nodded eagerly.

'Glenarvon Cole has completed the selection and authorisation for the twenty-six million Green Disciples and the Devout. This number was hammered out after heated discussions in Boulder Creek…' He said salaciously. Siddha enjoyed his moments of rapt attention from an audience. 'It represents one square mile of hospitable land to be monitored daily.' He sat up excitedly. 'It's no longer a secret, but I have to deliver my address at McFarland's New Year Celebrations. I will have responsibility for the central square mile of McFarland, and all other UltraViolets™ will have a square mile allocated at random - as we don't want to be accused of favouritism. Of course, there will be logistical issues to be ironed out, but globally every square mile of hospitable land will have a person to watch over it. Now there are some discussions about titles. At first, Guardian was considered, but I believe we will choose Caretakers with the emphasis on care.'

Lizzie said, 'This is the first I've heard of it.'

'I know.' Siddha said triumphantly. 'I imagine that most of the time, there will be little to do. Hop in a FusionPlane™, check everything's ok and then back home. If there is a problem, then we can call on others to help.'

'What problems?'

'Plagues, fires, floods - anything where humankind can give Mother Nature a helping hand.'

Samuel said, 'How did Glenarvon Cole have the time to recruit all those people?'

'It wasn't difficult. It was passed down the pyramid, so to speak. Cain had his allocation, which he parcelled up and handed over mine. I put forward seventy-five McFarland citizens, of which sixty-eight were approved.'

'Who was not approved - the other seven?'

'They were late converts to the products of Brady Mahone Entertainment Enterprises when his son Bill Mahone came selling his wares like a snake-oil salesman.' He folded his arms. 'More evidence, if it was needed, of the misery which Brady Mahone has inflicted on the Greens with his corruption, temptation and lies.'

'Lies?'

'Yes. He was telling every Green he met that the UltraViolet™ wasn't worth waiting for - that it was no more than an outer coating for the NanoSuits™. Only a cynical mind could conjure up that ruse. They have learned the hard way that they paid a thousand years of life to satisfy their lust for second-rate Trad entertainment.'

Samuel said, 'These hunger strikers and the other Green rebels - do you think they will come around? It doesn't look like a phase they are going through to me.'

'I'm deeply concerned about them.' Lizzie said. 'It's heartbreaking to see my old students succumbing to this nihilistic rhetoric. I hope Bodhi does something about it soon. It's going to be such a shame to see the Centenary celebrations tarnished by their misery.'

Siddha stroked his chin as if he was deciding whether he could share his inside information. 'You haven't heard this from me, but I have it on good authority that Bodhi will offer everybody the UltraViolet™ in the last days of December.'

'But that still might be too late for some…'

'Maybe you could spread some rumours of your own. I don't want to be a Disciple with my own dead citizens on my watch. Personally, I think we've been given this information to use it in this manner. I'm not the only one who knows, and the word is spreading.'

'What should I say?'

'That Sattva Systems™ have taken on their concerns, and they will receive the UltraViolet™ with no strings other than they give up their hunger strike.'

'That might placate them.'

'Being told you've won has that effect.' Siddha added, 'On a more positive note, I know they want everybody to use the Yellow™ to its most outlandish uses on the New Green Year Party. Genesis Garcia has been tasked with putting plans together on the themes of the colours of the rainbow to mark the completion of the distribution phase of the NanoSuits™.'

Samuel laughed, 'I can't be the only one who dislikes being forced to dress up. I am just fine as I am.'

'I think most of the older Greens feel the same. It's comforting staying as one outward persona. However, the younger Greens like showing off, and if it brings back a sense of peace and Green harmony, then one night of dressing up is a small price to pay.

25: THE BOYS ARE BACK IN TOWN

Thanksgiving had become a guilty pleasure in the Green States of America. It was conducted furtively in the homes of the Greens, who celebrated it. The main difference from the Trad times was it was a wholly Vegan affair. There was nothing furtive about the celebrations in the Mahone residence, even if Brady or his sons had little idea about the details of its origins and traditions. All that concerned Brady was that it was a big deal in the Trad days, and he did it as one-in-the-eye to the Greens.

His sons all returned in time for the feasting and Debrock's fresh supply of dabs, and it was time to eat, talk and get high.

Brady made a point of seeking out Helgarth. 'Hey, Raelynn will be ok, y'know. Tyrone is a good guy. I've known him for years, he's kind, and he's crazy about her.' He added, 'For what it's worth, she loves him.'

'I know. But I'm going to miss xyr.'

'Come here.' She fell into his arms, and he squeezed her tightly. He held her until she had finished sobbing. 'If it's all too much for you, and you want to leave the table, I'll understand...'

'No. No, I'll be fine. It will be good to have the family back. Don't worry about me.' She kissed him on the cheek, smiled, and made her excuses for being needed in the kitchen. Brady knew she had never cooked a meal in all the years she had lived in his Malibu home - that's what the Green staff were for, but he didn't challenge her.

At the Thanksgiving meal, the whole family was together. His five sons had returned from their fact-finding missions across the globe, and they excitedly interrupted one and other with confirmations or contradictions to the other's reports. Amie, Helgarth and Lucy-Ian seemed subdued, but occasionally Brady could see them quietly discussing what he assumed was the Tyrone and Raelynn situation.

Bill attempted to summarise the discussions to date, as the elder and therefore the unelected spokesman for the boys. 'We've compared notes to try and find out what the Greens are up to, and there are one or two things which we all agree on.'

'Let's hear it.'

'We all managed to find everybody except Rhea Laidlaw and Glenarvon Cole.'

'I'm sorry, Pops.' Rocky said, 'they are always on the move, and I'm not even sure if Bodhi even knows where they are half the time.'

'No problem, son. I know you tried.' Brady wasn't going to embarrass the boy in front of his peers and say that he had recently spent the day with Rhea. Thinking of her stirred strange emotions of the loss of Tyrone and Raelynn, his friendship with the Bear and whatever it was with Rhea. He didn't like using the word love, even in his inner monologue. It felt like the kind of word a weaker man would use. However, it seemed hard to deny when he remembered that kiss.

Bill continued, 'The ones we did find, all let us talk to them. And that was the funny thing about it - there seemed to be a kind of pattern to our meetings.'

'Go on.'

'It was as if they knew we were coming, and they had a playbook. We found them real easy. They greeted us and ensured we were seen to be meeting them. There were lots of people around, but they spoke to us in private.'

'What did they talk to you about?'

'Absolutely nothing, really. They pretended not to know anything about voting. All they talked about was how great the New Green Year's party was going to be.'

Brady Mahone's sons nodded, and even Amie, Helgarth and Lucy-Ian had suspended their own separate conversations to listen into these updates.

'There was something else. In the last couple of days, the atmosphere around us changed. Nobody said or did anything - you know what the Greens are like when they get angry - they kinda shun you - quietly.'

'Spoken like a true Trad, boy.' Brady laughed.

'It wasn't just the Disciples and the Devout. When we first arrived, we saw a lot of protests and even hunger strikes...'

'Yeah. I've seen those too. The young Greens were skinny to begin with, but now - well, let's just say they didn't look like they had too long to live.'

'I know Pops. I've never seen anything like it before. None of us had. Anyway, when we first got there, they couldn't wait to tell us what they thought of Bodhi - none of it good. They were making all kinda plans to protest about the New Green Year Party.'

'That's interesting.' Brady rubbed his head. 'And what do these protests look like?'

'One thing Rocky did succeed in doing, was finding out from someone on the inside,' Bill looked at Rocky and smiled, 'that the New Green Year Party is going to be a Festival of Colour, based on the symbol of the rainbow.'

Rocky added, 'It's all about using the YellowSuits™ to the max - they think it will appeal to the younger Greens.'

'Yeah, I was there at the launch of the YellowSuits™, it was fucking weird if you ask me, and fucking unmanly.' Brady said this in a tone which stated he would be disappointed if his boys took part in this fey activity.

'Anyway, when we first got there, the Green rebels were talking about wearing sackcloth and ashes at the Centenary celebrations.' Bill said. 'They had this grand protest all worked out. They were going to march across the globe dressed in black. And to top it all, they were planning to commemorate all the dead, *including* the Trads who died as their sacrifice and contribution to saving the planet.'

'Fuck me. I would have loved to have seen Bodhi's reaction to that when he was first informed.' Brady laughed heartily.

Amie said, 'Hey, Brady. Don'cha think Lucian and Mary-Lou would have loved to have witnessed a parade like that.'

'Yeah. And Pops.'

'It ain't happening.' Bill said. 'That was the weird thing. The Hunger strikers caved, and the protests were called off. It was like somebody had flicked a switch, and it was like nothing had ever happened.'

Hawk said, 'I was waiting for Hunter to disappear for a moment, but it was the same here. He wanted everybody to know that I was talking to him, but only when we were in the Vehicle Lot. He said nothing of any importance, but he made it look like we had some kinda top-secret conversation. I don't get it.'

'He wants it to look like you are up to no good, even if you're not.' Amie said, 'Oldest trick in the book. It's a set-up.'

'You're right. They are trying to fit Brady Mahone up for a crime he didn't commit. Well done, Amie. You're right. I know it.'

'There is no vote. There is no meeting of the so-called thirteen.' She said quietly but authoritatively. 'They are destroying your business by character assassination. I bet the Green rebels are being told that this was all some kinda misunderstanding, and they were being played by you. It doesn't matter if it's the truth. I'm wondering what your crime is going to be.'

'Gonna be something big - to go to all this trouble.'

Bill said, 'Unless they just used you and us, to manipulate the Greens. They've done it before. Bodhi is the great listener, the man of his word, but you are always the outsider who shouldn't be trusted. I think he has killed off the business. After this, who's going to buy from us? The Greens who forked out a few Green Credits at a time, hell, some of them even got our products for free - well, they just learned that it nearly cost them a thousand years. I wouldn't take that risk again, would you?'

Brady nodded, 'I would rather go into rehab than lose a thousand years, and that's saying something.'

The gathering around the table laughed. Troy said, 'Do you think we'll get the UltraViolet™ now?'

'Yes. Precious didn't mention any exceptions.' Wilder intervened. 'She didn't say what was happening, but she kinda prophesied that everything would be ok and that I shouldn't concern myself. I didn't understand, but it makes sense now.'

'Well, at least we get to keep the money. There's plenty to last a thousand years, that's for sure,' Troy said.

Brady was still uneasy, but he didn't want to trouble his family any further. He thought, *I'll mull it over later when I've had a chance to let this information sink in.* 'Cheers, everyone. You've done well for the old man, and it's very much appreciated. Happy Thanksgiving.' He raised his glass of old moonshine made with his Pops' secret recipe and drained his glass. 'I think that's enough business talk for today. Let's start our month of partying, we've got all your birthdays to plan for, and I know you like your New Green Year celebrations. Let me declare here, and now, I don't want you boys to get your hopes up. I'm not giving away any FusionPassengerJets™ this time. I think we may have run our last sales competition. However, let this be a time for new beginnings.'

26: A MEETING OF MINDS

Brady spent the next few weeks in a dabaholic haze. He occasionally got so confused in his highs that he thought he was back in Cupertino with El Duque and his Brady Bombs. He had moments of clarity when he returned to the words of Amie about him being set-up, and he always decided to do something about it - tomorrow. But tomorrow showed no sign of turning up any time soon.

He was so stoned that he handed over the organisation of his sons' and Lucy-Ian's birthday party to Hunter. He even left the gift-giving for Hunter to organise. His brain seemed to be thinking that he no longer had an unlimited amount of cash to spend, so he may as well get his money's worth out of Hunter and his staff.

The thought of being, maybe, one-hundred and forty-three years old on January 1st, 2185, made him laugh hysterically. He had never known how old he was, he never knew his birthdate, he couldn't tell for sure if he had been born in 2041 or 2042. He tried to work it out using his fingers, but soon gave up. *It doesn't really matter, he thought. Who cares if I got it wrong? It don't mean a goddamn thing to me.* He laughed uncontrollably in his altered state of mind when he wondered whether he even had his hundredth birthday party in the wrong year. He didn't notice the hours passing on this circular inner monologue.

In the Mahone household, this was the final party of the season. There were the family birthdays on the 30th, the New Green Year's Eve on the 31st, and then to welcome in the New Year, it was time to give thanks to the head of the household and the family business - the great Brady Mahone - the self-proclaimed King of the Trads, the Last Man Standing.

Tomorrow arrived in the idea that he would have it out with Bodhi Sattva. It was the dabs talking, and if he were in his right mind, he would have cleaned himself up before flying up to Boulder Creek. But Brady wouldn't have recognised his right mind if it came up and shook hands with him. The only morsel of logic that prevailed was that he had to do it before the big parties. And that meant leaving today. He wondered whether tomorrow had been and gone in the blink of an eye because he was now in his FusionPlane™ and it seemed to be flying itself. He giggled like a schoolboy as he wondered whether Brady Mahone was flying himself.

He was utterly confused as the autopilot delivered him to the Sattva Systems™ HQ in Boulder Creek. He believed he should be in the Park in Cupertino. His vehicle was parked outside the Main Entrance, and there was a touring party leaving the cafeteria. He fell out of the FusionPlane™ and landed with a thud on the floor. He stood up woozily and examined the grazed skin on his left forearm. One of the Greens in the party turned away, as it had been years since anybody had seen blood.

Brady looked at her and then back at his arm, and he seemed fascinated by his wound. He then laughed, and then he staggered into the Main Entrance. His reputation preceded him, and everybody gave him a wide berth. He stood at the banner with the thirteen promises and swayed dreamily. Minutes elapsed, and Brady barely moved.

Sissy had been alerted and informed of his injuries, and it took her a few minutes to locate an old First Aid box which was a relic of a distant age. She approached Brady warily.

'Hi, Brady. You've injured yourself. Let me help you.' She examined his saucer eyes and deduced he was on old-fashioned psychedelics. She lifted the dead weight of his heavy arm and examined the deep grazes. She wiped away the blood tenderly, 'I want to apply some NanoHealing™ spray. Is that ok with you?'

'Huh.'

'Your wound. On your arm.'

He looked at it.

'I don't want it to become infected. Have I got your consent to apply NanoHealing™?'

There was a small but curious group of Greens watching this interplay with Genesis Garcia and Brady Mahone. He stared at them. 'I always did heal real quick.' He laughed hysterically and yelled, 'Do ya hear that! I always did heal real quick.' His startled audience backed away and headed for the exit as it dawned on them that this might be the predicted terrorist attack. They could easily have intervened, but Bodhi had ordered them to let him be.

Brady's laughter subsided as he watched his audience float away like dandelion seeds in the breeze.

Sissy repeated softly, 'I'm going to apply NanoHealing™ to the wound, and then I'll apply a dressing to it.'

'Yeah. I heals real quick. I want to see Bodhi.'

'Ok, Brady.'

'He's fitting me up, y'know.'

She said softly, 'Now, who told you that?'

'Amie. She's got more going on upstairs than you think.' He pointed in the general direction of his head.

She sprayed on the NanoHealing™ and bandaged his arm. 'There. That should do it. I'll take you to Bodhi. He's cancelled his meeting for you when he heard of your arrival. You mean that much to him.'

Brady accompanied Sissy to Bodhi's office. He moved with a mixture of stoned staggering and occasional attempts at dancing, complete with pirouettes. He spoke in a jumble of words that made little sense to Sissy.

Sissy didn't knock when she reached the office as she had a falling over Brady to contend with. Brady staggered over to Bodhi's desk and rested his palms upon the screen covering. He felt like it was hard work to lift his head. Sissy pulled up a chair to the back of Brady's legs and cajoled him into sitting down. She checked the responses of Brady's pupils, which were like pinholes, and said to Bodhi, 'I'm not convinced that Brady even knows he's here.'

Bodhi said, 'What has he ingested?'

'I believe it's most likely a particularly potent form of marijuana in the form of dabs. The younger and more rebellious greens call it Mother Nature's Seed.'

'I suppose the branding is on message,' Bodhi said, 'Hello, Brady.'

Brady looked at him, but he just giggled.

Sissy said, 'Do you want me to leave?'

'No. Not at all. This could be fascinating. I have nothing to hide. I'm not sure I could say the same about our friend here.'

Brady laughed and muttered, 'Hide and seek.'

Sissy pulled up a chair and sat at the end of the desk so that she could clearly see both their faces. She was curious to see Bodhi's reaction to his gate crasher. She edged back a little as she didn't want to engage in head tennis, and she tried to view their responses discreetly.

Bodhi snapped, 'You've got me. I'm all yours. If you can get your act together, I will answer anything you want. That is why you've come all this way to see me, isn't it?'

The sharp words seemed to penetrate Brady's haze, as intended, and he sat up in his chair. 'Whoa. Wow. This is crazy, man. It almost feels real.' He touched the desk and then examined his finger as if he couldn't believe he had the sensation of touching something in a dream.

'Something is troubling you.' His tone had softened to that of a concerned doctor dealing with a psychiatric patient.'

'Yes. Yes, there is. You don't treat me with respect.'

'I apologise. Do you accept my apology for the offence I have caused you?'

'Yeah.' Brady shook his head, 'I suppose so.'

'I know you've got a lot on your mind, and I want to ease your burden. I can't have an unhappy Brady Mahone spoiling the party now, can I? What is it that you would like to know to make you more comfortable with your predicament?'

'Are you going to steal my money?' Brady pointed at Bodhi as if he had worked out that Bodhi might give him a trick answer. 'Or my sons' money. I earned those Greenbacks.' Brady made a pathetic attempt to appear in control of both his mental and physical functions.

'Nobody is going to steal your money or your business. However, your profits will grind to a halt in the New Year, as our people now fear the cost of doing business with the Mahones. But on the plus side, you will still be exceedingly rich by Green standards.'

Brady wobbled in his chair, 'Cross your heart and hope to die - and no crossing your fingers.' He wagged his index finger at him.

'Cross my heart and hope to die. I will not involve myself in your business affairs.'

Brady chuckled. His mind groped for more questions, but he couldn't find a coherent string of words. He was frustrated but also thought it was funny. He couldn't remember being this stoned. 'This is some strong shit.' He muttered. 'Whoa.' He rubbed at his face, 'Are you trying to make Green souls?'

Sissy looked at Bodhi in bewilderment.

'What an interesting question. Brady, you surprise me.' Bodhi sat up straight. 'You are going to have to develop this line of questioning further. You have my complete and undivided attention.'

Brady smiled, 'There was this ghost, except she wasn't a ghost, and she was looking for you, but she couldn't find you, and she tried to grope me…ugh…fucking slimy…' He laughed, 'She wasn't my type.' He giggled at his joke. 'She was more your type.' He laughed uncontrollably. Sissy was dismissive of Brady's ramblings, but she could tell that Bodhi was taking it seriously. Brady recovered, 'You've got her, haven't you? She's been recycled. I know it's true, you think I'm dumb…'

'I've never thought you were dumb, my friend. I have always had the highest regard for your cunning. You are talking about Mrs Wilson, aren't you?'

Brady stabbed the air, 'Yes. That's right.' This affirmation energised him.

'Were you tempted to try on her NanoSuit™?'

Brady shuddered at the thought. 'Would it have worked? Y'know, been all indestructible…'

'It was an incredibly rare event, with me being temporarily unavailable - that and the delay to her funeral - but yes, it would have been possible to use her recycled Suit™ until I returned. Her Suit™ would seek out the nearest match to me, I'm guessing. Which raises questions. Some would be obvious…' He looked closely over Brady. 'My Father had a vasectomy after my birth, and I have the proof, and I know my Mother didn't have any other children, of that I'm certain. However, I'm wondering what trickery Professor Chu got up to…'

Brady was surprised to hear Bodhi dredge up Professor Chu's name from the past. He hadn't been obviously connected to Bodhi. 'He was a kind and considerate man - unlike John Kane - and he was a Trad.' Brady stated this as if this was all the proof he needed. 'If he had been a Green, you would have searched his soul. You would have crept around inside him like a sneak thief, stealing his knowledge.'

'It is common knowledge that we recycle the old NanoSuits™…' Bodhi waved his hand dismissively at the suggestion.

Brady slammed his fist on the screen, which covered Bodhi's desk. 'But is that what they really are? Or are they Green souls? You've got the soul of Mrs Wilson in you.'

'There is no such thing as a soul. It is a scientific fact. I have the life history of every dead Green within me, to access their reasoning and observations. It is a waste of a life and resources to let all this just rot in the ground.' He said to Sissy, 'I'm sure our friend here is emerging from his drug-induced haze quicker than possible for a Trad.'

Sissy replied, 'I applied NanoHealing™ to his arm. He grazed it badly when he fell out of his FusionPlane™.'

'Where on Earth did you find that? We haven't needed NanoHealing™ since before the Green Revolution.'

Sissy laughed, 'In an old First Aid box - it was almost a museum exhibit. It was the only thing I could think of to tend to an injured Trad - well, that and a dressing, of course.'

Bodhi rubbed his chin, 'It's been so long, I can't recall if it would have additional healing qualities...'

'The early versions had additional healing qualities. Remember the NanoBubbles™ for the holidaymakers?'

'Ah yes. You're right. Thank you for reminding...'

Brady felt like he had been forgotten about while Bodhi and Sissy tripped happily together down Memory Lane. He wanted answers, and he'd got Bodhi talking. 'Did she take a long time to find you? She was ok, y'know. Mrs Wilson, in case it had slipped your mind.'

Bodhi didn't appreciate having the functionality of his faculties questioned. 'Yes, I had a number of dead to accommodate when I emerged from the Sensory Deprivation Chamber. It was a challenging time. She liked you, and I was fascinated to have the full details of her first encounter with Brady Mahone, an ex-con, on the run...'

'I didn't just fall through the NanoShell™, did I?'

'No. You were genetically engineered. Your DNA sequence was modified at birth as part of the NanoIVF™ studies at Stanford University by Professor Yuan Chu under the patronage of my Father, John Kane. Unfortunately, they had a falling out, and my Father had him removed. My Father was a perfectionist, and he wasn't happy with his work.'

'John Kane...' Brady's wobbling hand touched the side of his nose knowingly. 'Didn't want the Trads to have any more babies. That's why he got rid of him.' Sissy kept her eyes on Bodhi when she didn't understand the signal which Brady had given Bodhi. Brady continued. 'I don't know what it means when you say I was genet.. whatever, engineered. I'm still a Trad, right?' Brady's mind wandered as he considered Professor Yuan Chu and whether he was related to him in any way. After all, he had contributed to Brady's development before he was even born. He would never know, but he wondered whether John Kane had sabotaged Project Brady to punish the Professor.

'Yes. You are still a Trad. Your genes were edited to remove inherited diseases and purified. Therefore, you have led an extraordinarily long life.' He added, almost as a note to himself, 'He may have seized the opportunity...' He stopped himself from going any further with this line of thought, for now. However, Sissy was considering the possibilities.

Brady rubbed his eyes. He knew why he had these Green abilities; he just wanted to know if Bodhi had arranged it. Apparently, he hadn't been fully aware until now. Brady suggested his own ignorance by asking a redundant question. 'So, this is why I can go where the Greens go?'

'Maybe. It is the most likely explanation.'

'But I'm still a Trad. I'm still a human being, y'know, a straightforward guy.'

Bodhi smiled, 'Yes. Undoubtedly.'

'Cool. I can live with that.'

'Are you feeling better, now?' Bodhi asked with mock sympathy.

'Yeah. I'm still me.' He added, 'So, I keep my money, and I'm 100% Trad, and you've got no plans to take my sons' inheritance off them?'

'None at all. You have summarised it perfectly.'

Sissy intervened. 'Why did you use the term 100% Trad?'

'It's just a figure of speech. We know what he means.' Bodhi grimaced.

Brady shook his head and then his whole body to shake the fogginess from his mind. 'I've heard people talk like that.'

'I don't understand.'

'Shutting the conversations down. It's what the criminals do when they don't want you to find out what they're planning. I've done that when one of my gang was starting to brag about our next job, and they were blabber mouthing.'

'I'm not a criminal, Brady.' He shrugged.

'It's an inside job, and you're the inside man.'

Sissy said, 'In Trad terms, I was a corrupt politician, and Bodhi was defrauding the US Government out of trillions of dollars, and yes, in that world, we would be criminals. But we only did it to save the planet from destruction, and we are in the Green world now. We are not the lawbreakers here; we are the promise-keepers.'

'Ok. So now you don't want to know what Brady Mahone thinks. I don't blame you. Once you get in my mind, you might not find your way out.' He looked into her eyes.

'I do want to know. What did you mean by using a percentage term?'

'I'd have thought it was obvious. I think every new layer of NanoSuit™ you get, you lose more Trad. I suppose, that's the same as saying that if I'm 100% Trad then 100% human. I guess if you've got nine NanoSuits™, then I'd estimate that you were at least 90% Green by now, or to put it another way, you'd be 90%+ Nanoparticles. You're losing your humanity, baby.'

Sissy looked sharply at Bodhi and was about to challenge him; then Brady put his hand up and laughed at her. 'Well, I suppose that's still a trace element of humanity left, looking after number one, only thinking about what this means for you. You should be looking at him.' He pointed at Bodhi, who reclined in his chair, either relaxed about the topic or in a gesture of resignation. Brady stated, 'He's Pure Nano. He ain't human at all. That's my theory.'

Sissy said to Bodhi, 'These are the ravings of a lunatic. Tell me it's not true, and I'll believe you. We can't let him go around making accusations…'

Bodhi said, 'Do you feel the same? Are you still Genesis Garcia? Your children's Moppa? Do you still have all the same emotions of love and fear?'

'Yes. I am still the same person as I ever was.' Her mind raced to search for confirmation that her diagnosis was correct.

'Then you have the answer you need.'

Brady attempted to stand but slumped back down again. His mind may have recovered its clarity, but his central nervous system was still stoned. He said sarcastically, 'Sissy, baby. Way to do denial. Total masterclass.'

'Hey, Bodhi, man…' He chuckled, 'Never thought about it before, sounds like Bogey Man.' He giggled away for a while, but the solemn look on Sissy's face brought him back to reality. 'Admit it, you are Pure Nano.'

'I'm interested to know your reasoning.'

'No, you're not. You're stalling. You can't kid a kidder.'

Bodhi smiled and spoke as softly as ever. He remained on brand. 'I like your term, Pure Nano. Maybe Sissy would have labelled it in that way.' He looked at Sissy. 'You always had a better way with words than me.'

Brady interrupted, 'Hey, but don't worry, one day you'll die, and then he'll inherit your soul.' He stared at Sissy as if he was imploring her to come to her senses. Brady knew he was stoned, but to him, Sissy was the one who had lost her mind.

'I've never called it Pure Nano, but I'm assuming you took it as a logical extension of Pure Green.' Bodhi was keen to bring Brady's intensity back to him and off Sissy.

'Yeah, that's what I was thinking. What did you call it?'

'Project X.'

'That's a crappy name. No logic there - I recall Libby talking about John Kane having a Project X, Y and Z. Is that where it came from?'

'I've never heard of that. You've got me at a disadvantage. No, it is perfectly logical. After UltraViolet™ comes X-Ray™. I'm wearing the X-RaySuit™.'

'And you are not human?'

'I would disagree. I would argue that I am the next step of human evolution. I have human form and thoughts. The only difference is that every human cell has been imitated, replicated, and replaced. All the human susceptibilities to illness and death have been modified and improved. I could operate for millions of years.' He looked at Sissy, 'I don't do this out of self-importance. One day in the far-off future, Mother Earth will need saving from the threat of the expanding Sun. She will need beings like me to save her. She is unique within the universe.'

She said, 'But you made that choice. Did we?'

'It's your choice, now. You could be the next to take the X-Ray™. Trust me, you won't feel any different.'

27: PARTY TIME

Sissy had Brady wheeled out of Bodhi's office, and then she put Brady in his Fusion-Plane™ and waited until the autopilot was set for home. When she was convinced that he was ok, she watched him leave. The questions raised were almost too big to contemplate. Sissy wanted to take her mind off them for now, and she needed reassuring and an overwhelming desire to be with family. She had the unsettling sense of being duped, but she hoped her unconscious mind would work on the issues in the background tasks of her brain and come up with more palatable and digestible answers to these most fundamental questions about humanity. It was the same pragmatism that had held her in good stead as a politician. She had learned to trust her process.

She used her Satt™ to call her partner, Annabelle and asked her to arrange a dinner party for her three children who were still on Earth. She added that their own partners and grandchildren would be more than welcome. Annabelle suggested a Vegan barbecue as it was easier to arrange, and Sissy acquiesced. She thought of Century Brady Garcia, her youngest, starting his life on another world far away from Earth. She recalled that he had taken the UltraViolet™ before he left for Mars, and therefore, he hadn't escaped her predicament. She pondered whether it was more human to rebel than succumb to the wishes of Bodhi Sattva - the unelected leader of the Green World.

The young grandchildren lifted her spirits as they hugged her and talked excitedly about the trivial things in the world that brought them so much joy. They were thrilled to have the opportunity to play in the extensive gardens in the Californian winter sunshine. She watched them play their imaginary games for many minutes before attending to her own grown-up children. She had never felt guilty about having this home to herself and Annabelle. She had earned it, and Bodhi had sanctioned it. But she always knew that the other Greens wouldn't understand.

At least I'm not greedy like Pinar. God knows how many homes xe's got around the world.

Annabelle was delighted to host a party, and she doted on their children and grandchildren. Sissy mixed with her family, but she never entirely shed her political skin enough to eliminate the sense that she was canvassing them. It gave her an affectation of aloofness which made her appear colder than Annabelle. Therefore, most relationship issues reached Sissy through Annabelle's filter.

Sissy asked the same questions of each family member but in such roundabout terms so as not to make plain her anxieties. Her questions to the young children were about if humans were animals. And what animals would they like to be, but this delved into how the creatures behaved and what they might think.

With the adults, she explored philosophical themes of what it meant to be human and even covered the general discussions about the history of the Trads. As Brady was known to all, he couldn't fail but to have his name appear in the conversations.

By the time that her extended family had drifted away, she wondered whether this had been an exercise in futility, as if she and everybody she asked were mostly Nano-machines as Brady had suggested, then was she or anybody else suitably qualified to ruminate on what was or wasn't human. If she was a machine, she could only answer in the same way as a computer…and then she contemplated whether she was an android. It amazed her that she had never considered this possibility before.

As she wiped away the mist on the bathroom mirror after she had showered, she forced herself to remember that she was more than one-hundred and fifty years old. The fact that this was a commonplace occurrence had removed any sense of abnormality about this. She then remembered her old political analogy about the frog not noticing it was being boiled to death if you put it in cold water and increased the temperature so slowly it never knew when the temperature reached boiling point. They had taken the NanoSuits™ freely, one at a time, and sometimes with more than a decade between each new upgrade, and each one only replaced a fraction of their physical being.

She got into bed next to her exhausted partner after a days' entertaining, and she thought about the journey she had been on. She recalled the heady days as a successful politician with firebrand views on tackling climate change. The victory was intoxicating and life-changing, not just for her but for the world. The only focus on the RedSuits™ was that these additions to the outer layers of their skin had brought them victory. It was the OrangeSuits™ and the SecurityProtocols™ that troubled her most in this darkening hindsight. These two developments at a stroke removed the need for doctors and the police. This was the moment when any investigations into what was happening to humanity had ceased. She deduced that everything which came next just completed the takeover one Suit™ at a time.

Sissy slept fitfully, tossing and turning, kicking away the bedclothes, which weren't necessary with the Suits™ but were kept as human comfort. She flipped over her pillow for the umpteenth time before Annabelle finally woke up. Deep down, she wanted to wake her.

'What's with you tonight, Genny? Just go back to sleep.' Annabelle turned to look at the face of her partner and lover. Only Annabelle called Genesis Garcia, Genny.

'I can't.'

'Do you want to talk about it?'

Sissy smiled. 'Yes. I need a sounding board.'

'I've been called worse things - usually by you.' Annabelle laughed softly.

'I had a meeting today.' Sissy said, 'You know you're not to…'

'I think you've only told me a thousand times over the years.'

'Sorry. Anyway, Brady Mahone staggered into the HQ today to see Bodhi.'

'I've always thought that odd, that people can wait years for an audience with Bodhi, but he drops everything when Brady Mahone comes to town.'

'I think I've gotten so used to it that I barely give that a second thought anymore, like so many other things.'

Annabelle sighed, 'Look, little old Genny, honey, tell me all about it, you know I like a little bedtime story.'

'Brady raised a very big subject at today's meeting, one I dismissed as the ramblings of a stoned Trad at first, but as the day has gone on, it's troubling me more and more.'

'Ok.'

'You're going to have to promise not to laugh. It's going to sound quite ludicrous at first, but trust me, it's incredibly important, but I don't know why. It's life-changing in a way, but at the same time, it doesn't alter our everyday lives. It's a philosophical puzzle…'

'You're losing me. I did notice you were getting deep and heavy with the family today.'

Sissy winced, 'Do you think they noticed?'

'A little. But they know you've got a difficult job.'

'I'm sorry.' She hugged Annabelle and then lay back on her pillow. She let out a deep sigh, 'Brady questioned our humanity. He believes that the UltraViolet™ Greens are in excess of 90% Nanomaterials, and therefore we are no longer human.'

'Wow. That's some claim. Tell me again about this man who is qualified to pontificate over us. Humour me, what are the characteristics of the esteemed King of the Trads with his kingdom consisting of, let me count…oops…' She raised one finger, she laughed as it was her middle finger.Sissy laughed and then recounted the stains upon Brady Mahone's personality, 'Let me see, he's an ex-convict, murderer, thief, drug addict, misogynist…'

'What about his bad points?'

They both laughed, 'I suppose I should try and be fair.' Sissy added. 'There are people that are fond of him. He has some Greens who have been friends with him for many years. By all accounts, his family love him. And over the years, he's won over the Pure Greens, but this is more out of their own misgivings about menial work they are required to do, rather than Brady actively wooing them.'

'Century had a more nuanced view. Remember, xe didn't see why expanding the mind through movies and music was borderline illegal. Xe wasn't lazy or entitled. You could argue that xe has opted for hardship on a hostile planet to be a part of something different.'

'I tried to explain that xe was exchanging the possibility of a shorter life here on Earth than a longer one on the hell of Mars. As it turned out, xe would have got the UltraViolet™.'

Annabelle turned over onto her side and brushed a stray hair away from Sissy's face. 'It wasn't about the UltraViolet™. Xe used to confide in me because xe knew you would disapprove. Xe was enthralled about Tia Cassandra reinstating the internet, streaming, smart devices and all the other Trad-cons. Tia had no use for Files in her brave new technological world. I think that upset xym more that xe had to leave xys precious collection of BMEE Files behind, but xe was promised more content than xe could ever watch on Mars. Apparently, Tia had her Server Banks rescued from under the Mojave near Cima and transported to Mars.' She watched Sissy's expressions as she didn't want to upset her, 'Century wanted to be a part of that culture, not working in fields, and examining landscapes every day for the rest of xys long life. Xe felt that Bodhi made the rules before xe was even born, which made xym feel disenfranchised.' Annabelle smiled as she pushed her fingers through Sissy's hair, 'Xe still loved you, y'know.'

Sissy said, 'I understood Bodhi's logic at the time, that nostalgia for the old days could be corrosive to our plans. After all, there was an immense amount of work to do with Operation Clean-Up. We had a planet to repair, but…'

'Maybe, it was a little over-the-top to ban entertainment…'

'But it was all so binary and full of racial stereotyping. I don't just mean American culture. The entertainment industry across the globe was wholly exclusive, whether in China, India, Russia…they all pushed their own dogma. To complete the thirteen promises, the old ways had to be outlawed.'

'No wonder you can't sleep.' Annabelle sighed as if trying to get Sissy to echo her calm manner. 'You should listen to yourself. It's all defensiveness and justification.'

'I know. You're right.' She said, 'Brady might be bad or let's be kind and say he's flawed, but there aren't any doubts that he qualifies as human.'

'I suppose so. I'll concede that.' Annabelle used the opportunity to bring up something that had always troubled her. 'Did you have an arrangement with Bodhi Sattva to plant xys seed in you in a physical manner?'

'No. Absolutely not. I promise. Century was conceived via NanoIVF™. You were there at the *freely* given and received ceremony.'

'But Genny, honey. These things can be faked.'

'You know something,' Sissy wasn't angry. She wanted to allay Annabelle's fears, 'With it being Bodhi, if xe had asked, I would have considered it.' She put a finger softly to Annabelle's lips before she could respond. 'But this was a Trad method, in xys mind, and I believe xe wouldn't consider it. Bodhi has never shown interest in anybody, sexually, in all the time that I have known xym. It's only in the light of what we've talked about tonight that it seems weird now.'

'Century doesn't know who his Father is. I've never disclosed it. I kept the official line that it was an anonymous donor. I often wondered if xe would have a primal instinct that it was Bodhi.' She laughed softly, 'It's funny, but the only person that had any kind of impression on xem, in that way, was Brady Mahone.'

'That'll be the name. Century *Brady* Garcia.'

'True. But still…' Annabelle smiled, 'Xe's happy, you know. Xe's made some friends on Mars. Century loves Tyrone and Raelynn.'

Sissy said, 'I think he felt bad about taking Tyrone's place. I'm glad that it worked out ok for Tyrone in the end. I just can't figure out how Samuel reversed the decision. I should have been aware of this change.'

'Family finds a way.' She added, 'He's proud that he lives in a world where the Greens and the Trads, or Originals, as they are called on Mars, all live together and share a common goal of building their new home together.'

'I'll have to call xem. I've left it too long. I've been busy with the end of year preparations…'

'Sssh. None of us is perfect.'

Sissy sighed, 'What about Bodhi Sattva?'

Annabelle laughed, 'Well, you're the one always complaining about xys decision making…'

'Yes. Agreed. Xe's not always right…in my opinion.' She paused before asking, 'What if I told you that xe is now Pure Nano, 100% made up of Nanomaterials. Would xe qualify as human or would xe be something else, something new?'

'In theory?'

'No. Bodhi admitted to Brady that xe is now X-RaySuit™. Apparently, UltraVio-let™ wasn't the last Suit™. Bodhi has remained one step ahead. Xe claims humanity has evolved with xym.' Before Annabelle could answer, Sissy added, 'And I could be next? All I have to do is ask.'

Annabelle said without thinking - and this made Sissy believe that the love of her life was speaking with her human heart and not her Nano brain. 'No. I couldn't bear that. I couldn't love and share my bed with another *species*. You have to refuse.'

28: CELEBRATION DAY

At the Malibu residence of Brady Mahone, the Green staff had been made to work harder than ever to make the birthday party for his sons and Lucy-Ian and Rae-lynn in absentia the best ever. Brady was acutely aware that he had given his staff a relatively easy ride over the years, but now the Green Credits were slowing to a trickle, and his fortune would have to last his boys for a thousand years or more, he was going to get his money's worth out of his, or more accurately, Bodhi's staff of spies.

The banners were everywhere in the massive dining room cum ballroom, celebrating the birthdays of everyone, individually, in the family. And Brady even had netting erected from the ceiling with hundreds of balloons from Libby's old storerooms blown up. He didn't tolerate excuses about holes and leaks in the old stock. Instead, he had them painstakingly repaired with NanoFixant™. He took particular pleasure in sending Hunter out to find more NanoFixant™ when the home stocks had run out.

Brady had started the day with a workout in the fully equipped gym with his boys. He believed that they worked out every day, whereas they now only did this when their Pops was in residence. Brady was wearing only sports shorts and a sleeveless T-shirt, which left his natural South Sea tattoos on show on his shoulders and biceps. He was still in great shape as Brady worked out most mornings before breakfast. Despite all the theories about his origins, he always believed that physical strength training was one of the best things he ever did to remain this healthy into old age.

He always went back to his prison days when he worked out. Jail wasn't a significant hardship for somebody of Brady's criminal stature, and the one thing he enjoyed inside was the time given over to exercise with the weights.

He noticed Wilder blowing hard. 'Come on, boy. Harder. Faster. You've got decades on me.'

Wilder was pushing his legs on the exercise bike but was out of practice, and his lack of pace and coordination was betraying him. 'Aw, come on, Pops. Why do we have to keep doing this? The point of the Yellow™ and BlueSuits™ is that we can look any way we choose.'

'You know why. I've seen the shrunken bodies inside those Suits™. You want to maintain your own muscle. Anyway, it won't do you any harm, will it?'

'I suppose.' Wilder huffed.

'Trouble with you boy is you do too much thinking and reading and not enough doing.'

He watched Wilder gamely try to pick up the pace, and he was more impressed with his other sons' efforts, especially his eldest, Bill, who was pumping iron with gusto.

Brady shouted encouragement. 'Come on, boys, push it. I want you in great shape for the party tonight. You might be Green and all, but Brady Mahone boys are still real men.'

Alcohol was a rarity in the Green World, but Brady had his homemade stills, and he checked that these were ready before the birthday parties. He was proud of his handiwork, and he was sure that his Pops would have approved. He took a snifter and gasped at its potency. What he couldn't do with PassengerFusionJets™ he would make up for by having the most fun party in the world. It made Brady feel young again, thinking about the fun they would have tonight. There had been a bright young party animal who had been flirting with him for the last few days. She was part of Debrock's crowd. Debrock might even have put her up to it, but he didn't care. He was thrilled at the prospect of getting lucky tonight.

By the early evening at the start of the party, he was already thrilled at the effort the partygoers had put into the evening's celebrations. His sons, Bill, Rocky, Wilder, Troy and Hawk, along with Lucy-Ian, and the mothers of his children, Amie and Helgarth, with the room, packed out with Debrock and his crowd of around forty Green rebels and freaky friends packed the room. Hawk had cranked up the volume of the old Trad Electro Dance tunes, and everybody began to party hard. Drink and Dabs were being consumed like there was no- tomorrow, and Brady danced away with his latest companion.

He had his own plans for the night. He would drink moonshine, dance for a while, as where he led his guests would follow. He had to remain reasonably clear-headed to give his speech to his birthday boys at midnight. Then he would have sex with this woman friend of Debrock's. Brady hadn't asked what her name was yet. And then he would have a couple of Debrock's super-strength dabs and then maybe sleep until lunchtime tomorrow. The New Green Year celebrations meant little to Brady Mahone, but he wouldn't stop his family from taking part.

Bodhi had asked, politely, for all Greens to sleep at their allotted time slots to ensure they were fully refreshed for the long process of receiving the UltraViolet™ at the New Green Year's celebrations, tomorrow, but the partygoers in Malibu had other arrangements, and sleeping was not part of their plans. It was 9:30, and the party was just heating up - there was zero possibility of anybody here retiring to their bed chambers at the preferred Green and non-UltraViolet™ sleeping slot by 10pm.

Hunter and his team of staff looked on from the edges of the party impassively. They stood to attention, waiting to attend to every need of the esteemed guests of Brady Mahone.

Brady was about to ask his companion her name when the music was turned up even louder. He smiled instead, and she twirled and danced suggestively next to him and then moved around him. Hawk raced into the centre of the makeshift dancefloor, and his brothers joined him. Brady guessed that it was Hawk who turned up the volume. The boys went into a jokey dance routine which clearly brought back some knowing memories for them. Brady laughed, but nobody could hear him within this din. He glanced at his watch as it just turned 10pm.

And then everybody collapsed.

Brady thought this was an elaborate prank at his expense. He looked around the room, and the only people left standing was Hunter and the staff. The music was still booming, but his boys, Amie, Helgarth and Lucy-Ian - he looked over the scene, waiting for somebody to jump up and cue the laughter on how they got Brady with this practical joke. If this was a joke, then they were incredibly well-disciplined. Even Debrock and his friends were utterly still. He looked down at his girlish companion at his feet, and then he knew that they were all dead.

He was frozen for a moment, and then he signalled for Hunter to cut the music. A staff member was dispatched, and without the music, it seemed eerily quiet. The lights went up, and a wrong switch had been pressed because the netting on the ceiling was released. Hundreds of balloons fell on the dancefloor. It was then that it hit Brady. He raced from body to body, checking for pulses or any other signs of life. He shook Bill and yelled at him to wake up, to no avail. One by one, he checked his family. He then cradled Amie in his arms and sobbed.

Brady looked up from the dead bodies and the balloons and into the face of Hunter. Hunter would have appeared expressionless, to most people, but to Brady's eyes, there was a definite smirk. It was an act of provocation, and Brady fell for it. He jumped up and hurled himself at Hunter.

Brady, deep down, knew it would never work, so he wasn't as surprised as he should have been to find himself doused in SecurityFilm™.

This is NanoRespect™, a trademark of Sattva Systems™. A crime against humanity has been committed. The welfare of our consumers is our highest priority. Please inform the nearest Disciple to remove Brady Mahone and dispatch xem to Sattva Systems™ with immediate effect. Thank you for using Sattva Systems™. Together, we save the world.

Hunter waited. He studied at the figure of Brady Mahone, suspended within the SecurityFilm™ with amused detachment. His Satt™ rang out. He fiddled with it and put it on the speakerphone. Brady guessed that he was supposed to hear whatever came next.

'Hello, Siddha. This is Hunter. Brady Mahone is captured and awaiting dispatch. Xe is technically under both our jurisdictions as I am the Malibu Disciple, and you are McFarland's. How do you propose we deal with this?'

'There is no need to instigate an Operation Clean-Up. The NanoPathogens™, which Brady had installed by persons unknown onto every File ever produced, will decompose the dead rapidly. I think it's appalling that he made a point of targeting our Green children with his free samples. I think it's xys revenge for the sterilisation programme of the Trads.' Siddha sighed mockingly.

Brady recalled his visits all over the world. He had given away thousands of free samples to children from Green Beijing to Green Cape Town to Green Quartiere Aurelio in Rome, he vividly remembered the young girl telling him that she loved him, and now she was dead because he gave her a File. He winced at the memory.

Siddha continued, 'There isn't going to be a trial. A Trad has no peers to judge xym. But the good news for Brady Mahone is that Bodhi will forgive xym, as it is part of the cultural identity of the Trads to destroy the things they don't understand. Is xe still there?'

'Yes. Xe can hear you. I'm not sure whether Brady Mahone has the intellectual capacity to fully comprehend the enormity of xys crime. Xe has murdered nine-hundred million in xys act of Green genocide. Even I struggle to digest such horror.' Hunter again looked into Brady's eyes with his subtle smirk taunting Brady. 'I know this man. Xe will deny it all and plead like a baby, but the trouble is, nobody will listen to the words uttered by a low-life Trad criminal. It's time Brady began to realise that xe has no friends and in addition, xe has zero credibility.'

It seemed strange to Brady that his mind was wandering and picking up on all the xe's and xym words in his time of utter despair - it was as if even language had evolved and left him behind.

Siddha said, 'Spoken like a true X™. Are you X™ as well?'

'Yes. My team have also taken the X™. We've earned it.' Hunter asked, 'What do you think will happen to xym?'

'Knowing Bodhi, I think he will let xym go. He knows Brady will travel the world trying to plead his innocence and throwing around baseless accusations, but these will be the ravings of a mad man. Bodhi will show mercy due to his extreme old age for a Trad, and I expect the X and the UltraViolets™ who survived his attack to shun xym. After all, those that are left are the Disciples and the Devout. They have always been wary of Brady Mahone, the Deceiver, and Corrupter. My guess is that xe will die alone. I'm presuming your service contract to Brady has been terminated?'

'Yes. We have served for more than a hundred years, but now we have been given a million years of life as our reward. We will now only serve Bodhi and Mother Earth. To tell you the truth, it's quite a relief to be leaving this den of iniquity.'

The Satt™ signal was silent for a moment, and then Siddha's voice re-emerged. 'Is there anything you need from me?'

'I would be grateful if you could tell Bodhi to expect the delivery of Brady Mahone, as I have our leaving arrangements to attend to.'

'Consider it done.' Siddha hung up.

Hunter took a deep breath, savouring the moment. He approached the Security-Film™ of the enwrapped, grimacing figure of Brady Mahone. He reached out his hand slowly, and then he touched the Film and Brady was sent away at high speed to Boulder Creek.

29: GHOST DANCE

The howls of the dead could be heard around the world. The decomposition of the Greenly Departed was swift, as there were no burials to be conducted. The recycling of the nine-hundred million NanoSuit™ layers had begun. As they emerged like husks, they saw the dead bodies of their loved ones, and they howled in the agony of their loss.

Many wandered in a confused state until they located their beacon. Some were thousands of miles away. Others found a stronger pull, as the genetic ties to Sattva Systems™ were strong, and they made swifter progress to join with their maker.

The screech of the death wails drove Brady crazy, and it even seemed to affect the progress of the SecurityProtocol™, which had captured him, as it strayed from its route as if a more substantial magnetic presence had interfered with its bearings. Brady wanted to scream to drown out the wailing, but he couldn't move a muscle in his filmy confinement. He watched the NanoSuits™ emerge from houses as the SecurityProtocol™ made its way tracking Highway 99 beneath him. The NanoSuits™ moved in their weird clockwork rotations as if they were driven by a system of cogs. Others flew like hatching flying ants moving straight up to the sky. He watched the sky changing colour to an unnatural shade of Electric Blue. And all the while, the howls of the NanoSuits™ got louder and louder.

Brady wondered whether he had died and was going to hell. He then saw an opaque NanoShell™ over the Sattva Systems™ HQ. It too was Electric Blue, and his SecurityProtocol™ slowed, almost to a stop. He watched the NanoShell™ open one at a time to let a single NanoSuit™ through to join with Bodhi. They were pressing against the NanoShell™, and now Brady could see that the smog of Suits™ had restricted his vision to no more than a few yards ahead. His SecurityProtocol™ merged with the NanoShell™ and then slowly slid through to the other side.

Compared to the chaos outside the NanoShell™ inside the Sattva Systems™ HQ, it was tranquil. The inside of the NanoShell™ had the usual forest scenes that a guest would have seen before. He was carried into the Main Hall. The people who were waiting for him were people he knew. Many of them he considered friends. They were in deep discussion, and those that glanced in his direction soon looked away either in disgust or embarrassment.

He tried to listen in, but a lot of the conversations merged into each other. *We should have known...It was a mistake to let him go about his business unchecked...I can't believe he could do such a thing...All those poor people...I lost friends, even children...And just a day away from getting their UltraViolet™...Life can be so cruel...I blame Bodhi...Brady must have had help, maybe it was a cell...We knew he was planning something, so why...*

He looked around. His heart sunk when he saw Samuel Beardon the Third in deep discussion with Lizzie and Siddha. To Brady's eyes, he looked like he was agreeing with them and not pleading on his behalf. Rhea and Glenarvon Cole were standing outside the main group. They were whispering conspiratorially as far he was concerned. He vaguely recalled the Regional Swedish Disciple, he knew her name was Bridgett something, but he also knew that she hated the sight of him.

Brady also made out the sounds of soft crying and commiserations, as some of their extended family members had lost loved ones who hadn't obtained the UltraViolet™ in time. It made him think of Tyrone and Raelynn and how they had only just escaped in time.

The loss of the sounds of the wailing dead Suits™ seemed to bring him back to his senses. He began to watch the room with a more strategic eye. He guessed Siddha was right that Bodhi might just let him walk out of here, but it made sense to case the joint for other potential escape routes. He eyed the group of Precious, Professor Pinar Dogan and Genesis Garcia suspiciously. He felt like they had a hand in framing him for this.

Cain wandered around alone as if he was deep in thought. It made Brady wonder if he wasn't wholly included in this inner sanctum.

Hours went by while the debates and discussions continued. There was movement from group to group. Brady thought his trial or whatever they had planned for him was about to start when Bodhi Sattva walked into the hall. He watched another NanoSuit™ dead soul merge with Bodhi. But all that happened was Bodhi had informed them that lunch was provided in the cafeteria. Brady watched in disbelief when they disappeared for another hour. The only thing of note that happened in this period was when Hunter arrived.

Brady assumed he'd left the packing to the rest of his staff while he made his way here. Hunter smiled at him and then placed an old antique pistol on the table near the suspended Brady Mahone.

At first, he was confused. Anybody leaving a gun for Brady Mahone in this predicament could be construed as trying to help him escape. However, Brady knew that an old gun couldn't inflict any damage on a Green. He looked around as best as he could from his confinement, and the Main Hall had nothing worth shooting at - even if he could shoot at a window or a pipe, he expected it to be Nano protected in some way. Also, he dwelled on the out-in-the-open placement of the gun. If Hunter was trying to help him, then there were plenty of places to conceal the weapon. He could have taped it to the underside of a table or a chair.

It then dawned on him. He was giving him the opportunity or the hint that he could commit suicide. Brady considered this option. He had no family; the world was full of dead NanoSuits™, and he would be made to be the patsy for a crime he didn't commit while he had to endure their sanctimonious crap about what a terrible person he was. He chewed it over and considered the speed at which his misery could be ended. Just one little squeeze on the trigger and bang - game over.

He knew for sure that he would have his opportunity. He knew how Bodhi schemed by now. Every Mafia hood he'd ever had the pleasure of talking to always spilt the beans on the foibles of their Godfathers. It was a way of proving their connections to the mighty and the powerful - the way they had their rivals murdered - there was always a little marker - the personal touch. He knew Bodhi would engineer a scenario where Brady would escape like a violent ex-con on the run. Brady could almost hear Bodhi saying, 'Oh dear, Brady has somehow got free, and look, he's got a gun. Everybody, stay out of his way. There's no telling what he's capable of.' Brady imagined the mock horror on their faces as he left and went into hiding, forever.

Another couple of dead NanoSuits™ wandered into the Main Hall, and they appeared like conjoined twins, and then another head appeared of a child merged with its two parents. Even from this vantage point, they looked like members of the same family. They were pulling in different directions, and they seemed to be attracted to Brady. They weren't wailing - they were still communicating with each other. *It's this way... No. It's over here... I was right about banding together to punch through the Shell™, wasn't I? ...The pull is coming from this direction... Are we nearly there yet? I want to go home.*

Brady watched the family move around the Main Hall like pieces on a giant Ouija board. Then they began their clockwork turning manoeuvre, one cog at a time, as one and then sped off in the direction of the cafeteria.

The gun on the table pulled Brady's attention back to his present problem. He determined that he wouldn't be a player in any game devised by Bodhi or Hunter. Instead, he wondered whether it might buy him valuable time if he got the chance to take himself hostage. He didn't know how they would react if he pretended that he was on the verge of suicide. They couldn't be seen to egg him on, but also, they wouldn't panic him. He knew they wanted to be free of any connection to this atrocity, and that meant that Brady Mahone had to take the cowards way out - by killing himself or running away. There had to be another way.

He relaxed. He let the SecurityFilm™ take the weight off. *Maybe, the biggest mistake they are making is giving Brady Mahone the time to develop a plan.* He examined the layout.

Another dead NanoSuit™ came into the Main Hall - again, it came close to Brady before concluding that he didn't smell quite right. It spoke to itself, like a demon communicating with hell. 'The families that bond together can puncture the Shell™. We will not be denied access to the Creator.' Brady shuddered at this sound of this twisted Suits™ voice and was relieved as he watched it glide away in the direction of the cafeteria where Bodhi was holding court.

There was the sound of murmuring and chattering, and then the selected Disciples and the Devout entered the hall. Brady knew it was no coincidence that these were the same people as logged on Professor Pinar Dogan's list. The surroundings were the opposite of grand, as each member of this caucus pulled up a simple chair made from recycled materials. There was no apparent hierarchy, but Brady noticed the little cliques that formed within the gathering. Even Bodhi sat among them and not at the front and centre as expected of a Trad leader.

Out through the Main Hall, Brady could see outside to the interior of the Nano-Shell™, but everybody else had their attention firmly fixed on Brady Mahone. Faces fixed firmly forward.

Yet another dead NanoSuit™ found Bodhi, and as it merged with him, Brady thought it strange that the group no longer found this weird. Perhaps, it had happened so often in the past that it was no longer a thing.

In the meantime, he took comfort from the apparently bright Californian sunshine from within the HQ boundaries, but he hadn't forgotten that it looked markedly different from this from beyond the Electric Blue NanoShell™.

Bodhi made a lowering gesture with his hand, and the SecurityProtocol™ placed Brady on the ground, and the SecurityFilm™ around him melted away. Brady was physically in good shape. Although he was emotionally unstable, he was grieving for his family whilst at the same time simmering with rage at his treatment. There had been plenty of occasions like this in his life, where he had been judged for the crimes, he had committed, and he never felt anger towards the prosecution lawyers, the jurors, or the judge - he thought of Judge Audre Jefferson and how she became his friend in her later years - the post-Revolution years. He never saw himself as the good guy. He knew he was bad and that he knew the game of risk and reward he was playing. It was his job to get away with it, and their job to catch him if they could - and if they did, it was a fair cop. He knew the people judging him on those days were the good guys, and therefore, he had no animosity to them. But this wasn't how he viewed his current situation. Brady wasn't used to being the victim.

Brady inched toward the table and picked up the gun. It had been a century since he last held one. He couldn't remember for sure, but he guessed that the last time he held a pistol in his hand was when he escaped from the Modern Ridgecrest Supermax Penitentiary back in 2084.

He pointed it at Bodhi for a moment, and then at Siddha, he made a gesture pretending to fire it, but his audience remained silent and unmoved. He began to wonder whether he was on show for entertainment purposes. He looked at Samuel Beardon the Third, but he seemed to be reciting a prayer, and scanning past Cain and Lizzie, he looked at Rhea, trying to judge whether she loved or loathed him. Her face gave little away, but he drew comfort from the fact that her eyes had a hint of sadness.

Over the audience's heads, he was convinced that the NanoShell™ around the Sattva Systems™ HQ was distorting. And then he saw a writhing form of a massed group of NanoSuits™ creeping up behind the audience. He saw the heads protrude and retreat as if there was a battle for leadership to find Bodhi Sattva. The audience couldn't see them, but Brady could.

One of the heads emerged, and he recognised Bill, his son, and it wailed, 'I've found him.' The rest of the audience had long since taken no notice of the recycling of NanoSuits™. The mass moved closer to Bodhi. Brady was appalled at the sight of this monstrous mash-up of his family. He guessed that this was what they were waiting for. He couldn't stand it any longer. He raised the gun to his temple, and then he heard a howl of anguish. Brady saw the screaming head of Amie emerge. 'Brady. No!'

All eight heads protruded grotesquely from the conglomerate of eight dead NanoSuits™ in a muddy mess, and they leapt on Brady. The audience watched in utter confusion as they shouldn't be attracted to Brady. He heard the ghostly greetings from all of them simultaneously. It was difficult for him to home in on one voice.

Hey, Pops, you're still alive...Don't do it...What have they done to you? You must fight...We can help...Use our Suits™...

'I'm not taking the Green. I'd rather die...'

No...Please...We haven't got long...Bodhi is pulling us back to him...Don't resist... We will be your tool...We can't stay with you even if we wanted to...You must hurry... Tell them the truth...

'They won't listen to me. I've already been judged.'

Then be someone they will listen to...Speak up...We will become them...You must hurry!

He watched the figure of Hawk being stretched out of the formation with Wilder wrapping himself around his younger brother, fighting desperately to keep him with the rest of his family. He dropped his gun and began to speak.

'I had been through all kinds of tests. My eggs had been engineered to ensure I had a boy.' Amie's body moved to the front of the writhing mass, and she took the form of Libby Skye as she was depicted in the movie poster at her Malibu home.

'The doctors and nurses had been well rewarded for working on the Millennial Eve, but what I didn't know was that they were offered bonuses which would make them rich for life if they induced me to have the first baby in the world born on the Millennial Day. They even had a registrar ready. I should have wondered why I had to go to Tonga to deliver the baby. You could say that they were highly motivated. The only rule was that I couldn't have a Caesarion section. I must have a vaginal birth.'

Bodhi stared at her, and it seemed that he might have the power to extract the vision of his dead Mother from the clutches of the other NanoSuits™, but they resisted in this ethereal tug-of-war.

'They were brutal with me. As the clock ticked down, they tried everything to bring Xavier into the world, and then as the clock was about to strike twelve, the surgeon butchered me. He sliced me up, and they used a ventouse and pulled him into the world on the first second of the new Millennium. I cannot find the words to describe the agony they made me endure. I suppose I should be grateful that they stuck around for the emergency surgery I needed afterwards. If I'd have known, what John's plan was, I would never have agreed to it, not even for this place. I have massive scarring to this day - even after the best cosmetic surgery you could buy back in those primitive times.' She wailed so loudly that it drew an echo from beyond the HQ's NanoShell™.

'Xavier's education began even before he was born. John had his teachers come and talk to the baby inside me. Can you imagine how weird that was, having to let complete strangers hover over my stomach and recite science and business lessons to a foetus? Every single day I had to let them do that to me.'

Bodhi yelled to drown her out, and Libby sprung back into the writhing forms. But she re-emerged. Amie was even more determined, and now she shone brightly in a stark white vision of Libby Skye.

'I talked to my unborn baby. He could hear me day or night. I used to say, "Xavier, this is your Mother. Whatever anybody should say to you, you must always protect your Mother." I must have looked like I was insane, but I talked to my unborn baby boy all the time, day and night. I had to keep my bond with my baby.'

She spat out, 'But he was Daddy's little science project, and he let me die. He could have saved me, but he didn't. He killed his own Mother.'

The gathered assembly began to murmur. The vision of Libby Skye turned spectrally clear, and, in her exhaustion, she fell from the mass and walked serenely over to the seated figure of Bodhi and merged into him.

Another ear-piercing wail went up, and this time it was from Helgarth. She emerged in the form of Tia Cassandra. 'We had a source from inside the FBI - she was on our payroll - and she gave us the crucial lead to Samuel Beardon the Second. He gave us the information we were looking for before he could give it to the authorities. Our source kept it from them. She was well rewarded for her silence.' Rhea shuffled uncomfortably and looked around for possible escape routes.

'John Kane despised humanity. He viewed them as worse than animals - actually, he loved animals, but that's hardly relevant here. He blamed humans for trashing the planet, and therefore he used humans for his experimentation. He was fascinated by nature, and he believed that humans were unnatural. He conducted little side experiments to understand the effects of nurture on virtually identical embryos.'

Rhea pretended to cough. She waved her apologies and stood up and headed slowly away. It was then that she saw the outer NanoShell™ stretching to breaking point. She couldn't see beyond the Shell™, but she knew it had to be a mighty force to be able to do that. She looked back at the distorted vision of Tia Cassandra.

'The first child he had was Xavier Kane, the person you know as Bodhi Sattva. He bred him to be perfect. From the moment he was conceived, he was hot housed to be the perfect heir to Sattva Systems™. The next child was born in the UK. He was indoctrinated with socialist values from before he was born. John Kane had people bombard the foetus with socialist doctrines and then raised by left-wingers. His name was Glenarvon Cole. Brady Mahone was his third experiment.' She answered a question that the audience couldn't hear. 'Closer to identical triplets. And Libby Skye is the mother of all three of you.'

The vision of Tia Cassandra laughed and howled at the same time. 'He strung her along. John Kane incentivised her and her friends to talk to you as a criminal while still in the womb. He had a script for them to follow, as they weren't particularly bright. This process continued until after you, Brady Mahone was born, and then your Mother, so to speak, died of a drug overdose.' She laughed hysterically, 'and then he placed you with a paedophile.' The exhausted NanoSuit™ of Helgarth fell as if there was nothing of substance for the others to grab onto. She completed her walk to Bodhi to recycle her Nanomaterials.

The NanoSuits™ of his sons and Lucy-Ian seemed to have lost their critical mass. Brady felt them fall away from him and sensed their utter exhaustion from their efforts to help him. They made one last effort to divert themselves away from Bodhi by leaping on Glenarvon Cole, maybe to confirm their story, or perhaps it was to apologise. Brady wondered if he would ever get to find out.

Brady saw Rhea pointing outside, and Brady watched the cracks appear in the outer Shell™. He remembered his conversation with Professor Pinar Dogan. He looked at her, and Brady raised his right arm high above his head. He clenched his fist so tightly that his skin turned white, and then he released it with a flourish in a gesture that suggested an explosion.

Pinar smiled, but she was obviously puzzled. She looked behind her. She seemed to be in shock for a moment until she threw her chair aside and fled for her life. Brady ran into the crowd, imploring them to follow her. Siddha and Hunter tried to restrain him, but Glenarvon Cole implored Bodhi to set him free. Bodhi didn't understand the sudden commotion. He watched with bewilderment as Professor Pinar Dogan raced into the building instead of away from it. Bodhi waved his hand dismissively at Siddha and Hunter, and they let Brady go free.

Bodhi's arm flopped back down by his side as if it was too heavy to hold up. Glen checked his own movements, and he sensed he was either getting weaker or heavier. Glen said, 'Where is Pinar going?'

'To the Sensory Deprivation Chambers.' Brady still wasn't sure if he could trust anybody here, but there wasn't time for assessing the motivations in an emergency. 'She's certain that Bodhi can't recycle nine-hundred million Suits™ within his body. He's Pure Nano now - he's not human, the whole things going to blow, and your NanoSuits™ aren't going to protect you.'

'Of course, they will. They have never failed.'

'I've seen it at Cima. If the same Nanomaterials are blasted at you. You will die. You must trust me. I'm begging you.' He added, 'Why do you think Pinar ran?' As if her actions were louder than her words.

The surge of black Nanomaterials began to ooze through the outer NanoShell™, and the California sunshine had turned to the black of night. The ooze moved like lava after an eruption, and it was all heading to Bodhi for recycling.

Siddha said, 'Don't listen to him, Glen. He's lying. Bodhi is going to be a God, and I will be at his right-hand side. You can't lose faith now. He's always kept his promises.'

Glen looked at the black mass and knew it was madness to stay. 'You do what you gotta do. For good or ill, my fate is tied to Brady's now.'

'Then, you are a fool, Glenarvon Cole.' Siddha turned away in disgust and moved toward Bodhi with Hunter alongside him. Brady kept his eye on Siddha. He never did trust him. Hunter whispered in Siddha's ear, and then Brady watched Siddha sneak away in the same direction as Pinar. He wondered if he was going to save himself, after all.

'I'll take as many as I can. Some will want to remain here. When I get to the Sensory Deprivation Chambers, I'll set the comms channels open. In case you didn't know how they worked.' Glen thought over the logistical issues. 'I'll tell the others to seal the Chambers for twelve hours, and then I'll be the first to check if it's safe to re-emerge. No point risking everyone.'

Brady said, 'What do the comms things do?'

'Obviously, once inside the Chambers, you are supposed to be isolated from external stimuli, but in this situation, we are going to need two-way communication. I will set this up, and then we can communicate with others secured within the Chambers and also communicate with the outside. We will need to know what's happening...' He felt pulled to the floor. 'I'm weakening.'

'Let's move.' Brady raced off. He yelled to the others, 'Come on. Go to the Sensory Deprivation Chambers...' He watched Bridgett dismissively wave Glen away, but he then saw that he had persuaded Precious to leave. Brady wanted to go to Rhea, but Glen had got to her first, and she was helping with the evacuation. He watched her arguing with Lizzie. He then saw the disconsolate figure of the Bear slumped in his chair. He was alone. Brady rushed to him.

'Hey, brother, you've got to go, y'know, save yourself.'

'My Alicia is going to die. How can I justify living if I can't protect my daughter?'

'I know, man. It's real hard, but she wouldn't want you to die as well. You know she wouldn't.'

'No. You go - save yourself. My time is up.'

'Isn't that for your God to decide - and what about Tyrone? Are you going to let me take the blame for not saving you when I had the chance? What kind of a friend would that make me?'

The Bear didn't answer.

'Look. Just save yourself today. For me, as a favour, and tomorrow you can do what you want. How does that sound? Couldn't we make a deal?'

The Bear didn't answer, but he did rise to his feet. Brady grabbed him by the arm. They started to race away when they heard a large crack, and the deluge of Nano-Suits™ began to fill the Main Hall. Brady looked ahead and saw Glenarvon, Rhea and Lizzie make it to the corridor. He looked behind, and the only ones who were staying back were Bridgett, Hunter, and Cain.

'Hey, brother. You go on ahead. I'm going to try and persuade Cain to come. He's kinda been ok with me.' He shook the Bear. 'You promise you won't do anything stupid, old man.'

'I won't.'

Brady moved freely through the Black Goo, and he was surprised how light it was. It hardly impeded his movement. However, the Bear seemed leaden-footed and seemed to find it a struggle to move freely. Brady rubbed the dry film from his bare forearm. He expected his white T-shirt to be stained black, but the residue fell from it as if it was being repelled. He guessed that the thick clouds of NanoSuit™ materials were magnetically attracted to the Greens, and they were weighed down by the accumulations on their own Suits™. He checked out the condition of Bodhi in the distance, and he couldn't spot any signs of movement. He was alive, but he had the appearance of a man who had gorged on a massive feast of NanoSuits™. Brady felt static in the air raise the hairs on his skin, and he tingled all over. This latest addition to the evidence of his senses wasn't reassuring. He had to move quickly.

Cain seemed barely conscious when Brady reached him. 'Hey, man. Can I help a brother out?'

Cain gazed vacantly at Brady with his crystal green eyes. 'I'm ok. I deserve to die.'

Brady laughed, 'You can be a stupid fuck sometimes, but you've always been ok with me. Now come on, your friends are waiting for you. Let me help.' Brady tried to help Cain to his feet, but he didn't seem to have the strength to stand. 'I ain't got time for this, man.' Brady swept him up in his big arms as easily as if he was picking up a bag of feathers. He marched through the dead NanoSuits™ as if they weren't there, but he could hear them howling.

I can't move...I'm being crushed...He's here. I can feel him...

They tried to attach themselves to Brady, but they were repelled from his body and even his clothes.

That's not Bodhi...Where's Bodhi?

Brady resolved to ignore them as he carried the frail, white-robed figure in his arms. He wondered if he was running out of time as the air was thickening and the light seemed to be disappearing into the massed black souls. The screaming from the crush intensified.

Brady reached the storeroom, which contained the Sensory Deprivation Chambers. To Brady, it looked like the storage facility of a Funeral Home. The first line of matt black coffins were wholly sealed. He investigated the coated glass plate on the first one, and he saw Lizzie, who looked alarmed to see Brady peering down at her. 'No. No...' He readjusted Cain in his arms.

'Hey. I saved you. Talk about gratitude...' He peered into the gathering darkness and heard a fight within the wails of the Dead NanoSuits™. He went to investigate. He passed more sealed coffins, but then he found the broken ones.

Glen and Siddha were fighting but without any energy, as they were both utterly exhausted. Siddha grabbed the open lid of a Sensory Deprivation Chamber and heaved it back against the locks, and it fell to the floor, like all the others.

Brady muttered, 'Where the fuck are the SecurityProtocols™ when you need them?'

Siddha headed for the next of the last two undamaged coffins. Glen grabbed Siddha's ankles with the last of his strength. Brady quickly but carefully placed Cain on the ground, picked up a broken coffin shell and ran at Siddha. He knocked Siddha off his feet, and he put him under the lid like catching a bug in a glass. Brady piled more lids on him until he was sure he wouldn't have the power to escape the weight.

He went back to retrieve Cain, and he put him in a Sensory Deprivation Chamber. Cain was too weak to either protest or thank Brady, all he could do was stare at Brady like a helpless child. Brady closed the lid, and it sealed over Cain.

Glenarvon Cole was close to death. Brady picked up his brother.

Glen said, 'There's only one left. You take it, I should die like my GreenRev comrades…'

'Are you kidding?' Brady laughed and looked at Glen as if he was a dying soldier on the battlefield. 'I hate solitary. Brady Mahone has spent too much of his life being locked up. I'm damned if I'm going to volunteer for incarceration.' He scooped Glenarvon Cole in a fireman's lift and then dumped him unceremoniously into the coffin and sealed it before Glen could protest. He didn't have time for sad goodbyes. Brady shrugged as he muttered to himself, 'I may as well see out the end of the war. Let's hope they put on a good show.'

He heard a voice emanate from a speaker from a neighbouring Chamber. 'Your only hope is to get high…'

'Ain't that the truth, sister.' Brady joked.

He peered into the chamber, and he saw it was Professor Pinar Dogan. She said, 'It's theoretical but with a high possibility…'

'I don't think we got time for this…'

'Ok. Yes. You need to find a FusionPlane™, get as high as you can, but not directly above Bodhi. Go…Now!' She added, 'Hurry!'

Brady raced down the corridors through the black mist through the Main Hall. He tried to get his bearings in the deepening gloom. He saw the banner with the thirteen promises, and then he spotted the exit. He sprinted through the door, and he caught the sight of a FusionPlane™, but it was privately owned by one of the Disciples and, therefore, was unresponsive to him. He passed by a few other vehicles until he found Rhea's rental. He climbed inside. He took over the manual controls and vertically took off as fast as he could. He switched everything onto maximum power. All he could see was black as he ascended through millions of expired NanoSuits™.

He wondered whether he would ever see daylight again, but finally, he did rise above them. He set off due south just as day turned to night, and he watched the light being sucked into the Sattva Systems™ HQ. The hundreds of millions of Dead Souls were sucked away in a fraction of a second. This was followed by utter silence and stillness, and then there was a blinding flash of light. In a moment, the California winter sun returned, but it was eclipsed by a tower of light which reached to the skies and then spread in flashes all over the skies from horizon to horizon, creating a strobe light effect which lasted a few minutes.

Without even making the decision, Brady started to fly to McFarland. The sky had turned to an unnatural Electric Blue, and then as if the Hands of God had been placed on a Van Der Graff Generator, the electrical storms began. He saw thousands of people below him who had come out to witness the strange astral phenomena. He watched them all being eviscerated with unerring accuracy. Each lightning bolt was attracted to the identical NanoSuit™ signatures as the Dead NanoSuits™ coating the upper atmosphere.

The lightning bolts lit up a grid system about one hundred metres above ground level, which stretched to the horizon. The grid crackled and fired off millions of sparks, followed by mini-explosions, and although he had never seen one, and the only person that claimed that they had - Vance, who likened it to catching the picture at the heart of a Magic Eye puzzle out of the corner of soft eyes - Brady knew that these were the Security Protocols™ being wiped out by the storms of heaven. He fought the urge to whoop and holler at this awesome display of power, as instantly, he remembered that millions were being murdered in these same minutes.

He dwelled on why the Security Protocols™ were targeted. Until he made the mental leap that these were created from the same materials as the NanoSuits™. He also guessed that they had some cloaking mechanism that kept them from the sight of humans. If the Greens had been able to see the millions of these at once, they might have been more concerned. As it was, they only appeared infrequently, and at times of trouble, this gave them the brand image of Guardian Angels as opposed to mind-controlling machines. He vividly recalled being inside the goo they covered him in after the death of his family and friends in Malibu, and he thought that the goo was probably a kind of viscous version of the Nanoparticles the Suits™ were made from. He shuddered at the thought of this being a close relative of the dead NanoSuits™.

Brady thought of Alicia as he watched the thousands of people being turned to charred ashes beneath him in horror. It was only then that the enormity of what had transpired hit him. He slowed his FusionPlane™ to a slow glide, almost as a mark of respect to the dead. Everybody was dead. He reminded himself that this wasn't strictly true. Many of his chief tormenters and enemies might be alive in their protective coffins, but as the lightning strikes continued from all horizons, he wondered how long it might be before they could be released. This could go on for hours, or maybe years.

He headed to McFarland. His home in Malibu was the sight of the massacre of his family and friends, and it held no prospect of comfort for him. He became aware that although there were thousands of lightning strikes in the distance, they seemed to have slowed around him. Brady hovered over his ranch for a while. He didn't know if he was safe. He considered that the FusionPlane™ might be protecting him. As he lowered his vehicle, he noticed that there were birds, and then he spotted other animals behaving as if nothing had happened.

Over by the old bunker, he saw the doors move. He didn't land. He watched closely. The doors opened slowly, and then a couple of Greens who watched over the place in his absence emerged, blinking into the sunlight. One of them spotted Brady and waved to him. Brady waved back. He was concerned that they would be fried by the heavenly fires, but nothing happened.

Oh, man. If only Pops had been around to see that he was right about his bunker all along. He always said it could withstand anything mankind could throw at it.

Brady wondered who else might have survived - maybe in caves or onboard Nano-Submarines™…

He manoeuvred his FusionPlane™ to head back to Boulder Creek. He flew quickly, and he kept checking the skies for lightning and the ground for any other signs of Green survivors. He didn't see any. Finally, he landed at Sattva Systems™, and he was surprised at the lack of damage. *It must be one of those death by electrocution kinda deals like they used to do to us good 'ol boys in the old days.*

There wasn't a single sign of the black NanoSuits™ of the dead. He went over to the resting place of Bodhi Sattva and if Brady expected any precious metals to be left behind. Something he could have made into a manly piece of jewellery, then he was to be disappointed. All that was left was dirt. He moved his fingers through it. He sniffed it on his fingers, which reminded him of coal dust.

The height of Green technology and it's turned to coal dust.

Brady removed his Sattva Ring on his Pops' silver chain and placed it on the black dust.

30: ELECTRIC BLUE DAY

Brady opened each of the Sensory Deprivation Chambers and helped them climb out as they were still feeble. It wasn't a coincidence that the first one he rescued was Rhea Laidlaw.

'I suppose you're going to arrest me now. That'd be just my luck.'

She laughed, 'No. You're free to go. Brady Mahone.'

'But what if I don't want to go?'

She dug him weakly in the ribs. 'Maybe, I'll bring you in for questioning later.' She looked around at the other Chambers. 'I think we should let them out. They will all want to know what happened, and then we need to plan for the future.'

Rhea didn't have the energy to release anybody, so Brady helped to lift them out. At first, he put them on the floor, where they sat with their backs against the wall. He went to the Main Hall to bring them all chairs, but the air reeked of coal dust, and even though it rolled off him like water droplets off his old, waxed Poacher's coat, he wondered whether it was potentially dangerous to the Green survivors. He returned empty-handed. Glen asked, 'What happened?'

'It's bad. I don't think many survived. I'll tell you later. You all need to get outside as I don't think it's good for you in here. There's a lot of dust in the air - I think it's the same stuff that's making you real weak.'

Glen struggled to his feet and started to help the others to their feet. He hadn't the strength to assist the Bear, so Brady went to him, and he needed all his power to raise him, as he was almost a dead weight now. 'Any news about my Alicia?'

'She's gone, like nearly everybody else. I'm really sorry, man.'

'You're not one for doling out false hope, brother.'

'Words were never my strong point - you know me. Now come on, you're going to have to be strong for the others.'

The Bear smiled knowingly; he knew Brady was trying to instil a sense of purpose in him. He appreciated the attempt. Brady made several trips to carry a survivor and place them in the fresh air of the Californian winter sunshine, which had re-established a semblance of normality. Brady looked up curiously at the Electric Blue sky. Professor Pinar Dogan followed Brady's sightline and was puzzled and then profoundly concerned.

Brady Mahone, the last Trad on Earth, looked over his exhausted Green survivors - Rhea, Precious, Lizzie, Professor Pinar Dogan, Genesis Garcia, Cain, Glenarvon Cole and Samuel Beardon the Third. Those that found sufficient energy grieved for their lost loved ones. He was surprised to see Genesis Garcia weeping so openly as, for some reason, he thought that politicians didn't cry real tears.

'Cain?'

He roused from his inner thoughts. 'Yes.'

'Are you X-Ray™?' Brady added, 'Bodhi, Hunter and Siddha were. I'm guessing, as part of their crew, that you would be as well.'

'No. I hesitated and asked for more time to consider.'

Brady turned to the group. 'Anybody else?'

A few hands went up hesitantly. He studied them. Professor Pinar Dogan, Glenarvon Cole, and one that took him by surprise until he revisited the connections - Lizzie.

'And yes - we still can issue X-RaySuits™.' Pinar answered before Brady even thought of asking. Pinar scanned the scene. 'The facilities are untouched.'

'From what I witnessed, massive electrical storms produced millions of lightning strikes which seemed to seek out the Greens. It didn't touch me, the FusionPlane™ or even the wildlife.' Brady knew he was removing any last vestiges of hope for them with this statement.

'And Moses and Aaron did so, as the LORD commanded; and he lifted up the rod, and smote the waters that were the river, in the sight of Pharoah, and in the sight of his servants, and all the waters that were in the river were turned to blood. Exodus 7:20.' He had used his reserves of energy to relay his sermon with as much power as he could, but his breath was laboured, and then he lay down on the grass verge near the Main Entrance of the Sattva Systems™ HQ. The Bear visibly wilted.

Brady shook his head. He was as interested in Religious Education lessons as he was in Science. He only had one thing he desperately wanted to know, and that was whether these Greens would clear his name and accept responsibility for the deaths of their own kind. 'You know I had nothing to do with these deaths, don't you? Does anybody actually believe that I would kill my own family and friends?' He studied each of them. 'Look. I know, I ain't no saint. I killed people, bad people in my eyes, but I didn't have anything to do with this.' He raised his arms as if to indicate the world. 'Come on, people. Put a guy out of his misery, here.'

Pinar said. 'One of the side projects which John Kane instigated, decades before the Revolution, was developing Nanoparticles as a pathogen.'

Brady wasn't going to stop Pinar talking by asking what a pathogen was.

'It had a working title of NanoTaint™. It was a method of transferring Nanomaterials to the centre of the brain. These particles were inert and undetectable unless we activated them. John had a twisted sense of morals and would not conduct these experiments on animals, but humans, especially children, were fair game. I won't lie, I knew everything, but I was gaining an insight not afforded to other more regulated branches of the scientific community.'

Rhea interrupted. 'I was working for the FBI at the time, and Marjorie was with Military Intelligence, while her husband was with the CIA, we were investigating the deaths of children, and he had put together a case on the mysterious deaths of children in Pakistan. We had links to John Kane.'

Sissy said, 'I didn't know you were in the FBI...'

'Why would you? There was no FBI. It gave me a sense of purpose - I enjoyed my old life, I wanted to know how you did it.'

'I've still got those files.' Brady stated. The others were puzzled, but Rhea was intrigued. 'I stole them from the Los Banos Police Department. I've seen those dead kids. Judge Audre Jefferson went through them all. She made me a summary that even I could understand. However, I never saw anything in there that mentioned this NanoTaint™ crap.'

Glen looked over to Pinar, and it was a look of a colleague who'd been kept in the dark. Pinar said, 'With a complex magnetic switch, we could instantly but painlessly terminate a subject. He was keen to try it out on the Files used by his paedophile ring if they ever tried to blackmail John Kane. Each file was coated with NanoTaint™, and it was ingested through the fingers. It was a prototype technology which was eventually used in Distors™.'

'That actually makes sense. I tried to give one of these Files back to Bodhi - long story, I was blackmailing him.' He waved away any attempts to get him to continue. 'That's a story for another day.' Brady was puzzled. 'So, why didn't I die? Nobody handled them more than me.'

'Bodhi was a natural birth. By the time you and Glenarvon Cole's conception in the lab, you were genetically engineered to repel NanoTaint™. The last I saw of John Kane; he was going to bring you back for tests. There had been a memory distortion as a child with Bodhi, and John wanted Xavier, Bodhi to be perfect. You were one of two perfect donors. You were the most dispensable due to your conditioning.'

'Thanks for reminding me.' He peered into Pinar's face with her brown eyes. He wasn't sure whether he was talking to a machine or a human. 'If I was to take responsibility for all these deaths, and it was designed to keep Bodhi Sattva's impeccable reputation intact - then he couldn't have got somebody else to do it for him, say Siddha, for instance…'

'Bodhi did it. And I was the only other person in the world who knew he had the means. Bodhi thought he was doing it for the right reasons. He was saving the planet, and he wasn't going to waste *Her* resources on Greens, who were unwilling to work for a thousand years. It was simpler to blame it on you.' Before anybody could comment, Pinar raised her hand, 'I may as well tell you how it was done with the final details. Bodhi grasped the opportunity for the disloyal to self-select themselves for elimination when he watched Brady grow his business - all he needed to do was take over the manufacturing to enable worldwide distribution. The NanoTaint™ was placed on the head of every Diamondback Rattlesnake.' She looked only at Brady. 'We didn't concern ourselves with your original homemade sales, as you were utterly persuasive at making your customers want more.'

Pinar looked back at the group and raised her hands. 'I know what I've done - I'm guilty. I never believed Bodhi would be so decisive.' She looked up at the sky and pointed, 'This is an extinction-level threat. I will try and make amends by helping to solve this.'

Genesis Garcia had been reflecting on how she helped design the BMEE logo with the snake twisting through the letters. 'Ruthless - not decisive. He instilled into each of us here, never to touch these files, as he would consider that as an act of giving in to the temptation of nostalgia for the Trad world. We now know why.'

The others muttered in agreement but were interrupted when a Satt™ rang out with an unfamiliar tone to everybody but Rhea. They all looked at her. She answered and then put it on speakerphone. 'Hi, Tia. You're on speaker. There are only a few survivors. You can talk freely.'

She said to the others. 'There will be a short delay. Tia is on Mars, but one thing she is a genius at is communication technology. The delay in transmissions will make regular conversations tricky, so I'll resort to using the term over when I have finished my sentence.'

Tia said, 'Our observatories witnessed the Earth appearing like a pulsar for a few minutes. Of course, I know it wasn't a pulsar, but I'm using the terminology for descriptive purposes. This was followed by a worldwide thunderstorm, and we tried to communicate but received no answer. It's good to hear your voice again, Rhea. Over.'

Rhea was about to answer, but Pinar pleaded with her to let her speak to her first. Rhea gestured, ok.

'This is Professor Pinar Dogan. We need your help. In the aftermath of the quantum mechanical black hole's rapid evaporation, it has created a layer of carbon particles in the stratosphere. The amounts are significant enough to change the quality of light reaching the Earth's surface, damaging vegetation. I'll continue with my work here, but it would help if you can get some of my old colleagues working on the problem at your end. To use round figures, there were approximately one billion people, each with eight NanoSuits™. These are polluting the Earth's atmosphere. The sky has changed colour substantially. Over.'

They all looked up at the Electric Blue sky. If they had noticed it before, they put it down to becoming accustomed to the light after their trauma, but Pinar was right - the colour change was unmistakable.

Glen said, 'We haven't done this for nothing, have we? I don't believe this.'

'You shall have no other gods before me...' Samuel Beardon the Third muttered his response in reproach to his own sins.

Pinar said, 'Science and humanity are strange bedfellows, with every new discovery comes the means of man's salvation and destruction. Science has given us this problem - fortunately, it may also have the solution...' Pinar muttered, 'Science will help fix up what its users fuck up.'

The Satt™ caught up with the transmission. 'Our Laser-Induced Breakdown Spectroscopy has confirmed your analysis. We will send whatever resources you need. I'm in the observatory with the man who first observed the Earth's disturbance. He claims he heard his uncle's voice on the speakerphone. I'll put him on for a moment...'

'Was that you, Uncle Sam? We are ok up here. Raelynn and I are having a baby. I'm going to be a Dad...sorry...over.'

'The bad news can wait. Let him have his moment.' Brady shook his head and pointed up to the heavens.

Rhea said, 'You can talk with him in private afterwards. You can use my Satt™ for as long as you wish.'

The Bear nodded and whispered, 'Thank you.' He then shouted as if he had to physically make his voice carry all the way to Mars. 'That's wonderful news. Pass on my love and congratulations to Raelynn.'

Brady shouted, 'Way to go, man. You tell Raelynn that I'm mighty proud of her.'

Rhea smiled and spoke into the speakerphone. 'Over and out.' She said to the group. 'I'll leave the Satt™ on the reception desk. Anybody can use it, but I suggest we take turns monitoring it for incoming calls.'

'I think we should take a bit of time to recover...'

Brady looked at his watch and said, 'What the fuck is the time? My watch says 75:10.'

'I'm sorry, Brady.' Pinar shrugged. 'Everything's been set for the GreenMetric-Time™. It's the least of our worries. You'll just have to get used to it. In old money, it's just after 6pm.'

'Ah, for fuck…'

Rhea took hold of Brady's hand, 'I don't mind teaching you…unless you don't want me to…'

'Yeah. Ok. Deal.' He laughed.

'Let's say we get out of here.' She said to the others. 'Shall we all meet back here in a couple of days and make some plans for the next steps. The old Satts™ should still be working if we need to contact each other.' Rhea led Brady to the Fusion-Planes™, and she opened one.

Brady said, 'Hey, that was your rental?'

'Yes.'

'I might not have got out of here in time if it wasn't parked up. All the others were Private…'

'So, are you telling me I saved your life?'

Brady laughed, 'I wouldn't go that far…' She gave him a look of mock disappointment. 'Ok, yeah, you saved the life of Brady Mahone.'

'And what's your life worth?'

'What do you want?'

'Let's start by letting me have a look at those Los Banos Files of yours.'

Brady laughed, 'There are dozens of boxes of them. You might have to stay over to get through them all…'

'That's fine by me. I don't mean to impose.'

The FusionPlane™ lifted off vertically, and Brady set the autopilot to the Mahone Ranch. 'On one condition…'

'And what's that?'

'That you read them slowly. I wouldn't want you to miss anything.'

She held his hand, smiled, and then kissed him. As she pulled away and sunk comfortably into her passenger seat, the sky's Electric Blue colour caught Brady's attention.

He said, 'The sky looks kinda cool.'

'Yeah, if you discount the tons of carbon dust threatening to destroy all life on Earth.' She teased. 'Hey, Brady-kins…'

'Brady-kins!'

They both laughed. She asked, 'What are your plans?'

'What do you mean?'

625

'Well, as far as I can tell, you've only got a few Brady Mahone Entertainment Enterprises customers left, and I don't think your millions of Green Credits are going to be of much use anymore.'

Brady shrugged, 'I suppose I'll just have to retire.'

'So, you wouldn't be interested in going back to work, then?'

'I dunno. What could I do?

'Is that modesty I hear, Mr Mahone?'

'We both know I'm not cut out for Green work...'

'What would you say if I told you that a certain Fleet Captain Marjorie Hampton is planning to return, and she thinks you would make a great LeviathanLifter™ pilot?'

Brady gasped, 'Oh, man. That would be cool.'

'Marjorie believes that the LeviathanLifters™ will be called into action to spray the dust clouds from the stratosphere. Do you want the job?'

'Hell, yes.'

Rhea laughed, 'If I was still an undercover TV reporter - I think my intro would run something like: Brady Mahone saves the world!'

Brady roared with laughter. After a minute or two, he calmed down, and he remembered those he had lost along the way. 'You know what's real funny?'

'Go on.'

'If my Pops were alive today, I would have to have told him that we've just invited a bunch of Martians to invade the planet.'

THE END.

ACKNOWLEDGEMENTS

I'd like to give my heartfelt thanks to my family, Cathy, my wife and my daughters, Beck and Katie, for their love and support while writing (and recording) this book.

A Small Request...

If you have enjoyed this book, do please help to spread the word by putting a review or a rating on your favourite bookseller or Goodreads; by posting something on social media; or in the old-fashioned way by simply telling your friends or family about it.

Book publishing is a very competitive business these days, to a saturated market, and independent publishers such as ourselves are often crowded out by big business.

Support from readers like you can make all the difference to a book's success.

Many thanks.

MORE FROM JIM LOWE

Previously published by Jim Lowe: The New Reform Quartet

Book One: New Reform

Tatum had learning difficulties and had a brutal home life, but one thing to emerge from her living with a family of gun runners was that she learned to shoot with unerring accuracy.

When she finally escaped her family, she found friendship and camaraderie with a sisterhood of feminist activists until many of her friends were killed in a deadly terrorist attack.

It was then that Tatum spiralled into a state where the only solution was to take revenge on their killers…

The New Reform series was conceived in 2013 (before Brexit and Trump) and was a darkly satirical look into future political influences.

Not only did it play with the idea of corrupt populism, but also militant feminism, marketing, hacking, viral content, social media influencers, new money combined with dark desires - and even what could happen to the latent power of the aristocracy and the liberal elite if their power was turned inwards to ignite a potent force.

The four books have different themes but are interlinked, and by the end of the final book, all the plotlines are neatly gift-wrapped and presented with a tightly knotted jet-black bow.

Set in the fictional city of Arlington, this alternative history spans decades beginning in the eighties.

The story begins with Tatum waiting and watching - something she is exceptionally good at. In fact, she could watch and wait for England - and beyond…

Book Two: The ODC (The Online Death Cult)

Denise was a soulless sociopath with money to burn and urges to satisfy, and then she met Brandon. He was a celebrity seeker with a love for her, but with no regard to the trail of destruction, he would be willing to cause to make her his own.

Book Three: With Two Eyes

Nadie was only seeking the truth for the family of the man she had loved, but instead, she found herself treated as a travelling freak show. But as she doggedly continued in her lonely quest, little did she know that she was changing the world one step at a time.

Book Four: Fourth Room.

Bob had all the power and money he could want, but all this gave him was boredom and frustration at his perceived lack of freedom. Would he stand in the way of those who would use his position to start a new world order in his name…

All titles will be available, wherever possible, on eBook, paperback, hardback, and audiobook.

If you want to know more about my writing and recording, please visit my website at jimlowewriting.com.

Thank you.

Milton Keynes UK
Ingram Content Group UK Ltd.
UKHW010007131023
430461UK00006B/185